Linda Holeman is the author of the international bestsellers *The Linnet Bird* and *The Moonlit Cage*, as well as eight previous books, both novels and short stories. She lives in Winnipeg, Manitoba.

Acclaim for Linda Holeman's previous novels:

'A stirring tale of one woman's search for fulfilment' *Woman & Home*

'Compulsive reading . . . [*The Linnet Bird*] succeeds in being more than just a historical saga; it is a rites-of-passage tale with a very convincing and resourceful heroine' *The Lady*

'An epic story of passion and determination' *Good Book Guide*

'This tale of love, loss and redemption is impossible to put down' *Yours*

'[Linda Holeman] is a master of dramatic tension and of seducing a reader's attention . . . There is a beautiful imagination at work here and a touch of genuine narrative magic that makes the book a one-in-a-lifetime read' *Globe & Mail (Toronto)*

In a Far Country

LINDA HOLEMAN

headline
review

First published in 2008 by HEADLINE REVIEW
An imprint of HEADLINE PUBLISHING GROUP

First published in paperback in 2008 by HEADLINE REVIEW
An imprint of HEADLINE PUBLISHING GROUP

1

Cataloguing in Publication Data is available from the British Library

ISBN 978 0 7553 3110 9

Typeset in Bembo by Avon DataSet Ltd,
Bidford-on-Avon, Warwickshire

Printed and bound in the UK by
CPI Mackays, Chatham ME5 8TD

Headline's policy is to use papers that are natural, renewable and
recyclable products and made from wood grown in sustainable forests.
The logging and manufacturing processes are expected to conform to
the environmental regulations of the country of origin.

HEADLINE PUBLISHING GROUP
An Hachette Livre UK Company
338 Euston Road
London NW1 3BH

www.headline.co.uk
www.hachettelivre.co.uk

For Zalie, Brenna and Kitt,
as always, with love

*We may worry about death but what
hurts the soul most is to live
without tasting the water of its
own essence.*

Jelaluddin Rumi, thirteenth century

PROLOGUE

Bombay, 1885

IT IS THE ELEVENTH day, and Ganesh is about to be immersed in the Arabian Sea.

I am on my way home, but have come down to Bombay's seafront to watch the immense images of the elephant-headed god lowered into the murky water.

The many Ganeshes of varying sizes have been paraded through the streets, and their bearers are now converging along the wide, sandy curve of shore. It is alive as many gather for this final ritual of the Ganesh Chaturthi Festival.

I watch the sea. Nobody notices me; I have worn a sari and oiled my hair, braiding it in a thick plait that hangs over one shoulder. This is the garb I choose for my work, as the women are more comfortable when I visit dressed as one of them. And I, I have worn many disguises.

The sea is shallow here, the waves slow and gentle, washing up on the ribbed sand. The first young man, his Ganesh carefully cradled in his arms, walks into the water. Chants waver through the still evening air: *Return early next year, Oh Victorious Lord Ganesh. Oh Father Ganesh, come again next year.*

In Bombay, the Hindus have their many gods, the Muslims pray to Allah, the Christians worship the Father, Son, and Holy Ghost, the Zoroastrians stand in devotion before fire.

The water is my altar.

I pick up a necklace of red lotus blossom, dropped from a decorated Ganesh, and walk to the water's edge. I take off my sandals and shift my heavy bag to my shoulder. A tiny, panicked gecko darts from between two rocks, and runs over my bare feet. Holding up the edge of my sari, I join the throngs, wading in to the cool water. I throw the flower necklace as others throw their own flowers, or small sweets, or coconuts, into the sea, making their *puja* to Ganesh.

My hand empty, I stand still, looking up. The sky holds faded ribbons of pink.

Suddenly I am weary. I see a little girl, perhaps seven or eight, tightly holding the hand of a woman who is surely her mother. The woman smiles at the child as they stand at the edge of the water. The little girl suddenly jumps up and down, her neatly braided hair bouncing as she points towards the carried Ganesh. Her sari, a cheerful yellow, is clean and crisp, and small bangles jingle on her wrists. The woman's smile broadens, and the obvious love she feels for her child makes something small and mean pinch my chest. At this child's age I had worn a stained charity frock, and my hair had been untended, hanging long and matted down my back. I had run about the mission wild, unnoticed. I knew my mother had never looked at me as this mother looks at her child. She had never held my hand with such easy ownership, such pride.

And then the child looks up at her mother, and I have a clear view of her little face. Although her eyes shine with excitement, her features have a calm confidence, one borne of the knowledge of her place in the world. She knows, I thought, who she is, who she belongs to. And how she is loved.

I offer a silent prayer that she will never know what I knew. That she will never experience the pain of losing all who protected her, the terror of abandonment, the taste of fear. That those clear, bright eyes will never see what I saw, and that she will never have to stoop as low as I did, in order to find my own place in this world. And finally, that she will not view it – this world – with the same loneliness that once clouded my vision.

I tell myself it is only fatigue, after a long day, digging up the old sorrows and resentments, the old shame. I take a deep breath and look away from the mother and child, and away from my secrets, at least for the moment.

I watch as Ganesh is submerged into the murky sea. Slowly, the lapping water covers the long trunk, symbolic of deep scriptural wisdom. Next it hides the large ears, ready to listen to the Lord's *katha* – his tale – with the greatest of zeal. Then the eyes, small in order to view the deity minutely. The water goes over the large forehead, developed for great intellect to realise the Lord. Finally, the top of the head is swallowed. If I still believed in the Christian dogma, I could imagine that the Hindu Ganesh is being baptised.

Although I rarely think about my own attempted baptism, half of my lifetime ago, again the memories come, and I am suddenly once more at the mission, on the banks of the Ravi River. As I look back on my life, I wonder if this was when my story really began, on an August day much like this one, when the water closed over my head as it does over Lord Ganesh's now.

But unlike today, it was not a time of celebration. There were no chants of joy, no gifts, no offered prayers. My baptism had been lonely and grim, performed with brute force, and created out of false hope. Intended to wash away my sins.

CHAPTER ONE

Church of England Medical Mission
The Punjab, India
Year of our Lord, 1871

I CAME PERILOUSLY CLOSE to drowning during the baptism. It was my second; the first, performed when I was an infant, obviously hadn't 'taken'. My mother insisted that my father, being a man of God, perform this repeat baptism in the late summer, just after my fifteenth birthday.

It was the end of August in the Punjab, a time of weary overabundance. The monsoons had flattened the rubbery red and green leaves of the hardy crotons, untended and growing wild around the verandah. The rains sent twisting rivulets down the inner walls of the house and infirmary, the thick, thatched roofs unable to withstand the pounding beat. They drove the family of bandicoots living behind the manure pile to grow even bolder, running across the courtyard seeking shelter, their long ratty tails shining eerily, their greasy coats standing in spikes.

The summer corn had been harvested, and now the stalks crackled and swayed in the wind: the lonely, empty sound of paper crumpled in the hand. Or the sound of fire, licking and destroying. Roving packs of jackals skulked through the rows at night, scavenging for rotted ears, snarling and snapping at each other over the remains. The last unpicked fruit: mangoes and apricots, figs and citrus, had long ago fallen and burst, and the crows picked at the decaying fruit with furtive, stabbing motions, their expressionless eyes darting.

And the Ravi River, which ran a benign, lazy course in summer, shrunken to a thin ribbon, now eagerly swallowed the offering of the monsoons. The endless rain had turned the normally turgid waters into a fast-running river with a surprisingly strong new undercurrent, and, swollen with its own importance, it had grown wide and bold, grabbing and pulling in anything that dared to venture too close to its thundering edges.

The whole mission had a sad, ruined look in the steady grey rain. And what more fitting time for my mother to declare me, as well, ruined, and to try to turn back time, try to re-create me and turn me into a more acceptable image of a missionary's daughter?

I didn't know my parents' plan until the storeroom door was flung open. I heard my mother coming; her heavy footsteps across the verandah always gave me time to hide my illicit book and sit up straight, the Bible open in my lap and my features manifesting false piety and contrition. I had learned that without this expression I would not be let out for another hour.

On this dark, humid afternoon, the skies heavy as they always turned just before the low, black clouds opened, my mother had again shut me in the storeroom at the back of the mission house. Her instructions were the usual: to memorise three passages from the scriptures. This was how she had seen fit to punish me from the time I was six years of age, and able to read. I had spent many, many hours in the storeroom with a Bible in my hands. Probably months, if one added up the twice- or thrice-weekly punishments over the last nine years.

She would not accept the young woman I had become.

She couldn't comprehend that no matter how many Bible passages I read, how many scriptures I knew by heart, my nature would not be changed. And the older I grew the more insulted I became at her basic assumption that if I studied the Bible long enough, eventually I would become a different daughter, one that a missionary and his wife could be proud of.

I knew with complete certainty that it would never happen.

This last time, when my mother discovered me 'running wild with heathen friends' – her description – she had had enough. Something more drastic must be done to ensure that I would not burn in the everlasting flames of hell, and continue to embarrass her.

The monsoon was gathering strength as my father dragged me by the arm across the back garden of the mission house and then continued on, through the remains of the harvested corn and sugar cane fields all the way to the swirling waters of the Ravi River that ran a quarter of a mile behind the mission.

My mother followed; in spite of the wind I could hear the sudden catch of her breath as she tripped on the hard, broken stalks, her uneven gait as she struggled to keep up with my father's – and my – hurried pace. I didn't want to look back at her and have to see the smug justification I knew would be there.

And I didn't want her to see the uncertainty I knew was on my face. For a long time now it had been important that my mother should not read any form of weakness in my expression. Especially not fear.

Yet I cannot explain how unexpectedly frightened I was: not of the wind, or the impending rain, or the river itself – there was nothing unusual about these things determined by

God. It was my father's strange behaviour which made my breath come quick and panicked, my feet leaden with dread. My father was kind and soft spoken. He protected me from my mother's wrath, and I had never seen him act in a violent manner. But today it was as if his mood suddenly reflected the weather.

The Ravi churned with a dull, rhythmic pounding as I was pulled into it, the current sucking and grabbing at my skirt. Although not as cold as it would become in the next few months, the water was choppy and dirty, filled with what it had dragged in from its banks.

'Father,' I said, 'look.' I pointed, with my free hand, at the bloated carcass of a small black dog, on its back with its legs straight up as if they were masts stripped of their sails and yet still hopeful of catching the wind. That same wind whipped my hair loose from its ribbons and blew thick strands across my face. The carcass swirled, briefly, in a small eddy only a few feet from me, and then was swept away. The dog's grey tongue was caught between its scissored teeth. I thought the sight of the dead creature might make my father relent; he was always moved by the dead, whether human or animal.

'Don't make me put my face under this water, Father. Please.' Mushy cobs bobbed past, and a long, winding strip of threadbare black fabric, a Sikh's lost turban, surely, slapped against my skirt, which billowed up around me: a brown serge mushroom. In the next second the black cloth was torn free and hurried after the dead dog as if in pursuit.

I pulled back on my arm, putting on my most pleading expression, but my father only gripped my wrist more firmly. My father, so mild, often distant. *The meek shall inherit the earth.* But there was nothing meek about my father this day. His hand, encircling my wrist, was like an iron manacle, cold and locked. How had my mother convinced him to carry out her ridiculous demand?

'Father,' I asked, one more time, 'why are you doing this?' I had asked him the question twice as I'd stumbled behind him. He hadn't answered. But this time he blinked with a rapid staccato, as he always did when perplexed or upset. When he finally spoke, his normally gentle voice had a rough quality, although this may have only been caused by the wind. It was as if some of the words were ragged, torn.

'Your mother saw you,' he said, 'with Darshan and Jafar.'

'What of it?' I said. Darshan and Jafar were the sons of Sanosh, our cook. They lived in the neighbouring village of Tek Mandi but often came to visit their father at the mission. Darshan was two years older than me, his brother a year younger. 'Father, what of it?'

'She said . . . she said she saw you . . .' he stopped.

'Saw me what?' I questioned, my own voice now as raw as my father's. 'I only talked with them, asking about the goings-on in Tek Mandi, about the cricket match they played, of their sister's up-coming wedding.' I was shouting to be heard over the wind and rushing water. 'And they played one game of *goli*; I just watched. Jafar took all of Darshan's marbles. I did nothing wrong, Father.'

'I want to believe you, Pree,' he said, and looked back at the riverbank, where my mother stood. She lifted her chin, and my father's eyelids fluttered. And then, his other hand gripping the back of my neck, he slowly forced me down.

My fear was joined by shock — utter disbelief that he would actually do this to me, and yet just before the water swirled over my face I found the presence of mind to squeeze my eyes shut and take a gulp of air. I closed my mouth tightly and held my breath. The water had an oily texture to it.

My father held me under for only a few seconds, then brought me up. 'Do you renounce Satan, and take unto you the Lord's name?' he asked.

I opened my mouth to say *Yes, yes I do*, in the same

9

reflexive manner as when I echoed my father's words and amens at our morning prayers. But as my lips parted, water ran into my mouth, and I tasted it, tasted that tepid, brackish water of the Ravi, knew that it carried things dead and useless, and hesitated.

'Go on, Pree,' my father said. 'Say it. Now. The rain is coming.'

I stared into his thin face, seeing how the skin around his narrow nose had grown white. His well-formed lips were bluish under the sandy moustache. There was no green in his hazel eyes; they were brown and muddy as the river, with no hint of compassion.

Did I take the Lord into my heart? Did I really want to? And while I remained silent for that long moment, the skies opened and rain was dumped on to us as if from huge buckets.

Was this the answer I had instinctively waited for?

The hard rain drummed upon the surface of the water and stung my face and neck. I looked at the shore as my father held me in the dirty water up to my waist.

The others who lived at the mission were gathering there, surely having seen the strange spectacle of my father forcing me through the courtyard and into the dead fields.

Glory, my mother's ayah, came from the field to the bank, her dark blue headscarf over her nose and mouth. Following her was Sanosh; he held something in his hand, but I couldn't make out what it was. Finally came Pavit, our leper, slowly hobbling to join the others. He walked with great difficulty, his deformed hands using the knobbed sticks of mango wood to help him make his way on wrapped feet. He usually didn't venture out in the rains; now his soaked bandages would have to be changed.

My mother stood at the front of the tiny, forlorn assembly, arms hanging limply at her sides, her hair blowing wildly about her head, long orange strands lifting and dropping, lifting and dropping. She shifted from foot to foot, hunching her shoulders against the punishing rain.

And then I saw Kai, alone to one side, his arms crossed over his chest. His white dhoti and shirt clung to his hips and chest. His thick, dark hair was flattened against his scalp. Even from a distance I could see the set of his shoulders, the lift of his chin. He stood straight, unmoving, watching with no expression as if he were one of the Hindu stone idols, impervious to rain and wind.

Kai. I hadn't seen him for three days. And now he was here to witness this humiliating exhibition. I closed my eyes in shame.

'Pree,' my father said, again, in that new, painful voice, and I opened my eyes and looked back into his face. 'Pree, take unto you the Lord's name.'

I shook my head, my mouth still firmly closed.

'What do you mean by defying me, Pree? Renounce Satan. Take the Lord Jesus as your everlasting saviour. Say it, say that you take the Lord Jesus into your heart. Say it,' he demanded, his voice competing with the hammering of the rain. 'Say it so I can tell your mother you've repented.'

'I won't,' I shouted, my words blown up and over my head, racing down the river with the same speed as the dead dog. 'I have nothing to repent of.' Of course this was a bald-faced lie; I knew my many sins. 'You can't make me. You cannot force one to undergo baptism, Father. I am no longer an infant.' I raised my voice even louder. 'When I was a baby you chose to baptise me. But this time it's my choice. Mine. Not yours. And especially not Mother's.'

He stared at me as if confused, and then he glanced towards the shore again. I looked, too; my mother came closer to the rushing bank, her eyebrows meeting as she lifted one hand as if to question why my father looked at her, and

11

what, exactly, was happening. The rain was now lashing sideways; I knew it would be my fault when her joints ached tonight.

'You will say it, Pree,' he said, his face now so close to mine that he no longer had to raise his voice. I smelled cumin. I knew I shamed him in front of the others, knew that all I had to do was say that simple word. *Yes.* That was all. *Yes, Father.* But I couldn't. I realised I didn't believe it. I didn't believe that I could take Jesus into my heart; I didn't want Him there. I wanted to be the soul possessor of my own heart. Had I always known this, or was it a revelation that suddenly came down upon me in the same way the rain did, sure and swift, with an unmistakable pulse?

Squeezing tighter now, his long fingers closed almost entirely round the back of my neck and throat – I felt their pressure on my Adam's apple, making me gasp for air – my father took his other hand from my wrist. In one swift movement he placed it, the palm flat, on my chest, and forcefully plunged me backwards into the water. Choking from the pressure on my throat, and shocked by the unexpected and disturbing fact of his hand on my breasts, I didn't take a breath before the water covered my nose and mouth. He held me under for a longer period. I felt as though my chest would rupture; bubbles burst from my nostrils. I tried to stop him, my waving arms and clawing hands ineffectual, able to only grasp, with my fingertips, the sodden cloth of his jacket.

When he finally pulled me up, lessening the pressure on my throat, his hand no longer on my chest, I sputtered and gasped. My father's eyelids fluttered rapidly, surely his vision, like mine, blurred by the rain. But in a sudden rush of understanding I realised he was having one of his chest spasms; now his eyes were rolling upwards. I could see the veined whites and just the bottom curve – crescents of brown

– of his irises. And then he shuddered, and his eyes rolled down, back to their usual position. He said nothing, simply looked at me with an expression I had never before seen, as if I were a stranger, and not his own child.

I met his stare before I was plunged under the surface again and again.

He held me under the water even longer each subsequent time, and finally, as I was brought up into the air after the fifth or perhaps the sixth time – I could no longer keep count – my arms fallen limply at my sides, I heard someone screaming. Was it my mother? The voice was thin, as if coated in wool, and called my name. Except the name I heard wasn't mine, wasn't *Pree*; it was something else, and yet still I recognised it. I went back under the dark, swirling water, and this time the front of my head exploded with a pain I had never before known.

And then . . . everything was red. *Sara lal hai, sara lal hai.* All is red. The Hindi words came to me in the same woolly, muted voice as my name.

All is red.

My father's hands released me, and I understood, with dull confusion, that I floated just under the water's surface, the current sucking, pulling me with its flow. Why didn't I stand, or raise my head into the air? I sunk, my heavy skirt and petticoats and boots weighing me down as if they were made of lead. There was spongy softness of reedy mud under me; I knew I gently floated along the bottom of the river, and yet I no longer felt any sense of urgency or my earlier panic. I could see myself, drifting peacefully, hair around my head like a starfish, like Medusa.

The red burst in my head was even brighter now. I was a spinning nebula, preparing to give birth to new stars; I was a brilliant flame, one of the lamps lit for *Diwali*. I was a coloured kite, my string sparkling with dangerous glass in the sun, flying over the flat roofs of Lahore for the festival of *Basant*. I was part of everything, of the earth and the skies, spiralling out of control, faster and faster, shooting off luminous sparks. The pulsing roar of that splendour filled my ears.

I'm dying, I thought, but it was a strangely exhilarating sensation. My own *atma* was only one of the many souls, another spirit on the wheel of Karma, waiting to be reborn.

I had never felt so pure.

And then, with a shocking, whooshing rush, I was yanked down from the skies, the bright glow of my sunlit glass deadened, cold, in an instant. And in that second of time I was sorry, disappointed to be taken from my moment of wonder. Before I could grieve any further, a flat hand, a fist, I couldn't tell which, pounded between my shoulder blades with powerful blows, the dull yet urgent thudding reverberating through my body. My mouth stretched wide, soundless at first, and then, with a long, sighing gasp, I pulled air into my lungs. I tried to open my eyes, but they refused to do my bidding. Now my lungs flamed as if they truly had been touched by burning glass, and I retched, spitting up the Ravi, gagging as that same strong hand pulled my jaw so that my head turned to one side. I emptied myself of the river water in coughing, gagging, explosions. And when only a trickle belched from my throat I was carried. The rain pounded against my face as the fist had pounded my back.

The jarring motion of my head bouncing against a solid chest brought back some far, distant memory, forgotten until now. *Sara lal hai.*

All is red.

CHAPTER TWO

M Y MOTHER BENT OVER me, attempting to undo my bodice, but her fingers felt huge, clumsy, as she fumbled with the small bone buttons, and I pushed her hand away.

'Come, Pree. Rouse yourself. Take off your wet clothes.'

I tried to focus on her face. I held my breath against the stink of her rotting gums. On my back with my arms at my sides, my hands palm down on the bed, my fingers touched something unfamiliar beneath me. Someone had placed a woven mat over the bedclothes to protect them from my soaked clothing.

'What was it preventing you from accepting the Lord into your heart?' my mother asked, stepping back, holding the ever-present handkerchief to her lips. Above the square of stained white cotton her eyes flashed in the dim circle of light from the lamp.

It had grown dark – was it evening, or simply the heavy clouds blotting out the daylight? How much time had passed between my time in the river and now? The naphtha lamp hung from a hook suspended in the wall over my bed, swaying slightly in the damp, chilled air that whispered through the half-opened louvres. The lamp's flame, even though protected by the smudged glass, flickered.

I could hear rain, although the fury had lessened.

'Pree? Why would you not do your father's bidding? Answer me.'

Long wet strands of my hair were wrapped over my chin and throat, and I weakly reached up to pull them away, lightly pushing away my mother's hand as it returned to hover over my bodice. She moved back a second time, feeling for the wooden chair beside the bed. I heard the creak of its spindly legs as she lowered herself to its cane seat. My unexpected silence obviously surprised my mother. I always had a ready – and usually sharp – retort for her questions or demands.

'Because although some Indians and half-castes do embrace Christianity,' she said, into the quiet room, 'led to it as easily as a wasp to sugar water, you – the daughter of a Church of England minister – refuse to open yourself to our Lord.' She stared down at me pointedly.

Still I said nothing. What she said wasn't true; conversion of the natives appeared impossible, at least for my father. I studied the dancing shadows from the moving flame thrown on to the rough walls with their peeling whitewash. The rhythm of the shadows unexpectedly reminded me of the terrible and brutal dance to the goddess of death, Kali. I had seen a devotee spinning by hooks cut through his back in Lahore the year before. His face wore a look of pious beatification as he whirled over the heads of the crowd, the cruel hooks pulling his skin into sharp, pointed shapes. Triangles, tents, pyramids, I remember thinking, his skin no longer flesh but something else: transformed, sinuous fabric. I had stood with my hands over my mouth, unable to look away from the stretched skin and the man's face. His mouth had been open in a silent cry, yet his eyes, staring and glazed as crystal, were filled with joy, as though witnessing some magnificence unseen by the rest of us.

Now I squeezed my eyes shut. The disciple mutilating his own body, the naked sadhus renouncing all worldly possession and slowly starving themselves to death, the Christians facing the lions, all the suffering for one's beliefs and spiritual attainment whirled through my head.

I didn't want this suffering. Even though my parents were missionaries, I didn't want to be trapped within the confines of religion, forced into their beliefs simply because I was their daughter. I was only fifteen – I wanted to be free to make up my own mind, in time.

I opened my eyes and my mother moved, blocking the moving shadows, slamming the door on my images of the swinging Hindu and the excitable and deadly teeth of the lions. I blinked.

'Well? What do you have to say for yourself, Pree? This wouldn't have happened if you had answered your father as was only proper. I am in complete despair over you. Why are you so stubborn about accepting the Lord's ways?'

I continued to stare at the wall. 'I don't know, Mother,' I said quietly. Perhaps I had used all my energy. I was indeed overcome with the weariness of the struggle. Not just today's struggle, but the one that had gone on for so long – the struggle between my mother and myself, between the Lord and myself.

And I was not only weary, but wary, deeply disturbed by the fact that my father could have given in to my mother's unreasonable demands, and treated me in such a frightening manner. I couldn't lose the image of his crazed, wind-blown appearance, the combination of confusion and unfamiliar fury on his usually placid face.

While I had witnessed his anger a very few times – and these were when he had been trying to prevent ill-treatment of man towards man or animal – he had never mistreated anyone. Although certainly he had been distressed with my behaviour on many, many occasions, it was my mother who disciplined me firmly, with hand and with stick, as well as with confinement in the storeroom. My father's only reaction to what he referred to as my antics was a long, sorrowing look and the usual questions, to which I had to give the proper responses.

'Where do sinners go, Pree?'

' "The wicked shall be turned into hell, and all the nations that forget God," Father, Psalm 9: verse 17.'

'And Pree, how can you escape this hell?'

' "Believe on the Lord Jesus Christ, and thou shalt be saved," Acts 16: verse 31.'

He would nod, then, and turn away.

From the time I was ten years old I had known, with sad certainty, that although my father was kindly and well meaning, he was weak of character. He was bullied by my mother. He could not stand up to Glory or Sanosh, the servants. Even Marta, our water buffalo, would lower her head stubbornly when he attempted to hitch her to the cart. And he had no influence, spiritually, over the natives who came to our mission for medical help. In my memory he had been unable to harvest Christianity in even one of them, except for our own Pavit. I saw now that apart from reading his Bible and presiding over morning prayers, he spoke little about anything of a religious nature. He carried out his work in the infirmary, helping those who came. But he no longer exhibited a desire, or even interest, in speaking to the patients about evangelism.

No, it was my mother who carried the power and strength in our family, who made me endlessly repeat the scriptures to her, ensuring herself they were firmly fixed in my head. As the wife of a minister it was not behoving that she be unable to effortlessly bring forth simple scriptures, and yet I saw, more and more, her struggle in trying to recall Bible verses. It appeared that her memory was not as it once was, and this angered her.

She carried this anger over many things: the dead babies in the graves behind the mission, the ants in the flour, the creeping rot on the walls, her own ill health. Anger for not being able to force me to be the kind of young woman she wished me to be.

I witnessed her anger, and while I was young I was a victim of it. I didn't attempt to understand it, but simply accepted it, in the way of a child. But that time had long passed, and I would not allow her to treat me as she treated my father and the others at the mission. *I* had not brought her here, to this miserable run-down mission on a dusty, narrow country lane running off the Grand Trunk Road. I had not chosen for her a life of pious poverty. I was not responsible for her misery. And I would not be blamed for it.

My mother was tall, almost as tall as my father, and raw boned, her wrists and collarbones knobbly. Her hands were large and permanently red. Her thick, curly hair, once a bright red-orange, was now faded ginger, falling about her face and shoulders in fizzled strands. Unlike my father, and in spite of her ginger hair, her skin didn't burn, and she rarely wore anything on her head. She was covered in freckles which seemed, as she grew older, and with the constant exposure to the sun, to run together, giving her skin a darkened, blotchy appearance. She usually wore a limp, wrinkled cotton frock with no stays, no adornment at all, not even a lace trim on her collar. When she was working in the infirmary she often unbuttoned her collar and cuffs, and on rare occasions even rolled up her sleeves, exposing her sinewy freckled wrists and forearms. Once I observed my father speaking to her about this in a low voice.

'Mother?' he said. He always called her Mother when we were alone, and Mrs Fincastle in front of anyone else, including the natives who couldn't understand English. He glanced at the doorway and nodded: two Hindu men, one limping heavily and helped by the other, stood on the verandah. 'Your sleeves,' he said, with a quiet, firm tone.

She raised her chin. 'We're not in a drawing room in London, may I remind you, Reverend.' She chose to call him Reverend both in public and private. 'I'll keep my sleeves rolled up if I so wish.'

This is how it usually was between my parents: he requested, she defied.

And yet in spite of my mother's lack of respect for my father, she still wished to discuss her health with him. She constantly demanded attention from him on this topic, seeking his sympathy. Her health was her favourite topic; she stressed that she wasn't well because of the horrors of living in India. She discussed cases from the medical books in the infirmary, pointing out her similar symptoms, determining that she'd contracted a certain illness, occasionally trying to convince my father to bleed and purge her.

But at her pleadings he would only shake his head in a resigned manner, obviously dismayed at my mother's requests for invasive treatments to rid her body of toxins. And although he also told her not to swallow any more medicine, she still drank liquid calomel. When I had, a few years ago, asked my father what this was that I often noticed my mother dosing herself with, he explained that it was a chalky mixture of mercury and chlorine. He shook his head, looking out at the fields with a grim expression. 'In spite of all that I tell her, she believes it protects her from many illnesses, or will cure the imaginary ones she has. And she continues to acquire it from someone in Lahore, although I no longer order it. I've never discovered where she gets it or keeps it.'

He looked from the fields to me. 'It's what's caused the problems with her mouth.'

Up until then I simply accepted the state of my mother's mouth as rotting teeth or a gum disease; I'd seen many of both at the infirmary. But now I understood that it was because she'd taken the calomel for so long that her saliva came too readily to fill her mouth. This was why she had to hold a handkerchief to her lips – to mop up her constant drooling. But the handkerchief covering her mouth was also vanity, because the calomel was slowly rotting her gums. At times they bled, and her teeth were brown and softening, and couldn't remain too much longer in her head. All of this created, in her mouth, the odour of decaying meat. I had too often been the recipient of that hot, stinking breath, sometimes peppered with frothy saliva, upon my face as my mother grabbed me and pulled me close, scolding me for various disobediences.

'Will her mouth grow worse?' I had asked my father.

He nodded. 'Eventually. And it can also . . .' He stopped, looking away from me.

'It can also what?' I prompted, but he would speak no further of it.

The look on his face made me go out to the infirmary with a candle that night, and spend a long time looking through his line of musty books. Eventually I found what I was looking for in Buchan's *Domestic Medicine* – the properties and usefulness of calomel. I read, pulling the candle even closer, that while calomel does have healing qualities for cholera, and is a cathartic, it should only be taken in small doses for a short time because of its effect on the mouth.

But the most chilling discovery – something my father couldn't bring himself to speak of – was that the mercury in calomel can also affect the brain, slowly resulting in fatal madness.

Lying on my bed in my wet clothes, all fight had gone out of me. On that particular windy evening as the monsoons swept through the plains of northern India, I had no energy left to spar with my mother. Surely my unfamiliar lethargy was a direct cause of the ordeal I had just suffered.

But, feeling as I did, maybe I had a glimmer of understanding of my mother's discontent. Was this the way she always felt? I looked at her; she was studying me with an odd, somehow careful expression.

'You don't know why you can't accept the Lord into your heart? That's your answer? You don't know? You, the daughter born of missionaries, born into a home which has always revered the Lord most high, which supports itself through that devotion, don't know why you can't feel as your father and I do?'

'Yes. I don't know,' I repeated, suddenly annoyed – no, angry – with her persistent questions. Especially after what I'd just gone through. I found my old strength, and sat up. 'I don't know. And I can't. I simply can't, Mother.' My voice rose to a dangerous level as I stared at her. I know she saw that I did speak the truth, for her look was suddenly sharp, and troubled, and this brought me further strength. And also a strange, slightly guilty pleasure, to witness her dismay.

'How could Father have treated me so cruelly?' I asked, growing ever louder. 'I almost drowned,' I said, trying to sound indignant. But perhaps it came out as simply petulant. I undid my bodice, then pulled down the top of my dress, wriggling out of it.

My mother rose from the chair, the dry wood giving a tiny shriek of relief. Her shoulders were high and stiff as she turned so that she wouldn't see me undress. 'Really, Pree. You are too immodest,' she said.

I stopped in the middle of peeling off my wet petticoat, suddenly remembering the strange statement my father had made about Darshan and Jafar. 'What did you tell Father about me with Sanosh's boys?' I asked. 'What lies did you make up to convince him that I must be baptised again?'

She didn't turn to face me, and I heard the sucking sound she made when she tried to swallow her excess saliva.

'Mother?'

'You're too old to be running about with boys,' she said.

'Running about? I haven't run about – as you call it – for some time, Mother.' When I was much younger I *had* been a rather wild and unkempt child, I suppose. My parents were always overly busy, and I had no ayah to watch over me like the English children in the Lahore cantonment.

But those days had long passed. And so for my mother to insinuate that I was still that bedraggled, careless child was insulting.

'Darshan and Jafar stopped by to visit their father; I was only talking with them, watching them with their marbles. I've known them all these years, ever since Sanosh came when I was so young. You know that. They're my friends.' I tossed my ruined boots to the floor with an angry thud.

My mother whirled around at the sound. 'They are most certainly *not* your friends. And you shan't have anything more to do with them. We shall speak no more of it, but you are forbidden to associate with those young men.' She snicked her tongue. 'Cover your paps.'

Ignoring her request, wearing only my linen under-drawers, I sat on the edge of my bed as I rolled down my stockings. I opened my mouth to argue as she crossed the room, but then closed it as I studied her.

'Mother?' I pulled my nightdress from under my pillow. 'Mother,' I repeated, more loudly, putting the nightdress over my head and slipping my arms into the sleeves.

She was at the doorway, but looked over her shoulder at me.

Under my nightdress, I stepped out of my drawers. 'What happened? Why did Father let me go?' Now I remembered the thin screams. I slid the damp mat from the bed on to the floor and lay down, still watching my mother's face.

Her expression underwent a change; it was as if she were

debating with herself. 'Your father had one of his . . . turns,' she finally said, and I suddenly remembered how his eyes had rolled upwards as his face contorted. 'He . . . he couldn't hold you any longer, and let you go. You know how it comes over him,' she said, stressing each word in an uncharacteristic manner.

When his periodic chest ailment occurred, my father's heart bucked and jumped in an irregular dance, and a weakness overtook him, drenching him with sweat, and he had to sit, tearing at his collar and gasping to breathe.

'And he let you go,' my mother repeated, slowly, each word very formed and clear as she stared at me as if I were partly deaf and needed to study her lips to understand. 'He had to. He himself fell forward into the river. Sanosh and Kai rushed out and supported him, dragging him back to the shore. You . . . you were just . . . standing there, I'm sure of it. I'm sure I saw you standing,' she said, too loudly now. Defensive. 'We were concerned for your father. But then . . . we didn't know . . . Sanosh and Kai were still helping him out of the water, and I didn't . . . I was concerned about him, of course, while you—'

'While I what?' I interrupted. 'While I was *not* to be concerned about?' *I could have drowned.*

'It all happened so quickly, and the rain made it difficult to see, but Kai – it was Kai who realised – who ran back into the water, and found you, lifting and carrying you back to the house.' She spoke rapidly, her voice as hard and angry as mine, now that I had challenged her. She dabbed at the saliva snaking down her chin

She moved into the darkness near the door, and I could no longer see her face. I lay in a circle of light. A silver moth fluttered about the lamp, then touched the glass, trembling in ecstasy before falling to the folds of my nightdress.

'You don't remember Kai bringing you back here?' she

asked, and in that instant I wondered if it were really she who had screamed. Could it have been me? Or was it just inside my head, the effects of struggling to breathe? What had I been thinking as I sunk under the surface of the river? Something disturbing, something . . . a memory.

'Make sure you stuff your boots,' she said, in the open doorway now, 'or they'll shrink.'

'I'm never going back into the storeroom,' I said, although quietly. I needed her to understand what this day had done to me. 'I'm no longer a child to be punished in such a silly way.'

She didn't respond, closing the door behind her.

I picked up the dead moth by its still wings, studying its shape. I couldn't remember its Latin name; I would ask Kai tomorrow. I leaned over and set it on the stack of books on the floor on the other side of my bed.

'I almost drowned,' I said again, although more quietly, into the empty room. What if Kai hadn't returned, this very day, from wherever he had gone? How long would it have been before my mother, or Glory or Sanosh or Pavit noticed that I had disappeared? Would my mother have sent Sanosh back for me, or would she herself have waded into that filthy, rushing water to search for me, only to discover it was too late, that I'd been swept downstream?

I knew my father would not be able to live with it should I have drowned. It would surely be the final blow to his already shaky beliefs; I couldn't imagine how he'd carry on. But would my mother feel any responsibility, any guilt? She would mourn the loss of her only living child, oh yes, but would she accept it as the Lord's decision, and consider it simply another pillar of her martyrdom?

I pulled up the thin coverlet and turned on to my side. My pillow was already sodden from my thick wet hair. In the flickering shadows I looked at the heap of my soaked clothing, the heavy scuffed boots, their high edges already curling.

I tried to remember what it was that had seemed so real and frightening just as I had sunk into that strange, brilliant state under the surface of the Ravi River.

I thought of Kai, carrying me. It was his chest I had rested against. I wanted to remember the feel of his arms, holding me.

And then I thought of my father's face, looming over me, his pale hair around his head in a crazed nimbus. I had trusted him, and he had failed me.

My eyes burned, and I squeezed them shut, but hot tears – angry, confused – came, and I couldn't stop them. I only wanted to sleep, and have this terrible day over.

But sleep wouldn't come. I cried as I counted the times a mynah called in the dark, wet air. Sixteen.

CHAPTER THREE

I WAS ALWAYS COUNTING. Eight was my favourite number; when I found something adding up to eight – whether in nature or contrived by man – I was sure it was a harbinger of good luck. Any multiples of it might – possibly – also herald a positive outcome.

I counted the number of steps I took, the clouds above me, the bright green parakeets gathered in the peepul tree in the courtyard each morning, the gleaming copper pots Sanosh lined up outside the *rasoi* where he prepared our food, or the times Marta bellowed as she waited to be milked each morning. I counted how many pins were in my mother's hair; I counted how many times my father used the phrase *Praise the Lord* during morning prayers.

Until recently my father often spoke to me of various issues; he informed me of events taking place in the Punjab that he heard about in Lahore, and sometimes even asked my opinion. I realised he treated me with a certain respect; this was why his attempts to baptise me, against my will, were all the more shocking.

The morning of my attempted baptism my father had uttered *Praise the Lord* eleven times, always an unlucky number for me. Now I wondered if it were a portent of what had happened: that my father, in an attempt to make me a better Christian, had instead pushed me ever further from his beliefs.

My father was the Reverend Mr Samuel Fincastle of London, and had established this particular mission outside of Lahore when I was a little over two years old.

His own father had been just prosperous enough to allow his son to choose a craft; my father attended the Royal College of Surgeons in London, where he learned the workings of the organs inside the body and how to set bones and deal with a variety of ophthalmologic and skin disorders. He said he imagined this would be his life's work. But one day, he had told me, in a dreary cellar in East London, working over the torn body of a child trampled by a team of runaway horses, he received the calling. He would never speak much of this, simply saying he knew with complete conviction as he gazed upon a curious light filling the dying child's face, that he was needed to help the poor heathen souls find their true salvation through evangelicalism. He then studied theology, and caught the fervour for what he saw as this strange and chaotic land through the stories of a senior minister who had lived here for twenty years.

He was not young when he came to India; all his studies had taken him into his thirties before he was able to find the means to marry my mother, younger than he was by fifteen years. And so he arrived in India in 1849 to spread the word of the Lord and to minister to the sick. His first mission was a small one in the city of Allahabad, situated halfway between Calcutta in the south-east and Delhi in the north-west. Although my parents had been married for a year before my father left England, my mother's difficult confinement had prevented her from accompanying my father.

Baby Elijah had been born in England four months after my father left for this country. Although my older brother lived for close to two years, he had been born with a twisted spine and weak lungs, and his health was so delicate that it was impossible for my mother to take him on the long and arduous sea voyage to India. When he finally succumbed to his frailties, my mother, after a period of mourning, sailed to India and joined my father at the end of 1853.

They had been apart for almost four years.

Together they maintained the mission in Allahabad for another three years; my sister Alice Ann was born and died there, and I was born there as well, on August 17, 1856. We had moved north, to the Punjab, to start this mission in 1858, after the last flames of the two-year rebellion against the English in northern India by the sepoys – Indian soldiers employed by the British army – had been smothered.

Since my parents had been unsuccessful in converting the Hindus and Muslims who lived in the area surrounding Allahabad, they felt their chances might improve here, in the northern Punjab, when this part of the country was still unsettled from the recent bloodshed of the rebellion. They imagined that they could build on the possible introspection of the natives on the crimes committed against the Europeans. Constructing the mission with its infirmary on a strip of countryside, granted to my father by the Church of England, we were a three-hour cart ride from the grand city of Lahore.

Following the course of the next few years at the new mission came my other siblings: Elizabeth, and finally Gabriel, born when I was six. Like Alice Ann, neither Elizabeth nor Gabriel lived beyond infancy. I don't remember Elizabeth, or much of anything before that, but it seems all my memories started shortly before Gabriel died. I can clearly recall his shock of orange hair, the same colour as my mother's once was, and his tiny, wan face, pale as chalk. His high, trembling call was like that of a weak kitten. His cries went on day after day, night after night, endlessly, it seemed to my child's ear. And then one morning when I awoke I realised the sound I heard wasn't my little brother's usual thin cry, but my mother's wail. And with that I knew he was dead and had flown up to heaven on his glorious wings to be with the others, Elijah and Alice Ann and Elizabeth, another child to sit with the lambs at the feet of Jesus. Another angel to look down upon me.

Gabriel had lived longer than the two little girls born before him: he had survived almost four months before this land claimed him. Although Elijah was buried in England, and Alice Ann in Allahabad, there were four headstones at our mission cemetery, for my mother could not bear to leave her memories behind. The white marble headstones were small and square, with the children's names chipped into the smooth face. They stood in a fenced area in the shade of a sheesham tree in a cleared space of field behind the mission. The recessed names turned green in wet weather, mossy and damp, and I often ran my fingers over the furry pattern. One of my weekly jobs was to weed the tiny cemetery and trim the mounds of red and pink and white impatiens, planted by my mother and growing in abundance on each grave, as well as wash the white stones of both summer dust and muddy monsoon splashes.

Four Fincastle children, all dead. And me, just me, christened Priscilla but called Pree, very much alive in this shabby mission in the alternating rotten lushness and dust of the Punjab.

The morning after my failed baptism, I took the tiny hand mirror with its enamelled handle – one of my discoveries from the latest charity box – and studied my reflection. I looked first at my brown eyes, flecked with gold, then moved the mirror downward to my nose and mouth, then my chin, and, finally, to my throat. The darkening bruises of my father's fingers were there, purple-fresh, as if pansies had pressed their faces against my skin. I placed my own fingers over the rounded, petal-like shapes, wondering how my father and I would behave towards each other this morning.

In spite of my shock and anger at him, some small part of me pitied him. I knew he didn't wish to hurt me, knew he would be horrified to see the evidence of brutality, never before demonstrated, on his only living child. But there was nothing to be done about the marks. I currently possessed three frocks, and none had a collar high enough to cover my bruised throat.

I heard movement from the other side of the thin wall that separated my bedroom from my parents': my father's usual dry cough upon arising, the dull rasp of my mother's voice. My tiny room was almost filled by the narrow bed with its high wooden spindles, draped with greying mosquito netting in the hot and wet months. The sagging mattress was felt stuffed; every year I had to open it and take out the hard, flattened felt and re-stuff it. A scratchy coir mat covered the uneven floorboards on one side of the bed, and on it sat the brittle cane chair. The only other furniture was a high dresser of mango wood over which was propped an image of the Red Fort painted on to wood that Kai had once given me after making a trip to Delhi. My frocks and petticoats hung from nails in the wall.

Still touching my throat, I moved to my bedroom window, looking out into the back garden with the three simple one-room huts belonging to Glory, Kai and Pavit. Built of bricks of lime, molasses, brick-dust and cut hemp, called pukka, they were formed wet, and became harder and tougher than stone when dry. Each hut had a woven curtain over the low doorway, and one uncovered window at the back.

I wanted to thank Kai for what he had done yesterday. Thank him for saving me, not as my father wished to save my soul, but for saving my life. I grimaced at the realisation that it was Kai who, as he held me and pounded my back, had seen me belching and spitting up the revolting river water. I hoped he was at the mission today; more and more he disappeared for days at a time, and when he was gone it was as if I waited in some strange, suspended emptiness. I watched for him, listened for the sound of his whistle as he walked up the road, his arms swinging in quick time with his step. I sometimes surreptitiously checked his hut before going to bed, wanting to reassure myself he was lying on his charpoy, reading or studying one of his maps.

There was no sign of him this morning.

With one more glance at my bruised neck in the tiny mirror, I silently opened my bedroom door, which led directly into the dining room.

The dining room held a rectangular table of stained pine, which was at all times covered with a threadbare damask cover, to hide its poor quality. Around it sat four Queen Ann chairs with padded seats of faded burgundy velvet. There was a sideboard with an assortment of mismatched china and a silver tea service on its tray. A doorway led into the sitting room, and on the opposite wall was a side door leading to the same verandah which ran from the front in an L-shape around the side of the house. The shuttered windows in both the dining room and sitting room faced the road.

My father was at the table, his back to me, head down as he read from his Bible. The idea of sitting across from him at the silent table, the marks on my neck shouting out what had happened the day before, was deeply unsettling.

Although dressed for my work in the infirmary, in my simple cotton frock and white apron, I was barefoot. I hadn't stuffed my boots as my mother had instructed me, and when I tried to put my lisle-covered foot inside, the leather was still wet and cold, too tight. I could not force my foot inside, and so I'd taken off my stockings and crept behind my father, wanting to slip out the side door. I was almost at the door when the floorboards, swollen with damp, creaked.

I looked at my father almost guiltily – although what, I asked myself at the same time, did I have to feel guilty about? His head rose in a quick, bird-like way at the sound, and he turned, and then stood and came to me, putting his hand on my arm. I looked down at his hand, trying to stay angry, trying to dredge up all the shock and rage I had felt the evening before as I lay on my bed, going over my father's strange behaviour. But I couldn't. I stared at his fingers, so long and pale, seeing a few sparse, straight hairs on them, and couldn't retrieve that anger.

'Pree,' he said. 'Please.'

I took my eyes from his fingers, and looked at his sleeve. He wore his black jacket instead of his usual daily one. He had two – this one, his better one – and a threadbare tweed. I knew he had on his Sunday jacket because his tweed would still be damp from yesterday. Nothing dried during the time of the monsoons. By tonight the tweed would carry a faint threading of green mould which would have to be briskly brushed away before he could wear it again.

'I . . . I wish to ask your forgiveness. I'm not entirely . . . not sure what came over me yesterday,' he said.

Finally I looked into his face. His eyes were red rimmed, and the circles beneath them, the same violent purple as my bruises, stood darker than usual. I knew he hadn't slept well, if at all.

'You're a difficult child, Pree,' he said. 'No. You're no longer a child. You're a difficult young woman. And this is why we – your mother and I – expect more of you.'

'That's no reason to treat me as you did,' I said, my voice toneless, and I lifted one hand, my free hand, to gesture at the dark flowers blooming on my throat.

His eyes slid to my neck and he winced as if his chest pained, but I knew it was the sight of his own fingerprints on my skin. 'Yes. You're absolutely right. There was no reason for any of my behaviour.'

'You only did it because Mother told you to.'

I wanted him to agree, to blame my mother for his actions.

'No. I also believed that it might help your wayward spirit if you—'

'But Mother put you up to it,' I interrupted.

He took his hand from my arm. 'Sit down now, Pree, and eat your breakfast,' he said. 'Will you accept my apology?'

'Yes.' I had forgiven him when I looked at his fingers on my arm, the ghostly hairs somehow evoking sympathy. 'But didn't she force you into it? You would never—'

'That's enough, Pree,' he said, his voice slow and heavy as he went back to his chair and picked up the Bible. 'Come. Come and sit down.'

I went to the table but didn't sit, standing behind my chair and gripping the back of it.

'We won't discuss this any further,' my father said, raising his chin at a sudden shuffle. 'Hopefully that's Sanosh with the porridge. He's late this morning.'

But it wasn't Sanosh on the verandah. It was my mother, emerging from her bedroom into the sitting room. Her hair was down, tangled, and she still wore her dressing gown as she passed through the sitting room and leaned heavily against the door jamb of the dining room.

'Where's Glory? She hasn't been in to attend to me yet,' she said, with weary annoyance.

'Help your mother, Pree,' my father said, his voice so exhausted, somehow grief filled, that I silently turned and followed my mother back into her room. I couldn't start this day with another act of rebellion, another pique of temper.

What my father had said was true; I was no longer a child, but a young woman.

It was difficult to brush through my mother's hair – even though it appeared to have grown thin of late – using her prized tortoise-shell brush with its boar bristles. Her hair needed washing; it was lank and gave off an oily odour. And because it was so dirty it was difficult to pin it up into the arrangement she preferred. The strands slid this way and that under the tiny metal clamps she handed up to me one at a time.

'You're not doing it properly,' she finally complained, taking the dish of hairpins from her lap and slamming it on to the top of her dressing table. Some of the pins scattered on the worn surface. She hadn't commented on my marked throat; did she even notice? 'Fetch Glory. Although she's generally useless, at least she's capable of doing my hair as I wish.'

I left the room, passing my father, who now had his head bent over the bowl Sanosh must have brought in. I saw his scalp, too pale. He still read, slowly spooning the thick, steaming porridge into his mouth. No matter what the season, my father ate his hot oatmeal every morning.

I went to Glory's hut. She was lying on her bed on her side, propped on one elbow, idly trying on glass bangles. A half-eaten *roti* lay on the cover of her rope charpoy.

'Please, Glory, my mother needs you,' I told her, and she looked at me with just the slightest hint of insolence, pulling off the bangles. They clinked and chimed as she set them back into their box with deliberate but annoyed movements.

At the sight and smell of the fresh *roti* my stomach contracted with hunger, but I didn't want to sit in the dining room with my father. And I didn't want the bland porridge, with its pat of butter and sprinkling of salt my father said gave it flavour.

Instead, I went to the *rasoi*, the kitchen hut off the side verandah where all the food for the mission was prepared. Sanosh didn't look at me, as he was busy making more *rotis*. He pulled the dough into balls, flattening them by tossing them from hand to hand, then slapping them on to the top of the clay oven. As I so often had as a child, I crouched beside him and fanned the flames with a cluster of thin dried stalks to keep the heat intense; each *roti* took only a few minutes.

As I fanned, I looked at the road that ran in front of the mission house, separated from our courtyard by a wooden fence. Fences which separated the farms and kept animals enclosed at night were hardened mud, but ours was wood, befitting, I suppose, what my parents deemed to be suitable for a Christian mission. I watched a farmer with his bullock cart piled impossibly high with hay rumble by. A few *koss* in one direction lay Tek Mandi, and in the other direction was the village of Dipha. There were other tiny nameless clusters of mud and thatch homes where the farmers who worked the surrounding fields lived; it was these farmers and their families who made up most of our patients.

I doubted Kai was on his way to one of the villages, for there could be nothing of interest in any of them for a person such as he. Surely he had gone south, only a ten-minute walk to the Grand Trunk Road, and was now on his way to Lahore.

In the opposite direction to Lahore, hundreds of miles north, the road led to Rawalpindi and into the North-West Frontier and the city of Peshawar. And beyond Peshawar lay the Khyber Pass, entrance to Afghanistan. Although I had never travelled further than Lahore, when young I had studied the map of the world my mother unrolled once a week for my geography lessons. She had eventually given the map to Kai; to this day it hung on the wall of his hut, creased and worn, the country marked in Indian ink by Kai in some pattern I didn't understand. He had many maps, rolled into long cylinders and tied with twine. I often came upon him poring over one, his finger tracing the lines of roads and rivers and his lips moving as if arguing with someone unseen.

When the last *roti* was baked, I silently watched Sanosh begin to prepare *sookh aloo*, the flavoured potatoes I loved. He pulled out his clay bowls of spices and seeds. Without looking at me he placed a small pile of bright yellow turmeric seed on a heavy stone and passed it to me. With another stone, I ground it while his deft fingers chopped cooked potato.

I had acted as Sanosh's *masalchi* always; he had taught me to grind the spices, placing little hills of greens, browns and yellows on the stone and demonstrating the motion necessary. I loved doing this, the easy, repetitive movement, the smells of the turmeric and coriander and ginger, the cloves and cinnamon and nutmeg and black pepper filling my head. Sanosh was kindly and patient; I could always count on him to slip me something tasty when I passed the *rasoi*. Although his home was in the nearby village of Tek Mandi, Sanosh stayed at the mission during the week, sleeping on a woven mat in the *rasoi* beside his pots, making sure the foodstuff was untouched by wild animals or thieving *dacoits*. One afternoon a week he went to his village – his wife had died some years earlier, but his oldest unmarried daughter cooked and cleaned for him and his sons – after he had finished scouring the pots and had left dinner prepared.

Now he heated oil in a heavy pan, and after a few minutes dropped in a cumin seed. It sizzled and floated; the oil was hot enough. He dropped in asafetida, stirring it, and then more cumin and fennel and mustard seeds. When the seeds popped he added the chillies and stirred everything until it was darkened, the chillies swollen. He dumped in the potatoes, then, still watching the pan, he put out his hand. I gave him the stone with the turmeric ground into a fine paste, which he scraped into the gently bubbling mixture. As he stirred it gently, I took a square of potato and popped it into my mouth, making a sound of pleasure. Sanosh looked up at me, smiling, and I returned the smile. But then his smile faded, and I realised he had seen my neck. I put my hand over the marks.

Immediately Sanosh lowered his head and went back to his stirring, saying nothing. Steam rose with the sizzle, and Jassie's nose appeared.

Jasmine was my dog, named after my favourite flower, although I called her Jassie. Her nose in the air, sniffing the odour of the cooking food, she slunk out from the hollowed space under the wooden frame of the *rasoi*, her tail between her legs. She was not a pariah dog, but had probably briefly been owned by someone. Wary, she would come close enough to take the food I set on the ground for her, although not allowing me to touch her. She had either been driven away or run off, and had arrived in the courtyard one evening, gaunt and cowed, when I was about nine.

She had dug out a space under the *rasoi* when she was carrying her first litter of puppies at the mission, and since then had claimed the safe, hidden hollow as her home. But she would never drop her litter there; I don't know where she went to have her puppies, nor what happened to them. She would simply disappear for two or three weeks, and then return, her dugs already withering. I could only assume the pups died, although once she brought one back in her mouth, keeping it under the *rasoi* with her. He grew into a fat little thing, friendly and confident, and I loved him. I was able to carry him around and he had no fear of me. But then, one night, when he was a few months old, I was awakened by the snarls and growls of jackals, Jassie's panicked barking and high-pitched squealing.

The next morning the pup was gone. Jassie's muzzle was bitten badly, and she was missing part of an ear. She lay with her head on her paws for the next two days, staring into the cornfields, the torn remains of her ear festering.

She had fought hard, and I shed tears for the puppy, and for her.

I had just finished my breakfast at the *rasoi* when I heard a rustle. Kai was sitting outside his hut studying an unfurled paper; he was at the mission, after all. The unease I'd carried since yesterday disappeared at seeing him.

Tossing Jassie the last of my *roti* – which she swallowed whole with two furtive gulps, her bony spine humped in her fearful haste to finish – I went to Kai, taking him a bowl of the spicy *sookh aloo*. 'What are you doing, Kai?' I asked, holding out the bowl and wooden spoon. He looked up as if startled, folding the paper he had been reading with hurried, almost furtive movements.

'Nothing of interest, Pree,' he said, offhandedly, tossing the paper into the doorway of his hut. His actions belied the studied indifference of his voice. He reached for the bowl. 'Thank you,' he said, and I saw that his fingers were stained with something dark – was it ink? He had a fresh cut on his cheekbone, and one eye looked slightly puffy.

'I . . . I wish to thank you. For yesterday,' I said, and he looked at my face, then my neck, and simply nodded. 'I don't know what would have happened if you hadn't returned. Hadn't been here.'

He busied himself stirring the *sookh aloo* to cool it.

My mother pounded out the determined melody of 'How Sweet the Name of Jesus Sounds' on the pianoforte in the sitting room. Its off-key strains filled the courtyard.

'My father . . . I don't understand what came over him,' I said, hoping Kai would comment, but he appeared consumed with stirring his food. 'You've been gone for three days,' I went on, slightly louder, and, perhaps at my tone, he looked up. 'What happened to your face?'

He touched the newly scabbed, crooked line. 'An accident.'

'Kai,' I said, 'you never tell me anything any more.'

He shook his head. 'Because there's no need for you to know,' he answered, his voice suddenly hard and quick, as if I were an annoying child.

But I wasn't a child. I was fifteen, past the age most Indian girls are married, and many with more than one child.

I studied his injured face, and thought of what I had witnessed, only the week before.

It had been early evening, and I had gone for a walk along the road, Jassie a few paces behind me. I heard distant drumming, and cut across a field to the sound, thinking it might be villagers celebrating some event. As I drew nearer to the rhythmic sound I saw, through the sugar-cane stalks, the flames of a dancing fire, and around it moving bodies in the clearing. Men's voices rumbled, too low for me to hear, and instinctively I did not wish to be seen. I crept closer but stayed low, hidden by the canes. And then I saw Kai. He was with three other young men. One drummed, with rapid, almost frenzied beats, and Kai and the other two men threw between them what I thought was the body of another man. But I quickly realised it couldn't be a human, for they tossed it too easily, as if it were of little weight. Squinting, I saw straw protruding from the loosely wrapped cotton in the shape of a head.

The figure was dressed in the clothing of an English soldier: the red coat, the black trousers. Kai then held the figure over his head with both hands. He shouted something; the noise of the flames blocked his words. He threw the form into the fire and rose his fist above his head, his mouth open as he continued to shout, his voice joined by the others.

The flames danced eerily on his face, and his eyes held a look I had never seen. I turned and ran, suddenly confused, wishing I hadn't witnessed the scene. Kai's face held grim joy, yet also obviously hatred.

I shivered now, thinking of him in that unexpectedly frightening situation. My face must have reflected the distress of that memory, for Kai, surely thinking I was hurt by his sharp response, immediately set down the bowl and stood, facing me. 'I'm sorry, Pree,' he said. 'I just mean . . . it would only bore you.'

'I don't think so,' I said, and as he lifted his arm to brush his hair from his forehead, I smelled the scent of him, so familiar.

'Your mother has come to the verandah.' He watched over my head. 'Shouldn't you go to prayers?'

I left without speaking further, feeling, as I always did now, that there was something unsaid, something in the air between us that disturbed me in a way I couldn't name.

It had never been this way until a year ago. Was it he who had changed, or I? Or perhaps it was both of us.

Kai was Glory's son, and six years older than I. I had been six when Gabriel was born, and I remember him clearly. So Kai would have known my every move: my first step, my first words. I had so many memories of him holding my hand as we walked together to the Grand Trunk Road, or him taking me to the Ravi in the warm weather, where he showed me how to make flat stones skip across the smooth surface of the water, and told me the names of the ducks that floated and bobbed on the surface. He said that in Lahore, love songs were sung on the banks of the Ravi, and haunting strains could be heard in its murmur. 'Do you hear them, Pree?' he would ask, and I would go to my knees, leaning towards the water, trying to hear the mysterious songs. Sometimes I said

41

Yes, yes, I hear one, Kai, and he would laugh kindly, and nod at me.

When I was a child I had tried so hard to please him, to make him proud of me. Then I thought of him as my brother; I even sometimes called him by the respected Hindi title: *bhai* – big brother. He had stepped in to protect me from the bullying of the older children who accompanied a parent to the infirmary, and he sometimes hid me from my mother when she looked for me, wanting to punish me for one of my many childish misbehaviours. During the monsoons, the courtyard's hard, baked earth that cracked and fissured during the blazing heat of summer turned to sour-smelling, churned mud. Some years it was so deep that when I was small, Kai occasionally had to pull me free from the sucking grasp that swallowed my boots to the ankle. I so loved the feel of his arms around me as he struggled to release me that occasionally I purposely waded into the thick ooze so that I could call to him, wanting to have him appear with a concerned look on his face as he came to my rescue.

And while my mother had taught me to read and parse and scribe and do sums, it was from Kai that I learned so much about the world around me: about the people we lived amongst, the creatures of the earth and the air and the water, the rhythms of the seasons, the constellations in the night sky and the wonders of strange, foreign lands. Over the years Kai had also taught me to read and write Hindi and Urdu, as well as speak a good deal of Persian, simply because I begged, when I saw him under the peepul tree with his pen and paper and books. I thought, often, of all the times I had sat beside him, sometimes leaning my head against his arm, as he taught me.

In fact, my mother had also taught Kai to read English when he was a child, but she said that by the time he was ten years old she could no longer teach him anything. He had always spent a great deal of time on his own, away from the mission, and none of us knew where he went or with whom he might associate. Glory paid little attention to her son.

As I grew older I was aware of the confusing aura of servant and family around Kai. Because Glory had been my mother's ayah since she arrived in India, Kai had lived at the mission since he was little more than a baby, and my parents knew him almost as well as they knew me. And I sensed that this is what made not only my mother, but more especially my father, treat Kai with a strange mixture of pride and sympathy, as if they, too, couldn't draw the line at thinking of him as simply an Indian servant.

While Glory and I did the laundry, carrying our clothing and bedding to the Ravi and beating it on flat rocks with stout sticks, then wringing it and carrying it back to the courtyard where we strung it on bushes, and my mother and I did what was necessary in the house and infirmary to keep things as tidy and clean as possible, Kai did all the hard physical work at the mission. My father, feeble due to his unreliable heart, was unable to lift and carry, to climb on to the thatched roofs to repair them, to spend all day in the sun, whitewashing the buildings. He couldn't tug Marta by the rope around her neck over to the ox-cart and get her in the traces and then attach her lead, or dig out the root vegetables from the garden, or replant and weed and carry water, bucket after bucket, to keep the vegetables we relied on from drying in the baking summer heat. Holding a hoe for ten minutes and slowly pulling it through the clumped earth immediately caused raised, raw blisters on the smooth palms of his hands. Carrying a single bucket of water made beads of sweat stand on his high, reddened forehead. Even the simple act of reaching up to fix a dangling shutter on to its hook forced him to sit in the shade of the deep verandah, mopping his streaming face and taking quick shallow breaths, while I brought him a glass of water and sometimes fanned him with a tied cluster of guinea fowl feathers.

My father looked at Kai with a trace of sadness, I realised, watching his eyes follow Kai. Shirtless in the heat, the muscles in Kai's bare back rippled smoothly as he bent over the furrows, throwing huge clods of dry earth behind him as though tossing pebbles. He clambered on to the thatched roofs with a quick nimbleness, gripping with his bare toes; the muscles of his calves, visible below his white *dhoti* or *panjammahs*, standing out in relief. I thought that the expression I saw on my father's face was due to his own sense of failure over his physical inabilities.

But there was also admiration in my father's expression. Sometimes he shook his head, slightly, as Kai effortlessly picked up yet another forkful of dried straw to throw to Marta, or whitewash a wall with tireless speed, as if he – my father – couldn't believe Kai's strength. And yet I also knew that Kai was not simply a strong back and pair of arms; because of Kai's quick and powerful mind, I could sense my father wished to speak to him of more absorbing issues than menial chores. Sometimes – in the same manner as he spoke to me – he asked Kai's opinion on the increasing postal rate, or the linking of the electric telegraph lines to more isolated areas, or tried to engage him in a conversation about the state of the railroads.

But it was Kai who held back, who, when my father called out some question, would answer with a monosyllable, his head turned away slightly, making it clear he didn't wish to have a discussion, or even meet my father's eyes.

Until I understood, I thought it was respect of servant for master, or simply the respect of a younger man for his senior. But recognition came later, after many things were revealed.

CHAPTER FOUR

As Kai had told me, my mother was waiting on the verandah. I crossed the courtyard to the ringing of the little bell that summoned the others. By the time I climbed the steps and took my place between my mother and father, Pavit and Glory were already kneeling on the wet ground.

Sanosh was a staunch Hindu and did not join them. And Kai . . . he did not attend the prayers either; he had long ago defied my father by refusing to attend. Did he carry religion within his heart? Sometimes I wondered if he could truly be godless.

As I knelt in position between my father and mother I noticed a battered wooden crate on one side of the verandah: another charity box. It must have come yesterday when we were at the river, or as I lay on my bed in exhaustion. I hoped it would have a few books; the last box had been disappointing.

Some of what I knew of the English world I learned from my parents' infrequent stories, and from the former visits in the English cantonment in Lahore, but my knowledge came mainly from the discarded books that came in the charity boxes. Because of the absence of older English children in India, the books I pulled out were never children's stories, apart from those moral tales for the very young, which held no interest for me. What I found were the books read by the English women and men of the upper classes living in India.

And so from the time I could understand the adult tales, I discovered the elegant drawing rooms of the wealthy, and the sordid hovels and cruel factories of the working poor; country lanes and wild moors; tales of orphaned children who were eventually taken in by a wealthy benefactor, adventures of men who could be nothing but heroes, and all the unexpected twists that finding true love could take. I read lurid penny novels of cheap paper from the works of the Brontë sisters to W. M. Thackeray, from George Eliot to Anthony Trollope to Wilkie Collins. I read Elizabeth Gaskell and Mrs Henry Wood. I read tales of Gothic Horror and the works of the Graveyard Poets.

And I also read books that were not prose or poetry, but fact, dealing with the world. There were always fewer of these than the novels; I ignored the more tedious ones on tiresome subjects, but did find it interesting to read history and astronomy and those on anthropological and geographical topics, as well as discourse on popular themes.

From these latter books I discovered the first arrival of the British in India, and their slow but steady rise to rule in much of the country. I always offered the books to Kai when I'd read them; he wasn't interested in literature, but he eagerly accepted the volumes on political theories and figures of power, as well as those on historic battles, adding them to his own that he bought, second-hand, in Lahore.

My father's only reading matter was his Bible, and my mother was too weary of an evening to read. She often just sat on the verandah in the dusk, rocking in the broken cane chair, or, in inclement weather, in the chintz chair in the sitting room.

The money paid to my father by the Church of England Ministry in Lahore was only enough to purchase the barest necessities of foodstuffs which we couldn't supply for ourselves through our garden, our chickens, and Marta's milk:

tea, sugar, flour, a bit of goat or mutton. But like all missions, the rest of our needs – our clothing and household items – were supplied by the wealthy English families in India. The charity boxes were delivered to our verandah three or four times yearly. The worthwhile boxes, in my opinion, contained a good selection of books and perhaps some other treasures – a small mirror, a working fan of Chinese silk, a tiny enamalled box – but, unfortunately, mainly consisted of cast-off clothing. There were well-worn frocks, discoloured petticoats and darned stockings, scuffed boots and limp bonnets, all ill fitting, which constituted a wardrobe for my mother and me. It didn't matter to me what I wore, as long as it was comfortable, and for much of my younger life I had barely glanced into the spotted and cracked mirror that hung over the wash basin on the side verandah.

The Ministry provided the medical supplies my father listed; they were delivered four times a year. The rupees paid to him every six months also allowed for a few servants; these, as well, determined by the Ministry. They calculated that every mission be allowed a cook, an ayah, and one general servant to carry out the physical labour. And so we had Sanosh, Glory and Kai.

Sudras, the untouchables who came to dispose of the contents of the noisome, buzzing enclosure behind the house, referred to as the convenience – where I daily dumped the china chamber pots from our bedrooms, as well as the soiled bandages from the infirmary – were paid in food for carrying away our refuse. Sanosh wrapped leftover *rotis* and lentil curries in broad leaves and left them on a high post near the front gate for the two bone-thin, ragged men who came weekly.

I had always known that missionaries lived on the charity of others; my mother hadn't ever attempted to hide the fact that it was saved souls we worked for and prized, not shining

47

coins or material possessions. And yet I was sometimes bitter that life at the medical mission was one of endless work and, to a certain degree, isolation and penury.

I had recognised this early on.

I had just turned eight, and accompanied my mother to the opulent home of the Wyndhams in Lahore. Their daughter Eleanor was a year younger than I; I suppose I was taken along because of her.

I had often visited Lahore before that. It was my father who particularly loved the city, and I had a number of memories of trips to Lahore with him. He would hold my hand as we explored the ancient city. I admired the three gilded domes of the Sunehri Masjid, and I often begged my father to tell me the story of Mir Mannu, who was supposedly beaten to death with slippers by the women attendants of a lady he had insulted within the golden mosque. I always laughed; surely soft slippers could not kill a man.

I loved the Palace of Mirrors, with its inlaid floral patterns in semi-precious stones set in marble, and Wazir Khan's Mosque, with its huge courtyard always alive with fluttering pigeons, and the Badshahi Mosque, one of the splendours, my father said, of Moghul architecture.

My father also explained to me that in every Indian city of a certain size the English built a special enclave for themselves, and called it a cantonment. It contained barracks, bungalows, churches, clubs and cemeteries, and the architecture of the cantonment was European, with little or no attention to native traditions. And it was on this first trip to visit the Wyndhams with my mother that I observed what he described: this newer part of the city was nothing like the narrow labyrinths of lanes and alleys and bazaars of old Lahore. The streets were wide and shaded with tall trees.

There was a huge green space in the centre, known as the maidan. And there were no natives walking about, apart from ayahs pushing their small charges in English prams. Natives were not allowed to have their own homes within the boundaries of the cantonment. The domestics working in the houses of the English may have stayed in huts in the back gardens, or returned to their own homes in the old city or even nearby villages.

I had known little beyond the cloistered life at the mission, and the bustling excitement of the streets of the old city of Lahore. The only buildings I had been inside of – apart from the glories of Lahore which my father had introduced me to – were our mission home and infirmary.

Both were bungalows of stone and wattle, whitewashed inside and out annually. They had thatched roofs with green weedy growth sprouting from them, and small creatures – mice and lizards and the tiny copper-headed house sparrows – lived in its thick, roughly woven matting, and occasionally unknowingly burrowed right through the ceiling. They would fall to a floor or table or bed, then scurry or flap about in panicked circles. While my mother seemed to find grim pleasure in whacking the offending creature to death with a twig broom, my father, using the furled black umbrella that stood in a tall brass cylinder by the front door, would try to shoo the unlucky little being, unharmed, outside to the verandah through the open door or one of the windows.

But the home of the Wyndhams! While my mother visited with the other ladies, I ran with Eleanor through the house and into the garden with its wide green lawn and carefully appointed flower gardens, speechless and stumbling with excitement and awe. At one point, in the house, I looked over my shoulder, and saw Eleanor's ayah panting after us, her lined, kindly face shining with perspiration, her bare flat feet slapping on the stone floors. She held up the bottom of her sari in an attempt to run, her wide body swaying heavily from side to side.

Afraid of being scolded, cautious of my mother's stern demands that I behave properly at all times, I stopped, saying, in Hindi, 'I'm sorry, Auntie. Do you wish to play with us?' and she looked at me oddly. Eleanor called to me, impatient, and I expected the ayah to tell Eleanor to slow down or stay in one place, but she said nothing, wheezing heavily, except to make a shooing motion with her hand to me. I turned and again followed Eleanor, with the silent ayah ever present behind us.

Seeing the plethora of servants, all busy at their assigned tasks, in the house and on the back verandah and in the cooking house and garden, I thought about Sanosh and Glory and Kai at home. I knew that Glory would be taking advantage of my mother being away, and was probably sitting in the sun outside her hut. Kai might be wandering in the garden, hacking at a few weeds, or perhaps sitting on the fence that ran along the front of the mission, reading. Sanosh would, at this time of day, be taking a nap on the mat in the *rasoi*.

But here, in the Wyndhams' manor, it was a humming hive of activity.

I saw the *chuprassi* in his white *panjammahs* and *kurta* and red sash, standing at the front door to admit any callers. Even at my young age I knew this would have been wasteful for us, for rarely did anyone come to call at the mission except the travelling box-wallahs, who brought their tin boxes of wares to the side door. We had no *dhobi* to wash the clothes or *durzi* to mend them or make new frocks. We had no *mali* to cut the grass — well, we had no grass, just the mud courtyard — or to brush the paths with a twig broom, to pick up leaves fallen from trees or trim the hedges. We had no *bheesti* to haul water. We had no *chowkidar* to keep watch outside the house, and no *punkah wallah* to pull the fan over the dining table in the hottest of weather. No fly-whisk child to stand behind each chair and assure no insects landed on the person seated there.

And we had no *khitmutgar* to wait table, giving seemingly silent orders to a fluttering group of boys to clear away each used dish and return it to the outside kitchen of the *biwarchi*, the cook, with his many boys to help. And it was clear to me we had no need of a *khansana*, a head bearer, to watch over all the others and make sure they carried out their jobs in the manner expected of them.

On that first, long-ago visit, Eleanor and I had eventually been gently guided by her ayah to the nursery. I watched and listened, my mouth open, while Eleanor spoke to her. 'Bring us our tea here, Kasi, and we'd like extra biscuits. Wouldn't we, Pree?' she'd said, looking at me, and I could only stare from her to Kasi. She continued on in this grown-up voice and manner, while the ayah bowed her head and nodded at everything Eleanor said.

Under Kasi's watchful eye, we ate our meal and drew pictures on Eleanor's slate board with chalk and then played at mothering Eleanor's porcelain dolls. We drank pretend tea from miniature painted china teacups. Eleanor bossed me about and once slapped my hand when I reached for the teapot without asking her permission. I realised she spoke to me in the same manner as she did to the ayah, lifting her chin just the slightest as she told me what I must do and when to do it. She had red-gold hair that, although tied in green dark satin ribbons, sprung loose in wild curls, and her pale green lawn frock was smocked with tiny yellow stitches. It's strange how one remembers such details.

I don't know if I was filled with admiration or frightened of Eleanor; I only know that I couldn't wait to return to the house on the broad, clean street. I wanted again to play with the beautiful dolls whose clothing was far finer than mine, and eat the light, sweet jam-filled biscuits.

But shortly after that Eleanor had been sent back to England for her schooling, as were all the English children once they reached six or seven. I had never seen her again, although we had, a few times, returned to the Wyndhams, and had also been guests of other families in the English cantonment. Although I was sent to play with the younger children – those under seven – I quickly grew weary of what I saw as their baby games, and chose instead to sit beside my mother in the finely appointed sitting rooms. I listened intently to the conversations. I learned the name of the latest royal child born to our Queen, imagined walking through the grand iron and glass Crystal Palace with all its marvels, and saw myself standing on the banks of the Thames gazing at the wondrous bridge spanning the city, or watching the tall sailing ships which came up the channel to dock at the London Port.

At those times I longed to be part of that world – the English world that was, through my parents, my own.

It became perfectly clear to me that these families, living in the grand homes built in English fashion, were not in India because they had heard the call of the Lord, like my parents, but had chosen to live in India because of the political and business opportunities the country provided. They had arrived in this country already prosperous, and grew ever more so; India provided a lifestyle of luxury for them which would have been unattainable in England.

I don't recall when our visits grew less frequent. But I do remember meeting these same families at the English bazaar in Lahore – the ones whose homes we had once been invited to. They nodded and smiled at my father and mother in a polite and formal way, but didn't stop to chat or invite us to join them at their tables as they sat in the open windows of Willis' Fine Tea Room.

Perhaps my parents' presence stifled them, and they were forced to think upon their language and comments more carefully. Or perhaps it was my mother's growing oddness, which I had noticed disturbed the ladies. But by the time I was ten, there were no further invitations issued, and never did anyone ride to the mission for a social visit.

By that time I came to understand the hierarchy of the British class, and our place – or perhaps our absence of place – as missionaries. We were English, and yet carried none of the weight of the Wyndhams or Rollings-Smythes or McCallisters. And as I grew older still I experienced combined humiliation and anger over the obvious lack of respect for my parents – especially by the ladies towards my mother, although she never spoke of these social slights. Every time we met any of the English on the streets of Lahore I smiled my prettiest and put on my best manners, curtseying and keeping my voice pleasant and modest. Naïvely, I realise now, I hoped that I could somehow convince those stylish and sweet-smelling ladies that my mother, in spite of her wet mouth and dusty clothing and occasional inappropriate comments, was, like them, a lady from England, and I was a girl like their own daughters who no longer lived with them.

But they paid me little heed, seeming impatient to go about their business, and each rebuff added another layer to my sense of confusion over where I belonged.

The uncertainty was also present at the mission. Although the natives willingly came to us for medical attention, we were always seen as foreigners, and treated as such, in, again, a polite and yet distant manner. And while playing with the Indian children who accompanied their parents to the infirmary, or while wandering into the nearby villages, I so often wished to share a kinship with the people. I wanted to identify with their beautiful and at times indecipherable religions and beliefs, and be joined to the long, ancient roots of India, so firmly anchored into the solid earth of the great subcontinent.

I felt the push and pull of both worlds. And the older I grew the more deeply I felt the overwhelming need to fit, to be part of a greater picture, but to whom and where I couldn't quite name.

Now, on my knees and pretending to pay strict attention to the morning sermon, I stole glances at the latest charity box. My father droned on: the familiar frustration over his lack of converts.

' "They shall go forth," ' he stated – Isaiah 66: verse 24 – with utmost conviction, staring into the sky, ' "and look upon the carcasses of the men that have transgressed against me: for their worm shall not die, neither shall their fire be quenched: and they shall be an abhorring unto all flesh." ' One fist was clenched against his waistcoat as if the prayer came from his disappointed belly.

It was such a familiar sermon; I knew what he would say by heart. At least it was one of his livelier presentations, peppered with frightening images.

Even as a very small child I was fascinated by the more gruesome of my father's scriptures. Anything to do with kindness and love, those scriptures talking of the Lamb of God, of little children and forgiveness, flew from my head. But the ones that conjured unpleasant images, oh, those stayed. And they were encouraged by my mother.

Although my father had given up all earthly pleasure for the gentle Jesus, my mother did not share his thoughts in this matter.

I'm not certain why she filled my head with violent details. When I was a small child the stories she chose to tell me – biblical and those based on her own knowledge of life both in East London and in India – gave me nightmares, and

I would often run into my parents' bedroom crying in the night. And yet it was not my mother who comforted me at these times – she, who created my wretched dreams – but my father, who took my hand and led me back to my bed, sitting on the edge of the narrow cot patiently, until next I opened my eyes to daylight, again alone in my tiny room beside my parents'.

The story that haunted me the most deeply, causing the most nightmares, was that of the *Bibighar* – the Women's House – at Cawnpore. It was one of the tales of the atrocities committed against the Europeans by the native soldiers during the Sepoy Rebellion, which had begun a year after my birth.

I was eight years old when my mother told me this sad tale, and the images it created remained with me always.

'It was the same month as now – July. Cawnpore is hundreds of miles south of Lahore, and that far-south summer is so much hotter than here, Pree,' my mother had said, staring at me. 'Cawnpore was an important garrison built by the British on the banks of the Ganges.' We were sitting on the verandah of the house; it was late afternoon, and too hot for any patients to come to the infirmary. Pots of drying, scraggly plants, spinning in an occasional breath of stifling breeze, were suspended by thick twine from the roof beams. There was the rush rocking chair with its broken arm and three woven chairs and a few low tables.

As she spoke, my mother handed me a copper bowl of long yellow beans; I put it in my lap and snapped each bean into three sections, dropping them back into the bowl. Mother fanned herself with a small whisk of donkey tail as she moved back and forth in the rush rocker, which creaked on the splintered floor of the verandah.

She shifted, trying to find a comfortable spot in the sagging woven seat; her joints caused her great torture.

She began to tell me the story, and as she did so, my brain brightened, in the way of a flame fed by air, and I saw it, saw the wavering, dancing shapes in the front of my mind.

'The women and children had been held captive by the sepoys, crammed into the *Bibighar*, the walled dwelling,' my mother said now, her eyes holding mine. My fingers worked of their own accord, snapping the beans rhythmically as I watched my mother's face. 'Most of the husbands had already been shot with the Ensign Rifles distributed to the British army, murdered by the very cartridges which are said to have been the final straw in the uprising. Wrapped in paper lubricated by grease derived from both cow and pig, the sepoys were forced to use their teeth to tear open the cartridge before inserting it into the long muzzles of the muskets. This was an affront to both Hindu and Muslim: an obvious attempt by the English to further denigrate their religious beliefs.'

A particularly ripe bean gave a loud, popping snap, and I jumped, but my mother didn't stop.

'Surely those women and children suffered terribly in the unforgiving humidity. There would be no sanitation, and they would be tormented by flies. It's said they existed on mouthfuls of putrid water and thin lentil soup for three weeks. Many had already died of dysentery and cholera; many more were desperately ill. There's nobody more qualified than I to describe how terrible it is to be ill in this country,' my mother said, her fan slowing as the rocking chair also stilled. 'What with all my ailments. Do you suppose the women's deliriums took them home, back to the cool safety of England, Pree?' She leaned forward, and I leaned back just the slightest, unnerved and yet mesmerised by the odd look on her face. 'Did they look down upon their wasted, silent children, praying for their salvation, or for their own forgiveness, for bringing children to life in this land that would now attempt to kill them in the cruellest way?'

I knew my mother thought of her own dead children. And I knew she didn't wish me to speak, even though she questioned me. Suddenly she rocked again, and waved the fan before her face.

'The house must have been filled with the stench of despair. The small group of rebel sepoys now remaining at Cawnpore had received word of the approaching army, and agreed they must kill all survivors so that no one remained to tell the tale. When the sun had fully risen to its high, white height, burning up all the blue and creating dreamy, shimmering images in its glare, the last three British men were dragged from their captivity and shot in front of a silent crowd of Indians and Eurasians gathered on the walls surrounding the courtyard of the *Bibighar*. The English women heard the gunshots.'

A camel pulling a cart loaded with corn stalks rumbled by on the road, and the rhythmic chirping of the cicadas filled the air. I could imagine this same sound in the courtyard in Cawnpore.

'The women rushed to the verandah. Immediately the sepoys tried to drag them to the courtyard to execute them, as well. But the women clung together, their arms wrapped around the verandah pillars or each other's waists, their wailing children clustered for safety between their skirts. Those brave women sang hymns for courage.'

Here my mother stopped again, staring into the courtyard and the road beyond. Sweat ran down her temple. She mopped at her wet lips with her handkerchief, and then sang, in a quavering voice, '*Praise, my soul, the King of Heaven; to His feet thy tribute bring. Ransomed, healed, restored, forgiven, Evermore His praises sing.*' Her mouth closed. I had dug my hands into the bowl of beans, feeling their soft, waxy surface.

'Well?' she said.

I opened my lips. '*Alleluia, alleluuu-lia,*' I sang, obeying her unspoken demand, but it came out a croak. '*Praise the everlasting King.*'

She nodded, one curt, reflexive dip of her head. 'And then the women ran inside, locking the doors. But the natives who had, until only months earlier, worn the scarlet jackets of the British army, would not be stopped. Unable to break down the heavy doors, they smashed through the window shutters with the barrels of their muskets. The women and children crouched helplessly on the floor or crawled behind furniture and pillars when the sepoys opened fire on them.'

My mother's eyes glowed. 'And then they began to work with their scimitars. They swung their heavy curved sabres again and again, slashing and mutilating.' She quickly, jerkily mopped her lips again. 'Finally, as darkness fell, it appeared that every movement, every voice, was stilled, and the butchers left the scene of mass murder.'

My mother was still staring at me, her head cocked to one side. I realised my right hand held a bean, wet and crushed in my fist. My left hand was over my mouth. What did she want now? Was I to sing again?

'They were all dead?' I whispered into my fingers. They smelled of the beans. 'Even the children?'

A small, strange smile came to my mother's mouth, and she leaned back. 'Early the next morning the burial scavengers moved in, and made the decision to dump the dead down an empty irrigation well in the courtyard. The well was huge, nine feet wide and fifty feet deep, with steps leading to its rim. These men hauled body after body – it's said that they dragged the dead women by their hair – from the house and courtyard. They left a bloody trail through the long grass, dry and yellowed from the heat, leading to the well. Before dumping the corpses over the lip of the well, they stripped them of any clothing and jewellery they considered worthwhile.'

I moved my hand from my mouth to cover my eyes, although of course the images were inside my head, and would not be stopped.

'Pree,' my mother said, 'you asked about the children. Look at me.'

I took away my hand. It seemed I could feel the heat from my mother's eyes, so intent was her stare.

'They discovered a cluster of children, from infant to those five or six years old, hiding in the deepest shadowed corners of the house. Imagine how weakened they would have been by their weeks of captivity. They would have spent the night alone surrounded by the bodies of their dead mothers.'

I tried to swallow, but, unlike my mother, I had no saliva.

'But the will to live is strong, Pree. It is very strong. You know that, don't you?' she asked, and I nodded.

'And so they ran. Those children ran. There were reports of a little girl carrying a baby who was already dead. A toddler had its arms and legs around the neck and waist of the oldest boy; he couldn't have been past seven, or he would be safe, at home in England,' she said.

I was barely older than the children my mother spoke of. My dry throat constricted at the pictures I made: the girl with the lifeless infant, the brave boy, leader of the tiny group, running in a lop-sided gallop with the small charge on his back. I envisioned Kai as that boy, me the girl with the dead baby. I knew the panic and horror on their white, pinched faces as they tried to escape. I was panting now, as if I, also, ran in the breathless heat.

'But there was nowhere to run,' my mother went on. 'They were caught as easily as kittens in a knitting basket, and then flung, alive, down into that black, hellish hole. They were left to perish on the lifeless bodies of their mothers.

'They were strangely quiet, it's said,' my mother continued, her voice growing ever louder. 'There was not a sound from the deep well.'

Both the rocker and the fan moved faster and faster, although she said nothing more. Finally I couldn't bear the silence any further. 'Did any of them live? Any of the children?'

'No,' she said, her voice mercifully quiet again. The chair and fan grew still. 'Some of the Eurasians who witnessed the horror were all too eager to give full reports and descriptions of the murderers. And some of those murderers were caught by the British, and later blown to pieces, alive, from the mouths of cannons. Their flesh and blood rained down on the watching crowd.'

She raised her eyebrows at me, her mouth curved up in a small smile. A smile. 'Well? What do you think of that?' she asked, but I couldn't bear to look at her face, and bent over the bowl of beans. I scrabbled through them, but they were all snapped. In fact, most of the pieces were tiny and many crushed; I must have broken them, over and over. My nails were rimmed with their yellow pulp.

When I remember her expression, and her decision to frighten me with that terrible story, I wonder now: did only a black stone sit behind her ribcage? She had told the story with no emotion save for the rising pitch of her voice.

CHAPTER FIVE

T HE MARKS ON MY neck were fading; it had been five days since my father's attempted baptism. Kai was gone again. The rains beat on throughout the day and night, stopping as suddenly as they started, then beginning once more.

I didn't know how long I'd been asleep when I was awakened by my mother playing the pianoforte. Or not so much playing as simply hitting the keys, slowly, over and over again. It was completely dark in my room; I had closed the shutters tightly before going to bed. The rain had stopped for now, but in the far distance thunder grumbled. I lay still, listening: middle C, three times. D, four times. Again. Five times, then six. E flat. E flat. E flat. Over and over. Finally the sound stopped, and I rose and went to the sitting room. There was no light, neither candle nor lamp, although the moon shone through the opened shutters and front door, swung wide, which led to the verandah. Why was the door open? In that ghostly light I could see the hands of the clock on the mantle: three-twenty.

It was cold in the sitting room, and I closed the front door and then, crossing my arms over my chest, I went to my mother. She hunched over the birdcage pianoforte, her hands poised. I could make out the faint gleam of the curly, faded gold script, just above the keyboard: *Robert Wornum, London*.

'Mother,' I said, but she didn't appear to hear me. And then her index finger lowered and raised, lowered and raised.

Plink, plink, plink. Still E flat, but faster, harder. Where was my father? Did he not hear her?

'Mother,' I repeated, this time touching her shoulder. It was rigid, as if made of stone. She didn't stop. Finally I stepped closer, putting my hand on hers, hovering on the ebony key. I felt the soft netting of her veins. She looked down at my hand, then up at me, and in the long narrow slice of moonlight which slashed over the left side of her face there was a horrifying blankness in her visible eye. Was she still asleep, living within a dream while moving within the world? Her chin shone with spittle.

'What's wrong, Mother?' I asked, moving from the direct line of her breath. At least she had stopped hitting the note.

But still she didn't answer. She pulled her hand out from under mine, absently using the sleeve of her nightdress to wipe her chin, then calmly resumed her plinking of the key, as if I weren't there.

I went to the bedroom to fetch my father, but the bed was empty.

'Where's Father?' I asked of my mother's back, not expecting an answer and not receiving one. Perhaps he'd gone to use the convenience, I reasoned, and went through the side door. But before I could start down the three verandah steps and walk to the path leading to the tiny structure, I saw my father approaching the house. He didn't come from the convenience, but from the direction of the pukka huts. In the cool, wet night air he wore his nightshirt, and his feet were bare. I never saw my father so; he was always carefully dressed before he emerged from his bedroom each morning. I was embarrassed, somehow, by his bare feet.

'What's happened, Father?' I asked from the verandah, and he gasped, putting his hand on his chest. His hair stuck out at one side of his head.

'Pree. You startled me. What are you doing out here, in the middle of the night?' He glanced behind me at the house. And I looked behind him, at the huts.

'I was looking for you,' I told him.

He ran his hand over his face, clearing his throat. 'I was . . . attending to Pavit,' he said. 'Why were you looking for me? Is something wrong?'

'Is Pavit ill?' I asked, watching my father come up the steps. His feet didn't make a sound. I worried that he'd seen Pavit's idols.

'He has more pain than usual,' he said. 'Now go back to bed.'

'But . . . it's Mother,' I said. 'Listen.' But now there was only silence. 'She was at the pianoforte. Not playing hymns, but simply hitting the keys. Did you not hear her? It woke me. She's acting strangely.'

'She's awake?' he asked, frowning, stopping beside me. 'But I watched her; she took her—'

He fell silent, as if he shouldn't continue, but of course I knew what he had started to say. My mother had terrible difficulty sleeping, and before retiring at night she took a large dose of laudanum. Thunder was rolling, low and distant, and I knew another lashing rain would be upon us.

I spoke loudly, to be heard over the grumbling from the night clouds. 'It wasn't effective, then,' I said. 'And she wouldn't speak to me. She looked . . . how she sometimes appears. When she's not herself.' It wasn't the first time I'd seen the strange emptiness on her face.

My father closed his eyes for a moment. 'You know how playing her music comforts her when she's disturbed.'

'I know. But she's never done it in the middle of the night.'

My father leaned into my face so unexpectedly that I drew back. 'I don't have all the answers, Pree. Now stop

pestering me. Go back to bed.' His voice was uncharacter-
istically loud; I knew he was upset.

We went inside together. My mother still sat on the
spindly chair in front of the pianoforte, although she was
unmoving, her hands limp in her lap. My father took her
hand and led her to the bedroom. She followed, docile, her
white nightdress giving her a ghostly appearance in the
shadows.

Later, much later, thinking back to that night, I knew that
my father's surprisingly sharp tone wasn't caused by concern
over my mother. It was the result of guilt. But as I went back
to my own bed, listening to the rain start again, I understood
why this day had been particularly hard on my mother. As
well as the discomfort in her joints brought on by the wet
weather, a young woman had come with her infant to the
infirmary in the early afternoon. The child had a raging fever,
and his mother quietly explained that he had taken no liquids
and had watery stools since the evening before.

'But it has stopped now,' she said, hopefully, though I saw
how limp the baby lay in her arms, and saw the hollows
around his eyes. My mother pressed her fingers on to his tiny
torso with its minuscule, rapid flutter, and I saw the laxness of
his flesh, and knew he would not live. 'Intestinal poisoning,'
she murmured to me, giving the woman a tincture of sweet
oil.

She instructed the young mother to try to feed her baby
a spoonful of the oil every hour, and bathe him in warm
water.

'The oil will do no good,' she told me, 'but I couldn't
admit to the case being hopeless. The child will be dead by
nightfall.'

The death of a baby always affected her in this way; I
knew it was because it brought back the memories of her
own dead children.

★ ★ ★

The next morning at prayers I glanced at poor Pavit, thinking of my father tending to him in the night. His disease was eating him away at an alarming rate now. He was old; I doubt even he knew his true age. I saw how he tried to clasp his remaining wrapped fingers together, and felt a fresh surge of annoyance at my father. He insisted that all of us, including Pavit, lace our fingers and bow our heads over them as he prayed on.

Pavit was our only charity case; although other missions might have a number of orphaned children and a few widows, and were paid accordingly by the Ministry for their support, apart from Pavit those in need had not come to our courtyard seeking shelter in return for conversion.

Pavit had told me that before he managed to cover the distance from his village to our mission, six years ago, he had been ostracised, sleeping curled in hidden shadows, his extremities beginning to rot while his begging bowl remained empty. The villagers, while willing to give to beggars outside the small temple to increase their chances of improving their karma, knew Pavit to be made untouchable by his disease, and of absolutely no benefit in helping.

All Pavit had had to do to earn this new life of food and shelter at the mission was convert to Christianity. While I'm certain my father must have rejoiced over his only convert in all his years in India, in actuality Pavit hadn't given up his beliefs. He had dutifully undergone a baptism, and faithfully tried to mumble along with the morning prayers, but I knew he was still a Hindu.

'More gods are better,' he always said to me. And so he still maintained a little elephant-headed Ganesh, for good fortune, on the edge of the inside door frame, and under his charpoy kept his whole collection of idols he himself had fashioned from clay, including a cross with a round ball on the top.

The first time I had asked him the name of that last one, the only one I didn't recognise, from where I sat in his doorway as a child, watching him line up the little clay shapes and touch each one reverently, he had looked at me quizzically. 'But this is your father's God, Missy Pree,' he said. 'The one on the front of the black book.'

Now I looked away from him to Glory. Clearly bored, she absently dug in her mouth with her index finger; she often suffered from toothache and usually smelled of the cloves she chewed in an attempt to keep the pain at bay.

My father and mother never opened their eyes during the tired prayers and admonishings. They didn't see that Glory and I paid little attention, and since Pavit's knowledge of English was minimal, he couldn't have taken much from the daily ritual. I watched the first patients arrive at the infirmary, and rubbed my fingers, still greasy from the *roti*, on my skirt.

Of course both my parents could speak some Hindi and Punjabi after so many years in India, but they spoke the phrases hesitantly, flatly, as if their lips and tongues were stiffened with cornstarch. My father used a twisted combination of Indian and English words which was a language unto itself, and usually confused the natives. While my mother had more of an affinity with the vernacular, I was often called on to translate for them, running between the front and back verandahs to explain what a patient was saying or asking, or what my mother or father were telling them.

This had been the beginning of my medical knowledge.

I spoke Hindi, Punjabi and Urdu with ease; the only people with whom I spoke English were my parents or the other English people I encountered on my occasional visits to Lahore. And with Kai. Kai and I had always communicated with each other in English.

I loved Kai's voice. It was almost pure English, like mine, although there was a tiny difference, maybe the sound of

Hindu music. He sounded nothing at all like his mother, with her *chee chee*.

I thought of the many evenings my father had been saddened at losing what he thought might be a convert, a man who had listened intently to his garbled speech, head waggling slightly with what appeared to be agreement and approval as he watched my father's face. ' "Verily I say unto you," ' my father would always finish his hopeful speech, quoting from the Book of Matthew, ' "Except ye be converted, and become as little children, ye shall not enter into the kingdom of heaven".'

There would usually be more enthusiastic nodding from the patient. But once my father had finished dealing with the complaint the convert-to-be had come to the mission about, the man would back away. Bowing and making *namaste*, the head that had only moments earlier appeared to agree now shaking, slowly but pointedly at my father's outstretched hand, holding the black leather Bible, its cover creased and softened by years of use. My father was a tall, slender man, his blond, thinning hair a little too long at the back. He always wore a topi while outside, for his skin burned easily. Yet even so, his high forehead had a permanently reddened, peeling patch of rosacea. His face was usually calm, still — as if waiting to hear an inner voice.

My mother blamed my father's gentleness for his failure to convert. She said he was too weak, that he had no back-bone, and even heathens could see this, and didn't trust that he was capable of speaking the truth. I hated when my mother spoke critically of my father, who simply looked away, lean and pale.

At these times, after he'd left, I tried to stand up for him, even though I knew it would only anger her further.

'What about Pavit and Glory? They've converted,' I once argued.

She shook her head, frowning. 'For Pavit, converting was better than sleeping in the streets, kicked and starved, wasn't it? And as for Glory,' here my mother made a face as if she'd bitten into a rotten egg, 'your father is a man of God. He couldn't turn away a destitute half-caste with a hungry child in her arms when she came begging for shelter in return for work. But he knew what kind of woman she was. She agreed to conversion, like Pavit, in exchange for shelter and safety, only because she had no alternative. And your father was weak to allow her to stay, simply weak. A strong man would have sent her away to atone for her sins elsewhere, and only accept her back when she'd made it clear that she'd left her whoring ways behind her.'

I was shocked at my mother's use of the word whoring, although this came at a time when her odd behaviour was making itself known more and more often, and I accepted it as this.

I knew that Glory had been hardly more than a girl at the mission in Allahabad when my mother arrived. She often said how my father had expected my mother to be pleased with an ayah waiting to serve her. After all, my mother had always done the serving; she had worked at one of the ragged schools in London's Spitalfields. Her own parents had died when she was young; she was raised by an aunt, and had found solace for her loneliness in helping with the dirty, abandoned children of the back streets. She tried to teach them the simplest of lessons, handing out a slice of bread and cup of thin soup every morning to encourage the children to come to the ill-equipped but well-intentioned schools. She also played the piano for the hymn singing at the end of each day.

My father said he'd first seen her when he stopped in at the school to examine an outbreak of skin lesions amongst the students. She'd had a glow about her then, he said, when he first saw her pounding out a tune on a wobbly spinet. 'A glow that came from within,' he'd said. 'Her hair like a glorious red cloud. We both dreamed of helping others find the wonders of God, and in leading the uncivilised and barbaric heart towards the knowledge of Jesus. This is what united us.'

But my mother would speak little of that time, and in spite of my father's description of her glow, I sensed that even then there was an inner darkness she tried to cover.

'No matter how distasteful it is to have one with such a low character nearby,' she went on now, 'your father says we cannot turn out Glory.'

I had many times heard my mother implore my father to tell Glory that because of her very slovenly and disrespectful behaviour she could no longer have a job and a home at the mission, and had also heard my father refuse. These were the only times he stood up to my mother.

To cast her out, he argued, after she had taken the Lord into her heart, had renounced all her idolatrous gods, would not be a Christian act at all. 'And what about Kai? This is the only home he knows. Do you wish him to leave as well, if Glory were to go?' At this my mother fell silent.

Kai appeared to be my father's trump card.

I knew my mother cared a great deal about Kai, although she didn't demonstrate it in any direct manner.

There was a great deal about Kai that made him different from the other native young men I saw at the infirmary and in the neighbouring towns and villages and in Lahore. I couldn't remember Kai ever behaving in the manner of Sanosh's sons, Darshan or Jafar; tall, rabbity boys with arms and legs thin as sticks, endlessly making jokes and overly concerned about their cricket scores. Kai had always been serious, thoughtful, a slight crease between his eyebrows, his lips firm. But when he occasionally forgot himself, throwing back his head and letting out unselfconscious whoops of laughter, his face was transformed, and I loved to see him in this playful manner.

Eurasian through his mother, his skin wasn't as light as hers, but his eyes bore the same colour, a pale green, quite startling in his dark face. His thick hair was shiny and black, and curled over his ears and on to the collar of his long white shirt, which he wore over white cotton *panjammahs* or a wrapped dhoti. He kept his clothing so clean and bleached that at times it was almost blinding in the pure sunlight.

And he wasn't a half-converted Hindu like his mother. He was a full Christian; he had been baptised as a very small child by my father, my mother told me, in exchange for allowing Glory to keep him with her at the mission.

But the main difference between Kai and the other young men of the area was that Kai didn't know his father, which was indeed a shameful thing. Not only for him, but even for my mother. She seemed more troubled by the fact that her ayah had a bastard child than Glory herself. I didn't know whether Kai's father had been English or Eurasian; I knew with certainty that Glory wouldn't have ever lowered herself to be touched by a native, even a high-caste Brahmin. She was full of snobbery, was Glory. I had for some time believed that Kai's father might have been a Rajput – he had the height, the slender yet strong build, and the regal features that spoke clearly of that tribe.

But there came a time when I put together certain facts, and thought I knew, with certainty, who Kai's father really was.

He wasn't a Rajput after all, but an Afghan.

CHAPTER SIX

I HAD KNOWN THE Afghan a long time before this thought came to me. I had first seen him when I sat with Kai beside the Grand Trunk Road.

The Grand Trunk crossed India's breadth. Much of the road, Kai told me, had been built in the sixteenth century, and it stretched between Calcutta and the city of Kabul in Afghanistan. I always thought the road rather stately, with its sheltering shade trees filled with twittering birds. The English had rebuilt great lengths of it with pukka, the stones heaving and buckling and then resettling with the ravages of the weather – the heat or cold or wet. The sounds of those travelling the road echoed, on a still day, all the way to the mission, and were familiar and safe: the faint voices and shouts of men, a sudden thin, high shriek of female laughter, the noise of the animals – the whinnying of horses, bellowing of cattle, the plaintive call of goats and sheep, the disgruntled roar of camels – as well as the ringing of hooves against the uneven stone. And through it all, there was the muted rumble of the wooden wheels of the bullock carts, the screeching of their axles, and the barking of dogs running alongside them.

When I was quite young Kai had often taken me with him to sit under a banyan tree, watching life stream by, south to north, north to south. It was ever changing and ever interesting. Kai pointed out various sights, and it was at these times that I had learned much about the life that surrounded me. There were the Hindus: the men in their simple loincloths and shirts or jackets or shawls, depending on the season, and the women in saris, with their nose rings and bangles. The married ladies had a dusting of vermillion powder on their hair-parting, and the widows were in white. Both men and women often wore the smear of red paste – the blessing *tikka* – on their foreheads. Kai taught me to recognise the castes and sub-castes by their appearance: the knot with which a dhoti was tied; whether a moustache was trained upwards, downwards or across; the high-caste Brahmin with his waxed moustache and saffron turban, the white turbans of the middle class, and the lowest sweeper in colourless tatters. Even on the wide road the caste rules were observed: the lower castes moving to one side or even off the road, bowing their heads or kneeling, making *namaste* to the higher. A *sudra* would sometimes beat a small drum to warn of his approach so the others could make sure he didn't pass too closely.

There were bearded Sikhs with black turbans, a sharp *kirpan* tucked into their belts, and the occasional Parsee with his small round white cap. The Muslim men were identifiable by their square-cut beards and thin white skullcaps; the women by their covered faces.

There were the mendicants, ash covered, sometimes naked and sometimes wrapped in rags, clutching begging bowls. Their hair and beards were long and matted, their fingernails uncut, and they often raised one hand in a blessing as they passed us.

I saw the English in their covered carriages drawn by two horses, and occasionally a palanquin carried by four bearers, the English woman inside protected from the dust and view by the swaying curtains, the accompanying man on horseback alongside.

And there were the Afghans, standing out above the crowd on their tall, proud horses. Some wore billowing trousers and shirts and vests, others the soft white *kurta-salwar* – the trousers and long matching shirt – of the far north. And they always wore leather boots, which distinguished them further from the Indians, who were barefoot or in simple woven sandals.

And one afternoon – I may have been eight or nine at the time – the Afghan rode up on his golden Arabian as Kai and I sat under our favourite banyan. Kai rose, hailing him as a friend. The Afghan was a Pushtun, and although I knew his language would have been Pushto, he spoke to Kai in Urdu. It was very clear, although there was a slight, unknown accent in it. His hair was covered by a turban, and he had a light brown beard; I assumed him to be a Muslim. His eyes were very dark, his cheekbones high, and although much older than Kai, he was still straight and slender.

I watched them speak, obviously at ease, as if they had known each other for some time. I came up beside Kai, respectfully greeting the Afghan with *Assalamu alaikum* as I reached toward the horse's golden coat.

'May I touch him?' I asked, and the Afghan nodded, unsmiling, watching me with his dark gaze as I stroked the beautiful creature's velvet nose. I smiled at Kai, and then the Afghan, wishing I could some day ride such a creature. I had only ever ridden on Marta's broad, swaying back.

Over the next few years I regularly saw the Afghan on the road. I didn't question why he so often travelled the Grand Trunk. While he and Kai talked, I stroked the horse's nose or fed it long grass I pulled from the side of the road. And then, finally, one day the Afghan asked if I would like to sit on his horse. I nodded, and he helped me put my foot in the stirrup and I swung up into the curved, decorated saddle. The horse shivered beneath me and I grasped the pommel, nervous to be so high above the ground. The Afghan continued talking to Kai, but once he glanced at me, and I smiled broadly at him, lightly tapping my heels against the horse's broad sides. He stopped, mid-sentence, his lips, within his beard, suddenly uncertain, and I thought I had angered him with my heels, and immediately stopped.

I realised then that he never smiled. Later, I knew that what I had seen on his face wasn't anger, but sadness. He didn't return for a long time after that. I made up a story about him, about how he had loved a beautiful *rani*, but she had been kidnapped. And every night he looked at the moon, and recited a poem of love for her.

It was a full year later — I must have been eleven at that time — when I was sitting outside the *rasoi*, peeling turnips. I looked up at the sound of hoofs, and at the sight of the familiar golden Arabian rose and ran to the fence, remembering how tall and straight the Afghan was, and how easily he sat in his tooled leather saddle, the heels of his boots hooked into the stirrups.

It was the first time I had seen him at the mission.

As I ran past the peepul tree towards the fence, the Afghan leaned forward just the slightest, picking up the reins that had fallen loosely against his horse's neck as the animal grazed at the weedy growth at the side of the road. He looked at me with an expression I didn't understand. His face was open, and his eyes too bright. Had I really remembered them as so sad, or had I only imagined it?

'*Salaam*,' I said, hoping he'd let me sit in the saddle again.

The Afghan nodded, then his face changed, back to his usual guarded expression. As if wary, he looked past me, to the house. 'I've been in the north,' he said. 'Is Kai at the mission?'

'No. He's been gone since yesterday,' I said. 'I don't know

when he'll return.' I climbed on to the fence, sitting on the top rail and stroking the Arabian's sleek coat. Its skin rippled under my hand.

Suddenly my mother called to me, sharply, from the verandah. Before I turned towards her, the Afghan pulled abruptly on the reins, and dug his heels into the horse's flanks. The horse's head jerked up, and he gave a whinny of surprise, but immediately pulled away from the fence and trotted off.

The Afghan didn't look back, and within the next moment urged the horse into a gallop. I stayed on the fence, but in only a few moments they were too far for me to see any details, just a dark shape and a cloud of fine yellow dust.

'Pree!' my mother called again, more demanding, and I climbed from the fence and went to her.

'What were you doing?' she asked.

'Just talking to the Afghan.'

'Who is he?'

'Kai's friend,' I said.

'I don't like you speaking to strange men. If he returns, stay away. That man will be up to no good. Kai does not have the best judgement in choosing those he spends time with.'

'What do you mean?'

She didn't answer, dabbing at her mouth with a sour look.

A week later, as I sat on the verandah, the Afghan came again, and this time Kai, walking through the courtyard with a basket of freshly washed clothing, put it down and went to him. The Afghan swung his leg over his horse and slid to the ground, leaning against the gleaming beast with his arms crossed over his chest, and the two talked at length.

The Afghan took something – a book – from his saddlebag, and opened it, and Kai leaned forward, looking at it. I watched them, and saw the way Kai stared, so intently, with such interest and respect, into the Afghan's face as the older man spoke. They were of the same height, and had the same dignified posture. Although the Afghan's eyes were so dark, it was from Glory that Kai had inherited his eye colour. And it was at that moment that I came to the conclusion that this could indeed be Kai's father. After the Afghan rode away Kai returned to his basket, taking out a wet shirt and shaking it. I went to his side.

'Kai?' I said, and he absently glanced at me, draping the shirt over a bush.

I took a deep breath, and said what I'd been thinking about. 'Is he . . . the Afghan . . . is he your father?'

Now he looked at me sharply, his hand still. 'Why do you ask that?'

'Just the way . . . you seem at ease with him.'

'You ask too many questions,' he said. 'And you should mind your own business.' His voice surprised me: distressed, almost heated. 'Who he is should not concern you,' he said, now bending to pull out a wet sheet. I took the other end, sorry that I'd upset him. Without looking at each other we snapped the sheet to straighten it before laying it over the hedge to dry.

Surely I had guessed the truth. Why else would Kai react in this way, angry and yet secretive? The only piece of the puzzle that didn't fit was Glory. I couldn't imagine a man like the proud Afghan choosing to be with a woman like Glory.

What my mother repeatedly said about Glory was true. She was not a good ayah. Yes, she brushed and pinned up my mother's hair every morning, and she tidied the bedroom where my parents slept, and made sure my mother's few dresses were clean and pressed. She heated water for her baths in cool weather, and filled the copper hip-bath with tepid water in the summer months. She attended any of the small private needs my mother might have. But she performed all these duties with a slightly put-upon air. She never anticipated what my mother might need, as I had seen other ayahs attend to their memsahibs in the English houses in Lahore. Instead, she had to be asked, sometimes almost cajoled, to do her expected duties, and she didn't seem to show any indication of wanting to act as a companion to my mother, in the way of a treasured ayah.

She was pretty, small and well formed. From her English father she had inherited skin the colour of milky tea. Her mother, she told me, had come from Goa, on the Arabian Sea, far to the south-west, and had been part Portuguese, as were so many of the Indians there. Her parents had never married; she carried her mother's Portuguese surname: da Silva. From her mother came her shiny black hair that, when freshly washed, fell in waves below her waist. Her nose was long and narrow, and she had arched brows and thick, dark eyelashes which framed her pale green eyes. But her chin receded, and this, combined with a slight overbite – although her teeth were straight and only slightly tinged pink from chewing betel – kept her from actual beauty.

Still, it was hard not to notice Glory when she walked past. And she knew what impression her appearance made.

And I had liked Glory when I was young.

She taught me how to tie a sari: she held the six yards of silky material in her small hands, deftly wrapping it around her, tying and tucking it just so to emphasise its border, and when she was done it flowed to her feet with graceful folds. She had me practising, laughing at my clumsiness, but helping me until I could do it almost as quickly as she could.

I didn't question why she had so much jewellery – two large tin boxes of brooches and ear bobs and nose rings and bracelets and anklets and rings and necklaces. She would empty the boxes on to her charpoy and we would sit together, me with a sari over my frock, and try on the assorted jewellery, except for the ear and nose rings, for of course I had no punctures.

Glory's hut was far more civilised than Kai's or Pavit's. As well as her charpoy, Glory had Kai put up rough wooden shelves to hold her tin boxes of jewellery and make-up, and he'd driven nails into the chinking between the stones to hold her saris as well as her few English frocks.

And Glory had a chair. This chair, old and spindly and made of teak, with a brocade seat that had once probably been scarlet but now was faded and worn to a streaky pink, was of utmost importance to Glory. Sometimes when I would go to her hut and call her name through the curtain I heard the rustle of her clothing, and knew she had risen and moved, in one swaying, sinuous movement, from her charpoy to the chair. She would call out for me to enter, and there she would be, her back straight, head inclined in an imperious manner, as if she were indeed Queen Victoria receiving a lowly member of court. At some point I realised that Glory felt this chair gave her dignity, and spoke of her English blood.

I will admit that I quite liked Glory when I was still young and naïve. But as I grew older I came to recognise certain truths. The fact that she lacked education was through no fault of her own, but none of the village people who came to the infirmary were formally educated either, and yet most of them did not carry her particular arrogant crudeness. My mother referred to her as coarse, and this was her greatest criticism of Glory.

Secretly I was glad, at the time, for what my mother called coarseness. It made Glory exciting; she was unlike the other ayahs I had seen in the English houses in Lahore, with their lowered eyes and scrubbed faces and white, shapeless outfits, their sliding, soundless movements. Comparing Glory to them was like comparing a beautiful butterfly to a cabbage moth.

When I was twelve I asked Glory her age. She told me she was thirty-one; it sounded very old, but then I realised that Kai was eighteen, and I calculated that she had had him when she was not much older than I was at the time. And, in actuality, she appeared very young, so much so that she and Kai could, with a quick glance by an undiscerning eye, pass as brother and sister.

In that same year Glory had begun to whisper different secrets to me – not just about the lives of the villagers now, but specifically about men. She told me they were all like soft clay in the hands of a woman who knows how to treat them. 'It is water over stones,' she said, her delicate fingers moving through the air, 'making them smooth. So simple, these men. I can get whatever I want, from whatever man I want.'

My parents gave Glory one day a month when she was not required to be at the mission, and on this day she would dress in her best frock and bonnet and slippers and go all the way to Lahore, rising in the dark to walk to the Grand Trunk Road and beg a ride from a passing cart. She would be gone the entire day, not returning until sometime long after I'd gone to bed. In the morning she wore a sleepy but somehow pleased expression, her lips forming into a slightly puffy smile. A day or two later she showed me gifts – the new sari or frock, bracelets or rings – and would put her finger to her lips, saying, 'Don't tell *Abba* or *Mata*, Pree, because they do not like that I have such lovely, lovely things.'

I wondered where she got the rupees to buy these things, for I knew she received only a minimal twice-yearly wage packet from my father. But one day I suddenly put her sly stories about men together with her many pretty possessions, and realised that Glory did not have to buy anything.

And I understood, then, my mother once saying that Glory's true gift was her ability to bewitch and beguile. From that point on I saw her in a different light. I particularly noticed that she wasn't at all maternal to Kai; she treated him as she treated Sanosh, with a kind of resigned, casually friendly manner.

And I could also understand why Kai didn't even call her *Mata*, but Glory.

The fascination I once had with her had long fled. She was lazy. Some days her *surma* was ground into her cheeks from the night before, signifying she hadn't even washed herself before bed or in the morning. She laughed too loudly, her mouth wide open, emitting a puff of betel and cloves. Even her jewellery, which I'd once considered beautiful, now appeared to be nothing more than tarnished tin and winking glass.

'Why does Glory put on such airs?' I'd asked my mother one day. 'She's a servant, and yet she treats me as though I were beneath her.'

'Glory,' my mother spit out the name, 'is a terrible ayah and a woman of questionable morals. What can one expect of someone with her dubious pedigree?' she had muttered. 'It's the fighting of the mixed blood; you can so clearly see her mongrel traces. Much as she wishes to be thought of as English, she's nothing but a Chutney Mary,' she added.

My mother often called Glory a Chutney Mary. I thought of the many Eurasian women I'd see in Lahore over the years, women born of an Indian mother and English father. They belonged to neither world, and some of them tried to pass as English. Although I'm certain a number could not be identified if their skin was light enough and they'd mastered English and the mannerisms well enough, still, the majority of them were immediately and easily spotted. They tried too hard, fawning over each other and especially any Englishman, fluttering their eyelashes and laughing shrilly at anything and everything. Like Glory, their clothing and hairstyles were slightly overdone, their English subtly accented.

And they were looked down upon by both races. The Indians were disgusted by them because of the women's lack of respect for their mother's culture, and the English dismissed them because of what they viewed as laughable attempts to assimilate their father's culture.

Of course no one would ever marry Glory; she was as scorned as a Hindu widow, being a half-caste who had borne a child without benefit of a husband. Glory knew she had little recourse than to stay on at the mission as my mother's ayah, and yet she had a disturbing confidence, a lack of respect for both of my parents.

I occasionally wondered why she felt so secure in her position. Glory held far too much power at the mission, although it was a long time before I understood the reason for this. For her purpose.

And what of my own purpose? I thought about this more and more of late: how did I belong? Oh yes, I knew that I was of importance in helping in the infirmary. I knew I was the daughter of missionaries, helping the heathen in India.

But wasn't there more? What of my future?

Needing to know how I fitted into this world in which I lived, split down the middle between the English mission and the Indian country, haunted me. I was often pensive, wishing to speak to someone of my fears. Kai was the only person I could imagine doing this with, and yet more and more he wasn't near.

And more and more my mother spoke longingly of home. Often now she sat in the yellow chintz chair in the sitting room in the evening, the lamp drawn close, and looked through two old and tattered books. They depicted scenes from the English countryside – one of sepia daguerreotypes and the other of watercolours.

'Do you remember, Reverend,' she'd begin, her hand on one of the images, and when my father would look up from his Bible she'd simply gaze at him.

'Remember what, Mother?' he'd ask, and she'd look at him quizzically, her head tilted to one side as if she was listening for the answer. Eventually he would again lower his head over the Bible, my mother still sitting there, unblinking. At these times I might play the pianoforte to try to cheer her; she had long ago taught me to read music using the hymn book. My favourite was 'Christians Awake' and, although a Christmas hymn, I played it loudly, and with unconcealed zeal, throughout the year. Once it had made my mother smile. But no longer.

I knew that my parents, even after spending so many years in India, still considered themselves visitors to this land, and reminisced about England and its green, misty climate as if it were a dear, dead friend. To them, India was a land of sorrow and disappointments.

Yet India was my country. I knew no other life but that of the mission, the nearby villages, and the city of Lahore. And I loved it all: the sudden, brilliant dawns and glorious red dusks of summer, the look of the sky as the first monsoon blew in, the winter fog that crept, low, over the fields. I loved the green breath of the palms in a sudden, cooling breeze, the churning browns of the river and the way the sunlight played on it, turning it golden. I loved the bright spot of a distant turquoise sari on the dusty road. I loved the smoky odour of dung fires which hung over everything, and the searing smell of hot mustard oil and the sweetness of jasmine and sandalwood. I loved the country sounds: the cooing doves, the screeching of lime and crimson parrots, and the distant baying of pariah dogs. I loved the village sounds of the chants and bells of the Hindu temples, the calls from the muezzins, the bellowing of the decorated, revered cows that roamed the narrow lanes, the melodies created by the twanging strings of the *shnai* and beating on the stretched animal hide of the *tambour* leading a Hindu wedding procession.

I loved the way the languages of the country fell from my lips without thought.

These were the things I knew; the things I couldn't find in the English books.

I belonged to India, and it to me, and I loved it.

I was the daughter of missionaries, and at some point, I realised, it was assumed I would carry on missionary work.

As time passed this filled me with a huge, yawning dread. I was consumed over what my future would hold.

Over what – who – I would become.

CHAPTER SEVEN

WITHIN THE NEXT few months I had more and more responsibility in the infirmary. My mother often stayed in the mission house, not rising from her bed, complaining about her various real or imagined pains, saying I must deal with the women and children.

I craved the unexpectedness each day in the infirmary brought. Who would come through the gate, and with what condition? Although I was always distressed at the sight and sound of another's pain, once I began to deal with the situation a certain detachment came over me, and I was able to attend to the sick and injured with concentration and efficiency.

On this particular day, with the rains finished now, and the air quite warm for October, there were three adults and two children on the verandah of the infirmary.

One was an elderly man with a dirty strip of cloth wrapped around his ribs, and another a middle-aged woman with a large watery growth on her cheekbone. A younger woman, close to my age, held a toddler on her lap and a new baby on her shoulder. The toddler coughed with great whooping, breathy sounds; the mother patted his back, her face creased with worry.

As I came up the steps the man and two women looked at me expectantly, rising out of respect and making *namaste*, and this gave me an unfamiliar stab of pleasure. Was it pride?

If so, I knew I shouldn't feel it — *Pride goeth before a fall, Pree* — but I liked the unmistakable feeling of authority. I smoothed the skirt of my frock on my thighs, and cleared my throat. Suddenly I wished I weren't barefoot.

'*Namaste*,' I said in return, pressing my palms together in front of my chest. As I bowed my head I saw that my toenails needed trimming. 'The Sahib will come soon to attend you,' I then told the old man, speaking in Punjabi, recognising by his dhoti that this was his dialect.

I led the women to the back verandah, and told the young mother that her son had chin-cough, giving her a spill of salt of tartar and telling her how to mix it in warm water and dose the little boy with it every few hours. Then I took two dried figs from my apron pocket and handed them to him; he stared at me solemnly and then took them, jamming them both into his mouth. The mother smiled hesitantly at me, and pulled a small twist of fabric from within her sari folds. I smelled saffron, and took the spice, nodding my thanks.

She left, and I turned my attention to the older woman with her growth.

The Muslim women who were allowed out of *purdah* came to the mission in their veils, or even in a covered cart, accompanied by a brother, a son, a husband or father. The Hindu women came with other women. And of course these women would only discuss and show their bodies to another female. Their choices in their villages were to be tended to by a midwife who had general knowledge of the female body and a selection of plant and herbal remedies and cures, often built on superstition, or to send a male related by blood or marriage to the *hakim* in a larger town to describe their ailments. The *hakim* — a local man trained in medical ways — could only listen to the symptoms and pass on information on how to deal with the illnesses or injuries of their wives or mothers, sisters or daughters.

Although many were treated successfully by age-old remedies – and in actuality, my mother also used some of the Indian remedies, although my father did not believe in them – other villagers, when finding no relief in the attempts of the midwife or *hakim*, chose the foreign medical help. The women and young children were ministered to on the back verandah by my mother, while my father dealt with the men on the front verandah. There were always far more female and child patients than men. Some of the patients arrived empty handed; others brought a squawking chicken or small sack of lentils or a twist of seeds in a torn strip of cloth as payment.

Although my father had not trained as an apothecary, and wouldn't have been allowed to dispense medicines in England, who was to prevent him doing so here? He was able to obtain what supplies he needed through the Ministry in Lahore, who ordered for him what he listed; no one questioned his need for the instruments, the bandages, and the variety of tablets and liquids to help the suffering.

I believe my mother must have, in her younger years, been a quick learner, for hadn't she learned the rudiments of basic surgery – stitching torn skin and setting broken bones – with no more training than carefully observing my father and asking many questions? She had long been his helpmate in the infirmary, and, in actuality, I saw, even in my early years, how deep her interest was. She regularly read the medical books kept in the infirmary, and was far more adept at diagnosing skin ailments and infections of the eyes and mouth and distresses of the intestines and bowels than my father. She actually understood more of the physician's role, dealing with problems within the body, while my father, in a determined, unimaginative manner, dealt with the surgeon's duties of simple repairs to visible concerns.

At some point, connecting body and spirit, I considered that perhaps my father was unable to minister to inner physics in the same way he was unable to successfully pass on inner beliefs.

The only thing my mother would never do was amputations; oddly, my father, for all his apparent gentleness, would carry these out as if almost excited at the prospect, although thankfully he wouldn't do them at the mission. If he determined there was no cure for the gangrenous limb, or one too badly crushed or injured through accident, he would go to the home of the patient and carry out the unpleasant act there.

As well, my father and mother would treat the *sudras*, who were not allowed near the midwife or *hakim*'s home because they would defile it by their presence. But they could only come to the infirmary in the evenings, when it was certain that no other patients were present. And they had to be treated in a special corner near the convenience, far behind the house, away from the infirmary and courtyard. Otherwise the other castes of Hindus would no longer come to the mission and be in contact with polluted ground, and my father would lose even that tenuous thread of connection with the people of the villages.

From my earliest memory I had seen people coming to the infirmary, and had witnessed any number of disturbing physical ailments and disabilities and injuries. And in the way of these things, because I had always seen them, they held little horror or fear for me. And, as my mother had, I learned the craft by watching and listening and, in time, poring over the handful of books on medicine and healing my father had brought with him from England.

I understood the role of quinine and laudanum, oil of turpentine and chlorine and sulfur. I observed that the needles used to stitch through torn flesh must first be held

87

over a flame. I learned that to avoid allowing miasma into an open wound the dressing must be soaked in carbolic.

I learned how to treat Pavit's suppurating sores with gurjon, chalmugra and marotty oils. I had taken over his treatment last year; I went to his hut once a week, and, as my father had demonstrated, first wrapped my own hands in clean muslin before touching Pavit's bandages. I put the used bandages into a tin pail and later dumped them to be burned. I applied the oils to Pavit's rotting limbs with a smooth flat stick. It was my mother who instructed me to tie a clean strip of muslin dipped in attar of roses around my nose and mouth to help stave off the odour.

I learned about fumigation and purging. I understood the cause of fungal infections, and about intestinal worms and how to rid the body of them; how to treat the flux that tormented so many babies in hot weather, dehydrating them and sometimes contributing to their deaths. I watched how torn flesh was stitched closed, and how broken bones could be mended with splints. I learned that attempting to wash blood from fabric with soap only created a slimy mess, and that cold water alone would do the job. I saw how boils were lanced and afterwards treated with Venice turpentine, and burns were soothed by a mixture of oil and powdered ginger. I folded paper spills and counted out tablets into them, handed my mother gauze and scissors, threaded needles, rolled long strips of muslin into bandages, and washed instruments.

I had always considered the work I did in the infirmary as simply another of my daily chores, like washing clothes or feeding the chickens or sweeping the verandahs or bringing in brass lotahs of water for washing down the floors of the house. But it was five months earlier that I had begun to help in earnest, performing my own first surgery.

The patient was Lalasa, my best friend.

★ ★ ★

It had been the middle of May, with the heat of summer full upon us. It sucked the vitality from the trees, the gardens, even the animals; the goats on the road standing with their heads down, and the chickens disappearing into the dusty ragged hedges. Marta folded her legs under her and refused to move for hours on end. Red dust swirled through the air on harsh winds, filling my nostrils and coating my throat, giving my damp, sweating skin a gritty feel. The dust and dirt was driven through the cracks in the mission walls, piling in small drifts along the floorboards. White ants had eaten through the book I was in the process of reading: Bulwer-Lytton's *The Last Days of Pompeii*, destroying it, the morocco cover crumbling in my hands as I took it from the shelf over my bed.

As was usual in the hot season, we had no patients after tiffin, our noon meal. Most came in the slightly cooler early morning hours, or waited until the worst fury of the daytime heat was spent.

My mother and I were inside the infirmary, silently rolling bandages, when an ox-cart, pulled by two young water buffalo, rumbled into the courtyard. I went to the verandah; a thin, middle-aged man jumped off and went to the flat back of the cart to lift down a young woman. Another woman climbed from the cart; I didn't recognise the man, and the woman had her azure headscarf wrapped around her face so that only her eyes showed.

She followed the man, weeping loudly. The girl made no sound as she was carried to the back verandah and set on the curling piece of matting. She had the end of her own headscarf — it was orange — balled into her mouth, and bit down on the soaked cotton as her head turned from side to side. Her eyes were squeezed shut, and tears ran from their outer corners, down into her ears.

'Lalasa,' I breathed, recognising, with a jolt, my old friend. Her shin bone protruded, horribly white and sharp, through the torn skin just below her knee. Lalasa was a year younger than I was and had often, through the years, come to the infirmary with her mother. Her mother suffered from lesions of the skin, which were helped by regular treatments of sulfur. I had never before seen her father.

As a child, Lalasa had been tiny and delicate, with huge dark eyes always ringed with *surma*. She had a broad forehead and a small, pointed chin and open smile. Over those earlier years, while her mother had waited for my mother to attend to her, Lalasa and I had played endless games of *lattoo*. I had grown deft at spinning one of the two tops Lalasa always brought. They were made of burnt earth and had a pin at the bottom. A string was wrapped round the lower part of the *lattoo*, and I quickly learned how to give the string a hard jerk as I tossed the *lattoo* to the ground. Mine usually spun the longer; Lalasa didn't mind that I so often won.

At other times we crouched in the tall, rustling rows of corn behind the infirmary, pretending we were hiding from the Afghans who were known for kidnapping beautiful *ranis*, taking them back to their camps and tents to be their own Indian queens. Lalasa tried to make me fearful of the Afghans who passed on the road, but she couldn't frighten me. I had my own Afghan and knew they were not all of the nature Lalasa believed.

There was only one thing about Lalasa that spoiled my pleasure at seeing her. She had a doll, an English doll with yellow hair and porcelain skin, which she carried about with her. She had received it as a present, she said, although she couldn't remember who had given it to her a number of years earlier. Each time she came to the infirmary she put this doll into my hands as if offering me the loan of a brilliant gift. I took it, holding it gingerly, because the doll made my chest tight and my jaw clench. She made me feel, at those times, the way Eleanor Wyndham made me feel. And again, I was filled with the sensation that I belonged to neither world, not Lalasa's Indian world, and not in the world of Lahore's English cantonment.

I pretended to Lalasa, for I loved her, that I admired the doll, but in the darkest places of my heart I wanted to never see it again, and was angry with Lalasa for forcing it upon me. I suppose it was simple childish jealousy: a Hindu village girl possessing a beautiful English doll, while I, a true English girl, had never had a doll of my own.

Eventually, when it no longer mattered to me, Lalasa stopped bringing the doll. And then one day it was not she, but her younger sister, who accompanied their mother to the infirmary. The sister said Lalasa was too busy at home, cooking for their father and caring for the latest baby sister, and could no longer waste a morning or afternoon at the infirmary. I missed her terribly.

Now it had been at least two years since I'd seen her; although still delicate, today her face had a grey pallor, and was wet with sweat and tears of agony. Her *surma* was smeared over her cheeks.

'What happened, Lalasa?' I breathed in Hindi. But she didn't open her eyes. I stepped out of the way as my mother leaned over, her hands on her knees, looking at the injured leg.

Then she turned to me. 'It's a clean break, Pree. You look after this one. My head is playing up with the weather today; I haven't the energy.'

My heart gave one heavy knock, and then beat with a hurried thudding, but I nodded, pulling my mother's low, three-legged wooden stool from against the wall for her to sit on. Plagued by her rheumatism, it was too painful for her to lower herself to the patients as they sat or lay on the floor.

Then I went into the infirmary and returned with a bottle of laudanum and the supplies I needed. I knew what had to be done — but I had never done it myself.

Kneeling beside Lalasa, I poured the first spoonful of laudanum. Her father lifted her head — less than gently — and yanked the cotton from her mouth. Lalasa opened her eyes.

'*Kripaya, Abba*,' she said, *Please, Father*, and it was clear that she was frightened — not only of the pain, but of her father. She looked at me, and her eyes grew even wider. I realised she hadn't even heard my voice when I first spoke to her.

'Rest easy, please, rest easy, Lalasa. I'll help you,' I said, although my hand was trembling slightly, and two drops of the laudanum dripped on to her sari. I gripped the handle of the spoon more firmly and directed the liquid to her mouth. She swallowed it, grimacing, and I gave her another two spoonfuls.

'That's enough, Pree,' my mother said, watching from her stool. 'The next supply doesn't come for two weeks.'

I put the stopper in the bottle, and as I waited for the medicine to numb the worst of the pain I sat beside her, talking to her quietly, asking unimportant questions: was her sari new, how was her sister, did she still have the old doll — trying to occupy her mind.

But Lalasa was in too much distress to answer. Or perhaps she was afraid to speak. She only shook her head restlessly, her eyes shutting again.

'How did she break her leg?' I asked her father, taking a deep breath and pouring carbolic over the blood-caked flesh around the wound. Lalasa cried out sharply, pulling at her hair, and her father, with obvious annoyance in his voice, said that she'd fallen from the roof of their house, where she'd climbed up to repair an opening in the thatch.

'Because I have no son, she must do the work of a boy,' he said, looking reproachfully at the mother, still weeping behind her own headscarf. 'And she is clumsy, always hurting herself,' he added. 'Useless, this girl.'

Finally the laudanum began to work. Lalasa breathed more slowly, and her head no longer thrashed. She opened her eyes and looked at my face again; her pupils were huge.

My mother stood and used her boot to move the stool along the verandah floor. The wooden legs made a long screeching cry as the stool was shoved into place behind Lalasa's head. My mother again lowered herself on to it. She nodded at the father as she firmly placed both hands on to his daughter's right shoulder. He did the same to the left.

'Hold her other leg,' I said to her mother. She shook her head, her wet eyes wide, but at a barking command from her husband she let go of the ends of her headscarf and knelt at her daughter's undamaged leg, placing her hands tightly around the slender ankle.

And then my mother said, 'All right, Pree,' and I took a deep breath and gripped the swollen, spongy leg and shoved the bone into place. Lalasa screamed, a long, shrill cry that seemed to come from not only her mouth, but her whole body, her head rising from the mat. Her mother shrieked with her. Then Lalasa's head dropped back, and while the mother continued to wail, Lalasa made only small panting sounds in her throat. Her chest rose and fell, rose and fell as I held a short splint on one side of her leg, and then the other, wrapping them with strips of muslin above and below the open wound so that the bone was held firmly in place. When I had finished my back teeth ached, and I realised I had clenched them so tightly that I felt tension radiating down my spine.

Lalasa was moaning now, and I gave her another spoonful of laudanum, in spite of my mother's protest, and stitched the jagged opening in her shin. The sharp needle went through the flesh as though through heavy cotton; I was surprised that the skin yielded so easily. It was no more difficult than stitching the edges of the endless handkerchiefs my mother used on her mouth; it had long been my job to cut white cotton squares and hem them for my mother's needed supply.

When there was a neat, narrow path of small stitches, I tied the thread and nipped it with the small steel scissors, then covered the long wound loosely with gauze held with more narrow strips of the fabric. Lalasa's moans diminished to a low, rhythmic hiccupping.

I stood, rubbing my hands on my apron, and held out a paper spill to her father. 'You must give her one sulfur tablet three times during the daylight hours, and do not allow her to move her leg. She cannot do any work for thirty days,' I said, glancing at my mother, and she nodded. 'Thirty days,' I repeated, and the man glared at his wife as if it were she who had made this demand.

'If you make her rise and work before that,' I continued, 'the bone will not mend. It will break again, and come out through the skin, and you will have to bring her here once more and I will do the same thing. But the next time she won't be able to work for much longer,' I told him. 'Maybe more than sixty days.'

He muttered something I couldn't hear.

'Or she will be lame for the rest of her life, and of even less use to you. Perhaps unmarriageable,' I said, adding that last sentence for effect.

He scowled, narrowing his eyes as he looked down at this daughter. 'She is to be married in six months,' he said. 'The date is set.'

'Auntie,' I said, turning to her mother, 'every day you must remove this bandage,' I pointed to the gauze, 'and wash the wound with this.' I handed her the bottle of carbolic, as well as a fat roll of gauze. 'Then wrap it in a fresh bandage. At first she will cry, because it will sting and burn, but you must do it, or the stitches will become rotten. Do you understand?' She nodded. 'After fourteen days you must bring her back,' I said, once more, for effect.

Then I called my father. He glanced down at the leg in the splint. His normally pale face was florid in the heat and Lalasa's mother's face grew fearful at his countenance. She pulled her headscarf down over her eyes.

'I did it,' I said, wanting his approval.

'Fine,' he said, in a distracted manner, disappointing me. I had expected some praise higher than that one word. And then he and Lalasa's father used the carrier we kept for this purpose – a strip of tightly woven cane tied firmly between two bamboo poles – to carry the girl back to the cart.

When they had left, my mother nodded at me, reaching up to pin a limp strand of hair back in place. 'Well, you didn't make too much of a mess of that,' she said. It was more of a compliment than my father had seen fit to give me. 'Although it's doubtful that girl will be allowed to heal fully. We'll be lucky to see her again, or, if we do, she'll be a cripple.'

My smile faded, and I went into the infirmary to clean the needle and put away the supplies I'd used. My mother knew how to spoil everything.

CHAPTER EIGHT

THE YEAR FOLLOWING my botched baptism passed with regularity: the winter months of December and January were predictably cold, and some mornings when I emerged on to the verandah I'd see Pavit huddled in shawls over the tiny twig fire he'd lit outside his hut.

It was in January, after the Maghi Festival, that I learned one of Kai's secrets.

Celebrated at the culmination of winter, the people of the Punjab rejoice at the last sowing of the winter crop, and the festival was held to ensure fertility and prosperity. I went, with Sanosh, to the Maghi festival in Tek Mandi. My mother didn't wish me to go, but my father allowed it. Kai had been gone for much of January.

In Sanosh's village, a bonfire was lit, and both men and women danced around it. Sanosh gave me handfuls of popped corn to throw into the fire, offering sacrifice so that, in turn, the villagers would be blessed with a rich harvest. Many of the villagers wore new clothing, and I laughed with Darshan as he joined his father and I in a shuffled rhythm around the fire.

As the fire burned down and the villagers made their way to their huts, Sanosh and I walked back to the mission. He went to the *rasoi* to sleep, but, still excited by the evening, I didn't wish to go into the house. Instead, I sat under the peepul tree. As I sat in the still night air, I heard voices from Kai's hut.

Pleased, I hurried towards his hut, anxious to see him after his last few weeks of absence. But as I approached, I heard low moans, and answering whispers. There was the clink of glass; a lamp burned in the hut, and behind the screened mat that covered the door I saw movement.

'No,' a man's voice came. 'Leave it.'

'Kai?' I said, softly, and the hut was immediately quiet.

Kai pulled back the mat, and I was shocked at his appearance. He wore no shirt, and his chest was bruised; there was a deep gash on one of his shoulders. His face was haggard, his nose strangely askew, and shreds of dried blood were flecked around his nostrils. His lips, even in the dim lamplight, were chalky.

'What's happened?' I asked. 'Kai, who did this to you?'

Kai motioned with his head for me to enter.

A young man – a Sikh, in his black turban – lay on Kai's charpoy. I could immediately tell, by the strange position and protrusions of his lower arm, that both the radius and ulna were broken. He cradled the broken arm with his other. There was a slash across his neck; luckily it hadn't gone deep enough to cut the jugular vein, but I could see that Kai had been trying to staunch the flow of blood. There was a bottle of chlorine and a bloodied rag on the charpoy. A *kirpan* – the Sikh's sword – lay on the floor. The man's face was contorted with pain as he spoke. 'Who is the woman?'

'She's all right. She won't say anything. And she can help. Pree, can you look after his arm? And the worst cuts?'

He stared at me intently, and I knew it was not the time to ask questions. I nodded, then told Kai what to fetch from the infirmary. With his help, I set the man's arm and cleaned and bound his neck. None of us spoke, although the man hissed through his teeth and made sounds deep in his throat as I worked on him.

When I had finished I stood back from the charpoy.

'Thank you, Pree,' Kai said. 'Now leave us.'

'Let me tend to your shoulder,' I said. 'And your nose is probably broken.'

'Never mind. I'm fine,' he said. 'Please. Go.'

I did as he said, knowing he would have to tell me, the next day, what had happened.

During prayers the next morning I kept looking at Kai's hut, wondering if he still hid the other man there. On my way to the infirmary I stopped outside his hut, and called Kai's name. At the low reply I pulled aside the door cover. Kai was alone. He lay on his charpoy, on his back, staring at the ceiling.

'Are you all right?' I asked, and he said, very softly, 'Yes, yes, Pree, just leave me.'

Later that day, when I saw him, slowly and stiffly forking straw into Marta's enclosure, I went to him.

'Will you tell me where you've been, Kai? And what happened, to you, and to your friend?'

He looked at me then, studying my face, and gripping the pitchfork. 'Have you heard of the Kukas?' he asked, and I nodded.

'My father has spoken of them. Sikhs. They cause trouble throughout the Punjab, he said, committing various crimes.'

Kai's jaw shifted. 'Is it a crime to want the rule of our own brothers? Is it a crime to work towards the expulsion of the British? Since 1857 they have done nothing but divide the country, Pree. They consider themselves virtual masters of our land; they are governing through a strategy of divide and rule, creating conflict among us.' His voice had grown louder, and I held my breath, seeing on his face the same grim look as the night around the fire in the field, when he burnt the effigy of a British soldier. Was he forgetting my father and my mother and I were also the British he spoke of with such venom?

'The Kukas are not troublemakers. They are torch-bearers in India's freedom struggle,' he said, through his teeth. He stabbed the pitchfork into the ground with such force that the handle vibrated, and I stepped back.

'But ... but you're not a Sikh,' I said, as if I told him something important he didn't know. 'How can you—'

'They are in need of able-bodied men to help.' He absently wiped his lips, and winced as his knuckles came in contact with his nose.

'How were you – and your friend – hurt?' I asked.

He didn't answer, pulling the pitchfork out of the ground and turning his back, resuming his work.

A few days later, as my father and I sat on the verandah in the evening, I asked, my voice deceptively carefree, 'Have the Kukas created more conflict of late?'

My father closed his Bible. 'It's odd you should ask about the Kukas. Only today I heard, from one of the men who came to the infirmary, that there was a great disturbance at Bhaini Sahib, near Ludhiana. Apparently a group of Kukas attacked Malerkotia; many were captured. Some were killed by cannon fire and others sentenced to life imprisonment.' He shook his head. 'Everything possible is being done to stop them. Their goal is to erode the faith in the British legal system. Of course they will never succeed. A new rule has been created; now it's against the law for more than five Kukas to ever gather in one place.' He ran his hand over the cover of his Bible. 'Did the natives not learn from the disaster of the Mutiny in '57?' He opened the Bible. 'What made you ask about them, at this particular time?'

Kai walked across the courtyard, and I quickly stood,

blocking him from my father's view, as if I had put Kai in danger. 'Oh, nothing, nothing at all, Father. Just idle thoughts.'

Only when he bent his head over his Bible did I take my seat again, following Kai's movements as he left the mission with a quick, purposeful stride.

The short but lovely spring, February and March, brought fresh winds and a burst of colour from the fields. Summer descended like a woollen canopy in May, the suffocating heat lasting through July, and then the rains came again.

Now each time Kai left the mission I worried, imagining him being caught in some illicit activity, and meeting death, blown to shreds, at the mouth of a British cannon. And yet after a few days he would return, and I was always relieved, not only to see him, but to notice that he never again appeared injured in any way.

My mother's behaviour grew evermore erratic; my father and I didn't speak of it, but it was a constant concern. On the bad days she didn't even play the pianoforte. And then suddenly, like a pale sun after a long rain, she had days when she acted quite well. After each of these days of normality I went to bed hopeful, thinking that perhaps whatever plagued her had passed. But within a short time the strangeness would return: the blank stares and stopped conversation, the nonsensical statements and confused placement of objects in the house and infirmary.

The strange times lasted for longer and longer periods, and I had more responsibilities in the infirmary and in the garden. I had little time for reading or dreaming, and I mourned the loss of the small freedoms that had been so important to me.

The downward spiral had a firm grip on the mission by my sixteenth birthday.

On the morning of 17 August, after morning prayers, my

mother and father both wished me well, and gave me my usual gift: a new pair of stockings.

I thanked them, trying to force an enthusiastic note into my voice. But as I fingered the hated lisle, an oppressive weight descended on to my shoulders. I thought of turning twenty, and then thirty, a spinster missionary, perhaps wearing spectacles, my eyes weakened by reading tiny script in poor light for so many years. Living here, in the lonely mission off the Grand Trunk Road, treating patients and talking about the Lord's wonders and never having a convert. And every birthday receiving a new pair of lisle stockings from my stooped, white-haired parents who presented me the yearly gift with trembling, spotted hands.

I thought of Lalasa; she had never come back to the infirmary after I set her leg, but I had heard, from Sanosh, that she had married a boy named Balin and now lived in the village further down the road with her husband's family.

Would I ever marry?

'What's wrong, Pree?' my father asked, and I realised my eyes were burning with tears.

'Nothing,' I said.

He put his hand on my shoulder. 'I'm sorry there is never money for anything more, Pree. If we could, we would . . .' he stopped, looking at my mother, as if unsure of what they would actually do. What they would give me as a birthday gift if they could afford more than stockings? Did they know me at all?

'Mother,' my father said, touching his own chin, and my mother slowly raised her handkerchief and swabbed away the shining saliva that had run from her loose bottom lip.

'So although I'm sorry there's little we can give you,' he continued, looking back to me, 'I've arranged for your mother and you to go into Lahore tomorrow. I heard, the last time I was at the ministry to collect my wages, that Mrs

Wyndham is having an Afternoon Tea. I took note of the date because it was the day after your birthday. You'll be welcome to attend, and I'm sure you'll enjoy yourself. Apparently Eleanor is finished school now, and here on a visit. You remember Eleanor,' he said, and I nodded. 'It will be a birthday treat,' he went on. 'And I'll instruct Sanosh to make you *ladoos*,' my father said, smiling stiffly. 'You'd like that, wouldn't you? I'm sure you like *ladoos*.'

Again, I nodded. 'Thank you, Father,' I said, returning his smile, trying to make mine more natural than his.

The sticky Indian sweet was indeed my favourite, but I didn't know my father knew this. He was trying so hard. But instead of cheering me, it only made me feel worse.

As my parents turned from me I looked at their backs. I must love them, surely, but at this moment I could feel little but growing panic. My father with his broken-down holiness, my mother with her weary bitterness and weakening grip on reality, their combined unhappiness . . . suddenly they filled me with fury. Was it hate I actually felt for them? They were blocking me — obliterating my vision, and my future. I wanted to be able to see around them, past them, even through them, and assure myself I was not like them. Would not become like them.

I knew my thoughts were uncharitable and small of spirit. I knew they did their best — for me, for the villagers, for the Lord. Compared to so, so many I had seen, in the villages and in Lahore, I had a life of excess: clothing to cover me, a sturdy house to keep me from the elements, a full stomach every night. I was sound in body. I loved my work in the infirmary, I loved to read my books, I loved Jassie. Sanosh and Pavit treated me with respect and kindness; I cared deeply about both of them. Glory was of little consequence. And then there was Kai.

I watched my parents leave the verandah and cross the

courtyard to the infirmary. My mother slipped in the wet mud; my father gripped her arm, helping her the rest of the way.

Happy Birthday, Pree. You selfish, ungrateful, hateful thing, I told myself.

Later, Kai presented me with a beautiful morocco leather journal.

'Kai! I love it. Thank you,' I said, stroking the soft cover and smiling at him. This smile was genuine, unlike the one I'd presented to my parents.

He returned the smile, his rare, open smile. His eye-teeth, slightly pointed, were a fraction of an inch longer than his front teeth.

'I thought of you when I saw it in Lahore, last month, and knew it would be perfect for you. To record your thoughts.'

'But . . . it must have been so dear. Where did you get the money?' I asked, and was immediately sorry, for his smile dropped away, and his face closed. 'I'm sorry,' I quickly added, 'Thank you again, Kai.' I picked up his hand and closed my fingers around his to show him how pleased I was. He squeezed my hand briefly, then tried to let it go. I clung to his fingers for a second longer than I should have.

'Happy Birthday, Pree,' he said again, taking a step back and disengaging his hand. 'I've been meaning to tell you something.'

An unknown look on his face filled me with trepidation. 'What is it?'

'I'm planning to leave the mission,' he said.

I felt the blood drain from my face. 'Leave the mission?'

He nodded. 'I'll look for work in Lahore. Perhaps as a clerk.'

'A clerk?' Why did I keep echoing his words? I knew I had paled; did Kai notice? 'You would be a clerk?' I said again, and a shadow passed over his face. I couldn't imagine Kai on a stool, hunched over a ledger in a dim, dusty room. Even though he was Eurasian, he wasn't anything like so many of the *babus* I'd witnessed, bowing and scraping to their English supervisors. 'You couldn't be happy as a clerk, Kai,' I said, shaking my head.

He said nothing, and I thought of the tiny, flickering change I'd seen on his face. No one else may have noticed it, but I knew Kai too well. He was lying. He wasn't going to be a clerk at all.

'What will you do, Kai?' I said again, so softly, and this time he turned his face from me, so I could no longer read what I saw there.

'There are things I must do, Pree. And I cannot do them while I am caught in the web of the mission.'

'The web?' Everything he said was somehow disconcerting.

He said nothing more, but I saw the blood beat, steadily, in the vein on his temple.

I don't want you to go. I wanted to say it aloud, but was fearful of appearing desperate. 'When do you propose to leave?' I asked, striving to keep my voice light.

'Before too long,' he answered, maddeningly. Did this mean in a week, a month? Next year?

So here was a further reason for dreading my future at the mission: losing Kai.

The next day my mother and I made the journey to Lahore, leaving late morning so as to arrive by early afternoon.

I had been able to sleep only fitfully, thinking about Kai leaving, and my eyes felt raw as we left the mission. I tried to find the usual excitement I experienced over going to Lahore a few times a year. But it was difficult. My heart heavy, I drove Marta down the Grand Trunk Road. We were fortunate to have only a bit of soft rain throughout the whole three hours, and by keeping our shawls over our heads my mother and I stayed fairly dry.

The road wasn't overly busy this day, and I barely had to touch the leather straps to Marta's back to keep her walking a straight path. We went along the raised road through fields of wheat stubble and yellow mustard. Dragonflies of red and orange swooped along the sides of the road. Clumps of mud villages appeared and disappeared, always with ragged or near-naked children running alongside the cart; women bent over fires or swayed gracefully between the huts with earthen or brass water carriers on their heads. A group of leathery water buffalos stood under a thorn tree, small white cattle egrets on their backs.

Suddenly my mother cried out. 'Stop! Stop the cart, Pree,' and thinking she had to relieve herself, I pulled on Marta's reins.

We were at a quiet, shady juncture, where a smaller road ran off the Grand Trunk. There was a rough, domed stone cenotaph between two trees; my mother hurried to it. She put her hand on whatever was carved there. As she reverently stroked it, I climbed down and joined her. I saw that the crumbling monument she touched was a *chattri* – one of the *sati* stones marking the site of some long-forgotten sacrifice occasionally seen along the Grand Trunk Road. My mother was caressing the primitive figures carved into the chipped and mossy stone. I could just make out the shapes of a man and woman, and knew this was the spot where a widow, long ago, judging by the state of the *chattri*, had sacrificed herself by climbing on to her husband's funeral pyre. By burning herself alive with her dead husband, she was ensuring the husband's successful rebirth. I knew that the wives who had done this throughout history in India – although it had been outlawed by the English forty years earlier – also believed that in joining their souls with the goddess Sati Mata, they would bring good luck for seven generations to not only their own families, but also their villages.

There was a small pile of rain-soaked marigolds at the foot of the stone, and smears of vermillion running down one side; someone had recently decorated the *chattri*, perhaps in a ceremonial gesture.

I stood beside my mother for a few minutes, then took advantage of the secluded spot, going behind the clustered stones, but when I had finished and returned, my mother was still in front of the little shrine. I grew restless, making designs in the mud with the toe of my boot. Finally my mother touched her lips with her fingertips and then placed them against the bosom of the stone woman.

'Such dedication,' she said, turning to me. Her eyes were bright.

'Yes. But the younger widows would have most likely left small children behind, orphaned,' I said.

'But they would live for ever under the honour of their mother's selfless death. It was a gift, possibly the only gift they could leave the children. As widows they would be useless anyway. They were more good to their children dead than alive. Don't you see, Pree?'

Of course I understood, but was perplexed. This was so unlike my mother, revering a Hindu custom. 'I suppose so. We still have a long way to go,' I said, and she followed me back to where Marta waited patiently, pulling weeds from the roadside with loud, rasping tears.

As we started again I opened the tin box of food Sanosh had packed for us: *katlamas*, the fried *roti* stuffed with minced goat meat and lentil paste; curried potato and okra samosas, and roasted chickpeas. My mother took only a handful of the chickpeas; she had never grown used to Indian food. I thought about what delicacies we might be served at the

Wyndhams', urging Marta into a lumbering trot so that we would arrive at Lahore sooner.

I sat straighter, gripping the reins as we approached the outskirts of Lahore, seeing the glorious towers and high, gilded cupolas of the centuries-old architecture. I manoeuvred Marta through one of the city's twelve gates; we passed rope makers and men hammering silver and brass. Then the streets grew evermore congested, and it was difficult to drive Marta forward. We constantly had to stop for other carts and animals, for horses and people, all crowded on to the narrow streets. There were cloth sellers and weavers, men cleaning other men's ears with long sticks, or cutting hair. Finally I urged Marta into an area of carts and bullocks and water buffalo, paying a small boy an anna to sit in our cart and wait for our return.

From there we took a rickshaw to the English cantonment; it had been a number of years since we had been invited here.

The rickshaw-wallah ran down the wide avenue of poplar and tamarind trees, passing beautiful, gleaming white bungalows. They were separated from each other by shaded gardens and spacious lawns of green which caught the watery sun that suddenly emerged from behind long gauzy clouds, covering everything in a silvery light. Along the drive that we turned into at my mother's request were brilliantly coloured oleander and hydrangea growing in tended profusion, thriving in the wet air.

My mother paid the rickshaw-wallah and we went to the high double doors with a gleaming brass knocker. The knocker had barely touched its brass pad when the door was opened by a *chuprassi* in a wide red sash.

Bowing, he admitted us and held out his hand for our shawls. I realised the shoulders of my frock were quite wet.

It appeared that the Wyndhams' opulent home hadn't changed to any great degree in the last few years. It was I who had changed. When I had last been here, I had been an innocent, excited child. This day, standing in the formal entrance, I was suddenly cautious, unsure of my presence here. My mouth was dry, my stomach churning. Now I knew I was certain I wouldn't be able to consume anything after all.

When we were ushered into the drawing room the conversation stopped and all eyes turned to stare at us.

'Oh,' Mrs Wyndham said, rising swiftly, standing still for a moment, and then crossing the room to us. 'How lovely to see you again, Mrs Fincastle. And . . . my, Miss Fincastle, haven't you grown up,' she stated, although her eyes raked over my face in a frankly disturbing manner. I wondered if I had a smear of dirt on my cheek, or a crumb of the *roti* I'd eaten on the way stuck to my lip. I resisted the urge to touch my face with my fingertips.

'We've just begun to serve the tea,' she said. 'I wasn't aware you—' She stopped, glancing at the woman nearest her, and by the look on her face I knew we hadn't actually been invited. Had my father said this – that an invitation had been extended to us – or had he simply heard of the social afternoon? Surely, judging by Mrs Wyndham's reaction, it had been the latter. My face burned; I couldn't look at my mother. Did she understand this, and the terrible breach of propriety?

'Do take a seat, Mrs Fincastle. And just look, Eleanor, here's Miss Fincastle. It's been . . . how long? Nine years, I would think, since you girls have seen each other.' She looked pointedly at a young woman sitting on a delicate tapestry chair of petit-point roses.

Eleanor didn't rise. 'Yes. I remember Miss Fincastle. Although I don't think I would have recognised her,' she said, her voice high and light.

I didn't know how to respond to this statement. I only knew I was suddenly too hot, aware of my limp and damp dull green frock, my heavy boots. Eleanor wore pink satin slippers.

'Please, sit here, Mrs Fincastle. And Miss Fincastle, just there, beside my Eleanor. You young ladies will have a great deal to talk about. Now, what can I offer you? Tea? Or some orange squash?' She clapped her hands and a number of servants holding silver trays emerged from the corners of the room.

I sat in the glorious room, looking at the paintings lining the walls: mountains and castles and lakes and stern gentlemen, all in baroque gilt frames. I took off my gloves and ran my fingertips over the satiny damask-cushioned seat of the chair on which I sat. The tables in front of me and to each side were ivory inlay and highly polished dark wood. Through an arched opening into an adjoining room I saw glass-fronted shelves with hundreds of books, and a grand pianoforte of gleaming mahogany. I wished I were alone in this house for just one day, and could do whatever I chose. I would play the pianoforte – surely it was in tune – and sing as prettily as I could; I would look at every book on the shelves; I would take off my boots and run barefoot on the carpets that appeared to be plush velvet; I would call up into the high, vaulted ceilings, call my own name, *Pree Fincastle*, and hear it echo and bounce around me.

But of course I kept my back straight and my knees and ankles together and drank orange squash and managed, after all, to eat a lemon curd horn and a thimble biscuit, with its depression of sticky jam in the centre, served to me by a stout, bare-footed Hindu in a spotless white uniform. The pastries were delicate and tasty, but I didn't enjoy them as I'd imagined. One of the other guests gave me a small booklet of navy silk. It was called *Basic Instruction for the Beautiful Table*, the latest instructions on proper table settings in England just now, she said, and every young woman should have one. She had given a copy to Miss Eleanor as well, she told me.

I put the book on the table beside me; at one point when the conversation was all around me but I was not included, I picked it up and looked through it. There were simple illustrations of folding serviettes into various shapes so that one was able to set a cut rose into a fold or make a little basket to hold what looked like wrapped sweets. It was a silly book I had no interest in. When I returned it to the table I saw that my fingers, greasy from the thick, buttery biscuits, had left dark marks. I realised that in spite of the book's subject, I hadn't even used the serviette still folded in my lap.

By the end of two long hours I was exhausted and wished to be gone. The women – Mrs Wyndham and the other twelve ladies whose names I had somehow forgotten after being introduced – had clearly ignored us. But it was Eleanor who made me feel truly terrible; had she not been there perhaps my later unforgivable behaviour would not have occurred.

CHAPTER NINE

'WHY, I CAN'T keep track of all of Eleanor's beaus. She cannot attend a single soiree without her dance card filled weeks in advance,' Mrs Wyndham announced loudly, beaming at her daughter. Eleanor smiled demurely, a dimple I hadn't noticed before appearing, charmingly, in her left cheek.

I was relieved Mrs Wyndham didn't bother to enquire how many beaus I had.

As her mother boasted on and on about Eleanor's accomplishments, I stole glances at her. She had inclined her upper body just a few inches in the opposite direction of my chair, and this slight movement made it perfectly clear she did not care to associate with me. She was no longer the girl with fuzzy curls and a wide smile with missing front teeth. Now everything about her was smooth and perfect. She was a highly groomed, eloquent and worldly young woman, while I . . . I was the same Pree, wearing cast-off clothing, my hair in unstylish, childish ringlets that my mother had somehow convinced me were necessary, winding and tying my freshly washed hair in tight rags the night before.

I knew I appeared completely wrong. I was unsophisticated and unfashionable, and I wished I were back at the mission. I didn't want the Wyndhams' pianoforte or books or carpets after all. I wanted to take off my high boots and feel the hard ground beneath my bare feet; I wanted to scrape my silly hairstyle back into one long plait; I wanted to pound out the old hymns on the piano, singing loudly and knowing no one paid any attention.

I had never felt so out of place and embarrassed for both myself and my mother, who, like me, appeared dowdy and awkward amongst the other women with their frocks of glorious, rich-looking fabrics and silk slippers and winking jewellery and elaborate hairstyles.

And my mother said nothing. She had a curious expression fixed on her face, nodding throughout the tedious conversations, her handkerchief to her mouth. Neither of us had spoken. Nobody asked us our thoughts or opinions, although, really, what could either my mother or I have added to the simpering talk of the latest frocks and hats, the terrible, endless duty of dealing with incompetent servants, or the anticipation surrounding the upcoming events of the social season?

The stout Hindu again bent low in front of me with his silver tray of biscuits. There were three of the thimble variety, four ginger, three shortbread, and one lemon horn. Eleven. I declined.

'We had an interesting case at the infirmary, just last week,' I stated, loudly, when there was a moment's lull in the conversation.

All heads turned towards me. I glanced at my mother; she looked startled, her hand on her throat and her eyes widening over the handkerchief.

'It was a virulent form of boils. Usually one only finds a single boil. But this appeared to be a spreading form. By far the worse case I've ever seen. But I managed to lance them all. The poor woman; it was so dreadfully painful for her. Of course, now she may succumb to a sepsis infection, what with all the open wounds. Bathing them daily with vinegar water and keeping them free of flies will be the key, I should think.'

I heard my mother clearing her throat roughly, but I refused to look at her. Other than that, complete silence had fallen on the room. I knew I was acting in a manner both coarse and inappropriate, and yet I seemed unable to control myself. I had no idea I was going to speak of boils. I only knew I was miserable and embarrassed and determined that someone notice my mother. And me. I couldn't sit, still and silent, any longer, knowing my mother and I were pitied and ignored, as unimportant and insignificant to these women as the servants they ordered about.

I wanted to be given even a moment of respect. But while I knew that talk of boils and sepsis would not bring this reaction, I couldn't stop. It was as if my voice belonged to someone else. 'Miss Wyndham?' I asked Eleanor, forcing her to turn towards me. 'What is the common remedy for boils in England?' I stared at her. 'Some here believe that wrapping a boil in the leaves of the tamarack may draw out the poison, but I think a quick slash with a sharp scalpel is the only real way to allow the foulness to escape.'

Eleanor covered her mouth with her lace napkin, shaking her head.

'Do people not get boils in England? From my medical studies, I believe them to be a universal misery, not particular to India,' I said.

Mrs Wyndham stood. 'Miss Fincastle,' she said, firmly and loudly, in the otherwise quiet room, 'we really must find you something to take home.' It was painfully clear that the visit – at least for my mother and myself – was over.

I looked up at her, suddenly sickened by what I had just done, unable to speak. Unable to look at my mother.

'Is there something you particularly need at the mission, Miss Fincastle?' she asked, her voice still louder. 'Something we may give you before you leave? We do believe in helping the cause of the poor heathens.'

'At the mission?' I finally echoed, standing. 'Yes, we should be going. Mother?' I turned to her. She sat unmoving, her face blank, and I held out my free hand. 'Come, Mother. There will be a number of patients awaiting us.'

My mother blinked, as if bringing herself back from some distant place, looking at my hand. Without taking it she rose, dropping the handkerchief. Her lips were lax, wet, and she swallowed noisily.

In order to cover the noise of her sucking and swallowing, I said, 'I feel positively slothful, enjoying a lovely and relaxing afternoon when so many are in need of our aid.'

There were a few agreeable, although stilted, murmurs.

'Being a missionary is selfless work,' I said now, quickly, feeling I must keep talking so there was no silence, no opportunity for anyone to comment. I went towards the door, hearing the dull swish of my mother's cotton skirt behind me, the important rustle of Mrs Wyndham's silk. 'One mustn't think of oneself, but of others. After the Lord, of course.' I heard the obvious bite in my voice as I spoke of slothfulness and the Lord in this room full of women who lived indolent, easy lives.

And then I realised that what I was now feeling was not embarrassment, nor humiliation, but a hard, stinging pleasure, a sharp knot of satisfaction. I turned back to the room. 'Good afternoon,' I said, dipping my knee.

Again, there was only murmuring, the dull buzz of bothersome insects about the ears at night.

When we were in the entrance – my mother, Mrs Wyndham and I – Mrs Wyndham said, 'I remember you always enjoyed taking a little something home, Miss Fincastle. Do you still like ginger snaps?'

I stared at her. I couldn't understand what I saw in her face. Did she mean to belittle me further? Did she honestly think I was the child I had once been, beaming over a painted tin canister of ginger snaps or a faded picture book or a cheap glass brooch? 'No. I – and the mission – have everything necessary,' I said, with firmness.

'Nonsense. I know you must – Eleanor, Eleanor,' she called, and Eleanor appeared in the doorway. 'Run and get that bonnet. You know, the one that—' she stopped. 'The pink one, Eleanor. Get it for Miss Fincastle. Now,' she added, with the same firm tone I'd just used.

Eleanor disappeared down the long wide hall. The ladies in the next room began a vague chatter, while my mother and I stood silently. I studied the pattern of the rug beneath the scuffed toes of my boots. Eleanor returned with the bonnet. It was indeed pink, a soft pink, with matching satin ribbons and a cluster of tiny felt violets just over the brim.

'I'm sure it will be lovely on you, dear,' Mrs Wyndham said, and set it on my head.

I had little recourse but to stand, like a wooden mannequin, while Mrs Wyndham tied the ribbons under my chin.

The ladies' voices grew louder as they returned to their former subjects. There was obvious relief in their voices now that I was safely silenced by Mrs Wyndham. Eleanor had returned to her seat, her back to the doorway.

'Well, fancy that,' Mrs Wyndham said to my mother. 'With my Eleanor's bonnet, her face framed just so, she's quite lovely, isn't she?' She sounded surprised. 'Do have a look, Miss Fincastle,' Mrs Wyndham said, turning me towards the looking glass on the wall behind me.

But instead of my own reflection, I saw my mother's face behind me. Her false smile was gone, and now there was something I didn't recognize in her expression. After a second I realised it was fear. Or something close to fear. Dread, perhaps.

I undid the ribbons of the bonnet. 'It's a bit large for me,

115

Mrs Wyndham,' I said. 'Thank you, but I shan't be able to wear it.' I began to lift the bonnet from my head, but Mrs Wyndham stepped in front of me.

'Nonsense,' she said, pushing it back down and pulling the ribbons tighter under my chin. I tried not to wince as she made a firm knot, catching a tiny fold of skin within the satin bow. 'There's no point in putting it in a charity box when there's a young woman in obvious need of a good bonnet. You must wear it always, dear. You've already let the sun darken your skin to an unflattering shade. Surely your mother has instructed you on such folly.'

I glanced at my mother, suddenly seeing how worn and lined her own skin had become, how her hair had faded so that now it had a dull, rusted appearance. She never wore a topi or bonnet at the mission; it seemed ridiculous that she move between the house and the infirmary wearing a headdress, whether strictly functional, like the topi, or for fashion, like a fancy bonnet.

'We really must take our leave,' she said, speaking for the first time. Her words were oddly slurred. 'It's a long ride back to the mission.'

'Yes, of course,' Mrs Wyndham murmured, and my mother and I went outside and climbed into the waiting rickshaw. As soon as we were seated I pulled off the bonnet and threw it to the floor between us. My mother picked it up.

We collected Marta and the cart. I held the reins, and we rode home in rocking silence, neither of us speaking for the whole journey. I tried to concentrate on the countryside, on the stream of people and animals on the road, on the sky. It started to rain. We both put our shawls over our heads again; this time the rain was slanting sideways, causing the full potholes in the road to bubble.

All I could hear in my head was my own voice, loud and rude, shocking everyone with my inappropriate statements. I could see the disdainful way Eleanor looked at my frock and boots, my unstylish hair. It all blurred into a nightmarish quality of jumbled words and images.

I needed to blot it out, to forget it had happened. I wanted no reminders of this miserable day; I would make sure of that. As soon as we rumbled into the courtyard I jumped from the cart, grabbing the bonnet. As I stomped across the courtyard towards the *rasoi* in the rain, my mother called to me.

'What are you doing?'

I stopped and looked over my shoulder at her. She was limping stiffly after me, Marta standing still hitched to the cart, her head down. My mother's eyes were fixed on the bonnet, which I dangled by its ribbons as I dragged it through the mud. 'What do you think you're doing?' she repeated.

'I'm going to burn it. I hate this bonnet and will never, ever wear it,' I told her.

She shook her head as she reached me, firmly taking the bonnet from me by its ribbons. 'You'll not burn it. It's a good bonnet.'

'I'll never wear it,' I repeated. 'I hate it, and I hate them all. Everyone in that house.'

'You're not six years old any more, Pree,' my mother said, her voice low and hard. 'And you won't speak of hate, as if you are indeed the mannerless young woman they think you are, and that you proved you were, with your silly, badly chosen conversation. It was disgusting. You were outspoken and clumsy, and I was ashamed of you. Ashamed and sickened.' And then she slapped me, first on my left cheek, and then on my right.

It happened so suddenly and so unexpectedly that I was shocked speechless, putting my hands on my cheeks, which immediately throbbed from the strength of her hard, calloused palms.

'You may be grateful for this bonnet some day,' she said. 'There may be a day when a bonnet such as this is exactly what is needed. *When the Lord sent me forth into the world, He forbade me to put off my hat to any, high or low.*' She turned then, taking the bonnet with her, patiently and meticulously brushing off the clinging mud as she slowly limped to the house.

'That's not a scripture,' I called after her, determined she wouldn't have the last word. But my voice trembled; I was fighting to hold back tears from both the sting of my cheeks and my own knowledge that what my mother had said about me was true.

'No. It isn't,' she called over her shoulder, continuing towards the house.

I watched her, seeing her slumped shoulders and her head forward on the thin stalk of her neck, as if it could barely support the weight of her skull. My hands were still on my flaming cheeks. I hadn't deserved such treatment, I inwardly raged, and yet somehow I couldn't find the usual anger for her I so often carried.

It was because I understood. The day had been as difficult for my mother as it had been for me. She was reacting out of anger and shame at the way the fine English ladies of Lahore had treated us. And she was also reacting out of disappointment in me, knowing that she would never have a beautiful, educated and courteous daughter like Eleanor Wyndham.

I lowered my hands, letting my tears come as I clenched my fists, wishing I, too, had something or someone to slap, and turned my face skyward, letting the rain soothe my cheeks.

When I lowered my eyes I saw Kai, sitting in front of his hut beyond the *rasoi*, sheltered by the rain from the thatch overhang. He was pointedly studying a pamphlet he held, his head lowered over it. But surely he had seen my mother slapping me, and my moment of pathetic self-pity as I stared at the sky.

Even more humiliated, I turned and ran back to Marta, unhitching her and leading her into the enclosure. There, hidden behind her, I leaned my head against her warm, broad side and finished my weeping.

Two months later, at the end of October, came the cool weather; through the stifling hot summer and the wet monsoons we waited for this time, before winter set in, when the skies were blue, the foliage lush after all the rain, and tempers even. It was late afternoon, and there were no more patients at the infirmary. Although I had laundry to do, I was sitting under the peepul tree, playing with the leopard gecko who slept, during the day, under a large jutting rock near the convenience.

I had my first pet leopard gecko when I was a small child. They were common; I had always seen them scurrying about the courtyard or on the thatched roofs, but on that day I found one curled in sleep in the shade under a bush. It didn't move when I touched it with my finger. I called to Kai, and he came, squatting beside me and looking at what I pointed to. He gently picked up the creature; the gecko stirred and blinked sleepily with its moveable eyelids, but didn't struggle or attempt to bite.

'Leopard geckos are gentle,' he'd said. 'They don't mind humans at all. A female,' he continued, turning her over and pointing to her unmarked underbelly, and then, holding his hand over her length he added, 'and full grown.'

I stroked her smooth belly. 'Can I play with her?' I asked, and he smiled.

'If she lets you. But she's a wild creature. You must allow her to live her life as she chooses. You mustn't ever make a prisoner of a living thing. Here,' he said, and put the gecko in my hands.

I named her Rujjie. I worried about her when I went to sleep; it was only in the darkness that she would hunt for her food, and, I also knew from Kai, that she was in danger of being caught by one of the night birds of prey. Between breakfast and prayers each morning I checked that she was back, safely, under the bush to sleep through the hottest daylight hours.

If I had any time to amuse myself during the day I might wake her and take her from under the bush. I fed her spiders I caught, or tiny crumbs of *roti* and bits of fruit, and watched her crawl over me with her long, nimble legs. Rujjie never strayed far; proving Kai right, she easily grew attached to me. Sometimes she would settle comfortably on my shoulder for up to an hour while I read.

And then one day Rujjie was simply gone. I had cried to Kai, and he put his hand on my head and said I mustn't cry, that Rujjie had gone off to be married and lay gecko eggs, and this was how it should be. He said she would be sad if she didn't do what nature told her to do. And even though his words had comforted me, I put my arms around his hips and cried, my face leaving wet marks on his bare stomach. He had let me; I was seven, he thirteen. Within a week he had found me another. I named her Rujjie as well. And even now, so far from being a child, I had a pet leopard gecko. Kai still brought me a female when I told him the last one was gone, and I named each one Rujjie.

This day, as my latest Rujjie lay on my thigh, her eyelids moving lazily in the dappled sunlight while I finished the final chapter of *Jane Eyre*, I absently stroked the soft, crepy skin of her back: dark brown spots on a yellow background. This gecko had twenty-four spots: very satisfying.

I read the last paragraph and closed the musty book, then

ran my fingers over Rujjie's tail, which had obviously been pulled off by a predator before I had her. It had grown back, as was usual for the leopard gecko. This new tail – short and wide – was less elegant than I knew her original tail would have been, but I liked to examine the place where it had re-grown, and marvel at this ability. I had often thought of this re-growth, watching the misery suffered by Pavit as he lost more and more of himself.

Now I fingered Rujjie's tiny claws, and her tongue emerged, slowly touching the fabric of my frock, as if tasting the dull nankeen, and I saw how her neck moved when she swallowed. I wondered if she were thirsty, and as I reached for another tiny piece of fig to feed her, heard footsteps approaching. I looked up, hoping it was Kai. In spite of his talk about moving to Lahore, he still hadn't left.

But it was a soldier, an English soldier, in his fine red jacket and tight black trousers and high, gleaming black boots. A tilted, peaked black cap, decorated with braid, shielded his eyes from the sun.

'I'm attempting to find a Miss Fincastle,' he said.

I stood, surprised, holding Rujjie against my chest. 'I'm Miss Fincastle.' The soldier's eyes went from my face to the gecko.

'Oh. But I'm looking for another Miss Fincastle. She told me she lived at the Christian mission. She has . . . light eyes. Rather green, if I recall. And . . .' he didn't seem to be able to describe her further, but of course I knew whom he meant.

He was perhaps in his late twenties and quite attractive, with wide, pale blue eyes and skin burnished by the sun.

'You must mean Glory.'

'Yes,' he said. 'Miss Glory Fincastle.'

'Don't you mean Glory da Silva?' I asked.

'She told me Fincastle.'

I frowned at her lie. 'Well, Glory isn't here. I don't know

where she is,' I said, although I knew full well she was in the house. I'd seen her carrying fresh bedding, pulled from where it had been drying over the bushes, only fifteen minutes earlier. I'm not sure why I told the soldier I didn't know where she was, although it crossed my mind she was in some kind of trouble. That might be why she'd lied about her last name.

Kai came around the corner of the house. 'Kai,' I called, more loudly than necessary. 'This soldier,' I emphasised the word soldier as Kai came nearer, 'is looking for Glory.'

Kai stepped up to the man. Although they were the same height, I saw that Kai's shoulders were wider. 'Why are you looking for her?' he asked, staring into his face.

The soldier frowned. 'Stand back, boy. It's no affair of yours.'

'It is, sir,' Kai said. 'She's my mother.'

Now it was the soldier who took a step back. 'Your mother?' The man's voice held a note of surprise as he looked at Kai, a full-grown man. Younger than him, but surely not that much younger.

'Yes. And my mother is engaged in her work. She's an ayah for the memsahib of the mission.'

The soldier made a sound in his throat.

'She'll be busy the rest of the evening,' Kai said. I saw the clench of his jaw. 'So there's no point in you waiting for her.'

'All right, then,' the soldier said, and he turned to leave. 'Tell her Captain Durham called round.'

'Did she do something?' I asked.

The soldier stopped and looked back at me. 'Do something? What do you mean?'

'Is she in trouble?'

He studied my face, then looked at Kai. 'She knows where to find me,' he said, and climbed on his horse and rode out of the yard.

Kai and I watched him go, and then Kai started towards the garden.

'Will you tell Glory about her caller, or shall I?' I called after him, knowing I shouldn't, knowing it was better to say nothing. Of course Glory wasn't in trouble. Did I assume she only spent time with Eurasians like herself?

Kai didn't answer, but as I watched him attack the hills of potato plants, digging up good-sized potatoes, he hacked with such vigour that clods of dry earth as well as the potatoes flew up around his legs, and I worried for his bare toes.

Later that day I told Glory about Captain Durham coming to see her. She said nothing, but stared at the road, touching her lips with her fingertips. The next morning, after prayers, I heard her asking my father for her wages. I noticed she had waited until my mother had gone to the infirmary.

'But it's not time yet, Glory,' he said, running his palm along the edge of the Bible.

'It is only another few weeks,' she argued. 'And I need some things. My day off is in four days. I will need it by then; I will go to Lahore and must have it.' She stared at him, and he blinked and then looked away.

'I suppose so, then,' he said, and she lifted her chin and smiled.

When he left, I asked, 'Is Captain Durham your beau?'

She looked at me sharply. 'That is not your business.'

'I just asked,' I said, remembering the soldier's blue eyes, and the surprise in them when Kai said he was Glory's son.

Three days later, when I went to Glory's hut to tell her she was needed, she had her frocks – there were six of them – laid out on the charpoy.

'Are you picking what you're wearing to go to Lahore tomorrow?'

'Yes,' she said shortly.

'I like the lavender one; the lace on the bodice is so delicate.'

She laid the frocks on top of one another.

'What do you plan to purchase when—'

But she brushed by me before I could finish, her bracelets clinking as she hurried towards the house. I stood in the doorway for another few minutes, looking at her frocks. I wished I owned one even half so pretty.

CHAPTER TEN

THE NEXT DAY Glory was gone before prayers; I knew she left at sunrise to have as much time as possible in Lahore. Although she wasn't in her hut when I went to bed that night, I knew she'd be there the next morning, creeping back to the mission in the middle of the night or even as the sun rose.

But she still wasn't back at prayers the second day. I saw my father talking to Kai as he worked in the garden, and knew he was asking about Glory. But Kai didn't lift his head, and I only saw the quick shrug of his shoulders. Later that day I went to her hut, and discovered all her frocks and saris gone, as well as her jewellery and pots of rouge and *surma*. I knew then that Glory had gone to be with the soldier, and wondered whether to tell my parents about him.

'Do you think something's happened to her?' I asked my mother.

My mother's lips tightened. We were sitting in the infirmary, filling spills with tablets. It was one of her good days. 'Well, you know Glory. Most likely she's with some man.'

I didn't have to mention the soldier after all. 'But would she really go without saying goodbye, even to Kai?'

'She has before. I don't suppose she even considers him.'

I nodded, thinking of an earlier time when Glory had left. 'When I was about seven,' I said, reaching for another bottle of sulfur tablets.

'Yes, but there were two other times before that,' she said, surprising me. 'The first time Glory left was back in Allahabad. Kai was far too young to be on his own; he was just over three. I couldn't leave him in Glory's empty hut, so I was forced to bring him into the house for a week or so, until we found another ayah who helped me out and took over caring for Kai.'

She set down the empty paper cone. 'He was so quiet. Unnaturally quiet for a toddler. It was six months before Glory came back. He didn't cry when she left, nor did he cry when I – or the other ayah – looked after him. He didn't cry when his mother came back and the ayah handed him over. Unnatural,' she said again. 'And then, some years later . . . how old was Kai then?' She blinked, as if counting. 'He must have been about eight or nine, because we hadn't been settled here very long, when Glory left again.'

'So I was a baby?' I asked, and she nodded.

'That time he acted up; getting into trouble. I thought he was old enough to stay by himself in the hut at night – he still shared it with his mother – but then we heard reports from the villages that he'd been seen running around in the dead of night, getting up to all sorts. So I had no alternative but to put down a mat in the storeroom and lock him in every night. To protect him from his own mischief.'

I thought of Kai locked in that shadowy room, hung with cobwebs, the floor busy with all manner of creeping, crawling things. Had the dusty sword at the back of the tallest shelf been there even then? I had found it while exploring during one of my long afternoons of imprisonment. The sword was enclosed in a silver scabbard, decorated with coloured glass of crimson and turquoise. So often I had held it, wondering how the old and yet still dangerous weapon came to be hidden in a mission storeroom. Now I realised it had probably been Kai who had put it there. I imagined him all alone in the dark, lying on a woven reed mat thrown on the hard floor. Was it summer, or the time of monsoons, or winter? Did he swelter or shiver through the long nights, or listen to the crashing thunder and try to find a dry spot where the roof didn't leak?

I knew the howls of the jackals at night, the scuffling of nocturnal animals along the sides of the buildings, the sudden scream of an animal attacked by the birds of prey that hunted in the dark. The fury of a storm. All of the sounds that had frightened me when I was very young, and had made me cry out from my room; my father always came.

At that moment I hated Glory for leaving him; I hated my mother for putting him in the storeroom. Then I thought of the high window; surely Kai had climbed through and hadn't actually stayed there at night. Yes. I could see Kai as a boy; he would never stay where he was told. And he wouldn't have been afraid the way I had been. I had an image of him running through the fields at night, lightning flashing in the broad black sky, thunder booming. And he was smiling. I again remembered his expression, the dark, grim excitement I'd seen in his eyes as he watched the burning effigy in the field, and thought of his involvement with the Kukas, and was troubled anew.

'But within a month I'd made my point, and Kai had learned his lesson. He stayed in the house with us after that. In your room. You still slept in a cot in our room.'

Now I tried to imagine Kai sleeping in my bed, looking at the same walls I looked at as I fell asleep and awoke.

He had been treated as their own son. I hadn't known this.

'And Glory stayed away for two whole years that time. Two years. Imagine. Well, it didn't hurt Kai; on the contrary, I believe it set him on the right road. Firstly, he wasn't under her influence, although she gave the boy no direction at all. And so your father insisted I teach him. He was sharp as a whip; he learned almost effortlessly. The only thing that gave him trouble was his penmanship. Your father instructed him in the scriptures, and even spent time every day giving him elocution lessons, correcting his language and speech patterns, although I wondered at the point of that. I think your father went so far as to enjoy his time with the boy. After two years we certainly didn't expect to ever see Glory again. We assumed she'd abandoned her son, and since we were a mission, and our job was to help the destitute, caring for Kai – teaching him to be a clean and God-loving person – was simply part of the burden we willingly carried for our Lord.

'And then, lo and behold, who should show up again but Glory. I wanted to run her off for good; it had been hard enough to take her back the first time she left. But your father, well, you know him. He wouldn't allow it. He said she could stay, if for no other reason than that she was Kai's mother. And, frankly, I needed more help than the little village girl I'd hired could provide.'

She raised her eyebrows. 'It was clear to me, although obviously not to your father, that the one who suffered the most with her return was Kai. It was almost as though he didn't remember her, or didn't want to remember her. It was as though he thought he was . . . well, we all – your father and I – we had more or less started considering him part of . . .' she stopped.

'So Glory's return was difficult for us all. And to make it even worse, she was furious at Kai for not welcoming her back with open arms. And then she blamed your father for driving out her memory. Of course it wasn't true; we simply never spoke of her, nor did he. I remember seeing him cry the first night she was back, when she insisted he go back to her hut, instead of sleeping in the mission house with us, as he had for those past two years. It was the only time I saw him cry – apart from when he hurt himself when much younger. He was always a stoic little fellow. I admired him for that.'

I stayed perfectly still. My mother so rarely talked at length about anything, that I didn't want to disturb her thoughts by asking a question or commenting on anything she said.

Her hands grew still, and she gazed at the scarred table top. 'Your father had grown to love the boy, I realised later.' Her voice was soft, as if speaking to herself. It occurred to me that the same thing had happened to her, although she wouldn't admit it.

Long moments passed, and when she started counting out more tablets I knew she didn't plan to continue.

'I remember the last time she left,' I said, not wanting the conversation to end, wanting to hear more about Kai when he was a child.

Glory had left just before Christmas the year I was seven; my father had wanted Kai to come into the house and join us for the goose Sanosh had prepared for our Christmas meal, but he politely shook his head. Thinking of him alone in his hut had spoiled my dinner for me, even though the crisp, greasy bird was a treat.

Now I wonder if his refusal to join us was embarrassment, but at the time I was upset, thinking he was angry with me. Finally my mother, annoyed with my sulking, told me to take a plate out to him. He accepted it; I also gave him one of the two striped hard sweets I had received as my Christmas gift.

And that year was also the spring of the Maypole. 'Kai was thirteen,' I said.

'Yes. Of course he was old enough to fare perfectly well for himself without his mother. And although he always had a certain streak of wildness, and every once in a while went back to his younger ways of stirring up trouble in the villages about this or that, it seemed he settled down that time.' She shrugged. 'Well, there's nothing we can do about it. I don't think there's one of us – you or your father or I or even Kai – who cares that Glory's gone off again.' She made a tsking sound. 'Glory and her ways, dressing up as some low character's fancy woman. A real Chutney Mary,' she said again.

'It was the year we did the Maypole, that last time,' I told her. Did she remember? It was one of my best memories – one of the only ones where I remember my mother acting in what I call a playful manner. She told me it was a custom in England that we would celebrate this day, 1 May, and directed Kai to pound a tall, thin sapling, stripped of its branches, into the earth of the courtyard. Then Kai and I, acting on her directions, ripped muslin rags – some white and others dyed an orange-red by soaking them in water and iodine – into long strips.

My mother told Kai to firmly tie the strips around the top of the sapling, and then demonstrated how we were to wind the strips – me the white and Kai the red – in a tabby weave around the pole.

Kai walked around the pole in the opposite direction to me, shuffling his bare feet with a concentrated look of boredom as he wound his muslin over and under mine, but his lips turned up just the slightest. Just enough for me to know he wasn't as disinterested as he tried to appear. I scampered under his arms, attempting the skipping jig my mother showed us.

I'm sure my father wasn't at the mission; he would never have approved of dancing. In fact, I'm surprised, now, that my mother acted in such an unpious way that day.

I can recall her watching us, clapping her hands and singing. I had never before heard her sing anything but hymns in her flat, raspy voice, and I grew giddy at the unexpected play and her undivided attention.

Now, sitting with my mother at the table in the infirmary,

a fresh breeze coming in the open windows, I concentrated on the song we had sung over and over that day, Something about mead and cheer and dreams and a pretty maid. Except my mother sang *prithy* maid.

'*For the Lord knows we shall meet again,*' I suddenly said, '*To go Maying another year. A branch of May I brought you here . . .*' I faltered. '*A branch of May I brought you here . . .*'

My mother nodded. '*While at your stand I keep. 'Tis but a sprout all budded out by the power of our Lord's hand,*' she said, and then stopped. 'I can't remember any more.'

I repeated the last line in my head, and then the final words came to me, all in a rush, '*My song is done and I must be gone, no longer may I stay. God bless you all, the great and small, and send you a joyous May.*'

I smiled at my mother, trying to remember the woman she had been that long past first of May, trying to bring back the feelings I had had for her as that light-hearted seven year old.

I wondered if Kai remembered it at all.

About a month later I saw Glory in Lahore. I had gone into the city with my father; it was the six-month date to collect his wages, and my mother had given me a written list of items I was to purchase. Usually she accompanied us, but this day she complained about a strange voice in her head, warning her that danger awaited her should she attempt to traverse the Grand Trunk Road.

I didn't look at my father as she told us her dire predictions. I couldn't. I didn't want to see his face. We hadn't spoken of her on the journey, and I'd waited for him in the wagon when he'd gone into the Ministry. He emerged a few minutes later, and we walked to one of the bazaars. He went off in one direction and I in the other, both of us with our lists.

I stood in front of a stall, breathing in the delightful mingling odours of the various oils and crushed petals, then picked up a slim phial, taking off the top and smelling it, idly watching the people coming and going around me. And then there she was, Glory, clinging to the arm of a gentleman in a fine wool suit and moulded topi. He was old – older than my father – his face seamed and lined by age and, judging by the deep, pale crevasses fanning from the outer corners of his eyes, a life in the sun.

Glory was dressed in a frock I didn't recognise – it must have been new. It was dark rose with a deep plum trim. Over her shoulders she wore a wool plum-coloured cape with satin ribbon edging it. Her whole outfit, like the gentleman's, was obviously of good quality. Unfortunately, she spoiled the impression by too much face paint, her lips and cheeks heavily rouged. And she'd hennaed her hair; now it glinted dully with reddish streaks under her rather extravagant hat, trimmed with silk roses.

Since I had assumed she'd left with the handsome young soldier who'd come looking for her, I was surprised to see her with this older Englishman.

'Glory!' I called, and she turned. I thought she would startle, would ignore me or hurry away, but instead, a smile wreathed her face, and she held out her arms as if she would embrace me.

'Pree, my darling girl, Pree,' she said in English, and I blinked at this odd greeting. She came towards me, pulling the gentleman by his arm. She smiled from him to me and back to him again. 'Here is Miss Pree Fincastle. My good friend, whom I spoke to you about, from my home. Pree, please to meet Mr Evans.'

My mouth opened. She had called me her good friend. The man removed his hat. Although he had a fringe of yellowed, greying hair, the top of his head was bald and shiny with perspiration. As he held out his hand I extended mine. He took it and placed his lips upon my glove.

'I can certainly see where you have acquired your beauty,' he said to me, and again, I looked at Glory, closing my mouth now. 'It's obvious it runs within your family.'

Within my family? What had she told this man? Was she calling herself Glory Fincastle, as the soldier had referred to her? And how could this man compare me to her? Did he not see our differences, that I was English, and Glory . . . I stopped myself, surprised that I would react in the same way in which I had witnessed my mother occasionally behaving. And now my judgement was as uncharitable as hers.

'Good afternoon, Mr Evans,' I said, politely, with a very small curtsy. 'Glory. We didn't know what happ—'

She interrupted before I could say anything further. 'And how do all go at home? All very, very happy?' she asked, as if she hadn't left the mission, and her son, but was simply an infrequent visitor there. As if I were part of her family; she of ours. Her voice was lower than usual, and slower, and I could see she was taking great care to speak in her most proper voice.

'Fine. Everyone is fine, Glory. But Kai—'

Again she cut my words. 'It is being very lovely to see you. Say my hello at home,' she said, and then lightly tugged on the man's sleeve. 'Come, Mr Evans, come. Now we will take tea, as you have said.' She looked at me once more. 'At Willis' Fine Tea Room, in the cantonment,' she added, raising her eyebrows slightly.

I watched her leave, seeing the slow, sensuous sway of her walk.

CHAPTER ELEVEN

T WO DAYS AFTER I'd been to Lahore I was in the courtyard, filling the brass lotahs with water in the late afternoon. There were no more patients at the infirmary, and I had decided to scrub down the verandahs.

I looked up at the pounding of horse's hoofs on the hard-packed yard. A young man, his head bare, jumped down from a sweat-lathered horse and ran to me.

'Much bad,' he said, in halting English, panting, his face twisted in distress, 'much hurt. The baba . . . no come out. Lalasa . . . please, come. Help Lalasa,' he cried out, his hands together in front of him in supplication.

'You're Lalasa's husband?' I asked in Hindi, and he nodded, a flicker of relief crossing his face at his language.

'I am Balin,' he said. 'Come, please. She asked that I bring the Mem; she said you and the Mem will know what to do.'

My mother had come from the house. 'When did the pains start?' she asked in English. 'How long has she been in labour?' She made a sound of annoyance when Balin stared at her, blinking as he tried to understand, and I translated.

'Yesterday, early morning,' Balin said, still panting, licking his dry lips. His tongue was furred with grey.

'But . . .' My mother stared at him. 'It's almost evening. Lalasa has been in labour all this time – almost two days, and you're only now coming for my help? Why?' She pushed past him.

Again, Balin couldn't understand most of her words, but her anger was clear. 'My mother, she says this is normal,' he tried to explain to me. 'She says it isn't the husband's business.'

'Didn't you call anyone — a midwife, or your sisters, or Lalasa's mother?' I demanded. 'Why didn't you get someone — even your own mother — to help her?'

The man shook his head. 'My mother says we must leave her, for it's only through pain that one learns strength. My mother says she will catch the baby when he comes, but Lalasa must be strong, like her, and do it alone. But Lalasa started screaming, screaming, and I couldn't listen any longer. I couldn't listen.' His eyes filled with tears, and even though I was furious at him, I knew he was exhausted and afraid, and had tried to do the right thing, caught between his obedience to his mother and his concern for his wife. 'My sisters won't disobey our mother. But I can't listen any longer,' he repeated. 'I can't let her suffer so greatly. I asked her, asked Lalasa, what can I do, and she cried go to the mission house. And so I came. You'll help her?'

'Lord have mercy,' my mother said, muttering something else under her breath I couldn't hear. 'Hurry, Pree, go ahead with him on the horse. Do what you can until I can get there.'

'I haven't ever—' I started, not knowing what it was I should do, but she interrupted.

'I have to take the cart. I don't know where your father or Kai are. Tell this fellow to hook up Marta for me, and run to the infirmary and get the bag. Bring scissors, lots of clean flannel and muslin, a needle and thread, and disinfectant.'

All I could think of was Lalasa, but in that moment I was relieved at my mother's clearness this day, her decisiveness and authority.

Balin did as I told him, and I got what my mother asked

and ran back outside with the carpet bag as Balin was helping my mother climb into the cart. 'Tell me where to go once I get to the village,' she said, and I translated Balin's directions.

Then she slapped the reins on Marta's dusty back, urging her into an ungainly gallop.

I bunched up my skirt and Balin lifted me on to the bare back of the horse before swinging up behind me. The journey – the horse galloping the whole way – took a short time, but it felt endless.

When Balin pulled the horse up in front of a small house built of pukka, I heard Lalasa's scream before we even reached the courtyard. Balin leapt off the horse, not waiting for me, and I ran after him. Four young women silently crouched together at one side of the courtyard – his sisters or Lalasa's friends. An older woman – obviously his mother – rose from a carpet beneath a feathery tamarind, shouting at Balin in anger, waving her hands in the air, but we both ignored her and ran through the house to the room he shared with Lalasa.

I stopped at the door as Balin went to Lalasa's side, stroking her forehead and whispering to her. She was panting, and even from the doorway I could see that she was unnaturally bloated, her bare legs, so lithesome in the past, now thick, the ankles indistinguishable from the calf. I saw the pale, shiny line of the scar on her shin. Lalasa's eyes went to me, and then rolled up, her mouth opening, and I rushed to her. As the next scream tore from her, I saw that her mouth was bleeding, ripped at the corners. Her knees were bent and her thighs trembled violently, and then her whole body was taken over by a convulsive spasm. Her scream died away as her body shook and trembled, finally slowing. Lalasa's irises returned, and she blinked as if confused. I wiped the blood from her lips; they had a lavender hue now.

'Pree?' she said, and I tried to smile, but my mouth

wouldn't work. She gripped my hand, although weakly. 'Pree,' she said again. 'You came.'

'My mother's coming as well; she'll be here any moment. She'll know what to do, Lalasa. She'll help you.' I spoke convincingly, but feared there would be little my mother would be able to do. If Lalasa had been in labour this long . . . and she was too small; her body was too small. 'Balin, fetch hot water,' I told him, knowing it was unimportant, but I wanted him to do something, to make it seem that we were helping Lalasa in some way.

I stayed with her through the next convulsions, unable to do anything but stroke her forehead and whisper encouragement to her when she was conscious. Balin brought the water in a basin and paced up and down the room. Finally my mother arrived, rolling up her sleeves, and, glancing over her shoulder at Lalasa, plunged her hands into the waiting water, scrubbing them. Then she came to the bed and smiled at Lalasa.

'Your son shows his strength,' she said in her halting Hindi, but her smile faded as she watched Lalasa's eyes roll up again. As her body convulsed my mother looked at me. 'It's probably septicaemia,' she said. 'Her body has gone into shock. Take Balin outside.'

I did as she told me, instructing Balin to wait with his mother until we called for him. The old woman wouldn't look at me, muttering under her breath as she chewed her betel.

I went back inside. Lalasa's body still laboured and convulsed; her eyes were open, but she no longer screamed. She made no sound at all, except for the grunting that came from her involuntarily.

'Is there nothing we can do?' I cried, crouching beside Lalasa's charpoy and looking up at my mother.

'The head is right here,' she said, bending over Lalasa, her hand between the girl's legs. 'I can feel it. But she has no more strength to push the baby out. It slips back between each pain.'

'Can't you pull it out?' I asked, angry at my ignorance, at not knowing what to do, how to help Lalasa. I knew the internal female anatomy from the medical books, and I had seen a man reach inside a bellowing cow with both hands, and then his arms, right up to his shoulders, digging and tugging, finally pulling out two long, narrow legs, followed by the calf's head before the rest of its body slithered out. I knew a woman wasn't made the same way as a cow, of course, but . . . 'If it's so close,' I ended, my voice faint. 'Isn't there some way to get it out?'

My mother's lips tightened, and then she opened her carpetbag and pulled out a small, sharp knife. She instructed me to hold it over the flame of the lamp that burned in the corner. I did, handing it back to her. 'Help me sit on the edge of the charpoy,' she said, and I held her arm while she painfully settled on the low bed with a suppressed moan. I looked away as she pushed Lalasa's limp legs apart and bent between them.

I didn't want to think of the knife cutting into Lalasa's soft, secret flesh.

At a sudden exclamation from my mother I turned. 'Come. Come now and help me,' she said, and I went to the end of the charpoy and saw, in the mess of bloody fluid, my mother's hands wrapped around a tiny head, also bloody, and moulded into a peak. Her fingers working into Lalasa's cut edges, she manoeuvred out one rounded shoulder, and then the other, and, much like the calf, the rest of the body emerged in one great rush. In spite of the blood – Lalasa's blood – covering the child, I could see it was a girl. As my mother held the baby with one hand she grabbed a piece of flannel and briskly cleaned out the tiny nose and mouth. The child made small mewling sounds, and my mother, spreading her own thighs so that her skirt made a hammock, motioned for me to throw another piece of flannel over her skirt, and then set the baby there.

At the sounds, Lalasa's mother-in-law appeared, peering over my mother's shoulder, and as soon as my mother had cut the thick cord and tied a thread around it near the baby's navel, the old woman rather brusquely took the now-crying baby, loosely wrapping her in the flannel, from my mother's lap. The child was still covered in Lalasa's blood.

As the woman carried the baby out of the room, my mother concentrated on Lalasa, pressing her ear to the girl's chest and rubbing her small hands between her own. She kept putting more and more flannel under Lalasa, but still the crimson spread.

'Prop up the bottom of the charpoy,' my mother said, and I did as I was told, placing large circles of the dried dung stacked against one wall to be used as fuel, under the end legs. As I did so, there was a thump, and I saw the china head of Lalasa's doll, fallen from where it had been wedged between the wall and the bed.

I tried not to think about Lalasa holding the old doll as she struggled to bring her own child into the world. 'How can she be cold in this heat, Mother? She's shaking.'

'It's the shock. Cover her and keep her warm while I wash my hands, Pree. Here, help me up.'

After I hauled my mother from the edge of the charpoy I tucked two sheets around Lalasa's small body, and as I did so, she suddenly stiffened. Her eyes rolled back into her head and her body jerked in rhythmic spasms similar to what she'd experienced before the baby was born.

'She's doing it again,' I cried out. 'Why is she having a fit even now?'

My mother shoved me out of the way, pushing a folded

piece of flannel into Lalasa's mouth. Her small white teeth clamped on it. After what seemed an eternity, the jerking stopped, and the girl's body relaxed and finally grew still. My mother bathed Lalasa's face with a damp cloth, murmuring to her. 'You're all right now, Lalasa. You're all right.'

Finally Lalasa's eyes focused, and I kneeled beside the charpoy so she could see me.

'Lalasa,' I said. 'It's over. The baby . . . the baby is here.'

'My child,' she said, her voice little more than a sigh. 'A son?'

My mother put her hand on my shoulder, and I looked up at her. She smiled down at Lalasa, although it was more of a forced grimace. 'Yes, Lalasa. It's a boy, a strong, handsome boy,' she said, in her stilted Hindi.

I sat back on my heels.

'Can you hear his cry?' my mother asked. 'Listen.'

I realised then that the baby was indeed howling, its voice loud and demanding from the courtyard, and I tried to smile at Lalasa.

Her eyelids flickered, and a faint smile came to her white lips. 'I hear him. My husband will be proud. Now my mother-in-law will find me worthy.'

'Yes, dear,' my mother said in the English Lalasa couldn't understand. 'You did well. You gave your husband a son.' She picked up her bag.

I took Lalasa's hand, but it was limp and cold. 'Lalasa?' I whispered, leaning closer. But it didn't appear that she could see or hear me. Her eyes fixed on the window on the opposite wall. A long, soft breath came from her partly opened lips, and then no more sound.

'Lalasa?' I said, again, my voice louder, but I knew it would do no good. I knew the look of death. The girl child had killed her. 'Mother!' I cried.

My mother moved in front of me, pushing me out of the

way and placing her fingertips on the girl's neck. She shook her head, her lips moving as I assumed she prayed. She gently put her hand over Lalasa's face, and when she removed it, Lalasa's eyes were closed.

I heard whimpering; I realised it was from my own throat.

'Prepare warm water, scented with elixir of roses,' my mother said. 'Get the elixir from my bag.'

I heard her, but couldn't do as she asked. My body was frozen, as still as Lalasa's. My mother shook my arm, her fingers squeezing it as she had squeezed my shoulder when she told Lalasa her baby was a boy. 'Prepare the water so that we can bathe her before her family sees her.' She turned back to Lalasa and pulled the thin sheet up and over her face. Lalasa's features were so small that her nose and chin barely made a rise in the thin fabric.

'Lalasa,' I whispered, and putting my hands into the Hindu *namaste*, lowered my head over them. I wanted to cry, for the pain in my throat was overpowering, my eyes stinging. And yet I couldn't. Then I rose and did as my mother asked, stirring a few drops of the elixir into a copper bowl of warmed water. I moved as if something heavy held my body and my mind with a massive, deadening force, as if it weren't me at all that stirred and mixed, but someone I watched.

I slowly handed the bowl to my mother and stood back – still with that strange, underwater sense of being in a deep, confusing dream – as she uncovered parts of Lalasa's body – a leg, an arm, her torso – bending over her and washing each exposed part and then replacing the sheet again.

'You brush her hair,' my mother said then, when she had finished with the cloth and rosewater.

I shook my head. I didn't want to touch Lalasa; I didn't want to think of her like this. I wanted to think of her as I had known her when she'd come to the infirmary with her mother: skipping nimbly through the yard, trying to coax Jassie to follow us as we ran to the fields, smothering her little sister's cheeks with kisses; her mother calling her *beti* – daughter – with such affection. She and I giggling as we hid in the high canes, pretending we were desirable *ranis*.

I could only imagine the anxious beauty of her face as Balin lifted the wedding veil last year, or her shy pleasure at telling him, a few months later, about the son she knew she carried.

I didn't want to remember her as a limp, torn body, an expressionless face. I pulled the doll from under the charpoy and lifted the sheet and put the doll into the crook of Lalasa's arm.

At a sound I turned, and saw Balin standing in the doorway. His face was naked with shock. He backed away, and then turned and left, and I realised, as I took the bowl from my mother, that the baby had stopped crying. There was no sound but the far-off lowing of a bull, the sharp squawk of a crow. My mother's hand touched my elbow.

'Come. We'll leave her to her family to prepare her further for her final journey.'

I looked at her. 'Why did you lie? About the baby?'

My mother briefly closed her eyes. 'You know as well as I that it would do no good for her to believe she died for a girl,' she said, her voice hard. 'Why not let her believe, in her last moments on earth, that her death was worth something?'

At that moment I saw something in my mother, something that showed so rarely that I wanted to breathe it in, draw it inside my body. I wanted to remember her always like this, caring enough to break one of the commandments out of kindness.

I followed her from the room, stopping at the doorway one last time to look back at Lalasa's still form. In the courtyard her mother-in-law sat on her carpet with her back against the tamarack. Balin was nowhere to be seen. Nor was the baby.

My mother slowly crossed the yard, her heavy bag dragging one arm lower than the other. She limped even more than usual. I took the bag from her, and when relieved of its weight she squeezed her hand tightly with the other as if to restore its circulation. As we passed Lalasa's mother-in-law, I stopped.

'Where is the baby?' I asked her, my voice low. I had never before seen this woman, but I hated her, hated that she could have let her daughter-in-law suffer for so long. 'I would like to see her.'

My mother kept walking.

'She is of no consequence,' the old woman answered, and my mother stopped and looked back at me. Something in the way her mouth suddenly pulled to one side made a prickle of anxiety run down my spine.

I turned my head in all directions, looking around the quiet courtyard. 'But where is she?' For some reason my voice came out with an uncharacteristic breathiness. 'I want to see her. I want to—'

'There is no baby,' the woman said, expressionless. She put an almond between her back teeth and cracked it. 'My daughter-in-law gave birth to a stone.'

'A stone? What are you talking about?'

'A useless girl, a stone. The same. She's dead.'

I gasped, and at the same time heard a sound from my mother, no more than a sudden inward take of air through her nose. 'Dead? But . . . no. I saw her.' My voice rose. 'How could she be dead? She cried, and waved her arms and legs. She—'

'She's dead,' the woman repeated, now picking the meat from its shell. 'My son has taken her body to be left for the jackals. In this way he will be ensured of the birth of future sons with a new wife.' She popped the nut into her mouth and chewed slowly, staring at me.

I blinked and opened my mouth, but it was as if my voice was a prisoner of my throat, which had closed. My tongue was suddenly too large, too dry, sticking to the roof of my mouth. I looked at my mother. Her face, for one frightening moment, looked as dead as Lalasa's.

'Come, Pree. We'll go home,' she said, and went out on to the road in front of the house, where the cart waited. I watched the slump of my mother's shoulders as she limped away from me. I heard another nut crack, and with that sound I jerked, and found my voice.

'No!' I cried, running after my mother. 'No. The baby didn't die. She didn't. You saw her. You know,' I said, pulling on her arm.

My mother stopped again, looking down at my hand on her arm. 'It's the heathen way. What can we expect? So many gods, and yet at times they appear godless. They worship everything but life itself.' Her words were venomous, but her voice was quiet, hoarse with weariness. 'And perhaps it's better for her. For the baby. An unwanted girl, her mother dead . . . it's better,' she repeated. 'She would have had a life unfit for living.'

I stood in the road, looking around me as if for an answer. I knew then that Lalasa's heartless mother-in-law had killed the baby. How? By pinching her mouth and nose? By placing her hard, gnarled fingers around the dainty throat? I closed my eyes at the image. And then I opened them, thinking of Balin, with his kind, weak face. He must have allowed it; in this, as it appeared to be in all matters, he had allowed his mother to hold the power, to dictate his own actions.

I heard the creak of wood as my mother climbed into the cart.

I stood there, looking around as if confused, searching for

something I'd lost. And then I saw, in a field with the sun sinking orange over it, a figure – a man – walking towards a thicket of trees. I could only see his back, but it was stooped, and he walked with a lurching sway, as if newly crippled. I knew with certainty it was Balin.

Without a second's hesitation I tried to run towards the field, after Balin, thinking that somehow the old woman had not carried out her vile act, that the baby was still alive, and I could convince him not to leave her for the jackals. I would take her, I would keep her safe . . . but my legs wouldn't work. They felt as if filled with liquid, formless – was it the shock of what I had just experienced? – and instead of running in the easy stride I always had, I stumbled, sprawling face forward into the dust. I hit my nose so hard that bright lights burst with the shocking pain. I lay there for a second, stunned, then slowly pushed myself into a sitting position. A man walked by, leading a donkey with a huge pile of straw tied on to its back. He looked at me with mild curiosity, but didn't stop. Blood, scarlet as Lalasa's, dripped on to my skirt; I tasted copper. I got to my feet, pinching my nose with my fingers to staunch the flow, wincing at the pain as I looked to where I'd seen Balin. He was no longer visible.

'Come, Pree,' my mother called from behind me. 'There's nothing more to be done here.'

I stood alone in the road while the sky was bathed in vivid orange. Then slowly, my legs still trembling, I walked to the cart and awkwardly pulled myself in. My mother handed me a wad of clean flannel. I held it to my nose as we rumbled home.

There truly was nothing more to be done.

CHAPTER TWELVE

THE NEXT MONTHS were difficult, thinking about Lalasa and her baby, feeling powerless and angry. The winter, and then the spring passed. Everything went on as usual.

I carried out my work at the mission with a quiet emptiness; Kai came and went, these days he was away more than he was at the mission. Even when he was home, we spoke little. My mother had her good days and her bad days; my father's prayers had become shorter and shorter.

And then, one hot day at the beginning of May, Glory returned, dragging two heavy carpetbags. She didn't wear an English frock, but a sari, draped loosely. And even swathed in the shapeless folds, it was immediately obvious she was large with a child.

She went to her hut, speaking to no one. She didn't come out for the rest of the day. The second day, at noon, I brought her a plate of lentil curry and a *roti*.

'I don't want it,' she said, when I moved aside her door covering and went in, allowing sunshine into the dark, stifling hut. She was lying on her side, facing the door, her hand under her cheek. There were new lines around her mouth, and she looked exhausted. 'Take it away.'

'You have to eat something,' I said. 'If not for you, for the . . . baby,' I said, making the first mention of the thing none of us had spoken of.

'All men are liars, Pree,' she said then, hauling herself up into a sitting position. I realised she was much larger than I'd thought yesterday. It looked as though she were ready to give birth, and I quickly calculated. If this was the case, she'd already been carrying this child when she'd left the mission last October. Was this really Mr Evans' child, or was it the child of the soldier who had come looking for her?

She took the plate and scooped up the curry with the *roti*. I sat on her chair.

'He promised to marry me,' she said, taking a bite of the *roti*.

'Who?'

'Mr Evans. He left me in the rooms he rented, and told me he was gong to prepare a civil service. I waited and waited. I waited two days, and then three. He didn't return. Finally a note was delivered by a *sudra*. An untouchable, Pree. He sent the note with an untouchable,' she said, tears filling her eyes at the devastating memory.

'What did it say?'

'I called in a scribe. I had to pay him five annas – the cheat – to come to my room, and read the paper upon the table without touching it.'

I waited.

'Mr Evans wrote that he had a wife at home, in England. That he was already married, and hadn't known how to tell me.' She looked into my face. Her *surma* had smeared, and black streaks now covered her cheeks. 'So he wrote that he of course couldn't marry me, and he thought it best – these are his words – he *thought it best* – that we were no longer together. These men. Always they lie,' she said. 'Always there is a first wife.' Then she turned away abruptly. 'Leave me now,' she said. 'Leave me.'

I couldn't imagine her despair, her grief. It had obviously happened with Kai, and now with a second child. Suddenly I felt a surge of pity for her. 'My father will allow you to stay here, Glory,' I said, not certain what, exactly, my father would allow. No. More specifically, what my mother would allow. Hadn't she made it clear she already found Glory a burden, a useless ayah who took advantage of my father's generous spirit? Would she really allow her stay on with another child?

I mentioned it at dinner that night.

'What will happen now?' I asked my father. 'Will you allow Glory to stay, once she has the child?' My mother hadn't come from her room this day; I was glad she wasn't with us as the uncomfortable subject of Glory and her condition were discussed.

My father didn't answer; he was pale in spite of the heat, his skin damp and waxy, the red patch on his forehead standing out in relief, like a scald. He hadn't touched his stew; I saw the tremor in his hand that held the fork.

'Father? Are you ill?'

He nodded then, rising and going to the bedroom. He shut the door, and I sat alone at the table in the fading light, the house baking in the evening sun, the rooster calling as if confused about morning and evening.

The next day my father remained in bed, and in a strange reversal of roles it was my mother who went to the infirmary. I helped her all morning; she stayed in the shade of the infirmary verandah to eat the boiled eggs and chopped cold potatoes Sanosh made for her and my father.

I brought a plate back to the house for him, but when I came through the front door I was shocked to see Glory sitting on the black Windsor chair in front of the piano.

'What are you doing?' I said. 'Don't touch my mother's piano.'

But Glory pressed two keys, making a soft, discordant sound.

'Don't,' I repeated. 'My mother wouldn't want you to do that.'

Glory just smiled. 'I don't see your mother.'

I wondered what had happened between yesterday and today to bring back her boldness. Yesterday she had been weeping and inconsolable. Today, apart from her bulk, she looked like the old Glory, with the same insolent smile.

I took the plate in to my father. As I set it on the chair beside the bed, I saw one of Glory's glass bangles, caught in the bedsheet. 'Has Glory been in to help you?' I asked, picking up the bangle.

He frowned. 'Leave me be,' he said. 'I don't want any food. Take it away.' His voice was petulant.

I took away the plate. Glory was no longer in the sitting room.

My father recovered over the next few days, slowly regaining his strength, as he always did. The summer weather slowed his progress; when he had an attack in the heat it always took him longer to recuperate. It was as if the hot, steamy air took away his breath.

I was on the side verandah early one morning a few weeks later, combing my hair. As I pulled a few strands from the comb's teeth and let them float up into the air, Kai came out of his mother's hut.

He stopped, looking at me, then came to the verandah. 'It's born,' he said.

I dropped my comb. 'What? The baby? Glory had the baby?'

He nodded. 'I heard its cry, only an hour ago. My mother was alone; she didn't call for help. She had the child alone.'

His voice was flat, unemotional.

'What is it? A boy or a girl?' I asked, clasping my hands, unsure of how I felt.

'A girl,' he said, and then turned and went back to his hut.

I ran into the house. 'Mother,' I called. She was sitting at the dining-room table, an empty plate in front of her. I don't know whether she had already eaten or hadn't yet begun. 'Glory had the baby. A girl, Kai says. Come. Let's go and see her.' I was suddenly strangely excited at the thought of the baby. There had been such a heaviness in me over the deaths of Lalasa and her little girl. This felt like a new beginning. 'Mother?'

She looked at me, but seemed confused, as if she didn't know of what I spoke.

'Glory's baby. It's here, Mother. Come.' I held out my hand. She looked at it, then put her own into mine. Hers was cold and dry.

My father came from the bedroom. 'What's all this about?' he asked, buttoning his collar.

'Glory's had a little girl,' I said, watching his face.

But it conveyed nothing. 'A girl, is it? Well, there's nothing to be done about it, I suppose.'

'Father,' I said, disappointed in his reaction, 'surely you can't feel the same way as the natives do about a girl. Isn't any child a gift from God?' *Did you feel this disappointment over* my *birth? Over Alice Ann's and Elizabeth's?*

He sighed, sitting at the table and picking up the black Bible he always left there. 'I just meant that there's nothing to be done about the fact that another unwanted child has come into the world.'

I led my mother out to Glory's hut. Glory lay on her side, facing the door, her knees together, drawn up under the thin coverlet. A pail sat in one corner; flies buzzed over it, and I smelled the unmistakable odour of blood. I knew the smell all too well, now.

'Glory? Where is she? Kai told us,' I said, and Glory made a slight motion behind her.

My mother and I both leaned over her. The baby lay there, between the wall and Glory's back, wrapped in a piece of flannel, her eyes shut.

'Did you tie the cord with thread?' my mother asked, eyeing the infant.

'Of course,' Glory said, sulkily.

'You could have called us, Glory,' I said. 'We would have helped you.'

'I needed no one's help,' Glory said.

My mother raised her chin at me, and I reached over Glory and lifted the baby. My mother held out her arms, and I put the baby into them, then had to look away at the sight of my mother's face. It had cleared, as if the strange mask that changed her features was moving aside, setting free her true spirit. I knew she must be thinking of her own babies, all the dead children, but instead of appearing sad, there was a joyful lightness in her eyes. I hadn't seen this look for a long, long time, and it filled my heart with gladness. She hummed, softly, and the baby stirred, stretching.

'I could take you, too,' my mother murmured. I thought of Kai, the little Kai, whose mother – the very mother who lay in front of me now, obviously as disinterested in this child, as she had been in her son – had run off and left him, more than once, for a number of years.

'Isn't she lovely,' I said, touching the baby's cheek.

My mother blinked, as if suddenly aware of where she was, of whose illegitimate child she held. 'A shame she's so dark,' she said slowly. 'Considering, if we're to believe her story,' she looked at Glory, 'that the father was white, and Glory herself is half—'

Glory now turned on her back, staring at the ceiling and pointedly ignoring my mother.

'Well,' my mother continued, 'one can never predict with what depth the tar brush will leave its mark. Here,' she said, handing the infant to me, 'clean her and give her back to Glory to feed.' She looked over at the pail. 'And tell Kai to take this mess and bury it in the field; he should put a stone over it so the jackals don't dig it up. They'll come from miles around if they smell blood, and I don't want them creeping into the courtyard. Filthy beasts.' Then she left the hut.

I crooned to the baby as I gently wiped her body with a damp cloth. Glory had bound the child's middle with a strip of gauze; a tiny spot of blood showed where the cut cord lay. 'What will you call her, Glory?' I asked.

Glory carefully turned on to her side, facing me again, making a small exclamation of discomfort. Although her eyes were closed, I knew she wasn't asleep. She didn't answer my question.

'You should feed her,' I said.

'When she cries,' she answered sullenly.

My mother returned with a woven basket. She silently put it on the end of the charpoy and stepped back. With one arm holding the quiet baby, whom I'd rewrapped in the length of flannel, I reached into the basket. There were squares of thick flannel for nappies and tiny lacy frocks and smocked shirts, all white cotton, little bonnets with yellowed but clean ribbons, and knitted booties.

'Did I wear these, Mother?' I asked, stroking the pleats of one of the frocks. She didn't answer, but turned and left. I knew she would be thinking her own sorrowful thoughts. I didn't know she'd kept the clothes that surely all of us had worn; they must have been packed way in tin-lined boxes at the back of her wardrobe.

When I'd dressed the baby – cautiously pulling her tiny arms through the sleeves of a dress, fitting the knitted booties over her minuscule toes, I sat outside the hut, holding her. She suddenly yawned, and then frowned as if with a sudden pain. Her mouth opened, but she didn't cry out. Kai came from the field, and I stood, holding out the baby to him.

'Look at how beautiful your sister is.'

He didn't ask about his mother, or take the baby, but he looked at her for a long time, and then reached out and ran his fingertips, so softly, over her fine dark hair. He let his index and middle finger rest on the soft, pulsing top of her skull. 'Poor thing,' he said.

I didn't ask what he meant. I already knew. I told him what my mother had asked that he do, and when he'd left with the covered pail, I took the baby back to Glory and tucked her on the narrow charpoy beside her mother.

I couldn't stop thinking about Glory's baby, her tiny pursed lips, her wrinkled fingertips. I wanted to hold her again, and I knew my mother was thinking of her as well. Each time we heard the thin, high hungry wail of the newborn through that first afternoon and evening, my mother would stop whatever she was doing, lifting her head with an instinct, an expression of concern in her eyes, as if it were her baby crying, needing to be fed. And when the baby's cries stopped, she lowered her head again, shaking it heavily, as if awakening from a dream.

The baby woke me that first night after her birth. I lay in bed, listening to the rhythmic, escalating wails. Why didn't Glory feed her? After a long time I got up, lit a candle, and carried it to Glory's hut. Kai was standing in the doorway, holding the infant awkwardly, her nappie and dress obviously wet and soiled. He looked at me, his face troubled. And then relief came over it as he held the little girl out towards me.

For a moment I found it hard to breathe. There was something overwhelming about the sight of him holding the child, looking at me with a sense of helplessness – perhaps the only time I had witnessed that particular expression. It was as if we shared the responsibility of the baby. Did he feel it? His eyes didn't leave mine as I set the candle on the chair inside the hut and held out my arms for her, and in our rather inexperienced attempt to pass the child and support her head we were, for that instant, so close, our faces almost touching as he bent towards me.

As soon as I had the baby securely in my arms he left.

Glory was lying on her back; I couldn't see if her eyes were open or shut. The baby screamed, her body rigid with distress and hunger, her tiny clenched fists waving. And yet I wanted to savour that moment, the moment I had shared with Kai.

I moved closer to the bed. Even in the wavering candlelight Glory was very pale, unmoving, her eyes closed, although she couldn't have been asleep with the baby's piercing shrieks.

'Glory,' I said. 'Feed the baby. You must.'

She opened her eyes. 'I'm tired,' she said. 'I need to sleep.'

'But the baby—'

'I don't want to.'

Did Glory imagine herself to be an uppity British memsahib, too delicate and prudish to feed her own child? What would she suggest – hiring a native wet nurse? I made an exasperated sound in my throat, quickly setting the baby on the charpoy and removing the soiled nappie, then binding a fresh one in its place. 'You have to. That's all. Do it now.'

What kind of a mother was Glory? Had I expected her to be any different in her approach to this child than she had been to Kai? I knelt beside her charpoy and put the baby into the crook of Glory's arm. Sighing, she fumbled with her nightdress, and only when the baby abruptly stopped crying, her head bobbing in tiny desperate movements as she latched on, did I go back to the house and my own bed.

* * *

Although Glory begrudgingly fed her baby when she cried, she was clearly disinterested in her.

'What are you going to call her?' I asked, yet again, when three days had passed and still Glory didn't refer to her as anything but *she* or *her*. I had bathed the little girl each morning, and changed her frequently through the day after seeing that Glory left her lying in her own mess.

Now she shrugged. 'I don't care.'

'You have to pick a name for her,' I said.

'You pick it,' she said, listlessly.

'Me? Name your baby?' I asked.

She didn't answer.

'Do you want a Hindu name or an English one?' I finally said.

At that she looked up at me. 'English, of course,' she said. 'She is the daughter of an Englishman. As I am.'

I thought for a full day, trying to decide on a name. Finally I named the little girl Adriana, because I'd just finished reading Shakespeare's *Comedy of Errors*, and I'd found that name to have a beautiful melody. My mother disapproved; she said the child should have a name chosen from the Bible in the hopes that it would contribute to her spiritual well-being.

I said nothing, but continued to call the baby Adriana, and within a few days this was the name everyone called her.

The following week a young man came to the fence twice, calling out to Kai. Kai spoke with him each time, and papers passed between them. I didn't recognise him; he was a Muslim. I asked Kai who he was but he only said, curtly, 'A friend.'

And then, exactly eight days after Adriana's birth, Kai announced he was leaving. I knew how angry he was with his mother, not only because she had brought this poor little female into the world, but also because now that she was here she showed no interest in her at all.

'Now, Kai? You're leaving?' Panic rose in my chest, fluttering like wings, making it difficult for me to breathe.

'Just for a while,' he said.

'For a while?' I repeated, my voice too high, staring at the bulging cloth bag in the dust at his feet. 'Is it because of the baby? Because of Adriana that you're leaving?'

He shook his head. 'No. There are other reasons . . . but because of her I've decided I won't leave for good. Not yet.' The wings hovered, then stilled, and I exhaled slowly. 'I know there's too much for you to look after, especially now, with the baby, and your mother . . . I'm sorry, Pree. But I've spoken to Sanosh, and he's agreed that one of his sons can help with the garden and any heavy work until I return.'

'How long will you be gone?'

'I can't say. It depends.'

'On what?'

'Pree. Just trust that I'll return.'

'But . . . without you here . . .' I didn't finish the sentence.

'I'm sorry,' he said again. 'I do know the extra burden this places on you.' He kept speaking of the physical work, as if that was why I dreaded him leaving. 'But I need to go, Pree. There are things that must be done. That I need to do. There are . . . wrongs. Wrongs that must be righted.' His jaw clenched.

I thought of the Kukas. 'But . . . you won't do anything that will . . . that could . . .' I stopped, unsure of how to continue. 'You won't do anything to create difficulty for yourself, will you, Kai? With the British.'

He stared at me, and then a strange smile – almost mocking – came to his mouth. 'There's no way to bring about change but through the banding together of individuals, those of us who believe in the same cause.' His voice had grown passionate as he stared into my face, and I was aware my palms were sweating. 'Do you not understand by now that I won't be part of the Empire? Ever. Ever, Pree.'

His manner had become so fierce, his voice rising on that last word, that I winced.

And at that he stopped, drawing a deep breath. 'I'm sorry, Pree' he said. 'I . . . I'm angry about a number of issues, about the way the British are running our country.'

'Will you go to Lahore, then?' I asked, desperate to have him speak of something else.

But now he looked away, and I sensed he didn't want to tell me an untruth, and so wouldn't tell me anything. 'You'll be all right here, then?' he said then, looking back to study Adriana, asleep in my arms.

'Of course. And my mother can also help see to the baby,' I said, relieved that we now spoke of ordinary issues. But a frown flashed across his features.

'Your mother? Do you think . . . ?'

I understood then. 'Even in her worst state, Kai, she wouldn't harm a child. When Adriana is near she grows calmer than I've seen her in some time.'

He nodded. 'Goodbye, then,' he said, and I turned my head to look out at the field, unable to speak.

'Will you not tell me goodbye, Pree? Are you that angry that I'm going?'

I wasn't angry. I was sad. I swallowed. 'Goodbye, Kai,' I said then, almost in a whisper, 'Hurry home.'

He looked around the mission. 'Home?' he said, and something in his tone made me feel infinitely worse. He slung his cloth bag over his shoulder. I followed him out on to the road, holding Adriana. He turned once, and waved. I waved back, pressing my lips on to Adriana's soft, dark hair, so like her brother's.

★ ★ ★

157

Glory announced that she would be unable to work for the next forty days; they were too dangerous, she said, not only for her own health, but for the child's. I knew full well that she only used the Indian cultural beliefs when they suited her, but said nothing.

From the day of Adriana's birth I had been filled with a fierce protection for the baby. Although Glory thought nothing of leaving her howling in her basket, I couldn't bear the sound of her cries. Glory was only too happy to let me take her, and I'd strap the little thing into a sling, like the native women, so she could rest against my back or chest when I worked at the infirmary or at my chores outside, and in the evenings I would bring her into the house. My mother and I would play with her as if she were Lalasa's beautiful porcelain doll, dressing her in different little frocks and endlessly pointing out to each other the strength of her chubby, kicking legs and the alertness in her bright eyes. I made simple dangling toys with yarn and buttons and laughed aloud at her serious but uncoordinated attempts to follow their movements as I gently swung them over her.

What I had told Kai about my mother was true; she had more energy with Adriana about. She stopped whatever she was doing when I carried in the baby. Holding out her arms, her face relaxed, and she forgot to cover her mouth, smiling unselfconsciously as she bounced Adriana on her knees, murmuring nonsense to her.

Those were the only times – sharing the care of the little girl – that my mother and I had laughed together in such a long time.

And so I kept Adriana with me at all times, only taking her to Glory for feeding, although she slept beside her mother at night so that she could feed when hungry. And after a while it began to feel that Adriana was my own – perhaps a sister, perhaps even what I imagined to be my daughter. I only knew that she was all I thought about, and I also realised that what I was feeling for her was love. I didn't know this sensation, having someone to love. Of course, I argued with myself, I had my parents, but whatever I felt for them was too twisted up in their own lost dreams and broken spirits; they created a muddiness, a swirling sensation of concern, sometimes anger and sometimes sympathy.

What I felt for Kai was too confusing – and perhaps fearful – to name. I couldn't let myself think about my true feelings for him. But Adriana filled the emptiness like a clear, shining light, a clean hopefulness that had no past.

Sometimes, watching my mother with Adriana, I wondered if she felt the same way as I about the child, wanting something to love. But she did have a husband and a daughter of her own. Had she ever looked at me the way she looked at Adriana, her face so warm and open? Had my mother ever felt this love for me? Had I ever fulfilled her the way I was fulfilled by Adriana? I wanted to think it was so, and yet when I watched her face change as I set Adriana into her arms, a distant thrum of melancholy ran through me. I sensed I had never brought this look to her face, this softening of her ruined mouth, this tenderness in her eyes.

But at the same time I believed Adriana to be our little saviour, sent to soothe some of the discontent that hovered over us. To bring my mother and me closer. With her in our lives, the mission became a better place.

CHAPTER THIRTEEN

ONE AFTERNOON, WITH no patients at the infirmary, I dug in the garden, weeding and pulling up root vegetables – there were always crops of radishes, and the carrots were a good size – while Adriana slept in the sling across my chest.

Humming as I took a brief rest, leaning on the hoe and absently looking at the road, I saw a familiar golden Arabian horse. My heart lifted; I couldn't remember when I'd last seen the Afghan.

How long had he been sitting there, watching me work? I put down the hoe and walked across the courtyard. As I approached I saw his eyes fixed on Adriana.

He wore the usual dark turban and white *kurta* and black trousers tucked into high riding boots, although this time he had a finely worked brocade vest of burgundy and navy over the *kurta*. As he studied the baby's head there was something unfamiliar, some stiffness, in his features. Or perhaps it was that his face had faded from my memory slightly?

He didn't even greet me. 'Is this . . .' his voice faltered. He cleared his throat. 'Is this your child?' he asked in Urdu, which we always spoke. Even his voice was hoarser than I remembered.

'No,' I said. 'She belongs to the ayah, to Glory,' I said, watching for his reaction. If he was indeed Kai's father, wouldn't the mention of Glory's name cause some reaction?

His face did change, slightly, and the tension in his shoulders lessened slightly. Now I could see that his hands trembled, ever so slightly. And he was thinner, surely.

'Have you been well?' I asked, then, because I felt something for him at that moment, with his sad eyes and nervous hands. Pity, perhaps. I suddenly remembered my old imaginings, the fantasy I had created about a lost princess. He seemed such a . . . I searched for the right word. A solitary man.

'Yes,' he said. 'And you?' Now his face was an impenetrable mask.

'I'm well, also. It's been some time since I've seen you.'

'I've been living in Peshawar this last while,' he said.

'Oh.' There seemed little else to say, and yet I wanted to talk to him. He was looking at me in such a strange way, and yet it didn't bring me any unease. Instead, as I looked up at him, so tall on his horse, a calmness came over me. I was somehow drawn to him; I wanted to put my hands over his, and stop their quivering.

'What is it like? Is Peshawar truly as exciting as I've heard?'

His face shifted, just the slightest, and again he cleared his throat. 'It's full of disease, and danger. The truce between British India and Afghanistan is uneasy, and Peshawar, because of its border position, is caught between the two powers. The summers are long and suffocating, the winters dry and cold. A difficult climate. But there is an intoxicating spring, filled with the scent of orange blossoms. It is a city of contrasts.'

I watched him; he grew less and less stiff, and as he spoke more easily I realised he had an eloquence with words. Again I thought of him reciting poetry. Like this, his face losing its intenseness, he appeared younger than I had always thought.

'Yes. Peshawar is a good home for me now,' he said.

'You describe it as a place I would like to visit,' I said. 'But before now? Did you formerly live in Kabul, or perhaps

Jalalabad? Herat?' I named the cities of Afghanistan I knew.

'I've lived in many places,' he said then. 'In Afghanistan, in India. And other countries.'

'Other countries?' I couldn't imagine him, with his turban and grizzled beard, his skin so dark and chapped by wind, living anywhere but the hills of Afghanistan or northern India. 'What other countries?' I suppose I was staring at him, possibly sounding too interested, for suddenly his face closed again, and I was sorry. He looked over my head. 'Is Kai back?'

'No,' I said, surprised that he would know that Kai had left the mission.

'He hasn't returned from Amritsar, then?'

I was further taken aback. Kai had never mentioned Amritsar, south-east of Lahore. How did this man know so much more of Kai's life than I? 'He didn't speak of where he was going, or when he would be back. But he said he'd return.'

The Afghan didn't answer, studying my face as if thinking of something else. 'He left when?' he asked.

Adriana stirred, and I put my hand on her warm back. She was almost two months old. 'Over six weeks ago.'

'Ah. Yes,' the man murmured, as if he understood something I didn't.

Suddenly I was filled with worry. 'Do you . . . is Kai still involved with . . .' I hesitated, hoping the Afghan would know what I spoke of.

But he waited, sitting very still.

'With the Kukas?' I said.

'You know of this?'

'He told me, briefly. Do you think he's in danger?'

He lowered his eyes, and his horse shifted. 'The Kukas were in the past for Kai. He has become involved in other areas. But there is no need for you to worry. Kai knows how to protect himself.'

There seemed nothing else to say then. Finally I asked, as the silence grew, 'Shall I pass on a message when he returns?' I looked into his dark eyes, and he blinked and didn't speak.

'Is there a message for Kai?' I asked again.

The man touched his heels to the horse's flank, and it lifted its head at that gentle prod. 'Just tell him I've been to Gwalior, as we discussed, and have now returned to Peshawar,' he said.

'I'll tell him,' I said.

He turned his horse, looking over his shoulder at me, down at Adriana, and then into my face. '*Khuda hafiz*, Pree,' he said, and something in his voice, saying the simple goodbye, made me draw in my breath. Perhaps it was that he had never before said my name. And I realised I didn't know his.

Before I could ask him, or say anything further, he rode off.

As he had promised, Kai returned, although he had been gone three long months. It was September, and the monsoons were over. My seventeenth birthday had passed, and Adriana had grown plump, her face wreathing with smiles whenever I murmured to her. Her hair was so thick and luxuriant that I'd had to trim it in a fringe on her forehead; it made her dark eyes even larger. She had laughed aloud for the first time only two days earlier, and gurgled and babbled in response to my singing and talking to her.

Kai rode into the courtyard on a dappled mare. I rushed to greet him, leaving Adriana propped against a pillow in her basket on the verandah. My heart pounded, but I held back from going too close, from flinging my arms around him, as I wished to do.

'What a wonderful horse,' I said, instead, standing well back as he dismounted and pulled his bag from behind the saddle. 'She's yours?'

He combed through her forelock with his fingers. 'Yes,' he said, looking into my face. His face was hollow, his hair longer. There was something wrong with one of his ears; was the earlobe slightly torn? The moment stretched.

'You must see Adriana,' I said. 'She's ever so big, and she smiles at everyone. You won't recognise her. Wait, I'll just fetch her,' I told him, because I felt so awkward standing there, him staring at me, and I hurried back to the verandah to scoop her into my arms.

Kai had already begun to groom the mare, but stopped as I brought Adriana to him.

'I think she looks like you,' I said, and he smiled, but in a distant way.

I held her closer, as if to put her in his arms, but he didn't react. Adriana reached out and grabbed Kai's shirt with one plump hand. He looked down at it, a dark star against the crisp white cotton, but said nothing.

'Don't you think she's beautiful?' I finally asked, taking her hand from his shirt and holding her closely against me again.

'Yes,' he said. 'You've managed, then, with everything?' He resumed brushing the mare's coat. She snickered with pleasure.

I didn't understand his studied disinterest in Adriana. 'It's been difficult,' I admitted. 'It's harder to keep Adriana occupied while I work in the infirmary now. Luckily she's content to be held by any of the women. Although I won't let her near a mother or child with anything infectious. But I've kept up the garden; last week I dug out all the carrots and turnips. The potatoes are growing well. And I managed to repair the roof of the infirmary; the thatch was damaged in the monsoon.'

I knew I was chattering, hoping for some reaction, perhaps a word of praise.

But Kai simply bent his head and groomed more briskly, and the mare's flesh rippled under the brushstrokes.

★ ★ ★

One morning, a few weeks after his arrival home, as I went out on to the side verandah, I felt the first breath of cool air, and breathed deeply. I knew that today Adriana was four months old. Thinking about her, I realised I hadn't heard her this morning. She was sleeping through much of the night now, but awoke with a hungry, demanding cry just as the sky was lightening with the first pink rays. I always heard her strong voice echoing through my bedroom shutters.

I looked at Glory's hut now. The last time I had seen her – or Adriana – had been early evening the day before. Glory had the baby in the sling and was walking through the courtyard to the road; I hadn't thought anything of it. She often took a short walk down the road, or went into one of the villages.

At that very moment the silence was shattered by Kai's voice. He was shouting; he so rarely raised his voice that I knew something was dreadfully wrong. And then he came out of his mother's hut, his face stricken, and hurried into the hard-beaten earth of the courtyard.

I rushed down the steps. 'What is it, Kai?' I asked, catching up to him and grabbing his arm. 'Is it Adriana? Is she ill, or—'

But he shook off my arm. 'Where would she have taken her?' he said, and I frowned.

'Taken who?'

He stared at me, and his hands folded into fists. 'Adriana. She took the baby and left her somewhere.'

I gasped, then turned and ran into Glory's hut, as if I had to see for myself that what Kai said was true. It couldn't be. Surely he was mistaken. Glory lay there, one hand under her cheek, looking at the doorway. 'You didn't, Glory,' I said. 'You didn't . . .' I couldn't finish the sentence, couldn't bear to think of what she might have done.

She sat up. 'A daughter only brings financial hardship. What dowry would I offer? I don't want to support her for the rest of my life. Better now, when she is so young. Better now,' she repeated.

I stared at her for another moment; the horror of it hadn't fully set in, and I didn't believe Adriana was truly gone. Surely she was just in the next village. We would get her back. I ran out to the courtyard where Kai was saddling his horse.

'We'll find her,' I said. 'Glory can't have walked that far. She must have taken her into Dipha. I saw her walking in that direction yesterday. I'll come with you. And if she's not there we'll go to Tek Mandi. She'll have to be in one of the villages.'

Kai swung into the saddle, and I held up my hands. 'Pull me up. Take me with you,' I repeated, but he shook his head, turning the horse towards the gate.

'Look through the corn, and the sugar cane,' he said, his voice low, and my mouth opened.

'But . . . but why would she . . . she wouldn't be there. Kai.' I said, not wanting to understand what he was saying. I couldn't bear to think of Adriana lying on the furrowed earth, screaming, attracting the wild animals of the countryside. I squeezed my eyes shut, trying not to think of Lalasa's baby.

'Unless she's killed her,' Kai said, his voice so filled with hatred, his words shocking me, and I opened my eyes and put my hands over my mouth, shaking my head. I kept shaking my head; the expression on Kai's face was so dark and frightening that tears filled my eyes.

He dug his heels into the horse's sides. 'Go,' I said, crying, my voice loud and shaken. 'Ask anyone you see. Don't stop until you find her,' I told him. 'Find her, Kai!' My voice had risen to a shriek.

He rode away without a word.

But we didn't find her. As evening drew near a pall settled over the mission; everyone – my parents, Sanosh and Pavit – knew that Adriana was gone. Kai had ridden back but didn't come to me, and now silently brushed down his horse. I was exhausted from the day's fruitless search. My hands and face were scratched from pushing through bushes and stalks. My boots were covered in mud from wandering along the banks of the Ravi. My hair had come loose and was matted with sweat and tiny twigs had lodged in it. My throat ached, and my voice was hoarse from endlessly calling the child's name.

I sat on the steps of the front verandah as darkness descended over the courtyard, my head resting on my arms, which were crossed on my knees. My mother, her face drained of colour, rocked with restless, quick movements behind me. My father stayed in the infirmary; Pavit sat motionless under the peepul tree. Even Sanosh's scrubbing of the pots was muted.

And Glory hadn't emerged from her hut.

Night fell; there was only a dim light from the infirmary. I didn't have the heart to trim the wicks and light the lamps in the house.

Kai came to the verandah, and I raised my head, studying his face in the shadows. 'Nobody in either of the villages knows anything of her, although a woman said they saw my mother climbing into a cart heading towards Lahore.'

'Did she have Adriana?'

'The woman didn't notice.' He shook his head. 'But it makes no sense for my mother to kill her. Glory only does things for her own benefit. Somehow she'll have made a profit from Adriana.' He walked quickly towards his mother's hut, and I followed.

Glory was still lying on her charpoy.

'Light the lamp,' Kai said to me, and I did as he said.

Then he grabbed his mother by the shoulders, lifting her off the charpoy and holding her so that her feet didn't touch the ground. He roughly shook her, hissing into her face.

'Have you killed the baby? Or left her somewhere to die? Is this what you've done?' He shook her harder. Glory's head flopped on her neck, and then her face hardened.

'Stop,' she whined. 'Stop, Kai.'

Kai's hands still held his mother's shoulders, but he did stop, and she hung limp under his grip.

'What have you done with her, Glory?' he asked, but I heard defeat in his voice.

'She's safe, in Lahore,' Glory said. 'She'll be well looked after.'

'But who did you leave her with?'

Now Glory's face twisted into a strange smile. 'She will be cared for,' she repeated. 'It isn't fair that I should be burdened with her.' Her smile wavered just slightly, although she struggled to keep her face fixed in a laconic outward show. 'She'll have a better life.'

'But who would want an Indian girl child?' I cried out. 'Who would want her?'

But Glory would say no more. I knew there were few options, unless she took her to another mission. And yet at the same time there would be no profit for Glory in handing her to missionaries. Kai thought in the same way as I.

He studied her face. 'And you, you too will have a better life, is that it? How much money did you get? Who did you sell her to? And for what purpose?'

'Leave me alone. You're hurting me. You can't mistreat your own mother,' Glory said in an angry tone. 'Show respect.'

Kai threw her back on to the charpoy, then grabbed up one of Glory's jewellery boxes. 'Respect?' he said, spitting the word in her face. He pulled off the tops of the boxes, dumping bracelets and anklets and earrings and rings on to the floor. 'Where's the money? How much did you get?' he repeated.

Glory, saying nothing, sat on the charpoy watching as Kai went through all her belongings, tossing clothing to the floor. And I stood near the lamp, watching Kai work through his rage.

But he found no rupees. Finally he stood in the middle of the hut, surrounded by clothing and jewellery, his face wet with sweat, contorted with anger. He stared at his mother for a long moment, and then left.

I hurried after him; he was walking through the courtyard, towards the enclosure that held Marta and his mare. 'Kai!' I called, almost running to keep up with his long strides. 'Could we go to Lahore, tomorrow, and look there? We could . . .' I thought of the options. 'Perhaps Mr Evans. The man — the baby's father — maybe she took Adriana to him? Or if we go to the other missions? Or could she have sold her to a temple, to be trained as a *devadasi*?' I knew the ancient custom of selling girl children into the temples to be brought up as virgin goddesses was now prohibited, but that some temples still took in girls. Although now they were used for prostitution by wealthy donors.

'Could we, Kai?' I said again.

Finally he stopped, and turned to me. 'She's gone, Pree. My mother would have made sure we won't be able to trace her. She's gone,' he repeated.

We stood looking at each other for that moment in the near darkness, united in our grief. His face was so angry, and I was crying, looking up at him, my arms at my sides. I just stood and cried, my face wet with tears, my nose running. Kai watched me, and his face softened, the anger changing to something I couldn't recognise. He swallowed a number of times. I longed for him to put his arms around me, to comfort me, and leaned towards him as he stepped closer. But then he stopped, pulling away, and it seemed that he fought with himself to not touch me.

'Go to bed now, Pree,' he finally said, so quietly it was almost a whisper. 'There's nothing more to be done,' and then he turned and went to the enclosure, and I knew he would saddle his horse, and ride into the night.

Still crying silently, I slowly went up the side steps and into the dark house. I was glad I didn't have to face my mother; I didn't think I could bear to look at her. As I got into bed and wept, thinking of never again seeing little Adriana, I heard the rocker on the front verandah. In another moment the mare's hoofs clopped out of the courtyard, and then immediately turned to a gallop. I knew Kai would ride her until she was lathered in sweat, down the empty road under the moonlight.

We each dealt with our grief in our own way: Kai riding himself and the horse to exhaustion, my mother rocking. I don't know what my father felt; he had treated Adriana in a rather distracted manner, occasionally smiling at her but never showing an interest in picking her up. As for me . . . I counted the frenzied creaks of the rocking chair until I spiralled into a dark sleep.

I arose with a pounding head the next morning. The sky was bright, and yet a darkness covered the mission. It was as if a death had occurred – and hadn't it? The child I had loved with a depth I didn't know I possessed was gone, as swiftly and shockingly as if smothered by the cold breath of cholera or the heat of smallpox.

When I went on to the side verandah I saw my mother, kneeling in the little cemetery. And in that instant I understood what she felt. Not, perhaps, as deeply, for I had not borne Adriana from my own body, and she was not a part of me, but I understood, for the first time, the grief of a beloved child torn from my arms, senselessly and unexpectedly.

I went to my mother, and knelt beside her, sitting back on my heels. My mother's eyes were closed in prayer, her head lowered over her hands, clasped at her chest. She didn't move when I joined her. I didn't join my hands or bow my head, but I closed my eyes, sending out a prayer for Adriana, a prayer that she not be harmed, that she was safe and clean and fed. That somebody would love her as I had.

My father rang the bell for prayers, and yet neither my mother nor I moved.

And then something unexpected happened. My mother's hand took mine, and held it. I didn't open my eyes, afraid that if I did she would let go. Her hand was larger than mine, and rough but warm, and she squeezed my fingers painfully.

I thought it would be impossible to cry after all the tears I had shed over the last day and night, but they came again, with that pressure of my mother's hand. I stayed as I was, my eyes squeezed shut, crying long after my mother released my hand, and I knew, by the sounds, that she had risen and left.

When I finally left the cemetery, I was relieved to see that no patients waited at the infirmary. I didn't trust myself to think clearly, and didn't know how I'd react if I had to deal with a baby. As I went to sit on the verandah I saw Kai, leaning against the fence, looking at the road, his hands hanging loosely over the top railing. He was very still, which was odd for Kai.

None of us spoke Adriana's name for the next few days. Glory wisely stayed silent, carrying out her duties but then returning to her hut.

But I wanted to talk about Adriana. I didn't want to act as

if she hadn't existed. I went to where Kai was sharpening a hoe in the garden.

He glanced up at me, then bent his head over his task.

'Do you think she's all right?' I asked.

Kai didn't answer.

'How could your mother give away her own child?' I stared at his profile, at his thin, straight nose, his thick eyelashes, knowing my question was pointless; we both knew the answer. 'She kept you.' Of course I knew why Glory had kept her son, but not her daughter. I knew, and Kai knew I knew, but still he answered me, slowly honing the edge of the hoe on a stone.

'She knows I'll have to provide for her. As a son, she expects that I'll eventually take her into my home, and my wife will care for her in her old age. It's my duty.'

I blinked, a strange, uncomfortable feeling flooding through me, for that instant taking away the pain. I thought of all the times Kai disappeared from the mission. I assumed he continued to carry out his work in aiding rebels. But I knew nothing of his friends. Or if he loved a woman.

I sat heavily on a rock at the end of the row. 'Are you . . . do you plan to marry?'

'Now? No,' he said, glancing down at me, and I let out my breath. I had realised I'd been holding it in while I waited for his answer.

What was this feeling between us? I wanted to name it. No, I wanted him to name it. When he was away I felt as though part of me were missing. And yet when he was near I was anxious, uneasy, as if always waiting for something unknown.

CHAPTER FOURTEEN

THE LONG WEEKS following Adriana's disappearance were empty and silent. The mission was too quiet without her occasional cries and new laughter; the evenings now empty without her to play with, to bathe and dress in the pretty little frocks that I had once worn. I couldn't remember how I had passed my time before she was born. And I couldn't bear to even look at Glory; every time I was forced to be in her presence I wanted to hurl cruel words at her, to strike her. But I knew there would be no point; I didn't speak to her, and kept my face turned away from her.

Some nights I wept for Adriana, unable to bear the thought that she might be neglected or mistreated. I knew she may have been dead. More than once I sat up in the dark silence, thinking I heard her cry. At those times fresh grief flooded over me. I forced myself to believe that somewhere, in this land where infant females were unwanted, someone had wanted her. That whoever Glory had sold her to – if she indeed sold her, and hadn't actually left her to die – would not misuse her, but treat her with love. I didn't truly believe my own thoughts – I knew that in reality Adriana did not have a future – but it was the only way I could get through that time of mourning. In the diary Kai had given me I marked the day I had last seen and held her. I didn't write anything more for a full month, my heart too heavy to put pen to paper.

At that same time – a surprisingly hot October day the month after the last entry about Adriana – we had visitors. Nobody had ever before come to call. I was sitting on the top step of the infirmary verandah, reading from my father's heavy copy of *Gray's Anatomy: Descriptive and Surgical*. There were no patients this morning, as was routine on the hottest of days. It was Glory's free day; she had left the mission, as usual.

I came down the steps as a fine carriage, pulled by a double span of high-stepping, gleaming black horses, driven by a bearded Muslim in a blue turban, came into the courtyard. A man and woman climbed out.

Before I could greet them, the man, looking around the courtyard and seeing me, called, 'Where is your memsahib?'

I opened my mouth, surprised not only at his words – that he would address me as if I were a native servant – but at the odd shape of the sounds. I had never before heard English people speak like this. 'Take us to the house, if you will,' he said.

I nodded – for what else was there for me to do? – and walked from the carriage to the front verandah, very aware of the man and woman behind me. I was also aware that I hadn't re-braided my plait that morning, and the thick braid was matted, with wisps standing out from it. I planned to wash it later in the day, but, in the meantime, had wrapped my head with a clean, large striped handkerchief I took from my father's drawer. My old frock was short, reaching only to the middle of my shins. It was too hot to wear stockings and boots; I felt my bare calves knot as if in embarrassment in front of these strangers. Suddenly thinking of Mrs Wyndham and Eleanor and their view of me, I was sorry to be seen in such a state.

Before I stepped on to the verandah of the house my mother appeared in the open doorway. She looked surprised.

No, I understood in the next second, not surprised, she was shocked, almost frightened, her features twisted into an expression I had never before seen.

'Good afternoon,' she said, her voice muffled by the handkerchief she kept firmly against her mouth.

'Mrs Fincastle?' the man said, pushing past me and extending his hand. He was not particularly tall or heavy, but rather broad. 'Allow me to introduce myself. I'm Mr Lang.' He reached for my mother's right hand; I saw she had her fingers clenched into a fist, but immediately opened her fingers and allowed Mr Lang to take her hand. He bowed over it, then straightened. 'And may I present my wife, Mrs Lang.'

Mrs Lang stepped on my foot as she strode past me. I winced, stepping back.

'Good day, Mrs Fincastle,' she said, bowing her head slightly. 'Excuse our unannounced arrival. There is simply no way to get word in this part of the country, is there? We're on our way to visit acquaintances in Amritsar. We spent last night in Lahore, and heard of your mission, and thought we would call. So terribly uncivilised, I know, to arrive with no prior notice – but what is one to do?'

'You're . . . you're not from the ministry in Lahore, then?' my mother said, something lightening in her face.

'Oh, no. We run an American mission in Peshawar. But there are so few whites in this part of the country; we must band together, mustn't we, and we thought, well, it would only be polite to stop by.'

An American mission. They were Americans, then, with their soft, stretched-out words. I had never met an American.

My mother nodded, dropping the handkerchief in what appeared to be relief. I saw Mr and Mrs Lang's eyes go to her mouth, and my mother immediately lifted the handkerchief again. 'Yes, yes, it is so lovely to have a visit. One does get terribly lonely for the company of others. Others,' she repeated. I was sorry to see that my mother, like me, hadn't bothered with her appearance this morning. She looked even more . . . how can I describe my mother that day? It was as if I were suddenly seeing her with new eyes.

As my mother stood there, again repeating the words *others*, she not only looked unkempt, but also very ill. Ill and worn, haggard in a way that wasn't caused only by hard work and climate and age. It was as if the edges of her very being were blurred: her eyes vacant, her mouth, under the handkerchief, slack, her hair faded and her skin sagging around her jaw and throat.

Mrs Lang patted her own throat with her gloved hand.

'Oh, please, do come in. Come in, Mr and Mrs Lang,' my mother said, blinking as if suddenly confused, or perhaps unsure of how to treat these unexpected guests. 'You're sure to be thirsty. And you will stay for dinner,' she added, and I glanced at the *rasoi*. As I did so, my mother caught my eye. She straightened her shoulders and took a deep breath. I knew she was trying very hard to organise her thoughts. 'Pree,' she said, 'run and inform Sanosh we will have company for our noon meal.' She stared at me with such intensity that I understood I must tell Sanosh to make sure we had enough food. 'And fetch the Reverend; tell him to come immediately to meet our visitors. Oh, there he comes now,' she said, lifting one hand. We all turned to watch my father come around the corner of the house. He wore the same worried expression my mother had worn only moments earlier, before she learned the Langs were not from the ministry.

Now my mother moved her handkerchief and smiled at my father, a strange, mincing smile, and I saw Mrs Lang's eyebrows shift, just the tiniest degree, at the sight of my mother's gums.

'And then return, Pree,' my mother added, and I nodded, hurrying down the steps and to the *rasoi*.

When I told Sanosh about the extra food needed he smacked his forehead and moaned loudly. 'But this is very, very bad. I have already made the goat stew. And there is simply not enough for another man and lady.'

'Add more water,' I told him, 'and make a lot of *roti*. I'll return to help you after I've spoken to my mother.'

Leaving Sanosh banging his copper pots in frustration, I went back to the house. Coming in the side door, I saw my mother going into her bedroom, and heard my father's voice from the sitting room, followed by the answering murmur of Mr Lang.

My mother motioned for me to go to her, and I followed her into the bedroom. 'I've just excused myself for a moment,' she said. 'Hurry. I must change, and have my hair redone,' my mother whispered, shaking her head. 'I'm ashamed to be seen like this.' She stopped and looked at my head, in its knotted handkerchief, and then down at my shamefully short frock, my bare legs and feet. 'As you should be.' She impatiently gestured for me to undo the row of buttons down the back of her dress.

Once she was in her best dress, the rather musty *peu de soie* of dull brown that she kept for the occasional trips into Lahore, I took down her hair and combed through it, twisting it into the fashion she considered becoming. As I worked she whispered to me in a constant, toneless stream, telling me to set the table with the good dishes, to help Sanosh, to be on my best behaviour, and so on, as though I were six years old, not seventeen.

Wondering what I might talk about with the American Langs, standing behind my mother at her dressing table with extra hairpins still in my mouth and her tortoiseshell brush in one hand, I heard the rustle of silk, and looked to the open doorway. Mrs Lang stood there, clutching a knitted bag with both gloved hands. The gloves were white, and of the softest leather I had ever seen. I wanted to stroke them, as I might a small, compliant animal.

'I'm sorry,' she said. 'I simply couldn't wait any longer. I'm in need of the . . .' her voice dropped to a whisper, 'convenience.' The woman's English was unhurried, flat and so velvety that I had to concentrate to understand her. When she said I, it sounded like *Ah*.

'Of course,' my mother said, grabbing her handkerchief and standing, knocking me out of the way. The pins fell from my mouth on to the uncarpeted floor. 'Allow me to direct you,' she said, with a flick of her hand, and for one instant the woman's eyes met mine. They had a strange expression, and were too wide, or perhaps a little confused. As my mother approached her, the woman put her gloved hand on the wall to steady herself, and I knew she was feeling ill.

I hoped the beautiful glove wouldn't be marred by the rough, chipping wall with its thick paste of whitewash.

I knelt and picked up the pins and began to set them back in their container, but, on a sudden whim, pulled off my kerchief and unbraided the messy plait and pinned up my hair in the same style I had just done my mother's, with a few soft wisps about my face. I turned my head this way and that, pleased with my new reflection. I was too old for the girlish braid. Then I went to my room and, like my mother, put on my other frock, my best — although of course it was one of the cast-offs of the good ladies of Lahore — a green sprigged cotton which hung limply. I wished I had looked for a petti-coat in the last charity box. And then I put on my thick lisle stockings and forced my feet into my cracked leather boots.

How long had it been since I had last worn them? A month, two? They had grown too tight. I tried to ignore the cramping pain in my toes as I set the dining table with our best china, not the everyday tin plates and mugs, and finally went out to the *rasoi* with the big china tureen. I held it while Sanosh poured the stew from the pot into it.

But as I turned to carry it back into the house, he stopped me.

'No, Missy Pree,' he said. 'It is not the proper way for you to serve with a *burra* sahib and memsahib here. Go and sit with them.'

I returned to the house. My parents and the Langs were already seated at the table. Four sets of eyes turned, looking at me as I stood in the doorway. Although I had put out a place-setting for myself, there weren't enough chairs – we only had four of the heavy old Queen Ann upholstered chairs with their sagging, dusty brocade seats of worn burgundy velvet.

In the silence I went to the sitting room, bringing back the spindly black Windsor chair from in front of the piano.

Again, that odd silence as I carried it to the fifth place-setting, beside Mr Lang.

'Well,' he said, as I put down the chair. He looked at my parents, and they looked back at him.

'I suppose one doesn't stand for formality in the countryside,' he continued, then rubbed his hands together. 'You'll sit here, will you then, my dear?' he boomed, shuffling his chair over a bit. Now he glanced at his wife, and then again at my mother, and finally at my father. 'It would give me great pleasure to be seated next to such a lovely miss.' He smiled broadly now, bowing his head slightly at me. His teeth, like his body, were quite square, and they had a definite grey hue. 'I have become quite tolerant of the unexpected ways of this country.'

His voice had the same drawn-out quality as the woman's. Although his dark hair appeared thick, low on his forehead and curling over the tops of his ears, I saw the bald circle on his crown before he straightened.

I sat beside him. Clearing my throat, I spread the heavily darned, ancient damask serviette on my lap.

'We have no difficulty with your ayah joining us, please be assured, Mr and Mrs Fincastle,' Mrs Lang said. 'Why, back home many of the servants become part of the family, after all.'

Blood raced up my neck to my face. I counted the beating in my ears. One, two, and then my mother's voice punctured the hot room. 'I'm sorry. I should have introduced you earlier. I thought I had, but . . . this is our daughter, Miss Pree Fincastle.' She looked at the empty plate in front of her. 'I'm certain I introduced you earlier,' she repeated. Her face was flushed, her lips wet yet cracked. 'We so rarely have company . . .'

Mrs Lang opened her small reticule and took out a fragile, pale blue fan, snapping it open. The snap spoke of embarrassment, or perhaps anger. 'I do apologise, Mrs Fincastle.' She didn't apologise to me. 'Well. It seems my husband has made a terrible blunder.' She raised her eyes and I stared at her.

'Sorry about the mistaken identity, my dear,' Mr Lang said, turning towards me. 'I simply assumed—'

'One of my husband's gravest errors,' Mrs Lang said, her words even slower, and a little slurred. 'Assuming.' She no longer had that wide-eyed, nervous look. Now she appeared quite relaxed and not at all ill. She in no way resembled the trembling woman I had observed in the hall outside my mother's room earlier. She touched her upper lip with a delicate lace handkerchief which she pulled from her sleeve, looking upwards. My father had remained silent through this horrendous exchange.

'Well, we've certainly experienced worse heat than this,' Mr Lang said, with a small, gruff laugh, again baring those grey teeth. 'We spent a year in Ceylon, trying to start a mission there, but were met with too much hostility. The Tamils are far less open to change, we found.' He wiped his moustache with his napkin.

I fixed my eyes on the tureen of goat stew Sanosh silently

carried in and set in the middle of the table. As he left I saw that his turban had come untied and its tail straggled down his back.

'As you have probably observed, we aren't allowed the luxury of many servants, due to the constraints of our mission.' My mother spoke rapidly, loudly, almost desperately, as if afraid of any more silence.

'You poor thing,' Mrs Lang said. It sounded like *pour thang*. 'But to not even have an ayah, Mrs Fincastle. I saw your daughter helping you, but—'

'I do have an ayah,' my mother interrupted. 'She's just . . . indisposed at the moment.' She looked at me, and I knew I mustn't speak. 'You know how lazy these women are. Bone idle. Hard to get a decent day's work out of them. Thankfully our daughter is a great help.'

Sanosh returned with a heaped platter of *roti*, placing it beside the stew. For some reason the conversation stopped as we all watched Sanosh. One of the *rotis* slid off the platter. He picked it up with his fingers and dropped it back on to the pile.

Mrs Lang looked away and turned to me. 'And how is life for you here, my dear, in such an isolated place?' she asked. 'It must be difficult, having returned from your schooling, leaving behind the friendships and the social milieu of England. Although I do admire your tenacity, coming back to help your parents. I assume you intend to carry on with missionary work as well?'

So many questions. I didn't look at my parents. 'Actually, I didn't receive a formal education in England. I have grown up here, taught by my parents. But I was wondering, Mr and Mrs Lang, were you on the side of the Rebels or Yankees during the recent Civil War?' Only last year Kai had talked to me about the war in America which had taken place in the preceding decade.

My father stood and reached across the table to ladle the stew into the individual bowls. His frayed jacket cuffs exposed his pale wrists.

'Oh, my goodness,' Mrs Lang laughed, rather too loudly, 'we certainly don't wish to discuss such unpleasant topics as war at table.' She accepted a bowl from my father, setting it down and absently pushing her spoon back and forth through the steaming dish.

'Kai . . . a friend, told me about it. He has a number of old newspapers and articles, and always lets me read them. Of course it was terrible that your president, Mr Lincoln, was killed, and—'

'You enjoy reading, then?' Mrs Lang interrupted. 'And what other studies did you find to your liking?'

'History, I suppose,' I said. 'And I love learning languages.' I took the bowl my father silently held to me.

Now Mr Lang took an interest. 'Greek, Latin?' he asked. 'Or perhaps Italian?'

My soup had a vertebra in it. I pushed it aside, hoping one didn't appear in Mr or Mrs Lang's dish. 'No. No, the languages of India. Hindi. And Urdu and Punjabi. Also Persian.'

'Pree is very competent in many areas,' my mother said, surprising me. She had never paid me a compliment. 'She also copes well in the infirmary. And yes, she'll carry on the missionary role.'

I started at my mother's words: *Yes, she'll carry on the missionary role*, she had said, so casually, the decision made for me without my knowledge. Without even a discussion on what I might do with my life.

'Mr Lang, please. Do take a *roti*,' my mother said, moving her handkerchief aside just the slightest as she lifted the platter and extended it towards him. 'I so wish we had a *khitmutgar* to wait table. I again apologise. And I'm also sorry if this humble repast is not what you're accustomed to, but we try our best in our little corner of India. Our cook naturally has some strange ideas, but we've worked diligently with him to try and perfect our favourite English meals. Although more than anything I miss bread. Quite an impossibility.' She was speaking too loudly, and had to frequently wipe the saliva from her lips.

'You should try to find a cook from Goa, Mrs Fincastle,' Mrs Lang said sympathetically. 'They're akin to you English having a French chef at home. A number of Goans, with all that Portuguese blood, are, while often regrettably Papists, wonderful cooks. And their religion means there aren't any restrictions on meat. And even better – they know how to bake bread. True bread, light and fluffy, risen from yeast.'

My mother stared at her as if she spoke an unknown language. Then she looked back to Mr Lang, both their hands now on the platter.

'Our ayah's mother was Goan,' I said, to fill the silence.

My mother finally let go of the platter. Mr Lang took a *roti* and then looked for a plate to set it on. I jumped up and brought small side plates for everyone. As I set his down, I saw him studying the goat stew in its gluey, odd-coloured gravy, bits of potato and withered carrots floating on the surface.

'I've come to enjoy a good masala curry, myself,' he said. 'Some damn good – oh, I do beg your pardon – there actually is some tasty Indian food to be had.' Beads of sweat ran from his hairline down to his jaw. He glanced at the ceiling. 'Could we have someone pull the punkah while we enjoy our meal?' he asked. 'It's quite warm for this late in the year.'

My father cleared his throat. 'Pree, see if you can find Kai to pull the punkah.'

I stared at him. The punkah had been unused for years. And to ask Kai to pull a punkah rope . . . it would be shocking and belittling. This was a job for the lowest servant, the youngest child.

'He's not here,' I lied.

'Then you go on, dear. Give the punkah a few pulls,' my mother said. I rose and took the rope, yanking on it, and the punkah came to life, creaking overhead. Dust flew from it, but at least it rose in the churned air, and didn't immediately fall on to the table. The wisps of hair that had, as usual, come loose from their pins and fallen down my mother's back, stirred in the slight breeze.

A heaviness grew in my stomach. These people had thought I was an ayah, even while dressed in my good frock and boots, with my hair pinned up. I continued to stand in the corner, the rope biting into my palm, while my parents and the Langs ate. The talk remained small and dreary. They spoke of food, of weather and problems with drought in Karela, the famine in Bengal. Mr Lang touched on the issue of past British economic and administrative policies, which led to restrictions on internal trade now, but it was clear that neither my father nor mother were able to comment on his statements.

'Oh, and we avoided one of those awful burnings. We were almost subjected to the terrible sight – well, of course we didn't stay to watch that good lady wife setting herself afire on the husband's pyre,' Mrs Lang said, 'only a few weeks ago, in Rawalpindi. "I declare", I said to Mr Lang, "well, Mr Lang, I don't rightly know how these people carry on with their preposterous imaginings." '

The room was still, except for the whoosh, whoosh of the punkah. 'They believe it to be a duty of honour, Mrs Lang,' I said. 'They see it as a final duty. Of love." '

'Oh, pish tosh,' Mrs Lang said, shaking her head as she looked at me. 'Silly superstitious nonsense, suttee. Gives me chills. In spite of the heat.' She sighed. 'Can you pull a bit faster, my dear? I'm not feeling much of the good of that fan.'

As I pulled harder I glanced at my mother, and was horrified to see her gazing blankly at Mrs Lang, her mouth open and saliva, coloured by the stew, on her chin. She blinked.

'Suttee?' she said, then said, more quietly, 'sati,' using the Hindi word. 'Sati,' she repeated, in a reverent way, and I couldn't bear for the Langs to see her in this state.

'Mother,' I said, going to her and positioning my body so that the Langs couldn't see me wiping her chin. 'Finish your stew.'

I went back to the corner and pulled the rope again. Nobody paid any further attention to me; while my parents ate with determined duty, the Langs took only small, tentative spoonfuls. My own stew sat untouched. I was hungry, and growing more and more angry at their obvious dismissal of me.

'Shall we retire to the verandah and leave the ladies to their talk, Mr Lang?' my father said, when it was apparent nobody was eating any more – my parents' bowls empty while the Langs' remained half full, but their spoons set down on the tablecloth.

Mrs Lang stood, and my father and Mr Lang immediately rose. My mother remained in her seat.

'I would so dearly love a cup of mint tea,' Mrs Lang said, with that full, soft voice that was so melodic it almost sounded like singing.

'Oh. Yes. Well, we could have some tea in the sitting room,' my mother said. 'Pree? Could you go out and ask Sanosh to prepare tea? I'm not sure we have mint, Mrs Lang. But our cook does prepare a lovely spiced tea.'

The woman put her head to one side. 'Whatever you have will be just lovely,' she said. *Jess luuvly.*

I nodded, starting back to the sideboard for the silver tray and its teapot.

'Do come back and join us for our tea, Miss Fincastle,' Mrs Lang called.

'I should return to my chores,' I said, although I had none. I didn't want to return. I didn't want to spend any more time witnessing my mother's despair.

'Come back, as Mrs Lang has requested, Pree,' my mother said, and I knew she was as uncomfortable as I; she didn't want to be alone with Mrs Lang.

'Yes, Mother,' I said, as if I were always this obedient daughter, then went out to the *rasoi* with the silver set and asked Sanosh to prepare his special tea, with ginger, cloves and cinnamon. He sighed deeply, as if the extra burdens heaped upon him today were almost more than he could bear.

'But Sanosh,' I added, 'no cardamom today.' Sanosh liked to infuse his special brew with cardamon, but he felt it was best chewed fresh and then spat into the pot. Of course my parents had no idea the tea they had grown to enjoy was prepared in this way, and instinct told me it was better to be safe with Mrs Lang's tea.

CHAPTER FIFTEEN

W HEN I RETURNED to the house, I felt Mrs Lang's eyes
on me as I came into the sitting room. She was on the
yellow chintz, and my mother on the sagging horsehair
settee.

'Come, Pree,' Mrs Lang said, waving at the only other
chair, the horsehair that matched the settee, as if she were the
memsahib of the house.

I crossed the room and sat where she indicated, my knees
together and my hands folded in my lap. I was aware of my
dusty, shrunken boots, the toes almost white, on the rug. I
heard my mother's heavy breathing, the swallowing of her
extra saliva.

Mrs Lang leaned forward. 'Now, you must tell me, Pree.
Do you go out among the heathens and deliver the word of
Our Lord?'

I licked my lips. 'No.' I looked at my mother, but she was
studying the termite-eaten leg of the tall, glass-fronted
cabinet containing my father's Bible collection.

Mrs Lang's eyes widened. 'So . . . although the daughter of
missionaries . . . and your mother said you will continue the
role – do you not wish to experience the deep rapture in
delivering His message to others?' Her eyes gleamed.

'I . . . no, Mrs Lang,' I said. 'I work in the infirmary. I don't
. . . well, I don't discuss the Lord with anyone.'

Now it was Mrs Lang's turn to look sharply at my mother.

'Do you not send her out among the village heathen, Mrs Fincastle? She could do so much. Especially if can speak their language fluently.' Her hands were very white and smooth, as white and smooth as the leather that had earlier encased them. They had not felt the touch of the sun. But now the tremor I had seen before our meal, slight, but noticeable, returned. She clasped her fingers to still them. 'Will the tea arrive soon, my dear?' she asked me now.

'Yes. Sanosh will bring it shortly, I'm sure,' I said.

'I hope so,' Mrs Lang said. 'My throat is terribly dry. But let me tell you more about my vocation. Mr Lang and I started the American mission in Peshawar just over a year ago.' I thought of the Afghan, and what he had told me about Peshawar. 'And while my disposition is not fitted to do any field work myself, and I don't have the facility for languages, I – with Mr Lang assisting me – feel it is my duty to be there.'

Sanosh came in with the tea tray, depositing it on a low brass-topped table near the window before slouching out. I fetched the good cups and saucers from the dining room and set them on the table beside the tray. I hadn't noticed, until now, that the teapot was streaked with tarnish, and dented on one side. The teacups didn't match their saucers.

Mrs Lang stared at the tray, but continued to speak. 'It was I who funded it, in other words. The mission employs a number of Bible women, young native women, orphaned and brought up as Christians in missions, to go to the women's quarters – the *zenanas* of the Muslim houses. Those poor secluded women aren't allowed out in public – a nasty business, isn't it? And of course – you know all too well, don't you? – they cannot be seen by any males, other than their own men folk. So our preachers are of no use to them. But the Bible women – because of their gender, and with the ability to speak to the women in their own language – are let in by the more progressive husbands. It's usually under the guise of medical help, or education, but of course, while there, they do their best to spread Christianity. Our girls have done some wonderful work, I will admit.' She placed one hand to her throat, wincing, as if it pained her, and my mother rose and went to the brass-topped table.

'Do you take sugar, Mrs Lang? I'm afraid we've only the very rough, brown variety, but—'

Mrs Lang shook her head, and my mother poured a cup and took it to her.

As the woman accepted it, the cup rattled in its saucer, tea splashing over the side. 'Goodness me, but I do need my medicine,' she said, setting the cup and saucer on the table beside her. She took up the knitted bag she kept in her lap the whole time, and from it withdrew a small silver flask. It gleamed, obviously newly polished. She uncorked it and added a generous amount to her tea. 'For my nerves, of course,' she said, with a look of chagrin.

Glancing away from the silver flask, my mother poured herself a cup of tea, stirring two spoonfuls of sugar into it and returning to her chair.

'I'm sure you also rely on help with settling your nerves, living as we must in this foreign land.' Mrs Lang pointedly stared at my mother, who pressed her handkerchief more tightly against her mouth. 'It's a difficult country, I'm afraid,' she went on, gracefully lifting her cup to her lips, and then draining it without stopping. 'Yes,' she repeated, 'a difficult country. Especially in your situation – well, the loneliness and isolation must be quite unbearable at times.' In the following silence, Mrs Lang's eyes scanned the room. 'And I can only imagine your workload. Do you have many converts?' she asked my mother.

'Allow me to pour you more tea, Mrs Lang,' I said quickly, rising and filling her cup again.

'There are so many small humiliations, don't you find?' she said now, and I was grateful she hadn't insisted upon an answer. 'It's often the ingratitude for our work I find the most intolerable. But Mr Lang and I consider the mission in Peshawar important,' she said. 'Our mission is very forward-thinking, actually run by women.'

My mother didn't respond.

Mrs Lang, calmed by the spirits she had put in her tea, closed her eyes, laying her head on the back of the chair. I knew it was dusty and saw the fuzzy streak of an old cobweb; would Mrs Lang find dead flies or the mummified remains of other insects in her collar later? The room grew quiet; I suspected she was falling asleep.

'Run by women?' I said, quite loudly.

Mrs Lang lifted her head, languidly smoothing her hair with those white, now-peaceful hands. 'As I said, it is truly forward-thinking. It's called the Women's Union Missionary Society, and is run strictly by women, like myself, from America. I have hired a very capable woman to be in charge, and she appears to have no need of male assistance.' She smiled again. 'I know it's hard for you, living here, as you do, to ever imagine that.'

I didn't like the tone of her voice when she said *living here, as you do*. I knew the mission – my home – had been very discreetly insulted.

'I've been lucky enough to live a very fortunate life, and I felt it important to share some of that fortune,' she continued now, as if with renewed energy. 'When my papa, bless his soul, passed on, I took a portion of the wealth he left me, and came, with Mr Lang, to do what good we could for the poor heathens of India. In a similar fashion to you and your husband, Mrs Fincastle,' she added, looking at my mother. 'Well now, that's not exactly right,' she continued, frowning and shaking her head. 'Not like you, because we all know,

190

don't we, that missionaries, even medical missionaries, simply don't have the same, well, I suppose you could say opportunities for . . .' Her voice died off.

My mother sat very straight, still holding her handkerchief to her mouth, the cup and saucer in her other hand, although she hadn't taken a sip while Mrs Lang spoke. Then she put down the cup and saucer and smoothed her hands on her skirt, over and over again, as if she were unconsciously wiping something from them. Seeing her red, rough hands with their knobby knuckles moving in an unconscious, repetitive movement, her hair again unkempt, her downcast eyes, the left eyelid jumping, I was suddenly sorry for her.

I looked at Mrs Lang in the shabby chintz chair with its torn arm. In her beautiful striped silk dress of deep plums and greens, her pristine gloves visible in the opening of her bag, her thick, styled blond hair, the winking ruby ear bobs, she indeed looked like a jewel herself; a glorious, costly jewel plunked on a dusty cabbage leaf. And for the first time I truly saw the long cobwebs in the corners of the sitting room, and the threadbare state of the rugs, chewed by white ants, over the rough wood of the floor. The furniture was all in various stages of disrepair, the wood either warped or splintered or marked by tiny mandibles, the horsehair cushions of the sofa and chair so ancient that they dipped in the middle, flattened by the years of other bodies occupying them before they had arrived at the mission. There were husks and shells and corpses of insects littering the windowsills. As in the dining room, here in the sitting room the overhead punkah wasn't ever used, and I saw it had a number of sagging bumps, which I knew would be small rodents or lizards which had expired in the cotton folds. And there was no rope to pull it. What had happened to the rope? What had it been used for?

The keys of the pianoforte were yellowed and chipped,

and the small fireplace still held a pile of grey ashes. Black streaks from last winter ran up its bricked front.

I saw the extreme poverty of the mission, and that my mother was deeply embarrassed of the way we lived.

'India does open one up so, doesn't it?' Mrs Lang murmured.

My mother stood. 'Excuse me, please,' she said, and went into the dining room. I heard the opening and closing of the door to the side verandah.

Alone now, Mrs Lang studied me again. 'How do you pass your time here, then?' she asked.

'I've told you, Mrs Lang. I work in the infirmary.'

'But . . . your poor mother.' She leaned forward, as if about to share a secret. 'It must take all of your energy, and patience. Is it Sand in the Head she suffers from?'

I blinked. I had heard of this name for the hysteria, or the alternate lethargy which sometimes afflicted European women in India. They lost track of themselves, and were unable to cope with daily life. I didn't know how to answer. My father and I, Glory and Kai, Sanosh and Pavit, had all lived with my mother's behaviour for so long. Perhaps we had stopped seeing the seriousness of it. Mrs Lang's comment now filled me with a horrid foreboding.

'I . . . I don't know. She has suffered from many ailments. And hardships,' I added, suddenly wanting to defend my mother to this imperious stranger. I felt I was back in the Wyndhams' sumptuous drawing room. But this time I would not let anyone criticise my mother. 'She has good days as well as bad, like anyone, Mrs Lang,' I told her, my voice hard.

'Oh, I didn't mean to cause offence, child,' Mrs Lang said. 'It was just an observance.'

I said nothing more. As we continued to sit in the heat, I saw that Mrs Lang again began to blink heavily, and I hoped that she would give in, and allow her eyelids to close all the way.

My mother returned and silently took her place on the settee. If Mrs Lang fell asleep, perhaps my mother and I could tiptoe out. I wanted to be away from her; I was exhausted by the charade we had to play, by her endless and uncomfortable questions. I was not used to foreign strangers in our midst. *Go to sleep, Mrs Lang. Sleep. Sleep, please,* I repeated in my head.

Suddenly she opened her eyes and looked at me. 'Have you ever been to Peshawar, my dear?'

I shook my head.

'It's a good journey, however they measure distances here, those silly *koss* that are so vague, but I'm sure, judging by the endless number of days it takes us, that it must be well over four hundred miles. A very arduous – and, I must admit, rather dangerous journey on the Grand Trunk. No decent places to stop at all apart from Rawalpindi and Gurjanwala; just those awful *caravanserais* alongside the road, crowded with animals and natives at night. Oh my goodness. The noise, and the smell. Quite unsettling. The English really must get to work on laying the railroads this far north, so that we don't have to be subjected to sleeping with all manner of people, don't you think, Mrs Fincastle?'

'I've only been as far as Lahore,' I told her before my mother could answer.

'Oh, well of course, Lahore is magnificent.' She spoke slowly, enunciating her words carefully. 'Those Shalimar gardens, and the Citadel, that Majarajah something or other . . . oh dear, what's the name?'

'Majarajah Ranjit Singh,' I said.

'Yes, well, that lovely marble fort. You know the one.' She fell silent again. 'But our mission . . . well, it's certainly nothing like this at all. There's a great deal of activity. Our young ladies do appear to love their calling. And their lives.'

I didn't know what to say. Why was she telling me this? The discomfort of the situation filled me; I was a seed, ready to burst from its pod. I had to leave. As I stood, Mrs Lang's eyes closed again, and her head gave one great dip, her chin towards her chest. The suddenness of it startled her and she lifted her head, a slight frown creasing her face as she struggled to raise her eyelids. 'This heat,' she said. 'The punkah . . . would you mind terribly, Miss Fincastle?'

But I didn't move. I couldn't pull it; there was no rope. In a few more seconds there was another dip and bob, and then another, and finally Mrs Lang's head fell forward, heavily, her chin against her throat, her breathing audible, deep and even.

I rose, glancing once at my mother. Her face held no expression. I half expected her to insist I stay; when she simply looked at me, I was relieved, and hurried out of the room.

I slipped out the side door, hearing the men's quiet laughter from the front verandah and smelling the odour of cheroot. I wanted to finish the infirmary preparations for the next morning: I had left instruments unwashed and we needed more rolled bandages. The unexpected visitors had upset our usual routine. And it would be good to be away from the house, from the stuffy, dirty sitting room and the strange Mrs Lang and her spirits and odd questions and insinuations.

The infirmary was warm and quiet, with insects buzzing in the louvres and the comforting smell of disinfectant. I worked for some time, but just as I finished, plugging a rubber stopper into a large bottle of quinine, I heard voices. Looking out the window, I saw it was Mr Lang and my parents. Mrs Lang would, surely then, still be asleep in the sitting room.

My father and Mr Lang were involved in some kind of debate. Their voices were loud, and carried a polite edge of dispute.

As they came through the door of the infirmary, I set down the quinine. My mother's face was wan, and neither she nor the men glanced at me. I backed away from the table, closer to the wall.

'Again, I must disagree, Reverend. It's been proven over and over. Don't tell me you English don't love Gall's theory. Why, it's common knowledge that the ruling class has long used it to justify the inferiority of its colonial subjects.' Mr Lang looked around the infirmary, his eyes stopping on me.

'Who's the native I just saw working in the garden?'

'Kai,' I said, slowly. I knew of Franz Joseph Gall's principle.

'Call him in here, please,' he said.

'Don't bother,' my father said. 'It's of no consequence.'

'You don't get off that easily with me, Reverend,' Mr Lang said, rather jovially, and went to the door. 'Boy!' he hollered, then turned to my father. 'Does he understand English?'

My father nodded stiffly. I could smell him. His wool suit, damp with perspiration, smelled like a dog with a rain-soaked coat. His face was wet, and he wiped the sweat from his forehead with his sleeve, inflaming the rosacea further.

Mr Lang shouted again. 'You, yes you. Come here.'

Kai came to the open door and stood there, facing Mr Lang. Kai was not a boy in any sense of the word, and I had never heard anyone call him *boy*, nor spoken to him in such an overbearing manner.

Mr Lang stepped closer to him. 'Can you understand me, boy?' he said, slowly, loudly, directly into Kai's face. I saw a drop of saliva jump from his lips to Kai's cheek.

Kai ignored it, although his jaw visibly tightened. 'I understand you perfectly, sir,' he said, his voice low and dignified.

Mr Lang looked startled. 'What is this? How is it a servant has such a pure tone?'

My father didn't answer.

'He's been with us since a babe,' my mother said. 'He learned from us.'

Mr Lang grinned and clapped my father on the back. 'Well, you certainly do train your charity cases well,' he said, glancing at Kai. 'I'm surprised you'd waste your time with speech lessons for even the black ones. This one sounds just like you, dear fellow,' he said, with a hint of insincerity.

'I am Eurasian,' Kai said, his voice controlled.

'Miss Fincastle,' Mr Lang said, ignoring Kai's statement, 'have any of your studies introduced you to phrenology?'

'Yes,' I said, dread filling me; I knew what he was going to do. I avoided looking at Kai.

'It's a well-researched method,' Mr Lang blustered, obviously mistaken in his belief that he was impressing his small, quiet audience. 'There are various aspects to studying the shape of the skull as an indication of mental abilities, character traits and moral faculties. Those with criminal personalities have a particular definition. I would think you, Reverend, as a surgeon, would be particularly familiar with the truth in this.' He lifted his hands towards Kai's head. 'Bend your neck forward,' he demanded.

I started at Mr Lang; I simply couldn't look at Kai as he was treated in such a disrespectful manner. I wanted my father to speak up, to tell him not to belittle Kai like this. But my father said nothing, and I knew that Mr Lang was simply acting the way I had seen the English people in the Wyndhams' house treat the servants.

Glancing over his shoulder at my father, Mr Lang said, 'You'll see. I'm sure I'll be able to determine that . . .' his voice dropped to a hoarse whisper, as if Kai were not standing in front of him, 'there's a degree of inferior mental capacity.'

Kai hadn't moved. His eyes shone a dangerous black, and had narrowed.

'*Ana, ana*, come along, boy. It won't hurt,' Mr Lang added, chuckling, reaching up.

Kai took a step backwards. His hands were clenched at his sides, but he hadn't taken his eyes from Mr Lang. 'I am not an experiment,' he said, quietly, but with the bite of carefully held-back anger. 'Sir.' The last word was uttered with obvious sarcasm, and I heard my mother's intake of breath.

'What? What sort of insolence is this?' Mr Lang demanded, finally lowering his hands, looking from Kai to my father.

Beads of sweat stood out on my father's forehead. He neither commanded Kai to do as Mr Lang ordered, nor did he berate him for his attitude. I didn't understand. His expression was as strained as my mother's had been, earlier, in the sitting room. Now it was she who stepped in. She laid her hand on Kai's bare arm.

He had rolled up the sleeves of his shirt, and I saw the raised tendon that ran up the inside of his arm.

'Go and ask Sanosh to make another pot of tea, Kai. I'm sure when Mrs Lang awakens she'll enjoy a cup. And Mr Lang,' she continued, 'if your wife wakes up alone in the sitting room, she'll wonder where we've all gone.'

Mr Lang was scowling.

'We must go back and join her,' my mother added, her voice now firm. 'Go on, Kai.'

I felt a surge of relief. There was authority in her voice, and it was as if my mother had shaken herself back into the assertive woman from an earlier time. And while I had always disliked her brusqueness, her commanding tone, at this moment I was grateful for it.

But Kai ignored her. He continued to stare into Mr Lang's eyes, then looked over at my father, who stood motionless. It appeared Kai was waiting for my father to say something, but when it was obvious he would remain silent, Kai lifted his chin.

'Reverend Fin? Is it your wish that my head be groped to show the lower intelligence of the native?' His tone was confident, carrying an air of superiority. 'Reverend Fin,' he said, more loudly, his fists still clenched. 'Can you say nothing? Will you never say anything?'

'Kai! That's enough,' my mother said, but for the second time Kai ignored her, walking up to my father. When their faces were only inches apart, he opened his mouth as if to speak.

'No, Malachi,' my father said, before Kai said anything more, 'I will not.'

Malachi? I had never before heard this name, apart from reading it within the pages of the Bible.

And at that Kai's mouth, although stiff, held the hint of a smile. And then he turned, his shoulders square, and we all watched him walk down the infirmary steps. His back was straight, his head high.

'You don't have much control over your people here, do you, Reverend?' Mr Lang asked, mopping his cheeks with a limp cotton handkerchief he took from his breast pocket. 'Can't see how you can allow such impudence. Such disrespect.' He shoved the handkerchief back into his pocket. 'I know people are more relaxed in the countryside, but really, sir, that was an outrageous display of insolence. It clearly demonstrates the problem with so many of the half-castes: if you plant the seed in the wrong soil, you will produce a substandard plant.'

'You may feel my skull, Mr Lang,' I said, not realising I was going to say it until the words had flown from my mouth. The three faces turned to look at me. 'Perhaps you can tell me something about my character.'

Mr Lang made a dismissive sound and frowned; it was obvious he was shaken and angered by Kai's behaviour, and by my father's lack of support.

'It's more effective on the male skull,' he said, in an offhand tone. 'It's a well-known fact the female skull is not as reliable in test situations. Now run along, my girl,' he added, and heat rose in me that he would dismiss me as if I were a silly child.

'Mr Lang,' I said, full knowing that I was further complicating the already tense situation, but uncaring, 'can you explain to me why, exactly, the female skull is inferior?'

There was heavy silence in the room. Mr Lang's mouth was slack. 'I said unreliable. Not inferior.'

I heard the wet sound of my mother's lips opening, about to reprimand me, and so hurried to finish, because I knew I wouldn't get another chance. 'Even so, Mr Lang, is it really a fact − as you've stated − which would suggest proof? I recently read an essay by Sydney Smith, on "Female Education" which instructed the reader to train her − or his − mind to distinguish a fact from an hypothesis or assumption. So I'm wondering: could this perhaps be another of your assumptions, referred to by Mrs Lang earlier? Could it just be your *assumption* that the female skull is of lesser reliability than the male skull?'

'You will leave immediately, Pree,' my father now said. 'But first you will apologise to Mr Lang for your impertinence and . . . and ignorance.'

I took a deep breath. 'As my father instructs me, I apologise for what he calls my impertinence, Mr Lang,' I said, and he raised his eyebrows, his thick fingers tapping on the table beside him. 'But I cannot apologise for my ignorance, can I? Ignorance is not my fault, nor is it a choice. I do not wish to be ignorant, but due to my life in this—'

Another sound from my mother stopped me, and I knew

I had gone too far. I turned from Mr Lang to her; her skin had a grey pallor in spite of her weather-worn complexion. I lowered my eyes as hers stared into mine, and then I turned and walked from the infirmary, much more slowly than my heart was beating.

And as I left I heard Mr Lang's laugh, low, but instead of what I expected to be annoyance, it was filled with obvious amusement.

CHAPTER SIXTEEN

W HEN I APPROACHED the huts, I heard movement from within Kai's, and went to his door.

'Kai?' I said, through the matting. 'May I enter?'

'Yes,' he answered, and I pulled aside the thinly woven hanging, hooking it back on a nail, and stepped in. On Kai's pallet were three shirts and two pairs of *panjammahs*, neatly folded. He was taking books from the low shelf under the window.

'What . . . what are you doing?'

He stopped, a stack of the books in his hands. 'I'm leaving, Pree. I should have left long ago. I realised, just then, in the infirmary, that I've stayed far too long.'

'But my father didn't make you do as Mr Lang said,' I cried, my voice high. 'Nothing has changed, Kai. Don't go.'

He looked down at the books in his hand. 'It's not just what happened today, Pree. There's nothing for me here. This place – this strange, mixed-up little world – isn't enough,' he repeated. 'I've known for a long time I would have to leave, but have stayed because I . . .'

He stopped, looking at me. I held my breath. It seemed he would say something important. Very important.

'You stayed because of what, Kai?' I asked, barely above a whisper. Please, I thought, please say what I hope you will.

The hut was silent. He stared into my eyes.

My chest rose and fell. Did his as well, or did I only imagine it? Wish it. *Say it. Say it now, Kai.*

Mr Lang's booming laugh broke through the fragile thread that joined Kai and me. At the gruff laughter, Kai blinked, then looked down at the books in his hands, and I knew the moment had passed.

A swift desolation came over me, and I sat heavily on the charpoy.

Kai busied himself with his packing. 'Only moments ago, in the infirmary,' he said, his voice normal, 'I knew with complete certainty it was well past time.'

My hand was on the small pile of Kai's clean clothes, which he had scrubbed himself, and hung on the bushes to bleach under the sun. I could smell them; they gave off the scent I associated with Kai, hot sun and warm wind. 'Where will you go?' I asked, watching my fingers trace the collar of the top shirt.

'Lahore. At least for now. I have friends there.'

I looked up at him as he took a large woven bag from a nail on the wall. And suddenly he looked like a stranger, a man I didn't know.

He had a life I didn't know about, a man's life, while I . . . I had just blindly gone about my own life at the mission. *This strange, mixed-up little world*, Kai had called it.

I had worked in the infirmary and, with Sanosh, I had tended to my mother's needs and read my books; while I thought about the whole world outside of the mission, I had never placed myself in that world. And yet today, after meeting the Langs, I knew something had changed in me. I knew I couldn't look at the mission, or even my parents, in the same way ever again.

And the presence of the Langs had caused something to shift for Kai as well as for me. 'Why did my father call you Malachi?'

'That's my full Christian name.'

'But . . .' I had never thought of Kai's name, although in the back of my mind I now realise I had assumed it to be the diminutive of Kairav or Kailash, Hindi names. Not a Christian biblical name. 'Your mother named you Malachi?'

'I assume so. Perhaps it was at your father's insistence,' he said, still busy with his hands, not looking at me.

'And you're going to live in Lahore now?' I asked, even though he had just told me this fact.

'Yes,' he said, in that same clipped way.

I wanted to recapture the emotion I had felt only moments earlier, before Mr Lang's laughter had spoiled it. I wanted Kai to say something meaningful, something that told me he would miss me as I would him. That he was not leaving my life in this way.

'Probably the Reverend can hire one of Sanosh's sons to help permanently with the work,' was all he said, in a distracted manner, as if that was what was important, as if that was what we would miss: a strong body to whitewash and haul water and mend the thatch and attend to the physical needs of the mission.

He put the books into the bottom of the bag and reached for his rolled maps.

'It's far.'

'Lahore isn't far, Pree.'

'But . . .' *Won't you miss seeing me every day? Won't you think about me, and wonder what I'm doing, as I'll think of you?*

'But what? As I said, I should have left long ago. I don't know why I stayed, under the thumb of . . . of him,' he said, nodding his head in the direction of the infirmary and tossing the maps beside me on the charpoy. He slapped a pair of woven sandals together, and a puff of dust rose in the air. He shoved them into the bag, then held out his hand, and I passed the maps to him. He stopped for that moment when both our hands were on the long paper rolls, our fingers a few inches away. He looked at them, then at me. 'It's different here for you, Pree.'

'Why is it different?'

'Because you're a woman. You won't have to go out into the world and prove yourself.'

'Why won't I? Do you think I'll be happy staying here, helping in the infirmary for ever? Listening to my father's empty sermons? Pretending to pray? Do you think this is my only future?'

He sighed, pulling the maps from my hand and sitting beside me on the charpoy. 'I don't know, Pree.' Suddenly he turned his head and looked into my face. 'Yes, I do know. This place isn't where I see you. You don't fit here any more than I do.'

'What do you mean?'

His face closed. 'Nothing. I chose the wrong words.'

'No. I want to know. Why don't I fit here?'

He smiled, a quick, impatient smile, and tapped my temple with the rolled maps. 'You know too much, don't you?' It wasn't a question, and I had no answer. 'And soon you'll need to know more.' He stood, shaking his head. 'No. You need more already.'

My chest filled with sombre joy that Kai *had* noticed my life and who I had become. It gave me the courage to ask my next question. I stood to face him. 'And so . . . Kai? What should I do? What should I do?' I repeated. I knew he didn't have the answer. But I didn't want him to leave. I couldn't bear for our connection to be broken, and yet I couldn't beg him, couldn't cry out that I couldn't bear for him to just walk out of my life.

Couldn't he see, on my face, in the position of my body, that I needed him here? That without him the mission would lose the last of its thin spirit and become an empty shell?

But he turned back to the bag, placing the maps along one side, then the shirts and cotton trousers on the top of the books and sandals. 'Your parents will make sure of your future, Pree,' he said.

I looked at the floor, not wanting Kai to see my disappointment should he turn around suddenly. 'My parents? You truly believe that?' I murmured. After today, comparing my washed-out, weary parents to the loud, bright Langs, I realised how colourless my father and mother were. They were fading into the Indian landscape. How long would it be before this happened to me, as well? Before I, too, became just another part of that backdrop, the colour of the rotted lushness, the dust?

'Of course.' He continued packing, although obviously he was thinking of my question. 'Soon, surely, they will . . .' he turned back to face me.

'Yes?' I said, embarrassed at how quickly, how eagerly that one word came from my lips.

'They will find you a husband,' he said.

I made a rude, angry sound. 'That's not what we're talking about, and you know it,' I said. I hated my voice, the high pitch, the breathless quality. The desperation.

Kai smiled, a smile I didn't recognise, and one which held no warmth. 'You will do mission work, like your parents. And yes, surely you will marry. Probably a young reverend looking to start his own mission.'

I sat again. 'Don't say that.'

'Why not? What do you expect your life to hold? You're no longer a child, Pree. You understand what I'm talking about.'

I couldn't look at him, and swung my gaze to the striped bag. Kai took down the square mirror that hung on a nail to one side of the door. He sat beside me again, holding the mirror so that both our faces were reflected in it. His hair was so dark, his eyes the astonishing green. My eyes had turned gold, as they did when tears threatened, and, ringed with my dark lashes like his, stood out in my face. And the hot sun had brought out the lighter streaks in my hair. I had forgotten that I had pinned it up.

'Look at us,' he said. 'Two lost souls.'

I didn't understand his sudden, troubling tone, the way he stared into the reflection of his own eyes as if searching for something. I looked into them too.

'Kai? Mr and Mrs Lang thought I was the ayah.' His pupils drew in, but otherwise his face remained completely still.

'The Langs are foolish people,' he said. 'He's puffed full of his own importance; she's addled by drink.'

'She asked if Mother suffered from Sand in the Head,' I told him, wanting him to tell me, again, that the Langs were simply fools, and didn't make any sense.

'You must care for your mother,' was all he said. 'She has been a better mother to me than my own.' He finished packing the last of his meagre belongings. Then he stood in front of me, and I rose. The top of my head came to his nose. 'Goodbye for now, little *bahan*,' he said, and put his hands on my shoulders. Instead of being pleased to hear him say the words I'd wanted him − asked him − to call me when I was so much younger, today they displeased me. I didn't feel like his sister at all, and I wasn't little. We were a man and woman, caught in the same trap, discussing our futures.

'Tell the Reverend and Mem Fin that I've left. That I've gone to Lahore for good.'

'You won't even stay to say a proper goodbye to them?' I asked, surprised, suddenly thinking of Glory.

'I won't face those Americans again.'

'But . . . will you come back to visit us, Kai?'

Not answering, he dug back into his bag, pulling out one of the books and a stick of charcoal he used to mark his maps.

He wrote something on the empty page at the back of the book, tore it out and set it on the charpoy.

'Should you ever need to find me,' he said, then leaned down and kissed my forehead. At that I threw my arms around him, holding him tightly. I lifted my head so that my lips were against his neck.

'But will you come back to see me, Kai?' I breathed into his skin. It smelled of something faintly spicy. 'Say you'll come back soon.' I could feel his pulse beneath my lips. It grew stronger, ticking faster now. One twothreefourfivesix — so fast I lost track.

Suddenly he put his hands on my upper arms and pushed me away. 'Goodbye, Pree,' he said, and turned and went through the doorway, the striped bag slung over his shoulder.

I heard the murmur of his voice, and knew he was saying goodbye to Sanosh and Pavit — did he bid farewell to his mother? — and when I finally heard the clopping of his horse's hoofs through the courtyard, I walked out, to the gate, and then on to the road, watching Kai. The sun, lowering in the sky now, touched the white of his shirt with a warm, soft glow of gold.

And then I was running, running down the road, calling his name.

He stopped, turning his horse, but didn't dismount.

'Kai,' I cried, still a distance from him. 'Don't. Don't go.'

He moved as if to swing down from the saddle, but then his shoulders straightened. 'Go home, Pree,' he called. 'Please. Don't do this.' His voice carried to me down the road; it seemed I could see his words dancing towards me in the air. I wanted to catch them and hold them to me. I wanted to feel them as I'd felt his pulse under my lips.

Then he turned his horse and as his heels kicked into its sides, it broke into a canter, leaving in a cloud of yellow dust.

I stopped running, watched Kai until he was just a small dark smudge on the long road.

He didn't look back.

I went to his hut and lay on his charpoy. I rolled over and buried my face in the light cover and breathed in his scent. Hot sun, warm wind. That unidentifiable spicy scent.

Surely my mother or father had kissed me when I was smaller. Surely. But at that moment I couldn't recall ever knowing the touch of someone's lips upon my skin. Now the memory of Kai's soft touch on my forehead remained, as did the frenzied ticking of the pulse in his throat against my own lips.

My body and head felt heavy, not with sleep, but with sorrow. I turned once more on to my back, picking up the folded paper Kai had left. I looked at the one line written there, then put it on my stomach, smoothing it over and over with my fingertips.

Eventually, I heard voices in the courtyard, and slowly rose and went to the doorway.

The Langs were leaving, saying their goodbyes to my parents. They crossed the courtyard to the carriage that had waited for them all this time. Shadowed in the doorway, I didn't care whether they saw me or not. But, unexpectedly, Mrs Lang stopped before she got to the carriage, looking purposefully around the courtyard, her hand shading her eyes in the late afternoon sun.

'Miss Fincastle,' she called, spotting me. Why hadn't I stepped back into the hut, pulling down the door mat? Why had I let her see me? 'Come along and bid us farewell.'

Still holding the paper, I went to the carriage. Mrs Lang had the relaxed, easy look again. So close to her, I smelled the harshness of fresh alcohol on her breath.

'I hope we may one day see you in Peshawar,' she said.

'You must come and visit our mission some time.' She leaned closer, and said in a conspiratorial whisper, 'There is more to life than this.' Her breath was like a living thing.

Although the later afternoon sun still shone, sprinkles of rain came from nowhere. 'Yes,' Mr Lang said. 'You must come to Peshawar.' He stepped closer, putting his hand on the back of my bare neck. His fingers were hot, and damp, and gripped my neck with a strange and urgent pressure. How dare he touch me? He had no right to be so uncommonly familiar. Perhaps Americans had different rules. Still, he was a rude man.

He looked skyward. 'A jackal's wedding. Isn't that what they call it here – this rain, when the sun shines?'

I didn't respond.

'A fine, well-spoken and obviously well-read young lady like yourself, well, you could be a bonus at the mission there,' he said. 'We need young women with a sense of independence to carry out our work. And as well as your religious upbringing, you have the added assets of some medical knowledge and the languages of the country. You could find a sense of fulfilment in training the Bible women. There are so many young ladies who wish to be welcomed into the closed zenanas and behind the *purdah* gates. We don't have enough people to train them.' His fingers pressed even deeper, and their touch repulsed me.

Mrs Lang didn't appear to notice. 'A rather odd and sometimes rough place, Peshawar,' she said. 'But we have grown to love it, haven't we, Mr Lang,' she stated firmly, her eyes finally moving to her husband's hand. 'Let's be off. I don't wish my gown to become damp.'

Mr Lang removed his hand from my neck and extended it to her. She put her own gloved hand into it.

I continued to stand, mute, while Mr Lang followed his wife into the carriage. Did they notice I hadn't spoken? The driver, who had sat for all these hours under the sun, slapped the reins against the backs of the horses, and they snorted, lifting their heads against the bits in their mouths. I watched the carriage and its passengers leave, suddenly exhausted by it all: the wearying afternoon with the Langs, the upsetting episode in the infirmary, and, very worst of all, Kai's departure.

I went back to Kai's hut; as I lay on his charpoy again I realised my legs were shaking. I closed my eyes, trying to recapture the feel of Kai's lips on my forehead.

But it wouldn't come. Only the hot imprint of Mr Lang's hand on the back of my neck remained.

'Kai,' I whispered, then covered my mouth with both my hands. The overwhelming sense of his loss – a feeling of abandonment – swept over me with a physical force, and I cried, keeping my hands firmly over my mouth so that no sound escaped.

CHAPTER SEVENTEEN

FOR THE NEXT two months I kept expecting Kai to return, glancing up from the garden or the verandahs and watching the road after dinner.

'Glory?' I asked her one evening. 'Do you miss Kai? Do you hear nothing from him?'

'He is a man, Pree. He does what he must.'

'Do you think he'll come back?'

She looked at me. 'He'll come back. I am his mother. He must return to care for me. When he has a wife and a home he will take me there.'

I don't know what upset me more, Glory's casual surety that she would always be cared for by the son she treated so poorly, or her statement about Kai marrying.

Of course he would some day marry. My lips involuntarily twisted, and I turned away from Glory, disgusted. She could sell her own daughter so she didn't have to be responsible for her, and yet she expected her son to be responsible for *her* for the rest of her life.

Adriana's little face was fading from my memory. I knew she would be growing, her features changing. She would be seven months now. Who cared for her? Who would know that shaking a dried tamarind pod so that its seeds rattled made her laugh? Although, I told myself, that was when she had been so small. Now she would need new distractions. How many teeth did she have? Did her hair still curl, like Kai's, when it was damp?

I wished I had an image of her, like the salt prints of English families in the photographer's window in Lahore. I had nothing to remember her by.

Jassie was expecting another litter. Poor Jassie. A litter of puppies every six months. She was always skittish as her time drew near.

And my mother grew more fretful. She was ever more distracted in the infirmary, losing track of what she was involved in, sometimes taking down the wrong bottle of medicine, or pouring the wrong tablets into the paper spills. Once she began to lance a boil without first sterilising the scalpel. I had to constantly watch her, ensuring she treated the patients in the correct manner.

The time for our twice-yearly trip to Lahore for my father to collect his wages approached. On the appointed day I dressed in my best dress. Fortunately, a recent box from the church in Lahore had contained a pair of boots; I could no longer fit my feet into the old ones. The newer ones were a fraction too large, and rubbed against my heels when I walked, but too large was better than too tight.

I had a cup of tea with my father in the sitting room in front of the fireplace; the small fire was welcome in the cold morning air. Then I went to see if my mother was ready. She stood in the middle of the bedroom in her petticoat, but turned sharply as I entered, so her back was to me.

'Mother?' I said, going to her side. 'Do you need help with—'

She quickly folded her arms over her flat chest, but in that split second before she hid her arms from me, I caught a glimpse of sores, some scabbed over and some with congealing fresh blood, on the insides of her forearms.

'What's happened, Mother?' I asked, trying to pull her arms from her body, but she glowered at me.

'Get out. Leave me alone. I'm trying to decide which frock to wear.'

'Your arms . . .'

'Go out and have Sanosh hook up Marta. Go, now,' she said, with such intensity that I backed out of the room. What had caused the sores on her arms? Was it an infection of some kind? Some variety of insect bite? And why would she hide them, as if ashamed?

We set out on the Grand Trunk Road early on that wintry December morning. A low fog hung over the fields, and long trails of steam flowed from Marta's nostrils in the cold air. But as the pale sun rose higher and higher in the sky, it burned away the fog, and by the time we were partway to Lahore the air had warmed enough for me to remove my second shawl.

We arrived in Lahore by noon. Throughout the time it took us to journey there, I had touched the reassuring rustle of paper in my small cloth bag – the folded page directing me to Kai.

When my father came out of the ministry and again joined my mother and me in the cart, he carefully sorted through the few bills and the many coins he held, his lips moving as he counted, then sat quietly, as if calculating. Finally he gave me a few annas.

'It's not much, Pree. But perhaps you can buy yourself some new hair ribbons.'

I thanked him. It was the first time I had been given money, and the first time I would choose a gift for myself. And I would see Kai. Nothing could spoil my excitement this day.

My father left our cart with others along a side road, securing Marta's reins to a post with the promise of one anna to a scabby-face child to sit in the cart and make sure the beast didn't pull free until we returned. Father left my mother and me for his own pursuits.

At the bazaar my mother seemed slightly confused, wandering, picking up a round melon or fingering a piece of silk. I knew she needed new hairpins, but she continued to pick things up and set them down. The annas clinked in my bag; the paper from Kai crackled. I wanted to be on my own, away from my mother and her endless dithering.

Finally she said she would sit and have tea at one of the English teashops, and allowed me to go off on my own, arranging for us to meet in a nearby square within two hours.

I had to ask a number of people about the address Kai had written on the paper. As I hurried down a narrow alley, I saw that one of the tiny shops held a few used English books, and paused to look at a small book on cartography.

It took me a few moments to bargain with the seller, an elderly man whose turban quivered with contrived annoyance when I refused to pay him what he asked. But eventually he agreed to my price, as I knew he would. Placing the annas in his hand, I put the book under my arm and hurried on down the alley, dodging fat cows with their gaily painted horns alongside scrawny three-legged dogs. They scrounged, the cows and the dogs, side by side, in the mounds of discarded rotted vegetables that lay along the foundations of the buildings.

I came upon the place I was looking for. It was a small, dark shop, selling sandals displayed on a low table. A young man, obviously a Eurasian by his skin and hair, sat beside the table, idly drinking a cup of chai. He stood when I entered.

'Yes, Memsahib? You wish to buying sandals?' he asked in English, now smiling broadly.

This was not where I expected to find Kai. 'No. I'm looking for Kai da Silva. Does he work here?'

The man's smile disappeared as he looked into his teacup.

'I'm a friend. My name is Miss Fincastle,' I said, wondering at his sudden change in demeanour.

'One moment, Memsahib,' the young man said, and went through a low door I hadn't noticed when I'd come in.

In the next instant Kai emerged, ducking his head, the other man following him. My heart thumped painfully, and I licked my lips, suddenly overcome at the sight of him.

'Pree,' he said, coming towards me. I'd forgotten how tall he was, how I loved his teeth. 'Is everything all right?' he asked, his eyes wide and his mouth grim.

I put my hands to my cheeks. They were hot, and I knew my face might give away my joy at seeing him.

'Yes,' I said, my lips trembling slightly. I couldn't smile. 'Oh yes. Everything is fine. I've . . . I've just come to see you.'

His face lost its tightness. 'Oh. Oh, good.'

We stood in the dusty shop. The distance between us was too great. I wanted to be close to him, to smell his scent. I wanted to know he felt the same way. 'And you're well?' I asked, looking at the table of sandals. 'You make – or sell – sandals?' I couldn't keep the surprise from my voice. Surely Kai hadn't left the mission to spend his days in a dull shop such as this one.

He didn't speak immediately, although he opened his mouth. 'Come through,' he finally said, and I followed him as he stooped to pass under the low doorway. Once we were in the next room he closed the door behind us. Here it smelled of ink and was stacked with paper. Lamps hissed on the walls, adding to the dim light that fell from the one high, barred window. Another young man, a Muslim, stood with his hand on the lever of a machine I didn't recognise. He stared at me without smiling. 'Let's go to the courtyard,' Kai said, and as he passed the man Kai murmured something to him in a voice too low for me to hear.

The courtyard was small, cluttered with stacked wooden crates. It was shaded by the shadows of taller buildings on either side. A dirty white dog sprawled on its side in the one small patch of sunlight. It lifted its head and looked sleepily at us, then flopped its head back on to the hard earth.

'You've come to Lahore with your parents?' he asked, as we faced each other.

'Yes. My father's collecting his wages and getting some supplies.'

'They're well? Does one of Sanosh's son's help at the mission?'

It was small talk, unimportant. I had thought of so many things I wanted to talk to Kai about over these last months, but suddenly they flew from my head like the flock of pigeons that rose from a rooftop nearby. They soared into the sky, going ever higher until they resembled pale scraps of rag fluttering in the blue.

'They're as usual. And yes, occasionally Darshan comes by to help. But this . . .' I gestured at the tilting back of the shop, 'this is where you work, Kai? A sandal shop?' Again, I tried not to let the surprise I felt be evident in my voice.

Kai reached up to brush his hair from his eyes. His fingertips were black, stained. It wasn't dye, from the sandals; it was unmistakably ink.

His face was veiled. 'We do other work as well.'

'Are you printing books, then?' I asked. That would make more sense. And yet I hadn't seen any in that back room. Just the stacks of paper.

'No. We print . . . daily news, of a sort. I live in a room upstairs. But never mind that.' It was obvious he didn't wish to speak of what he did, and this filled me with unease. 'So all is well?' he asked for the third time.

'Yes,' I told him again, and then handed him the book. 'I don't know if you are still interested in maps,' I said, feeling my face flush unexpectedly. 'And I'm sorry; it's rather musty.'

Finally he smiled at me, taking the book and opening it, flipping pages and looking through it. 'Thank you, Pree,' he said. 'You do know me.' He looked up, and I couldn't read what was on his face. 'I have something for you as well.'

He disappeared into the shop and returned a few moments later, leaving the door open, carrying something wrapped in newsprint. 'I planned to bring it to the mission when I next came.'

'It's been well over two months,' I said. 'I thought you would have come for a visit by now.' I kept my voice light, cheery in a way I hadn't felt as I'd waited for his return. 'As you once said, Lahore isn't so far from the mission. And you have a horse, after all.'

He nodded. 'I meant to come sooner. But I've been very involved. With my work.' He held the package out to me.

I took it; by the hard squareness of it I immediately knew it was also a book. 'You like your work?' I asked. I wanted him to confide in me, to tell me his purpose here in Lahore. I had never thought of Kai as dishonest, and yet I had long recognised that he was secretive and passionate. 'You are happy with your work?' I persisted.

But his face closed as it had moments earlier. 'Yes,' he said. 'But come now. Open the package.'

I didn't want to unwrap the crackling paper. I wanted to savour the moment, let the joy of being here with Kai, awkward as it was, last as long as it could. I pressed the package against my chest briefly, and then, not looking at him, unwrapped it and let the paper fall to the ground.

'Mary Woolstonecroft. *A Vindication of the Rights of Women*,' I read, and then looked at him. 'You remember how I once spoke of her. And it's new. A new book,' I said, caressing the beautiful marbled cover. I lifted it to my face and breathed in its fresh odour. 'I've never had a new book. Thank you, Kai,' I said. 'You know me well, too. Now I'm even more sorry that the one I gave you is so—'

'You look older, Pree,' he said, interrupting, and a strange heat came over me.

'I am older, by a few months.'

'I know. But there's something else.'

I tried to smile, although my mouth felt unnatural. 'Maybe it's just that you've never seen me away from the mission. There was a new box recently; this dress isn't quite so faded as most that arrive, and for once it's a proper fit. And I always wear my hair up now.' I was talking too fast, almost breathless.

He nodded.

'And you, too. You look fine as well, Kai.'

He nodded again, obviously as uncomfortable as I was, and then there was silence, and the unfamiliar unease between us grew. I opened the book to the first crisp page, and then another, but my eyes couldn't decipher what I pretended to read. Kai cleared his throat.

We stood in the cool December air, and the afternoon call for prayer came from a muezzin, reminding me of the time. 'I have to go. My mother will be waiting for me,' I added, a kind of despair filling me. 'I have to go,' I repeated. I don't know what I'd expected. I had come to see Kai, and I'd seen him.

He nodded. 'I have a great deal to do before the end of the day.'

This disappointed me. I wanted him to tell me to stay, that he wanted nothing more than to spend another short hour with me.

'I'd best leave, then,' I said, retrieving the paper from my feet and rewrapping the book, aware I was carrying on this parting too long. I moved towards the shop, and he followed me. Just before I reached the doorway I turned and put my hand on his arm, lightly, and he looked down at it. And then suddenly – was it unexpectedly, or had I wanted to do this all along? – I put my arms around him, still awkwardly clutching the book, and after only a second's hesitation, he did the same. We stood for a moment like that, our arms around each other in a light hug, our bodies not touching, just our arms. But suddenly, and I'll never know if it was Kai or me, one of us moved, and then I felt the length of his body against mine. We stayed like that for only a few seconds; I smelled the familiar spicy scent of his skin. I felt his cheek brush my temple, and then the cool touch of his lips on my cheek. 'Goodbye, Pree,' he said, quietly.

I couldn't stop myself; I turned my face just before his lips left my cheek, and put my own lips on his. I don't know where I found such boldness.

And he didn't pull away, although I felt him move with surprise. But he left his lips on mine for just a fraction longer than would have been an innocent, virtuous kiss, as one might kiss a relative, and in that tiny moment I felt heat flood into them. My body immediately softened, and I pressed harder against him.

But he gently pushed me away. I looked up into his face; he was looking over my head. I sensed someone behind us, the other man, surely, watching through the doorway.

'Goodbye, Pree,' he said, again, stepping even further away.

I felt as though something had been taken from me, something I wanted back with an urgency I hadn't known before.

'Your mother will worry about you,' he said now. 'Do you have an anna for a rickshaw? You shouldn't walk through the streets alone.'

'No one ever bothers me,' I told him, truthfully. No matter what any of the men – the Hindus and Muslims and Sikhs – thought of me, I was treated with respect because of my appearance. I was a young Englishwoman, wasn't I, and the English ruled the Punjab.

'So will you come to the mission?' I asked. I didn't say *soon*, or *ever*.

'Of course. Give the Reverend and your mother my regards,' he said, the formality of his words again emphasising the strangeness between us.

I nodded, and then, holding my book against my chest, I went through the shop, past the Muslim now turning the lever of his machine, through the second door and the table of dusty sandals and young man with his teacup. I turned once to wave to Kai. He stood, framed in the open doorway, and lifted his hand in a similar farewell.

When would I see him again?

On my return to the designated spot my mother and I had agreed to meet at, I found her pacing impatiently. She appeared oddly agitated, her lips twitching and her eyes unusually intense. She grabbed my arm. 'Hurry, Pree. Hurry,' she said, pulling me behind her. She walked more quickly – although jerkily – than I had seen her move for a long time. 'You've been too long. Everyone's speaking of it. We're going to miss it.'

'Miss what? Where are we going?' I asked, following her into a rickshaw, but she didn't answer. We were pulled through the city to one of the gates, but it wasn't the one where the bullock cart – and my father – waited.

When my mother and I climbed from the rickshaw outside the gate, I still didn't know what she had brought me to see. There was a huge crowd, and all I could see was the upper branches of a spreading banyan tree, with its long rooting tendrils growing from its branches, supporting the heavy mother tree.

'Let us through,' my mother said, pulling me by the hand.

'*Chala jana, chala jana,* move, out of the way,' she shrilled. The crowd of natives obediently parted, the men and women standing back so that we could pass through without touching. As we finally came to the front, I saw a funeral pyre in the shade of the banyan. I looked at my mother. She didn't hold her handkerchief to her mouth, and her lips were parted, a thin trickle of saliva running from the side of her mouth. Unblinking, she didn't appear to feel it, and an unusual flush gave colour to her sallow cheeks.

'Mother?' I said, raising my voice to be heard above the many voices. Her clutch on my hand was painful, and I struggled to pull my fingers away. My other hand held my gift from Kai.

But it was as if my mother were unaware of me, her own hand fixed on mine in an unconscious death-grip, and without warning my heart jumped, beating too rapidly.

In the next instant the crowd fell completely silent, and now my heart thumped painfully. I knew what my mother had brought me to watch. I made one last feeble attempt to pull my hand from my mother's, but it was futile. I shook my head, *no, no,* to no one in particular.

In the silence a camel roared, and then they came. The woman led the way; her round face was strangely peaceful, her eyelids heavy. Her lips turned up in a benevolent smile. Had she been given something, opium, perhaps, to put her into this strange, sleepy state? Or was it simply the strength of her love, and her spiritual ecstasy? She was dressed in red wedding finery, her hands newly decorated with bridal henna, her gold bracelets and anklets shone in the afternoon sunlight.

It was clear that she was younger than I.

Following her, six men bore a woven charpoy, and atop it lay a figure shrouded in gold fabric. The husband.

When they reached the pyre the widowed wife stepped

away from the others and circled the piled logs and twigs, slowly and reverently. Her lips moved as she silently prayed. Her husband's family passed in front of my mother and me to raise the body on to the logs, and for an instant I saw the uncovered face. He looked to be no more than twenty, and was handsome even in death, his long lashes resting on his cheeks, his top lip a boyish bow.

And then there were drumbeats and intoned prayers, and the wife stopped her circling. A man and woman – surely her in-laws – stepped forward to gently, respectfully, take her arms and help her climb to join her dead husband.

I watched, transfixed, as she settled herself comfortably, lovingly placing her husband's head in her lap and putting her hands on his cheeks. Her hennaed fingers looked like a child's, and the nails were bitten. There was an awed hush; behind us the sounds of the city were muted, as if from far away, and I felt as though the universe had narrowed to this one spot. I was alternately hot and then shivering as if with chill. I don't know if my mother's hand still held mine, as I could not feel my body. I was only aware of the girl's calm face; it grew closer and then receded, closer and receded, pulsing like the sun, and my eyes burned as if I indeed stared into the sun, but I couldn't look away.

I grew aware of a sly crackling; I hadn't seen the kindling being lit, but the sound grew in intensity. And then it caught fully, and the flames, fanned by the winter wind, blew upward in a sudden whooshing rush. The drumming and chanting grew louder, and the crowd joined, their voices rising. I simply stared.

'She is truly a saint and a goddess,' my mother whispered, turning to me, now clutching my arm.

Finally I could move my eyes, and looked away from the girl, and at my mother. I had never seen her face so soft, apart from when she had held Adriana. Now it appeared that she bore the look of one sated, of desire fulfilled. Her mouth opened, and as the tip of her tongue emerged to touch the underside of her top lip, I felt ill. It was as though I was witnessing something of an obscene nature, something highly personal and intimate.

I looked back to the pyre. The flames surrounded the girl, and she was no more than a wavering shadow caught between them. She was unmoving; whether she cried out or not I don't know, for those watching sighed and murmured and shouted and sang with approval.

And yet I sensed she was silent.

And then the flames caught and feasted on her sari, her hair, her flesh, and rose upward in a gleeful burst as a collective gasp came from the crowd. My mother slumped against me, one hand still tight on my arm, the other folded against her flat bosom, and her lips moved, repetitively, and I knew she was saying *yes, yes yes yes*.

Terrible hissing and popping now came from the pyre. I didn't want to think of a burst skull, melted organs, charred bones, and yet it was as if I could see through the flames, and watch as the girl, not even as old as I, was slowly consumed from the outside inward.

I closed my eyes tightly, willing myself to be somewhere else, willing this to be a terrible nightmare, but knowing it was all real, and that I was a part of it. And I felt a deep shame, not only at myself for being a witness to this, but for my mother. For her enjoyment of this unbearably cruel ending to a young life.

And for the first time in my life I thought of being away from this – from all of it – the tragic beauty of the beliefs and customs I had always known. I wanted to be somewhere safe and predictable, somewhere where I would not be subject, almost daily, to suffering and cruelty and death. Was this my Christian side surfacing, then, the part of me that didn't want to embrace this combined glory and destruction, so tightly wound together that it appeared impossible to separate one from another? Deep inside, did I truly long for a simpler set of rules, of a basic right and wrong, as my father preached?

The confusion of it filled my head; the smell of burning hair and roasting flesh, the floating of ashes, the adoration of the crowd and their cries surrounded me so that I felt I must escape, must run from this, run, covering my ears and closing my eyes.

I broke from my mother's grip, pushing back through the crowd and into the city again, not able to bear waiting for the fire to burn itself out, to reduce the young husband and wife who must have married so recently, and surely with such hope, to only ashes.

I had no annas for a rickshaw, and was suddenly confused as to where I was, even though I knew the city well. I ran through the narrow lanes of Lahore, rushing as if chased by Death who hung over the pyre, Death now bored and looking for another victim. People moved out of my way. In a detached, momentary glimpse I saw a Hindu woman pull her child close, a Muslim touch his amulet for protection. It was only a long time afterwards, thinking back on the day, that I realised how I must have looked, an English woman dashing through the streets with her skirt flying, her face smeared with tears and mucus, her hair dishevelled and coated in flakes of ash, her eyes wild as she held a wrapped package against her chest.

When I could run no further I leaned against a building, pushing at the pain in my side, leaning forward and taking deep, shuddering breaths. And then I lifted my chin and wiped my face with my free hand. When I pulled it away I saw that my fingers were black; the print from the newsprint wrapped round the book had transferred to my damp hand.

I bent over, lifting the edge of my frock, and scrubbed at my face.

Slightly calmer, I regained some sense of direction, and shortly afterwards found my way back to the proper gate. When I walked towards our cart, my legs trembling and my mouth dry, my mother was already there, sitting beside my father.

She turned her head, and spoke in a low voice that I knew my father, fussing with Marta's reins, didn't hear. 'Haven't you the stomach for real life, Pree?' she asked, coldly. She spoke as if I weren't her daughter, but someone she wished to insult. Were her eyes still glowing with pleasure, or was it my imagination?

I climbed into the back of the cart, unable to bear sitting beside her.

'Pree?' my father called. 'Are you all right? Where have you been? What is streaked on your face?'

I didn't answer.

'You haven't been bothered, Pree?' he asked, but still I couldn't look over my shoulder at him. Obviously my mother hadn't said anything to him about the horrific scene we'd witnessed.

There was a sati, I wanted to tell him. *She was not even as old as I, and Mother took me to watch. She forced me to watch.* But at the same time, a small voice in my head asked, *But did she really force you? Couldn't you have left?* And this unnerved me even further. Had I really wanted to be there, to watch that young woman kill herself?

I said, turning my face just enough so that my father could hear me, 'I couldn't find my way back.'

This must have satisfied him, for he then clicked his tongue to Marta; I heard the slap of the reins on her back, and the cart jolted forward.

The ride, throughout the next few hours, was mercifully

silent. I closed my eyes, blocking the sights of the countryside and road, trying to force my thoughts back to Kai, to the look on his face when he'd first seen me, and as he studied the book I'd given him. I tried to bring back the heated pressure of his lips on mine, the strength of his arms around me, the broadness of his chest against mine, the thump of his heart. But it was lost now. The image of that destroyed girl, with her strange, accepting smile, haunted me.

And, almost as disturbing, I couldn't stop thinking of my mother's reaction, her obvious excitement and yes, pleasure, at another's unbearable suffering.

Eventually I looked down at the book in my lap. The paper it was wrapped in was printed in Hindi; I absently read it. Report of violence against a Muslim by the British, urgings to not allow the passing of an English bill dividing farm lands in the eastern provinces, other angry cautionings, demands for freedom and rights and rising up against the British.

Kai was still involved, as I suspected.

I removed the newsprint from my lovely book, setting it on the floor beside me, and within moments the wind carried it away.

CHAPTER EIGHTEEN

A MONTH LATER, IN the full grip of January cold, my mother announced to me that she was expecting a child.

We were in the infirmary, putting away supplies after having just seen the last patient, when she said, in her usual perfunctory tone, that the child was due in five months' time.

My mouth opened as I glanced at my mother's gaunt frame. 'But . . . but Mother. You don't look . . .'

'That's what this country does to a woman, Pree. Wears one to the bone. But I can assure you that I'm certain of my dates. The child will be born in May.'

Adriana's first birthday, I thought, turning from my mother, deeply disturbed at her disclosure. She was so worn and aged, and was somewhere in her middle forties — I had lost track of her true age, as neither she nor my father ever noted their birthdays — but she hadn't yet reached the time of life where no more children can be conceived. I knew of her monthly cycles as she knew of mine; she and I lived in such close quarters. She had often, in the past, made reference to the physical discomfort her time brought. I tried to think when she had last referred to it; it was Glory who gathered my mother's laundry and would know whether there had been bloodied cloths.

But even more disquietening was the image of my mother and father, together. I couldn't bear to think of it. 'That's lovely, Mother,' I said. 'How exciting.' I tried to muster enthusiasm, and yet kept thinking back to only a few weeks earlier, and my mother's unsettling and worrisome reaction to the *sati* in Lahore. How would she cope with an infant?

And in that next instant I knew Kai's words about me leaving the mission could not come to fruition. I could never leave, abandoning a brother or sister. Because that's what it would be: abandonment. Neither of my parents could be trusted with a baby or small child. Oh, possibly physically, yes, they would feed it and keep it clean. But it was the playing of their minds that worried me, how a new and malleable little soul could be twisted by the sad realities of what was happening at this mission.

'That's lovely, Mother,' I said again, still not facing her. But the news was far from lovely. Far from it.

My mother didn't want any dinner, going straight to bed. Concerned over my mother's disclosure, I couldn't eat, either, and instead, I went looking for Jassie; I hadn't seen her for the last week. I got down on to my hands and knees at the edge of the *rasoi* and peered underneath, holding a sliver of raw chicken.

'Jassie?' I called, waving the bloody scrap in the opening. 'Come, girl. Come out.'

There was the sound of movement, and then Jassie crept out. It was obvious she had had her pups; she was again lean, her teats hanging low and swollen. I backed away and put down the meat. Jassie swallowed it in one gulp. 'Did you bring any babies back, Jassie?' I murmured, listening for the cries.

I never knew how many puppies Jassie gave birth to, or how many died. She somehow hid or destroyed the dead ones; occasionally I'd see one or two little yellow pups scampering after her, but apart from that one time she'd brought home the little male, she always led them away from the mission, into the fields. Every six months, like clockwork, she had another litter.

After dinner I sought out my father; he was in the courtyard, leaning on the fence and looking at the road.

'Father?'

He turned. He looked even older than usual, dark circles around his eyes, his cheekbones standing out in frightening sharpness. His shoulders, under his jacket, were bony and frail.

'Mother has told me. The . . . news.' I was unexpectedly embarrassed, finding it difficult to look at my father.

His face contorted as if gripped by a sudden, unexpected pain.

'Is it your chest?' I asked, stepping forward.

'No,' he said. 'No. It's not that. It's your mother. I'm terribly worried for her.'

'Because of what this birth will do to her? That it might be too difficult for her because of her age, or is it because you don't think this baby will live either?'

He ran his hands over and over his face, scrubbing as if trying to wash something away.

'Father?'

Finally he said, 'Your mother is very ill, Pree.'

'You mean . . . the baby?' I asked, slowly, sensing that wasn't what he meant.

He took a deep breath. 'There is no baby.'

An involuntary gasp came from my throat. 'But she just told me this afternoon, Father. Do you mean she's already—'

He couldn't look at me as he interrupted. 'There never was a baby. It's all part of her illness,' he said now.

'But . . . can you be sure?'

'I know with certainty that there can be no baby, Pree,' he

said. 'It's an impossibility. Do you understand? I'm her husband, and I know it cannot be,' he repeated, finally looking into my face, his eyes blinking rapidly.

I did understand. My mouth went dry; I was even more embarrassed to be discussing something of this nature with him. I looked away, nodding.

'It will pass, I'm sure, this notion your mother has,' he said, and left.

I went to my parents' bedroom doorway and looked in. My mother sat on her dressing-table chair, her legs apart so that her limp skirt fell between her thighs. With one hand she held an embroidered handkerchief to her lips; her other hand rested on her flat belly. She stared at the window with a vacant look.

I went to bed early, not even having the energy to read before sleep. I was so weary, not because of the long day's work, but by the sad confusion, palpable in the chilled, dead winter air of our four rooms.

It was only a week afterwards that I awoke to my mother's loud weeping. A chill went through me; suddenly I was six years old again, knowing that my infant brother Gabriel was dead.

I flung back my bedcover and ran to my parents' bedroom. My mother sat in her nightdress on the edge of the bed, rocking back and forth, sobbing, a tiny wrapped form in her arms. My father, fully dressed, stood at the window, his back to the room.

'Mother!' I cried. 'Mother . . .' I ran to her, looking at the stillness of the bundle she held. When she didn't speak I called to my father.

'Father, what's happened?'

He turned and looked at me. His hair stood out wildly, and his face was worn and sallow. He shook his head at me. 'Come with me, Pree,' he said, and crossed the room and took my arm, leading me into the sitting room.

'What happened?' I asked again, and a second time he shook his head.

'Your mother is ill,' he said, in the same deadened tone he'd used when we had last discussed her, standing at the fence.

'What's she holding, Father? Could it really be—'

'Pree,' he said, shaking my arm once, hard. 'There is no baby.'

'But she's holding—'

'There's no baby,' he repeated, his voice harsh.

I pulled away from him and went to the bedroom doorway, staring at the bundle of flannel in my mother's arms. She cradled the tiny form against her, weeping softly now.

'I don't know what to do with her,' my father said, behind me, his voice low and hoarse with sadness, with exhaustion, with despair. 'I don't know what to do,' he repeated, and I heard his footsteps, slow and hesitant, as he went out the front door.

I couldn't leave my mother, although I was confused and frightened. Who was I to believe? Of course my father was the logical one, the sane one, and yet what did my mother hold and weep over? She came towards me, still carrying her burden.

'Mother?' I said, softly, touching her arm, but she ignored me and went out the door my father had left by, only a moment earlier. I followed her; what else was I to do?

She went across the courtyard to the infirmary. I tried to go in with her but she closed the door in my face. I heard the sound of small, almost stealthy movements, and in a few moments she came out again, carrying a small wooden box. *Warner's Safe Cure* was imprinted on its side, but I saw, as she passed me, that the name *William Jamieson* was written on the top in India ink. My mother's letters were shaky, the ink splotched.

She went to the little graveyard, stumbling through the dried, yellow winter grass; again, I simply followed her, my hands hanging at my sides. I was overcome with a sadness so huge, although for whom or what I didn't know, that my chest ached.

I watched as my mother set down the little box that had once held a medicinal supply but was now a tiny coffin. Kneeling in her nightdress, she dug with her bare hands at the dry, hard earth beside the other four headstones.

I looked from my mother to the box, back to my mother, and again at the box. Finally, I knelt beside her. She didn't appear aware of my presence, scrabbling in the cold earth with a frenzied clawing, breathing heavily. Holding my own breath, I lifted the lid off the box. The small form was still wrapped in the square of white flannel. I touched it; it was stiff.

My father didn't lie, did he? And yet my mother's grief was so real. Her uncombed hair hung in long tangles. Her face was wet with tears, and now her fingernails were torn and bleeding.

I had to know.

I unwrapped the flannel. It was a small furry body, yellow, its eyes closed and delicate paws curled against its body. A tiny sliver of grey tongue was caught between the lips. It was a dead pup, surely one of Jassie's. Where had she found it?

I gently rewrapped it and returned the lid to the box. My mother, finally finished with her digging, took the little box and set it into the hole. Still kneeling beside her, I joined her in pushing the dirt to cover the box, and then I helped her stand. I had to support her, gripping her arm as she leaned against me and looked down at the mound of earth. She didn't cry any longer, but simply hung against me as if her legs didn't exist. She was limp and surprisingly heavy in spite of her emaciated state, and in the cool winter air my forehead was beaded with sweat from the effort of supporting her.

Her lips moved in silent prayer. There was the clatter of wings; a flock of dozens of Brahminy starlings flew overhead. The sound of their flight snapped like a startling burst of applause. My mother tore her eyes from the new grave and watched them. Her expression was eerie; it was as if she were one of the birds, for I actually saw her open her mouth as they dipped, as one, close to the ground before rising again, and something like wonder crossed her face.

'We shall send Kai to Lahore to have a stone carved,' she said, still watching as the flock wheeled away. 'A lovely white stone, to match the others. William Jamieson. My little William,' she said, in a dull, croaking voice that sounded as if she had not spoken in weeks, and I knew, with certainty, she had completely left reality.

Afterwards I helped her back to her bedroom, trying to get her to drink some warm, sweet tea, but she simply shook her head, her eyes on the basket sitting on a low table under the window.

The basket held the clothes she had given to Glory for Adriana. As she had instructed me a few days ago, I had taken them from the wardrobe. She had spent a long time looking through them, smiling as she patted and stroked the tiny dresses and bonnets.

My father once more stood at the window on the other side of the room, staring out at the back garden.

'Take the clothes away, Pree,' my mother said. She had pushed herself up so that she leaned against the head of the bed, and was still staring at the basket. 'Take them from my sight.'

I went to the basket and looked down at the tiny soft

white dresses, some smocked with different coloured thread, others with lace tatted at the hem. I remembered the feel of Adriana's little body as I held her, and a new ache went through me.

'What do you wish me to do with them, Mother?'

She covered her eyes with her arm. The sleeve of her nightdress slipped back, and before I could look away from the infected scabs and the fresher blood on the insides of her pale, freckled arms, she put her mouth to her arm and bit. The sight filled me with fresh horror; she had all along been doing this to herself. 'I don't care,' she said, lowering her arm. 'Give them to someone. I'll never need them again.' Her breath caught in her throat at that, and the soft weeping began anew. 'I need my baby,' she wept. 'I want my baby,' she repeated, over and over, in a quiet, defeated voice I didn't recognise.

'It's as before,' my father said, and I turned to look at him. 'She's acted in this way before, when we lost the others. But I fear that this time . . .'

When he said no more, I studied the tiny garments in the basket in front of me, stroking their softness as my mother had, only days earlier.

'I cannot go through this again, Reverend,' my mother said then, her voice hardly more than a whisper.

'Of course not, Mother,' my father said, still across the room. I wanted him to go to her, to show her some compassion. It was a dog which had died, not a child. I knew that, and he knew that. But to my mother the pain was as real and as fresh as if it were her own flesh and blood she had again put under the Indian soil.

'No.' My mother's voice was louder now, and firm. I looked up from the baby clothes. She caught her breath and wiped her cheeks, and something came over her face. Now it was perfectly still. 'I will not go through this again. You will have to accept that. It's over. That part of my life is over. There will be no more dead children.'

My father finally went to the bed and looked down at my mother. 'Don't think about this now, Eve. Weeping will only cause further distress.'

It was the first time I had heard my father address my mother by her Christian name. It sounded odd, and intimate. I felt as if I were a voyeur, and wished to be gone from the room.

'I will regain my physical strength, as I always do,' my mother said now. 'But I cannot – I will not ever again harbour the hope I've lived with these past months, only to have it once more destroyed. This is the last time. There will be no more opportunities for a child, Reverend.'

I sat perfectly still in the silence. I didn't wish to be party to this conversation.

'You will sleep in the infirmary from now on,' my mother said. 'You will no longer share my bed.'

I stared at the floor.

'If the Hindu aesthetics can suppress their natural desires using meditation, you, as a man of God, can also learn to accept celibacy,' my mother went on, her voice weak but her words forceful. 'You are a man of religious devotion and self-effacement, are you not?'

My father's voice was toneless. 'That's enough, Eve.'

'I won't allow you to touch me ever—'

'Eve! Stop it, Eve.'

Whenever I had said her name in my head – Eve – the first e drawn out, the v soft, it was a lovely name. But at this moment, as it came from my father's lips, it carried the hard knock of a stone thrown against a wooden wall. And then there was silence except for his harsh breathing. His face had grown paler still, his fists clenched, while my mother's open hands curled loosely on the thin sheet.

I knew my father was angry, but not at what my mother said. He was distraught, as I was, and angry at his inability to help my mother, at his inability to deal with her. To fix her. I saw that he knew he could no longer depend on prayer for this situation.

Now there was silence, broken only by Sanosh's low chanting as he thumped dough. *Om Namah Shiva*, he intoned, over and over again, keeping time with the thumping.

'Get out, both of you,' my mother said, and we left.

I wanted to run from the house out into the fields, or down to the river. I wanted to be by myself, to put my hands over my ears and open my mouth wide and scream into the sky, into the eddying waters, erasing what I had just witnessed. But my father touched my arm as I hurried out of the front door ahead of him.

'Sit down, Pree,' he said, lowering himself into the rocking chair.

I hesitated, one foot on the step. 'Sit,' he said again, and with one last longing look at the freedom beyond the courtyard, I sat beside him, on the smaller cane chair. I studied the fluttering leaves of the peepul tree. Pavit sat under it, covered in layers of shawls, his back against the grey bark. I was cold, and wrapped my arms around myself. From the corner of my eye I knew my father stared at his own fingers, clasped in the prayer position in his lap. I knew, without looking, how white the knuckles would be, that he was gripping his hands, holding on to himself as if to keep himself weighted in the rocking chair, weighted so that he would not float up, and away. Surely he wished for an escape from this misery as I did.

We continued to sit in silence. Finally I heard my father swallow a number of times, and then he spoke. 'You can see, Pree, what state your mother is in.'

'Yes,' I whispered. It wasn't a temporary case of Sand in the Head, as Mrs Lang had once suggested. With my mother's arms covered, I could stop thinking about the bite marks on her tender flesh. As long as she slept, long, long hours, some days not even rising, I didn't have to see the emptiness in her eyes. But I had been avoiding the truth for too long. My mother was utterly mad.

'I shall have to send her . . . take her to . . .' he stopped. 'She simply can't remain here any longer.'

'You'll send her back to England?' I asked. A strange emotion took hold of me. I licked my lips. 'But . . . will we go with her? She can't travel alone.' We still hadn't looked at each other, and spoke into the air in front of us.

My father didn't answer immediately, giving time for images to start in my head. Images of leaving the mission, and leaving India. I thought of Eleanor, of her mother, of the women in her drawing room. They were the people of England I knew. I couldn't live surrounded by others like them. I thought of Sanosh and Pavit, of Jassie and Rujjie. Of my life, the only one I knew.

Alarm grew in my chest; I thought of my father's heart, and its difficulty in beating with regularity. Mine, on the other hand, beat harder and faster in a quick, ticking rhythm.

I thought of Kai, and his pulse beneath my lips.

Could I leave all of this?

'No. Not to England, Pree. There's no money for even one sea voyage. Although perhaps if I go into Lahore, and talk to the church . . .' He stopped, and finally I looked at him. A variety of emotions were passing over his face. I didn't recognise one of them; he was a stranger at that moment. 'But even so, there's no one there left at home. No one to care for her. Not England,' he repeated, then focused on me. 'Sit back, Pree.'

I hadn't realised I'd been leaning forward so stiffly. At that moment I saw myself on the cane chair, hunched forward, my shoulders high, my neck extended, turned, to look at him. I was a vulture, a bird of prey, swooping high overhead, circling, watching for movement, head cocked. Trying to see, to hear.

I leaned back, lowering my shoulders, forcing the tension out. 'Where do you mean, then?'

'Delhi, perhaps. I made enquiries when we went into Lahore the last time. There are . . . facilities within the English community in Delhi. For those needing care, care that the family can no longer offer.'

Images of Bethlem Royal Hospital – Bedlam – from books I'd read, flooded my head. The filthy straw and the wretched creatures, half naked. Depravity, torture, wasted bodies. Visitors with long sticks to prod and tease through the bars, to enrage those known as *unfortunates*. Screams and gibberish from drooling mouths. Mouths like my mother's had become.

'No. Not an asylum,' I said, shaking my head, my voice too loud. 'You couldn't put her into an asylum, Father. Couldn't we just keep her here, and—' Again, descriptive passages filled my head. The mad Bertha, Mr Rochester's wife, locked away in the attic while Jane Eyre unknowingly lived beneath her.

'No, Pree. And of course I wouldn't put her into an asylum. I would find something . . . suitable. A rest home, where she could be cared for with respect, with concern. She's paid her debt to India. She deserves to be treated well by it. She's not a threat to anyone but herself. I worry . . .'

I knew he also thought of her arms; her own self-destruction.

'I will do what I must,' he said, and we continued to sit beside each other, while inside my mother lay on her bed.

A man and boy waited on the infirmary verandah. Glory wandered through the courtyard, her finger inside her mouth, grimacing. The smell of cardamom and saffron wafted through the air from the *rasoi*. Jassie trotted in from the road, nose high as she sniffed the air.

Pavit, his chin on his chest, had fallen asleep under the peepul tree.

CHAPTER NINETEEN

T HE NEXT DAY my father prepared to go to Lahore.
'The Church will surely support my request. I have
worked for them for twenty-three years. They will not –
cannot – deny me when I now need their help.' His voice was
firm and convinced, but his eyes didn't show the same
confidence.

He was gone for the full day, not returning until evening
was descending. Leaving Marta and the cart in the middle of
the court-yard, he went straight to the infirmary. I was
surprised he'd been away so long, and that he didn't unhitch
Marta, or give her food and water.

I undid the harnesses and led her to her enclosure, forking
out fresh straw and filling her large wooden water bucket.
Then I went to my father in the infirmary. He was sitting on
the bed, his hands hanging between his knees.

'What happened, Father?' I asked. 'What did the Church
say? Will they take care of Mother?'

He didn't answer, staring at his own hands.

'Father?' I touched his shoulder, but still he didn't respond.
Finally he raised his head and looked out of the window.

'They suggest I send her back to England.'

'But didn't you tell them there's no one there . . .'

'I was told we should put our faith in the Lord,' he said,
but not in the usual way he spoke of the Lord. This time his
voice was mocking, and it shocked me. He turned to me.

'Reverend Burgess said the Lord would surely care for His daughter, as she has cared for the heathens of this land.' And then he gave a short bark of laughter, which frightened me more than his tone.

'And so it is up to us after all, Pree. You and I – with the help of Glory – and, of course, with the assistance of the *Lord*,' again, that stress on the word, the twist of his mouth, 'will see that your mother is cared for.'

My mother deteriorated rapidly over the next three months, requiring Glory or myself to help her with even the simplest daily needs.

Glory was responsible for keeping her clean – for bathing her and getting her out of her nightdress and into a frock each day, for keeping her hair tidy. I worked in the infirmary with my father, but stopped to feed my mother at noon, and I again fed her in the evening. I got her ready for bed and made sure her bedclothes were fresh. Every few weeks she had a clear day, a day where she sat up and looked around her as if surprised to see where she was. On those days she spoke to me normally, asking about patients we'd once seen, and about small, unimportant matters relating to the mission.

One morning, as I passed my mother's bedroom, I glanced in to see Glory brushing my mother's hair. But she was brusquely ripping the tortoise-shell brush through the long tangles. My mother's neck snapped back with each jerk of Glory's wrist.

'Glory,' I said, crossing the room and stopping her hand. 'There's no need to be so rough.'

'She doesn't feel it,' Glory said.

'How do you know?'

'Look at her. It's as though she's asleep.'

I moved from behind my mother to her side, looking into her face. I had never before seen my mother's eyes wet, except

241

at the death of Gabriel, and then the horrid, more recent episode with the imagined baby. And although it may only have been a physical reaction to the tugging on her scalp, her tears filled me with an emotion I had never before felt for her. Even when she had buried the puppy she believed to be her child, I had been filled with a confusion that bordered on loathing for her bizarre behaviour. But now . . . to see her so broken, so weak and accepting, gave me a jarring sense of loss.

I took the brush from Glory. 'I'll do her hair. You put fresh bedclothes on the bed.'

Glory did as I told her. After that I also saw to my mother's morning care, letting Glory do the simple housekeeping.

My father was strangely distant through all of this. At times it seemed he'd forgotten about my mother, lying in her shuttered bedroom in the house. But if I mentioned her name he'd stop what he was doing in the infirmary, suddenly, looking at the window or door, his face distressed as if he'd just had tragic news.

He took his evening meal with me in the dining room, but sometimes ate very little, staring into his dish or bowl as if he was looking for an answer to a deep question within the food. He answered me in one or two words, and after a while I stopped trying to make conversation with him. As soon as the meal was finished he would return to the infirmary, and I assumed he went to bed, for I never saw a light shining from its windows.

One morning he came to me on the back verandah of the infirmary, where I was talking to a woman whose child's throat was raw and reddened.

'I have to go to Lahore,' he said.

Usually these trips were discussed beforehand. 'Now?' I asked, rising. 'But it's not time for your wages.'

'I have to go,' he repeated.

'Shall I make a list of what we nee—'

242

'No,' he interrupted, and abruptly left.

I heard the returning rumble of the cart late in the evening, and saw him unhitching Marta and putting her in the enclosure. But he went straight to the infirmary, not coming to the house to speak to me.

The next morning, when I went to the verandah for the usual morning prayers, he was sitting in the rocking chair. His Bible was on the small wooden table beside him.

'Father?' His waistcoat was stained with dried food and grease, his hair was brittle and dusty. 'Are you ready for prayers?'

He stared at me as if I'd just asked a puzzling question about sums. 'Prayers?' he repeated.

For one horrible instant I saw a blankness akin to my mother's in his eyes. Then he blinked, and put his hand on his forehead. 'No. No, Pree. I . . . what with your mother, and . . . and everything, I . . .' he stopped, as if words failed him. He had prayed through everything in the past. 'But you can say them. You can still say them, Pree.'

I shook my head, and went to the infirmary. A morning without prayers broke a routine I had known my whole life, apart from the few times my father was too ill to rise in the morning. And I found this – that he chose not to say them – more unsettling than I would ever have expected. I had always thought I hated the prayers. And yet now, without them to start my day, I felt strangely unattached. I was like a kite, its string broken, dipping and hovering before finally disappearing into the glazed brightness of the sky.

'What would you do, Pree, if you could go anywhere?' my father asked at dinner a week later. It was quiet, and there were just the two of us as usual. Mother was in her room lying still and flat.

'In India, you mean?' I asked, a forkful of stringy mutton halfway to my mouth.

'Yes. In India. Where would you like to go?'

I put down my fork and smiled. 'I would like to go to Benares with its burning ghats. I would like to see the Hanging Gardens and the Tower of Silence in Bombay, and the Taj Mahal at Agra. The pink city of Jaipur.'

My father held up his hand. He didn't return my smile. I noticed his lips were white and flaky. 'I meant one place. Just one place, Pree. If you could live anywhere else, where would it be?'

I leaned my chin on my hand, my elbow resting on the table. There seemed little concern for the usual table manners these days. I twirled a piece of my hair around one finger. 'To actually live? I don't know. Not Lahore.' I thought of Mrs Wyndham and the others there. 'I don't think I'd like to go to Calcutta. But maybe Madras? No. Too hot. Bombay. Yes, I think Bombay, and the Arabian Sea. I would like to live near the sea.' Again I smiled at my father. 'I would like to see the ocean, and smell its salty spray.' It felt good to talk about pleasant things. It had been so long since I'd spoken of dreams, or plans. They were the things Kai and I had once discussed, so long ago. Now he was out in the world, living his dreams, while I was still here at the mission, with its heavy aura of hopelessness.

My father nodded, although he appeared distracted and not really listening. 'Do you remember the Langs?'

'Of course.' The memory of Mrs Lang's slurred speech and Mr Lang's hot hand on my neck came back. It was because of Mr Lang that Kai had fought with my father, and left for good. 'Why?'

'They're still in Peshawar,' he said, very slowly. 'I heard, while in Lahore most recently, that they're doing all manner of good works, especially with Muslim women. What do you think of Peshawar?'

I thought of the Afghan. The last time I'd seen him was when Adriana was still with us. And he'd said he was going back to Peshawar. I remembered the strange way he'd said goodbye to me. Had I ever given Kai his message? 'What makes you talk about the Langs?'

My father was watching me intently. 'They were very impressed with you.'

I shrugged, taking a forkful of daal and putting it in my mouth. I chewed carefully; Sanosh sometimes didn't pick through the lentils carefully enough, and I had once chipped a back tooth on a tiny pebble. My father didn't appear to notice that more and more I was bringing in Indian food for our dinner.

'There may have to be some . . . changes here. Shortly,' my father said. He pushed his plate away and put his hands together as if he were about to pray.

I swallowed the daal. 'Changes? What do you mean?'

Now my father lifted his clasped hands and pressed them to his forehead. He pushed so hard that when he eventually removed them there was a white imprint in his already pale skin. His eyes fluttered.

I stood. 'Father? Are you ill?' His eyes closed, and he leaned back in his chair, pulling at his collar.

'Water,' he croaked. 'Bring me water, Pree.'

I hurried to him with a full glass, putting my hand under his chin as though he were a child, and pressing the glass against his lips. He drank, grimacing and rubbing his left arm.

'I must lie down,' he said. 'Help me.'

I helped him to stand, and then, his arm draped heavily across my shoulders and mine firmly around his waist, I half dragged him to the settee in the sitting room. I had to bring his legs up for him. He lay on his back, clutching his left arm with his right hand, his breath ragged and his face the colour of putty.

I sat for a while beside him, then, seeing he appeared to be more comfortable, letting go of his arm and breathing more normally, I went to the dining room and gathered the leftover food and dishes. I carried them out to the *rasoi*. Glory was there, talking with Sanosh.

He looked at the full plates. 'You did not like the daal?' he asked, as if insulted.

'No, no, it was fine,' I said. 'But my father became unwell, and couldn't eat.'

'He's ill?' Glory asked.

'He seems to be a little better now. He's sleeping, in the sitting room.'

'I will go and attend to him,' Glory said, surprising me. She never volunteered to do anything.

'No,' I said. 'I told you, he's asleep. Let him be.'

She stared at me, and there was something in her face I couldn't recognise. I knew it wasn't because I'd just given her an order; she was used to that.

Later I helped my father to my bedroom. 'Sleep here tonight,' I told him. 'I don't want you alone in the infirmary while you're ill,' I said.

He nodded weakly, and I helped him take off his jacket and waistcoat and pulled off his boots, then I took an extra blanket and spent the night on the settee.

The next morning I went to the *rasoi* and, standing, ate a bowl of *kedgeree*. Afterwards I attended to the one woman who came to the infirmary. My father had been asleep in my room, my mother in hers on the other side of the wall.

After I'd dealt with the woman and her lacerated palm, I returned to the house. As I came in I heard Glory's voice; I assumed she was with my mother, as was her job. But I found her in my room, perched on the edge of my bed. My father was sitting up, leaning against the wall. His colour had returned to normal, and he was smiling at something Glory had said.

When they saw me my father cleared his throat. 'Thank you, Glory,' he said. 'You may return to Memsahib now.'

Glory stood, brushing past me with a strange, pleased smile.

'What was she doing?' I asked, wondering at her smile. Her attitude towards my father was usually a studied act of disinterest.

'I . . . I called out for water,' he said.

I looked at the chair beside my bed, and at my dresser. There was no glass or jug.

My father swung his legs to the floor. 'The pain is gone,' he said. 'Are there patients to be seen to?'

'No. Only one woman, earlier,' I said.

He breathed deeply. 'There are fewer and fewer patients,' he said, and I nodded. Surely it was the spreading word of my mother's strange behaviour that was keeping the highly superstitious villagers away.

Tinkling sounds came from the pianoforte. I turned my head to listen. Was my mother up, then? For her to go to the pianoforte would mean she was indeed feeling well. It had been so long since she'd touched it.

'I'll just rest for another moment,' my father said.

I went to the sitting room. But, as had happened the earlier time when my father was ill, before Adriana's birth, it was Glory at the pianoforte, pressing the chipped yellow ivory, one key at a time.

'You shouldn't touch my mother's pianoforte without her permission,' I told her. But again, she looked at me with a slightly pleased look, that same tiny smile I'd seen moments earlier.

'She won't play it again,' she said.

'You don't know that,' I argued, although inwardly I couldn't imagine my mother's fingers ever making sense of the keys. 'Please, Glory. Leave it be. It may upset her.'

But Glory openly ignored me, turning back to the keyboard. In the next moment my father appeared in the sitting room doorway, pale yet clear eyed, his waistcoat unbuttoned and his jacket over his arm, his hair long and wild. My mother had always cut it for him. Glory smiled at him.

'Listen. I play,' she said, suddenly banging her fingers on the keys, making a terrible racket.

My father winced at the discordant sound, but did not tell her to stop. Instead, he simply backed away and left.

The strangeness of that tiny scene troubled me.

The next week I was in the infirmary, counting supplies, when I heard the rumble of a cart. I went to the verandah and saw two men in a large, sturdy cart pulled by a pair of black Brahmin bulls, driving through the courtyard towards the house. Once in front of it, they climbed down, carrying ropes.

Alarmed, I hurried out. My father came from the house and motioned for them, and they followed him inside.

I ran in the front door. The men were tying the ropes around the pianoforte. 'Father? What—'

But he simply put up his hand, and within moments the men dragged the pianoforte across the room, its legs screeching on the sloping floorboards. At a command from my father I held the door open, and the men got the pianoforte on to the verandah. Sweating and muttering to each other, they manoeuvred it down the steps and into the open back of the cart, lying it on its side.

I watched, my mouth open. As they left, my father brushed past me, and I caught his sleeve. 'Father,' I said, 'I don't understand. The pianoforte . . .' I was both angry and saddened to see it go. It was the one thing my mother – and I – so loved. That had brought us happiness.

'We need the money,' was all he said, not looking at me and pulling his arm away as if annoyed. He went to the infirmary, and I stayed in the house.

Suddenly the sitting room appeared empty, even though all the other furniture remained. The floor where the pianoforte had sat was unfaded. I stared at that rectangle of darker wood, wishing I had played the pianoforte more frequently. If my father had only told me what he was about to do, I might have spent the prior evening enjoying it one last time. The unexpected loss of the pianoforte was an abiding ache.

That evening, reading a book I'd brought in from the infirmary, Buchan's *Domestic Medicine*, in the circle of light from the lamp in the middle of the dining-room table, I heard my mother in the sitting room. I went to the doorway and watched her. She first sat on the settee, then, obviously agitated, went to the yellow chintz chair and sat on it, as if she couldn't find comfort.

'Mother? Are you hungry? Or thirsty?' I asked.

She ignored me, studying the blank wall where the pianoforte had been until that afternoon. The spindly Windsor chair was still there, pushed to one side. She rose and sat on it, looking at the wall quizzically, the way Jassie did when she watched me eating, waiting for the tid-bit I would drop for her. After a moment my mother put out her hands, as if blind, moving them back and forth in front of her, her head cocked, listening for sound.

It was difficult for me to watch, and I was relieved when she finally stood and, without looking at me or speaking, slowly went back to her room and closed the door.

I returned to my book, but was unable to concentrate. I went to my own bedroom and like my mother, quietly closed the door behind me.

★ ★ ★

A few days later I found Pavit weeping until the peepul tree. 'Are you in pain, Pavit?' I asked in Punjabi, crouching in front of him. He supported his left wrist with the stump of his right hand.

He shook his head. 'I'm frightened, Missy Pree.'

'Frightened? Of what?'

'It is Glory. She tells me that I will have to go back to the streets of my village. But I cannot go back there, Missy Pree. I cannot.' His face was wet with tears, his half-eaten lips twisted into a cruel line. The gauze around his right wrist was dark with moisture from his decaying flesh. 'Even the blind and the feeble minded do not allow me to sit and beg with them outside the temple.'

'Glory told you that? What did she mean?'

'I only know what she told me, that soon the mission will close. You will have to go back to your old home, Pavit, she said, and sit with your begging bowl again, hoping someone will give you a grain of rice.'

Why had Glory told Pavit this lie? What was she talking about? Something nagged at the back of my mind, and in the next instant I remembered. Just before his last attack my father had said that things would change. But surely he meant because of my mother. What did Glory know that I didn't?

'Don't worry, Pavit,' I said, clicking my tongue. 'The mission won't close,' I added, briskly. 'You won't have to leave. Glory is simply stirring up trouble.'

'I know I had many sins in my other lives, Missy Pree,' he said. 'This,' he held up his bandaged stump, 'is my punishment. I am deserving of my pain. It is perfectly just.' He announced this calmly. 'And it will be better in my next life. I make my *pujas* to all the gods, even your father's. And next time I will be in a higher caste. Before I was like this, I always bowed to a Rajput or Brahmin; if I had sandals I removed them in their honour. I am always trying to be good,' he said, 'but I do not know how I will bear to be so alone again in this life.'

'You won't have to be, Pavit,' I said. 'And in the next life I know you will be successful and well.'

'I will make another *puja* today,' he said.

'Do you want me to help you?' Everything was so difficult for him now. He nodded, and we went to his hut and took out his idols and phials. While he watched from his charpoy, I wiped the clay figures with a clean cloth, and anointed them with saffron powder. I touched their feet and chests with red tikka paste, and then splashed water on their mouths. Finally I ran out to the courtyard and picked up a few fallen blossoms and sprinkled them over the gods.

'Thank you, Missy Pree,' he said. 'I feel better now.' His lungs sounded like bellows. I knew he was growing weaker. I couldn't bear to think of him worrying about having no home and no one to care for him.

'Rest now, Pavit,' I told him.

He nodded, carefully lowering himself to his charpoy, pulling his collection of shawls tighter around himself, even though the hut was hot, the warm April sun beating on its thatched roof.

That evening, like the rainbow after the monsoon, Kai returned.

CHAPTER TWENTY

I T WAS NOT AS I imagined it would be; I didn't see him coming up the road, didn't run to him and throw my arms around him.

I was on the side verandah; my mother was in her bed, as usual, and my father had retired to the infirmary. The night air was sweet. I had set a lamp on the table on the verandah, thinking I might sit there and read for a while; I didn't feel ready to go to my bed.

And there was Kai, crouched outside Glory's hut, talking to her as she sat with her back against the wall.

'Kai,' I called, dropping my book and running down the steps. 'Kai! You're home.'

He stood, and although I rushed towards him, something in his posture made me stop when I was a few feet from him.

'You're home,' I repeated, although quietly this time.

'For a short while,' he said, his eyes dropping down my body for the merest instant. I wore my nightdress, and suddenly was aware that I was silhouetted by the light from the lamp on the verandah behind me. I was self-conscious in a way I had never before been with Kai, and crossed my arms over my chest.

'For a few days,' he said.

'Only a few days?'

'I'm leaving Lahore,' he said.

I didn't speak.

'I'm going down to Madras. A friend of mine is there. He told me about the opening of new offices; they're looking for translators. It's a good opportunity, more interesting and better wages. I just came back to tell . . . everyone where I was going. And that I might not be able to come to the mission again, at least for quite some time.'

I noticed that Glory had a paper packet in her hand. Kai had brought her money.

Now there was a different feel to the mission; I awoke anxious to face the day. Kai was back, if only for a short while, and the old and comforting rhythm had returned. He worked diligently, repairing the buildings and, by his very presence, made the mission feel alive again. I didn't eat dinner with my father, but went out to the *rasoi* and sat on the ground with Kai and Sanosh and Glory. Pavit was in his usual spot under the peepul tree, but he didn't eat. When had I last seen him taking a plate to his hut? Out of respect he never ate in front of us.

While we shared our meals Kai talked about life in Lahore, and I told him about people who had come to the infirmary. He laughed at some of my stories. For the first time in a long while I laughed as well. I refused to think about him leaving, about not seeing him again for a long time. He acted in the old way, friendly and interested, but that was all. Watching his hands as he ate, his mouth as he spoke, I thought about how he had put his arms around me, the feel of his lips on mine, in the courtyard of the shop in Lahore.

Did he not think about it as well?

The fourth evening we sat under the peepul tree together. Pavit hadn't come out of his hut except for a short time, in the morning. Sanosh had cleaned his pots and was asleep. Glory had gone into her hut, and a few moments earlier her

253

candle had been extinguished. Both the house and infirmary were in darkness.

'I'm leaving tomorrow, Pree,' Kai said.

I knew this had to happen, and yet I was overcome with a swift, unbearable sadness. A small cry escaped from my lips.

He didn't look at me.

'I wish you didn't have to go, Kai,' I said. 'And all the way to Madras . . . I . . . I can't bear to think of you being so far away.'

He still didn't speak. The silence grew. Finally he said, 'This is the path I've chosen.'

I thought of Glory's past words, about Kai starting his own life with his own family. 'Do you . . . are you planning to marry?' I knew I'd asked him the same question another time.

'Marry? I couldn't support a family now.' He stood, looking down at me. 'And I want – need – to be on my own. There are things I have to do without anyone depending on me. I can't have anyone in my life right now.'

I got to my feet and faced him. My heart thudded. I wanted, with such desire, for him to put his arms around me that my breath came in short huffs. I kept my mouth closed so that he wouldn't hear how his presence affected me.

'Do you understand, Pree?' he asked then.

I understood his words, yes, but not his reasoning.

'Can you understand?' he asked again. 'I can't . . .'

He didn't finish his sentence, and I stood, silent.

'We'll say goodbye in the morning,' he said then, and turned to walk away.

'Kai,' I said, 'wait.'

He stopped and I stepped close to him. I couldn't see his face. Although there was a moon, we were under the leaves of the peepul tree.

I held my breath and put out my arms, but as my

fingertips brushed his sleeves he shook his head. 'Good night, Pree,' he said, softly.

I watched him go into his hut, my arms still outstretched. I was by turn hot and cold, embarrassed by both my forward behaviour and his polite but clear rejection. I had humiliated myself. I squeezed my eyes shut for a moment, then opened them and walked through the moonlit courtyard and into the black house.

Something woke me. My nightdress was damp with perspiration, my hair plastered against my neck, but the air wasn't particularly hot. My shutters were open, and the sky, although still dark, had lost its blackness. I went out to the front verandah, and as I sat in the rocking chair, letting the night air dry my skin, I made out a shape under the peepul tree. At first I thought it might be Jassie, but almost immediately knew it was too big. I went down the front steps, and as I approached the tree I saw that it was Pavit, slumped against the trunk. Had he also found the night somehow oppressive, wrapped in his bandages and shawls, and come out in search of air?

As I drew nearer something about his position struck me as odd, and he wore only an old pair of *panjammahs*, ragged at the hems, and a loose shirt. It was the first time in many months that he had given up his shawls.

I studied him in the dimness. Not only had he taken off his shawls, but he had unwound all his bandages. I cupped my hand over my nose and mouth as the smell rose up to meet me. But in the next instant I lowered it with the realisation of what I was seeing.

Pavit's time had come.

I looked at the grotesque cavity of his missing nose, at his bottom lip eaten away to expose the roots of his few remaining teeth, at his eyes, still mercifully untouched, open and staring. I put my fingers on his forehead; the skin was still pliable and I thought I could sense a tiny degree of warmth. It was very recent, his death. Had it been this – his spirit, on its way through to the next step on the wheel – that had awoken me? I put my head back and looked up through the latticework of the soughing peepul leaves, as if I might see the wheel, spinning as it carried Pavit to his next incarnation. Surely, as we had spoken about so recently, he would be rewarded for all his suffering in this life. I thought of his *atma*, his spirit, slipping as if a wisp of fog through his skull. How free he would be.

'Pavit,' I whispered, suddenly overcome with sadness for him. I noticed that beside the old man's left hand lay a copper vessel. It was one of the dented, well-used kitchen copper jugs; why did Pavit have it?

I lifted it, hearing the slosh of liquid. Sniffing its contents, I smelled tamarind, and saw, on the mouthpiece, remains of the tamarind paste Sanosh used to clean copper and brass. I lowered myself to the soft earth beside Pavit and sat, holding the container, for a long time, the understanding coming slowly. Then I emptied out the water and set the vessel to one side, again gazing at what was left of Pavit's face, and saw now not the ravages of his disease, but his expression. He was more peaceful than I had ever witnessed. But instead of being pleased at this calm look, I was deeply troubled.

Pavit had not believed me when I told him he would be protected here. He had told me, directly, that he could not go back to starving on the street, to be spat on and stepped around, to be stared at with revulsion.

Tamarind paste, combined with water and left in the sun in a copper vessel, had the ability to create a deadly combination. While most of Sanosh's cooking and serving pots were layered with tin on the inside to prevent poisoning, he always ensured that he never allowed any of the paste to get inside the few uncoated containers he used.

'Old friend,' I murmured, tears filling my eyes. Pavit had chosen to die here, in the safety of the mission. And the terrible realisation came: he had organised his death as a direct result of my careless reaction to his worries. I had failed; I hadn't reassured him enough that Glory's spiteful threats would not become reality. Because I had dismissed his fears, he had taken his life.

I shivered, suddenly cold in the spring air, and then went to Kai's hut, calling his name softly from the doorway.

He immediately sat up, as if he had not been asleep, but waiting.

I stepped into the hut, and Kai sat very still, staring at me. His expression was one I didn't recognise. 'No, Pree. Please.' His voice was a low murmur, but there was something else in his tone, something in the word please . . . 'Don't make this so difficult for me,' he continued, in that same low tone, as I stood only a few feet away. 'You must know I—'

My cheeks flamed. 'It's Pavit,' I said. 'He's dead, Kai.'

In the instance of silence following my announcement Kai's features changed. I realised what I had seen in his face a moment earlier was an unfamiliar softness. Was it desire?

Kai threw back the coverlet.

'I'll fetch my father,' I said, looking away from his bare chest, his *panjammahs* gleaming whitely in the darkness.

'No,' Kai said, so quickly and loudly that I started.

'Why not? He must know. We can't leave Pavit in the courtyard. The jackals . . .'

'I'll go and wake him. You stay with Pavit,' he told me, reaching for his shirt hanging on a nail. 'Just let me put on—'

But now I was confused, possibly angry with Kai: first for his assumption that I would come to him, to his hut and his bed, as if I were an immoral woman like his own mother. And secondly that he would dictate to me where my father was concerned.

I turned and ran across the ground, the soft dust under my bare feet still warm from the day's sun. I went up the steps of the infirmary and through the open doorway, blinking as my eyes adjusted to the inside darkness. The shutters were closed.

When I pulled back the thin curtain in front of the charpoy, there was my father, asleep on his back. And beside him lay Glory, her head on his chest. My father's arm was around her, his fingers cupping her elbow, lightly and yet with full possession, as if it were a piece of fragile porcelain he must protect. Glory's hand, fingers spread, lay on my father's chest, over his heart.

I stood, looking at them for a few seconds, then stepped away. I couldn't think clearly. My father and Glory? And yet somehow . . . in some way I was not as shocked as I expected. There had been too many signs. My father in the dark yard in his nightshirt, when I'd gone looking for him, worried about my mother over a year ago. Glory's bangle in the bedclothes, and her sly smile as she sat beside my father the last time he was ill. Had I already known, but refused to let it come, let the image grow clear and strong in my head? And Kai . . . he knew too, then, surely he knew, by the way he had attempted to stop me from coming here, to the infirmary.

I reached down and prodded my father's shoulder. Startled, his eyes grew wide as he sat up and saw me. He quickly turned to look down at Glory, opening his mouth as if to speak – to explain? – but I didn't give him a chance.

'Pavit has died,' I announced. 'Kai is with him in the courtyard. We can't leave his body there.'

'Oh. Oh, I see,' he said, moving to sit on the edge of the bed in his white nightshirt, and the way he positioned his body was an obvious and pathetic attempt to block Glory. Did he really imagine I hadn't seen her?

She stirred then, making a small, questioning sound in her throat, and, seeing me, sat up in a lazy, undulating motion. She was naked, and didn't attempt to cover herself. I saw her breasts, high, full, the nipples small and dark. She put her hand on my father's arm, gently, her long slender fingers a stain on the whiteness of his nightshirt. She showed no shame.

I could not imagine my father cupping my mother's elbow with such delicacy. Their obvious familiarity with each other, their intimacy, made my voice hard.

'Don't bother yourself, Father,' I said, my words clipped. I was overwhelmed with emotion: sadness that the old leper I had known so long had taken his own life, inviting death, so alone; furious that my father and Glory would be so blatant, carrying on their unlawful act with my mother across the courtyard in the mission house. And I was angry that Kai knew, and had tried to protect me from this knowledge.

I walked stiffly to the door, my bare soles slapping the warped floor, then stopped and turned back to look at them. They were both sitting up in the tangled bedclothes, their shoulders touching as if they were husband and wife.

'You're sinners,' I said, my voice low and deep. 'You call yourself a man of God, Father, and yet you commit the sin of adultery. And with . . . with her,' I continued, my voice rising. 'You both sicken me. My only comfort is the future you are both aware of. You will rot in hell.'

Then I left, running down the infirmary steps and back to the peepul tree. Kai, the blanket from his charpoy around his shoulders, was sitting beside Pavit's body. Sanosh was there as well, crouching behind Kai. Kai looked at me as I sat, cross legged beside him, but said nothing. My mouth trembled with the shock of what I had discovered, but I would not speak of it to him. And I was so cold; now my whole body shook. Again I realised I wore only my thin nightdress.

Kai pulled off the blanket and put it over my shoulders. 'Pree?'

What did he want to hear? I looked at him; the light from the low, waning moon collected around his head like finely spun wool. I knew my eyes were hard as stones. He turned away, and we sat beside each other, silent.

My father came down the steps of the infirmary, fully dressed. Glory didn't show herself.

I looked back at Pavit, and, for the first time, visualised what the diseased old man may have looked like when he was young, when he had been whole, and full of hope for his future. Again tears came to my eyes. I put my hands to my face and wept.

I wept for Pavit, and his lost life. I wept for us all, in this place of sin.

I had known, from the first realisation of what had happened, that I would tell no one that Pavit had taken his own life. If my father knew that Pavit had chosen death he would pray about the wrongdoing of taking one's own life, the transgression of suicide. My father, whose own life was a sin, and a lie.

He did attempt to pray for Pavit that morning, after the sun had risen, washing the sky in pink.

We were on the verandah, as usual; Pavit's body was on his charpoy in his hut. I had roused my mother, and although I didn't have the strength to dress her, had wiped the sleep from her eyes and combed her hair and wrapped her shawl around her shoulders before I led her to the rocking chair on the verandah.

Glory hadn't come from her hut, and for this I was glad. But just after my father began his prayers, Kai came and knelt on the ground in front of the verandah. It was the first time in many years that he had done this, and I knew it was out of respect for Pavit.

But my father kept forgetting his train of thought, pausing, clearing his throat, and looking down at the black Bible he clutched. Never once did he allow himself to look at me, although I stared at him the entire time. My mother sat with her chin on her chest, her eyes closed. I didn't know if she was asleep or simply lost in whatever tangled thoughts rang in her head. Her hands were upturned on her thighs, the palms cupped as if waiting for something to fall into them.

' "*He will swallow up death in victory; and the Lord God will wipe away tears from all our faces, and the rebuke . . .*" ' my father started, then stopped in the middle of the verse, and simply stood, looking at the now brightening sky.

My mother suddenly raised her head. 'Is someone dead?' she asked, with an unfamiliar quickness in her words.

'Pavit,' I said. I had already told her this when I had helped her rise.

She nodded. 'Ah. He sorrows, the Reverend. He sorrows for the dead soul.'

I bit hard with my back teeth, wanting so badly to say that it was not sorrow which made my father stop his prayer, but guilt. The guilt — not only of his adultery, but at being found by me — was what made him stumble in his prayers.

'Dig the plot outside the cemetery fence, lad,' my mother said then, staring at Kai. Had she forgotten his name? 'Of course Pavit can't be buried in the sanctified ground of our Christian cemetery. He's a heathen.'

'He was converted, Mother,' my father said. ' "*And He said unto him, Arise, go thy way: thy faith hath made thee whole.*" '

Kai looked at him, then at me, and then back to my mother. 'I believe Pavit would wish to be cremated, Reverend,' he said.

'Do whatever you wish,' my father said, putting his hand

to his forehead and feeling behind him for a chair. He sat down heavily.

'Oh, oh yes, of course,' my mother said, rather vacantly. 'Of course,' she repeated. 'Yes, he must be cremated,' she said, and then chanted: '*He shall come again with glory to judge both the living and the dead, at whose coming all men must rise with their bodies and are to render an account of their deeds." '*

That afternoon Kai gently lifted Pavit's wrapped body into the back of the cart, and led Marta through the fields towards the Ravi. Sanosh had earlier taken the cart and gone to purchase the wood sold for cremations. He had also brought back a length of yellow cloth to wrap Pavit in; I had seen Kai giving Sanosh money as he left.

I carried Pavit's idols in their cloth sack. I had gone to my father, speaking to him for the first time since I had discovered him with Glory the night before. 'Kai and Sanosh and I will cremate Pavit,' I said, unable to look at him as he sat on the infirmary verandah. I studied the railing. 'I'm sure you don't wish to be part of a heathen ceremony.' His head nodded as I left the infirmary.

My mother slept in her room through the cremation. As for Glory . . . she simply didn't appear.

Kai and Sanosh cross-stacked the short logs upon the largest flat rock we used to beat our laundry, and laid Pavit's wrapped body on them. They piled smaller sticks upon his chest and legs. I put the sack of idols beside Pavit.

'Do you wish to light it, Sanosh?' Kai asked, but Sanosh shook his head.

'This duty should fall to you,' he said. 'Like the eldest son, you must light the pyre to open the way to heaven.'

Kai knelt and lit the dry wood.

As Kai and Sanosh chanted together and Pavit's yellow shroud caught fire, I tried not to think of my father and

Glory, tried to drive out the images of them in bed together, of her bare breasts pressing against my father's arm, his hand on her elbow.

Kai's voice was beautiful, deep and filled with true sorrow as he spoke prayers in both English and Punjabi. *Ram Naam Satya Hai*, he then chanted in Hindi, and I joined in. I hoped Pavit's soul would hear all the prayers and chants, and take comfort from them. I said my own prayer, wishing that Pavit was not lost, due to his suicide. His next life would have to be better; surely he had suffered enough in this one.

The flames crackled, and all around it the countryside and river blurred in the wavering heat. I knew the fire was cleaning Pavit of all disease; the smell of him, in death, was sweeter than in life. We stayed on the bank until the fire burned itself out, tendrils of smoke spiralling into the air. Bits of fine ash drifted over us. I looked away from the remains of skull and bone.

And then we returned to the mission, where Sanosh sat staring at his pots, and Kai disappeared into his hut.

CHAPTER TWENTY-ONE

M Y FATHER SAT ON a stool at the infirmary table, pouring tablets out of a large bottle on to the table. He had been counting them; they sat in small piles. He looked up as I came in. I must face him, I knew, and this time did not look away.

'Pavit is . . .?'

'Yes. He's been cremated, in Hindu fashion, the way he would have wished. He was never a true convert,' I said, wanting to hurt my father. He looked back at the tablets. 'And now I must speak, Father,' I told him. 'Of what . . . of you and . . . her,' I said, unable to utter Glory's name.

The patch of rosacea on his forehead stood out, angry and red as if he were branded. I thought at that instant it was a pity it was not in the shape of an A, such as Hester Prynne's, as would have been fitting.

A feeling – was it hatred? – surged through me as I looked at him. Everything was changing – my mother going mad, Pavit dead, and now . . . now this. My father sharing himself with dirty, mean-spirited, selfish and immoral Glory.

He was not the man I had thought him to be; he was one of small compass, I told myself. A charlatan.

Apart from the patch on his forehead, my father's face was waxen, drained of any colour. It had a faint sheen, the lustre of pearl but with no beauty. He wiped his hand over his lips. 'Water, Pree. Could you fetch me a tumbler of water?'

'Not now,' I said, angry that he would think to ask for a drink when what I faced him with was so important. 'Father, I have held my tongue this long and terrible day. But I cannot hold it any longer. I must speak of you and Glory.' There. I had said her name.

But once uttered out loud, the image came clear again: her nakedness, her fingers over his heart, the way he had held her as they slept, and I felt my face contort involuntarily, as if I had been slapped.

My father had the decency to drop his gaze. 'You don't understand, Pree,' he said, addressing his knees. 'You can't possibly—'

'I understand,' I interrupted. 'I know what I saw. I know what you and Glory do.'

Sweat ran from his hairline, down in front of his ear. 'Do not use such coarseness, Pree. It is not fitting for a daughter to speak so to her father.' He attempted to wipe away the sweat, but as he lifted his arm it suddenly came down heavily on the table, knocking over the bottle. White tablets scattered across the tabletop, on to the floor.

'Why not? You behave coarsely. Indecently.' My voice rose. 'Do you really believe you have the right, at this moment, to reprimand me?'

Unexpectedly he stood, although he stooped, slightly, as if protecting his upper body. He put his right hand on his left arm. 'I am your father, Pree. I tell you again, you may not speak in this way. Please. Please bring me some water. I . . . I am afraid I . . .'

I shook my head in annoyance. 'Father. Please don't act as though you're having one of your spells, simply to stop me. I won't be stopped. This is not something you can pretend hasn't happened.'

He turned to me then, with a look of confusion on his face. His open lips were chalky, the darkness behind them a wound. The hand that had been gripping his arm fell as if he were a marionette, the string suddenly dropped from the master's hand, and then, as if released entirely from the hands that controlled him, he crashed to the floor with a heavy thud.

Later, I asked myself if I could have been responsible, if it had been me who brought on the attack – one I accused him of fabricating to avoid my confrontation – which would be his final one. I tried to remember how he had appeared as I'd walked into the infirmary. Had he already been in pain? Would it have happened even if I weren't there? I wanted to comfort myself with the thought that it was not my fault, that I could not hold myself accountable for what happened.

If I had not goaded my father, I asked myself so many times after that, would my life have sunk to its eventual depths?

I had, of course, immediately gone to my knees beside him, touching his white, damp face, lifting his cold hand, the fingers limp and unresponsive.

'Father?' I cried, loosening his collar, undoing the buttons of his vest. 'Father.' I looked around the empty infirmary, as if expecting some unknown figure to come forward to help me. But of course there was no one. I left my father and ran to Kai's hut, calling his name. He emerged with his hair shorn. Like a dutiful Hindu son, he had cut his hair out of respect for Pavit.

'My father is ill,' I said. 'Please. Come and help me.'

Kai ran beside me into the infirmary, and, as easily as he had lifted the wrapped shell of Pavit's body, lifted my father and set him on the bed.

'Maybe it's my fault,' I said, crying now. 'I upset him and—'

But Kai interrupted me, his lips tight as he took off my father's jacket and tie, pulled off his boots and took the nightshirt from the end of the bed. 'Don't blame yourself,' he said. 'It's simply another attack. There's no direct cause.' He sounded strangely uncaring, and looked so different without his thick, curling hair, his eyes even larger, his face thinner. It was almost as though he were a stranger.

I turned away while he put my father into the nightshirt.

And then he left; I vaguely wondered whether he actually left the mission, or simply went back to this hut, and I sat by my father's bed. Eventually he opened his eyes, and I raised his head and put a cup of water to his lips. I had debated with myself over putting laudanum into it, but was unsure whether it might hurt his heart further, so chose not to.

He managed a few sips, and I bathed his face. When I knew he was sleeping, his breathing no longer so laboured, I stood, stretching out the stiffness from sitting so long in one position. I pulled a light cover over him, and leaving a candle burning in the fading light, walked down to the river.

Jassie lay curled in the pile of Pavit's remains, enjoying the lingering warmth. She raised her head and looked up at me. Then she slowly thumped her tail, once, twice, three times, and the ashes rose around her.

I returned to the infirmary and stayed with my father in the dark for the next hours, sometimes sitting on the floor beside the bed, sometimes on the stool with my head on my arms on the table. And then I heard light footsteps on the verandah, and the tinkle of bangles, and Glory came into the infirmary.

'What do you want?' I asked, whispering harshly.

'I will sit with him,' she said.

'No,' I said, although, truly, I was so weary I could

barely keep my eyes open. I knew it was long after midnight.

'For a few hours,' she said. 'Go and sleep.'

I was too tired to care any longer. I went back to the house and fell asleep, fully clothed, almost immediately.

When I awoke I lay still for a moment, my head aching dully. I glanced at the clock; I had slept for a full six hours and it was now after eight, so much later than usual. I was slightly shocked that I could have slept so deeply after the horror of it all: Pavit's death, the discovery of my father and Glory, Pavit's cremation, my father's illness.

Not bothering to change, I splashed water on my face and ran a comb through my unbraided hair. I glanced in my mother's room before I went to the infirmary; she lay still, obviously asleep.

As I crossed the courtyard I saw Kai milking Marta; he was still here, then. A man holding a small boy with his wrist in a make-shift sling sat on the infirmary steps. The door behind him was open.

'We can't help you today,' I told him. 'I'm sorry.'

He nodded and, carrying the child, left.

I stood in the doorway of the infirmary. The curtain wasn't pulled across the end wall, and Glory lay, in full view, on the bed beside my father, holding his hand. Had the villager seen this?

I was infuriated anew.

'Glory,' I said, in a low voice, 'leave my father now.'

'Your father wants me here. Don't you, Samuel?' she said, not even bothering to call him Reverend. By the way the name slipped so easily from her lips I knew it was not unfamiliar for her to do this.

And to distress me further, my father weakly murmured. 'Yes. Let her stay, Pree. She brings me comfort. Would you deny a dying man comfort?'

His words made me more uncomfortable, although I don't

268

know if I felt anger or sorrow. Was he dying? Or was this a further plea for understanding, wanting me to accept what he had with Glory? I came inside, shutting the door and closing the shutters halfway, so that the room was shadowed in striped gloom. I didn't want any other villagers witnessing this spectacle.

Standing at the side of the bed, I crossed my arms over my chest, looking down at my father. That he would die hadn't occurred to me. He had been ill so often before, although, I knew now, never as seriously as this. But surely he was saying this for effect, to protect himself from my anger. 'She brings you comfort?' I asked in a soft voice. 'And who brings my mother comfort, Father? Who brings your *wife* comfort?'

Glory sat up, running her fingers through her long, loose hair, but stayed on the bed, sitting on its edge.

'Don't tell your mother, Pree. Don't tell her about this,' my father said.

I hated him for that, bringing me into all of this, asking me to lie, or at least to omit the truth. 'I don't think she could even understand it,' I said harshly, thinking of her, lying in her own filth, not even remembering my name some days.

'She was a good woman,' my father said, speaking slowly and taking deep breaths between sentences. 'I tried to love her. I did love her, once. In England. I loved her in England. But there were all those years between us, with only the contact of letters twice a year. And then, when she finally was able to come to India she had changed, surely from the strain of dealing with Elijah's illness and eventual death while so alone. She was no longer the woman I had married.'

I leaned against the table. Let him make his excuses.

'She became more and more hardened. And it seemed she blamed me for everything. The deaths of the children. My inability to convert the heathens. And then, for these last years, I felt she even blamed me for her own . . . for her illness.'

I wanted to hate him, wanted to scratch his face, to shout that he was evil, deceitful, that I couldn't understand how he'd done what he did. But at that moment I couldn't hate him. I knew he had, in his own way, tried to be understanding of my mother. But she made it so difficult for anyone to love her.

And I had been there when she'd cast him from her bed. I knew he had been lonely. That wasn't a reason for adultery; there couldn't be a reason if one was strong, I told myself, believing, at seventeen, that I knew enough about the world to make this judgement.

But I also knew Glory, so willing, so flirtatious. I reasoned that if my mother hadn't put him aside maybe he wouldn't have fallen for Glory's charms. I believed completely that this wickedness had only occurred in the last few months.

'But, Father,' I said. 'The Bible says that even thinking about adultery is a sin. Matthew 5: verse 28: "*That whosoever looketh on a woman to lust after hath committed adultery with her already in his heart*." But for what you've done . . . Do you not believe you will burn in Satan's grip?'

My father's eyes closed. 'I surely will, Pree. For all my wickedness I will surely never meet my Lord. I have accepted this. "*Every man shall be put to death for his own sin*." I am as one already dead. I know this, Pree.'

Footsteps dragged up the verandah stairs. I opened the door to tell whoever had come seeking medical help that they must return another day. But when I pulled back the wooden door, it wasn't a native.

'Mother,' I said, with dull surprise, glancing behind me to where Glory still sat on the edge of my father's bed. I moved into the doorway, hoping to block her view as my father had tried to block me from seeing Glory only two nights earlier.

'You shouldn't be out of bed in your nightdress and bare feet. Let me take you back to the house.' I tried to step out and close the door behind me, but my mother shoved me aside with unexpected strength.

'What's happened?' she said, and her eyes were clear. I knew then she had a glimmer of comprehension today, that it was one of the days when she awoke and could make sense of things. Why now? Couldn't she have remained in her bed for one more day, until my father was better, until we could pretend that everything was as it had always been?

'What are you doing here, with the Reverend?' my mother said, coming into the infirmary, walking unsteadily and yet directly to the bed and Glory.

I expected Glory to rise, to make some excuse. But she didn't. She stayed where she was, smiling almost sweetly at my mother. Then she reached out and put her hand on my father's.

'Your husband is needing very much a woman to care for him,' she said in English. 'You are no longer good for this. Not for so long time. Maybe never, Mem Fin.' She was still smiling.

My father closed his eyes.

'So I am doing caring for him,' Glory said. 'I am always caring for Samuel, as he wishes.' Her words, combined with her smile, made her meaning perfectly clear.

And my mother understood. I could see it in her face. She just stood there, looking from Glory to my father, saliva running from one side of her mouth. She slurped, wiping the back of her hand across her lips. 'How long has this gone on, Samuel?' she finally asked, in a strangely accepting tone.

I stepped forward. 'Mother, come away. Don't upset yourself further with—'

She shook off my hand as if I were a bothersome fly. 'How

long, Samuel?' she asked, in that same, straightforward manner.

My father didn't open his eyes. He was afraid, I knew, weak and afraid.

But Glory was neither of these. 'I am already telling you. For always. Since before you are coming,' she said.

I stared at her. Outside Sanosh chopped something. I counted the thunk of the knife on wood five times before my mother spoke.

'Before I came where?' she asked, slowly, as if not sure of the language.

'Before you are coming to India,' Glory said. 'Always it has been this way between us, between Samuel and me.'

Children shouted to each other, passing on the road.

'I gave him a son,' Glory said, casually. Callously.

A son?

'A son?' my mother repeated dully.

My father moaned, moving his head from side to side on the flattened pillow. 'No, Glory. Stop. Don't.'

'It is time,' Glory said. 'Always, always she is thinking she is big lady with me. Always she is being *burra* memsahib, looking at me like I am dung beetle. But no more. Now she will know.' She stood and walked the few steps to stand in front of my mother. 'I gave him living son while son you made died,' she said, their faces only inches apart.

'When my son died? Gabriel?'

Glory smiled more broadly, but her lips were cracked and dry. 'Son in England. First son.'

My mother swayed. I saw the matted state of her hair; I could make out the odour of her oily, unwashed flesh. Her nightdress was shamefully stained. I put my hand on her arm.

'My children don't die. My children strong. You – you,' Glory said, with venom, 'can't give him living child.'

I was trying to understand it all. Glory had had a son, all

272

those years ago. Of course my mother had given him a living child. I was proof. I was not a son, but ... I let go of my mother's arm and leaned back against the table again, staring at my father.

From somewhere my mother found a new energy. 'Shut your mouth, Glory,' she said. 'Shut it now. Say nothing more. You're a liar and a dirty whore.'

It was all too much. Glory's loud statements, my mother speaking in such an unfamiliar way, my father neither agreeing nor denying.

Someone said, 'Kai? Is it Kai? Are you Kai's father?' It was my voice.

My father put his arm over his eyes in the darkened corner. I could see us all as if I hung from the ceiling on a giant web: my mother, shaking and gaunt, her large reddened hand gripping the table; Glory, looking at her with that pleased, cunning smile; my father, cowed, hiding his face, and me, standing with my mouth open and arms hanging limply at my sides.

If what Glory said was true, my father had lain with her when she was little more than a child, twelve or thirteen years old. A sour taste flooded my mouth. I swallowed it; it burned my throat. Could it be? Could my father be Kai's father? 'Mother? Can she really speak the truth?' I asked. She didn't answer; her face was losing the clarity that had been there only moments ago.

I had sudden flashes of memory. The way Kai had faced my father when he was belittled by the Langs, asking my father if he would speak up. My mother telling me how my father had treated Kai as a son when Glory abandoned him, how he'd shown a tenderness – perhaps love – towards the child Kai. And how my father always allowed Glory back to the mission, no matter how long she'd been gone, no matter what she'd done.

I knew, then, that what Glory said could indeed be true.

And that meant that Kai was my half-brother. I thought of the warm firmness of his lips on mine, the way they lingered for just a second too long, and then how he put his hands on my arms, stopping me. The way he stepped back, an unreadable expression on his face.

'Does he know?' I asked her, my voice too high, strangled. 'Does Kai know, Glory? Does he know who his father is?'

Glory looked from my mother to me. Finally she stopped smiling. 'Oh, yes, my son knows,' she said. 'Of course. He knows this always. From small boy time he knows,' she said.

I closed my mouth; my breath came through my nose in short, hard bursts. I looked at the floor, at the toes of my boots. Then I looked at my mother. She was slumped against the table, her expression troubled and confused, as if she had been lifted from all that was familiar and set down in a strange land, with people she had never before seen.

But then she moved in a fitful, sluggish way, in the way of one awakened from a deep dream. She jerked upright as if pulled by a fishhook in her skull, and straightened her shoulders. She watched her own hand as it reached out and closed around Glory's wrist, gripping it so tightly that her knobbed knuckles stood white. Glory looked down in surprise, wincing at the obvious pressure.

I know that it would have been an easy feat for Glory to rip her wrist from my mother's grasp; she was so weak after all this time in bed. But I think Glory was as astonished as I was. My mother then shook Glory's wrist as if she were a terrier with a rat in its jaws, and stumbled towards the bed, dragging Glory with her.

My father had lowered his arm; his breathing came hard, rasping in his chest. One thin hand rested on the coverlet. His fingernails had a purple hue.

'Samuel,' my mother said. 'Samuel, sit up.'

My father's eyelids fluttered, and with great effort he rose first on his elbow, and then managed to prop himself against the wall.

'Is Kai your son?' my mother demanded. 'Did you father Kai with Glory? Did you dirty yourself with this whore while I was trying to keep our son alive in England?'

My father's eyes closed again, but my mother wouldn't stop. She dropped Glory's wrist and with a dull thud fell to her knees at the side of the bed. She usually moved with such stiffness, and I assumed her joints had seized; this sudden movement was surprising.

Her face was inches from my father's, and I could only guess at the stench from her mouth as she breathed into his. 'Samuel,' she said again, now shaking his arm, roughly, as she had just shaken Glory.

A flicker – pain, distress, or, I thought, more likely fear – crossed my father's face. And then his head slumped to one side, his eyes rolling away from my mother, and up at Glory.

'Answer me. With your dying breath, Samuel, you will speak the truth,' my mother said, her voice little more than a low growl. 'You will not die without speaking the truth. Is Kai your son?'

His eyes went back to my mother, and his lips attempted to open, although a thick, gluey substance at the corners made it difficult. Finally he was able to whisper. Just one word, the word I knew, with certainty, I would hear.

'Yes,' he said. His lips and his eyes closed again.

My mother sat back on her heels. She looked at Glory. I did as well. In spite of her chin's weakness, somehow Glory gave the impression of lifting it. In triumph? A new look, one of superiority, was now in her eyes as she looked down at my mother on her knees.

'I held him, like so,' Glory said, putting out her hand, palm upward. 'Always. While you' — she shook her head — 'held only air.'

'If you held him, it was because he was weak. He's blameless,' my mother said, slowly, and I stared at her. Did she really believe this? 'Women like you are capable of trapping an innocent man with lascivious behaviour. Even a good man can be poisoned by these sorceresses,' she said, her voice now a shaky whisper. 'Look at Jezebel,' she murmured, her eyelids strangely heavy, as if she were on the verge of sleep. 'Witness the wife of Potiphar. Witness Delilah. Witness . . .' Her voice trailed off, and she lowered herself to the floor beside the bed, her arm outstretched and her head resting on it, although her eyes remained open.

But still Glory wasn't finished, although now she switched to Hindi. 'He loved me. He begged me to come away with him, many times, to leave the mission and you,' she said to my mother, who lay unmoving.

And leave me? Would my father leave me so easily?

'He made many plans, as he lay beside me, trying to convince me. He made the plans, over and over, but I would not do it.' She looked at my father again. 'And do you know why? You are right, Mem. He is weak. Always too weak for me. I need a man with strength in his arms and in his head. He' — she now clicked her fingers at my father — 'was of no use for anything. Except for pleasing me in the ways of a man when I had no one else.' She smiled again. 'He took me my first time, when I was a girl, hired to help at the mission in Allahabad. And I thought this is how it was. But then, when I had another Englishman, a man strong and exciting, who showed me what it could be, I knew I had wasted myself with Samuel. He was too weak in all ways, in his body and also his thoughts.'

She stopped, her face unreadable as she now looked at the shutters. Who was she telling this story to? My mother

276

appeared to be comatose; my father lay near unconsciousness.

'But I always allowed him to come to my bed. Because it made my life simple, because I was bored,' she said.

I was sickened at her words. I couldn't bear to listen any more, to be in this room with the poison swirling around us. It was difficult to breathe.

'Out of boredom,' she repeated, touching my mother's still body with her bare foot. She wore a sparkling ring on her second toe. I watched it press against my mother's hip.

'Leave her alone,' I cried, rushing at Glory, her boldness breaking my stunned inertia. I pushed Glory, hard, and she stumbled against the bed. It shook, and my father's body moved slightly, but he didn't open his eyes.

'Leave us all alone. Go away. I hate you. I hate you,' I said, the last words rising to a near shout.

Glory looked at me, that same small smile returning to her mouth. Then she looked at my father. 'I planned to go,' she said, 'after I spoke my truth. Goodbye, Samuel,' she said. 'You are no good to me now.'

I saw the tiniest flicker of my father's eyelids, and the left side of his bottom lip tugged downward. He heard her, and understood. When she turned away from him, in my direction, I slapped her cheek, as hard as I could. The blow left my palm stinging, and immediately her cheek reddened, but again, Glory looked at me in that same insolent manner.

I knew that nothing would touch Glory. In that moment I saw how she had played us all, had tricked and deceived not only my mother, but also, in a different way, my father. She had no heart. She didn't care about him, just as she didn't care about Kai or the baby daughter she'd abandoned. She cared only for herself. I'd always known this, but I hadn't realised the depth of her self-absorption.

'Get away from us all. Leave,' I tried to shout, but my voice had lost its strength now, much as my mother had lost whatever brief energy she had dug from deep inside herself. Now she lay on the floor beside the bed, her eyes still wide, staring blankly, a trickle of rust-coloured saliva running from the corner of her mouth.

I was the only one left, the only Fincastle with a voice.

Glory turned, and without a backward glance, walked from the room.

CHAPTER TWENTY-TWO

I STAYED WHERE I was for the next little while; I lost all track of time, sitting there on the stool at the table, my mother's inert body on the floor, my father's in the bed.

Finally I stood. My legs were unsteady. I went to the courtyard, past Sanosh, who looked at me and opened his mouth as if to speak, but then closed it again. I went to Kai's hut. He wasn't there, but his bag lay on the charpoy.

I looked for him in the fields, and then at the river. It was there I found him, sitting on the ground beside Pavit's pyre of grey ashes. He stood when he saw me.

'How's your father this morning?' he asked, in his usual voice.

I couldn't speak for a moment. 'Do you know nothing of what's gone on?' I asked then, fury growing in me at his ordinary demeanour.

'What do you mean? I slept last night, and this morning came here, to say my last prayers for Pavit. I'm about to leave. Is it your father? Is he worse?'

I stepped up to him and slapped him, hard, across his cheek, as I'd slapped his mother.

He stepped back, shocked, his hand on his cheek. 'Pree,' he cried, his voice and eyes alarmed. 'What's wrong? What's happened?'

'You're . . . all this time. You knew. You knew my father

was . . . he's your father. All this time,' I repeated, crying now, 'you knew, and you didn't say anything. About Glory and my father.' *About you and me.*

All colour save for the dull red imprint of my fingers drained from his face.

'Glory told us. My mother and me. She told us, and my father admitted it. It's too horrible. Too horrible, Kai.' I covered my face with my hands, weeping. I felt his touch on my shoulder and jerked away, lowering my hands.

'How could you? How could you not have said anything to me? How could you let me live my whole life, not knowing? How, Kai?'

He just stood there.

'Well? Answer me,' I shouted.

'What would you have done about it, Pree?' he asked then, in a quiet voice. 'What good would this unhappy knowledge of the Reverend being my father bring? And think of your mother. Would you have wanted her to know?'

I was breathing heavily, although no longer crying.

'But you're . . . you're my *brother*,' I said.

He turned then, and as he walked away from me, I called after him, 'Are you just going, then? Just leaving, leaving me to deal with it all?'

He didn't look back.

'I hate you!' I shouted. 'I hate you!' Again, I was treating him exactly as I'd treated his mother. Suddenly I thought he might be more like her than I'd ever dreamed. 'You're a coward. I'm glad I didn't know you were my brother. I would never want such a coward for a brother.'

I was weeping anew. My voice was high and shrewish. I watched Kai's back, his close-cropped head, his long neck.

I didn't hate him; I could never hate him. That was what made all of this so much more difficult. And of course he wasn't a coward in any way.

The only truth in all of this was that he was my half-brother.

Nothing had changed in the infirmary when I finally returned, stumbling through the field, trying to make sense of all that had happened. My head ached from weeping; my throat was raw from shouting at first Glory and then Kai.

I pulled my mother from her stupor, dragging her out of the infirmary, and Sanosh ran to help me get her into her room. Then I went back to check on my father; I spoke to him and tried to rouse him. I lifted his head and held a cup of water to his lips, but he didn't have the strength to drink; not a muscle of his face indicated that he felt my ministerings.

I turned at a rustle behind me. Glory stood in the doorway, a bulging carpetbag on either side of her. She was dressed in her finest frock, although her hair was unbraided and hung to her waist in a thick curtain.

She bent over my father and ran her fingertips along his cheek. At her touch he opened his eyes, and this pained me deeply. He had not been able to find the strength within himself to acknowledge me, and yet with the tiny pressure of Glory's fingers he pulled himself back from whatever distant place he had been hovering.

'Samuel,' she said. 'Samuel, I go now.' She leaned further over him so that her hair, black as a crow's wing, spread across his chest. He slowly lifted one hand – what effort it must have taken – and put it on that silky length.

'I have always loved you,' he whispered. 'Always.'

He seemed unaware of my presence, even though I stood beside Glory. Perhaps he just didn't care. The pounding in my head grew even more painful. I moved to the shadows at the foot of the bed.

She didn't respond to his declaration of love.

'When I am gone —' he murmured, and stopped. 'When I am gone,' he said again, now weakly taking her hand in his, 'tell me you will not speak of the girl. Promise me.'

Glory glanced at me.

'Promise me, Glory. Before I die, you must promise.'

'Yes, yes. I do not speak of it, Samuel.'

The girl. Adriana? Could this be? In spite of Glory making it appear that Mr Evans had fathered Adriana – and I remember thinking it might have been the soldier – had it, in actuality, once again been my father? She had already been with child when she left the mission. Of course.

And so, like Kai, Adriana was part of me. She was my little sister.

My head threatened to explode. There was too much pain, constant new pain. The disclosure about Kai, and now this. My father hadn't even been strong enough to prevent Glory from giving away – or selling – his own flesh and blood, *my* flesh and blood. I was stung, sharp needles all over my body. How could he have stood by and allowed this to happen? Who was this man who spouted Bible verses about goodness and mercy, about the precious nature of little children, the lambs of God?

I stayed where I was. I wanted my father to look in my direction, to ask for me. I wanted him to apologise to me, apologise for allowing me to see him for what he truly was. For destroying all my beliefs about him, for the disillusion of this virtuous existence he'd pretended to have while in India.

For the sickening fact that I was the daughter of not only the ruin my mother had become, but of a man who had lived so much of his life as a lie. Who could allow his illegitimate children's lives to be dictated by a woman incapable of love.

As I continued to stare at him, I knew that while I wished he would ask for my forgiveness, in reality there was only one thing I wanted him to say. All I wanted him to say, as he had said to Glory, was *I love you. I love you, Pree. In spite of the dreadful, unthinkable muddle I have made of our lives, I have always loved you.*

But he didn't. What he said, his voice growing stronger as if finding some hidden reserve of strength, was, 'My beautiful, beautiful girl.'

At that the pain in my head receded, just the slightest, and my heart lifted, filling as though with the very atmosphere, for here, now, he would read my thoughts and say what I wanted to hear. I was his girl. I took a step out of the shadows, ready to put my arms around him, but at that moment his eyes fixed on Glory's face. Not mine.

'I'll never forget the first time I saw you, when you were just a beautiful girl. And because of you I've known what it truly means to love. I've loved you from the day I first saw you.'

I didn't want to hear this, didn't want him to speak of love so openly to Glory, Glory, with her dirty ways, her low character. Her lack of morals, her carelessness as a mother. How could he still love her? She'd made it so clear she'd only used him, and never loved him. Did he not remember – or perhaps understand – her tirade in Hindi, only hours earlier?

'I know, Samuel,' Glory said. She paused. 'You have some rupees?'

A sound – outrage – burst from my throat, and for the first time, my father looked at me.

'I go far, Samuel. I need rupees.'

My father looked away from me, and then shook his head. 'There is no money, Glory,' he said, and I don't know whether he told the truth, or whether he had suddenly realised that I was in the room, watching and listening. 'I'm sorry,' he breathed, shutting his eyes, and at that Glory let go of his hand, putting it on his chest.

And then she left.

I stayed where I was for a long time. I don't know how much time passed, but suddenly I realised my father was very still. I wondered, almost idly, if he had died. I went to him and put my fingers against his neck. Nothing. Then I put them on the underside of his wrist. Here I felt the tiniest pulse, as if the movement of a sleeping ladybird.

He was still alive, then.

I was suddenly aware of my own body: I was thirsty, and needed to use the convenience. Leaving my father, I first went to the convenience, and then to the well, where I drank two cups of water. Glory and Kai were gone. Pavit was dead; my father lay near to death. I looked at the house; what of my mother? I wandered, as if in a strange twilight, to the verandah. I heard movement behind me; it was Sanosh.

'The Reverend . . .?' he enquired.

'He still lives.' My voice was like dry leaves. 'Could you make tea, please, and bring it to the house?' I asked him, and he silently bowed his head and backed away.

When he brought it I drank the steaming liquid as if it were a magic potion, one that would make the world clear, would show me understanding. It scalded my tongue, my throat, and I held on to this pain, for it gave me something to think about, something other than everything that had occurred.

When I finished the second cup I poured another and took it to my mother's room. It was dark, the shutters were closed, and it smelled of urine. She lay on her side; I opened the shutters and sat on the edge of the bed.

'Tea, Mother,' I said, and she pushed herself up. I held the cup to her lips as I had to my father's. She drank like an obedient child, and then lay down again. Ignoring the wetness of the bedclothes, I simply drew the coverlet over her. Then I went to my own room. I couldn't bear to go back to the infirmary; I needed to shut my eyes.

I had just drifted into an uneasy sleep when I heard my mother's voice, shrieking. I jumped up and ran through the front door, following the sound of her voice. There she was, resembling a madwoman in her filthy nightdress, her hair a scrambled nest, walking up and down the length of the verandah. She waved her arms and screamed, shouting about the Reverend lying with Glory, about Kai being his ill-begotten son, about the devil having claimed the mission as his own, that here was the fire and brimstone of hell. 'I come not to call the righteous, but sinners to repentance,' she shouted. 'For this mission is truly Gethsemane, where betrayal is the only truth.'

People on the road – those walking, those on donkeys or horses, those leading camels by their braided ropes, those sitting in carts pulled by oxen – had all stopped, and were watching my mother. How many of them could understand English, could understand her screeching proclamations?

Please, I thought, as I grabbed her arm, please don't let them comprehend what she's shouting. But even as the thought formed in my head, I knew with certainty that someone – it would only take one person – would under-stand, and would translate – into Hindi, into Punjabi, into Urdu, into any of the other languages of India. The story would cross and criss-cross, its edges overlapping, and everyone would know. I could imagine the expressions on their faces; the disgust and wonder – *these crazy anglos, crazy, no pride, all their talk of their God, and how we must behave.*

I shook her, striking her once on the shoulder to try to draw her attention to me, to stop her banshee screaming. As I dragged her – she had found a shocking, mad strength – through the door, I was aware of murmuring. It was a low, underwater sound from the road, a swelling like the Ravi in the monsoon, and I knew with certainty that what my mother was screeching at the top of her lungs would be the conversation in all the villages along the sides of the road by nightfall, and by tomorrow it would be common knowledge on the Grand Trunk, and then into Lahore, and perhaps even further.

Once inside, I tried to put my hands over my mother's mouth. She pushed them away. But eventually, her voice raw, her screams stopped. She still mumbled and whispered, but was exhausted, and lay on her bed in a deep stupor.

For the rest of the day I went back and forth, between the house and the infirmary, between my mother and my father. I was stretched like a strip of India rubber, pulled and twisted to such thinness that I knew I would soon rip in two.

Darkness fell and I closed the shutters in the infirmary against the night air, lighting a candle. When it burned down I lit another, simply sitting on the stool, watching my father.

At one point, by the stiffness of his features, I imagined his spirit had left his body. I went to him and placed my fingers on his wrist, trying to feel the pulse of his blood. But my fingertips were calloused, and I couldn't tell whether I actually felt movement within his narrow wrist, as I had earlier, or whether I just imagined it. And so I held the lit candle in front of his slightly open mouth, and only by the sway of the thin, bluish flame, little more than the tiniest rhythmic flicker, did I know he still breathed. He didn't move nor open his eyes during that long night.

As the first glow of light poked long fingers through the cracks in the shutters, I rose and opened them, flooding the infirmary with brightness. Even though the air was warm, I was cold, and let out an involuntary, audible shudder, my back to my father. And in the next instant I heard a similar sound from the bed.

I turned; my father's eyes were open. 'Father?' I whispered, for it was as if too loud a voice would disturb this moment, might make his eyelids lower once more.

He blinked, once, heavily and slowly, and I moved so that I was in his line of vision. 'Father? I'm here,' I said, kneeling beside his bed. I wanted him to say something, to tell me something, something I could remember, could carry with me, always. I wanted him to somehow erase the horror of these last few days, of his last words, to tell me it had all been a lie, of course it had been a lie, that he wasn't capable of such deceit, such behaviour. That he loved me too much, even if he didn't love my mother, he loved me, and would never have done something to confuse me, to haunt me throughout the rest of my life. That he was still the same father who came to my room when I cried out in the middle of a thunderstorm as a child, and sat with me until the worst had passed, the same father who allowed Sanosh to slip me illicit sweets, the same father whose face showed sorrow when he could offer nothing but lisle stockings as a birthday gift.

But he didn't speak. Instead, a long, rattling gasp came from his lungs, from somewhere deep, deep inside. The horrible sound rose, and then there was another, hollow echo of the first, and then . . . nothing. Silence. I took up the candle, now little more than a feeble flame in a pool of tallow, and held it in front of my father's mouth.

It blew out, extinguished so suddenly and sharply that I cried out in surprise, jerking so that a splash of molten wax fell on to my father's cheek, just beside his nose. His eyes were still open, but now fixed. I knew the look; I had seen it before, on Lalasa, and on Pavit, only . . . could it only have been two days since Kai and Sanosh and I had cremated Pavit?

It felt as though months, years perhaps, had passed in these few days.

The dawn draught from the open window breathed on my bare neck, and I knew then that it had only been this that had killed the flame.

I sat back on my heels. 'My father is dead,' I said, aloud, as if by speaking those words I would know it to be true. 'My father is dead,' I repeated, looking at him, the teardrop of wax now hardened on his unmoving face.

I told my mother. 'Father's gone,' I said, unable to utter the words *dead* or *died* to her. I could say them to an empty room, but not to her.

She stared at me.

'Do you understand? Father . . . is gone to the Lord,' I said, knowing this, too, was a lie. Surely he was firmly in the clawed grip of Beelzebub. I shook my head, wanting to remove this image from my head.

'Oh?' my mother said, in a small, surprised voice, the tone she might have used, when she was still in her right mind, if I had told her the apricots were ripe, or that Sanosh had made a chicken biryani for dinner instead of the usual chicken stew.

'Can you understand, Mother? Father . . .' I had to say it. She had to show some reaction. I had been too cautious. 'Father is dead. He died,' I said, more loudly than necessary.

She nodded. 'I understand,' she said, and this shocked me. She understood, but had no reaction.

I studied her face. There was no expression. Did she feel as I did, lost, confused, unable to sort out the interwoven emotions of anger and sorrow? Or did she feel nothing? When she had slipped, finally, into true madness, had she lost not only her senses, but her ability to feel? Already it was clear that this was the case physically: she didn't appear to have hunger or thirst, feel heat or cold, and her body voided itself without her knowledge.

'What . . .' I was about to ask her what I should do, what

we would do, but before that first word was out of my mouth I knew she would have no answer. She would never again have any answers.

I went out to the *rasoi*. 'Reverend Fincastle has died,' I told Sanosh, my voice firm and my eyes dry. 'My mother and I will remain here. Will you stay, and continue to cook for us, Sanosh? I . . . I will somehow find the money to pay you. The Church will provide for us, I'm sure, until we know what we'll do next.'

He nodded, tears running down his withered cheeks. He was a faithful servant who genuinely cared about our family. I didn't think he would simply walk away, even though he now knew the whole sordid story. 'I weep for your father's soul,' he told me. 'What will become of it? It will be so low on the wheel.'

I had no heart to argue with Sanosh, to remind him this would not happen in my father's afterlife. My father would have no chance of rebirth, even as a reptile. He had made his choice, and for this would burn eternally.

'I shall fetch the *sudras*?' Sanosh asked. 'To clean his body?'

Already − so newly dead − my father was no longer referred to as a person, but a body. 'No. I'll do it. But could you please request them to dig a . . . a hole. In the graveyard,' I said, turning to look at that small fenced plot. 'With his children,' I added, unnecessarily. 'We will bury him there.'

Sanosh nodded.

'I would like him to have a coffin,' I said, using the English word. There was no Indian word I knew of for coffin: the Hindus and Sikhs cremated their dead, the Muslims buried them in a shroud, the Parsees left the body for the vultures.

Sanosh stared at me.

'A box. To put him into, when he goes in the ground.'

But Sanosh shook his head. 'Not for my business, Missy Pree,' he said, switching to English, as if the foreignness of a coffin forced him to speak in the language not his own. 'Not good. No Hindu, Muslim, no one make box for dead.'

If Kai were here, I suddenly and unexpectedly thought, Kai would make a coffin. Kai would know what to do. I blinked at the realisation that it wasn't only my father who had died. It was Kai's father as well. Would he hear about it? Where was he?

Sanosh was waiting for me to instruct him on what to do. That this was my role now.

'I have made the porridge,' he said, gesturing in a slightly confused way, at the pot sitting to one side of the fire. *Who will eat the porridge now?* he seemed to say.

I looked down into the pot of congealing oatmeal. And suddenly the enormity of my father's death came upon me with full force.

I hadn't wept when I looked down upon him as his spirit left his body. I hadn't wept when I forced my mother to understand the fact that he was gone. I hadn't even wept when I discussed his body and burial with Sanosh.

It was the porridge which created that first rush of deep sorrow, and it unexpectedly rose within me in one swift movement, bursting out in a choking sob. I stood beside Sarosh, looking down into the pot of oatmeal, crying.

'As you say, Missy, as you say,' Sanosh told me then, his voice sorrowful, and his sympathy further fuelled my tears. 'I will summon the *sudras* to dig a hole. Beside the children.'

I nodded, turning from Sanosh and running back into the infirmary. I knelt beside my father's body, weeping quietly, my arm over him, my head on his chest in a final embrace.

No matter what he'd done, how he'd betrayed us all and sinned, he was my father.

CHAPTER TWENTY-THREE

S OMETHING STRANGE CAME over me for the next two days, a frightening, intense energy that didn't allow me to sleep. There was so much to do.

My mother had risen from her bed, mumbling confused prayers and wandering around in the courtyard. I had to bring her into the house twice. I had no time to attend to her; she was still in her soiled nightdress, stumbling about barefoot as if blind, and I hated that she was seen in this way by those on the road. I knew I should care for her, bathe her and try to get her to eat, but I had to look after my father.

He still lay in his bed, wearing the nightshirt he had died in, his clothing on the floor where Kai had left it when he undressed him. There was no choice; he would have to be buried in the dark wool suit. But it was spotted and smelled strongly of perspiration. I didn't want to put him to rest in it; it was somehow disrespectful and hurtful to him, even though of course it was not he who was aware of it, but I.

I used the naphtha for the lamps to try to clean the jacket, dabbing at the stains, hating the gassy reek burning my nostrils as the oil soaked into the wool, mingling with the smells of my father's body. Although when I was finished the suit looked more presentable, I tried to mask the odour – which I would for evermore associate with death – with the attar of roses from my mother's carpetbag. But the two strong smells mingled in a cloying, suffocating way. I despaired at the idea of my father going into the ground smelling so falsely. For one mad moment I imagined dressing him in a blinding white *kurta* and dhoti, starched, pressed, smelling of air and sun.

I thought of Kai again.

I had Sanosh heat water, and, with a hard square of tallow soap, gently washed my father's face and neck. I pushed up his sleeves and washed his arms and hands. I washed his feet. I dampened his hair and combed it neatly, the teeth of the comb leaving their marks in the thinning hair. I shaved him.

I couldn't bear to see his nakedness; staring at his still face, I struggled and worked the nightshirt up and over his head, having to drag his arms — so thin and yet so heavy now — out of the sleeves. And then, in one swift movement, I simply pulled the white sheet he lay on around his naked body.

I combed his hair again; it had been ruffled by the nightshirt.

I looked behind me, at the stinking suit laid out on the infirmary table, and then threaded a needle with thick cotton. I leaned over my father and stitched the sheet closed, from his bare feet — those long, pale toes — to the top of his head. It was better that he should be put into the ground like this, I told myself, clean at least in body. Naked as he had been born. Before I completed the final stitches to close the sheet over his face, I gently placed my fingertips on his forehead. Without the blood coursing through him, the damaged skin there no longer stood scarlet; now it was simply a roughened patch of flesh, as devoid of colour as the rest of his face.

After he was sewn into his winding sheet I felt calmer. It was as if he could rest now, could sleep, finally.

And perhaps I could, as well.

The noise in my ears abated. Darkness covered the mission as the shroud covered my father. I took the suit to the courtyard and burned it. There was a full, bright moon. I watched the sparks shooting upwards, clean and strong.

Then I wandered about the house, still restless; my feet needed to walk. I lit a lantern and went to the edge of the Ravi, remembering my childhood here; how Kai had taught me to skip stones, how he had pointed out the teal-headed ducks with their tails in the air, bobbing for plant life, how he laughed at me when I asked for an anna to throw into the water, for Lalasa had told me the legend that anyone throwing money into the Ravi will receive back ten thousand times the amount. He had laughed, but the next day had given me an anna, and stood beside me, his face serious, watching as I drew back my arm and threw the coin with all my strength, my lips moving in a small plea. And then he had smiled, and said – strange that I suddenly recalled his words after these years, when I hadn't thought of that moment for so long – *even if the fortune you wish for is not to be, Pree, surely some reward will come from your determination.*

Where was Kai now, when I needed him more than ever before?

Still watching the slow-moving Ravi, I pushed away the thoughts of my attempted baptism there, and the frightening stranger's face my father had worn that day. I made myself think of Kai again, but now I couldn't recapture the good memories. Instead, all I could think about was that Kai was my half-brother, had been my half-brother all these years, and I had never known.

My father had committed adultery. My mother had gone mad, and now blasphemed. Even Kai had committed the sin of omission; he had known – always – that I was connected to him by blood, but had never told me. Had never spoken the truth. He had kissed me, knowing he was my half-brother. He and I were more evil than my father and Glory – was not incest worse than adultery?

We were all sinners. The mission was indeed a place of sin, as my mother had proclaimed.

I spent much of the night there, sitting beside the Ravi, not wanting to return to the mission. It was clean there, by the water, the air fresh and undisturbed. But eventually the sky lightened and the first morning sounds began – the sleepy twitter of birds, the distant lowing of an ox, a faint voice calling from somewhere down the river. I slowly went back to the house, knowing I had to prepare for the next few days. There was little time to dally; with the warmth of the late spring my father's body would soon begin to rot. It was up to me to decide on the funeral ceremony. It would be a tiny, sad event, but it would be my final goodbye to my father, and I wanted it to feel proper.

But I had great difficulty planning the passages I would read. Most of what I might have so easily chosen now rang with hypocrisy. Throughout that day I sat at the dining-room table, flipping through page after page of my white moiré Bible, through verse after verse. Shadows grew; feeling more and more agitated, I lit the lamp, trying to find exactly the right scriptures.

I was vaguely aware of Sanosh creeping in and out the side door; I heard the clink of a spoon on a tin plate, heard his murmur to my mother. At one point he set food beside me; I looked at the chicken masala as if it would speak to me, but had no appetite and left it untouched.

Twice I had to relight the lamp when the wick burned low. I wouldn't go to bed until I found the right words for my father's funeral. But the further I searched the more distressed I became, and finally I wept in frustration and, I suppose, exhaustion, lying my cheek on my open Bible. The lamplight dimmed in the morning brightness, and still I wept on to the thin page. But the tears seemed to belong to someone else. I didn't feel anything at that moment – neither sorrow nor anger. Not even hunger or weariness. My thoughts raced as I cried, silently; I couldn't seem to sort things out properly. I only knew that today the *sudra*s would come to dig the grave, and tomorrow my father would be lowered into it.

Since my mother had shrilly shouted out the sordid history of what had gone on at the mission, about the Reverend Fincastle's indecent behaviour with our ayah, and that her bastard son was his, nobody had come to the infirmary seeking attention. It was a dull relief to be left alone. The infirmary doors were closed, hiding my father's body, and I couldn't imagine speaking to anyone of injury or illness with his still form so near.

For most of the day I simply wandered about the fields, not wanting to be present while the *sudra*s dug in the cemetery. As dusk fell I sat on the steps of the infirmary, and a huge weariness settled over me. Such was the need for sleep, finally, that with feet that felt as if they were made of the thick clay Pavit had used for making his rough idols, I slowly crossed the courtyard to the house.

Passing my mother's door, I stopped. She was sitting upright, bathed in the moonlight which shone through the window, and had taken on an even more frightening appearance. Her hair, unwashed and uncombed for so long, had, in the white yet shadowy light, the look of Medusa's reptilian horror. 'Mother,' I said, loudly. 'Lie down. Go to sleep. Tomorrow we will bury Father. I'll help you bathe in the morning.'

The thought of hauling water and heating it, scrubbing my mother from head to toe, dressing her in clean clothing and arranging her hair, and then having to put my father into that hole in the earth, wrapped only in his cotton shroud, was too much.

I turned from my mother's blank stare and lurched to my own room, sitting on the bed and managing to unlace my boots and pull my feet from them, but not having the energy to undress. The room was cool, but the distance across the floor to close the shutters against the night air appeared too far. I fell back, dragging my coverlet over my shoulders, thinking, for an instant, that with my own untended hair and clothing worn so many days, that I probably resembled my mother more, at this moment, than I ever had.

I sat straight up in bed. My room was oddly lit; I rubbed my hands over my face, trying to understand what caused the strange orange glow, brighter than sunlight. And then I heard Sanosh shouting, calling my name, and there were other noises, unidentifiable crashings and whooshings. I leapt from my bed, dizzy for the first seconds, the smell of smoke strong in my nostrils, and ran outside in my stockinged feet.

The infirmary was ablaze. I stood as if frozen on the verandah, mesmerised by the sight of the building crackling, flames shooting out of the windows. The dry wood of the verandah had caught, and fire trembled, tripping in a delicate dance along the top railing. The thatched roof was only smoking at this moment, but those flames reached longing arms towards the dry edges.

My father, his shroud in flames, his skin puckering and blackening, came in horrifying images. 'Father!' I shouted, 'no, Father!' The lucid part of my brain knew that his soul was already in hell, burning. He would be tortured by fire for evermore. And yet the idea of that part of him still left on earth – his physical body – being licked and caressed by burning tongues sickened me to such an extent that I leaned forward and gripped my abdomen as a sudden wretching spasm twisted my intestines. Then I ran across the courtyard, bent slightly, one hand gripping the front of my frock.

Sanosh was tossing sprays of water from a bucket hopelessly on to a wall of flames. 'What's happened?' I screamed, grabbing his arm.

He turned to me, his face smeared with ash. He shook his head and set down the bucket, shaking his head. His eyes were wide, but I couldn't read what I saw there.

I looked from him to the now empty bucket. 'Get more water, Sanosh,' I cried. 'I'll get a bucket too. We'll—'

But he shook his head again. 'No good, Missy Pree.'

I shouted at him. 'It's not too late. It's not, Sanosh,' and then I ran closer to the infirmary. But at that moment the thatched roof caught in an explosive rush, and the force of burning air threw me back. There was sly crackling: the wattle between the stones. The verandah was now completely consumed. Sparks shot high into the dark sky. I watched, too close, my face baking. It was as if I were shrinking, also consumed by the fire, growing smaller and smaller. It was too bright; I couldn't look away, even though my eyeballs felt as though they were seared.

In one swift, unconscious gesture I put up one hand to shield my eyes; I was being blinded. I saw it all on the inside of my eyelids: my father's eyeballs and hair gone, the last of his flesh melted away, and his bones — ulnas, femurs, fibulas, the clavicle, scapula and sternum, pelvis, the snaking spinal column, his ribcage a rounded arc, his skull with the teeth a terrible, smiling curve — all soon to be blackened and then charred. Strong hands pulled my shoulders, dragging me away.

'No,' I cried. 'My father.' But Sanosh gripped me with surprising force, and the heat lessened, and I could open my eyes again.

There came a low, stealthy, somehow pleased groan, and in the next instant the roof of the infirmary collapsed inward.

A wail rose from somewhere deep inside my chest, and I

opened my mouth, sucking in the hot air as I screamed. And then there was another sound, reflecting my drawn-out screaming, and I was momentarily shocked. Could I create this animal-like cacophony? Looking behind me I saw her, Jassie, her eyes brilliant, reflecting the inferno, and as I looked at her she raised her head and howled as if she were one of the pi-dogs that tormented her.

Had she – as I – grown momentarily wild by the frightening violence of the flames?

'Come, Missy Pree,' Sanosh shouted, pulling at my arm, 'come.' I fought him for an instant, although what I was fighting I don't know. But he would not relinquish his grip, and finally I allowed myself to be led from the hissing and crackling to the *rasoi*.

As Sanosh and I stood in front of the hut, his hand still gripping my arm, I realised how my chest hurt with each breath, and so I breathed shallowly. Jassie stood off to one side of the *rasoi*, trembling as if poised to run, alternately whining quietly and throwing back her head to emit uncontrollable howls.

I felt the pressure of Sanosh's hand on my arm. I looked down; his hand and fingers were burned, already blistering. His other hand was burned as well.

'Missy Pree?' he said, 'Missy Pree.'

I looked from his hands to his face. I opened my mouth, but nothing came out. I thought perhaps my throat had been damaged from the heat and my screaming. Perhaps I just couldn't form words.

'Missy Pree,' Sanosh said, yet again, and I studied his eyes. 'You strong memsahib.' He spoke in English.

What did he mean? Ash floated down, softly, coating my hair and shoulders and skirt. Sanosh was also covered. I was reminded of Pavit's cremation. I looked down at my stockings, filthy, my big toe poking through a rent in the cotton.

'No girl now. You Memsahib,' Sanosh said, and I nodded absently at his strange statement, wondering why he spoke English when we usually conversed in Punjabi. He hadn't removed his hand from my arm. It was the first time Sanosh had ever touched me.

'Your *mata*,' Sanosh said now.

'Yes,' I said, but had to clear my throat, as it came out an unidentifiable grunt. 'Yes, I'll tell my mother,' I said, my voice raspy.

'No, Missy Pree,' Sanosh said, and taking both my arms, looked intently in my face. '*Mata* . . .' he stopped.

I watched his face. He looked away, back to the burning infirmary.

'Your *mata* . . . I tell to you . . .' He pulled his gaze from the building back to me. His eyes were wet, streaming, as were mine, from the smoke. I watched him dully, waiting.

Suddenly he lowered himself to his haunches and put his face into his hands. 'Very bad, Missy Pree,' he murmured, his voice obscured by his burned hands, and I stared down at his bowed, thin shoulders. 'Too very bad for Sanosh.'

My legs trembled suddenly, from the shock of the fire or from something else, some sudden instinctive dread brought on by Sanosh's behaviour. They would no longer support me; I sank to the ground beside him.

We sat in silence, the fire now a steady thrumming crackle. It sounded innocent, like nothing more than a huge bonfire.

Jassie, quiet now, slowly walked towards us, and sat near me. I looked into her face; she stared back, not nervously lowering her eyes as she usually did.

Finally Sanosh lifted his face from his hands. 'Missy Pree,' he said, and took a deep breath. He studied the infirmary again, as if he couldn't bear to look at me as he spoke. '*Mata* is sati.'

'Is sati?' I dumbly repeated, uncomprehending.

He nodded. 'I hear sound, come look. Already some fire I see. Inside. I run for water, I try to come inside. I am in door. Already too much fire. But then . . . then . . .' he stopped. 'Missy Pree,' he said, finally looking at me. 'I see *Mata*. With *Abba*. She sati, Missy.'

I looked from his earnest face to the infirmary, and then back to him. What was he telling me? Did I misunderstand? 'What are you saying, Sanosh? My mother is asleep. In the house. She's asleep,' I told him again. I had seen her, sitting on her bed, her eyes wide and staring. Senseless.

'I see your *mata*, Missy Pree. I try to get her, but no good.' He shuddered. 'I see Mem Fin, sitting on body of Reverend. She make fire on herself. When I see her, already she burn up. Alive, but burn. No sound. Smile. Like good Hindu wife. She smile. See me, and smile, all fire . . .' He shuddered again, and dropped his head.

My own head was shaking rhythmically, denying what he said. How dare he say these things? Did he mean to hurt me? *His hands.*

'No,' I croaked. 'No, Sanosh. You lie.' I ran back to the house, my stockinged feet pounding up the three steps, rushing into my mother's bedroom.

In the darkness I ripped the jumbled, stinking bedclothes from the bed, tore them off and threw them to the floor, stomping on them as if the flat shadow of my mother could somehow be hidden in the folds. I ran to the sitting room, staring about the dim, empty room, then continued on to the back passage, grabbing the key to the storeroom from the nail near the door. My fingers trembled so violently that I could barely fit the key into the lock, knowing she couldn't be in there. Still, I flung back the door; a long shaft of moonlight illuminated the dusty, vacant room.

I fell to my knees in that lonely place, the place where Kai had once slept as a little boy when his mother left him, alone and afraid; the place where my own mother had so often put me as punishment.

I covered my face with my hands, a long, thin wail coming from somewhere deep within my throat, a sound I'd never heard before and didn't think I was capable of, the cry of a jackal, a hyena or pariah dog, howling with loneliness. I was Jassie, I was an animal, baying at the moon. And in my head were my mother's words, from that day on the way to Lahore, when she stood in front of the *chattri*, touching it with reverence.

It was a gift, possibly the only gift they could leave the children. They were more good to their children dead than alive. Don't you see, Pree?

CHAPTER TWENTY-FOUR

JUST BEFORE DAWN a light rain started. It put out the last of the smouldering embers, creating a dank, sad odour. I felt as if I had been flayed of my outer layer of skin; it hurt to wash my hands and face, to brush through my hair. I slowly made two long plaits as if I were once again a small girl.

When I finally went out on to the front verandah in mid-morning, I saw a small group of people gathered at the fence, looking at the smoking remains of the roofless, still-standing blackened stone. I recognised many of them: people from the villages who had come to the infirmary to have us tend them. The woman whose palm I had most recently treated raised it in a half-wave, but no one else called to me or came near.

And then, one by one, they left, not looking back. They were curious, and surely fearful of the evil spirits lurking about the Christian mission. Like my mother's mad behaviour, word of the burned infirmary would be well known all the way to Lahore in a few hours.

But only Sanosh and I knew what had caused the fire.

I sat on the front verandah in the rocking chair, my back straight, and stared at the road that ran in front of the mission house. I know now that I was in shock, for I was unable to move. I simply sat, not even rocking, watching the road. Throughout the day people passed by. They all stopped, staring at the charred remains, glancing at me, and then moving on. When it grew dark Sanosh came around the side of the house, his hands wrapped in clean rags, bringing me a bowl of vegetable curry and a *roti*.

'You must eat, Missy,' he said.

I looked into his kind face, suddenly seeing his age, his leathery ears long, his shoulders slightly stooped. A huge, swooping panic rushed from somewhere, filling my chest so that my voice couldn't force its way out, and I was shaken from my stupor.

He took my hand and curled my fingers around the bowl. 'Eat, Missy,' he repeated.

With my free hand I clutched his arm as he had gripped mine in the dancing light of the flaming pyre the night before. 'Sanosh,' I finally said, my voice a strangled cry. 'You won't leave me, will you? You won't go away?'

'Eat, Missy,' was all he said, again, his own face unreadable, and then he left, going back around the house.

I set the curry and *roti* on the verandah railing, the thought of chewing and swallowing unimaginable. I went inside and lay on my bed. One of my plaits fell across my face; it smelled of smoke.

When it was completely dark I sat up, my stomach cramping. I went to the verandah; the food was still there. I ate the cold curry standing in the dark, holding the bowl under my chin and scooping up the congealed mush first with the *roti*, which I rolled into a cylinder, and, when it was gone, with my fingers, licking them clean when the bowl was empty. My movements were hurried, furtive. Again I thought of Jassie.

Then I went back to my bedroom.

For the next three days I only left the house to go to the convenience or to the side verandah to get the jug of water and whatever food Sanosh left there for me. Before I stepped out the door I always looked through the sitting-room window, waiting until the road in the front of the house was empty, so that nobody would see me, point at me, whisper about me and my cursed family. I moved slowly, back and forth to the convenience, or watching my own hand take the jug and bowl or plate, carrying it back to my room and sitting on my bed in the shuttered darkness, chewing and swallowing, bite by bite, without tasting, filling my stomach only because I knew I must not become weak.

I was in a strange netherworld between dreaming and waking; the edges blurred as images ran through my head, and I tried to distinguish between what had already occurred, and what might lie ahead.

On the afternoon of the fourth day after my mother's death I rose from my bed, standing in the middle of my bedroom, hands curled at my sides. Some inexplicable sense of feverish urgency gripped me. I had been inert too long; now I must act. Nobody would arrive at the mission to show me the way, to tell me what to do next.

I opened my mother's bedroom door, cautiously, as if her spectre might be sitting in the bed, looking at me with a death-head grin. Swallowing, I was disgusted anew by the lingering odour and the mess. I pulled open the shutters and tidied the room, making a fresh bed. It felt comforting to use my body, and as I worked, my mind was finally able to stop its pendulum swing between the past and the unknown. I focused on the immediate.

I went to the tin canister decorated with faded roses that was kept, along with my father's ledger, in a small cabinet in the sitting room. I ran my finger over the last written page of the ledger, noting the date of his payment from the church and his most recent expenditures. Then I counted the money in the canister. My father had lied to Glory, then. There were rupees, although not many. Hopefully enough for Sanosh to purchase food for perhaps a month. And then what?

I took my diary and pen and ink to the dining-room table. Dipping the nib into the India ink and sitting straight, I took a deep breath. I would determine to whom I might turn to for help.

Kai, I wrote. But he had said he was going all the way to Madras, on the Coromandel Coast of the Indian Ocean. I knew nothing about that area, except that it was close to the furthermost south-eastern end of the country, and the journey would take months by road. Perhaps there was a train running there from Delhi, but there weren't enough rupees, I knew, for this sort of huge undertaking. Even getting to Delhi would be a problem. And even, if in some unknown twist of fate, I could reach Madras, and find Kai, what good would that do me? I had shouted at him as he walked away, shouted how I hated him. Surely he would forgive me for that, given the circumstances. But even so . . . he had made it completely clear that he didn't want to be burdened with another person. What had he said? *This is the path I've chosen . . . I want – need – to be on my own.*

I crossed out Kai's name, pressing so hard the nib broke with a shocking crack. The ink, blotchy and thick, had the shape of a dead crow, flattened on the road by the wide wooden wheels of a bullock cart.

I took another nib and fitted it on to the pen. *Peshawar*, I wrote, *American Mission*. I thought of Mr Lang, and his hot, damp hand, his pleased chuckle at my outburst that day in the infirmary. Of Mrs Lang, with her uncertain mouth and trembling hands, her thinly veiled insults. No. Even though my father had made a subtle suggestion about them before he died, I didn't want that.

Just as I had with Kai's name, I crossed out Peshawar. Then I wrote *Lahore – English Cantonment*. Images of Mrs

Wyndham and Eleanor, of their friends, Mrs Rollings-Smythe and Mrs McCallister and other women came to me, images of the women who had cruelly judged us, who had made it clear we were so beneath them. How would they react now, knowing, surely, of the immoral minister and his half-caste lover and illegitimate son, of his mad wife?

Although that option filled me with distaste, I didn't cross it out. There were so few choices.

Finally, I wrote three more words: *Lahore Christian Ministry*. The Ministry hadn't helped my father when he went to speak to them about my mother, but surely they would have to offer some assistance to me now.

I put down the pen and went to the mirror beside the front door. I was seventeen, a woman now. A woman who could speak not only the Queen's English, but also Punjabi, Hindi, Urdu and some Persian. A woman who knew the Bible and Book of Common Prayer, but who also knew of the Vedas and all the gods of India. Who knew the manners of the English sitting room as well as the ways of the peoples of this land.

Would any of this knowledge help me now?

That night I was awakened by the howling of jackals. They sounded closer to the house than ever before. As I lay in the blackness, men's voices rumbled from the road. Were they simply farmers walking home late from visiting another village, or were they dangerous *dacoits* with their long sharp knives, ready to plunder the mission for anything they could use or sell? Would they then use those same sharp knives to get rid of me, so that I couldn't accuse them?

Everyone knew I was alone, didn't they?

But I wasn't alone. Sanosh was here. I swung my bare feet to the floor, breathing heavily. If Jassie was present she would bark if strangers came into the courtyard; she would alert

Sanosh. I thought of his stooped shoulders and slow walk. What could Sanosh do to protect me against a group of strong men?

I had long felt the distress and worry over my mother's declining health. I had known such grief over Lalasa and her baby, and had mourned even more heavily and deeply after Adriana's disappearance, for it were as if she were dead as well. I had sorrowed for Pavit. I had experienced revulsion at the discovery of my father and Glory. What had I felt for Kai through all of this? Whatever had been there before, the urge — and desire — to be near him, the strange breathlessness I felt in his presence the last year, was now masked with confusion.

I didn't know how to categorise my feelings over the loss of my parents; it was too new, and I was still immersed in shock and disbelief.

But I had never felt outright fear before, fear of being alone, of being helpless and in danger for my life. Without lighting a candle, I crept to the storeroom and, stepping on the bottom shelf of one of the cupboards, reached to the far back of the top shelf. My fingers found what I was looking for, and I took down the old sabre, covered in a thick layer of years of accumulated dust. I wiped off the sheath, then carefully slid the sabre out, studying it in the near-darkness. I went to the sitting room and opened one of the louvres and tried to see the road; the men's voices had died away. Now there was only the cry of the jackals. I returned to my bed, my fingers closed tightly around the handle of the sabre I put under the bedclothes beside me. But sleep wouldn't come.

I was still awake when the room lightened. Relieved that the long night was over, I sat up, rubbing my forehead with my fingertips. The familiar sounds of Sanosh starting breakfast preparations came through the window. This normal, everyday occurrence filled me with such relief that tears came to my eyes.

I slid the sabre under my bed.

307

The sky was still pink, and yet I had already taken heated water and bathed, washing my hair. I carried the scent of death, of smoke and despair.

I took my good dress from the wardrobe; it smelled musty and I sprinkled it with a bit of lavender water and shook it thoroughly. I knew I should press it, but I didn't want to take the time and effort to heat the flatirons. I dipped a rag into the can of blacking and polished my boots. Although my hair was still damp, I pinned it up. And then I went to my mother's room and pulled her dressing-table chair to the wardrobe. Standing on it and stretching to the back of the top shelf, I took down the tin hat-box. I blew the dust and cobwebs and dead insects from its lid and opened it, looking down at the hated pink bonnet I had seen my mother put there over a year and a half ago.

I took it out and held it, looking at the frayed ribbon ends. *When the Lord sent me forth into the world, He forbade me to put off my hat to any, high or low.* I remembered my mother's voice as she stroked the firm crown of the bonnet, standing in the courtyard. And then finally I was able to feel emotion, and to grieve over her unnecessary death. I sat on the dressing-table chair and ran my hands over the bonnet, crying for my mother.

When I had finished, I took a handkerchief from beside my mother's bed, blowing my nose and mopping my eyes. I returned the chair to the dressing table and sat in front of the looking-glass, studying myself. How strange was the shape of my mourning. It took a pot of porridge to make me cry over my father's death, and now a bonnet to cry over my mother's. Why was it that inanimate objects could bring tears?

Was something missing within me?

★ ★ ★

I hitched Marta to the cart and set off for Lahore. The rupees and annas from the canister were wrapped in a handkerchief in the small reticule of my mother's which I kept on my lap. I was loathe to spend them, but I took them with me as a precaution — against what, I didn't know, but it felt better to have money with me. Sanosh had given me a dented brass tiffin holder; in one compartment he had put potato samosas, in another a lentil masala, and in still another, three folded *rotis*. I smiled my thanks at him, although the smile was difficult to form.

It was even difficult to meet his eyes. Sanosh was a good and moral man. I was ashamed, even though they were dead, of my parents and their actions. And at the same time I was ashamed of myself for feeling this way.

Three hours later I left Marta and the cart at the outskirts of the city and hired a rickshaw to take me to the Wyndhams' home.

I knocked on the front door. The *chuprassi* who opened the door, a different man from the one I remembered from the last visit, told me that the Memsahib was, as usual at this time of day, at the Lahore Club.

I nodded and paid out another precious anna to have the rickshaw-wallah take me to the Lahore Club facing the wide, shady and green *maidan* where ayahs watched small English children play and women in fancy hats sat on benches, fanning themselves and talking. By this time I was hot and tired. And hungry.

Again I stood in front of double wooden doors, these even taller and wider than those at the Wyndhams' home. I knocked using the brass door knocker.

The door was opened by a Hindu in a high white turban, beribboned with red to match the cummerbund wound round the waist of his knee-length white jacket. He wore loose white trousers and woven reed sandals, dyed red.

'Yes?' he said, in English.

'May I come in, please?' I asked.

He frowned. 'Go away.' He started to close the door, but I put my palm on it.

'Wait. I'm here to see Mrs Wyndham. She knows me.'

Now he shook his head, again attempting to shut the door.

I wedged my foot between it and the doorframe.

'Your sort not being welcome here,' he said, annoyed now, his eyes travelling from my bonnet to my boots. His English was heavily accented with the Punjabi rhythm.

'My sort?' I asked, looking down as he had. I was sorry to see the red dust of the road gathered in the folds of my skirt, and that the darned patches on my white gloves stood clear; the thread I had used to repair them had a slightly yellow cast.

It was tempting to berate him in Punjabi, but I wouldn't lower myself. I knew, by his disdainful expression, that I needed to use any authority I could.

'I am not a "sort",' I said, in the most superior voice I could find, staring into his eyes. 'I am Miss Fincastle, daughter of the Reverend and Mrs Fincastle. I demand that you fetch Mrs Wyndham for me.' His eyelashes fluttered, and his head waggled the slightest. I knew he was suddenly unsure of possibly making a mistake, and this gave me further courage.

I raised my chin, stepping inside now. 'I shall wait here,' I told him, 'while you kindly fetch Mrs Wyndham. I'm sure she won't be pleased at your behaviour towards me,' I added.

He stared at me for another moment.

'Well? Go on,' I said, never lowering my chin. 'It's Miss Fincastle,' I repeated.

'Yes, yes,' he said loudly, although without his former imperious manner, 'just be waiting. I am calling upon Mrs Wyndham for you.'

I stood, my hands clasped on the handle of my reticule in

310

front of me, and looked at the pillared passages. There were potted palms in huge china pots, and hunting prints upon the walls. Through an open door I heard the clink of glass and men's laughter. I leaned forward, seeing leather club chairs and the stuffed heads of tigers on a wall. Cigar smoke wafted towards me, as well as a trace of cooked meat.

I thought of the tiffin carrier I'd left in the wagon, my stomach suddenly churning with hunger. I was sorry I hadn't eaten before I'd arrived in Lahore. The samosas and masala would be quite cold by now. Maybe Mrs Wyndham would invite me in, would offer me tea and something to eat. She was a mother; surely she wouldn't turn away a young woman the same age as her own daughter. Especially not one so touched by tragedy.

From somewhere within the inner reaches of the club a clock chimed, once.

Eventually Mrs Wyndham came down a long hallway, led by the *chuprassi*. When she stood in front of me he bowed and stepped to one side.

Mrs Wyndham had a nasty pink sty on the verge of erupting in the corner of her left eye. 'Well,' she said, putting her hand on the shelf of her bosom. 'I was surprised when the *chuprassi* spoke your name. Whatever are you doing here, my dear?' She was not unkind, but neither was she overly friendly. 'I recognise the bonnet,' she added. 'I knew it would suit you.'

'Could I . . . could I come in and speak to you?' I asked.

She drew back as if I emitted an unpleasant odour. 'Oh, that wouldn't be at all appropriate, my dear. The Club is for members only, so I'm afraid—' she stopped, looking me up and down, from my bonnet to my newly polished although now frightfully dusty boots, in the same manner as the haughty *chuprassi*.

'Mrs Wyndham,' I said, taking a deep breath. 'I don't know

if you've heard. My parents . . . both my parents, are just recently . . . deceased.' I stuttered slightly on the last word.

She frowned, a look of dismay coming over her face. 'Yes, Miss Fincastle, I had heard. We all have. And we are all so terribly, terribly sorry.'

Was the consternation genuine? She glanced down at her bodice; I realised she was looking at the tiny timepiece pinned on a ribbon there. 'And so I imagine you'll soon be going home?' She raised her eyes to me.

'Home?' I asked. 'I've just now arrived in the city.'

'I meant to England, Miss Fincastle. Will you return to England now?'

I shook my head. 'I don't know anyone there. This is my home, Mrs Wyndham. And . . . I was hoping that perhaps you could . . .' it was difficult to ask for help, especially from someone like her. 'That you might be able to be of aid. I am quite alone now, and I cannot, of course, stay on at the mission any longer.'

She blinked, licking her lips as if uncertain how to reply. Finally she took a deep breath. 'Well, we're always willing to help our own. Come around to the house later, when my whist game is over, say an hour? I'm sure I could find something for you.' She leaned closer and whispered, 'That frock, I'm afraid to say, is far too short to be decent, Miss Fincastle. And the state of your gloves . . . dear, dear me.'

She took my hand – in its shameful glove – and pressed it between hers, with that same simpering look of dismay. 'And I truly *am* so sorry about the Reverend and Mrs Fincastle,' she said, and then let go of my hand and stepped back.

I was rooted to the spot, not comprehending that she was dismissing me until the *chuprassi* opened the door.

'But . . . Mrs Wyndham. I have no means of support. I—'

A flicker of impatience crossed her face. 'What would you have me suggest, my dear? I'm sure it's up to the Church to find a way to help you. Good-day, now. I cannot keep the other ladies waiting. You understand.'

She turned and went back down the hall. The *chuprassi* cleared his throat, lifting his chin towards the door. I stepped outside – for what was there for me to do? and the *chuprassi* closed the door.

I stared at the polished wood for some time.

I went to the Ministry; there was a very shiny brass nameplate beside the door. The Most Reverend Burgess, I read. The nameplate was new; in this climate, even with constant polishing, brass quickly grew spotted. I pulled the small braided rope which hung from a hole in the wall beside the door, and heard the muted tinkling of a bell.

I was admitted by a stern old woman with eyes such a faded blue they were almost colourless. She studied me suspiciously when I told her my name and background and asked to see the Most Reverend Burgess.

In a decidedly cool manner she ushered me into a book-lined office. 'May I present Miss Fincastle,' she said. 'The daughter of the Reverend Fincastle,' she added, her lips pursed.

'Thank you, Mrs McNulty,' Reverend Burgess said.

The woman stood there, her lips still in that tight pucker. 'That will be all,' Reverend Burgess said firmly, and Mrs McNulty turned, stiffly, shutting the door behind her with an exaggerated carefulness.

'Please, sit down, Miss Fincastle.'

I smoothed my skirt beneath me, keeping my feet together and clasping my gloved hands in my lap. I stared at them. My stomach rumbled again; I hoped the Reverend Burgess didn't hear the embarrassing groan. 'I don't know if you're aware, Reverend Burgess, of the tragedy—'

'Yes, yes, Miss Fincastle. It is well known,' he said, not

unkindly, and at his tone I looked up, but his strained expression brought another wave of humiliation, similar to that which I'd experienced earlier at the Club.

'May I extend my deepest sympathies. I am sure this has all been terribly shocking for you. You are their daughter, I believe, Mrs McNulty said. Am I correct?'

I was confused by his voice, his odd question, and nodded, staring at my hands again. It was easier to not look at him.

'If I appear slightly perplexed . . . well, frankly, Miss Fincastle, I had not been aware that you were at the mission. It wasn't mentioned . . .' he stopped, and I looked up. He was studying me in a frank manner. 'I had sorted through your father's records after he came to see me, a few months ago, but there was no record of any offspring living at the mission. No record of funds being allotted to send you back to England for your schooling, which is part of our responsibility: to help our missionaries with their children's education.'

It took a few seconds for this to sink in. I could have been sent to England for schooling? My parents had never once mentioned any such possibility.

'Of course these records are not always up to date, and cannot be relied on, what with the movement of missionaries within the country. Records are lost, or inadvertently destroyed,' Reverend Burgess went on. 'The Most Reverend Parr, whom I replaced after his sudden death, surely knew the details of your family, but since I have only been here for the last year there is a great deal about the various missions scattered throughout the Punjab that I have not yet been made aware of.'

I nodded. It really didn't matter what he knew or didn't know about me. 'I've come to speak to you,' I licked my lips, 'of a very delicate subject. Although I found, in my father's papers – he was quite meticulous about recording debits and credits – that he did collect his last pay packet, in December . . . now that it is almost May, I . . .' I sat straighter. 'I would like to collect his wages for the last four months, Reverend Burgess. The last payment owed by the Church of England to my father.'

There was silence. My humiliation grew, and again I looked down at my gloves. Although my voice was firm, my words unquestioning, and certainly, certainly I had a right to what my father had worked for, I suddenly felt as though I were begging. I hadn't expected to feel this way; Mrs Wyndham had brought out a similar feeling of shame.

'Although of course my family lived simply, there are . . . expenses I must cover. Until I,' the words trailed off. Until I what? What would I do? I raised my face and looked at the Reverend.

'You don't know, then?' His voice was stern, but his eyes held something – pity?

'Know what?'

He drew a deep breath. 'Your father broke all ties with the Church.'

'What?' I forgot my manners, leaned forward and set my hands on the desk. 'What are you talking about?' My voice had a slight hysterical squeak.

'Last month,' Reverend Burgess said, 'your father came here, to see me. He said he was no longer fit to be a man of God. He confessed that he had broken vows, and that he could no longer, with any honesty, continue to represent the Lord in India, or anywhere. I remember our conversation all too clearly.' He suddenly pulled a leather-bound book forward and opened it, running his finger down a page. 'April the eighteenth. Yes, that's the date your father came to see me.'

I stared into the Reverend's eyes. I saw the murkiness of a cataract in the right one, and knew he was half-blind. I recalled the unfamiliar look on my father's face the last time he'd returned from Lahore. How he'd spoken to me of going somewhere else, suggesting the Langs in Peshawar. How Glory had frightened Pavit, frightened him into taking his own life, by telling him the mission would close. My father had told her, then, told Glory about his departure from the Church. Told her, but not me.

'And at that time he collected the wages owed to him. I paid him the four months, even though it was not then the end of April, as well as for the next two, to round out the full six months. As a compensation, for his long service. I also told him that out of respect for his past work he could stay on, living at the mission if he so wished – although of course we could not pay for the medical materials any longer. I told him he should apply to a foreign aid society; perhaps they would take over supplying what was needed to carry on medical treatment, with an added small wage. I'm afraid, Miss Fincastle, that nothing is owed to him. I am able to show you his signature on our papers if you . . .' He stopped.

The Reverend's eyebrows were thick and grey; the hairs at the ends of them stood out, like tiny curled wings. 'You really weren't aware of this?' he asked. 'Your father said nothing? For in spite of his abrupt cutting of ties with us, nevertheless, the ministry was willing to offer him – and his family – passage back to England. But he refused. He said India was his life; he had nothing to return to.'

Yes, India was his life. And Glory, he hadn't wanted to leave Glory.

'Miss Fincastle? Are you all right? I'm sure all of this is a terrible shock – your parents' death, and now this . . .' He rubbed his right eye carefully, slowly, his index fingertip gently circling on the lid as if to clear the maddening film. 'And so while there is no payment forthcoming, we could perhaps do something to help you. A steerage passage home for you,' he said. 'Not immediately – the paperwork, you understand – but perhaps in a few months I could procure—'

I pulled my gaze from his eyebrows. 'Home?'

'Well, I'm sure you'd rather be in England, with your own kind, now that you're so suddenly . . . on your own. I can't imagine you'd care to stay here, now that—'

'This *is* my home,' I interrupted. Just as I'd stated to Mrs Wyndham. Could no one understand this? The home the English spoke of with such reverence, such love, was not mine. It belonged to them. It held no memories, no past and no future for me.

A silence fell. 'I see,' he finally said, touching his right eyelid again. After another long, uncomfortable moment, during which he rolled his pen back and forth in his thick fingers, tapping on the blotter in front of him, studying the nib as if it held a secret, he finally spoke again. 'But what will you do, Miss Fincastle? Where will you go? Do you have friends within the English community here? Friends who can take you in?'

I stood. 'No,' I said, shaking my head, thinking again of Mrs Wyndham. 'There is no one.'

The Reverend stood as well. 'Then I think the only possible solution is for you to return to England.'

How could I return to a place I'd never left?

'And in the meantime we can find something for you here. The Church will not turn away one of its children. Mrs McNulty is the housekeeper for the manse, and of course there are the Indian servants, but there is always too much to do. Mrs McNulty won't, I'm sure, object to sharing her room with you, and in exchange you can help her with her duties until the funds have been allocated for your passage home.'

Now it was as if I were the one half blind, not the Reverend Burgess. I couldn't see properly; it was as if the vitreous humour of my eyes had suddenly grown thick and concentrated, blocking my vision. I felt for the edge of the desk, then reached out to touch the wall beside me. 'I will stay – may I stay – at the mission? Just for a short while. Until I can see my way clear.' I had the presence of mind to understand the black irony in my statement. 'Until I can . . . can . . .' *Until I can what?*

As if through a fog, or layer of smoke, Reverend Burgess came from behind his desk, towards me. 'Of course, Miss Fincastle. Of course. We shall try to find another minister to take over. Missions are loaned in perpetuity to the Church of England; no one will turn you out. These things do not happen quickly anywhere, but in India . . . well, it could be quite some time. Quite some time indeed,' he repeated. 'It's become more and more difficult to fill these positions since the Mutiny. There is such despair over the lack of converts in India. Missionaries are choosing other heathen lands to spread the word of the Lord.'

'Yes, yes,' I said. 'So I can stay there? As long as I want?'

'At this point, Miss Fincastle, yes.'

I had to get back there, claim it as mine. Look after it. 'Thank you,' I said, my hand on the doorknob. 'I must go.'

'Miss Fincastle, allow me to have Mrs McNulty make you some tea, give you a bit of a meal, before you head back. Don't leave in this state, Miss Fin—'

I turned the doorknob and ran out into the hall, leaving the door open behind me. I passed Indian servants, who moved to the walls as I rushed by, and, just before I reached the wide, thick outer door, I caught a glimpse of Mrs McNulty, watching me with a fishy glare from under hooded lids.

CHAPTER TWENTY-FIVE

I STOOD OUTSIDE THE Ministry. Nothing looked familiar. The sensation was similar to the one I had the day my mother had forced me to watch the sati; I was a stranger in an unknown place. I didn't dare spend even one precious anna to hire a rickshaw to take me back to Marta and the cart, and I wandered the streets, suddenly unsure of the way. Now Lahore had lost the beauty I had always associated with it. A stout turbaned man bared his teeth at me in a leering, blood-filled smile; the next instant I realised it was only betel staining his cracked teeth. An old woman with unkempt grey hair straggling down her back crouched in a doorway, smoking a *beedi*, the little roll of tobacco wrapped in a leaf glowing between her toothless gums as she stared up at me with hollow eyes. Pariah dogs leapt from late afternoon shadows, snarling over a rotting chicken head. A child dying of starvation lay across the lap of his mother. His round ribcage stood out like a loom in his tiny torso, his stomach distended, his knees grotesque knobs. A man approaching me blew his nose into his fingers and flung the glistening glob near the toe of my boot.

I fought to keep my panic within my chest. It was the same fearful sensation I had experienced hearing the men on the road outside the mission in the night. I ran, stumbling down dark alleys, panting. By the time I recognised my surroundings and found Marta, I was weeping. I climbed into the cart and slapped her back frantically with the reins, shouting at her. She stood still, looking over her shoulder as if assuring herself it was actually me.

'Go, Marta! Go home!' I cried, and finally she jerked forward.

The last of the evening light faded in the final hour before I reached the mission. I had never travelled the road alone before today, and never at night. It was deserted apart from an occasional man walking or leading a bullock. Banks of fog rose from swampy areas, lighter than the darkening air, creating a floating, eerie effect. Night sounds echoed in the still countryside: frogs gulped and the rubbery flap of bat wings rose from a copse of thorn trees. In the distance jackals howled. From the mud villages off the Grand Trunk, fires winked like dull sequins in the fog. Passing each one, I heard retching coughs and babies' wails and the gurgles of spitting as the village settled for sleep. The stones of the road gleamed faintly in the dull glow of the moon, partially obscured by night clouds. Unable to see more than a foot in front of Marta, I missed the side road leading to the mission; it was only when I recognised a village that I knew I'd come too far. I turned Marta around, straining my eyes for the narrow junction that led to the mission road.

Finally, with a long sigh of relief, I saw the familiar fence. The mission was unlit save for a small fire from the *rasoi*; there was still the dank, lingering odour of burned thatch. Fumbling in the darkness, I untied Marta and led her to her enclosure and water bucket; I threw an armful of dried straw down for her. As I crossed the courtyard, I heard voices from the *rasoi*.

I went to the cooking hut; Sanosh was crouched in front of the fire, slowly polishing a small brass pot with a bushy twig. But he wasn't alone.

Standing over him with her arms crossed, her two carpet-bags in the dust at her feet, was Glory.

Before I had a chance to speak she opened her lips in a thin, gloating smirk, a triumphant feline smile. I smelled cloves.

'I'm back,' she said in Hindi. 'I heard that the Reverend died. And the talk was that the Mem had also passed to her death because of madness.' She stared at me, shaking her head. 'I always knew she was possessed by a *preta*, a ghost from the spirit of one of her dead children who cannot rest. The little *preta* will always seek out a human to enter. They rule them, and make them sick. I knew this always; I told the Reverend, but he wouldn't believe me. Now I am proven to be right. She was possessed. When the Reverend died she allowed the *preta* to kill her.'

'Stop talking about my mother,' I said. 'Stop it.' I glanced at Sanosh, but his head was bent over the pot. I knew he wouldn't have told Glory how my mother died.

Glory shrugged. 'The Reverend and Mem are no more. So I will live here now.'

Hadn't enough happened today? I shook my head, my mouth open in disbelief. 'What are you talking about? Of course you can't live here. This is *my* home.' My voice was hoarse with fatigue. 'I don't want you here.'

'Do you think I care what you want?' she asked. 'You think you can stop me? The mission has always been my home as well as yours. Your father wished it to be so. You know that I speak the truth.'

'You can't,' I said. 'Sanosh, tell her she can't stay here.'

Still on his heels, Sanosh looked up at me, his hands held out, the pot in one and the polishing twig in the other, his usually placid face dark with what I recognised as anger. He didn't want Glory here either. 'It is not my business, Missy,' he said, and bent his head, working at the pot with renewed vigour.

Glory picked up her bags and walked towards the house.

'What are you doing?' I cried, running along beside her. 'I told you, you can't stay.'

'I will take the big bedroom,' she said. 'I have always liked a high bed with a true mattress. So much more comfortable than a charpoy.'

I followed her as she walked through the dark house and into my mother's bedroom. She opened the shutters so that long shafts of moonlight fell across the neatly made bed where, less than a week before, my mother had lain.

The very next morning Glory began ordering me about.

'Pick some lemons,' she called to me. 'Squeeze the juice of one into a mixture of a spoonful of kaolin clay – it's on my dressing table – and another of buttermilk,' she said. 'I just used the last of the Beckingham's Neroline; I'll get more the next time I go into Lahore. But for now I need something for my skin.'

My dressing table, she had said, with such an easy manner. But it wasn't hers, it was my mother's, as was the Beckingham's Neroline. I remember my mother finding the half-used container of the face cream in one of the charity boxes, and holding it up in triumph.

'Ah,' she had said, 'how many years it's been since my skin has felt English lotion. What a lovely surprise.' She had opened the tin and held it towards me; I had breathed in its scent. And yet I noticed that my mother only used the Neroline sparingly; the joy of it, for her, came from seeing the round tin, with its decorated cover of lilacs. Such a simple pleasure.

The container still sat on her dressing table, only a thin layer covering the bottom and rimming the edges.

And now – this very first day – not only had Glory used it up greedily, but she had also completely taken over my mother's room. As I stiffly lay in my bed the night before, enraged at Glory's boldness and angered at my own inability to force her to leave, I had heard thumping and the screech of furniture being moved, and had gone to the doorway of my mother's room. It was ablaze with three lit lamps, using more naphtha than we had ever used at one time, and there was Glory rearranging the room to her liking.

As I watched her, it came to me that she used everything that belonged to my mother – including my father – with no thought of the pain it might bring.

She saw me, and gestured for me to come in. 'Help me. The wardrobe is too heavy.'

I had simply stared at her, then turned and gone back to my own room.

'You will do as I say, Pree,' she called through the thin wall. 'Come and help me.'

I turned on my side, putting my pillow over my head and counting aloud. Except this time I counted nothing, just stating the numbers themselves, trying to find comfort in their familiar rhythm. But sleep wouldn't come, and I finally arose, exhausted, to face the morning when the first rays of light came through my shutters.

And now I was at the well, and she was on the verandah, demanding lemons.

'And cut one in half. I need them to soften my elbows.'

'Do it yourself,' I called back. 'I'm not your servant.'

She came down the steps, holding up the skirt of her new frock so that it didn't drag in the dust. She wore silk, peach-coloured slippers. 'Do you want to eat, Pree?' she asked, standing in front of me.

I put down the full pail I had just hauled up from the well. Glory stepped back so that the sloshing water didn't touch her slippers.

'Well? Do you want to eat more than what you can dig up in the garden? Do you want more than eggs? Wouldn't you like a *roti*? Do you have the means to buy flour, or meat? Tea or sugar? A supply of rice? What about oil for cooking and for the lamps? What of candles?'

I stared into her face.

'It would be an easy matter for me to hire someone to work here. I don't need you, Pree. Do you have any way to feed yourself, to buy yourself something to wear?' She looked at my frock; it was too tight, ripping under one arm and uncomfortable for working in the garden, for milking Marta and hauling water. I had already torn off the collar and I kept the top buttons undone so that I didn't feel as if it were choking me. There would be no more charity boxes.

'Well?' she said again.

I stood there for a long moment, staring at her.

'Where is the money to live going to come from, I ask you?' she went on. 'Not from you.' She studied me for another moment. 'But I have money. So you will do as I ask, and you will be grateful to me for providing you with a home.' She delivered these last lines quietly, with complete confidence. Although slightly shorter than me, and having to lift her eyes to look into mine, at that moment I saw that she felt much, much taller and far more powerful than I.

Silently I turned and went to fetch the lemons.

For the next week Glory continued to bully and threaten me. My feelings for her had turned to hatred. I knew I should not feel this, should try to accept what she was doing. She was right. How would I live here? The few rupees and annas were barely enough for food for the next weeks.

She knew I had no recourse, no options.

And so I did as she said, thinking that somehow I would come up with a way to make Glory leave, come up with a way to make my life meaningful. I let myself think of my parents; I knew that in spite of their frailties and the unhappiness surrounding us for so long, I would now give anything to have back my former life with them. I tried to concentrate on better times at the mission, but it was difficult. The destroyed infirmary, with the ashes of my parents under the rotting, creaking burned timber, sat like the hulking carcass of some great beast, reminding me, daily, of what had happened.

Sanosh was my only ally. I held on, that first week, to the thought that perhaps a semblance of normality could return to the mission. He would cook, given a salary by Glory, I would do the physical work needed to keep the mission from falling into further disrepair, and Glory – well, Glory would do nothing but enjoy the new status she had created for herself.

But soon, within the first month of Glory at the helm of the mission, our lives fell into a state I had never imagined.

The men came. They were English soldiers – members of the Lahore Punjab Battalion – from the barracks on the outskirts of Lahore.

It began simply, with Glory having a 'gentleman caller', as she described him.

When this first 'gentleman' arrived early one evening after I had eaten at the *rasoi* with Sanosh, and Glory had taken her meal on the verandah, I was sitting at the dining-room table reading.

I looked up at the sound of a horse entering the court-yard, and heard the low rumble of a man's voice, answered by Glory's higher one. And then they came into the house. The soldier paid little attention to me; he and Glory stayed in the sitting room, drinking the whiskey he'd brought. Finally, annoyed by Glory's loud laughter and their silly talk, I went to bed. But before I fell asleep they moved from the settee to Glory's bed, and I couldn't bear to hear, through the thin

325

wall, what I was forced to listen to. They didn't care that I could hear their loud play and embarrassing movements, and after ten minutes of the shameful sounds, I gathered my pillow and coverlet and spent the night on Kai's charpoy.

But even in the hut I could hear Glory's drunken laughter through all the open windows. As I had the first night that Glory had returned to the mission, I put the pillow over my head and counted.

After a few days I realised that what had happened with the soldier would continue; he came night after night, and I couldn't bear to be witness to Glory's wanton behaviour. There was also something far more worrisome than being subjected to the lewd sights and sounds. On the soldier's fifth visit, Glory had gone to the convenience, and I came out of my room to fetch the book I had left lying on the settee. The soldier sat in the horsehair chair, his cheeks flushed with drink, legs spread out in front of him, feet encased in heavy black boots. He watched me move across the sitting room, and I could feel his eyes on me, could hear his breathing.

'What's your name, then, little lass?' he asked, and I glanced at him, and then quickly away, unnerved by the boldness I saw there. The lazy smile, the half-closed eyes, the long fingers wrapped loosely around the glass of amber liquid.

I didn't answer, taking up my book and hurrying from the room, feeling the heat of his stare on my back. I closed my door and leaned against it, praying for Glory to return quickly. When she did, I let out a sigh of relief, and moved to my bed. But I didn't undress or lie down. I waited until I heard the familiar sounds on the other side of the wall, and then, my heart thudding, and with a number of furtive trips, took all of my belongings — apart from the bed and mango wood dresser, which I couldn't move on my own — to Kai's hut.

I still had the sabre; I put it between the wall and the charpoy.

Glory struck Sanosh a few days later. She had a stout branch in her hand, and was standing over him when I came out of Marta's enclosure after milking her.

Shocked, unable to believe what I was witnessing, I saw Glory raise the stick and pound Sanosh's poor old shoulders as he sat in front of his grinding stone. He flinched, putting up one hand to protect his face, and I set down the milk pail and ran to them.

'What are you doing?' I cried, grabbing the branch from Glory's hand and flinging it away. 'How dare you beat Sanosh?'

She put her hands on her hips. 'He has disobeyed. I told him I wished him to prepare English mutton with gravy. Instead, he has made his boring vegetable curry. I am the mistress of the house. He must do as I say.'

I looked down at Sanosh. Although his head was lowered, I could see that his mouth trembled, and tears came to my eyes. I knelt beside him and put my arm about his shoulders. 'Leave him alone,' I told Glory, looking up at her. 'Never, ever treat Sanosh with so little respect. Have you no soul?'

She lifted one eyebrow, smiling slightly. 'My soul has nothing to do with my appetite,' she said. 'And Sanosh will cook what I tell him. I am paying his wages, am I not?'

I had to look away from her expression, so chilling was it.

Without warning her slippered foot emerged, kicking over the pot of curry. It spilled on to the dirt. 'Make the mutton and gravy,' she said, and then turned and left.

Sanosh and I sat in silence, both of us staring at the curry as if mesmerised. His old body shook. Finally, my arm still around him, I said, 'Sanosh. You must leave here.'

Now he looked at me, his narrow face showing surprise.

'But I will stay for you, Missy Pree,' he said. 'If I leave, who will cook for you?'

'I know how to cook, Sanosh,' I said. 'You know that. I've learned from you.' I tried to smile at him, but it was just a twitch of my upper lip. 'You must go,' I said. 'Go back to Tek Mandi and live with Darshan and his wife. Sit in the sunshine and play with your grandchildren. You've worked hard for us all these years.'

'It is true I am old,' he said, as if to comfort me. He glanced at the house, where Glory now sat on the verandah, rocking lazily.

'You will cook for her as well?' he asked.

I shrugged. 'She has money, Sanosh. She'll have to buy the food we need, so at least I won't have to worry about that.'

Only a few days earlier, when I had asked Glory for money for the needed food supplies, she had unlocked a mother-of-pearl box and taken out a thick stack of rupees, waving them in front of me, a smug look of pride on her face.

I stared at it. 'That's my father's money, isn't it?' I'd said. She only stared at me with the same haughty expression, peeling off a few notes to hand to me, before very pointedly locking the box again with the key hung on a thin chain around her neck.

It was, with certainty, the six months wages my father had collected from the Most Reverend Burgess in April. Where had she found it? Had it been in the tin canister? It would have been an easy feat for her to rummage through the few belongings in the house and find it before she left that last day, when my father had told her he had no money to give her.

She was so devious that she'd left a few rupees and annas so I wouldn't suspect she'd found the canister.

'Please, Sanosh,' I said now. 'Don't stay here. You will make me happier by leaving. I don't want this to be your life.'

Sanosh didn't answer for a few moments, then sighed heavily. 'I think you are right,' he said. 'I think my time for working is through. But you will sometimes come to visit me, in Tek Mandi?' he asked. 'You will always be welcome in my home.'

'Of course, Sanosh,' I said, looking at his hands. Although enough time had passed for his burns to heal, the skin was scarred, raised and pink. I would never forget his consideration and sympathy, not just when my parents died, but always. I was deeply saddened at the thought of losing Sanosh's faithful, comforting presence at the mission, but now I was ashamed for him to be here, treated by Glory as a slave.

He looked around the courtyard, his eyes resting on the charred pile that had been the infirmary. 'Maybe you should leave here as well, Missy. It isn't good that you stay with that one.' He raised his eyebrows at the verandah. 'I think it is time you go and live in Lahore with the other English. There is nothing for you here any more.'

'Maybe,' I said, knowing full well it wasn't a possibility. I doubted that Sanosh would believe me if I told him there was also a caste system among Christians, and that I wasn't welcome with the Wyndhams and the Rollings-Smythes in their fine homes which lined the carefully maintained streets of Lahore's English Cantonment.

I missed greeting the villagers as they came to the infirmary, and dealing with their problems. I missed Sanosh and Pavit.

I missed my father and mother.

I missed my old life, and hated the new one, imagining it couldn't possibly be any worse.

I missed Kai.

A few days after Sanosh left, lying in Kai's old hut at night, of course I thought of him. Wouldn't he some day return to the mission, if only to see Glory, or bring her money? In spite of his lack of feelings towards her, he had told me he wouldn't abandon his mother. If only Kai would come back to the mission, somehow he would have the power to change things.

I began a new prayer: *Please, Heavenly Father, who watcheth over me, please bring Kai home. Please bring Kai home.* I'd found a simple string of beads – Sanosh's *japa mala*, accidentally left behind in the *rasoi*. Now, along with my Christian prayers, I whispered the *japa*: *Jai Shree Krishna, Jai Shree Krishna, Jai Shree Krishna* one hundred and eight times, running each bead through my fingers. I did these combined Christian and Hindu prayers five times a day, as the Muslims prayed: after sunrise, midday, mid-afternoon, sunset and evening. Five hundred and forty prayers every day to both my own God and the Hindu deity, respecting the Muslim's prayer ritual. This would surely have some effect, I told myself.

I carried on in this manner for two weeks. And then one night I heard my own voice, whispered and breathy, desperate, and was reminded, for one horrible moment, of my mother's voice as she prayed and wept over the dead puppy.

I threw the beads to the floor beside the charpoy, and turned on my side, abandoning all prayers, both Hindu and Christian.

Glory didn't even notice I'd moved out at first; I was unimportant to her, apart from cooking and doing the outside work that allowed her to live as she wished in the mission house. I did not clean the inside of the house for her, although I tried to whitewash the outside stones and repair the thatch as Kai had done.

After three weeks the first soldier was replaced by another. I was glad to see the last of that first one; after the night he had looked at me so intently I had stayed in my hut as soon as I heard his horse arriving most evenings.

Soon it became an ever-changing march of soldiers in similar uniforms but each decorated with different braid and stripes, depending on their rank. I would not call them gentlemen, as Glory did. And it didn't take me long to see that the first soldier had not been unique. More and more I was made uneasy by their presence as the next weeks passed. It had been two months since Glory had returned to take over the mission.

I didn't look at the soldiers as they rode into the courtyard each evening; depending on the weather I would either go to my hut or walk to the river or through the fields as soon as they arrived. One evening two came together, and just as I hurried past the house one spoke to me.

'Come and join us,' he called. 'You,' he said, more loudly, when I didn't stop. 'Where's Glory? Glory! Tell the girl to come back. She can join our little soiree.'

I didn't answer or look back, nor did I hear Glory. Holding my breath and walking primly until I was out of sight around the corner of the house, I ran into the field.

Something told me I shouldn't return to the mission that night. The air was soft and warm; eventually I lay down, hidden in the cornstalks. I had been driven from the mission house. Now I was not even safe in my own hut. How long could I live like this?

As I turned on my side, trying to curl into a comfortable position, I heard a familiar snuffling. I sat up again.

'Jassie? Is that you? Come, girl,' I said, and she slowly stepped through the stalks. At the sight of her dear, narrow head, I felt even more sorry for myself, and, unbidden, a sob rose in my throat. Jassie stared at me, her head cocked to one side, surely puzzled as to why I was in the cornstalks in the darkness.

'Lie down, girl,' I said. 'Stay with me.'

She hesitated, looking behind her as if she wished to leave, but then slowly, gingerly, she lowered herself to the ground a few feet from me. How I wished she would come near enough to touch. I wanted to hold her body close to mine. I wanted, so badly, to be near to something warm, something alive and breathing in that dark, lonely night.

But she stayed where she was, eyes wide and unblinking in the darkness, staring at me. Eventually she sighed and lowered her chin to her paws, her body losing its tenseness and her eyes closing. And that was enough for me: her very presence was a comfort.

When I opened my eyes at the first streaks of paling sky, she was gone, the only trace of her a swirl in the soft dust.

CHAPTER TWENTY-SIX

MERCIFULLY, FOR THE next few days no soldiers came. I breathed more easily, and told myself that the particular soldier who demanded I join them might never return. Glory took Marta and the cart into Lahore, and returned with the cart heaped high with purchases. When a soldier arrived that evening – an unfamiliar man – I watched, stealthily, from the doorway of my hut as he carried in chairs and lamps and wrapped articles. And the following day a pianoforte was delivered by two swarthy men in turbans. I had turned away when I saw what they were hauling up the house steps, the sight of the pianoforte filling me with something – an uneasy, strange mixture of sadness and joy – that I couldn't quite define.

'Come, Pree,' Glory called to me, once they'd left. I was mixing Marta's manure with straw and patting it into rounds that I slapped against the enclosure wall to dry in the sun. 'Come and see my new pianoforte.'

I didn't want to do as she instructed, but I wanted – needed – to rest my eyes on the pianoforte. Slowly I went up the verandah steps and stood in the open doorway of the sitting room. I hadn't been inside the house for the last month.

Although the old horsehair settee and chair were still in place, Glory had draped them with scarlet and turquoise fabric. The glass-fronted cabinet also remained, but Glory had taken out the yellow chintz chair – perhaps to her bedroom – and now there were three new chairs of cheap cane. There were also small, bright carved brass tables, on which had been placed lamps, dripping with gaudy glass. I saw porcelain ladies dressed in painted gowns, and sweet dishes of gold-edged English china. There was a big brass tray on mahogany legs in front of the settee. On it sat a jingle-jangle glass vase and, for some unknown reason, a sporting trophy – some equestrian win. The walls were crammed with poor watercolour copies of English rural scenes and the Royal family in cheap gold frames, the glass covering them already fly-blown, so I knew she had bought them used.

She had purchased all of these things with my father's hard-earned money, squandering it on unnecessary material goods and silly trinkets. It was the money I might have used to leave the mission – to go where, I didn't know – but it would have at least made me feel I had some power, some control, over my own life.

My parents had been dead only two months, and already the worn but familiar signs of their lives at the mission – all they'd worked for – were disappearing. The infirmary was gone, the people I had once loved were gone, and the one thing left – the house – no longer looked like the only home I had known.

My breath caught in my throat as a sweeping sense of desolation came over me. The enormity of it was so strong that I had to lean against the door frame.

I was not yet eighteen, and had nothing, and no one. I was alone, not only at the mission, but in my life. Kai was somewhere in India; I might never again see him, and yet I clung to his memory with the desperate hope of one drowning.

'What do you think, Pree?' Glory ran her fingers down the keys, and I took a deep breath and straightened up.

The pianoforte was indeed glorious. It was new, and of much better quality than the old one my mother had adored. It had a round matching stool. Glory must have had even more money than what she had taken from my father, to purchase a possession of such beauty.

Now she ran her hands over the gleaming top. 'Come, Pree, play something,' she said. 'I also purchased a book of music.' She gestured to the music stand. On it sat bound sheets. *Mendelssohn: Violin Concerto in E Minor*, I read, with annoyance.

In spite of my overwhelming sadness and fresh anger for Glory, my fingers wanted to be on the keys so badly that they moved involuntarily, remembering the feel of smooth, cool ivory, and I took one step into the room.

But Glory frowned as she studied me. 'You stink of dung,' she said. 'Go and wash your hands and when you are clean come back and play something,' she demanded, as if I were a small child.

It would give me pleasure to say no to her; she couldn't force me to play the pianoforte. And yet how I wanted to. I would do this for myself, not for her. I went to the well and scrubbed my hands, then came back to the sitting room. I put my fingers on the beautiful keys, caressing their unblemished surface. My nails were ragged, still rimmed with manure and dirt. I took a deep breath and played a simple C-scale. The pianoforte naturally was out of tune after its journey in the back of the cart, but not badly enough to spoil its sound.

How my mother would have loved a pianoforte like this. I doubted she had ever had the opportunity to touch one of this magnificence.

I ran my fingers over a few more scales, then played the first tentative notes of 'Christians Awake', not sure whether I would remember it or not. But once I started I played the song in its entirety – all six verses – the keys moving as if of their own accord. When I had finished I simply sat there, remembering so many other times I had played the beloved hymn in this very room.

Then I wiped my face, wet with tears, with the back of my arm and went back outside to finish making the dung cakes for the cooking fire.

The only thing I was grateful for was that Glory hadn't spoken during my playing, or afterwards.

The next day I couldn't rise from my bed. There was nothing wrong in my body; I had no pain anywhere. But a heaviness had come over me as darkness fell and I lay on Kai's charpoy, recalling playing the pianoforte. I moved my fingers on my thighs as if I might re-create the music, humming the melody in a cracked voice, and knew the sadness had started the moment I leaned against the door frame, studying the lovely pianoforte in the now unfamiliar room.

I slept poorly, awakening with a start many times throughout the night, and when daylight broke, my head was hot, my eyes prickly.

I thought of playing the pianoforte, but the joy of the familiar hymn and the happiness it had once brought me, again only emphasised how much I'd lost.

Perhaps it had taken this passage of time – these past few months – for the horror and grief to truly take hold of me. Perhaps I hadn't fully absorbed what had occurred. Had it been so overwhelming that I had pushed my emotions aside, had blundered on almost mindlessly? I recalled how, only a few days after my mother's horrific death, I had managed to march into Lahore and implore both Mrs Wyndham and the Most Reverend Burgess for help.

And when no help was forthcoming I had returned here, to watch Glory take command and Sanosh leave. And then I had carried on, working diligently and repetitively in the garden and mission in the way of a mindless ox that ploughs the furrows, thinking of nothing but the manger of hay at the end of the day.

But this morning, fresh, new sorrow came over me in a wave, as deep and pulsing as if I had just heard my father's last shuddering breath, as if I had just stared at Sanosh's freshly burned hands, choking on acrid smoke, unable to believe what he told me my mother had done.

'What will I do?' I whispered to the rafters. 'What will I do?'

Although my eyes burned, no tears came.

Glory pushed aside the door covering. 'What are you doing? Where is my tea and breakfast? Get up and cook for me, lazy girl.'

I stared at her. 'I'm sick, Glory,' I said, which was partly the truth. Is not a deep sadness, one which stills the body as if held with lead weights and grips the mind in a dark and hard vice also an illness?

'What's wrong with you?'

I turned to face the wall, not answering, and in a moment she left, muttering. I heard her start a fire, then the angry clatter of pots.

I first saw the Colonel a week later. A handsome man, he was tall and well built, with thick auburn hair and bright grey eyes, his smile easy.

Although I had lain in my charpoy for one more day of self-pity after the arrival of the pianoforte, eventually I had risen, disgusted with my own dirty hands and feet and unwashed hair. I took off my filthy, torn frock, bathed and washed my hair, and twisted it into two long plaits which I wound around my head and pinned in place. I put on an old kurta and pair of *panjammahs* Kai had left behind in his hut. If I were to act as a servant at the mission, I would look like one. And in this way I also hoped not to draw attention to myself when any of the soldiers were present.

I had especially noticed the man Glory called the Colonel because he stood out from the other soldiers who had spent time at the mission house with Glory. Obviously of a higher rank, indicated by the braid on his jacket, he was not only the most attractive of all of them, but he also carried himself with an air of authority, of one used to being in control.

The second evening he came to visit I was hauling water from the well, pouring it into a brass lotah.

'What's the girl's name?' I heard him ask Glory, who sat beside him on the verandah in one of the new rattan chairs she'd purchased only weeks before. 'She can't hide her looks under that boy's garb.' His voice, although low, carried across the courtyard. I glanced at him, then quickly bent my head over the well.

'Never mind her,' Glory said. 'Let's go inside. I'm bored. Pour me another drink, Colonel,' she said, in her sweetest, although to my ears, wheedling, voice.

The Colonel stayed where he was, ignoring Glory's request. I concentrated on hauling up the overflowing bucket, but was aware of him still studying me as I took the bucket to Marta's enclosure.

The third time the Colonel came he was accompanied by four others: two soldiers and two Eurasian women. It was immediately obvious, by their slovenly way of dress and the coarse mannerisms, that the women were of low breeding.

I watched the verandah, hidden in my dark doorway. The Colonel was charming and flirtatious, showering Glory with compliments. In turn she simpered and fawned over him, sitting on his lap, stroking his arms and his chest and, as she whispered to him, her tongue licked the curve of his ear. After the first few pegs of whiskey he grew ever more charismatic, laughing at everything Glory said, agreeing with her and again complimenting her. But by the fourth glass he became sullen, and by the sixth, angry and argumentative. I watched, holding my breath as he threw his glass on to the verandah floor in a rage, grinding the glass under his boot, and pushing Glory to the floor.

'Colonel,' she beseeched, standing and trying to caress him. 'You are mistaken. I meant only that I—'

He raised his hand and slapped her face with such force that she stumbled into another soldier, who caught and supported her. In the silence that fell over the courtyard I must have made a sound. Was it a small cry of surprise, a loud intake of breath? Whatever I did unwittingly, it drew attention to me, for suddenly I was aware that all eyes on the verandah had turned to me.

'Go and get her,' the Colonel said to one of the soldiers, who came down the steps. I moved back inside my hut. The soldier came to the doorway and moved his head.

'The Colonel wants you,' he said.

I shook my head, standing in front of my charpoy.

'Hurry up, girl. You don't keep the Colonel waiting,' he said, and took another step towards me.

There was a sudden shrill burst of laughter from Glory, and the soldier looked behind him, through the open door. Then, without another word, he turned and left.

Whatever Glory had done to make the Colonel forget about me, I was grateful.

The next morning the horses were gone, and the house was quiet, although the cheap scent worn by the women still lingered in the convenience.

That afternoon one of the women returned in a cart driven by a sullen-looking native. She and Glory sat on the verandah and drank whiskey, arguing quietly, their voices too

339

low for me to hear them from where I ground spices outside the *rasoi*. I glanced up to see Glory frowning and shaking her head, and then putting money into the woman's outstretched palm. And in that moment I understood what kind of house of ill-repute Glory was creating at the mission, and my heart grew heavier still.

The next evening I was outside the *rasoi*, preparing to eat a bowl of goat biryani and another of yogurt I had prepared. I looked up at the sound of hoofs, thinking it was another soldier, come to join those already here – the Colonel and a second soldier, who had brought one of the women from the evening before. They were inside the house; it was growing late, and lamplight already shone through the windows.

But it wasn't a soldier who rode into the courtyard. An Afghan sat tall astride a striking black horse with delicate legs and a luxurious mane. The man looked around the darkening courtyard. For one moment, my heart giving a high, light tap of unexplained joy, I thought it was my Afghan.

Almost immediately I realised my mistake, and my heart returned to its usual beat. I went to the man, the bowl of biryani still in my hand.

'*Assalamu alaikum*,' he said, wishing me peace in the traditional Muslim greeting.

'*Wa alaikum assalam*, and on you be peace,' I replied, and he nodded and swung off his horse, his face contorting for a moment.

Standing in front of me, he spoke rapidly in Pashto.

'I'm sorry,' I said in Hindi, hoping he spoke it, 'I do not speak your language, but you wish to drink, and water your horse?'

'*Ha, pani*,' he replied in strongly accented Hindi. '*Kripaya.*' Although he spoke slowly and with effort, he asked for water with politeness and quiet dignity. I nodded, studying his narrow, glittering black eyes, aquiline nose and high cheekbones which I associated with the Pathans who passed by on the road. They were an attractive race. Again I thought of the man I had once referred to as my Afghan, the one on the golden stallion. His nose hadn't been hawkish, like this man's, but fine, narrow. He had never returned since that last time, when I'd had Adriana with me; the time he had told me he was leaving Lahore, and going to Peshawar. 'I need water. Please. For myself, and my horse,' the man said again.

Gesturing at the well, I nodded. 'Take what you need.'

He led his horse to the well. He hauled up the bucket and set it down with contrived, awkward movements of his left hand, his right arm against his body. The horse immediately put its nose into the bucket and drank with great slurping and snuffling. The man glanced at the bowl I still held.

'I have food?' he asked, but before I had a chance to respond he said, 'I pay.'

I held the biryani out to him.

'I pay,' he said again, now reaching within the folds of his cloak, but slowly, carefully.

'No,' I said. 'Take it. May you never be hungry,' I added, remembering the Afghan salutation.

He winced as he leaned forward to reach for the bowl of biryani with his left hand. 'May you never be poor,' he responded, in thanks.

'Are you hurt?' I asked, seeing the stiffness of the arm he so pointedly held against himself, certain he was injured by the careful exaggeration of his movements, the strained expression.

He shook his head, but now, looking more closely, I saw a bright stain on the right sleeve of his shirt. It was fresh, and growing larger as I watched.

'You are. Your arm,' I said, and he glanced at his sleeve. 'May I see?'

His face grew rigid, as if both surprised and insulted at my forwardness. He shook his head, an abrupt and almost angry movement.

'Maybe I can stop the bleeding.'

He stared at me, his eyes dropping from my face to my kurta, to my *panjammahs* and bare feet, before coming back to study my face. 'What kind of woman? You are midwife?' he asked, and I shook my head.

'Not a midwife. But I . . .' I hesitated, then said, 'I am a woman of . . . *dava*.' I surprised myself. But it was true. I was a woman of medicine. If he was wounded, I could help him.

'*Dava*?' he said. 'You heal?'

I nodded.

He studied me for another moment, his thick, dark brows almost meeting, scowling as if unsure of how to react to this. Then, slowly, as if still deliberating with himself, he set down the bowl and gingerly rolled up his right sleeve and held out his arm with the underside up. There was a blood-soaked strip of fabric wrapped around his forearm, but it obviously was of no use in staunching the flow.

I stepped closer, peering at it, and put up my hands to untie the makeshift bandage. 'May I?' I asked, and he looked around the courtyard as if confirming that we were alone, obviously reluctant to be seen allowing himself to be touched by an unknown woman. Then he gave a curt nod. I worked the cloth free; part of it was sticking to drying, older blood. When I finally pulled the cloth away there was so much blood that it was hard to see what had happened. Using the edge of my kurta, I patted at the underside of his arm, and saw a fresh knife wound, long and gaping. I wouldn't ask what had happened. 'It's deep. It will keep bleeding. You'll soon grow weak. It should be closed.' I pressed the cloth back against it, and put his other hand over it to hold it in place.

He watched his left hand, holding back the blood steadily seeping between his fingers. His look was almost one of curiosity, as if the blood didn't belong to him. Then he looked at me.

'I can close it,' I said, nodding. 'I can sew it together.'

He studied my face again, the look of reluctance still there, and then gave the slightest of nods. I went into the house through the side door. Some of the shelves in the storeroom still held dusty bottles and medical supplies.

I tried to move quietly, not wanting to draw attention to myself, but I had to pass the dining room. Glory looked up from her hand of cards. I hadn't been in the house since I'd played the pianoforte. It was stifling, even with all the shutters open, and smelled of sweat and candle wax and cheroot smoke and alcohol.

Glory, facing the door, stopped dealing from a deck of cards. 'What are you doing?' she called, and I flinched as the soldier and other woman looked up from their hands, and the Colonel turned in his chair.

'Have you come to join our game of Loo?' he asked, smiling lazily.

'No. There's an Afghan in our courtyard,' I said.

'An Afghan?' the Colonel repeated, rising and picking up his musket from where it leaned against the table. His eyes went to the blood on my kurta.

'There's no need for that,' I said, nodding at his musket. 'He doesn't intend any harm. He just wanted water, and something to eat. And he's hurt.'

Now the Colonel stared through the open window. 'They possess a lot of energy, those Afghans,' he said. 'And shifty blighters, especially that sort, the Pathans. Never know what they'll do. Same mixture of arrogance and suspicion in the lot of them.'

'At least they have more heart than many an apathetic

343

native,' said the other soldier. 'Glory, play your hand.'

'Most probably because they haven't been ruled by the British for centuries, like the darkies,' the Colonel said. 'Good thing they're no longer against us.'

Glory looked at him, frowning. 'Come back to the game. I will take this trick.'

As the Colonel set down his musket I slipped into the storeroom, peering at the shelves in the dimness and taking what I needed. But as I stepped out of the room, holding disinfectant, flannel and gauze and a needle and thread, there was the Colonel in the passageway outside the storeroom. His unexpected presence, so close, made me start, and the roll of gauze dropped to the floor. The Colonel put his left hand against the wall of the passageway as if to prevent me from passing.

'Are you going to tend to the Afghan's needs?' he said, looking at what I held against my chest, then reaching out to run his right index finger down my cheek. He smiled, and I smelled the dusky odour of tobacco, but I could tell that he wasn't yet intoxicated.

I turned my cheek to pull away from his touch. 'He's wounded.'

'Perhaps when you've finished you'll tend to me. Will you, Pree?' he asked, too quietly, no longer smiling, and involuntarily I shuddered at his intensity. In the other room Glory argued loudly, accusing someone of taking one of her cards. 'Will you let me come to your hut, and you tend to my needs?' His voice was low, little more than a whisper, and his eyes stared into mine, unblinking.

'Please. Let me pass,' I said, trying not to look into his eyes. And yet there was something almost hypnotic in his gaze, and his eyes held mine. My heart pounded; he was too near, his voice too intimate in the narrow, darkened hallway. I felt the heat of his body, and had a sudden, sickening image of it on mine. I could not let that happen. As if reading my mind, the Colonel leaned closer.

'I will eventually take you whether you wish it or not, Pree,' he said, softly, with a hint of a smile that was almost benevolent.

A cry of alarm escaped from my lips. 'No!' I said, stooping and picking up the gauze. Ducking under the Colonel's arm, avoiding touching him, I hurried out the side door.

The Afghan's sleeve was still rolled up, and although he was pressing the soaked cloth over the wound, blood dripped from it in a steady stream. I put down what I carried and went to my hut to fetch a candle, lighting it so I could see clearly.

I gave the candle to the Afghan to hold in his left hand. Then I poured disinfectant over the wound and gently patted it as clean as I could with pieces of flannel. He didn't flinch or make a sound. I held the threaded needle over the flame of the candle while I counted to twelve, as I'd been taught, and sewed the wound closed. The man was completely still as I worked.

'Where do you live?' I asked, hoping to distract him from the pain of the needle biting through his flesh.

'Herat,' he said, naming the city I knew to be on the western border of Afghanistan.

'You're returning home now?' I asked, glancing up at him, the needle poised over this arm.

He nodded.

I knew he would have to pass through Peshawar on his way into Afghanistan. Again the man I had once thought of as my Afghan came to mind. He lived in Peshawar. As did the Langs.

It took sixteen stitches to close the wound.

When I had finished I again cleaned away the remaining blood and wrapped his arm with a clean strip of muslin, tying the ends.

'It will soon heal,' I said, realising how good it felt to help someone again, to use the needle and thread, to see something open and raw neatly closed and clean.

He simply nodded his thanks, rolled down his blood-soaked sleeve and crouched to eat the biryani.

That night in my hut I thought back to all the people who had once come to the infirmary, and the sense of purpose I had felt in helping them. I knew how I missed that, and how much of my emptiness came from no longer being useful to others. I pushed away the image of the strange encounter with the Colonel in the hallway, and knew I could never again put myself in a position to be too close to him.

In the morning there was no trace that the Afghan had been in the courtyard.

CHAPTER TWENTY-SEVEN

LATER THAT DAY Glory came to the *rasoi* where I sat cross legged, a plate in my lap, eating a piece of fish I had caught in the Ravi and fried in chickpea batter, along with a *roti* stuffed with okra and split peas.

'The Colonel is coming again tonight,' she said.

I looked up at her, chewing slowly.

'Stay away from him.'

'I don't wish to be in his presence,' I said truthfully, and yet I felt the tiniest shiver, the same unfathomable sensation I'd experienced in the dark corridor the night before.

Still standing over me, she reached down and picked a sliver of fish from the pan, putting it into her mouth and then licking her fingers loudly. 'I do not like his interest in you.'

I kept eating. *Nor do I*, I thought, *nor do I*.

'Perhaps you would like to earn money,' she said, studying me, her head to one side.

'Money? What do you mean?' In the instant I spoke, I saw the image of her putting coins into the Eurasian woman's hand, and held my breath.

'I could introduce you to your own gentleman, Pree. If you have your own gentleman, the Colonel will not want you. But, my goodness, you must find a decent frock. You are quite unattractive in such native clothing.'

I blinked, looking away from her, studying the flake of fish between my index and third finger.

'What do you think, Pree? Would you like to work for me?'

I understood her meaning, but couldn't bear to respond. After a moment I looked back into her face. 'I already work for you, Glory. If you would like to pay me for cooking, and for the rest of my work at the mission, I will accept money.'

She smirked. 'I will not pay you for these servant's tasks. But you could help me entertain.'

Slowly, my blood grew too hot. And then it ran, tripping like angry fire, through me, and I stood in a rush, my plate falling from my lap to the ground, the fish landing in the dust.

'For this you would be well paid, Pree.'

I couldn't speak, didn't dare speak. Instead, I simply walked away, down to the Ravi, and sat there for a long time, wondering how my life had come to this.

That night the Colonel and his followers again came to the mission. As soon as I heard approaching horses I ran into the field and, as I had before, sat among the new corn. The air was sweet, the sky still bright, and although I wasn't uncomfortable, after a time I grew restless. There would be another hour of light. I wished I had brought the book I had started to read the night before, Anthony Trollope's *The Warden*. Dare I go back for it?

I rose, making the decision with little thought, and then carefully slipped back towards the house. Seeing from a safe distance that Glory and her visitors were inside the house, I went more boldly towards my hut. But sitting on the top step of the side verandah was a young ensign, reading.

I had noticed him before, this young ensign who always accompanied the Colonel. He usually waited with the horses, grooming them and feeding them, or sitting on the fence along the road. He had never come to the house. There was a great deal of noise from inside: someone pounded on the pianoforte, and others sang a silly ditty through bursts of laughter.

I squinted, lifting my chin in an effort to read the title of his book as I went by. It was *The Count of Monte Cristo*.

He looked up and studied my face, a small, friendly smile on his lips. The smile was so genuine that I had to stop.

'Hello,' I said. There was no reason to hide from him; it was only the Colonel I was avoiding, and it was clear he and the others were well occupied. 'You're reading Dumas,' I said, and his eyebrows rose in his forehead. 'I liked that tale a great deal.'

He looked confused, and stood, removing his cap. 'You've read it?' he said. 'This book? You've read *The Count of Monte Cristo*?'

'Yes,' I said, smiling. 'Do you find that so odd?'

He looked confused, tucking the book under his arm.

'I'm Miss Fincastle,' I told him.

'Miss . . . Fincastle? I'm sorry, Miss, but I . . . I didn't expect . . . your English is . . .' He stopped.

'Proper English?' I asked, smiling again at his innocent, flustered demeanour. I looked down at the old *panjammahs* rolled to mid-calf, stained from kneeling in the garden that afternoon. The elbows of the *kurta* were threadbare. I'd taken the pins out of my plaits; they hung down to my waist. I knew my skin was darkened from constant work outside in the early summer sun, the muscles of my arms and legs hard and defined, and understood the ensign's uncertainty.

I no longer had the appearance of a Miss Pree Fincastle, daughter of missionaries.

'I've seen you working about the garden and courtyard,' he said. 'I thought you were . . .' He left off awkwardly.

'My parents were missionaries here. Before,' I explained. 'I appear this way because it makes it easier for me to work. And

. . .' I looked at the house, but didn't feel it would be proper to explain the other reason.

'But . . . why are you here?' he asked. 'Why didn't you leave with your parents?'

'They died here.'

He studied me. 'I'm sorry, Miss Fincastle.' He had to raise his voice to be heard over the boisterous laughter and shouts. 'But again, I must ask why you've stayed. With . . . with all that goes on here.' He tipped his head towards the house.

I stared back at him. 'This was my home. I have nowhere else to go.'

He nodded, a look of sympathy on his face, and then he shook his head slightly, and finally smiled again, that good, true smile. 'I'm Ensign Edward Halyard,' he said, 'although my friends call me Eddie. And I'm glad to know there's someone here with whom I can discuss *The Count of Monte Cristo*. Although you mustn't tell me the ending.'

I instinctively trusted Ensign Edward Halyard. Eddie, with the nice smile.

'Why do you come here?' I asked. 'You never . . .' I gestured towards the house as he had a moment earlier.

'The Colonel's orders. I'm to make sure he gets back to the barracks every night,' he said. 'As you've probably seen, he gets himself into quite a state. Some nights I have to tie him on his horse.' He smiled. 'But believe me, I'd rather be somewhere else. Anywhere, actually,' he added, with a small laugh. 'No offence meant, Miss.'

'None taken. So would I.' I laughed as well, but it came out as a strange croak. I hadn't laughed for a long time.

I said goodbye then, and hurried into my hut, snatching up my book, then waved at Eddie as I passed him on my way back to the field. I slept there again that night, using my book as a pillow.

* * *

350

The next time the Colonel came, I watched for an opportunity to talk to Eddie. I had come through Marta's enclosure to the fence, where he leaned.

'You've finished *The Count of Monte Cristo*, then?' I asked him, appearing beside him unexpectedly, and he turned as if startled, and then his face broke in that somehow familiar smile.

'Oh. Miss Fincastle,' he said, colour rising on his cheeks. 'Yes, yes, I finished it only yesterday.' We stood, leaning against the fence, and talked about the book for a few moments, then fell silent.

'Does the Ravi run beyond the fields?' he asked, and I nodded.

'Would you like to walk there?' he asked. 'I find it terribly boring simply waiting. And the Colonel won't wish to leave for many hours.' He looked up at the still pale sky, then back to me. Again, his face flushed. 'Unless you find my suggestion too forward. I completely understand if you prefer not to . . .'

As his voice trailed off, I realised I had never before spoken to a young Englishman. He was treating me with respect, as if I deserved respect, in spite of the way I was dressed, and the way I lived. What was the proper decorum in this situation? I knew that surely I should decline; walking unchaperoned with him after just meeting him could not possibly be how things were done in England. But this wasn't England. And, in this new and twisted life I found myself in, there didn't appear to be any rules I could refer to.

'I would like to go for a walk,' I said, straightening my shoulders, thinking of the Colonel's intense stare. 'But don't let's pass the house. Come with me; I know another way.'

He followed me down the road a bit, and then through a worn path in the field used by those who worked there. As we walked side by side on the narrow trail, Jassie appeared, following at a safe distance, and Eddie turned to look at her.

'That's my dog, Jassie,' I said, suddenly recognising that she was old now; she had grown large with only one litter of puppies last year, and had been away for just a few days. It was obvious her milk hadn't come in, so I could only assume the pups had been born dead. Her scarred muzzle had grown pale and bristly, and her back slightly swayed.

'Hello, girl,' Eddie chirped, squatting and holding out his hand, and I shook my head, explaining that she would never come near.

And then Eddie told me about his dog, back in England at his parents' home. We talked easily about nothing in particular: his life in England, mine here, books we'd read, things we'd seen. I knew that in spite of him having travelled halfway round the globe, he was naïve and somehow unworldly. We were the same age, but I felt much older.

Without noticing it, we dispensed with all formality; he called me Pree, and I called him Eddie. Was this because I was dressed as a boy, and had no feminine wiles such as I'd seen Glory demonstrate? As darkness fell and we sat on the bank of the Ravi, I studied him as he spoke. His appearance was boyish, with dimples and that hopeful smile that made his brown eyes almost disappear. His blond hair stuck up in an endearing way when he took off his peaked army cap. He was not tall, although slightly taller than me, and his wrists were delicate.

In those few hours I sensed that he, like me, was lonely.

The Colonel didn't come for a few days, although the two women arrived with other soldiers. I realised I was disappointed, watching for Eddie. Finally, three nights later, the Colonel did ride up, and as Eddie was wiping down the horses I went to him, again avoiding being seen from the house.

'Shall we walk by the river again?' he asked, without even

saying hello. He looked even more sweet to my eyes this evening. Over the last days I had thought of the many things I might tell him the next time I saw him; I knew how anxious I was to talk to someone, to have a friend.

He had a mango; as we walked to the river he cut into it with his knife and offered me half. I shook my head and he ate it all, laughing as he licked the juice from his palm.

As we stood looking at the river, I turned to him, suddenly, to ask him if he'd seen the fish that had just leapt from the water, and in a sudden rush his cheeks stained crimson. Without looking away from me he reached inside his jacket. 'I bought this for you in the bazaar.' He held out a small tiger's eye pin. The stone was brown, streaked with gold, and surrounded with smaller bits of topaz-coloured glass. 'When I saw it I thought of you. It's the colour of your eyes.'

I looked at it winking on his palm. I smelled mango, and raised my eyes to his.

'You shouldn't have done that,' I said, my voice little more than a whisper. Images of Glory's boxes of cheap jewellery, all those things she had shown me each time she had gone into Lahore, came to my mind. 'You don't need to buy my favour.'

His fingers immediately closed around the pin.

'I'm sorry,' he said. 'I didn't mean . . . it's . . . it's only a small gift. Please, take it.' He stuttered slightly, holding his hand towards me again and opening his fingers.

'Do you think I'm like Glory?' I asked, growing more disturbed, my voice slightly louder.

'Glory?' He looked genuinely puzzled.

'Glory. At the house. The woman who runs the house.'

His eyes widened. 'Of course not. I . . . I just received my salary yesterday. I don't have much to spend it on, and I wanted to buy something for you. It doesn't mean . . .'

But I knew too well, from living with Glory, the weight a gift could carry, and stood, studying my bare feet.

'Pree,' Eddie said. 'It's not . . . that. What you're thinking.'

I knew he told the truth, but somehow I couldn't look at him. The evening was spoiled. I walked back to the mission, aware of him following at a distance, and without speaking to him again, went into my hut and stayed there. But I couldn't sleep, and was still awake many hours later, when I heard him struggling under the weight of the Colonel, who cursed and grunted as Eddie urged him to try and walk.

Only when I heard the diminishing sound of trotting hoofs did I come out into the dark courtyard and sit under the peepul tree.

The next day was hot; summer had fully descended. It was mid-afternoon when Glory called to me from the doorway of the house, and I went up the verandah steps. She'd only recently awakened; although she was dressed and had styled her hair, her cheek was marked with the lines of her pillow.

'Pree,' she said, her voice sullen. 'The Colonel is very interested in you.' She licked her lips, looking around the room, then went to the table in front of the settee and picked up a glass. She drained the murky liquid left in the bottom and wiped her mouth with the back of her hand. 'He would like to make an offer.'

I stared at her. 'An offer? What do you mean?' I thought of my disappointment in Eddie's offer – the gift that I knew, in my heart, was a true and innocent present, but any joy I might have had in receiving it was spoiled because of this. Because of Glory and the life she had forced me into. Suddenly my disappointment turned to anger. 'I'm not a half-caste whore like you, Glory,' I said, quietly but firmly.

I waited for her anger, wondering if she might try to strike me, but she only looked at me, studying me from my head to my feet, then smiled and pulled me to the mirror beside the front door. 'Look closely, and tell me what you see, Pree,' she said.

I smelled alcohol – stale, from the previous night, and sharper, from the mouthful she had just swallowed.

I glared at her reflection, then looked at my own, something I rarely did now. I looked back at her. She was still smiling, the cat smile I hated.

'Well?' she said, and I again looked at our images, side by side.

Glory wore a pale blue frock of fine lawn, tightly drawn in at the waist. It swung prettily over her crinoline. Her face was pale with cream and powder, her eyes no longer ringed with *surma*. Her hair, which she always kept hennaed now, so it was no longer black but a shining auburn, was piled high, with wisps at her collar and charming curls around her cheeks. She looked almost – almost – like a respectable woman of uncertain heritage, although her age and the way she lived were beginning to show, and her face was slightly puffy.

My skin, darkened by the summer sun, was a shade deeper than Glory's, who never stepped outdoors except to sit in the shade of the verandah. This morning I hadn't tended to my hair, and it hung in tangles. My *kurta* and *panjammahs* were waiting to be washed in the Ravi, so I'd put on one of Glory's old saris; she had no interest in them now and had thrown them all out in a heap one day. I had sorted through them – just like I always had the charity boxes when the mission was still a mission – and decided to keep a few. The sari I wore today was dull yellow; the loose end of it was not pulled demurely over my chest and one shoulder, as it should be, but hanging down. The low bodice, a little too small because I was taller than Glory, exposed the tops of my breasts. I had been working in the garden under the hot sun, and the sari was streaked with dirt and perspiration.

Now Glory's smile turned to a smirk. 'Well? Do you see a half-caste whore in the looking glass, Pree?' she asked, and I pulled my arm from her, both angry and shocked at what the mirror reflected, and at what Glory had suggested.

'I will not have anything to do with the Colonel,' I said, straightening my shoulders and leaving the house. And yet I couldn't forget his words. *I will eventually take you whether you wish it or not, Pree*. I kept my back rigid as I walked away, and yet inwardly I was quaking, filled with fear at – again – the image of the Colonel brutally forcing himself upon me.

I tried to find comfort by going to the cemetery and sitting by the four little headstones, cleaning them with the end of my sari, and pulling out the ever-present weeds. I had long since filled in the empty grave once dug by the *sudra*s for my father, but there were now two round white stones, one on either side of the headstones. I'd hauled them from the river in the cart, depositing them in the graveyard and whitewashing them. They represented my parents. I knew I should have something more fitting than river stones to commemorate their deaths, and yet I had no means to purchase headstones and have them carved. I thought that some day – like the rest of my imaginings – I would somehow be able to do this for them.

I don't know how long I remained there, but eventually I heard horses, and knew Glory's visitors had arrived. I hoped it wasn't the Colonel – I didn't want to have to hide from him, and the discomfort I felt over what had happened with Eddie the evening before made me uneasy at seeing him as well.

I waited. I grew hungry; I hadn't eaten since midday, and now the sky was losing its light. The house appeared silent from this short distance. Finally, when it was completely dark, I went towards the courtyard, wanting to slip into the *rasoi* and take some of the cold chicken I had prepared earlier.

I heard no sound from the verandah, and so, encouraged, hurried past.

'Pree.'

Stopping, I closed my eyes and held my breath. The Colonel was indeed on the verandah, sitting alone with a full glass in his hand. For a moment I considered ignoring him, but when he said my name again, more firmly, I opened my eyes and turned to him. 'Yes?'

Glory came out of the house and stood beside his chair, holding her own glass.

He drained his glass and poured himself another from the bottle he lifted from beside his chair. 'Glory?' he said, holding out the bottle to her.

She shook her head. Her face was still, her mouth unsmiling, which was unusual when there was a man present.

'I've told Glory I'm interested in having you join one of our parties,' he said, smiling now, the charming, inviting smile.

I drew myself up, my heart thudding. 'I told her I wasn't interested.'

'You don't seem to mind spending time with Ensign Halyard. I've seen you two sneaking about. Is it that you imagine you're too good for me?' The smile had disappeared with the last sentence. He set down the bottle and glass, and came down the steps towards me, stopping close enough to speak directly into my face. 'You'll like what I have to offer,' he said, and I turned my face from the whiskey on his breath, shaking my head.

He didn't speak for a moment. Then he said, 'I'm not a mewling lad like young Eddie.' He put his arm around my shoulder, looking at Glory. I stiffened under the easy drape of his arm. 'Isn't that right, Glory?'

Glory didn't answer.

'Is she really still a virgin, as you say?' he asked her, but he turned to me in the next instant. My breath caught at his crude comment, and his nostrils flared, wolfishly, as if trying to draw in my scent. 'Or have you given it up to Halyard? Or maybe to others as well?'

I stared into his face, unable to speak, my chest rising and falling under the bodice of Glory's old sari. The Colonel's eyes dropped to my breasts.

Glory finally spoke. 'Oh no, that isn't being happening. My goodness no, Colonel. I am not letting anyone to touch her. I save her.' She talked rapidly, her English *chee-chee* more pronounced.

I clenched my teeth. She was saving me? She, saving me?

'And who are you saving her for?' the Colonel asked, now slowly rubbing his hand up and down my arm. I tried to step away from him, but his fingers closed around my upper arm.

'It is not for what man I am saving her, Colonel. It is for how much rupees. The right rupee price,' Glory said, her eyes on his hand. I saw the anger in her face, and knew it wasn't for him, but for me. Although she had made it clear she would like it if I brought in money in the same way she did – because I knew she would be sure to take most or all of it for herself – I also knew she had special feelings for the high-ranking Colonel, and didn't wish to share him.

'And what would that price be?' he asked her.

It was as if I didn't exist, as if I were invisible. And yet the Colonel's hand was strong and unmoving; I was held as if my arm was wrapped in a chain.

A slow smile came to Glory's mouth as her eyelids lowered in her usual coyness. But there was something different this time; she glanced at me, and I was shocked at the hatred I saw there. 'For one first time, cost would be high high. Twenty rupees.'

'Twenty rupees? Are you mad? Is she made of pure gold?' he asked, but his grip didn't lessen. 'That's twenty times what I pay you.'

'It is not being so very, very much for a man like you, Colonel,' Glory said. 'You before are telling me that you are wanting to pay for . . . unusual business. Maybe a virgin is unusual?'

As the Colonel relaxed his fingers to turn to me, I wrenched free. 'You can't sell me, Glory,' I said, trying to keep my voice firm, although my breathing was ragged. 'I'm not yours to sell, as if I were Marta.' I had backed away, out of the Colonel's reach.

The Colonel smiled now, a warm, pleasant smile. 'Of course not, Pree. Glory, she's right. We're treating her poorly. She is a young woman who deserves respect.' Just like that, any threat dropped away, and he smiled fondly at me, as if I were an old and very dear friend.

I was wary, knowing full well that he was simply pulling out his beguiling ways, encouraging me to trust him. When he was like this it was as if those near to him were bathed in the rays of the sun.

I stepped away, slowly, never turning my back.

Glory was staring at me, glowering, but I could see beneath the surface. Already she was letting go of the anger and calculating the new frocks and slippers and jewellery she could buy with twenty rupees. Of course she would keep the money.

The Colonel now had a sensuous, intimate look on his face. His eyes were fixed on mine; he was trying to draw me to him, as he had the night outside the storeroom.

Their expressions terrified me: the Colonel expected to have me, and Glory expected to be paid what she asked.

I went into my hut. I didn't glance at the fence, where I knew Eddie waited with the horses. Watching.

Pulling the sabre from its hiding place and holding it I sat, unmoving, on my charpoy, staring at the door. But the Colonel didn't appear, and I heard nothing more. When I awoke in the morning, my neck stiff from having fallen asleep slumped against the wall, the sabre still beside me, I knew I had been spared.

But for how many more nights, I thought. How many more nights?

CHAPTER TWENTY-EIGHT

THE NEXT DAY I sat at the *rasoi*, polishing a brass pot. I looked at the blackened stones of the infirmary; they had been washed clean by the late spring rains and already tumbled further upon themselves as the last of the wattle broke down. Saplings and weeds grew around them and through the crevices; in a bizarre way the infirmary now resembled one of the ancient Hindu shrines found alongside the roads.

I thought of the fire, and then of Sanosh, and rose, putting the pot into the *rasoi* and wiping my hands. Then I set off for Tek Mandi. I needed to feel, if even for an hour, that I was still the same person. I hoped that Sanosh could remind me of who I had once been.

Did I also hope that he might offer some help? Could it be possible that I believed he might give me an opportunity to find safety away from the mission?

He was sitting outside the home where Darshan, his wife and their two small children lived. Tears filled my eyes when I saw him, and I blinked them away. I longed to run to him and embrace him, but knew this would make him uncomfortable. He rose when he finally realised it was I who approached him, and for one instant his eyes showed surprise – at my appearance, or simply at seeing me? – but then his old face quickly wreathed in a smile, and he made *namaste*. I returned the gesture, and he welcomed me into his son's home. I followed him into the dim hut, and immediately sensed that his daughter-in-law didn't want me there. Of course, she, along with everyone else in Tek Mandi, and in the village of Dipha, and maybe beyond — would know of the brothel that had replaced the mission. I had been thoughtless to come, and to put Sanosh in this position. And how could I, for one instant, have imagined that I might stay here?

Sanosh spoke to his daughter-in-law, introducing us, and while she wasn't impolite, the atmosphere was strained. She served us tea and an earthen plate of figs as Sanosh and I sat across from each other. We didn't speak of earlier times, which would bring forth memories of my parents and the horrific tragedy. We didn't speak of Kai. We especially didn't mention Glory.

Instead I told him a silly story of Jassie's latest antics, and another about the number of tiny geckos I had found when I had so recently re-thatched the roof of the house, and he smiled kindly. He listened, concerned, as I told him that Marta was growing old, that something was wrong with her hip, and that I didn't know how much longer she would be able to pull the cart. He talked about his life with Darshan — whom I didn't see — and the blessings of his two grandsons. That he was fortunate to have an obedient and compassionate daughter-in-law. I learned what Jafar was doing, living in Ludhiana now. We spoke only of safe things.

'And you are happy, Sanosh?' I asked him, after we had again moved outside and sat in the sunshine with our backs against the simple house.

'Happy, not happy,' he said, lifting his shoulders. 'The question has no meaning. This is my life. Nothing more, nothing less,' he said, watching his daughter-in-law thumping dough over a tiny fire, smoke billowing around her face.

I couldn't understand his answer. Maybe, I reasoned, one had to be born a Hindu to feel this way.

★ ★ ★

A few days after I visited Sanosh, feeling lonely and restless, I took Marta and the cart into Lahore. Although I had no money to buy anything, I looked through a tray of used books in the English bazaar for the sheer pleasure of it. But when I raised my eyes I saw Mrs Rollings-Smythe staring at me, not far away. She pointedly looked away from me, whispering behind her fan to her companion, a woman I didn't recognise. The other woman stared at me openly, her mouth agape, shaking her head as her fan fluttered frantically at chest level.

I could only imagine what the English community in Lahore thought of me, and the way I lived. If they had looked down on me when I was a missionary's daughter, I shuddered to think of the brush they painted me with now. I vowed never to go to Lahore again.

Two evenings later I was emerging from the convenience when I heard the Colonel's voice. I ducked behind the convenience and crouched in the bushes there. I heard the Colonel, calling for Glory, then go straight into the house. I was weary; I had worked for hours in the garden, and had hoped that the Colonel wouldn't come that night: I wanted to sleep deeply, but wouldn't dare if he were nearby. The idea of spending another night on the ground in the cornfield was unappealing.

I planned to take my blankets and pillow this time; at least I would make myself more comfortable. I waited for an hour, hearing the Colonel's and Glory's voices on the verandah, and the Colonel shout for Eddie. Finally, when there was only the low, steady murmur of voices from within the house, and the courtyard was in darkness, I slipped into my hut, and gathered blankets and my pillow.

And then I heard Eddie calling my name. I didn't move.

He called again, and something I didn't recognise in his voice made me go to the doorway. He stood on the side verandah, only a dark form in the light from the open door behind him.

'Come here, Pree,' he called, and I realised that what I had heard was a slur in his words.

'What is it?' I whispered, mindful of the Colonel and Glory's loud laughter from within the house.

He beckoned to me in an odd, clumsy manner, and I started towards him, seeing, as I drew nearer, than he clung on to the railing for support.

'Eddie?' I said, surprised. I had never seen him take alcohol.

'You're supposed to come inside. The Colonel wants you at the party.'

I stopped. 'No,' I said.

'Pree.' Eddie came down the steps, his heel catching on the bottom one so that he stumbled against me. He righted himself, one hand on my shoulder. 'One doesn't refuse the Colonel. He's my superior. I have to carry out his wishes.' I could smell the whiskey on him. His hair looked as if he'd run his hand through it, over and over. 'Come, Pree,' he said again. 'You don't want me to get into trouble.' He held out his hand.

When I didn't take it, he leaned closer. 'If you don't he'll come to get you himself.'

'I'll hide. Tell him you can't find me.'

He stared into my eyes. 'He'll only beat me. And the next time he comes it will be the same. And the next time. You can't say no to him, Pree. But come with me. It's better if you stay with me.' His whisper was the loud, conspiratorial one of someone highly intoxicated.

What was I to do?

'Maybe I can tell him I want you, Pree. Then he'll leave you alone.'

Did I truly believe this about the Colonel?

'Pree. Please,' Eddie breathed, and I knew, looking at him, that what he said about the Colonel beating him was the truth.

I closed my eyes for a moment, then put my hand into his outstretched one and followed him into the house.

When we walked in Glory was sitting on the Colonel's lap, drinking from a glass he held to her lips. At the sight of us he stood, Glory half falling to the floor. She laughed loudly, merrily, as she awkwardly pulled herself on to the settee.

'Here they are,' the Colonel said, weaving where he stood, the amber liquid in the glass sloshing over one side. 'The pretty children. Come, lad, have another drink.' His eyelids were almost closed; I knew he was very drunk.

He held the glass in Eddie's direction. Eddie obediently took it and drained it, his head back.

Glory called out. 'Sit down, Colonel, sit with Glory again.' She heavily patted the cushion beside her.

'There's been enough sitting,' the Colonel said, and put his arm around Glory's shoulders, pulling her up to stand beside him. 'Pree, you must have a drink with us.'

I didn't move.

'Drink with us, Pree,' the Colonel said again, picking up the whiskey bottle. But it was empty. He flung it across the room, and it shattered against the wall.

I flinched, but Glory laughed. She put her hand on the Colonel's chest for support, playing with one of the gold buttons on his jacket.

'Yes,' she agreed. 'Too much sitting, too much talking,' she said. 'Too long talking.' She took his hand and led him towards the bedroom. 'Come with Glory, Colonel.'

He followed her, glancing over his shoulder just before he went through the door. 'You wait here, Ensign Halyard.'

But Eddie was sprawled on the horsehair chair with the empty glass in his hand, his legs stretched out, wide apart, his eyes closed.

'Yes. Good lad. You rest. And when I'm finished with this one, you can have her. And then I'll take the girl,' he said. I shook my head, unable to speak, backing away.

The Colonel lurched into the bedroom with Glory, and I breathed out in a long exhalation of relief, glancing at Eddie. But he was snoring lightly, his mouth open, already deep in drunken sleep. He could do nothing to help me should the Colonel attempt to carry out his threat.

I blew out the lamps and ran to my hut, looking at the blanket and pillow I'd dropped on the floor when I'd followed Eddie into the house. Did I want to go out and sleep in the corn? I was so weary, my charpoy so inviting. The hot summer night was still, not a breath of air coming through the small window or uncovered door. I suddenly sensed that no one at the mission would stir until morning. The Colonel had been so intoxicated.

I put on my nightdress and lay down with a deep sigh. I was being granted another night.

I was awakened by voices. Sitting up and seeing light in the courtyard, I knew it was Eddie, leading the Colonel to the horses to take him back to the barracks. But instead of fading, the wavering light came closer and closer. Feet stumbled on the uneven ground, and in the next instant the Colonel and Eddie stood in the doorway, flooded in the light of the lamp the Colonel held high.

The Colonel, wearing his trousers and boots, but without his jacket and his tunic unbuttoned, pulled Eddie in behind him.

'Come on, Ensign. Time you were made a man,' he said. 'Watch and learn from the best.'

366

I stared at Eddie. He looked as if he were sleepwalking; his eyes were glassy and his hair was damp with sweat and was plastered against his skull.

'A right joke, trying to sell her for a ridiculous sum,' the Colonel said, heavily setting the lamp on the seat of the chair. It tilted precariously. 'Of course she's no virgin, although I dare say she can't possibly have known as many pricks as the old girl,' he continued, slurring and weaving. 'Have you known many, little lady?'

I shook my head, my mouth too dry to swallow. The Colonel seemed even taller, wider, with the three of us crowded into the small hut, than he had in the house. The lamp cast monstrous shadows.

'Don't play coy with me, girl,' he said, staring intently into my eyes, although blinking heavily. 'Stand up,' he ordered, as if I were one of his soldiers.

I did, opening my mouth, not knowing what I would say next, but, trying to hide my terror, raised my chin, staring at him in the same way Glory had often stared down a man when she didn't like what he said.

But instead of ducking his head, or laughing in a slightly bemused manner, as I'd witnessed with Glory, the Colonel's hand shot up, and he slapped me across the side of my head. His force knocked me on to the charpoy, and I lay there, stunned, my ear ringing, my cheek throbbing as if burned by flames.

Eddie came out of his stupor and stepped in front of me, but he was unsteady, fighting to keep his balance. 'Please, sir. Leave her be,' he said. 'Don't hit her, sir,' he said. 'She didn't mean you any disrespect, sir.'

'She's a girl who needs a lesson taught, is what she is,' the Colonel said. 'Aren't you?' He looked down at me, his lips loose. He unbuckled his belt and fumbled with the first button of his trousers. 'Do you want me to show you how a real man does it, boy?' he said to Eddie. 'You can watch, and then take your turn.'

I pulled up my legs and pushed myself further on to the charpoy, my hand still on my ear. I was in shock. *Not like this*, I kept thinking. *Not like this*. My back was against the wall; now I drew my knees to my chest. Then I reached down, between the wall and the charpoy, feeling for the sabre. My fingers opened and closed on air.

'No,' I said. 'You can't.' I tried to make my voice sure, strong, but it sounded piteous in my own ringing ear. 'Don't,' I said, knowing how weak and ineffectual my words were. 'Eddie,' I called, staring at him, leaning against the wall now. 'Eddie, don't let him.'

Eddie straightened. 'Sir.'

The Colonel slid his belt from its loops in a long, slithering swoop of sound, his upper body swaying. The belt fell to the floor, the buckle clinking, and at that moment my still-grappling fingers touched the tip of the handle of the sabre.

'Sir. Let me. Please, sir,' Eddie said. 'I'd like to take her first, if you don't mind.'

The Colonel's hands – now on the second button of his black trousers – stopped. 'That's more like it, lad. That's what these women are for – to teach you how to do it. Learn from a cheap cunt so that some day you know how to please your good lady wife. Go ahead, then. This one's no unpicked flower; look at that face. Old Glory's only trying to trick me.'

I tasted the copper of blood; my front teeth had bitten into my bottom lip when he hit me. I pushed my arm down further, and was able to close my hand around the sabre's handle.

'Sir? I think I'm . . . I'm a bit nervous. I'm not sure I . . . with you watching, sir. Could I ask you to return to the house for now? I'll fetch you when I've finished.' Eddie's words were heavy in his mouth, as if he spoke around a mouthful of uncooked lentils.

The Colonel chuckled. It was a wet, sloppy sound, and I thought of my mother's mouth of saliva. 'Shy, are you, Ensign? All right, then.'

He stooped heavily and picked up his belt. 'All right,' he said, and I shut my eyes in relief, although my fingers didn't loosen their grip. 'I'll make do with the other again. But give it to her good, boy. I want to hear her moans all the way back at the house. And don't forget to come and get me when you've got her ready for me.'

Eddie saluted clumsily, and the Colonel, not even bothering to refasten his buttons, dragging his belt on the ground, took the lamp and left. I lowered my hand from my ear, staring up at Eddie. He sat on the charpoy with a slight groan, and in the next moment lay back, dropping his head on to my pillow. His legs were still on the floor; he looked at me, blinking heavily.

Did he mean what he had said to the Colonel? If he did, I knew I could stop him. He wasn't anything like the Colonel.

I stayed where I was, my back against the wall, watching his eyes watching me in the dark. I pulled my hand from the sabre, and heard its thud as it fell back to the floor.

Unexpectedly, Eddie reached out and put his hand on my breast. His fingers were hot through the thin fabric of my nightdress. His breathing grew heavier. I felt nothing. Nothing.

At that moment I knew with certainty that I could no longer protect myself here. And I couldn't continue to live in this fear, jumping at the sound of each horse, hiding, sleeping in the fields at night, waiting for what I knew was the inevitable act to occur. If not the Colonel – should he somehow lose interest and no longer frequent the mission –

it would be the next man. Glory would carry on, and I would never be safe.

I had nowhere to go and no one to turn to. This was my life. I would never become one of the whores who worked for Glory, but I would not be able to protect myself from anyone who chose to take me. And at that thought I realised that I would rather Eddie take my virginity – no, I would rather give it to him – than be raped brutally by the Colonel or another like him. Eddie would be kind. His breath was sweet, in spite of the whiskey, and his cheek not yet needing the scrape of a razor.

Now he was looking at his hand on my breast. He moved his fingers, tentatively, and my nipple rose, as if it possessed its own will, against his palm. He shut his eyes.

That tenuous lengthening of my nipple reassured me, even though I felt no pleasure. It would be all right with Eddie. I would take the pain I knew there would be. I would accept it. And losing my virginity would make me stronger. Wouldn't it?

Eddie watched his hand continue to move, softly, over my breast, and I didn't stop him. In the humid air I felt heat rise, in waves, from him, still in his full uniform. And suddenly he looked away from his hand and into my face.

'Is it as the Colonel says, then?' he asked. 'Are you really an old hand at this? You've only been pretending, all this time?'

Finally I also felt warmth run through my body, but it was not brought on by desire. 'No. No,' I repeated, shamed. 'Of course not. You believe me, don't you?' It was very important to me that he understand I wasn't like Glory. 'I have never been with a man, Eddie,' I said, forcing myself not to think of Kai's lips on mine. To drive away that image, I put my mouth on his.

Although his lips were warm and pliable, I still felt

nothing. It hadn't been like this with Kai. When Kai touched me I felt as though my body contained quicksilver, fluid and undulating. I had wanted to lean into him, to let his body absorb mine as a stream runs into a river.

I pulled my lips from Eddie's, and he took his hand from my breast. His face was lit only by a long sliver of moonlight that came from between the slats of the wall. I couldn't understand his expression, but it made me look away.

'Do you want me?' I finally asked.

'Yes,' he said, his voice faint. 'Yes. Of course. You're so . . . but . . . no.'

'No?'

'No, Pree. I . . .' He looked down at his own body, lifting a hand limply, letting it fall back by his side. 'Not like this. I've thought of it, yes, of course I've thought of it, of you, but . . .' His voice faded.

There was silence, and, in the next moment, a tiny rasping sound. I leaned up on one elbow. His eyes were closed, his lips slightly parted.

I watched him breathe, the slow, heavy exhalations of drunken sleep. How ironic, I thought, that when it was me asking for this to happen, I was denied. Did I feel relief? I don't know. I was exhausted, wearied by it all, this life that seemed to move forward in unexpected ways, dragging me along.

I pulled off Eddie's boots and hauled his legs on to the charpoy. He groaned again; his hair was even more matted with sweat, beads of it standing on his forehead and collecting under his eyes. The high collar of his jacket was cutting into his neck. I undid the buttons, struggling with his inert body, finally taking off the jacket. Then, with great effort, I managed to pull his tunic over his head. His chest was boyish, concave, and I thought of Kai's, how it had once looked like this. I put my hand on it, running my fingertips up and down the clavicle. His ribs rose and fell; the skin over them was soft, like the raised ribs of sand at the edge of the Ravi.

Then I put my head on Eddie's chest. I felt the low, jarring thud of his heart, and this gentle, even rhythm inexplicably made me weep.

At some point in the night I stirred, realising I had been asleep, and my eyes flew open in panic, thinking that the Colonel might return. But all was silent; I could only pray he had finally fallen in the deep unconsciousness of heavy drink beside Glory. Eddie's warm body was against mine. He still breathed heavily, and now lay on his side, facing me. I sat up and looked at his face. In the moonlight he looked so young, his lips full and slightly puffy, as if sated, his cheeks so smooth. His chest was also hairless, his belly flat and muscular. I put my hand on it; his skin, no longer heated, was cool and almost silky.

My cheek and ear were swollen and sore. I felt old, old and dirtied by all I had heard and been forced to witness since the downward spiral of my mother's madness and all that it and my father's illness had led to. I lay down again, turning to the wall so that my back curved into Eddie's body, fitting it against his. He muttered one unintelligible word and put his arm over me, his hand lying loosely at my waist. I thought he might be waking, but he didn't move again, or make a sound. After a long time I took his hand in mine and brought it to my face. It smelled of horseflesh, and I also sensed he had again eaten a mango that day. I pressed his cool hand against my hot, aching cheek and thought once more of Kai.

And for the second time that long night my eyes filled with tears, and I pressed my back more tightly against Eddie. He returned the pressure, but I knew it was involuntary; he was spent with the drink, and would probably not awaken for many hours.

I lay in that hot darkness, feeling a deep sadness that I had never known, not when my father died nor when my mother committed *sati*. Not in the horridness since then. I wept because of the overwhelming sad joy of being close to another human body. I pulled Eddie's arm more tightly around me.

It had been so long since I had felt kindness and consideration from anyone other than old Sanosh. I wept with self-pity, and because I was lonely and afraid, and because I knew Eddie was also lonely and afraid, so far from home. Because I wanted to love someone, and be loved in return.

But it wouldn't be Eddie. We were covered mirrors, unable to reflect each other.

I wept for us both.

CHAPTER TWENTY-NINE

I AWOKE TO THE first sleepy murmurs of the birds in the peepul tree. A grey light came through the window, although the rooster hadn't begun his first crows. I sat up and stroked Eddie's face. 'Wake up, Eddie,' I whispered, gently shaking his shoulder when he didn't respond to my voice or touch.

His eyes finally opened, and he stared at me as if confused. He sat up slowly, attempting to lick his lips, closing his eyes again.

I climbed over him and poured a tumbler of water from my pitcher. I wet a cloth, sitting beside him on the charpoy, and as the rope sagged he opened his eyes again and raised himself on one elbow, taking the tumbler with a shaking hand. He drained it and handed it back, not looking at me, then lay down again. I wiped the damp cloth over his face and neck as if he were a child. He obediently closed his eyes and allowed me to do this.

'You'll be late returning to the barracks. You must go and get the Colonel,' I told him.

He nodded, again rubbing his eyes and then letting his hand fall on to his chest. He raised his head and looked at his fingers on his own bare skin. 'Are you . . . is everything all right?' He didn't look at me.

I thought of his smell, horse and mango. 'I'm fine,' I said.

'I don't remember . . .' His voice was low, as if ashamed.

'You slept, Eddie,' I told him. 'That's all.'

He nodded, finally raising his eyes to my face. He made a small exclamation, reaching out to touch my bruised cheekbone. I winced.

'But now I . . . the Colonel . . .' And then he sat up, silently, and I handed him his tunic. 'I'm sorry, Pree. I'm sorry for all that you suffered. Although he won't remember anything. He won't remember that he forced me to drink, or that I brought you into the house. He won't remember that he brought me here, to your hut, or that he struck you. I've seen the state he falls into when he drinks so heavily too often. I've seen him take women and then have no memory of it.' He pulled the tunic over his head. 'The Blackness, he calls it.' He worked with his buttons. I didn't speak.

'I have manoeuvres in the south for the next month,' he said. 'Away from Lahore,' he added, unnecessarily, looking at me.

I nodded.

Again he studied my cheek, my throbbing ear. 'Will you be all right, here? Or is there somewhere, someone . . .' his voice trailed.

When I didn't answer, he picked up my hand, gripping it. 'I don't want to think of you here. What if the next time the Colonel comes for you . . .' he stopped.

'Thank you, Eddie,' I said. 'You acted bravely, stopping him.'

He gave a pained half-smile. 'It's a good thing he does lose all sense of what's gone on. I'm not allowed to override a superior. In any matter.' He picked up one of his boots. 'But you here, with Glory, and all the rest of it . . . it's an evil place for you, Pree.'

'It's my home, Eddie. The only one I've ever known. I'll be all right,' I said, because what else could I say? I couldn't depend on him – or anyone – to help me. 'I've always been all right.'

There was nobody to turn to; I had only myself.

He rose, standing in front of me as he worked his arms into the sleeves of his jacket. His face had a greenish tinge, and I knew how ill he must feel.

There was no more to say. I stood and lay my undamaged cheek against his. He put his arms around me and rested his temple on mine. I let myself soften against him; for that brief moment I relished simply being held, and feeling I was cared about.

'You'd better rouse the Colonel,' I said, quietly, 'or you won't get back to the barracks before your morning exercises, and he'll blame you.' I pulled away so that I could see his face.

He nodded. 'Goodbye, Pree,' he said. 'When I return from manoeuvres, if the Colonel still requests that I accompany him I'll be able to see—'

I put my fingers against his lips. 'Goodbye, Eddie,' I said. What had happened would make it too difficult to ever spend time together again; it was all spoiled by the violence and embarrassment. I knew it and he knew it. We could never again have the easy friendship we'd only begun to know.

He held my fingers, pressing his lips against them. Then he left.

I sat on my charpoy, the wet cloth against my ear. In ten minutes I heard voices, followed by the pounding of horse's hoofs on the hard ground, and only then did I lie back, my arm over my face, and closed my eyes.

I was shocked to open my eyes to bright light, and even more surprised to read the face of my clock and see that it was after ten o'clock. I had fallen into a deep, dreamless sleep of exhaustion after Eddie left with the Colonel, and it was only Marta's demanding lowing that woke me.

I arose, throwing on my *kurta* and *panjammahs*, knowing with certainty that I couldn't stay here any longer. I had to leave the mission – this place so ungodly that it was ludicrous to still think of it as *the mission*. And yet I couldn't utter the name of what it had actually become.

At the well I splashed water on my face, then hurried into Marta's enclosure. Her moans stopped as I entered, and she swung her head at me reproachfully. Her udder was so full she flinched as I took hold, kicking with her back hoof, but I leaned my forehead against her rough side and hurriedly milked her.

With the mindless, rhythmic pulling I made my plans. I knew that it would do me no good to just go as far as Lahore and try to find some means to live. I thought of the expression on Mrs Rollings-Smythe's face in the bazaar, and how by now surely everyone in the English community knew what the mission had become. I would not be welcome in any capacity. And I might come face to face with soldiers from the barracks who had come regularly to the mission – to say nothing of the Colonel – at any given time.

No. I had to go much further than Lahore. But in order to leave I had to have money. Although Glory always had rupees from the soldiers, I knew she spent them all on herself, on the new furnishings and clothing and jewellery and slippers, on whiskey and prepared sweets.

If I could somehow spirit the pianoforte out of the house, I would have sold that. I thought about what else was in the house. My father's Bible collection, still in the glass-fronted cabinet. I didn't know how much they would be worth, but some of them had exquisite covers and were very old and, I remember my father saying, quite valuable.

It was fortunate that Glory didn't know about books; it didn't occur to her that they could be sold. I knew she liked the book cabinet with its row of spines; I was sure she felt it gave the mission sitting room a certain English dignity.

My spirits lifted slightly. With whatever rupees I could bargain for the Bibles, I would go somewhere else, another city where no one knew who I was, and where no one had heard of my parents, or what had become of the mission. But where, exactly, would it be possible for me to go?

I again thought of the Langs and their mission in Peshawar. Suddenly the idea of working in a mission for them didn't seem as distasteful as it had originally. Now, knowing this life of debauchery with Glory, the idea of a clean and respectable mission was strongly appealing.

And the Afghan might still live in Peshawar. I thought of his kind face, his sad dark eyes. Surely I could find him. And he had seemed aware of Kai's movements. Perhaps he could even tell me news of Kai.

At that I shook my head. I was imagining too much; I didn't even know the Afghan's name, and already I was planning on finding him and having him talk to me of Kai.

But still, I would go to Peshawar. I would slip into the house and take the Bibles, pack my own few belongings, and drive Marta and the cart into Lahore and sell the Bibles. Then I would start on the Grand Trunk towards Peshawar. I could be away long before Glory even stirred; she never arose until mid-afternoon.

Finished, I set the pail of warm, steaming milk to one side and started through the open gate of the enclosure. But at the sudden hurried beat of approaching horses' hoofs, I stepped back, hidden behind Marta's broad back.

'Pree!' the Colonel bellowed, and I dropped to a crouch, watching from under Marta's belly and through the slats of the enclosure as the Colonel rode into the courtyard. He pulled sharply on his horse's reins, and then half fell from his horse, cursing at the unknown ensign who attempted to assist him. He was highly intoxicated – surely it couldn't be from last night. He must have continued drinking this morning.

I stayed perfectly still, holding my breath. He lurched towards the house, opening the front door and calling something unintelligible, then stumbled to my hut, again shouting my name, continuing with a barrage of coarse obscenities. He came out of the hut carrying my chair, and I watched in horror as he dashed it against the ground, the brittle wood easily splintering and breaking in his hands. Glory appeared on the verandah, calling to him in a cajoling and yet slightly confused voice, and he made his way towards her. When he'd gone into the house with her I jumped up and raced out of the enclosure and on to the road, past the ensign, who watched me, expressionless.

I kept running, all the way to Tek Mandi. I went to Darshan's home, and panted out to Sanosh that I was fearful of one of the men who came to see Glory, and that I could no longer stay at the mission. Sanosh patted my hand, and spoke quietly to his daughter-in-law.

Within moments she sullenly handed me a cup of tea and a plate of chicken and lentils. I couldn't eat, my stomach convulsing painfully with nerves. I sat across from Sanosh, picking at the edge of the woven mat under me, the untouched plate between us.

'Where will you go if you cannot stay there, Missy Pree?' Sanosh asked. 'To your friends in Lahore? I told you this before, Missy, I told you, did I not, that it is not right that you stay with that woman and her bad ways. You will go to Lahore?'

I shook my head. 'They are not my friends there, Sanosh.'

'But they are your people. They will help you, surely.'

'I'm going to Peshawar,' I told him.

He frowned. 'Peshawar? But that is not such a good place. Why would you go there?'

379

'There's a mission,' I said, 'where I might be welcome.'

He studied me, then shrugged. 'As you say, Missy Pree. You know what is the best place for you, it appears.'

I nodded and rose then, helping Sanosh's daughter-in-law with washing and cooking for the rest of the afternoon. We didn't speak and she didn't look at me, simply handing me what was needed.

As darkness fell and the village settled I spent the night on the floor of the house, tossing and turning, falling into nightmarish dreams. In the early morning I rolled up the blanket and mat, handing them back to the woman who looked younger than I. She held her baby boy on her hip, turning her face from me as I thanked her. I knew her honour with the villagers was at stake.

'I'll go now, Sanosh,' I told him.

'To Peshawar?' he asked.

I nodded. 'But first I must stop at the mission.' I couldn't leave without the Bibles, without Marta and the cart and my own belongings. I would be able to see, from the road, if the Colonel was there. If he was I would stay out of sight until he left.

'You'll return to the mission? But . . .'

I studied the faded rug at my feet. 'Just to retrieve what I need.'

He nodded, his forehead wrinkling.

'Thank you for your hospitality, Sanosh,' I said, and turned to leave, but he said, 'Missy Pree? Would you like me to walk back with you?'

I looked into his seamed face. He was old and frail, and I knew he would be of no physical assistance should I require it, but suddenly I couldn't bear to think of going back to the mission alone. 'Would you do that?'

'Of course. Come. We will walk together.'

★   ★   ★

I knew something was wrong as soon as we reached the fence. I had seen that the army horses were gone from far down the road, and at first I'd felt relief. Glory would still be asleep, and I could do what I needed to do without any disturbances.

But the mission was too quiet. Marta wasn't in the enclosure; I suddenly remembered running for the road, leaving the gate open. As we went through the gate I could see, from across the courtyard, that the front door of the house hung oddly. It was soon clear that it swung from only one hinge.

I hurried up the steps, Sanosh following more slowly. As I looked through the doorway my mouth opened in horror. The room was destroyed: most of the furniture was over-turned, one shutter was ripped off the window, and there was broken glass everywhere. The pianoforte was brutally smashed and lay on its side like a gutted animal, its wires ripped out, hammers and ivory keyboard twisted. The tall cabinet was tipped over, and the glass of one door smashed. The Bibles were strewn about.

I simply stood there, my hand to my throat, feeling Sanosh's wheezing breaths on the back of my neck. And then I heard a faint sound, little more than a whimper, from the dining room.

'No, Missy Pree,' Sanosh whispered, as I took a step into the room. 'It is very bad here. Come away. Come away,' he said, and pulled on my arm.

'Pree.' The gasping croak was Glory's voice, and yet not Glory's voice.

I went to the dining room and drew in my breath. The four Queen Anne chairs were destroyed, their legs broken and their seats slashed open as if with a sharp knife or sword. And lying under the table was Glory, on her stomach, her face turned to one side. She lay in a congealing pool of her own blood. One eye was swollen shut, but the other looked at me dully.

I pushed away the table so I could kneel beside her. I felt the sharp grind of glass under my knees. 'The Colonel did this to you, Glory?'

She didn't – or couldn't – speak.

I looked at Sanosh, his eyes wide. 'Come and help me,' I told him. We tried to lift Glory; she moaned in pain, gasping and whimpering. Sanosh and I half carried her to her bed.

Once she was on her back I caught my breath and again asked her, 'It was the Colonel?'

She made a small sound in her throat that I took to be a yes.

'But why? Why was he so angry?' I remembered him shouting my name as he pitched about the courtyard.

Glory lay still; a bubble of blood widened and thinned from one nostril with each breath. Her thin frock was ripped down the front and one sleeve hung empty, torn from the shoulder. Sanosh pulled at me and I left her, stepping over the furniture and debris, and followed him back out on to the verandah.

'You must go from this place right now, Missy Pree,' he said, and I nodded. 'It is a place of much evilness. Not a place for you.' The whites of his eyes were yellowed. 'I wish—' he started, then stopped. 'I wish it was possible for you to stay at Darshan's. If it were my own home, Missy Pree, you would be welcome.'

'I know, Sanosh. I know,' I said. 'But you're right. I'll leave, and go to Peshawar,' I said, although it came out weakly. I thought of the Bibles. How many had been destroyed?

'I have a few rupees saved, for my old age. But my son cares for me; I want for nothing. I will give them to you.'

'No, no,' I said. 'You've done so much for me, so much, with never any thought for yourself. I can't take your money.'

I attempted to smile at him. 'Thank you, Sanosh. I don't know what I would have done if you . . . without you.' I wished I'd had something to give him. 'How can I repay you, even in the smallest of ways?'

'There is no need of a gift. Only ensure me that you will find safety, Missy Pree,' he said. 'I cannot bear to think of you . . .' he looked at the house, and I knew his meaning.

He made *namaste*, and I dropped to the ground and knelt before him, touching his feet in respect as if I were his daughter-in-law.

'Please, Missy,' he said, obviously uncomfortable.

I rose. 'Goodbye, Sanosh,' I said, and he nodded, then left, stopping once to turn and wave. I lifted my hand in response.

I slowly went back into the house, stepping carefully over the broken glass to the Bibles. Without picking them up I could see that most of them were ruined, the pages torn, covers ripped off. I closed my eyes at the vision of the Colonel beating Glory, ripping the house apart in his rage.

I picked up a soft morocco-covered Bible, and then a smaller one with beautiful gilt pages. A plain, heavy one lay to one side, and I realised, with a knock of my heart, that it was not part of the collection, but the one my father had read from daily and always kept close at his side. I had never thought of it even when my father was alive; it had been familiar as my hairbrush or the dented silver teapot on its tarnished tray, and had held no interest for me.

I blew off the dust and ran my hand over it. It wasn't worth anything; it was an ordinary, well-used Bible with a plain black cover. I opened the book to the front page. On it was my father's name, *Samuel Emmett Fincastle*, written in his own delicate, upright script. Through the almost translucent onion-skin paper, I saw more of his handwriting. I turned the page.

Married: Eve Marion Allen, 26 January, 1848. Below the

marriage details, my father had recorded the family births and deaths. I read them in a detached manner:

Elijah Jarvis, b 9 September, 1849; d 13 November, 1851.

Alice Ann Margaret, b 4 March, 1856; d 16 April, 1856.

Elizabeth Rebecca, b 21 July, 1859; d 5 September, 1859.

Gabriel Charles, b 11 October, 1862; d 27 February, 1863.

I read through the list again, tracing each line with my forefinger now, reading silently but moving my lips.

Of course Kai's birth was not listed; of course not.

But neither was mine.

My finger went back to Alice Ann, the sister born before me. Her date of birth was 4 March, 1856. But my birthday was 17 August, 1856.

I heard my own breath, as if from a distance.

'Pree.'

I slammed the book shut as if guilty, or ashamed. As if I had been caught looking at the vile pictures of barely clothed women like those on the pack of cards I'd once unsuspectingly picked up from the sideboard after one of Glory's evenings.

'Pree,' came Glory's murmur again.

I didn't answer. I held the Bible against my chest, going over and over the two confusing facts.

My sister could not have been born in March, six months before me. And I was not listed among my father's legitimate children.

CHAPTER THIRTY

SOME TIME LATER — a few minutes, an hour, I don't know
— the sound of rustling came from the bedroom. Then a
low moan. And another. More rustling.

'Pree,' Glory breathed again.

I sat, unmoving, clutching the Bible.

'Pree,' Glory called, in a low voice now. 'Help me.'

'I'm here,' I finally said.

'Water,' she said.

Still holding the Bible against me, I went to the courtyard.
With one hand I drew water, poured it into the brass lotah
sitting on the edge of the well, and took it to Glory. The
bedroom was dark, the shutters drawn, and it smelled even
more strongly of sweat and blood in the heat of the morning.
I lifted a few louvres, and the bright sunshine made hard lines
of light across the floor and bed. I poured water into a tin
mug and took it to the bed. Glory shakily tried to push
herself up, but couldn't. With a groan, she fell back, but lifted
her head.

In the vivid light her face looked even worse than I'd
originally thought. Drying, sticky blood coated the side of
her face where she'd rested her cheek on the floor. As well as
the closed eye, deeply cut under the eyebrow, one cheekbone
was enlarged to a violent purple lump. Her lips were caked
with dried blood, the top one protruding like a puffy beak.
Her right ear was swollen and inflamed; the hole in her

earlobe from which an earring usually hung was torn through.

'Here,' I said, holding out the mug.

Slowly, as if half asleep, she reached for it with her left hand; I saw that her right wrist was swollen and dark, the hand seeming useless as it lay on the coverlet.

Holding the mug awkwardly, she lifted her head a few inches, cautiously putting the cup to her split bottom lip, wincing. I could have helped her; I didn't. Dribbles ran over her chin and on to her neck, finding their way down to her chest, snaking between her breasts. She may have tasted a few drops.

'Take it,' she said, exhausted by this simple effort, and I took the mug from her shaking hand. Her fingers were hot. She groaned as she lowered her head to the now stained pillow, shutting her eye.

'Glory,' I said, staring at her almost unrecognisable face. She didn't answer. I said her name again, more loudly, and she moved her head, just the slightest.

'Don't shout,' she finally whispered. 'Help me. I'm hurt, so hurt,' she added, unnecessarily. 'And it's your fault. The Colonel wanted you. He blamed me that you weren't here. How could you do this to me?'

'I need to ask you something,' I said. 'About this. Look.'

The one eye that could still open flickered and she stared, uncomprehendingly, at me. 'At what?' Her voice was little more than a breathy exhalation.

'This.'

Again, although her vision lowered to what I held, her glazed eye had the same blank stare.

'It's my father's Bible,' I said, speaking as if she were a small child, as if she wouldn't recognise the book. Her eye closed. 'But I need to ask you about what's written in it. And what's

386

not written. Glory!' I said, and a tremor passed over her features. 'I need you to tell me something.'

'Not now. I need to sleep. You stay here, and help me,' she mumbled.

As I turned to leave she made a sound, and I looked back at her. 'If the Colonel comes back, you will do what he wishes,' she whispered. 'Or this will also be your fate.'

I had a sudden image of the man's powerful fists, his neck, like a Brahmin bull's, standing thick, corded. The deep maroon of his face when he slapped me in my hut. 'I will,' I said, lying, 'but only if you promise to talk to me later. To tell me the truth, Glory,' I said.

'The truth.' She was simply parroting my words.

'If you don't promise, I'll go and leave you alone. Alone, with no water, no food. And the Colonel will come back. What will you do if he comes back and I'm not here again? What will he do to you then?'

Now the eyelid opened, and this time understanding was there. 'What truth do you ask about?' As she spoke, the congealed blood on her bottom lip cracked and opened. Fresh blood leaked out, slowly. Glory put out the tip of her tongue, touching it. She made a sound deep in her throat.

I looked around the room, then picked up a petticoat thrown into a corner. I tore a strip from its bottom, and dipped it into the mug. I put it to Glory's bottom lip, soaking up the blood. She didn't move at first, but then closed her top lip on the wet cloth, attempting to suck on it.

I pulled it away. 'Shall I leave you?' I asked, wanting to find some sympathy within myself. But there was none. I didn't care about her, but she was the only person here who knew me, knew of my past. Water dripped from the cloth on to the coverlet.

Her lips opened, unconsciously, as if she were an infant suddenly deprived of the warm, full breast. Her right front tooth dangled from a bloody, stringy tendon; the left one leaned back into that dark maw.

I touched the cloth to her lips again, and she immediately sucked. I took it away.

'Shall I leave?' I asked, yet again. 'Or will you tell me? Tell me about . . .' I stopped. About what? Would she know why my birth hadn't been recorded in the Bible? Was it just a slip of my father's hand – the dates of Alice Ann's birth and death? Had she been born and died a year earlier, in 1855?

Glory would know. She was in Allahabad at the mission when my mother arrived. Wasn't she there when Alice Ann and I were born? She would know.

And in that same instant a terrible thought struck.

My father had lain with Glory to produce Kai. And in spite of what she told me, I believed he was the father of Adriana. Could he not have fathered me with Glory as well? My stomach heaved.

'I will tell you whatever you want, Pree,' Glory said now. 'I will tell you. But water, more water.'

I dipped the rag into the mug again, and this time let Glory suck on it until she turned her head away. I left her then, taking the Bible to my hut. Lying on my charpoy, I put it beside me. I stared at the book as if it were something dangerous, something quietly breathing. As if it were a pulsing heart, holding secrets. Finally I turned on to my back, still wide eyed, watching a scorpion make its way along the rafter, eventually disappearing into the mouldering thatch.

Marta was gone. I traipsed through the fields and down to the river in hopes of finding her, but realised she would have probably wandered far by now, crossing fields or down the road, into someone's courtyard or one of the villages, and if she was being fed and milked she wouldn't return.

And I couldn't find Jassie. I called and called; I dumped

dried kernels of corn into a tin pan, rattling them as I called her name, walking between the rows of new, rustling corn, the tall sugar cane. But there was no sign of her. She would be in her time of heat, then; at these times – as when she had her pups – she disappeared.

It was a full two days before Glory could speak to me. During that time I didn't worry about the Colonel returning; I couldn't think of that. I moved as if through a dream, feeling no hunger, nor weariness nor sense of fear. I had something much larger to concentrate on: the strange discovery within the pages of my father's Bible. I had a raw, chilled sensation, inside and out, in spite of the punishing summer heat.

I worked in the garden, collected the eggs, hauled water. I kept busy at all times; if my hands were idle my thoughts made me feel I might lose my mind, as my mother had. I brought Glory water and plain weak tea and thin soup which I made with mashed carrots and lentils. I supported her shoulders and held the liquids to her swollen lips so she could swallow, painfully, around her loose teeth. I didn't dress her cuts, or help her on to the flowered chamber pot, even when she called to me, begging. She was forced to soil herself where she lay, and the room grew unbearably fetid.

I didn't care about her comfort. All I wanted was for her to recover enough to tell me what I needed to know.

For those next two nights I lay on my charpoy in the hut while Glory moaned in the mission house. Did I sleep? I don't know; all that circled in my mind, endlessly, was the question I needed answered: was I Glory's daughter? Occasionally there were footsteps or the slow, plodding rhythm of a horse on the road outside the mission. I took note of the sounds, but had no thoughts for my own safety. It was as if I were suspended in that circle of my thoughts and nobody, not even the Colonel, could break in.

Small things came to me, unbidden, as my mind wheeled

relentlessly. Mr Lang mistaking me for the ayah. Reverend Burgess having no record of my existence within my father's records. Even the sharp look my mother gave me, when I told her, after my father attempted to baptise me again, that I didn't know why I couldn't take the Lord into my heart.

I thought of my mother, and how she had cared for little Adriana. She would have been ripe with longing for a child to replace the daughter – Alice Ann, who had died only months earlier – and would have taken me into her arms, never suspecting that it was her own husband who was fathering the half-caste ayah's children. My mother had accepted me as her own because I was fair enough to pass.

Was I truly, then, a Chutney Mary, acting at being English while native blood ran through me?

I remembered how my mother had tonelessly spoken of the difficulty of relinquishing Kai to Glory after she and my father had cared for him for two years, assuming Glory would never return.

Kai. I sat up straight, my heart now beating so hard that it hurt my chest.

If Glory was my mother, Kai was not my half-brother, but my full brother. I put my hands over my face. And he would know. Of course he would know. He would have been six years old when I was born, old enough to understand his mother giving birth to me, and then me being raised by Mem Fin in the mission house.

I had lusted after my own brother. He had kissed me, in the print shop in Lahore. I had never forgotten the press of his lips against mine, warm and so briefly insistent, the pressure of his body.

It was difficult enough when I believed him to be my half-brother. But my full brother . . . I let out a low groan, then threw myself down on to my charpoy again, scrubbing my head against the pillow in an attempt to lose the image I had held so close through these last years.

That memory, like my whole life, had been a sham, a lie, an ugly blotch.

The only comfort I held on to, through that long night, was that my father's blood also ran through my veins. At least I was still my father's child.

That morning, the third day after Glory's beating, when I went into the house I heard her moving slowly about her room. Eventually she came to the doorway of the sitting room, where I had righted the furniture still serviceable – one of the cane chairs, the settee and the brass-topped table that sat in front of it. The foot of one of the table's legs was missing, but I propped it on a stack of the ruined Bibles. The pianoforte still lay on its side.

Now I sat on the horsehair chair while Glory stood in the sitting-room doorway, clutching the jamb with her left hand. She had managed to take off her filthy, torn clothing, but had obviously been unable to dress herself with the use of only one hand, and so had just wrapped a thin sari loosely around her, without knotting it. Her right hand – was the wrist sprained, or actually broken? – was supported in a torn strip of muslin she'd somehow managed to wrap over and around her shoulder. As she came nearer there was an unmistakable soiled, gamey odour about her. With her long hair half pinned up and half down, a clump matted with dried blood over one ear, she looked like a *churail*, the witch-ghost of Punjabi myths.

My mother, the witch. The temptress, whore, spit upon by righteous villagers, defying all gods, embracing no religion. No soul, and no heart.

I had studied myself in my mirror that morning. Every feature, from the thickness of my eyebrows to the shape of my ears, the formation of my teeth, the colour of my eyes, my skin, my hair. Was there a resemblance to Glory? I couldn't see it. But then I had never seen a resemblance between my father and Kai.

Glory slowly, carefully lowered herself to the settee across from me. 'I am hungry, Pree,' she said. She spoke English, in an odd, slippery way, and it took me a moment to realise she'd pulled out her dying, dangling front teeth.

'I've made daal, and mashed it, so it won't hurt your mouth,' I told her, my voice soft. 'And some wheat *rotis*. They're fresh. Can you smell them?' I watched her face. Could this woman – my mother – allow me to live like this? In squalor and immorality? Did she not care enough about me to try to protect me from men like the Colonel?

But of course I knew the answer. Glory cared only for herself, in the past, and now.

'Bring me daal,' she said, but I shook my head.

'Not yet.'

She attempted a frown, but this movement obviously hurt her face, and she grunted. 'I ask you for food, Pree. You must be good-good girl to me,' she said. 'I look after you.' Why was she speaking English in the sing-song accented English she used with the soldiers? She and I always spoke Hindi when we were alone. The missing teeth created a lisp. The end of her tongue was too visible.

I smiled. It was not a true smile, but a stretching of my lips into a square grimace. She was less of a mother than Jassie. Not only would she not fight to save her offspring from danger, but she also used them for her own purposes. 'You haven't ever looked after me. And I don't have to do anything for you. But I will. After you tell me what I want to know.'

I knew with certainty that I couldn't trust Glory, that once her stomach was full, and she felt stronger, I would have no control over her. But now, at this very moment, when it took all her energy to walk the fifteen steps from the bedroom to the sitting room, I held the trump card. For now I possessed the power.

'I'll heat water and bring in the hip bath,' I said. 'I'll wash your hair, and put salve on your cuts. I'll feed you the warm daal and a soft *roti*. Would you like that, Glory?'

She stared at me. I saw a glint from beneath the swollen lid of her left eye.

I reached forward and took the Bible from the low table in front of the settee. 'I will do all of that for you.' I opened the book. 'My father recorded the births of my brothers and sisters here,' I said. 'But there is no record of my name.'

She continued to stare at me.

'Why is that? And why is Alice Ann's birth written as only six months before mine?'

Glory blinked; and then, slowly, she smiled. It was a horrible smile, the missing front teeth and swollen lips created an impression much worse than the rictus I'd presented only moments before. Worse than Kali's smile. And there was something else, cunning, or even pleasure, that I saw there, and I was filled with foreboding. Suddenly I didn't want to hear the truth, the truth I thought I already knew.

Somewhere in my subconscious I'd simply wanted her to shrug, to say your father was a forgetful man, who knows why he made this mistake, or why he didn't write your name. But with that smile, I knew this was not what I would hear.

Still, she didn't speak. But it was as if the room was filled with noise that was only in my head: the roaring rush of water, the swirling, storm-filled clouds grumbling during the monsoons. 'I know you are my mother,' I said, my voice loud to be heard over the thick atmosphere. Over what, I realised then, was fear. No longer was I numb. The fear had returned.

At my words her smile increased, just the slightest, and I

hated her more fully than I thought possible. 'Your mother?' she repeated.

Something in her mocking, surprised tone sent a shiver of hope through me.

'Why you are thinking this, Pree?'

I swallowed. 'You had Kai with my father. You had Adriana with my father.'

She shook her head, just the smallest of movements. 'Adriana was not your father's child.'

'I heard him,' I argued. 'As he lay dying, he said you weren't to speak of the girl. Don't speak of the girl, he said. I heard him, Glory.'

The smile hadn't wavered. 'Yes. He said this. But he is not meaning Adriana. He is meaning you. You are the girl.'

Suddenly I remembered the way Glory had looked at me as he said this. 'I see,' I said, raising my chin. 'Because he wanted to protect me. To let me keep believing that the woman who had raised me was indeed my mother. Because he loved me. My father loved me.' My voice had grown even louder.

'Your father?' she said, and coughed, her features contorting with the effort. 'You want to speak of the Reverend Fincastle? You want to play this mother-father game with Glory? I will play.' A thin stream of blood trickled from her right nostril. She coughed again, and the stream grew thicker.

'It's not a game. I only want the truth. I deserve the truth, Glory.'

At least she wasn't smiling any longer. 'All right,' she said, putting the knuckles of her uninjured hand to her nose, then pulling them away and looking at the smear of blood. 'There is no reason for secrets now.' She lifted the edge of the sari and mopped at the blood. She closed her eyes. 'I am myself forgetting these things after so long. It no longer matters.'

She said nothing more then, and I thought she was

drifting to sleep, propped in the corner of the settee. When I could stand it no longer, I blurted out, 'But I guessed the secret, didn't I? That you're my mother? That when I was born my moth—' what would I now call the woman whom I had always thought of as my mother? 'That you gave me to her. You simply gave me to her, to raise as her own.' I had reverted to Hindi, wanting Glory to speak to me in her language. I hated her simpering English voice.

Glory had opened her eyes at my first sentence. Her face showed no emotion now. 'You need to know old secrets?' she asked, still in English. Suddenly her eyes focused on the smashed pianoforte. I looked at it too; the twisted keyboard had become a ghastly grin of broken teeth, like Glory's.

'Ayeee. My very lovely pianoforte.' Then she shrugged. 'So Pree wants to know,' she said, still in English. 'Even I don't think of this so-so long. I don't care. It is being nothing for me. And so long – how many years you are? Eighteen? Nineteen? So many years. You make me remember old stories. And so I will tell you. Why not? You are nothing now – you matter to no one. No reason for secrets for long time.'

My blood drummed in my ears. I sat very still, as if some fragile thing inside me might shatter if I moved suddenly.

'Nobody is caring now,' she repeated. 'Nobody is caring long time. I only keep secret when Samuel is alive because he tell me I must. So long ago, when you come to us, Samuel say to me, if you tell, I will make you go away. Leave Kai and go, go back to how you live before. I tell him, Samuel, if you make me go I will say to Mem Fin about Kai. And he say good-good, tell memsahib. Tell memsahib, leave Kai and go away. He is my son. Memsahib will be his mother.'

I saw it clearly in my head. The images of Glory and my father, blackmailing each other to keep their secrets. Glory letting my father take her whenever he wanted, knowing this was her power over him. And in return knowing he w never turn her out. Each of them playing their little game, each of them safe, knowing their own needs were fulfilled by the other.

When you come to us, Glory had said.

'So when you come I say yes, I make him what he wish, the promise. Mem Fin lives in the crazy spirit world, even then. Baby – Alice Ann – dies before, and Mem loses all her sense. She cry, cry, all night, all day. Samuel is sick, long time.' She touched her left breast. 'Sick as always, inside. He can do nothing. Mission at Allahabad is no good – Samuel sick in body, Mem sick in head. Only wants baby. Boy, girl, doesn't matter, only baby. But not Indian baby. Many Indian babies she can take; Indian baby girls everywhere. But she want white baby. English baby.'

The room was very still. Although the other, imaginary sounds of water and sky had died away, there was a true, loud buzzing: bluebottles caught between the louvres. The room baked under the midday sun; my face was wet with sweat. I reached up and wiped my forehead with the back of my hand.

Glory carefully licked her lips. 'Make me tea. Much hot milk. Sugar. And then I tell you how you come here.'

It was hard to think clearly. *When you come to us*. Not *when you were born*. She had said *how you come here*. Could I believe Glory when she said she wasn't my mother?

'Tea, now,' Glory said.

'There's no milk. Marta's gone,' I said, and went outside. My hands knew what to do without using my head, which felt as if there was a coating of something thick and sticky on the inside of my skull. It made it difficult to see, to hear, but still, my hands worked with the intensity of someone blind, unmindful of all else, concentrating on this chore and this chore alone. As if by making the tea I was passing a test, using a key to open something locked, and would soon be rewarded.

I started a fire in the brick oven. I took fresh water from the well and poured it into a tin pan. I sat. Finally I noticed it was boiling; I hadn't seen the first spitting at the sides of the tin, the slow gurgle, then the furious, angry bubbles rising to the surface.

I wrapped the sleeve of matting around my hand, grasped the edge of the pan and poured the water over the tea leaves I'd sprinkled into the old brass kettle.

I brought it and the tin sugar container back to the house. I set them on the table in front of Glory.

'I want a china cup,' she said, finally speaking Hindi. 'The tin mug you presented me with the last few days was very disrespectful.'

I noted, dully, that her hated air of superiority was returning.

Going into the dining room, I found a spoon and an unbroken flowered cup on the floor. I brought it back to the sitting room and poured tea into it, adding two mounded teaspoons of the coarse brown sugar and stirring it. I set it in front of her.

'No saucer?' she asked.

I didn't answer.

She picked up the cup with her left hand, attempting to curl her little finger, but it simply looked awkward. She brought the cup to her lips, blowing on the steaming, fragrant liquid.

I couldn't remember when I had last eaten or drunk.

I returned to my chair and sat, unmoving, while Glory took careful sips. One, two. Three, and then four.

'You know of the sepoys, and how they rose against the English,' Glory said, setting the cup on to the table.

I nodded, the old stories my mother had once frightened me with still clear in my head.

'Get me more tea,' she said again.

I prepared it and lifted it towards her.

'There was a battle cry the sepoys shouted,' she said, reaching for the full cup I held in my outstretched hand. 'I remember it still. *Sara lal hai*, they screamed. *Sara lal hai*.'

The cup slipped from my fingers and crashed on the floor, splashing tea on to the hem of Glory's sari and my bare toes. It burned. I thought of my mother in flames.

'Ayeee. You clumsy girl. Pour another cup.'

But I stepped away from Glory, my legs suddenly quivering, putting my hand over my eyes, rounding my shoulders as if expecting a blow. *Sara lal hai*. All is red. The waters of the Ravi closed over my face again; I felt its powerful surge, choked on its heavy coppery odour as it flooded my nostrils. *Sara lal hai*, I'd heard as I lost consciousness beneath that brown water.

'What's wrong with you?' Glory asked. 'Why do—' but I took my hand from my eyes, and held it up, stopping her.

'What does it mean? All is red. Why did they shout it?' I was breathing so heavily that it was difficult to speak.

She didn't appear to notice my discomfort. 'Red is the colour of the British rule, and blood. The sepoys planned the rebellion some months before the first attacks. Small printed papers were baked into chapattis and passed throughout the sepoys of northern India. The message was *Sub lal ho gaea hai*. All has become red – the British have taken our country, and now we will take it back. It indicated to prepare for bloodshed,' she said. 'At least that is the story.'

She continued, something about the sepoys, but I couldn't hear anything more she said; it was as if the thick, muddy water of the monsoon-fed Ravi had now come into my ears, filling them, making me dizzy, unbalanced, as if I were spinning through the air like the hooked devotee in Lahore.

With a strange detachment, I watched the floor between Glory's feet and mine. The warped wood rippled as if it were waves driven by wind, coming ever higher around my ankles. The sludge in my ears had a voice: it whispered something, and my mouth flooded with a sweet taste that was familiar, but I couldn't name.

The jarring motion of being carried as someone ran, the taste in my mouth, the thudding in my ears, the Ravi over my face . . . I leaned forward and gagged, emitting a mouthful of stringy saliva: there was nothing in my stomach. It ran down the front of my *kurta* and on to my feet, still wet with sweet tea, and all the while the voice didn't stop its whispering, whispering a name that was almost Pree.

All is red.

CHAPTER THIRTY-ONE

A THICK, SOUR SMELL rose from my *kurta*. Once more I sat on the chair.

'Dirty girl,' Glory said, and I looked at her dully. Glory, always carrying the rancid whiff of day-old face paint, the pungent odour of the last man between her legs. Glory, stinking now of her own soiled clothing. Glory, calling me dirty.

'Your name isn't in the Bible because you are not a child of the Reverend,' she said, then made a small, thick sound, as if clearing her throat of phlegm, or swallowing the last of the blood that may have trickled down from her damaged nose. 'And you are not *my* child.'

I blinked, staring at her. I believed Glory at this moment. For all of her immorality, her conniving and lying, I believed her now. She was not my mother. There was no reason for her to deny it. Wasn't I relieved? 'But . . . not a child of my father . . .' I stared at Glory. 'Do you mean that my mother,' I said then, slowly, lowering my gaze to my knees, unable to look at Glory any further as I spoke the unbelievable words, 'lay with another man and conceived me?'

There was a moment of silence, then a sound. I looked at Glory again, thinking she was choking on her own blood. But she wasn't choking. She was laughing, a bubbling, ugly sound. 'Mem Fin? With another man? She wouldn't even open her legs for her husband for many, many years. Don't you understand what I'm telling you? You were not a child of the Fincastles. They were not your parents.'

'Then . . .' It was too huge; there wasn't room in my head for it all. I put my elbows on my knees and leaned my face into my open hands. What was happening?

I heard the glugging of liquid, the rattle of a spoon against china. Glory had poured herself another cup of tea.

'So? Don't you wish to know from where you came?' she asked.

I looked up from my hands.

'The fighting took place all over northern India. Delhi, Meerut, Lucknow, Cawnpore. Many, many places,' Glory said, although I already knew this. 'And when it was all over, when there was no more fighting, a woman brought you to the mission at Allahabad,' she said, calmly, as if she told me the tea she had poured for herself was too hot, or she needed more sugar. 'A few months after the last fighting, in the summer of 1858.'

I let her words absorb into my thoughts. 'Was it the seventeenth of August?' I finally asked, quietly. My birthday. The date I was told was my birthday. 'Was that when I was brought to the mission?'

Glory shrugged. 'Maybe. I don't remember. It was the time of the monsoons. Mem Fin thought you must be two years, a little more or a little less, for although you were sickly and underfed, you walked about and carried yourself easily. I say no, you're too small, but Mem Fin said look, she has all her teeth.'

At that she moved her tongue within her own mouth, tentatively touching the empty space where her front teeth had been only a few days ago. She made a small sound of dismay. 'I will have gold teeth made,' she said, to no one in particular as she gingerly put her index finger to her injured gums. She no longer even seemed dismayed, as if she weren't the victim, but only a witness of her own tragedy.

'The woman who brought me,' I said. 'Who was she?'

Glory took her finger away from her mouth. 'She hoped to earn money. She asked for many rupees as payment for returning an English child to the English. You, of course.'

I nodded.

'But I say to Mem Fin the woman is surely your mother. She had relations with an Englishman, and wanted to be rid of the burden of a useless half-caste girl child. She was a low-caste Hindu.'

'A Hindu?' I said, slowing rising. 'But . . . no. I'm English. I'm . . . I'm white.' I held my hand out in front of her, as if to convince her. But as I looked at my sun-darkened skin, such a weakness came over me that I had to sit down again, heavily.

Glory gave that same frightening grin. Her words rang in my head. A useless half-caste girl child. Like she had been. As her own daughter had been.

'Are you so sure you are English, Pree? This is what Mem Fin said, that you were a lost English child from the Devil's Wind – the Sepoy Uprising. But I think you are like me. Like Kai. Like Adriana. You are simply a half-caste, not a lost child.'

'A lost child?'

'Of course. In all the killing and chaos, children were lost. Children are always lost at these times. They are orphaned or abandoned. In the case of the Uprising, when a white child was discovered alive, possibly with its dead mother and father, a native would return the child to the British, demanding payment.'

'And that's why that woman brought me to the mission in Allahabad,' I stated. 'Or maybe she was my ayah. I'm one of the lost British children.'

Glory slowly shook her head. 'I never believed it.'

'But is that what she said?'

'Yes. But she was a filthy beggar. She surely lied. You were verminous and of foul odour, wrapped in only rags. At first you didn't speak at all; you were silent for some months. Mem Fin said this was because of your fright. And then, when you finally began to talk, you spoke baby words, a mix of languages, some English, some Hindi, something else. None of us could understand you. So who can ever say if the woman really was your mother? And if she wasn't, no one will ever know where she found you, or who you were.'

Who I was. Who I am. Glory continued on as the shadows shifted and the light grew grainy, something more about my sorry state, how I cried out in terror at night for so long, but a heavy shroud seemed to have dropped over my brain again. Too much, too much. I couldn't think clearly. Useless, un-related thoughts came to me: how the mirror near the door had dropped to the floor, but hadn't broken, that the heavy mantle clock – the one in the mission as long as I could remember – no longer ticked. Where was it? Smashed some-where, perhaps underneath the pianoforte, or there, behind the broken bookshelf. That the last of my mother's . . . of Eve Fincastle's dishes were broken, apart from the cup Glory drank from.

From outside there was a stealthy creeping on the verandah, a low snuffling. I thought of Jassie. It must be her time of heat; a bold pi dog was sniffing out her scent.

I tried to focus on Glory again. She was still sipping her tea.

'Did the woman say that my name was Priscilla?'

Glory closed her undamaged eye. 'Who can remember after all these years? Mem Fin wished you to be called Priscilla. I don't know if it was your name or if she chose it.' She opened the eye. 'But now something comes to me.'

I waited.

'You would not turn at the name Priscilla. Would not

403

come to Mem Fin when she called you this; she said you were of a stubborn nature, even as such a small child. You — yes, it was you yourself, finally. You said another name.'

'What was it?' I prompted. 'What did I call myself?'

But Glory had no answer. 'It was something that sounded, to Mem's English ear, like Pree, and you were content enough with Pree.' She nodded, as if she'd just thought of something else. 'And you cried, cried, cried, always calling out a word.' She frowned. 'But how I can be expected to remember after all this time? Something you wanted, holding out your hands, especially when it was time to sleep. For so long you would not be comforted.' She closed her eye again, and her mouth fell slack. 'That's all I know about that time.' I could see the thick meatiness of her tongue in the open square of her missing teeth.

'And that's why we came here, far north, to this empty place,' she said, her eye still closed. 'Because Mem Fin feared someone would come looking for you. She never said this, but I knew. And also because she wanted to believe you were her own child; she wanted no one to know she took you from another woman's arms. Here, nobody knew anything. She could pretend.'

And then Glory fell silent.

I watched her, and knew she had nothing more to tell me, and that she had, this time, told the truth about what she knew of my arrival at the mission in Allahabad. Her face, with its swollen bruises, showed pain and exhaustion, but no trickery. She had nothing to gain by lying about this to me.

I stayed in the sitting room while Glory slowly limped back to her bedroom.

What can I say about my feelings during those next long hours when I sat alone, in the failing light? How does one react when one learns that one's whole life has been a lie?

I thought about the Fincastles. My parents. Of course I would continue to think of them as my parents; they had raised me as their daughter. I went to the mirror on the floor and lifted it. Its wire was broken, but I held it in front of me. In the early evening shadows, I looked at the young woman reflected there. She was suddenly a stranger. It was as if what I had just learned had transformed me: now I saw a woman who was neither English nor Indian.

But it wasn't only my outward reflection that was different to me now; inside as well I was someone else. My blood did not come from missionaries. Who was I? Yes, yes, I was still Priscilla Fincastle, called Pree, but also someone else. Someone hidden from my view, from everyone who looked upon me. Who were the people responsible for me being in the world? What had I inherited from them?

I put down the mirror and pressed my fingers against my neck, feeling the beat of my blood. If I listened deeply enough, would I hear something, find some clue as to who I really was? Something strange came over me. Knowing the truth – or at least the part of it that I knew, that I was not born of the Fincastles – brought on a certain anguish. But there it was. There it was, I thought, you don't know who you are.

And the feeling that followed was a release of sorts. Maybe now I could stop questioning things, questioning my own feelings. If I wasn't, by blood, the daughter of missionaries, could I now stop the guilt over falling so desperately far from what they expected of me?

Maybe I had suspected there was something puzzling, troubling me, for a long time, and yet there had never been anything tangible, anything to hold on to with certainty. I tried to re-create moments of my past, searching for unexplained comments, unexplained expressions. There were the old watery, distant and confusing memories that had come over me under the Ravi, and as Glory had uttered the words I remembered from somewhere. *Sara lal hai.*

Slowly, it all brought a dull, strange freedom. I was not the daughter of missionaries. I was the daughter of no one. I had come to the mission as a lost child, with nothing to tie me to my past.

And so now there was nothing to determine my future. I owed nothing to anyone. There was nothing more to lose.

I went to the storeroom with a woven mat and pillow, taking the lock and key and locking myself in.

Now I could think clearly again, lying on the mat in the darkness. And with that clarity my fears returned. Of course the Colonel would return. It was surprising he hadn't come before now. Here in the storeroom, I would hear him and be warned of his arrival. I could climb through the high window and slip out into the night before he might think of looking for me here, before he might kick in the door in his search for me.

For the moment I was safe. But I had to leave the mission, and go to Peshawar. With that thought I sat up.

And so Kai was not my brother in any way. Thinking that we shared the same blood had so distressed me, and yet now . . . did it really matter? Kai was no longer in my life. He didn't want to be, no matter what our relationship – blood or friendship or more.

I lay down again. I wouldn't think any further of Kai. I needed to think about getting to Peshawar. That plan hadn't changed. Even though I no longer needed to carry the heavy burden of my parents' legacy, I still had no other choice.

The remembrance of Mr Lang's hand on the back of my neck came to me. But after what I had now experienced, he would be no more than a bothersome fly. I could swat him and he would be gone. He was not a threat.

Peshawar was as good a place as any, and at least I would be given shelter. But now there was the new difficulty, and I tried to think how I could still bring this plan about. The Bibles were ruined; I couldn't sell them. And even Marta was gone, so I couldn't drive myself. It was a journey of well over four hundred miles. By ox-cart — the cheapest way — it would take close to two weeks. I would have to hire a cart and driver in Lahore, as well as pay for food along the way.

And for this I would need more than the handful of annas Glory might have in her reticule after her most recent shopping trip to Lahore. I needed a supply of rupees.

I lay in the darkness of the storeroom, looking at the high rectangular window, the window I had stared at through all my childhood punishments. A night wind shook and rustled the trees; their swaying branches created odd patterns on the storeroom walls.

My thoughts moved as the patterns I watched, shifting and changing. I had no possibilities. There was no way for me to procure the amount of money I needed; even old Sanosh's offer, while touching, would be nowhere near the required amount.

A sudden image came to me, so unexpected and shocking that I sat up, shaking my head as if arguing with an unseen force.

I lay down again. No. I wouldn't. Couldn't. The prospect was vile and disgusting.

I listened to the wind in the trees, and continued watching the gliding, almost sensuous movements of the shadows.

No. I could not.

The next morning before the sun was up I heated water. Sleep had been impossible, but I felt no weariness. Through-out the long night I had wrestled with my own thoughts, as surely as if I wrestled with the devil's dark forces. And I had finally succumbed. Was I not strong enough, or too strong? There was only one way out, as surely as the window in the storeroom was the only escape.

And in order to leave this place, I would face my worst fear. I would make real what until now had only been a frightful threat.

I bathed and then went into the house. Glory was sleeping heavily. I looked through her saris, and chose a beautiful silk of green, edged with bronze. I slipped at least a dozen of her bracelets on to each wrist, and a single gold one on to my ankle. Looking in the mirror, I lined my eyes with her *surma*.

I was on the Grand Trunk Road before eight o'clock.

I begged a ride from a passing cart, and when I reached the barracks outside of Lahore I spoke to one of the two ensigns who stood on duty at the gates. 'Please tell the Colonel Miss Pree Fincastle wishes to speak to him,' I said.

The young ensign eyed me suspiciously. 'Which Colonel do you mean?' he asked.

I blinked. 'I . . . I don't know. He's tall, and has light brown hair. Grey eyes. Oh, and a scar, just here.' I ran my finger under my bottom lip.

The ensign nodded. He showed no expression, ducking his head at me and leaving. I wondered if young women in saris often came to the gates asking for the Colonel.

I watched a vulture land at the side of the road where I waited, a dead rabbit in its curved yellow beak. It greedily ripped open the rabbit, pulling out its intestines and swallowing the long, stretchy grey rope in steady, rhythmic gulps. Its head swung up each time there were approaching footsteps or hoofs, the end of the intestine swinging from its deadly beak like a thick worm.

The Colonel accompanied the ensign back to the gate. I pulled my veil across the bottom of my face.

'Well. This is a surprise.' His face and voice held a barely concealed pleasure. He took my arm and led me away from the ensigns, into the barracks courtyard. In the shade of a wall he studied me, letting his eyes linger from the top of my headscarf to my bare feet with the single gold bangle around my right ankle. 'You're looking very attractive, Pree,' he said. 'Not at all like the rather careless girl you choose to portray at the house. And yet I knew what was there, under that shapeless, unattractive clothing. I'm a connoisseur of women. Women of all sorts. But I must admit I never imagined you'd scrub up this well.'

I dropped the end of the transparent scarf, raising my chin to meet his eyes. I saw his pupils swell, briefly, and knew this wouldn't be as difficult as I'd feared.

'What can I do for you?' he asked.

I smiled. 'I have business I would like to discuss,' I said.

He frowned in a playful manner. 'Business?'

'Can we go somewhere? Somewhere private?'

He looked even more surprised than when he had first seen me. 'All right. Come this way,' he said, and I followed him.

I was relieved that Eddie was away from the barracks on manoeuvres; if there had been a chance of him seeing me with the Colonel, without knowing my reasons for being there, I would have felt even more sickened at what I was about to do.

The Colonel led me to a row of officer's bungalows. I refused to look at the other soldiers who watched us pass. He stopped in front of one of the bungalows, opening the door and waiting for me to enter. But instead I faced him.

'Glory is very poorly,' I said.

He cocked his head. 'Is she?' he said, in an easy manner. 'What's wrong with the old girl?'

I stared at him. Did he really expect me to believe he didn't remember what had happened; what he had done?

'Because you beat her,' I said, and he blinked. Something passed over his face, then he shrugged.

'Have you come all the way here, looking so magnificent, to talk to me about Glory?' He gestured into the open doorway, again trying to usher me inside. 'Let's not have the whole place know our business, Pree,' he said. 'This isn't really approved of, bringing a woman to private quarters. Step inside. Please,' he added.

I stayed where I was. 'I'm here because you told Glory what you would pay for me,' I said. 'Twenty rupees. Will you pay it?'

His face was unreadable. 'So you've come to me for money?'

I raised my eyebrows and looked into his eyes. *What other reason would I come? Do you really think I desire you?* I wanted so badly to spit those words into his face, but I thought of the twenty rupees, and knew there was a game I must play.

'Of course that's not the only reason,' I lied, so smoothly that I surprised myself. 'I've missed seeing you, Colonel. And I thought about what you once said – do you remember?' I asked, tilting my head to one side and smiling, ever so slightly. 'That my first time should be with a man like you.'

It was the right thing to say. He picked up my hands and rubbed his thumbs over my calloused palms.

I kept smiling, a smile as false as my words.

He returned it. 'Twenty rupees is a lot of money,' he said, and I gently but firmly pulled my hands from his.

'Twenty rupees,' I repeated.

He nodded. 'All right. But only if,' he leaned closer, putting his mouth to my ear, 'you are as you say. Untouched.' He then pulled away and spoke into my face, his tone not quite as velvety. 'If not, well then, you'll not even receive the rupee I pay Glory, and any others like her. Because you won't make a fool of me.'

'I would never try, Colonel,' I said, and then went through the doorway. He took my hand and led me straight to his bedroom, not bothering with the false niceties of offering me something to drink or sitting to chat in the main room. I had only an impression of simple furniture on scattered rugs before we stood in the middle of his bedroom. It was orderly and clean, the walls of unpainted wood and the floor covered with a striped rug. Under mosquito netting was a tightly made single bed with a grey blanket and a thick pillow. Along one wall was a wooden desk and chair, on another a narrow wardrobe. The window had a louvred shutter over it; now he closed it. The room was dim and surprisingly cool.

'As well, you must wear the sheath,' I added. I had taken some from Glory's store of them when I chose the sari. She had chattered about them, once even showing me one of the thin sheaths of sheep gut, saying that she would never again bear a child, and that this was how to prevent it. To catch the man's seed in this barrier before it planted the child within the womb.

The Colonel shook his head. 'That's not part of the bargain.'

I put my hand on his chest, a gesture Glory so often used with her men. 'I've brought some with me. Of the largest size, of course,' I said, with an intimate look, surprising myself at how easily I fell into Glory's slippery talk. I wasn't even embarrassed by my own forwardness. I was play-acting, just acting. I wasn't Pree Fincastle. I was a lost girl, a girl of unknown origins, coming from nowhere, belonging to no one.

'There's no reason to protect myself if you're as pure as you claim,' he said. 'Isn't that so?' His face darkened, the lust there only a moment ago retreating. 'If you're clean there's no reason for it,' he repeated.

'Of course, Colonel,' I agreed quickly, pulling away the

end of the sari that was draped over my shoulder. He looked at the top of my breasts, and again, his pupils dilated. I worried that if I insisted on the sheath I might antagonise him, and lose my only opportunity to escape the mission. He wouldn't care about my concern, would he? I could only pray that the chance I was about to take wouldn't result in a child. *Prayer.* Did I actually believe in its power?

He was still staring at me, and I shook my head slightly, trying to smile. 'I was jealous of Glory when she was with you,' I lied shamelessly. 'It was only fear of her, fear that she would turn me out if I showed my interest in you, that made me stay away from you. And deny myself. But Glory is no longer of concern. You saw to that, didn't you, Colonel?'

I watched his face, looking for something – some admittance to what he'd done, even the tiniest shred of remorse. I could read nothing but desire now, his colour deepening and his breathing heavier.

'And when I awoke this morning and realised Glory no longer had any hold over what I wanted, I didn't want to wait.' I stepped closer, so that my thigh touched the front of his trousers, and knew by what I felt there that he was already prepared for me. 'I dreamed of you, knowing you would be the only man to satisfy me,' I whispered. The cloying smile hadn't left my face; I was sprouting words written by another's pen. I was a character in a book I had never read, but instinctively I knew her.

'Yes, yes,' he murmured, exerting pressure back against my thigh, swaying his hips from side to side slightly as he ground against me. 'I will satisfy you. But perhaps I'll spoil you for other men; once you know me others will be a disappointment.'

I could barely contain my disgust, but my smile didn't falter.

'Dressed so, with your eyes outlined, you have the face of

a beautiful Indian goddess,' he said, putting his arms around me and pressing his hardness even more firmly against me, and I had a stabbing moment of shock at the size of him.

'With the heart of Kali,' I added, although even to my ears my voice was weak.

He then took my hand and led me to the bed.

Who had I become?

CHAPTER THIRTY-TWO

I WAS AFRAID, MY palms wet and my heart pounding. Afraid and filled with dread, although it was clear the Colonel, sober, wouldn't hurt me if I did as he wished. And it was also obvious he was full of pride, wanting to impress me with his prowess.

From a life of watching and listening to women talk about their bodies at the infirmary, I was well aware of exactly what to expect. But I was shamed by the thought of this man seeing my nakedness, and putting his hands on my body. Although I strove for a brave front, I was, as well as fearful, horribly humiliated by what I was doing.

Sitting on the edge of the bed, my whole body was quivering slightly, and I could actually smell the Colonel's excitement. It filled the very air, like a presence. I had no option but to watch as he slowly, languorously, took off his clothes. Although my mother had firmly tried to impress on me that the naked body was a shameful thing, in the world I lived in it was impossible to avoid nudity, and I had seen the unclothed human body – both male and female – all my life.

I'd first watched with a child's naïve curiosity as my mother dragged me past the mossy bathing ghats outside Lahore, her head turned away from the naked children and the men and women with their thin, clinging wet dhotis and saris bathing on the steps at the edge of the river. I'd occasionally stared at naked holy men, the ash-covered devotees who had renounced all worldly possessions and paraded through the streets of Lahore and the villages as they proclaimed their dedication. I'd seen the exposed portions of the bodies of the men and women who came to the infirmary; although my mother made it a point to never venture on to the front verandah, or into the infirmary if my father was dealing with a male patient, I had run about freely as a child, largely unnoticed.

And since Glory had begun her business, I'd been the involuntary witness, more than once, to a naked soldier stumbling out of one of the doors to urinate over the verandah railing, too drunk or too lazy to go to the convenience.

The human body and its workings held no great mystery for me, although the actual sensations of the act I was about to partake in did.

The Colonel's chest was wide and solid, and covered with dark hair. His skin had a curiously rough appearance, and before he touched it to mine I knew it would be dry and unyielding. His arms and thighs were thick and muscled, his hips narrow, but a small roll of loose skin hung just over them, and his belly was softening, something not noticeable while he was in his uniform. A line of dark hair ran down from that belly, and I didn't want to follow it, but as he stood in front of me, stepping out of his trousers, it was impossible not to see what was at eye level.

What I had felt through his clothing was confirmed; I couldn't imagine something of that size fitting into me, and had a moment of sudden, outright panic, and had to close my eyes.

'Don't be shy, my little Miss Fincastle,' the Colonel said in a low voice. 'Surely you like what you see. Women always do. Come, open your eyes and have a look. It will only bring you enjoyment, and anticipation of what is to come.'

How had this man come to believe so fully in himself?

His vanity was almost as repugnant as his body. I took a deep breath and stood, opening my eyes to look at his face instead of that which he seemed so determined I study.

'So far you are demonstrating your avowal of purity well,' he said, smiling. 'Quite modest, it appears. Do I frighten you?'

I wanted to appear confident, and yet it was clearly obvious to the Colonel that I was crumbling. *You will do this*, I told myself. *Because if you can manage this, there is nothing you cannot do. This is a final test of your strength, and your will.*

'So. Is it fear I see, or simply excitement, Miss Fincastle?' he asked again, and I forced my lips into the smile I had worn earlier.

'A little of both, Colonel,' I said, with an attempt at playfulness, but my voice was little more than a piteous mewl.

'Good. Fear makes it better for me,' he whispered then, putting his arms around me and pulling me against his nakedness. The suddenness of his movement, and the tightness with which he held me caused me to draw in my breath so quickly that I choked, turning my head to one side against his chest. I suddenly felt ill. What if I were to be sick at this moment? I found it difficult to breathe.

'Now, now, don't be distraught, little one,' he said, running his hands up and down my bare arms. He buried his face in my hair. 'Come. I can't wait to see you,' he said, and although I thought it impossible, my heart beat harder, and the sickness in my stomach grew stronger.

The Colonel took his time removing my sari, unwinding it bit by bit, his breath growing louder. He stood in front of me, slowly undressing me, and his expression brought to mind a child with a coveted new toy, a dog with a stolen piece of meat. His pleasure was clear; he made sounds deep in his throat and occasionally leaned closer and licked my neck, and the sensation of his tongue was almost unbearable. And yet he used the charm I had seen with Glory before the drink turned him ugly.

'You're beautiful, so beautiful,' he murmured, uncovering my right breast. 'Your skin, untouched by the sun, is like silk.' He lowered his head and as I felt his mouth close on the nipple my stomach heaved, and yet I remained still.

You will do this.

He turned my body this way and that, removing the whole length of the sari, slipping off the jingling bracelets and kissing first one wrist and then the other, his lips moving up my arm until he reached my shoulder. Although I had thought of his lips as normal, rather thin, they suddenly felt large and wet as they slid over my skin.

Then he set me on the edge of the bed again, pushed my thighs apart, kneeling between them and pressing his upper body against mine. After a few moments he stopped, lifting my hands, which lay limply at my sides, to put them around his neck; his hair was thick under my fingertips, and I could smell pomade. It had a slightly cloying odour, and he also smelled of sweat, of leather and tobacco. He gathered me closer against him and then, in one swift movement lay me back on the bed and positioned himself on top of me. But he was so heavy. I couldn't breathe, and struggled under him, pushing at his chest with my palms.

'No,' I said, suddenly filled with terror. Everything was too real, too clear: his smell, his voice, his body. The hair on his chest and between his legs was thick and scratchy. For one instant I thought of Eddie, his smooth body and the scent of mango on his hands. Of Kai, with his light, spicy scent, his lips against mine.

I didn't want to be here with this brutal, thoughtless man; I didn't want this to happen at all. What impossible state had I been in to imagine I could do this? I felt as I had as a small child, locked into the storeroom that first time. Or awakening

417

in the darkness of my bed to crashing thunder. 'No,' I cried, loudly, gasping for breath.

'Shh, shh, it's all right,' he said, looking down at me, moving off me. 'You really are untouched, then? Or just a wonderful actress?' He cocked his head to one side. 'If this truly is your first time . . . Don't fight me, Pree. I'll try not to hurt you.' His voice was condescending, and his expression grew even more proud, like a teacher about to demonstrate some amazing fact to an unsuspecting student.

I took deep, trembling breaths, staring up at his face. I knew he wouldn't let me leave, and also that if I fought too much he would simply take me, possibly turning violent. I had no choice.

'Let your limbs go loose,' he instructed, and I forced my breathing to slow, and tried to lose the rigidity of my whole body. He ran his fingertips lightly up and down my arm. 'This is growing tiresome. Close your eyes, and let me do this.' But all I could think of, as he again positioned himself between my legs, his fingers running over and over my bare skin, dipping between my thighs, was how easily those hands had turned into fists, and what they had done to Glory.

My breathing slower but still ragged, I squeezed my eyes shut and gripped his hips between my knees.

And when he finally entered me, I first felt only a dull, rasping discomfort, and held my breath, and he stopped. Then he pushed harder, with steady insistence, and the pain grew in intensity, and I realised I was weeping, quietly, saying no, no, shaking my head back and forth. And as the pain mounted there was suddenly a new pain, so quick and sharp and unexpected that I felt as though I were one of Glory's sheaths, splitting mercilessly. I cried out, a loud, gasping cry, and opened my eyes.

At that jolt of pain and my cry he had stopped. I looked up at him. His eyes were open as well, and he was smiling down at me indolently, and whispered, 'Good girl,' as if I were Jassie. Then he moved inside me with a steady, unhurried rhythm.

I put my mouth against his shoulder, biting his skin so I didn't make a sound. Such was my feeling of distaste – of utter disgust – for him, but also for myself, that I was afraid I would wail, like a small, disappointed child, and I refused to give in to that. The jingling medallions he wore around his neck swept against my forehead with each of his movements. His skin, under my lips, tasted of salt. Dry and salty.

I couldn't bear to think of what was happening to me, and so instead I counted his thrusts as if counting the beat of a hammer on a nail head, but after a time lost track, and instead thought of the rupees. I counted to twenty a number of times before he finished, with a long, drawn-out hiss of pleasure.

Later, when he rolled off me and looked down at the small blotch of crimson on the sheet under me, he laughed. Not a cruel laugh, more the pleased laugh of a boy who has found a marble he thought for ever lost. I hated the sound.

'You did well for your first time,' he said. 'Took it without too much of a fuss. Did you like it?'

Did I like it? I carefully moved my legs away from him, aware of the wetness under me, blood and what the Colonel had left. *Did you like it?* he asked so casually, when inside I was screaming that I hated it, I hated him and what he had done, I hated his body and the vileness that came out of it into me.

Without waiting for me to answer he said, lazily lifting a lock of my hair and turning it around his finger, 'I could get used to having a woman like you.'

I raised myself on one elbow and stared down at him.

'I'm weary of used old slags like Glory. And I haven't the patience to play the games the younger Eurasians expect, with endless gifts and too much fawning. As for English-

419

women, well, we can forget about the single ones; they only have marriage on their minds.' Into which category was he putting me, or was I something completely separate? 'Occasionally a married woman whose husband is away will play along, but those affairs always end messily.' He let go of my hair, lying back and smiling at the ceiling. 'I don't know how it is you're different, but I could like you.'

He said this as if he were offering me a gift. *I could like you.*

Then he turned on his side and traced my lips with his fingers. 'Yes, I like this. Your well-shaped mouth, your fine eyes.' Now his fingertips were moving over my face as if he were one of Lahore's blind beggars, or as if he had never before touched me. 'And your body, although small, is too strong to be feminine. I find myself oddly drawn to it.' He ran his hands over my upper arms, squeezing them to ensure himself of the strength of my muscles, and continued on, whispering to me what pleasure it would give him to show me all the ways a man can please a woman, to teach me all the ways a woman can please a man. Although he seemed calm now, and no longer frightened me, I remained completely still.

He moved his hand, manoeuvring me so that my head was on his shoulder, his arm around me. He looked at the ceiling again. 'What are your feelings towards Glory?' he asked, his voice even.

With the same evenness I answered, 'Glory is nothing to me.' It was true; I had no feelings for her at all.

'Good,' he said. 'Can you get rid of her, then?' he asked.

'Get rid of her? What do you mean?' I stared at him, unable to read his expression.

'You should be running that place. Not her. You would bring some class to it.'

I shivered involuntarily, envisioning the mess of her face, and he drew me closer.

'Do you wish me to see to it?' he whispered into my hair. 'It would be an easy matter.'

And with that I knew then, that no matter how drunk he might profess to have been, he was well aware of what he had done to Glory. I didn't move.

'Think of the fun we could have,' he said, 'if you were to take Glory's place.'

I sat up, unable to let him see my loathing. 'I must be returning to the mission.'

'Not just yet,' he said, drawing a line down my naked back with his forefinger. I shivered again, and he laughed and pulled me to him. 'I'll ride out to visit you tonight,' he said, and I drew in my breath, holding it.

I hadn't expected this; I hadn't thought that he'd want to see me again. I thought he only wanted to feel the power of taking my virginity. 'But you'll give me my rupees now,' I said, my voice very calm, matter-of-fact, in spite of the anxiousness he had just created within me.

'Why do you need them right now? I can bring the money out tonight. Or better still, let me buy you something. Something worth far more than twenty rupees.'

'Oh no,' I said, forcing myself to smile as I moved from his arms, sitting up and facing him, running my fingers through my tangled hair. The room was too hot now, airless. There was a sheen of sweat on the Colonel's neck. 'I want to buy myself some new clothes. I had to wear Glory's sari today. I have nothing of my own. What would you like me to wear for you?' *Please, just give me the rupees and let me go.*

'I like you like this,' he said, putting his hands around my waist and again attempting to draw me close. 'No clothes at all.'

'I know,' I said, smiling at him. 'But I want to make myself look beautiful for you.'

'That's my girl,' he said, sitting up as well, pushing back my

421

hair and kissing my neck, just under my ear, the ear still slightly bruised by his own blow the week earlier.

'So you'll give me the rupees now? I'll buy something in Lahore before I go home.' I was glad he still had his mouth on my neck and couldn't see my face. 'What's your favourite colour?' I asked, trying to ignore his kisses, trying to not let the panic, rapidly returning, creep into my voice.

'Blue,' he said, his voice muffled against my skin. 'Yes, yes. You must buy a beautiful blue frock for me. For tonight.'

'All right,' I told him, looking down at the top of his head. I forced out a small laugh. 'But then you must let me be on my way. I'll need time to choose just the right things. It's been so long since I've been to the shops. I'll need slippers, and petticoats. And maybe a bonnet.' The lies rolled out in a pretty little voice I didn't know I possessed.

He laughed, finally letting go of me. The bed dipped as he got up and dressed.

I did the same, then turned to him, putting out my hand, palm up. 'My rupees, Colonel,' I said, smiling sweetly with my head to one side, as if slightly chiding him, and he again laughed in a delighted manner. He opened the top drawer of the desk and pulled out a handful of notes. He didn't count them. I could only hope there were at least twenty rupees.

'When you come tonight I'll be wearing a beautiful blue frock, chosen especially for you,' I said, taking the money and tucking it inside my bodice. 'Wait until dark so that you can see me in lamplight.' I wondered if I were going too far.

But he chucked me under the chin as if I were a child who had pleased him, and we went out into the early afternoon sunlight where he had an ensign summon a little mare for me. He also instructed the ensign to accompany me on my shopping rounds, back to the mission, and finally lead the mare back to the barracks. He obviously didn't trust me with the horse; did he think I'd sell it?

Actually it crossed my mind that if he'd allowed me to take it I would indeed have ridden her to Peshawar.

He helped me climb into the saddle. I had to bunch my sari under me to spread my legs across the seat, and sucked in a silent breath at the hot new pain as I settled into the leather. 'Take her wherever she wants to go,' he said to the ensign.

Then he reached up and tucked a piece of my hair behind my ear, smiling. 'Buy a bottle of whiskey as well,' he said.

I smiled back at him. 'All right.' I kept smiling, although my mouth trembled with the effort. I kept the smile on my face until I had turned, following the ensign away from the barracks. When I was sure the Colonel could no longer see my face, my mouth slackened as hot tears filled my eyes.

I pulled my veil across my face and wept beneath it, sickened at the images of the Colonel on top of me, aware of the new ache where my body met the hard saddle.

It was done, and could not be undone. I told myself it was the only choice, and therefore the right choice. What I had sacrificed was to ensure an escape from the living death that would be my life if I stayed at the mission. That is what I would concentrate on. Not what I had done, but the new life I would make for myself in Peshawar.

When I was in control of my voice I told the ensign I wanted to go directly back to the mission. He looked over his shoulder at me.

'Was I not to take you to the shops in the cantonment?'

'I told you I wish to go home. You heard the Colonel,' I said, my voice hard and unfamiliar. 'You are to take me where I wish to go.'

He nodded once and turned back.

At least the ride to the mission by horseback was so much faster than in a creaking bullock cart. I set the pace once we were outside the city gates, moving beside the ensign at a trot, and then urging the little mare to a gallop when the road was clear. The leather saddle chaffed my inner thighs and hurt my bottom and the new rawness as I bounced along rather gracelessly, but there was no time to saunter. As we galloped my headscarf blew off. I turned to see it float behind me; a flash of green and gold. The ensign called to me: did I want him to retrieve it? No, I shouted to him, pressing my heels harder into the mare's sides. We were at the mission in just over an hour; I was bathed in sweat. I slid off the mare and silently handed the reins to the ensign, never looking at him. Surely he wondered at my haste, but didn't speak.

While he led the horses to the well to drink I went to my hut, studying myself in my small mirror. There was a slight, reddened rash on my chin, caused by the Colonel's shadowed chin on mine as he ground his mouth against my lips. Other than that, I looked the same as I always had, apart from the slightly smeared *surma*. I had expected to look different. I felt different; older and dirty, disgusted with myself and what I had just done. As I stared back at myself from the mirror my eyes shone dangerously: luminous and glazed, as if I burned with fever, but I wasn't ill. It was combined anger and sorrow which accentuated their intenseness, the gold standing out against the darker brown like a bas-relief.

I was filled with anger at the Colonel, at his whispered demands and pleased, boastful laughter, but more so at myself. For allowing myself to sink so low.

And this caused the sorrow; sorrow over what I had lost – not just my purity, but my self-respect.

I pulled the rupees, damp from pressing against my skin, from my bodice and counted them. My fingers shook; I had to count twice. There were twenty-four.

'Good,' I said aloud, throwing the notes to my charpoy, as if I really were the wanton, careless woman I had acted this day. I heard the hoofs of the two horses as the ensign left.

424

And then I sat heavily on my charpoy, suddenly spent of energy. In the last week I had shared a bed with two different men; one innocently, out of loneliness, the other deceitfully, out of pure, calculated greed . . . although it was simpler, and caused less guilt, if I called it desperation.

I was a fallen woman; what I had lost could never be replaced. I tried to detach myself from this fact. 'What does it matter?' I asked the empty hut. 'What does it matter that I am no longer pure? I had no choice,' I said, too loud.

I smelled the Colonel, the scent of his body rising from mine, and the odour, slightly sour, brought bile up my throat which then filled my mouth. I left the rupees scattered on the charpoy and carried a full bucket from the well back to my hut, stripping off Glory's sari and bracelets and leaving everything in a heap on the floor. I scrubbed myself with a flannel. The water was cold; it was refreshing on my hot skin as I washed away the dust and grime of the road, as well as the last vestiges the Colonel's body had left on mine.

From the nails on the wall I took my mother's old petticoats and frocks that I'd once altered to fit me. They were drab things; I would have loved to have taken some of Glory's bright, pretty frocks, but they would be too small. I put on a dull navy cotton, and, sighing, the hated pink bonnet.

As I went to my knees and took the old carpetbag from under my charpoy, I heard the clink of the sabre. I pulled it out; it was far too long to fit in the carpetbag. I wished I could take it. What would await me on the road to Peshawar? I ran my fingers lightly over the decorated handle, then pushed it back under the bed.

I gathered my favourite novels: *Jane Eyre*, *The Mill on the Floss* and *The Rose and the Ring*. I took the Woolstonecroft book Kai had given me, my father's black Bible and my own white one. And finally, I picked up the tattered copy of *Gray's Anatomy: Descriptive and Surgical*, Mary Selby Lowndes'.

Medical Receipt Book, and *Domestic Medicine* by William Buchan – the books from the infirmary I'd had in the house when the infirmary had burned. I put all of these volumes into the bottom of the carpetbag. I wanted to take more books, but knew it would make the bag impossible to carry comfortably. I added the rest of the clothing, and then folded the blanket from my charpoy and set it on top. I stuffed my feet into my mother's old boots, and tucked the pile of rupees from the Colonel into a small drawstring bag. I tied it around my waist, under the skirt of my dress.

I hurried, thinking of the look on the Colonel's face. I was afraid he might decide to come early to the mission. As I stepped out of the hut, into the courtyard, I had had no intention of going back into the house – that place of such unhappiness now – but suddenly, surprising myself, I felt the need to look at it once more. I crept in, knowing it would be foolhardy to wake Glory – it would do her no good to know anything of what I had just done and what I was about to do. I didn't even start to allow myself to think what might happen to her when the Colonel came looking for me later.

Glory was asleep, propped up against one corner of the settee. On the table in front of her was a whiskey bottle with an inch of amber liquid in the bottom; she held a half-full glass of it in her good hand. Small, rhythmic snores came from her open mouth, a tiny whistle reverberating through the empty spot in her gums. In the unforgiving afternoon light her face was still a terrible mess, but some of the bruises were lighter around the edges, fading to green and yellow. And at that moment I felt a strange pity for her, and the disgust I had long carried for so many reasons – her sordid relationship with my father, her carelessness with her own children, her bullying reign over me here, and, of course, the position she had forced me into now – seemed to lessen. Perhaps it was because I was leaving this place, and she never would. Her future held only more of what had happened to her days earlier, while mine, although unknown, would have to be better than this. It would have to be, I told myself.

Snorting suddenly, Glory mumbled something unintelligible, and the glass tipped from her hand, rolling on to the settee. A whiskey stain in the shape of a eucalyptus leaf darkened the threadbare horsehair. I thought of the similar shaped stain — although scarlet — left under me, on the Colonel's sheet.

And with that, my fleeting pity for this ruined woman passed, and the familiar revulsion returned, and I was glad. If I were to continue to do what I must to survive, I could not let myself give in to any weakness.

Stopping once more to survey the room, I left the house and went to the tiny graveyard in the field. I knelt in front of the crumbling headstones, running my hand over each one. These little white stones were the only things I would miss when I left this place. I felt as though I were abandoning them, abandoning all that was left — their names in stone — of the four children who were not, after all, my siblings. Two of the small bodies didn't even lie under this earth.

Without my care, within a year or two the stones would topple in the wet soil of one of the monsoons. Green knotted tendrils would curl over them, and they would sink into the earth. There would be no further tangible trace of them, the children who had never had a chance to be, the children I had never known: Elijah and Alice Ann and Elizabeth and Gabriel Fincastle. They would truly be swallowed by India. I closed my eyes and said a Christian prayer for them, and then put a hand on each of the two peeling whitewashed river stones. Samuel and Eve Fincastle. My parents: the only ones I had ever known.

It was my father's weakness of character, allowing himself to hover between his carnal and spiritual desires that had

427

forced him into his ceaseless rounds of prayers, steeping himself in holiness to try to live with his guilt. Was this part of the reason I couldn't accept his prayers and believe his preachings with all my heart? Because instinct told me they were spoken with a false tongue?

Now I could understand more clearly my mother's endless attempts, through threats and punishments, to shape me, smooth me into a proper English girl. Now I understood the quiet desperation – and fear? – I had sometimes seen come over her features when I proved to her, over and over again, that I could not be tamed. Would not be tamed.

I squeezed my eyes shut; was the transgression I committed only hours ago not proof? There was movement over my hand on the stone, and I opened my eyes. A brilliant emerald green lizard darted down the side of the stone and disappeared into the dry, brown summer grass.

I wanted to weep for the sad, lost man and woman who had come to this country full of clear hope, and had gone to their deaths in a dark jumble of doubt and guilt and confusion. They had left nothing of themselves. Their ashes had sunk back into the earth – *dust to dust, ashes to ashes* – under the ruined infirmary, or perhaps had been blown, with the flames, into the wide Indian sky. In death they had become a true part of this foreign land as they had never been in life.

They had done what they could for the natives. For me. Could I not cry for them?

I stood, brushing my palms together, unable to pull forth sentiment, anxious to be gone. Stopping under the peepul tree in the middle of the courtyard, I put my hand on its rough, comforting bark, thinking of the times I had sat under it as a child, playing with Rujjie or reading, Jassie lying nearby on her side in the sun.

The bark was hard and ridged; as my fingers lightly ran up

428

and down it I thought of the Colonel's hands on me, and shuddered. I stepped away, knowing I mustn't linger any longer, but then heard a small yelp, a snuffle, from behind the *rasoi*.

Jassie.

I hurried to the cooking hut, thankful I would have a last chance to see the dog I had loved for so long, and bid her farewell.

But old Jassie wasn't alone. She was with a male, a spotted, mange-eaten pariah. The act obviously completed, they stood in the post-coital position, tails together, heads lowered patiently, waiting for the release.

'Jassie,' I said quietly, reaching towards her. If I could touch her, just once, before I left, it would bring me comfort.

She lifted that dear, sleek head, but instead of her usual gentle look, her eyes narrowed, and the corner of her black lip lifted, trembling. I saw a flash of yellowed eyetooth, heard the beginning of a rumble from deep within her throat, and I stepped back.

Jassie's expression was one of shame, and of open need.

She would survive; she always had.

'Goodbye, Jassie,' I whispered, and, without another backward glance, I left the mission and the only home I had ever known.

And I left behind the girl I had been.

Now I was a woman in every way, a woman of unknown origins. I had a right to find my place in this world, whoever I was.

I would never again allow myself to be ruled by another, by one like Glory, or the Colonel. I touched the reassuring thickness of the rupees under my skirt, and straightened my shoulders as I left the courtyard.

CHAPTER THIRTY-THREE

O UTSIDE THE MISSION fence I waved as a native family in an ox-cart came towards me. When they stopped, I told them I needed to go to Lahore. They nodded respectfully, and the mother told one of the boys to put my carpetbag into the cart, and move from the seat so that I might sit beside her.

For the second time that day I made my way back to Lahore. I watched the road steadily, wary of any redcoat on horseback, and lowered my head should one come into view. But we passed the barracks without any sign of the Colonel, and I breathed more easily.

Once on the other side of Lahore, I went to the row of carts and drivers for hire.

I chose a driver who looked cleaner than the others lined up with their carts and bullocks outside the Kashmiri Gate, leading north. I told him what I wanted in Hindi and Punjabi and then Urdu; he shook his head. 'Rajasthani,' he said.

I switched to English. 'Do you understand English?'

'Some, Memsahib, some.'

I repeated my request. 'I'd like you to take me north, to Peshawar,' I said.

He shook his head. 'Peshawar? Oh no, no, Memsahib. Not to Frontier. Very bad men. Maybe you go Gudjarala. Rawalpindi. Even Jhelum. I go those place.' I knew the fear many natives had of the Pathans. 'Jhelum good, Memsahib. Not Peshawar. Bad for you. For English.'

'No. It must be Peshawar.' Apart from what the Afghan had once told me, I knew little about Peshawar, in the most northern province of India, on the border of Afghanistan, other than that it was rumoured to be rough, filled with rather lawless men who came down from Afghanistan through the Khyber Pass. They lived by their wits and their weapons.

But there was also a large British population; Peshawar was an important outpost for the British military. After the first Anglo-Afghan War, when the English and Afghans fought over Afghanistan, the city had been under British rule.

This man standing in front of me, still shaking his head, was probably right; it might be dangerous. And yet maybe this would be my saving grace. Maybe there, in a city which knew a great deal of movement, of different peoples coming and going, nobody would be critical of, or curious about a young woman hoping to start a new life. And of course the Langs would give me shelter, and work. Peshawar was too far away for them to have known what had happened to my parents. About Glory. I could work for them, and start this new life where nobody knew anything about me.

Now the man's eyes studied mine. 'Why Memsahib go Peshawar?'

'Are you afraid to drive me?' I asked, hoping this would shame him. 'No one will bother you if you're with me.'

He digested this, nodding slowly. 'You pay more?'

'Yes.'

'How many you pay?'

Before I could offer what I thought reasonable he held up all his fingers. He was missing the end joint of his middle finger on the left hand. 'To go.' Another show of his fingers. 'Come back, Memsahib,' he said. 'Food. Us. And he.' He lifted

431

his chin in the direction of his bullock. He licked his lips, calculating. 'Night time pay in *caravanserai*.'

'Not twenty. I will give you ten rupees,' I said firmly, showing my ten fingers. 'Five to take me there, and five for your return. And I will buy whatever food we need, and pay for the lodging, as you say.'

Immediately he looked away. 'Ten rupee only?' He shook his head, not meeting my eyes. 'Not much, Memsahib,' he said, frowning, although his tone was respectful. 'More.'

'It is my offer,' I said. 'If you don't wish it, I'll find another driver.'

'Ten and . . .' he muttered under his breath, then held up eight fingers. 'Ten and this many.'

Again I shook my head. 'Not eighteen. Fifteen. Fifteen,' I repeated, making a show of fingers. After I'd paid for our food and to feed the bullock and our nightly tariffs I would be lucky to be left with a few rupees when I reached Peshawar.

He looked from my fingers to my face, finally nodding. 'As you say, Memsahib.' He glanced at the sky. 'Now dark soon. Next day we go—'

'No,' I interrupted. I needed to be away from Lahore and the barracks. The Colonel would be on his way to the mission at any time. 'We will go now,' I said. 'What is your name?'

'Chander,' he said, taking my carpetbag and putting it in the back of his cart.

I climbed on the rough seat beside him. 'I am Miss Fincastle. Now no more talk, Chander. Take me to Peshawar.'

He slapped the reins on the bullock's bony back. The flies and gnats gathered there dispersed, and clouds of dust rose from the thick hide.

We set off for Peshawar.

★ ★ ★

As we rumbled away from Lahore I watched, over my shoulder, as it diminished. The city glowed, its white towers and parapets and minarets and temples brilliant, so blinding they almost appeared to pulse.

Would I ever return? It was a place of such pale beauty, and yet it also held my darkest memories: the Wyndhams and the others in the English cantonment with their snobbery, the Most Reverend Burgess with his lack of understanding, and, of course, the Colonel. It seemed I could still smell him upon me, although I knew I was outwardly clean.

And further away still was Glory and the sad ruin of the mission, the tilting stones in the little graveyard.

I was leaving all I had ever known. But now what I thought I knew had changed. I was not who I had once believed I was. Between yesterday and today I had lost myself, first through Glory's story, and then through the Colonel's power.

I looked away, blinking rapidly. There was no time for sentiment, nor self-pity. On the wide dusty road, a watery mirage shimmered in the late-afternoon light.

Ahead lay the unknown, clean and new.

We passed rice fields with herons standing on their slender legs, the sun reflecting off the shallow water so brightly I had to shade my eyes. A man slowly ploughed a field with his bullock, small twittering grey birds following, digging in the earth newly churned by the blade. Beside the road sat a small boy, fanning a fire over which a brazier of peanuts roasted; he called out to us in anticipation of a sale as we passed.

We drove until it was time to stop for the night. But in those few hours I managed to firmly push away the last of my anxiety. The further we drove from the mission and Lahore, the straighter I sat, peering directly ahead into the warm, dusty dusk. I had no idea what awaited me, but I was suddenly calm. Calm and confident. I had made my choice; I would accept what it brought. On a whim I stood in the cart, stretching my arms in front of me as if embracing hope itself.

Chander looked up at me, and although I saw, from his expression, that he thought me slightly mad, as perhaps he thought all English people were, I didn't care.

I smiled at him, and he shook his head, but his lips turned up in the slightest hint of an answering smile.

Eventually Chander directed the cart into a *caravanserai*, one of the old rest spots built for travellers along the Grand Trunk Road.

As we drew nearer, the sounds and smells of the encampment echoed down the road to meet us. Voices talked, laughed, argued, and sang in a cacophony of languages; steady tinny music whistled from a reed instrument. Bullocks bellowed, horses whinnied, goats bleated, and the roar of a lone camel was joined by barking of dogs skulking about the *caravanserai* in the hopes of food. The wafting odour of dung fires and meat cooking made me realise how hungry I was.

We drove through a wide portal into the walled structure. Open to the sky, it contained a huge courtyard with a well, and along all the inside walls were stalls and chambers, large enough to accommodate animals and carts. The air was hazy with smoke, and men sat in front of small niches, selling food and tea and fodder. There were many carts, those open like ours and those canopied and shuttered or curtained, which I knew held Muslim women.

Chander directed his bullock into an empty spot and we climbed down. I gave him money to pay for the tariff and to buy straw for the bullock and food for us. I watched a fierce-looking Rajasthani woman in her red-and-blue-patterned sari, her arms covered with ivory bracelets to her elbows, leading a small girl by the hand towards a screened chamber at the far end of the courtyard. I followed her to the designated area for women, using one of the buckets there. As I relieved myself my flesh burned, still raw from the Colonel. Before lowering my skirt I saw a trail of darkening bruises on the insides of my thighs. I quickly washed my hands and face in the provided basins of water, and returned to the cart, anxious to forget about my discomfort, knowing food, and then sleep, would be soothing.

Chander handed me cooked goat meat in a *roti* wrapped in leaves. Two earthenware cups of tea sat on the seat of the wagon; he gave me one and rapidly swallowed his.

I was suddenly exhausted from what the day had held. Leaning against the cart, I ate the sinewy meat and oily *roti*, washing it down with the sweet, milky tea, my eyelids so heavy that chewing and swallowing seemed an effort. I sleepily watching the glowing cooking fires as they wavered and danced, sparks shooting into the still, darkening sky overhead. Men elbowed one another as they purchased sweetmeats and tobacco from the vendors. In the stall beside us a woman complained loudly about her mother-in-law to another woman, and told how relieved she was the old woman was going to stay with her second son for the next few months.

'Such a relief to a wife if her husband has a brother,' she said.

'Two spoons in the pot are always better than one,' the other woman agreed.

Chander fed and watered his bullock, rolled himself into a piece of burlap and lay under the cart.

I climbed into the back of the cart, taking off my bonnet and boots and spreading my blanket over the rough wood. Using a petticoat from my carpetbag as a pillow, I lay down. A burst of men's laughter filled the air, and dogs grumbled warningly to each other. In the trees outside the walls, I heard the chattering of a flock of plum-necked parakeets as they roosted for the night. There was the screech and thud of the only gate into the *caravanserai* shutting, the heavy rasp of iron clasps as it was locked. It would be safe from the thieves that haunted the road at night.

Eventually the noise lessened, and then the *caravanserai* was quiet except for occasional coughing. I was alone under the starred sky, surrounded by strangers, and yet I felt no concern. I refused to think about what I'd just left, pushing away the sudden and disgusting memories of the Colonel's body on mine, putting my hands over my eyes when I thought of what might be happening to Glory at the Colonel's hands at this very time. And I didn't allow myself to think about what my new life in Peshawar might hold.

As I fell towards the bliss of sleep on that warm summer night, the rustling from the tall trees outside the enclosure giving the sensation of a quiet melody, I was aware of an aura of freedom and peace that I hadn't had at the mission for a long, long time.

The *caravanserai* came to life at dawn. Muslim prayers were called, and the air was heavy with morning mist and smoke from the newly started cooking fires. A small herd of goats, bells at their necks tinkling, scampered across the courtyard as I sat up in the cart. Children cried out sleepily and birds whistled and screeched and trilled.

I stretched my arms over my head. I had slept the unmoving, dark and dreamless sleep of exhaustion, welcome after so many nights of tossing and turning and trying to stay alert because of my concern over my own safety, my distress at what I'd learned, and the decision I had to make as to what I would do.

Chander came to me with chai and *rotis*. I drank the sweet, spicy concoction and ate the hot, buttery *roti*, with deep pleasure. When I had finished I went to the chamber at the far end of the courtyard, and on my return Chander was waiting on the seat of the cart.

I had never known any sights except the countryside and villages which lay between the mission and Lahore. Now I swayed beside Chander as we rode along the teeming road, soaking in all I could. Fields unrolled on either side of us. This was more farm land, in some places even richer than that surrounding Lahore because of a series of shallow canals supplying water to the fields. I recognised the growing crops of wheat and sugar cane and maize and mustard. There was a crop I didn't recognise; I pointed to it and Chander told me it was tobacco.

We travelled along the Grand Trunk Road for the whole day; I jumped from the cart to find the privacy I needed in the bushes or massive banyan trees alongside the road while Chander would simply turn his back and relieve himself against one of the wheels. We passed endless women carrying brass lotahs balanced on a twisted rag encircling the top of their heads, and men bent double under loads of wood and branches they carried on their backs. Goats lay in the shade of thorn trees, and leathery water buffalos rested on their knees in the fields, gazing in front of them as their jaws swivelled in constant chewing.

Small villages of jumbled homes and a few shops periodically rose up alongside the road. They were all the same: the shopkeepers sat on their haunches, backs against the mud walls in the sun with their arms resting on their knees, chatting idly with each other as they sold grain or oil or rice, fruits or spices. A group of shouting ragged boys played cricket with flat pieces of wood on the weedy land behind them.

Sometimes, restless from sitting, I would climb down from the cart and walk alongside it. I picked up a shaft of sugar cane fallen from someone's bundle and peeled it, chewing its sweetness and then spitting the shreds of pith to the ground. Every so often a small child, naked or perhaps wearing a short *kurta* which barely covered his or her small belly, would appear out of nowhere and trot beside me for a few yards, holding out tiny hands to me.

A few times I heard rhythmic, rasping breathing, and would turn as four bearers, one holding each pole of a curtained palanquin, ran past with their shrouded passengers.

Chander and I didn't attempt to speak; he kept his eyes on the road and hands on the reins except for the times when he pulled out a small, circular *paan* box, deftly combining the betel and spices and tobacco stored in each wedge-shaped compartment, finally tucking the concoction inside his bottom lip. He sucked on this lump for some time, eventually expertly spitting out long, brown streams.

As the light changed and deepened and a low, even haze began to rise across the fields, the smell of wood smoke and food cooked on ashes made my stomach rumble. Small fires dotted the darkening landscape. Chander stopped at another *caravanserai*, and again we spent the night.

Over the next few days we continued on in this pattern. I was content to be part of this great chain of movement, and I felt my spirits continually rise. The journey was full of hope, the hope one feels after a weight has lifted. I didn't know what I'd find in Peshawar. Were the Langs still there? Of course I had to prepare myself for the fact that they might have left their American Mission, but even so, surely there would be some sort of Christian ministry that would take me in and allow me to work for my bed and food. They could hardly turn away one of their own.

We passed endless villages and small towns; when the roads grew busier I knew we were approaching a city. I saw Gurjanwala, the sun playing on its minarets and domes, and on the eighth day Chander stopped the cart, pointing towards a city in the near distance.

'Here is Rawalpindi, Memsahib,' Chander said. 'Clean. Many whites. Maybe you go 'Pindi?'

I knew he was still wary of travelling into Peshawar. I shook my head. 'Peshawar, Chander,' I said, and he frowned, shaking his head, and slapped the reins.

Over the next few days the landscape grew less lush and more rocky. We drove through valleys growing more wheat and cotton and tobacco, but also barley. And then, on the fourth day after Rawalpindi, Peshawar rose in the distance, backed by high distant mountains which appeared brown and barren. It was late afternoon. We had been travelling for thirteen days. I felt impossibly dirty.

I had Chander stop the next time I saw a small copse of trees, and changed from the stained, grimy dress I had worn for the entire journey into the brown *peau de soie* that had been my mother's good frock. I used the edge of my blanket to wipe the dust of the road from my boots. I put on the pink bonnet and the white gloves I'd kept in the carpetbag, not wanting to dirty them on the journey.

Suddenly anxious, wanting to find the Langs' mission, I fidgeted as we drove ever closer to Peshawar.

And then, there it was. Peshawar. City of bloody history, of beautiful flowers, of desperate men and hidden women. We had arrived. I had made this happen: I had lied and deceived and degraded myself to come to this place, which was my future. Unexpectedly my eyes filled with tears – of relief, of fear, of hope, of simple weariness.

We entered through a gate and were immediately caught in meandering streets with tiny dark passages of shops leading off them. The alleys were so narrow that there was barely enough room for two people walking side by side. There were the usual scrawny limping dogs and little herds of goats followed by a boy with a short stick, and the shouts of vendors and men driving mules and bullocks. Similar to Lahore, there were crooked, narrow streets and crowded, ornamented havelis, the homes of the prosperous, with bay windows and intricately carved motifs on their high balconies.

Rickshaws hurried by with frantic warning tinkles, and I saw the light, two-wheeled carriage pulled by a pony. I knew the fast-moving carriages to be called tongas; they had only recently been seen in Lahore as well.

'Where, Memsahib?' Chander asked, and I took a deep breath.

'Just keep going,' I said, and Chander rather listlessly directed the cart forward.

An Englishwoman pulled alongside our cart in a tonga, two little girls sitting in the back seat. The woman tugged on the reins of the prancing pony as a man's cart just ahead of her, loaded with some unknown variety of squash, turned over. I was pleased to see a woman out on her own, driving an open carriage; this city, while in no way as architecturally beautiful or physically pleasing as Lahore, was indeed less formal.

'Excuse me,' I called, and she looked over at me. 'I'm seeking a Christian mission.'

'There's a Presbyterian Board of Foreign Missions, as well as the Anglican Mission,' she said.

'Is there a mission run by the Langs? An American mission?' I asked, and she nodded.

'Yes,' she answered, in a rather non-committal voice, studying my face now. 'The Langs live not far from here, in the cantonment. It's only ten minutes by tonga or rickshaw; ask any driver to take you to them.'

'Thank you,' I said, the woman's reaction giving me a sense of unexplained unease.

The man ahead of her had righted his cart and the last of the squash was piled into it again. The woman's pony pranced, impatiently straining at the reins, and the carriage lurched forward with a toss of its head.

The little girls turned in the seat, waving at me.

I told Chander to pull to the side of the street. As I climbed down he pulled my carpetbag from the back of the cart.

'No. Leave it there, and please wait here for me,' I told him.

'Here Peshawar, Memsahib,' he said, with a confused expression.

'I know,' I said, 'but I have to find my . . . my friends before I take my bag.' I didn't wish to arrive at the Langs' mission appearing as desperate as I truly was. I needed to speak to them, and have them invite me. It was a matter of pride.

Chander set the carpetbag in the back again. I knew he would stay with my bag; I hadn't paid him yet.

'Wait here for me,' I repeated, and he nodded, glancing around anxiously. The streets were crowded with all manner of men, and, to Chander, they were surely unfamiliar and some of them understandably threatening. Jostling past us were roughly dressed men with their faces half obscured by the loose ends of their black turbans, and people from an Asian clan, their faces round and their eyes hooded to near slits. Other tall, fierce-looking bearded tribesmen hid their hands under the light shawls draped over their shoulders; some had muskets slung over their shoulders and cartridge-filled bandoliers crossed over their chests.

'You come soon back, Memsahib,' Chander said, frowning.

'Yes, yes,' I answered, beckoning to a passing rickshaw.

CHAPTER THIRTY-FOUR

THE HOUSE THE rickshaw-wallah brought me to was on a wide road that was reminiscent of the cantonment in Lahore; the houses were of the English style, made of white stone, and set apart from each other by blooming gardens. Tall cypress trees lined the road. I wondered that a mission was located in such a prosperous area, but then remembered Mrs Lang telling us she had started the mission with inherited money. She didn't have to rely on a ministry for funds. The rickshaw stopped in front of one of the fine bungalows, and I told the rickshaw-wallah to wait for me.

Two *chowkidars* stood guard on either side of the wide steps. I nodded to them as I passed, then rapped on the door. To one side of it was a gleaming plaque, and I was comforted to see the engraved name: *American Women's Christian Mission*. Two identical flags – the American flag, I knew, with its stars and stripes – flanked the door, hanging limply in the still, hot air.

The door was opened by a *chuprassi* in the usual white garb. I was somewhat surprised; I imagined a mission with the words Christian and Women in its title would be opened by one bearing both of those characteristics.

'You are having a calling card?' he asked in English, extending a white-gloved hand.

I shook my head. 'No. Please tell Mr and Mrs Lang it's Miss Fincastle.'

He admitted me, shaking his head almost imperceptibly,

442

obviously disturbed that I had no calling card. Then he left me standing in the front entrance of the pleasant bungalow, with its thick rug, gleaming wooden furniture, and a large painting of a man in a tricorn hat and military clothing standing proudly in the prow of a boat being rowed across choppy waters by other military men. It was a dark and somehow foreboding painting: the men were buffeted by the wind, and the boat appeared frail in the waves. The mission – although it seemed to me to be rather more of a luxurious home – was strangely quiet. Then again, I had no reference to any mission other than the one I had grown up in. No wonder Mrs Lang had found ours so backward.

Within moments Mr Lang came down the hall ahead of the *chuprassi*, smiling broadly. Those awful grey teeth; I'd forgotten. 'Well, well,' he said. 'Dear Miss Fincastle. It is indeed a treat to see you again.' He rocked on his heels. 'You're quite glowing,' he said, although I sensed he said it out of courtesy. Even in the best frock I owned, with my sun-burned face and my dusty hair shoved under the mismatched bonnet, I knew I looked less than presentable. And yet his sincere pleasure at seeing me gave me sudden faith.

He reached for my hand, and lowered his lips to my glove. But when he raised his head, he continued to hold my hand. His own hand was warm, enveloping mine, and he kept his face just a little too close. I drew back slightly, and eased my hand from his.

I had worried that the Langs were no longer here, or that if they were, they would have forgotten about me. And yet it was clear Mr Lang did remember me. He was welcoming, so much so, that I felt a shadow of doubt, subtle as a wing, passing in front of my eyes.

'This way, my dear, this way. Mrs Lang and I are just enjoying a cool drink on this warm afternoon,' he said.

I was thirsty; I could welcome a drink. And I was also hungry. It drew near the time Chander and I usually stopped at a *caravanserai* for the evening. I'd had only a *roti* and a cup of chai ten hours earlier.

'Look who we have here,' Mr Lang said, stepping aside, allowing me into a bright, spacious drawing room. 'The delightful little koel, our own Miss Fincastle from the Lahore mission.'

Mrs Lang didn't rise from her seat on the far side of the room, so I went forward, smiling, extending my hand. When I reached her she pointedly ignored my outstretched hand, reaching for a full glass from the table beside her chair. My hand hung in the air. Finally I let it drop to my side.

She simply looked at me, drinking from her glass as she did so. Mr Lang came to me, his hand on the small of my back. I could feel its heat. 'Have a seat, my dear, have a seat,' he said, ushering me to a small, green velvet tufted chair across from Mrs Lang. He sat beside me on a wide wooden chair with curved arms and a rush seat. I heard the groan of the woven reeds as he settled himself more comfortably.

I looked at him; his gaze was on my knees. I looked back to Mrs Lang. She was watching her husband.

'I hope you have been well, Mrs Lang,' I said, the smile still fixed on my face. In truth she did not look well at all. Fine spidery veins covered her cheeks, and the hair I remembered as bright now appeared faded. Her nose was larger than I recalled, and had a slightly purplish hue.

'I thought you might try to contact us after we extended our invitation,' Mrs Lang said then, looking from her husband to me.

I nodded. 'Yes. Well, that was quite some time ago, was it not!' I stated, my voice light and cheery, although the deception was difficult. I was wary and strangely unsettled by the woman's cool reception. 'Yes, it's been so long since you visited our mission. But I haven't forgotten your mention of my ability with languages, and my practical work with certain medical conditions, and, of course, being the daughter of missionaries, well . . .' I swallowed. The sound was too loud in the quiet room. 'Of course, I have solid knowledge of the Bible. You did say that all of these attributes might be of use to you in Peshawar.'

Neither Mr nor Mrs Lang spoke. A trickle of perspiration ran down my back. The room was so warm, and my mouth so dry with both thirst and nervousness. 'You had suggested that I could be of help here,' I repeated. 'At your mission,' I added unnecessarily, when the silence stretched. 'To help teach the Bible women you employ?' I finally said, although it came out as a rather weak question.

Why did they not speak? I could feel widening rings of perspiration under my arms. I had expected them to welcome me.

'I don't see any women about,' I said, in an attempt to fill the hot, heavy silence, and create a conversation. 'Are they all out working?'

'They stay elsewhere,' Mr Lang said. 'In the old city. We run the business side of the mission from here. This is our home.'

I nodded and turned back to Mrs Lang. It was obvious she was the one to whom I had to make my appeal. She continued to drink; her glass was nearly empty.

It was clear there was no offer forthcoming. I had no course but to be as forthright as possible. 'I am alone now, Mrs Lang. I don't know if you're aware – I don't suppose you would be – that both of my parents are deceased. And so I hoped I could perhaps . . . stay with you. Wherever the women stay, I mean. And work for you.'

'You've done the right thing in coming to us here, my dear,' Mr Lang said, reaching out to pat my knee. His fingers were thick, the ends spatulate.

'Don't be ridiculous, Henry,' Mrs Lang said, and I stared at her, surprised, not only at the venom in her voice, but also at the fact that she called her husband by his Christian name in my presence. 'Everyone has heard of you, Miss Fincastle,' she said now, speaking slowly, carefully, as if around something held at the back of her tongue. I knew all too well that she was highly intoxicated. The first time – the only other time – I had met her I hadn't understood her dependency. But what I'd so recently learned in the mission had taught me many things. Mostly things I wished I didn't know.

'The *brothel* you ran – run? – is common knowledge all over the Punjab,' Mrs Lang said now, and I started at the ugly words, a chill descending upon me in the warm room, splashed with sunlight. I opened my mouth to breathe, suddenly short of air. 'The ministry in Lahore has washed its hands of that polluted plot of land,' she went on in that same harsh tone. 'Surely you don't believe we could ever accept you here. Nobody in Peshawar will accept you. A woman like you, masquerading as one with the high morals of a woman of God . . . well, it's quite laughable, isn't it?'

I was shocked into silence. It had never occurred to me that anyone outside of Lahore would know what had happened at the mission. I tried to lick my lips, but my tongue was dry. I glanced at Mr Lang; now he studied the wall across from us, his eyes glazed in an odd, crystally way.

Mrs Lang was leaning sideways in her chair with her glass tipped in her hand.

Again I opened my mouth to speak, but had to close it and once more attempt to bring saliva to my mouth. 'Glory, yes, I will admit that Glory – the ayah who stayed at the mission after my parents –' my words came out in short, flannelled bursts, '– yes, she had visitors. But they were *her* visitors, Mrs Lang. Hers, not mine,' I said.

'You really mean to tell me, Miss Fincastle,' Mrs Lang said, speaking so slowly, with that obviously careful deliberation, and only stumbling occasionally, 'that you lived there, looking as you do, with that bold face, those knowing eyes – that you lived in a house of ill repute, and you are innocent?' She put her hand on her chest and coughed, bending forward as if in pain; the brief thought that it was the beginning of consumption came to me. Then she raised her head, and I realised she was not coughing. It was laughter. 'Well?' she asked, quite merrily now.

I had no response. My face bold, my eyes knowing? That was how I would describe Glory. Not me.

'What did you do there, then, Miss Fincastle? Did you hold daily prayer meetings with the . . . visitors, as you call them? Visit the sick or the poor in the nearby villages? Spread the word of the Lord?' Again, the damaged laughter.

I understood people gossiping in Lahore, but that my life with Glory had preceded me all the way here, to Peshawar, was like a hard slap across my face. My cheeks burned, and I put my hands to them. But of course, I realised, suddenly surprised at my naïvety – no, I corrected myself – my stupidity. The Grand Trunk Road was a direct line of communication. I lowered my hands. Had I not heard so many stories, tales of love and hate and revenge, gossip from all over northern India, as I stayed in the *caravanserais* for the last two weeks?

Rising, swiftly crossing the room, I stood in front of Mrs Lang, taking her hands in mine before she could stop me. But she immediately tugged them away as if I were an Untouchable, wiping them on her skirt.

I spoke quietly. 'I simply . . . lived my life. I didn't have anything to do with the men who came to see Glory,' I repeated, trying not to relive the memory of the Colonel astride me, his hips moving slowly, sensuously, while the silver medallions on the chain around his neck kept rhythm, swinging against my face. I squeezed my eyes shut. 'I did not live as Glory did, Mrs Lang. You must believe me.'

'Why did you stay, then?' she asked.

At the question, a curious weakness came over me. My stomach churned, empty and yet oddly heavy, while at the same time my head felt as though it were lighter. As if it might float from my neck. I looked behind me, at the green tufted chair, needing to sit down. Mr Lang hadn't moved; his mouth was open. *Why did I stay?* I went back to the chair as if swimming through turgid waters, and sat down, again looking at Mrs Lang. 'It . . . the mission was my home,' I said weakly. 'I didn't know where else to go.'

'You could have come here, immediately after the death of your parents, couldn't you? Or the instant you witnessed this woman – Glory? acting in a lascivious manner. Were you forcibly restrained?'

I looked at my fingers, now spread on my skirt, and shook my head.

'Then you must have wanted to stay. You must have enjoyed the sin of living among such filth, such degradation.'

I looked up. It was hard to focus on Mrs Lang. If only they would offer me a glass of water, a plain biscuit. I was so thirsty, and hungry. I couldn't seem to think clearly. 'I didn't, Mrs Lang. Truly, I didn't enjoy it. Not at all . . . but . . . I don't know what . . . it was my home,' I repeated, feebly, 'and . . . and . . . I suppose I thought Glory wouldn't stay. That she would leave, and the men would leave, and I would be . . .' *I would be what? What, exactly, had I been thinking?*

It was as if Mrs Lang, even in her drunken state, could see into my head. 'You would be what? A young woman, living in a desolate mission, alone? Whatever are you trying to make me believe, Miss Fincastle? It's all nonsense. Sheer nonsense. You came here wanting to use us, and our good reputation. For some reason you have tired of the game, and now wish to avail yourself of shelter in a decent place. It's as simple as that.' She tipped her head to drain the last of her drink and then stood, very carefully setting the empty glass on the highly polished table beside her. The wet glass slid a fraction.

'You may believe you have just travelled the road to Damascus,' she said. 'That your eyes have been opened to your past sins. But I think you are simply here because you have grown bored of that godless existence. Or found yourself in danger. For whatever reason you chose to come here, it's clear you haven't changed at all, and that you will bring your sinning into our mission.' She raised her chin, her eyelids lowering. 'I believe it's time for you to leave,' she said, crossing the room as if fighting a monsoon wind, thrown off balance by its force. She opened the door.

'Now, let's not be hasty, Mrs Lang,' Mr Lang said, standing as well. I remained in my chair, not trusting my legs. I knew that Mr Lang's insincere sympathy wasn't born of concern for me, but of his own inclinations.

She gave him a long look. 'Shut up, Henry,' she said, tonelessly, in that soft, slurry voice.

'Well, really, my dear,' he blustered, fussing with the buttons of his waistcoat. 'There's no need for—'

'Get out, Miss Fincastle,' Mrs Lang said, rather pleasantly, still not raising her voice. 'Be on your way, now.' If the servant standing outside the door didn't understand English, he might think she was telling me she was so happy to see me, and that I must come again, soon, to visit. 'There's nothing for you here, in Peshawar. Go find your own kind.'

'My own kind?' I echoed weakly.

She shook her head, slowly, in obvious annoyance. 'You understand me perfectly. You're a bright girl. I saw that the first time I met you. So don't insult me by pretending you don't know what I'm telling you. There are houses of the sort you're used to near to the barracks in any Indian city.'

In that instant I lost the fuzziness that had penetrated my head. I stood, finally, a slow anger coursing through me now, my hunger and thirst instantly gone. How dare she treat me in such a pompous manner, and insult me so openly? We faced each other for a few seconds, and in that time I gathered my strength. I called back the attitude I had found while presenting myself to the Colonel, remembered that I could be someone else. I wrote the words in my head, and they came from my mouth.

'Well. Of course I see your concern. But as a Christian woman, Mrs Lang,' I said, now forcing a pleading smile on to my face, 'would you not wish to help heal me of my . . . of what you see as my evilness? Is it not your Christian duty to take in one willing to be shown the light? Is this not the purpose of a Christian mission?'

She snorted. 'I know when it's not worth the effort. You're like one of the natives, aren't you, with their false smiles and lies, agreeing to anything in order to achieve their means. So just get out,' she said. Now she simply waved her hand as if unconcerned, lurching back to the table and picking up her glass, taking it to a side table which held a tray with tall bottles.

I straightened my shoulders. In spite of her intoxication, Mrs Lang had seen through my play-acting while the Colonel, blinded by lust and self-importance, hadn't.

I left the room, Mr Lang silently following me down the wide hall. On the front steps of the bungalow he took my hands in both of his. 'Well, this has all been a bit of a rum do, as you English say.' He flashed his grey smile. 'I apologise for my wife. She's suffering under the strain of her good works. And is not at all herself these days.'

My mouth twisted at his last words.

'But I can't see you go off like this. Where will you stay?'

'I'll be fine, Mr Lang.' It was simply pride speaking. Where would I stay? What would I do?

'Now I'm sure there's something – some arrangement – we could work out,' he wheezed, squeezing my hands more tightly between his own. 'A lovely young woman like yourself, well, I really couldn't allow you to wander about on your own. There are so many dangers.'

I stared at him.

'I could be your protector, Miss Fincastle,' he said. Sweat ran from his temples down his broad cheeks. I stared into his eyes, and he took this as encouragement. 'Yes, I could find you a little place in the old city where you could be assured no one would bother you,' he said. 'I could pay you regular visits, strictly to ensure you were all right,' he continued, so sincerely, as if I wouldn't understand what he was proposing. 'And please, my dear, pay no attention to Mrs Lang,' he huffed, leaning close, brave now that he was no longer in his wife's presence. 'She's not herself,' he repeated. 'This country . . .'

I smelled curry and tobacco on his breath. How I hated him. Pulling my hands from his, I thought of Mrs Lang, with her drunken leer, and my cache of rupees, owed to Chander, and put my hand over my mouth.

Mr Lang's face took on an expression of sympathy; he assumed I would weep. How wrong he was. It was an uncontrollable smile I was covering, a smile born of a hysterical reaction perhaps. He put his thick, hot hand on my waist as if to comfort me. 'Oh, my poor dear –' he began.

I looked down at his hand and the mounting hysteria fled, replaced by the anger I had felt only moments earlier. He was little more than a transparent fool, not even worth my rage.

I stepped away, out of his reach. 'Thank you for your time, Mr Lang,' I said. 'I can assure you, I will be quite all right.'

The moment I turned from Mr Lang and passed the *chowkidars* the shock came upon me. Where would I go? The rickshaw waited for me in the Langs' drive. I climbed in and dully watched the man's bare feet as he ran, the bell on his rickshaw tinkling. We left the wide shady boulevards with their clean soft roads and returned to the teeming, narrow lanes. The rickshaw-wallah neatly bypassed mounds of animal dung, ran around a black and white cow munching discarded vegetable parings, and past a frail old man lying on his side, one hand outstretched. I watched it all with a strange apathy, unable to form any true thoughts.

When he reached the cart I paid him, and then slowly climbed up and sat beside Chander.

I sat there for some moments, watching, without seeing, the activity surrounding us. Horses trotted by, people shouted, children cried. Somewhere a cockerel crowed.

Finally Chander touched my arm, and I looked down at his hand. 'Memsahib,' he said, and by the loud insistence I knew he had been trying to get my attention for some time. 'Now I go back Lahore, Memsahib?' he said. 'You say take you Peshawar. I take you Peshawar.'

I turned to him.

'Memsahib? You give me money. I go now.'

Nodding, unable to speak, I pulled open my bag and gave Chander the fifteen rupees I had promised. My hands shook, although he didn't appear to notice. He was anxious to leave, and after I'd climbed from the cart I'd hardly pulled my carpetbag from the back before he was shouting at his bullock and urging him forward.

As he disappeared from view in the busy street, I stood, my carpetbag in my hand.

I was alone in a strange city, with one rupee to my name.

CHAPTER THIRTY-FIVE

I WANDERED THE STREETS for some time, my carpet bag growing ever heavier. Again the faintness I had felt at the Langs' came over me, and I knew I had to eat. With difficulty, I parted with a few annas for some food and *chai* from one of the vendors. My carpetbag at my feet, I stood at the stall, chewing the grilled meat and swallowing two cups of tea, hardly tasting anything.

Evening was descending, and the markets were closing. All around me were shouts and calls, and I was occasionally jostled by the crowd. I moved to one side of the narrow alleyway, pressing my back against the cool stone, trying to keep down my mounting panic.

I was a woman alone in this dangerous and unknown city. I would have to find a place to spend the dark hours, somewhere were no one could see me. And if I did, what then? What would have changed when the sun rose tomorrow? I would still be alone, almost penniless, in a place where I knew no one.

I grew aware of a young man across the lane. Like me, he leaned against the building. His eyes were fixed on my carpetbag. I stepped over it so that it was between my feet, my ankles tight against its sides, watching him. His eyes darted up, studying my face, and I turned mine from his penetrating stare. I couldn't stay here, in this narrow alley, vulnerable and so obviously alone.

I thought of the other missions in Peshawar which the woman in the cart had spoken of, the Presbyterian Board of Foreign Missions and the Anglican Mission. And yet I couldn't go to them, for Mrs Lang's words still rang in my head: *The brothel you ran – run? – is common knowledge all over the Punjab . . . Surely you don't believe we could ever accept you here. Nobody in Peshawar will accept you.*

For one lonely, fearful moment, I wished to be back at the mission, with all its degradation; I wished I were in Lahore, where at least I was familiar with the streets.

And yet I knew that I had no allies in those places either. There was no one, anywhere, who thought of me, and worried for my fate. Were I to meet my death at the hands of unscrupulous thieves – perhaps that young man only a few feet from me – this very night, on this very street, there would be no one to care, to weep for me or say a prayer.

Taking a deep, shaky breath, I straightened my shoulders. Mine would not be that fate. I had come too far, at too much of a cost, to let myself sink into these pathetic thoughts. I looked left, and then right, then picked up my carpetbag and walked briskly to the right.

I walked purposefully, my chin forward, staring straight ahead as if I was going towards someone awaiting me. I turned this way and that, following the narrow, winding streets. The crowds thinned, and eventually only lone men or a pair of shrouded women moved silently past me. My abdomen cramped, my bladder suddenly painful. I cursed my decision to drink two cups of tea; I needed to find a convenience. Even this fact added to my panic. Of course there would be no convenience. I was in the middle of a city. I stared into every dark, twisting lane, and as my discomfort grew more intense, I grew desperate.

Finally I passed a short alley enclosed on three sides by dark buildings; there was no way in or out save the spot where I stood. It was empty but for a grey cat, sitting on a crumbling step, delicately licking its paws. No evening light filtered into the dirty, narrow place, and there was a pile of what appeared to be broken carts at the far end. I hurried toward them, squeezing in between the splintered wood and the crumbling walls of the building. There I was forced to do what I must, hidden by the carts.

I was sickened by shame, feeling little more than an animal in that dark, lonely spot. And yet, as I crouched behind the carts, I saw that one positive thing had occurred. I could let go of the worry I had carried since my time with the Colonel. The cramping was caused by my body's monthly time. I dug in my carpetbag for my supply of cloths.

The Colonel had left me with no burden save ugly memories, and for this I was grateful.

I spent the night in that dreadful place. I moved into the furthest corner, spread an extra petticoat under me, and attempted to sleep, my back against the wall and my carpetbag on my lap. I rested my forehead on my carpetbag, and slept fitfully. The night passed in a horror of staring into the dark, hearing unrecognisable rustling and movement – surely more cats hunting rodents – and drifting into an uneasy sense of dreaminess, only to lift my head and look around in quick, nervous glances.

When finally daylight came, I rubbed my eyes with the hem of my frock, tucked my hair under my bonnet again, then crept from that fetid spot, back into the streets of Peshawar.

I spent another anna on a *roti*; although I was thirsty, I wouldn't drink again. But the warm *roti*, along with the bright, clean sunlight pouring into the narrow streets, helped raise my spirits.

I would try the other missions; the worst that could happen would be that they would turn me away. Asking directions, I found my way to the Anglican Mission. I knocked, and the door was opened by a pleasant-looking, middle-aged Englishwoman in the dull garb of a missionary. Her hair was steel-grey and scraped tightly back from her forehead.

There was the smell of cabbage cooking. And an eerie quiet.

'How can I help you, my dear?' the woman asked. My heart rose at her kind tone.

'I . . . I'm looking . . .' I stopped, suddenly fearful of speaking the truth, of saying my name. If I did, would not her face close, and grow cold, as Mrs Lang had predicated? 'I'm in need of aid,' I finally said. 'I've come from . . . from the south, and am hoping to find shelter. In a Christian mission. I can work,' I added, my voice rising. We were still in the doorway; she hadn't invited me inside.

She nodded, her face never losing its look of concern, although now she studied my face more carefully, her eyes flickering to my bonnet, then down to my frock. I was deeply ashamed at how I knew I appeared, dusty and smelling of the road. Of where I had just spent the night.

'Of course,' she said, and I held my breath. 'I will direct you to where you will find the help you need.'

Her words surprised me. She put her hand on my shoulder, gently turning me so that I faced the street. 'It's not far. Perhaps fifteen minutes. Go left, just there, and then follow the street. Ask if you can't find your way.'

I stared at her. 'I thought . . . is this not a mission? I am the daughter of missionaries. I have medical training.'

She nodded, still with that look of concern. 'Of course. But the place you're looking for, my dear, is the Zenana Mission. They take in women,' she said, 'both native and Eurasian. They will surely offer you shelter.'

Now my mouth opened. 'But I—'

'First left, as I told you,' she said, smiling kindly and ushering me back on to the step. 'I wish you well, my dear,' she added, before closing the door.

I stood there for a full minute, letting her words sink in. I looked back at the heavy closed door. And then I went on to the street, turning left.

Twenty minutes later I stood in a dim, crowded alley. In front of me was a cross nailed on to a door, and under it, written in faded letters: *Peshawar Zenana Mission*. The building had a crumbling façade, and the wooden door frame and the one second-floor balcony were splintered and in need of repair.

I knocked. Nobody answered. I pounded, and finally heard footsteps. The door was opened by a young woman, possibly a few years old than I. The left half of her face was disfigured, the skin puckered and drawn, the eyelid pulled down so that there was only a glimmer from beneath the dragging lid. 'I help you?' she asked. She was native, wearing a plain grey frock with a worn and yellowed but neatly pressed collar.

'I've just arrived in Peshawar.' I said, as I had at the Anglican mission. I had no intention of telling anyone where I was from. Or anything more than a few facts. 'And I would like to speak to someone. Someone in charge,' I added. It was difficult to look at the woman's face. Her ear had been burned into the side of her head; there was only an opening beneath the dark upswept hair.

I realised I was staring, and lowered my eyes.

'Yes,' she said. 'Please come.'

I stepped into the hallway. There were muted voices, raised in song. The tune was familiar: 'On Christ Salvation Rests Secure'. From another part of the building came low chanting. A small child toddled down the hall, holding a half-eaten carrot, looking behind him and laughing. A girl of about six hurried after him, clapping her hands and giggling. I immediately felt comforted. Any place with happy children running about could not be all bad. I thought of the Langs' silent, spotless home, the muted Anglican mission.

'Follow me, please,' the woman said. Her English was heavily accented; I could tell her first language was Hindi. She led me to a tidy although sparsely furnished room with plain wooden chairs, large embroidered cushions and a few small tables. It was brightly lit by tall windows opening on to a courtyard. Two young women sat there, talking to each other in low tones. I didn't know with certainty whether they were native or Eurasian; they were dressed in similar plain frocks, their dark hair neatly pinned up.

'Rohana,' my guide said, 'please bringing tea for this guest.'

Both of the women immediately rose. As they passed me they smiled in an open manner, but I didn't move. I didn't trust my mouth to smile. Suddenly I felt I would weep at these small kindnesses – the offer of tea, the friendly smiles.

'Please,' the woman said. 'Sit.' She gestured to a chair with her right hand. I saw then that her left was withered, and held against her waist. The burns had fused the fingers together. 'Helena is lady for this Society. I will sending her to you.' She smiled, as the other women had, although only one half of her mouth turned up, and left me in the room.

I sat, my carpetbag at the side of the chair, listening to the sounds of the house. Music and singing, and children's voices. Footsteps sounded above me; I looked at the ceiling, then down at my hands in my lap. The palms of my gloves were filthy; I pulled them off, laying them on my lap so the dirt couldn't be seen.

Within minutes an older woman, English, entered and nodded pleasantly.

I stood, but before I could say anything she gestured for

me to sit again. 'Hello,' she said. 'I'm Helena. Have you been offered something to drink?'

'Yes. Thank you.' I had never known an Englishwoman to introduce herself by her Christian name.

She sat at an angle beside me, pulling the wooden chair closer than was usual for strangers, studying my face. 'You've just arrived in our city, Aimee tells me. What is the purpose of your visit to us?' she asked.

'I was hoping . . . to find work here,' I said. 'I'm the daughter of missionaries. And I know about medical matters.'

The woman made a surprised sound. 'Medical matters? Such as what?'

I was clasping and unclasping my hands, and now held them still. 'Setting bones and stitching wounds and lacerations. And I also know about infections – of the eyes and mouth and skin. Certain internal matters of the chest and stomach and bowel. And I speak Hindi and Urdu and Punjabi and some Persian.' I heard my own voice, too quick, too anxious. I stopped and took a deep breath, making myself speak with less desperation. I knew this was my last option. If I was turned away from this mission, with less than a rupee in my bag, what would I do?

A vision of myself as I had spent the last night, propped against the cold wall in the empty, dark alley, came to me, and I flinched involuntarily.

A deep rumbling came from my abdomen. I moved my legs, embarrassed, and surreptitiously pressed my hands against my stomach.

'Pashto?'

I stared at her.

'Do you speak Pashto?'

I thought of the Afghan on the golden stallion. 'No. But I could learn quickly, I'm sure. I'm also able to read and write in Hindi and Urdu.'

459

Finally Helena smiled. 'Well. We don't often have someone like you knock on our door. Most of our women come to us from Christian missions, where they've been raised and educated,' she added. 'But from your English, that doesn't appear to be your case.'

I swallowed. 'No. I *was* raised at a Christian mission – as I said, I'm the daughter of missionaries. English medical missionaries. I learned surgical procedures from watching them – and working with them when I was older. But I've lived in India all my life.'

'You weren't educated in England?'

I shook my head. 'My mother and father taught me.'

'But you're English.'

Was it a statement or a question? She was still studying me intently, and this made me uncomfortable. The woman at the Anglican mission had assumed I was Eurasian. And now Helena questioned me. I knew how dark my face and hands had become from my work outdoors and my days on the road. And yet still . . . This added to my insecurity. She had to let me stay.

'Would you like me to demonstrate something? Ask me to quote from any book of the Bible. Anything,' I blurted. 'I know so much by heart. Or perhaps I can explain the use of cobweb pills for biwar fever, or the benefits of sugar water when dealing with summer flux in babies. Not for the flux itself, but to keep them hydrated.'

Helena crossed her hands on her chest and laughed. The sound was open and honest, and I saw now she wasn't as old as I'd originally thought. 'Oh my goodness, no. I'm sure you're well versed in the scriptures, and it's obvious you have medical experience. And I can assure you that you would be a most welcome addition. We do have a desperate need for women who have more education, not only to train those here beyond what they know, but for simple medical procedures and advice. Most of our Bible women are able to teach a little English. Some of the more progressive Muslim husbands in the city don't mind their women and children learning English. In return we are able to spread a bit of evangelism. But sometimes the men are more welcoming to an outside woman for purposes of health than anything else. Many of the women in *purdah* have health problems, but of course they aren't allowed to be seen by men with medical knowledge.'

'Yes. It was the same at the infirmary, at our mission.'

Helena watched my face again. 'And your parents approve of your departure?'

'They've gone to the Lord. Not so long ago.'

Helena's face grew still, and she reached out and took my hands in hers. 'I am sorry for your grief, dear. So sorry.' Her hands were warm, larger than mine, and I returned their pressure. As I had earlier, I felt that I would weep.

'It must have been so difficult for you,' she said, in that same kind voice, and now tears did come to my eyes, and I drew in a stuttering breath. Was I weeping for my parents, or for myself, because I was so alone, and hungry, and frightened. I squeezed my eyes shut, and tears ran from beneath my closed lids.

'Come, come, my dear,' Helena said then, and in one swift movement put her arms around me. I smelled carbolic soap, and because it felt so natural, leaned into her from my chair, letting my head rest on her shoulder.

No woman had ever hugged me, not even my own mother. Eve Fincastle. I didn't want to move. I wanted to close my eyes and sleep like this.

Helena patted my back and then pulled away, taking a crisp handkerchief from her sleeve and extending it.

I took it, wiping my eyes.

'Well, I can assure you it would be wonderful to have

461

someone with definite medical training. And so you understand that most of our work is done inside the zenanas?'

I nodded.

'And you're comfortable with this? You've had experience with Muslims and their ways? *Purdah*, and so on?'

'Yes,' I said.

'Good. Well. If you're to work here, what may we call you?' she asked.

Did this mean I was staying? Unless she reacted as Mrs Lang had, when she heard who I was. But I knew she was nothing like Mrs Lang. Or like Mrs Wyndham and Mrs Rollings-Smythe. Although her clothing was unadorned and her hairstyle simple, there was a certain dignified attractiveness in her calm, direct gaze.

'We can certainly use more hands here,' she said, as if encouraging me. 'Your name?'

I took a deep breath. I had considered using a false name, but decided against it. I was so tired of defending myself. And I had lost most of my identity. My name was all I had. Still, I hesitated.

'Pree Fincastle,' I said, quietly, staring into her eyes.

'That's a lovely name.'

I didn't detect a change in her expression.

'Pree Fincastle,' she repeated. 'Is Pree your Christian name?'

'It's actually Priscilla.'

'But you prefer Pree?' she asked.

I finally let myself smile, a small and shaky smile. 'I prefer Pree,' I agreed.

'We don't bother with last names, or many formalities. We all use our Christian names here.' Her smile faded. 'There are some things I must make clear, though. And something I must ask you.'

'Yes?' I asked, suddenly anxious again.

The woman named Rohana entered, carrying a tea tray. She set it down on the table beside Helena.

Helena thanked her as the woman left, then poured two cups of tea and handed one to me.

'Thank you,' I said, and gripped the saucer tightly.

'A biscuit, perhaps?' Helena offered, holding out a small brass plate. Although I was so hungry, I knew I wouldn't be able to swallow. My throat felt impossibly small and tight. It was difficult enough to speak, such was my nervousness. What was she about to ask? Would I be able to answer truthfully, or would I have to lie?

I shook my head.

'What was I . . . oh yes,' Helena said. 'There are some things I must speak of to anyone who is thinking of becoming part of our family. Because that's what it is, Pree. We are like a family here.'

I nodded, and shakily held the cup to my lips, taking a sip. The sweet warmth flooded through me.

'Do you have other family, now that your parents are gone? Siblings, or extended relatives, elsewhere in India? Or even Afghanistan?'

Afghanistan? Of course; it was just across the border. Again I shook my head. My face must have shown a certain hesitancy, for now Helena leaned even closer.

'And you are not betrothed? Or otherwise . . . involved? With a man?'

I shook my head, staring into my cup. Unbidden, images of Kai came to me. And then Eddie. The Colonel. I shut my eyes again.

'And is there any particular reason you've come to Peshawar, from . . .?' She stopped, and I knew she expected me to say where I'd come from. I opened my eyes but didn't answer. I drank my tea, continuing to look down at the cup as if the act required all my attention.

'Peshawar isn't a place one comes to without much deliberation,' she continued, when it was clear I wouldn't respond. 'Especially now, with – are you aware? – the current upheaval with the political situation, and the rumblings between the people of India, both Indians and the British – and the Russians, over Afghanistan. Many Europeans are leaving, and yet here you are, arriving.' Her eyes dropped to my waist, and I looked down, to see what she was looking at.

'And so we sometimes have young women coming to us in time of need. When they find themselves in a certain condition. We always help them, Pree. There is no need to keep secrets; in fact, I prefer to know, so that it is clear to everyone what to expect.'

I nodded, understanding what she was asking.

'Children born here stay with their mothers. As I said, we are their family, and as long as the rules are respected, and the work is carried out, the women and their children need never fear they will have to leave,' she went on, as if I might need prompting. 'Of course some women choose to leave after a time. They marry, or decide to live elsewhere for a variety of reasons. I demand consideration. The only women I have ever asked to leave the house are those who demonstrate an uncharitable nature to the others here. We are able to pay each woman a minimal sum each month, very minimal, I'm sorry to say. But you will have no expenses while living here; everything is provided. As well as our work in the zenanas we all assist within the house, taking a turn in cooking and cleaning and helping with the children. We do not employ servants; we serve each other with the same love with which we serve Our Lord.'

I couldn't speak. My cup was empty, but still I held it to my lips to hide their trembling. My throat worked painfully. I couldn't weep again, or Helena might think me unstable. But she had no inclination of how she was making me feel. Only half an hour earlier I had nowhere to go, and no one. Now, in so trusting a manner, she was speaking as if I were already part of what she called the family here, at the zenana mission.

'I encourage everyone to speak English as much as possible. Of course many of the women slip into their native tongues with each other, which is fine. It's just that their English must be proper enough to teach it. There are a few women who haven't been able to master it. The woman who let you in, for example. Aimee. She didn't learn English until later in life, unlike the majority of the girls who grew up in the Christian missions. You can be helpful on a daily basis to someone like Aimee; it's good for her to converse with someone whose first language is English.'

I thought of Aimee's poor face.

'And the only other reason women may not stay is if they act in a manner not befitting to a Christian home. If one finds oneself becoming . . . involved . . . with a man, I insist on marriage. If marriage isn't forthcoming, then the woman can no longer stay. There can be no poor examples. No secrets,' she emphasised again.

'Of course,' I said, although I had secrets. Ugly secrets. 'There is definitely no . . . condition . . . that will prove itself in time,' I told her. As of yesterday I could be completely honest about this now. 'And I simply want . . .' What did I want? 'A new beginning,' I said. 'I want to do the work I know. And I do want a home, Helena. I do.' I set my cup and saucer back on the table. 'I have no family. If this could be my family, then . . .' Suddenly I clasped the handkerchief to my nose and mouth, unable to stop the tears this time.

'I'm sorry, I'm sorry,' I said, the handkerchief still over my mouth, and in that instant I thought of my mother, speaking through her handkerchief, and this made me cry harder. 'Please, Helena, I only weep because . . . it's been a long journey here, and I . . .'

She again patted my hand. 'I know,' she murmured. 'I know, Pree,' and I knew that she did understand. How had she become so compassionate? What hardships had she known, to have made her so empathetic?

We sat in silence. She held my hand until I could finally take a deep breath and mop my face.

Then she smiled, nodding, and said, 'Welcome, Pree. I shall introduce you to the others at dinner tonight.' Her hand was so warm as she gripped mine. Then she turned it over. She studied the deep scar along my left thumb – an accident with the scythe – and, on the palm, under my fingers, the hard ridge of callouses that now seemed a permanent part of my skin.

'Did you bring anything with you?' she asked, releasing my hand.

'Just this,' I said, looking at my carpetbag.

'Fine.' She rose and went to the door, opening it and speaking quietly to someone. In another moment Aimee arrived. Helena spoke to her in that same quiet voice. I couldn't hear what she said, but Aimee turned to me, and smiled her broken smile, and I smiled back, blinking.

CHAPTER THIRTY-SIX

AIMEE SHOWED ME my room on the second floor, which I would share with her and Rohana. There were three narrow beds, divided by curtains. One window looked out on to the courtyard. The walls were whitewashed and the floor was made of rough boards covered with simple rugs. A wardrobe stood beside the door, and there was a small fireplace in a corner. I wondered how cold it became in winter, this far north. I peeked behind a screen in another corner and found the washstand and chamber pot.

'There is also washing room down hall,' Aimee said. 'With convenience, and for cleaning all over. Helena says I be with you,' she said. 'I show you Peshawar, and taking you to zenanas.'

'That's fine,' I said, looking around the plain room. I was so weary, but Aimee appeared excited, anxious for me to see everything, and I forced myself to show enthusiasm.

On one wall there was a large unframed canvas, depicting Jesus with Mary Magdalene bathing his feet; on another a similar painting, this one of Jesus surrounded by children. Below this painting was a low table of plain wood. An unadorned white cross was propped against the wall; a small candle burned beside it, even though there was still daylight.

Aimee pointed at the painting of Jesus and the children. 'Rohana is painting. Artist,' she said, proudly. 'She is making all house pretty.'

I nodded, looking longingly at the narrow bed with its Indian cotton cover. I wanted so badly to bathe and take off my filthy clothes. I wanted it to be evening so I could put on my clean nightdress and lie in bed with a lit lamp and read. I thought of the three novels in my carpetbag; I had read them so many times.

'Are there many book stalls in the bazaar?' I asked. 'Maybe in the English cantonment bazaar.'

Aimee looked at me quizzically. 'Book stalls?'

I fought back the impulse to speak Hindi to her, remembering what Helena had said. 'To buy books. English books.'

Aimee took a small black Bible from her pillow. 'We having Bibles. You having Bible?'

'Yes. Yes, in my bag.' I had both my father's and my own white moiré.

'Now we pray,' Aimee said, and knelt in front of the small table, looking up at me.

'Oh. If . . . if you like,' I said. Of course I still whispered and thought my own vague prayers. But I couldn't remember when I had last said – or heard – an actual formal prayer. Not since before my father died. I knelt beside Aimee.

'Dear Lord in Heaven,' she said, her eye tightly shut, her good hand curled around the withered one at her waist, 'thank You for Your hand on Pree, for she is coming the path to our door. Thank You for she is having new life with us. We are praying to You please making her safe and she sees all glories in Peshawar, and You are making to guide her to help who needs help, as You are helping us in our needs. Dear Heavenly Father, thank You for gift of Pree. Amen.'

'Amen,' I echoed, quietly.

Aimee opened her eye and looked at me and smiled. She didn't even know me, and yet in her broken speech she thanked God for bringing me to her home.

I knew I mustn't let her – or any of the others here – ever

know what kind of woman I really was, and what I had done in my life.

There was a loud gonging from the courtyard. 'Dinner,' Aimee said. 'Come.' She held out her good hand as if we were children.

I took it and we walked down the stairs together.

'Your name from Priya?' Aimee asked. 'I like Priya. And you *are* pretty,' she added.

'Thank you. But no. Pree is short for Priscilla,' I answered, glancing at her. Looking at her straight on was disconcerting, but as she walked beside me, I could only see the unmarked side of her face. She would have been quite lovely . . . No. I thought of her welcoming and heartfelt prayer, only moments earlier in our room. She *was* lovely. I told myself that I must try to remember to be good and charitable.

'Helena says to me my name is meaning friend,' she said. 'In other language, not English.'

'It's a good fit, then,' I said, honestly.

'I am not liking my Hindu name. Aimee is Christian name,' she went on. 'Some Eurasian women here like Hindu name, some Hindu women like Christian name. What are you, Pree?' she asked with such candour that I stopped. She turned to face me, waiting for my answer.

Suddenly I was so weary that I had to put out one hand and support myself against the wall. It wasn't just from the travel, and the last horrid twenty-four hours in Peshawar, but of everything that had occurred before that. The danger I had felt at the mission. The troubling details I had learned from Glory of my unknown heritage. How I had debased myself in order to escape the mission.

'I . . . I am . . .' I stared into her waiting face, leaning my shoulder against the wall.

'You are sick, Pree?' Aimee asked, peering at me, her brow furrowed. 'You looking sick. You need I helping you?'

I shook my head, although weakly. 'No. I'm not ill. But I . . .' It was coming over me in waves. Her simple question: *What are you, Pree?* made me realise there was no simple answer. I didn't know what I was. Who I was. Yes, I was Pree Fincastle, but who *was* she?

'I . . . I don't know,' I finally said. 'I don't know.'

Aimee, in her uncomplicated, agreeable way, nodded. My answer was enough for her.

The dining room was filled with long tables of scrubbed wood; the seating was benches on either side. Women and children milled about, taking their seats, and a few other women carried in huge wooden plates and bowls from a door that led to the courtyard.

I sat beside Aimee, and everyone settled and grew quiet.

'Aimee,' Helena said, 'would you please introduce Pree to the others?'

Aimee stood, speaking loudly enough for everyone to hear. 'Here is Pree. She is joining our family.'

She touched my shoulder, and I stood. I found it impossible to look up as a chorus of hellos and welcomes sounded through the air. I think – I hope – I smiled, although my eyes were fixed on the table in front of me, and I quickly sat down. There was a prayer to bless the food, and then we ate. The food appeared plain but was filling: a thick vegetable soup, *rotis*, and great rounds of goat's cheese.

I put my spoon into the soup, but didn't lift it to my mouth. I felt that others were watching, judging me, and sat like this, my head lowered, until Aimee gently touched my arm. I looked at her.

'Eat,' she said, and I glanced from side to side, and then up, and saw that nobody watched me. They simply ate, helping the smaller children, and spoke of daily events. It was my own fear causing the discomfort.

I took a spoonful of soup. It was rich and delicious. I ate quickly, trying to control my movements, but I was so hungry, and the food so good. In only a few moments everything in front of me was gone. And then, although my stomach was full, my head was too full as well. I was overwhelmed by the level of chatter and laughter and movement. I rose with everyone else, and followed Aimee's instructions to help with the washing of the dishes and tidying of the dining room.

Then I sat in the courtyard and cut up mounds of fruit. All around me women talked and laughed; my hands worked without thought, and I watched my fingers, busy with the long knife, as if they belonged to someone else.

When we had finished Aimee took me back to the sitting room where I had spoken with Helena. Aimee gave me a Bible, and while she laboriously read, her lips moving and her finger following line after line, I just sat. The Bible was open in my lap, but I couldn't concentrate. Perhaps I dozed. Suddenly Aimee was saying my name, and I stood, the Bible falling to the floor.

Again we went into the dining room for a simple evening meal of more *roti* and cheese and the fruit I had helped prepare. And then there were evening prayers back in the sitting room, the women – some with small children on their laps – on the plain wooden chairs, and a few older children sitting on the floor in front of their mothers. I could barely stay awake. I had hoped everyone would disperse when the final amen was uttered, but then one woman stood and blew on a little pitch pipe. 'Our first hymn will be "Grace Taught Our Wandering Feet," ' she announced, and inwardly I was filled with despair at the idea of another hour of singing along – or at least moving my mouth – to the familiar hymns I hadn't sung for so long.

My face must have reflected my weariness, because as the

voices rose around me, Helena came to me. 'I'm sure you're tired after your recent travel,' she said. 'You may be excused for the rest of the evening.'

'Thank you,' I said, and went upstairs and then along the darkening hall, finding my room. I was filled with relief to have even an hour alone. I used the washing room, sighing with pleasure at the freshness of my scrubbed skin and hair, and put on my creased but clean nightdress. Back in my room I lit the lamp and got into bed, combing through and plaiting my heavy wet hair slowly with my fingers; the flock mattress was flat and hard, and reminded me of my childhood bed. I would have preferred a charpoy.

My eyes burned, and I knew it would be futile to attempt to read. I left the lamp lit for Aimee and Rohana and turned on my side, looking at the open window, hearing the sounds of the city as it settled for the night. From my bed, I could see the spires of four minarets. Four was a good number.

I thought I had no tears left, but they came again. I had found a place where I would be sheltered and fed. Where I did not have to fear for my safety.

Did I cry out of relief? I don't know.

The next morning, after prayers and a simple breakfast, Aimee took me into the streets of Peshawar. I followed her through the winding alleys and narrow lanes and bazaars smelling of ripe fruit and roasted meat and tobacco smoke. She delighted in showing me everything, struggling to find the right English words; I gently corrected her when it was appropriate, and she always smiled her thanks.

'Tomorrow we go to *havelis*,' she said, as we walked through the crooked lanes of the Qissa Khawani Bazaar. Water carriers sprinkled the streets to settle the dust; following them came sweepers with long brooms. I looked at the food stalls with their colourful pyramids of fruits: figs, apricots and pomegranates alongside bananas and oranges. There were tiny baskets of brilliant spices, and those more drab, with mounds of chickpeas and peanuts. Bangle-sellers showed off their glass or beaten silver hoops on long smooth sticks. Little boys scurried past with poles over their shoulders, carrying wooden cages of clucking and squawking chickens. I saw tiny brass phials filled, supposedly, with Ganges holy water from Benares, and the intricate boxes inlaid with tiny polished semi-precious stones from Agra. There were delicately embroidered wall-hangings and prayer cloths. I touched many things, the vendors leaping up from the ground or their low stools to eagerly show me their wares; each time I shook my head apologetically.

'Come, come, Memsahib,' a toothless man said, holding out a bolt of glorious aqua silk, unfolding it so that it fluttered like a solitary wing. 'Best silk for you,' he said, nodding vigorously, and when I protested, he pulled forward another, this one gaudy pink. I shook my head and kept walking, Aimee chattering beside me. She pointed out the peoples of Peshawar who had come down from Afghanistan, recognisable by their facial features: the Hazaras – the people I had seen yesterday, with the distinct eye-folds of the inhabitants of Mongolia; the dark-skinned Uzbeks; the Tajiks, tall and lithe and with pale skin and eyes, rather European-looking; and of course, everywhere, the Pushtuns, as Aimee called them. 'Is name they say. Pathans is English word,' she explained. While for the men there didn't appear to be any particular formality of dress, most of the native women I saw were Muslim, and so were veiled or completely faceless, gliding by in their draped *burkas*.

'You know this name? Qissa Khawani?' she asked me, and I shook my head.

'Street for telling stories,' she said. 'Long ago. Street where men talk about war. About women. Two favourite stories for all men. Other men listen, listen. Many stories, Helena says.'

I looked upwards; towering over the streets were tall, narrow buildings of two and three storeys, built of unbaked bricks set in wooden frames. Many had carved, overhanging balconies. All the roofs were flat. I moved aside as a small herder shouted and slapped his three water buffalos as he made his way through the streets.

'Is *havelis* for rich Muslims,' Aimee said. 'Tomorrow we go,' she told me again. 'You want tea? Helena give me annas, say you have tea. First time in Peshawar special time, Helena says.'

I looked at the tea-shops with their huge brass samovars and hanging teapots and tiny clay teacups. Outside men squatted, drinking tea. One also ate what looked like grilled goat and onion on top of a crisp round of bread. 'Yes, yes, please,' I said, again thinking how kind Helena was. How I should be so grateful to be here.

'We have Pushtun *khawa*,' she said, purchasing two cups, and we stood under the torn awning in the bazaar-labyrinth and sipped the scalding, sweet green tea. Only dappled sunlight filtered through the awnings and balconies of the shoulder-to-shoulder buildings. 'You know Pashto?' she asked, as Helena had asked me yesterday.

'No.'

'Soon you learn. I learn. Learn English, learn Pashto. Little both. Is better I know more, not just Hindi and Urdu, Helena says.'

I was realising that almost everything Aimee said ended with *Helena says*. I wondered how she had been so disfigured, and how she had come to the Peshawar Zenana Mission. Last night, looking at the mix of faces over dinner, I knew that every woman there had a story, her own story.

That night in my bed, I told myself it was only the newness of my surroundings that gave me the same strange sensation

I had experienced the evening before. I wanted to feel comfort, to feel that now all would be well. I told myself I would soon grow accustomed to the ways of the mission.

I didn't want to admit the truth nudging at me. While I was hugely relieved that I had indeed found a safe place to live, with women who were genuine and kind, I was disturbed at the idea that someone would tell me when to eat, and when to sleep. Would dictate my movements throughout the days and nights. That I would never have privacy, even as I slept.

In only two days I clearly understood the shape of this life. Every day would be like the former. Eat, pray, visit the zenanas. Return to eat, pray, sleep.

I would no longer have the choice to move about at will as I'd had most of my life. I had been free – before Glory took over the mission – in a way I hadn't realised. Yes, I'd worked hard, but there had always been time to wander to the Ravi, or down the road into the villages. I could sit under the peepul tree and read. If I couldn't sleep I could rock on the verandah in the night air. I had been alone for so much of my life, and I liked it. I liked having time to dream, to create stories in my head, to imagine what life might some day hold. I remembered my dreams about Kai, about his touch on me. How I had wanted that touch to mean something deeper, how certain I had been that he, too, had felt what I had.

I realised I was only thinking of the happier times, and that those thoughts were of a young and naïve woman. And although still not old, I was no longer naïve. The mission was no more; it hadn't been a mission since my parents died. It had become a place of ugliness. I would never see Kai again.

Pree, I told myself, you must always give up one thing for another. You must be grateful for this new life. I considered saying a prayer of thanks, but I seemed unable to find the right words. It appeared I would have to relearn how to pray.

This, the Peshawar Zenana Mission, was my home now. I had grown past the time of dreaming of what life might hold.

This *was* my life now.

And, as Helena had said, this was my family.

The next day, as promised, Aimee took me to the first zenana, in the *Haveli* Abdur Jan.

'Most best zenana,' she said. 'Husband – Abdur Jan – very good Pushtun. He is wanting his wives – four – and many children learning English. But youngest wife very sick. He is sad. Midwife don't know what makes sick. Helena say you know sickness, Pree. You look wife, maybe know.'

We walked toward an arched, pedimented gateway carved with relief sculptures; it was truly a grand *haveli*, its wooden balconies even more elaborately carved than most. Behind them were long latticed windows. As we approached I caught a fleeting glimpse of figures moving behind them: the women of the zenana. Through these grills they could watch the movement of the streets below, but not be seen.

We were admitted by a stern-looking Muslim, who nodded at Aimee and stepped aside for us to pass. Obviously familiar with the layout of the *haveli*, Aimee confidently led me down dim passages and then out of a high doorway into a beautiful garden in the centre. The huge building had been built in a square, with the garden courtyard in the middle. There were inner balconies facing the courtyard on all three floors.

The garden was truly breathtaking, full of trees and greenery and colour, with a splashing fountain at its centre. The cries of parrots and peacocks rang through the air, sweet with the scent of the flowering bushes and riot of plants.

'How lovely,' I breathed, and Aimee nodded.

'Abdur Jan is powerful man,' she said. 'Come.' I was

sorry to leave the shady, fragrant paths and re-enter the *haveli* on the other side. Aimee took me to a second floor, where a young woman lay still on a long divan, half covered with a gold brocade cloth. A serving woman sat beside her, massaging her hands with perfumed oil. Sunlight streamed in a latticed design through the delicate frets of the window.

'*Assalamu alaikum,*' Aimee murmured, and the serving woman repeated the phrase. The young woman, perhaps my age, opened her eyes.

Aimee said something in Pashto, and the young woman looked at me.

It was obvious she was very ill. Her face was drawn, her body thin, and her hair, thick in places, was patchy in others. Her eyes were dull.

'May I speak to you in Urdu, Bibi?' I asked her, addressing her in the polite form for wife or lady of the house, and she nodded slightly, murmuring '*ha*'.

'How long have you been ill?'

She blinked slowly. 'I don't remember. It started after the birth of my baby. But slowly. It's become worse and worse.'

'How old is your baby?'

'Almost a year.'

'Are you sick in your head?'

'*Nahi,*' she murmured. 'My stomach. I can no longer eat, but only drink a little, although even that is becoming difficult.' She gestured weakly at a heavy white goblet with a silver rim, filled with orange liquid, sitting on the floor beside the divan.

'May I touch you?' I asked her now, and again she weakly said yes. I pressed on the skin of her bare upper arm, then picked up her limp hand and exerted pressure on her nail beds. Her hands, trembling almost imperceptibly, were small and soft, smelling of jasmine from the fragrant oil. I watched

477

how fast the blood returned to her nails after the pressure, thinking about a problem with circulation.

I asked to see her tongue; it was slightly furred and grey, but this was usual for one with an ill stomach.

'Is your monthly time normal?'

'*Ha*,' she said. 'The same now as before the baby.'

'Is there a hardness in your stomach?' I asked, thinking of the tumorous growths I had, with my mother's hands placed on mine, felt under women's skin. If the growth was in the breast or abdomen, the women usually died, eventually.

'No, no,' she murmured. 'You see. Please.'

I gently probed her concave abdomen through the silk gown. There was nothing. I smiled at her then, because I didn't know what else to do, and she managed a tremulous smile in return. I placed her hand back on the brocade coverlet. I left her with the serving woman, and went with Aimee to see the children on the top floor.

'You know her sickness?' Aimee asked me.

'No,' I said, thinking about the abnormal darkness of her gums as she attempted to smile, and my mother's decaying, bleeding mouth. But the bibi's breath had smelled of nothing but mango juice.

I couldn't concentrate on it further once we entered the children's quarters. This was a huge, bright room, filled with painted wooden toys and satin quilts and bolsters. There was an infant and a baby about a year old asleep on the quilts as a nursemaid fanned them, and other children, one toddling about and the others appearing to be between two and five years old. I quickly counted: thirteen in all. I knew that there were a number of older children elsewhere in the *haveli*, as Aimee and I had passed by a half-open door and I'd heard the chanting of young male and female voices as they followed the instruction from a learned *munshi*. Abdur Jan was indeed not only productive and forward-thinking, but also prosperous, to be able to support such a huge family in this luxury.

Some of the children ran to greet Aimee, clustering around her skirt and saying, in English, 'Hello, Miss Aimee, hello, Miss Aimee.' They knew her well.

'Here is Miss Pree,' she said to them, also in English. 'Say hello, Miss Pree.'

They dutifully parroted her words, and I returned the greeting. I hoped other women from the mission also spoke to the children; it wouldn't do for them to learn Aimee's form of English.

'We say Pussycat to Miss Pree,' she said, and the children nodded their heads. Aimee lifted her good hand, saying, in a slow, metered beat, 'Pussycat, Pussycat, Where have you been?' her hand pumping with each syllable, to which the children chorused in a heavy beat to the rise and fall of Aimee's hand, in the same flat and rather tragic tone, 'I've been to London to visit the Queen.'

Then Aimee turned to me, smiling, and all the children beamed proudly.

I clapped my hand over my mouth to hide my smile. It felt good to smile. Dear Aimee. Dear children. I took away my hand and, my smile turning shaky, unexpectedly fought back tears. I crouched to the children's level, clapping my hands. They all clapped with me.

Before it was time to turn out the light that evening, I pored over pages in my medical books, trying to discern what might be causing the young wife's symptoms: the nausea, the hair loss, the shakiness. Again thinking of my mother, I referred to the pages on poisoning.

Reading various studies, my breath quickened as I read one in particular: along with many other symptoms, including the ones I'd seen today, the evidence of a bluish line

479

along the gums indicated toxicity from lead.

The next day I returned to the *haveli*; again Aimee accompanied me. In the young wife's room, I asked her if she'd been taking any herbal remedies. None, she told me. I didn't know if foods contained lead, but when I asked her about any changes in her diet she said she had eaten nothing new or different, when she could still keep food in her stomach.

She licked her chapped lips, and spoke in Pashto to her serving woman. The woman went to a table and poured pomegranate juice from a jug into the same white goblet I had seen the previous day. The jug matched the goblet, and was elaborately carved, with a silver handle and the same silver rim. As the servant helped the woman to drink it, I looked back at the jug, then went to it, picking it up. It was very heavy.

'Do you always drink from this?' I asked the wife, still holding the jug, and gesturing at the goblet.

She nodded. 'It was one of the many gifts my husband presented me with after the birth of our son,' she said. 'I keep all my juices in it; its thickness helps them retain their coolness. He brought it back for me from the Far East.'

I looked at her; her words reminded me of something, something that I wanted to relate to her illness, but I couldn't quite place what it was.

'Why do you ask about the jug?' she asked.

I ran my hands over its smoothness, then lifted it to my nose and sniffed. I could only smell the sweetness of the pomegranate it held, but I saw that the inside was also covered with a thick coat of the same smooth white lacquer as the outside. And then I remembered what was playing on my mind: last year I had read a book by Charles Dickens, a book of short stories entitled *Uncommerical Traveller*. And one of the stories, 'A Small Star in the East', made mention of the women poisoned while working in London's white-lead mills. I thought of Pavit and the tamarind paste in the copper vessel. My mother and her calomel. The various ways poisons could be introduced into the body, all at once or leaching in very slowly, over time.

It was only a very minor chance, but I could think of nothing else that might contribute to the woman's symptoms. 'Could I ask you, Bibi, to stop using the jug and goblet?' I said, and she looked at the goblet in the servant's hand.

'Why?'

'I don't know with any certainty,' I said, worrying suddenly that I might cause trouble by my uninformed opinion, 'but maybe they are made of poisonous material.'

Her eyes widened. 'My husband would wish to poison me?'

'No, no, of course not.' I grimaced. I shouldn't have spoken my mind. But there were no other clues. 'Sometimes, perhaps the danger is simply found in the very container itself. Unintentionally. It is beautiful and decorative, but . . .'

There was silence in the room. The bibi then spoke to Aimee in Pashto, and by her tone I knew she was questioning Aimee as to whether I could be trusted. Aimee spoke in a soothing voice, nodding.

'All right,' the young woman said to me. 'But I cannot tell my husband. He would be very angry.'

'Of course. Only drink from something else for the next week, and see if you feel better.'

She nodded weakly, and the servant gently drew up her coverlet and returned the goblet to the tray.

Within two weeks the young wife's health was returning. She came to the children's quarters as I sat there one afternoon, putting drops of warmed oil into one of the children's sore ears. Although still weak and moving slowly, she looked less wan, and smiled at me as she sat on the floor, leaning against a satin bolster. Her baby son crawled to her, and she pulled him on to her lap.

'*Allah hu Akbar*,' she said, 'God is Great.'

I nodded at her.

'I believe your words were true,' she said to me. 'I have been able to eat a little again, and my stomach no longer pains. I will see to it that you are rewarded. My husband is very pleased that I am no longer so unwell. Although I didn't tell him the cause of my illness, I said you were able to cure me.'

I shook my head. 'No, Bibi. I only told you what I thought. I did nothing.'

'Maybe you saved my life,' she said. 'If there is something my husband or I can ever do for you, you will tell me.'

'Yes,' I said, and then once more bent over the child with her head in my lap.

CHAPTER THIRTY-SEVEN

OVER THE NEXT few months I surprised myself, slowly growing to enjoy the camaraderie of the other women in the Zenana Mission. I didn't like the daily structure, and knew I never would, but I also realised it was necessary, with more than thirty women and children living under one roof. I now responded to the routines without thinking.

Helena always had the news from England, and sometimes spoke to us of the latest events around the table after dinner. No one but Helena had ever been in England, and even though many of the women carried some degree of English blood, the decisions made in that country, so far from here, seemed to lack a sense of reality or have any direct effect on us. And yet she insisted on keeping us informed.

Most recently Helena had spoken about how the prime minister to the Queen, Benjamin Disraeli, had dispatched a new viceroy, Lord Lytton, to Delhi last year, and this viceroy was demanding a British mission in Kabul, Afghanistan's capital. But Afghanistan's amir, Sher Ali, rejected this on the grounds that the Russians might then demand the same. There was a great deal of tension, Helena had told us, between Russia, lying on the northern border of Afghanistan, and England. Each wanted to establish themselves in Afghanistan. 'There are numerous rumblings of dissention,' she had said, shaking her head. 'And Peshawar is in a dangerous position again, as it was in the last Anglo-

Afghan war, caught on the border of British India and Afghanistan.'

I liked Helena; she was intelligent and concerned, not only over the women and children in her own zenana, but over the state of the city and the country. I began to feel a bond with her. Little by little we grew closer. Sometimes we found ourselves alone in the sitting room of an afternoon, and we talked. Or rather she spoke, and I listened. I still wasn't comfortable — and perhaps would never be — talking about what I had experienced.

'How have you come to Peshawar, Helena?' I asked her one afternoon.

'I loved a man,' she said, simply.

Her statement surprised me. Somehow I had expected that she had been a spinster missionary all her life, and had devoted her existence to good works, with little time for a personal life.

'We married in England. He came to India — he was a soldier — and I followed. We lived in Murree, and I had a child. But I hadn't wanted to leave England, and was unhappy here. I complained, loudly and often. I was not of a gentle spirit when younger.' Her voice portrayed nothing; she spoke as if about one of the other women.

'And then, during the Sepoy Rebellion, my husband was terribly injured. It did not appear he would live. I had said . . . unforgivable things to him before the Rebellion. I said I would do anything to leave this land, and that if it weren't for him I could be home. And then, when it appeared he would die from his wounds, I underwent a terrible awakening. It appeared I had made this thing happen. He would die, and I could leave.

'I knew how evil I had been. I went on my knees and made a promise to God: if He would allow my husband his life, I would devote my life to His teachings, and to bringing

484

His word to the unknowing of this land. My sacrifice would be that I would stay here all the days of my life.'

I watched her face.

'And shortly after my prayers and vow to the Lord my husband rallied. He lived,' she said, after a long silence. 'But now it was he who wished to return to England. He could no longer be in the army, due to his injuries, and wanted to start a new life. I told him of my promise, expecting he would understand and stay.'

She stopped, studying the window behind me.

'But he chose not to. He took our child and . . .' Again she stopped, and closed her eyes for the briefest of seconds. 'He returned to England. I stayed, and carried on as I knew I must.'

Finally I said, 'Do you . . . do you regret the choice you made?'

Her face clouded for a moment, then she straightened her shoulders. 'One should not make a promise one doesn't intend to keep. I understood fully what I was doing. My prayers were answered. God is good. That is what I must always remember.'

Her face was composed, dignified, but I sensed that she was not as certain as she tried to portray, and for this I felt a quiet surge of sympathy for her.

'But I can never stop thinking of my child,' she said, so softly. 'He is a man now, of course. But it still pains in the same way. There is no deeper agony than losing a child.'

We both sat quietly then, and I thought about those other parents – the man and woman I'd never known. Or at least had no memory of. The thoughts I had of them were shapeless and colourless, vague, because I couldn't picture them. I didn't know if they truly were European, or if I was the product of a European and an Indian, as Glory insinuated.

Did they still live? And did they still mourn my loss?

But even if they did, they were dead to me, and I to them.

I found my thoughts of this unknown man and woman playing within me more and more deeply.

When it wasn't my turn to cook or clean or teach and tend to the children at the mission, I looked forward to my visits in the various *haveli*s accepting us through their doors. Helena had given me rupees to buy simple medical supplies in the cantonment, and I now carried a small carpetbag containing them. Although most of the women in the *zenana*s spoke Urdu, and others were eager to use the smattering of English they were learning, I was steadily growing more proficient in Pashto. I was happy to leave the evangelical side of our visits to one of the other women from the *zenana* who always accompanied me – we went in pairs – and mainly attended to small medical crises amongst the women and children. I especially enjoyed the children; sometimes I taught the little ones a verse of a simple hymn as I tended to them.

And I had begun to feel very comfortable in Peshawar. Nowhere near as large as Lahore, and really not a lovely city structurally, it nevertheless had more of an attitude of acceptance, and I felt more at ease here than I ever had in Lahore. I understood why it had once been known as the 'Jewel of the Pathans'. It was an invigorating, yet challenging city, quite pulsing with the intrigue of both Central Asia and the mysteries of India. And yet, as I had been warned by everyone from Chander to Helena, it was not a safe time to be in Peshawar. Everywhere I went I heard men, over their chai, discussing the struggles that brewed in Afghanistan, its entry a mere twelve miles from Peshawar.

There were many British in Peshawar. And resentment against them grew ever stronger. Helena cautioned us all to be wary in our travels through the city; before we left each morning she warned us of any areas where she had heard there had been small skirmishes between Pushtuns and British; killings of both British and Afghans were occasionally reported.

As usual I thought of Kai, and his involvement against the British. But he was in Madras, at the other end of India.

I had time, during our walks to the various *haveli*s throughout the city, to become familiar with every turn in the numerous bazaars – the Bazaar Qissa Khawani, the Bazaar Mochilara, or the Street of Shoe-Makers, the Bazaar Bater-Bazan, the Street of Partridge Lovers. Here hung hundreds of the woven, conical cages of the Black Partridge, a favourite of the Muslims, who believed the bird's song to be in praise of Mighty Allah. The trilling calls competed with the nearby pounding of craftsmen's hammers.

Although I could rarely purchase anything, I knew what each bazaar sold, from exquisitely engraved brass and copper, to worked leather belts and the sandals known as *chappal*s, to the blankets and shawls of hand-spun wool from the long-tailed sheep of Kashmir. There were cloth and pottery bazaars, bazaars selling beads and bells and baskets.

One afternoon I spotted Mr Lang, haggling over a silver teapot with one of the merchants in the bazaar. For my first while in Peshawar I had fretted that I might see Mr or Mrs Lang, worried that they might create difficulty for me. But watching Mr Lang now from a distance as he tried to bully the vendor, I felt nothing. I knew I had become part of the city, and that I need no longer feel concern. I had been firmly accepted into the Peshawar Zenana Mission, and I knew that Helena would never be swayed by another's words.

The Bala Hisar, towering some distance on a rise to the north-west of Peshawar, was the city's massive fort. Its height, on the low hill, gave it a commanding view. It was a frowning brick structure with ramparts and battlements, now occupied by the British as military headquarters and an army garrison. I recognised the Persian name of Balahisar as meaning high fort. And of course, as in every large Indian city, there was the newer English cantonment, which I'd seen my first day here, seeking the Langs. But that day I had been in a state that had prevented me from seeing it clearly. Now I recognised its grand, gracious administrative structures, sprawling bungalows and spacious gardens.

One windy early autumn day on our way home from one of the *haveli*s, I convinced the woman with me – Marianne – to come to the large Christian cemetery in the cantonment. She didn't wish to enter, but waited while I walked through its elegant lych-gate covered with creeping bougainvillea. It was quite a lovely place, with tall sheeshams and old peepuls, the leaves rustling with that urgent, papery sound that heralds the approach of cooler weather. I read the words engraved on the stone and marble squares and crosses and obelisks, understanding even more about the role of the British in this city through the history recorded here. The markers held not only names and dates, but causes of death. There were soldiers who died in action during the first Anglo-Afghan war and in unrelated skirmishes: *Fallen for his Country*; *Stabbed to Death*, or *Shot by Tribesmen*. There were men who worked for the administration, with their less violent deaths: *Drowned*, *Tragic Fall From Horse*, *Climbing Accident*, as well as the predictable, for all the buried Europeans throughout India: *Enteric Fever*, *Heat Exhaustion*, *Malaria*, *Dysentery*. There were the stories of the wives and children who had followed the men to this far place, also told in a few words: *My Darling Sally*, *She Tried*, and the heartbreaking *Our Seth, aged two years. We loved him well. God loved him best*. My thoughts went, naturally, to the tiny plot behind the mission house, and the little ones buried there.

I realised now there were long stretches of time when I

actually forgot about the Colonel, and about Glory. It was harder not to think of Kai, especially when I saw a tall, slender man striding through the bazaars.

Many times I thought I saw my Afghan, for here the streets were full of similarly dressed Pushtuns. Occasionally I even touched one on the arm or shoulder, but when he turned to me it was never the familiar face.

I thought, more than once, how thoughtless I had been to not enquire his name. It would be good to see someone from my past who knew me without judgement. And he had been Kai's friend.

The late autumn brought Ramadan, and the Muslims fasted during the daylight hours. The *haveli*s were quieter; the children slept more during the day, waiting for sunset. Only those ill and the youngest, still taking their mother's milk, were exempt from the rule of fasting while the sun shed light. And then, after the thirty days had passed, there was a time of great celebration. All of us from the mission were invited to the various *haveli*s we visited to share the days of feasting. Along with Aimee and Marianne and Rohana, I was invited to *Haveli* Abdur Jan one afternoon, and we went together.

In the women's quarters we spoke quietly with the women and played with the younger children and listened to singing and poetry recitations in Pashto and Urdu from the older daughters. We were served a variety of delicious foods; I thoroughly enjoyed the hours we spent there. As the afternoon was drawing to a close the serving women circulated with a final dish on immense brass trays.

I took a spoon and small silver bowl from the woman who bent with her tray before me, and dipped the spoon into the pale, creamy substance.

As the sweetness soaked into my tongue, I closed my eyes. 'Mmmm. Delicious. What's it called, Marianne?'

'It's a special dessert; all the Pushtuns love it. I'm not sure of the exact name. They just call it *Peshawari kulfi*.'

I took another spoonful. It was very rich. 'I recognise the *falooda*.' The noodle, thin as thread, ground to a paste and lightly cooked in boiled milk, was popular in Lahore. 'But there are other tastes. Something nutty.'

She nodded, licking her spoon. 'Ground pistachio. Rosewater, and some flavoured honey.'

Suddenly, on the third bite, the sweetness was cloying. My stomach roiled, and I set the dish on to the low table in front of me.

'Are you all right, Pree?' Marianne asked.

I nodded, wiping my lips with my fingers as I stood. 'Yes. Yes. I just want to rinse my hands.'

I went to the small private room the women used for their ablutions. I breathed deeply, cupping my hands and drinking cool water. Something about the taste of the dessert had made me feel ill. It brought back some old memory, something I couldn't name.

But after a few minutes I felt better. I splashed water on my hot cheeks and returned to the other women.

But even in bed that night, after I'd cleaned my teeth thoroughly, the taste of the *Peshawari kulfi* lingered.

Winter came. It was colder than anything I had experienced. Winds from the snow-covered distant peaks swept into the city, groaning down the chimneys and causing people to hurry through the streets. Some mornings even the piles of animal dung were frozen where they had dropped, but the climate was too dry for snow. For once I was happy to wear my stockings and boots. Helena gave me a warm shawl, which I wrapped around my head when I went outside. The people of Peshawar swathed themselves in heavy Kashmiri blankets and shawls and the men wore big black felt boots and stomped their feet as they stood in small clusters outside the tea-sellers' stalls, drinking their steaming green chai sprinkled with almonds and cinnamon, which they believed further warmed the body. Women's veils and burkas streamed and snapped in the frigid wind.

We celebrated our Christmas, the children each receiving a small gift and a piece of wrapped English toffee that Helena procured from somewhere. We had a special meal and I lead the hymn singing with, of course, my favourite, 'Christians Awake, Salute the Happy Morn'. And it truly was a happy day. I had much to give thanks for.

That night I sat on my bed, thinking of the people I had loved. Did old Sanosh still live? I hoped so. And what of Adriana? Was she with Christians who celebrated this day? If so, did she receive a sweetie, or a new toy? Or was she being raised a Hindu? On this special day I allowed myself to imagine her happy. I allowed myself to imagine she still lived.

And Kai: surely, surely Kai was alive and well somewhere, perhaps in Madras, perhaps elsewhere. Did he think of me today? Did he remember that long-ago Christmas when I brought the plate of crisp goose and the striped sweet to his hut?

'What you think about, Pree?' Aimee asked. The curtain separating us was open, and I turned to her. 'You smile,' she continued, 'but not like always smile. What you think?' she repeated.

'Just . . . of my home. And other Christmases,' I said, looking into her face.

She nodded, her own expression melancholic.

'Do you . . .' I hesitated. 'Do you have happy memories, Aimee?'

Her face darkened further, and I realised I had been clumsy, insensitive. 'I'm sorry,' I said, quickly, but she shook her head.

'Not be sorry. I have many thoughts. Some . . . yes, some happy. From long, long time gone.' She attempted a smile. 'Please to keep happy in your thoughts,' she said, pulling the curtain between us. 'To keep happy thoughts is very good, Pree.'

I silently agreed, and went to sleep thinking of Kai, trying to remember his features with clarity.

Screams woke me. I sat straight up, thinking I was back at the Lahore mission, hearing my mother's mad howls. I threw back my cover, wild eyed as I looked about in the darkness.

It was Aimee, on the other side of the curtain.

I rushed to her side. Rohana was lighting the lamp. 'Shh, shh,' I said, leaning over Aimee and pushing back her hair, wet with sweat. She was on her knees, trembling, her good eye wide and glittering.

Rohana sat on her other side. 'It's all right, Aimee,' she said. 'You're safe. It's all right.' She looked at me. 'She sometimes has nightmares.'

I brought Aimee a cup of water. She took it, her hand shaking so that I had to wrap mine around it and help guide it to her lips. Within a few minutes her breathing returned to normal.

'Thank you,' she said, looking from me to Rohana, then lying down again.

'Shall I leave on the lamp?' Rohana asked.

'Yes, please. For only a few minutes,' Aimee said.

We went back to our own beds. When I awoke in the morning Aimee was already dressed, humming 'Our Thanks to God Most High' as she pinned up her hair. She didn't speak of the nightmare.

A few months later it happened again. When I woke to her cries I rushed to her. Rohana wasn't with us; she was sitting up with one of the children who had been ill all week, giving the child's mother a chance to sleep.

492

I wrapped a shawl around Aimee's shoulders and rubbed her back. She was quiet, but shook violently.

'It is a hymn?' she finally whispered.

I stopped rubbing her back. I was unaware that I was singing under my breath. But it was one of the soldiers' ditties from my days with Glory. It had nothing to do with goodness.

'No. Would you tell me what the nightmares are about?' I asked her.

She shook her head. 'Please, Pree, stay here, with me,' she said, and I did, crowding into her narrow bed. In the darkness her breathing became slow and steady; from within the house a child cried out, and was immediately comforted. I thought Aimee had fallen asleep, and was about to go back to my own bed when suddenly she spoke.

'My burning,' she said, in Hindi, 'sometimes comes back to me, in a dream.'

I sat up and looked down at her. In the moonlight the scars on her face stood white.

'I lived in a small village, far to the south of here. Like the others, I was betrothed from the time I was born. At six years old I was married, but I only went to my husband when it was time for the marriage to be consummated, when I was twelve.'

I was shocked. I had never before heard Aimee speak Hindi; in her own language she was fluid and articulate. I realised that all along I had thought of her as simple minded because her command of English was simple.

'I bore him sons. Two. And a daughter.' She smiled, a brief, trembling smile. It disappeared as quickly as it had surfaced. 'When I was eighteen, my husband was in the field, cutting sugar cane. You know how the cobras like to hide in the dense clumps. One bit him. Even though we all prayed for him, making *pujas* for two days and nights, he suffered much, and then died'. She stopped, closing her eyes. 'He was a good man. He cared for me, and I for him. If he hadn't gone to the fields that day . . .' She drew a deep, shaky breath, and her good eye was wet. 'His mother told me it was my fault; I was a despised *ghar-jalani*. She said I could not change, and I would continue to bring misfortune and death to the family. The only way to stop the chain of bad luck I had started was to perform *sati* on my husband's pyre. I said "no, no, please".' Her voice rose. 'I begged, "no, no!"' The final word was a desperate cry, and then her voice returned to its usual tone. 'But not for myself. It was for my children, Pree. I didn't want to leave my children to be raised by my mother-in-law. I told her I would be a good widow: I would shave my head and wear only white and sleep on the floor. I would do all the jobs of an Untouchable. But my mother-in-law beat me and told me if I didn't do my duty my husband's soul would not be released.' She rubbed her good hand over her scarred face in an unconscious gesture, and I saw how she shook, reliving the terrible time. 'I was so afraid. And I didn't want to die. I didn't care if I had to live my life as a widow, I didn't want to leave my children.'

I nodded, although she wasn't looking at me.

'My mother-in-law and my husband's aunts dressed me in my wedding sari, and decorated my hands and feet as though I were again a bride, and anointed my hair with the sweetest oils. I remember that my body shook so violently that I was slapped, for my trembling made it difficult for my mother-in-law to line my eyes with *surma*.'

'And your parents? They . . . they didn't try to stop it?'

Suddenly she turned her head to look at me. Now her face was still, almost hard, an expression I had never before witnessed. 'What do you mean? A daughter never belongs in the house she is born into, you know that. She is only a guest. I was no longer their responsibility; I belonged to my husband's parents.'

'Of course,' I murmured.

'I tried to run away, but was held firmly. And then I was lifted on to the unlit pyre. I screamed and again tried to escape. I saw my children, watching. I will never forget their little faces.' She fell silent, and when she continued, her voice had lost all emotion. She spoke in hurried, flat tones, as if she wished to finish, as if she wished she hadn't disclosed her story to me. 'And then someone hit me on the side of the head with one of the pieces of wood, stunning me. The fire was lit, and after a few minutes my head cleared; I smelled the smoke and heard the flames. For the first moments I tried to stay still, to be obedient, to accept the fate that was mine, but I couldn't. As the fire caught my sari, I scrambled out, and ran as nimbly as if I were a cat. But my sari was already flaming, and my oiled hair caught as well.'

I had to close my eyes, putting my hands over my face as I imagined the scene.

'I think I was chased at first. I'm not sure. I don't know if I heard voices or if it was the fire eating my hair. But then they must have let me run; now I know that they were sure I would die.'

I opened my eyes and looked at her again. She was watching me.

'I remember falling, and seeing my veil wrapped around my arm and hand, and the silk melting into my skin.' She lifted her useless hand with the other as if to show it to me. 'I hung between the earth and the sky for a long time,' she said. 'I don't know how long, only that I left my body many times, and floated with no pain. But then the pain would come back, even stronger, and I heard my voice screaming, and I knew I wasn't dead. But I wished to be dead; I wished then that I had died quickly, on the pyre. I knew I deserved the suffering. I hadn't accepted my fate.'

'But you were only—'

'A man cared for me,' she interrupted. 'Somehow he found me; maybe he heard my screams. It was a man with white skin and a long black dress. He had the cross on a rope around his waist; it was the first time I had seen the cross. *Aimee, petite aimee*, he said over and over again, as he put something wet – mud, leaves, I don't know – on to my burnt skin, and gave me water to drink. When finally I could eat, he fed me. He tried to soothe me. He sang to me, and he always sat beside me and spoke. I think now he was praying. I'll never forget his voice, even though I couldn't understand any of his words.

'And then one day, when I no longer cried from the pain, and could bear to move, he brought me here, in a cart, and left me with Helena. He knew Helena.' She stopped, and looked at the painting of Jesus with the children. 'I lost my children as surely as if I had died, except now they have been disgraced. My poor children.' Her voice trembled suddenly, and she beat her fist against her chest. 'My children,' she repeated, and tears ran from her good eye. 'My children,' she whispered. I could think of no words to comfort her. Then she took a deep breath and wiped her face with her sleeve. 'I've lived here ever since. Eight years. It's a good place for me. I could no longer live the Hindu life. I was evil in that life.'

'You weren't evil because you didn't want to die, Aimee.'

But Aimee shook her head. 'No. It wasn't right. My place was to be sacrificed. It was my predestined fate. And I changed that fate, and my karma was also reversed.'

'I don't think *sati* should be anyone's destiny.' I thought of my mother. 'That's why it's prohibited.'

'It was prohibited by the English. Not by my people. It's a duty of honour. And I ran from that duty, and from honour, and for that I knew I would carry a burden all my life. But one day, listening to what Helena told me, over and over, I knew I didn't want to carry that weight any longer. I knew I could give it to Our Lord God and He would carry it for me. And so I became a Christian. But it was through cowardice.'

'You weren't a coward, Aimee.' I stroked her knee through the thin fabric of her nightdress. 'Fighting to live isn't—'

'Not about being afraid to die. I was afraid that if I didn't convert I would be reborn as the lowest of reptiles. Perhaps a slimy bullfrog that cries out his loneliness from the mud. Or a scaly lizard, whose only pleasure until she is eaten by a chameleon is the sun upon her back. Maybe even lower. Maybe I would be reborn as a dung beetle.' She looked at my hand on her knee, then back into my face. 'I didn't want that, Pree.'

'I know,' I said.

'So I gave up my burden and the Lord set me free. I will never again marry, or know my children. But I have the love of the women here, and know the joy of holding the children of others. And when I die I will go to Heaven, and sit at His feet. And I will no longer be hideous. I will be whole again.'

'Yes,' I said, wiping my nose with the back of my hand.

'Don't cry for me, Pree. I'm happy.'

We sat in silence, and finally Aimee lay down.

'I can go to sleep now,' she said, turning on her side. 'Thank you, Pree. The Lord will bless you for your kindness to me.'

I tucked her blanket around her and put another piece of wood into the fireplace. Then I pulled my own blanket from my bed and wrapped it around myself and sat in front of the fire.

Hearing Aimee's story, and then listening to her as she spoke with complete faith about her trust in the Lord, had deeply disturbed me. She was a true Bible woman. She believed with her whole heart in the scriptures she read, in the prayers she uttered. She accepted what had happened to her, and knew what the rest of her life would hold. And was grateful for it.

Scarred and knowing she would live out her life helping others, with nothing of her own, Aimee was complete. While I — my thoughts were human, and base. I thought with longing of the pretty frocks I saw in the English shops in the cantonment. Instead of using my earned annas to buy biblical tracts, I bought English novels. I was so self-absorbed I even planned to be in a particular zenana during their afternoon meal, so I could have the treat of eating food much tastier than our usual plain meals here. And worst of all, I still dreamed of Kai's lips upon mine, and more. Of his body on and in mine.

Perhaps Aimee and I were alike in that we had both sacrificed a part of ourselves for a certain freedom. But what I imagined I had suffered could not be compared to Aimee's terrible ordeal. What I had lost could never match her great losses. I admired her for escaping her own death, and then carrying on with the only life possible for her, thankful in spite of both her physical and emotional pain.

And yet I . . . I could not accept this life in the zenana mission as my final stopping place. As my home, and my future. I knew I was still waiting, still yearning for more. I needed so much more than this.

My heart was not full of thankfulness. It was full of greed and self-pity and blame, blame for my lot in life.

I was a sham as a Bible woman, and not at all a good person.

CHAPTER THIRTY-EIGHT

WINTER EASED INTO spring. Flowers were everywhere; now I knew why Peshawar derived its name from the Sanskrit word *pushpapura*, meaning the city of flowers. They bloomed everywhere, taking away some of the usual drabness of the workaday city. I smelled orange blossoms, and thought again of the Afghan, and what he had said about Peshawar that long-ago day at the mission.

And then one beautiful May afternoon, as I sat on one of the balconies of *Haveli* Abdur Jan with four of his small children – three boys and one girl – smelling the sweet spring air blow down from the Himalayas as I instructed them in simple English words, I suddenly thought of the Maypole song, and taught them a few lines.

A few days later Helena came to me where I worked in the courtyard. It was my week to help with the food preparation, and I was stirring a huge vat of boiling vegetables. 'Pree. There's a messenger from Abdur Jan's *haveli*. You've been summoned there, and are to go immediately.'

I wiped my hands on my apron. 'Is someone ill?'

'I don't know. The messenger is waiting.'

I pulled off the apron and took my medicine bag, then climbed into the waiting tonga with the tall Muslim.

When we arrived the door was opened immediately, and a serving woman stood waiting.

'Who is ill?' I asked her in Pashto, but she just shook her

head. I climbed the stairs in front of her and started down the hall to the women's quarters, but she touched my arm and led me in the other direction. She opened a door and indicated I was to go in. I'd never been in this chamber before. It wasn't for the women; there were no latticed screens. There were many thick, brocaded cushions, and the furniture was made of sandalwood.

My eyes, after the dim passage, were dazzled by a blaze of sunlight falling through the open windows. I blinked, clearing my vision, and saw a nursemaid, Iba, as well as one of the younger children, a sweet-faced little girl of about four. She was sitting on a tasselled pillow, eating a *jalebi*. Her lips were smeared with honey, and she smiled at me, holding up the crispy coiled sweet.

'*Salaam*, Anjum,' I said, smiling back at her. She didn't appear ill in any way.

'Miss Pree,' she cried, running to me. I kneeled, setting down my bag, and she put her arms around my neck.

'Hello, my little star,' I said in English, translating her name, and she parroted my words. She was my favourite among the children, although I attempted not to give her extra attention. I knew why; she bore a resemblance to how Adriana might appear. As I knelt, my arms around her, I suddenly realised there was someone else in the room. A tall man stood at the window to my left, gazing at the courtyard below. I saw the back of his head, the thick, wavy dark hair touching the crisp white collar of his *kurta*. His black trousers and the long white *kurta* were of fine fabric, and he wore gleaming black riding boots.

The blood drained from my head with a rushing sound, leaving me momentarily faint. Anjum was a dead weight in my arms.

'*Ji*,' Iba said to the man, respectfully, 'this is the woman.'

Still, the man didn't turn. But he didn't have to.

From the open window came the sounds of the garden below: the off-key singing of a serving woman, the soft splash of the fountain, the sudden screech of a peacock. When the silence within the room spread, Iba said, softly, from behind me, 'This is the Memsahib you requested to see, *Ji*.'

I set Anjum down, and she went back to the cushion. And then I walked across the room, my movements studied, purposeful and yet slow, as if fighting the current of water. When I was a foot away I stopped, and he turned.

His hands were clasped in front of him, the fingers laced as if forced into the old Christian prayer position by my father all those years ago at the mission. He studied my face, showing no emotion, and then reached behind him, putting one hand on to the sill of the window. That was the only indication of his feelings. His hand, trembling almost imperceptibly, reaching for the sill as if to support himself.

'I couldn't be certain. Others might know the song. Mem Fin's song,' he said.

I stared at his face. He hadn't changed, except that he was no longer bone-thin. His eyes were just as startling, the colour of the sea, although there was something darker in them now that had nothing to do with their colour. I opened my mouth, then closed it. Kai. Here.

I found my voice. 'It was Anjum you heard singing the Maypole song?' I asked, glancing at the little girl again.

He nodded, and we both were silent again. Behind me, Anjum sang under her breath.

'Iba,' he said now, quietly again, in Urdu, 'take the child and leave us.'

Iba and Anjum left, and Kai and I were left alone, in the room smelling of sandalwood and honey.

We didn't touch, although the instinct drawing me closer to Kai was so strong it was as if my whole body was vibrating, just the slightest. Why didn't he reach for me, if only to hug me in the way of old friends?

'I thought I would never see you again,' I said, now staring at his hand on the sill. There was a pale scar running across the knuckles of his right hand. It was as if he were made of stone, or part of the carved wood of the sill. I wanted to pick up that hand and lay my cheek against it.

'I have business with Abdur Jan. We are old friends,' he said, and gestured towards the cushions. 'Sit, Pree. Please,' he said.

I lowered myself to the cushion Anjum had been sitting on; there was a blob of honey on the corner tassel. I touched the golden drop with my index finger, as if in a trance, then joined my thumb to the stickiness, opening and closing on that tiny resistance. Kai stayed at the window.

'Why would you come here, to Peshawar, Pree?' he asked. 'It's not safe. Especially not now, with all the unrest.'

Had the mission been a safe place? I didn't know how to answer.

'I thought that if you ever left the mission you would go south, to Delhi. Or perhaps all the way to Bombay. You always spoke of seeing the ocean,' he said.

'We can't always predict which road we'll follow. Or why. I didn't ever dream of Peshawar, and yet here I am,' I said. There was silence. 'I came here when I had nowhere to go.' More silence. I had a sudden thought. 'Do . . . do you live here, Kai?' Could this be possible – that I had been here all these months and not seen him?

But he shook his head. 'I come and go,' he said, and I was reminded of something similar the Afghan had told me, the last time I'd seen him. 'I travel much of India,' he continued, 'and occasionally visit Peshawar.'

His voice somehow held me firmly on the cushion. It had a curious closed sound; there was little of the warmth that I had heard when I thought of his voice. It was as if he was a polite stranger. I know that the last time I had seen him I had shouted at him, slapped him and told him I hated him. But surely, surely he had understood; I had just found out a shocking truth. He couldn't believe I meant what I'd said, couldn't possibly think that I hated him. But why did he demonstrate this reserve, this odd, cool manner?

Neither of us had smiled.

Kai looked at the figured carpet under his high, polished boots.

And then I couldn't stop the question which had been shouting in my head since I had seen him at the window. The question that had been waiting for an answer, at the back of my mind, since the day he had ridden away, as the man I thought was my father – and *was* his father – lay dying.

'How is it you never came back to see me?' The words burst from me as if shot from a cannon. 'To see if I was all right? If I needed help? Why, Kai? Why?' I said, hearing my voice rise unpleasantly, with almost a shrewish quality. I thought of his mother, of Glory, and how for this last horrible moment I sounded like her, and covered my mouth with my hands.

Kai didn't speak, nor look at me, still studying his boots on the carpet. Light of summer – the colour of the honey between my fingertips – illuminated him.

I took my hands from my mouth, calming myself, speaking more quietly, slowly. 'I thought you cared enough about me to come back to the mission, even once.'

He raised his face, looking at the ceiling. His neck was long, and smooth. He swallowed before he spoke, and his words shocked me. 'I did come back.'

'But . . . no. You didn't.'

'I did come.'

I shook my head. 'What are you talking about? Do you think I wouldn't remember if you'd been there?'

Now he drew his gaze from the ceiling to my face, and took a deep breath. 'On the day I left the mission, when your . . . my . . . father lay ill, your mother shrieking like a—' He licked his lips. 'My own mother demonstrating her lack of guilt – of conscience – all I wanted was to get as far away as possible. I only thought of myself, and leaving that place where I'd known so much unhappiness.'

Even after all this time the words hurt. *I only thought of myself.*

'The mission hadn't felt like a home to me for so long. Maybe it never really had. But it was your home. It was where you belonged.'

'And you really didn't think of me? At all?'

'Pree.' He looked and sounded angry, but I knew it was directed at himself. 'I was caught up in my own . . . my own thoughts. I didn't know whether my father lived or died, and I was filled with such fury that I thought I didn't care. I had no way of knowing what had happened to your mother.' His eyes slid away from me. What had he heard? 'I assumed you lived on, at the mission, as you always had.'

Kai still thought we shared the same father.

'I didn't care about my own mother; she was dead to me. I'm not a good son, Pree.'

'She wasn't a good mo—'

'And I'm not a good man,' he interrupted. 'Do you understand what I'm saying?'

I stared at him.

'In spite of her behaviour, my duty was to my mother. Instead, I thought only of myself, and what was best for me.' Again he licked his lips.

'I don't consider it selfish to want to make a life for yourself,' I said. Hadn't I said something similar to Aimee,

504

only a few months ago? Was I defending his actions – as I'd defended hers – because they were also mine? Because of what I had done to get away from the mission?

He finally left the window to sit on a cushion across from me. 'I had no idea what had happened to the Fincastles, how the mission had fallen into . . .' Kai stopped. 'I didn't know you'd been left on your own.'

Would you have come, if you'd known? I wanted to ask.

'I returned, Pree. To Lahore. And I was on my way to the mission. To see . . .'

I didn't understand his hesitancy. I waited.

Suddenly he appeared impatient, or angry. With himself, or with me? 'I planned to go to the mission, to take my mother's money. And . . . I hadn't been able to stop thinking about you, Pree. I needed to see that you were all right. I hated the way we parted.'

Tears came to my eyes. It was Kai speaking now, the Kai I knew. I wiped my eyes with my palms.

'But it was there, in Lahore, that I heard about the deaths of both the Reverend and Mrs Fincastle. And I also heard other things.'

I nodded, breathing heavily.

'I didn't believe what I was told. How could I believe such stories? My own mother . . . well, yes, I could imagine it. But you, Pree? You?' He rubbed at his scarred knuckles with his left hand. 'I had to see for myself, prove that people were mistaken. Not you.'

I sat, unmoving, watching his mouth as he spoke.

'I went to the mission.' He looked away again, still rubbing his knuckles in that repetitive, rhythmic movement. 'I saw horses, horses of the Queen's regiment. I heard music, laughter.' Now he let go of his hand, and both rested limply on his thighs. 'The mission looked terrible, with the burned-out infirmary, the garden overgrown, the house not touched by whitewash, the thatch sinking in places. I went to the house, and saw my mother,' he said. 'Saw how she lived, and what she did.'

The silence stretched. Finally I could bear it no longer. 'And did you see me as well?' My words came out in a whisper. Had he seen me, but not made his presence known? I stared at him. 'When, Kai? When were you there?'

'You had already left,' he said, and I closed my eyes in relief. 'My mother wouldn't speak of you, except to tell me you had indeed worked for her. As one of her . . . women. But then you had stolen everything from her, and run off. Of course I have never believed anything my mother says. But the others, those in Lahore . . .'

'But Kai . . . surely you know . . . not me, Kai. Not me. I wasn't part of your mother's evil ways,' I repeated. 'And I left when . . . when the situation grew dangerous for me. When I couldn't protect myself any longer.'

I stared at him now. Suddenly I remembered trying to explain my situation to the Langs, heard the same defence in my voice. But Kai was not the lecherous Mr Lang, nor the drunken Mrs Lang. He knew me. He would understand. 'Surely . . . surely, Kai,' I said, more insistently, as he turned his face from me again, 'you would know I couldn't behave in such a way.'

He blinked then. 'Yes, Pree. I know you.' And as he looked into my face, I felt it heat. He believed me, and I lied openly to him. I was professing my innocence, and yet I had committed that great sin with the Colonel. I had moved, purposefully, that one morning, into his mother's sordid world.

It had been easy to tell lies to others. Maybe even to lie to myself. But to see that I could also be dishonest with Kai . . . I dropped my gaze.

'Pree. Look at me.'

I raised my head.

'Do you think I don't understand the ways of the world?'

What was he saying? 'I know that you seek the truth, Kai. That's what you once told me, so long ago. That you seek the truth, and believe only that which you know to be true.'

There was a long silence. I was suddenly exhausted.

'So much has happened,' he said. 'I don't remember talking to you about truth. If I did, it was when I was younger, and idealistic, when I imagined myself worthy to propose such grand statements about truth. But since then I've learned—'

The door opened, and Aimee came in. Kai stood.

'Pree?' she said, looking from Kai to me. 'What you do?'

I got to my feet. 'This . . . this is an old friend,' I said, and Kai nodded at Aimee. 'Mr da Silva. And this is Miss Aimee, from the Zenana Mission.'

There was only a moment of hesitation before Aimee said, in her best English voice, 'How do you do?'

'It's a pleasure to make your acquaintance,' Kai said.

'Were you looking for me?' I asked, flushed and uncomfortable, as if I'd been caught doing something secretive and private.

'Helena send me. She said maybe there is problem, and you need my help. I look to the children first, but don't see you. Iba tells me you are here.'

'Yes. Well,' I said, straightening the collar of my frock, although I'm sure it was in place.

'I am going to see womans now. You are coming?' Did I hear a slightly different tone in her voice? Surely she couldn't find fault with me talking to an old friend.

'I'll meet you there in a moment,' I told her.

She nodded, slowly, then looked at Kai again. 'Good day, sir,' she said.

'Good day, Miss Aimee.'

She looked at me once more, then stepped out, closing the door quietly.

What had Kai been saying? Something of importance. I wanted to recapture the moment earlier, but the spell had been broken. We stood, facing each other. 'And – now what, Kai?' I said. *Now what?*

'Will you meet with me, tomorrow?' he asked.

I nodded, perhaps too eagerly.

'I have work I must do here,' he said, and I opened my mouth to ask him what work, what was he doing in Peshawar, but before I could speak he said, 'I can only remain in the city another week.'

Seven days.

'What was so urgent?' Helena asked me when I returned with Aimee. 'Was someone seriously ill?'

I had tried to compose myself after Kai left, joining Aimee. She hadn't spoken to me about Kai. Now she stood beside me as I looked at Helena.

'Was a child ill, Pree? Or one of the women?' she repeated.

I opened my mouth and said, 'It was a simple matter with one of the children. I'll go back to check on her tomorrow.' So. Already the lies began. I don't know why I didn't tell her the truth: that someone from my past had returned, and I wanted – needed – to see him again. But I had been completely silent about my former life for close to a year while I lived here; I wouldn't know how to begin.

As I spoke I glanced at Aimee, begging her not to say anything.

Helena simply nodded, unconcerned, and I felt even worse at her complete trust in me.

I avoided being alone with Aimee, hurrying to the bedroom before her, closing the curtain between us and blowing out the lamp so I could pretend to be asleep when she came in.

But I could barely sleep that night. The anticipation at seeing Kai again filled me with an excitement I couldn't describe, even to myself. But I had to keep it hidden, and not let Aimee notice.

The next morning, holding her Bible, Aimee stood behind me as I put a few bottles into my medical bag. 'I too am coming you to *Haveli* Abdur Jan,' she said. 'I am talking to children about Jesus today.'

'I'll talk to them after I've seen to the child. Why don't you go to *Haveli* Hamid Kahn today? There's no need for both of us to be in one place.'

'Who is ill child at Abdur Jan's? The one you say about to Helena yesterday?'

Why was she forcing me to lie? Couldn't she mind her own business? 'Anjum.'

'What is it ill?'

'Just a rash.'

'Rash? Not pox? Pox very bad.'

My hands were busy as I bent over the open bag. 'No. There are no other signs.'

'Why today is your good frock?'

'Aimee!' I whirled to face her. 'Just go. I'll see you at dinner.' I refused to acknowledge the surprised hurt in her eye.

She left, and I hurried out.

CHAPTER THIRTY-NINE

I MET WITH KAI, as we'd arranged, in a tea shop frequented by Eurasians in the native quarter. He looked even more handsome today, in another well-made outfit, Indian for all but the boots. Had he, like me, worn his finest clothing for our meeting?

'Hello,' I said, crossing the room, suddenly shy.

He smiled, standing, and reached across the table to take my hand. His touch filled me with joy. But it was clear that he was somehow anxious. Or nervous.

'I only have an hour,' he said, letting go of my hand, and the joy was replaced by a dark feeling. It was as if he was letting me know that his time was precious, and he was giving this small piece of it to me. He called to one of the servers to bring us chai.

There were nine tables in the tea shop.

I couldn't think of anything to say, and was relieved when at last he spoke. 'You look as if this life suits you. This life as a Bible woman. Although I never thought you . . .' he smiled again, even more warmly. 'I didn't think you would continue the life of your parents.'

I wanted to tell him they weren't my parents. I wanted him to know my father wasn't his father. We were in no way related. But it was too soon.

'It's what I know, Kai,' I said. 'And actually almost all of what I do with the women and children in the zenanas is medical, or teaching English. I leave the evangelical duties for my sisters at the Zenana Mission. You're right. That never was my strong point.' I made a wry face. 'But it feels comfortable, living in the mission house here and visiting the zenanas. Although . . .' I stopped.

'Although?'

'The women in the mission embrace those in the house as family.'

'And you don't?'

I shrugged. 'It's different for me. I've known a real family. Most of them were orphans, raised in missions, and—' I stopped. I had been an orphan, or at least a lost child, raised in a mission. 'Raised in a group, without parents,' I said, awkwardly. 'So the circumstances are what they've always known. I miss privacy, being alone with my thoughts. I'm never alone. Still, it isn't unpleasant. And it's . . .' I searched for the right word. 'Clean. It feels clean. Especially after . . .' I stopped.

Kai's face had changed subtly, and I wondered at my foolishness in bringing up the unpleasant topic of the old mission. 'Once the infirmary burned, I missed working with people,' I quickly went on. 'I like being able to help the children, and the women.'

Why did I feel this awkwardness? I tried to think of something more to say; why was there nothing to speak of ? Perhaps his work. 'What do you—' I asked, and at the same moment Kai said, 'How did you—' and naturally we smiled.

'Please,' I told him, 'go on', as green chai and thick slices of walnut cake were set in front of us by a man who silently appeared and just as silently left. I didn't think I could eat; my stomach was unsettled by being with Kai.

'I was about to ask how you decided to come to Peshawar,' he said.

I didn't want to mention the Langs and bring forward that

other unpleasant memory. What could I speak of that didn't conjure up something negative?

Of course. 'It was actually the Afghan – your friend, from the Grand Trunk Road – who told me he lived here. He described the city, and I liked the sound of it.'

Kai was very still.

'And it seemed a good place to . . . to disappear into. Kai?'

He was staring at me intently. 'Have you seen him?'

I blinked. 'The Afghan? No. I don't even know if he's still here.' I couldn't understand Kai's expression. 'Is he?'

He didn't answer.

'If I knew his name, perhaps I could find him. What's his name, Kai?'

But Kai looked away from me now.

'When I arrived,' I finally said, when I realised he wouldn't answer my question, 'I was told of the Peshawar Zenana Mission. They welcomed me, and so I've stayed most of a year now.'

'And you'll continue to live here, and work as a Bible woman?'

I stared at my untouched cake, his question distressing me. Now that he was here, now that we had again found each other . . . why was he asking me this? Did he think I could be content committing my life to this, like Helena or Aimee? No. I wanted something of my own. I wanted what I had once had. A family. Even at the end of that life, when things had gone so badly, and my parents were both so damaged in different ways, I'd had a home, and a family. Somewhere I belonged. Someone I belonged to, even though the belonging hadn't been the true connection I'd thought it to be for my whole life.

And I wanted that again, the feeling of being part of someone, of knowing I was important to someone, not for whatever skills I possessed, but for me. Until I'd seen Kai, yesterday, I didn't know where I belonged. I had nobody. But now he was here. I looked up from my cake to him.

'You're planning to make your life here?' he asked again.

'Kai,' I said, shaking my head. 'I don't know.'

Kai broke off a piece of cake and put it to his mouth, but before it touched his lips he set it on the plate again. It appeared he couldn't eat, either. The tension between us was raw. I took a sip of my tea. It was very sweet.

'I'm sorry about your parents, Pree. I know it must have been terrible for you.'

This was the time to speak of them, of the people he thought were my parents. I watched his lips. Again, the memories came to me: our kiss in the crowded courtyard of the printing shop in Lahore, my attempt to be near him that final time at the mission. 'I have to ask you something,' I said, and he nodded, crumbling the cake on his plate.

'Did you turn away from me in the past when I tried to be . . . close to you – because you thought I was your half-sister? That we shared the same father?'

His hand grew still among the broken bits of cake. I wanted to touch him, and I wanted him to touch me again.

'Turn away from you?'

'Yes. When . . . when I came to see you in Lahore, and you gave me the Woolstonecroft book. And even that last time you were at the mission.'

I couldn't read his expression.

'I'd forgotten about that book,' he said. Was he also saying he'd forgotten I'd come to see him in Lahore? That he'd forgotten about kissing me, even so briefly, in the courtyard there?

'Was that the reason?' I asked, picking up my cup and swirling it. I watched the circular spin of the hot liquid. 'Because', I took a breath, still watching my cup, 'the Rever-end wasn't my father. And she – my . . . mother – wasn't my real mother. They weren't my parents at all. They took me in as a foundling. And that means . . .' I kept on watching the liquid. 'Well, you and I. We aren't at all related by blood. The Reverend wasn't my father,' I said again, unnecessarily. 'I have proof,' I added, maybe too quickly, thinking of my father's Bible in my room at the mission house.

I finally dared to look up.

I had expected some exclamation, a look of surprise, or shock. But he simply sat there, looking at me.

'I found out, from your mother,' I hurried on, 'that I was brought to the mission as a two year old. That . . . nobody knew who I was. Am.' Again I waited for something, a word of disbelief, an expression of confusion. But he simply pushed his plate to one side, and picked up his tea.

'Kai? Do you understand what I'm telling you? The Fincastles took me as their own. But . . . now I don't even know if I truly am English. Obviously many see me . . .' I stopped. 'I don't know where, or who, I'm from. Kai? Why don't you speak?'

He took a drink and then put down the cup. 'I always knew you weren't the Fincastles' child.'

Now it was my turn to be silent.

'I was almost eight years old when you were brought to the mission at Allahabad. Of course I knew.'

I thought of the death of my little brother Gabriel. I had only been six, and yet I remembered the day clearly. Why hadn't I thought of this when Glory told me the story of my arrival at the mission? 'But . . . you never said . . .'

'Pree. I was a child who said little as it was. And I had enough of my own to think about.'

Glory leaving him, returning, leaving again. Knowing the Reverend was his father, but never being claimed by him. The confusion he must have experienced.

'I never really thought much about it. You were simply little Pree. The Reverend and Mem were your parents. It was only when you rebelled against them, when you were older, that I suddenly thought of the possible reasons for your behaviour. In particular, it was the day the Reverend tried to baptise you, during the monsoon. You simply weren't the earnest, mild-mannered sort of young woman one unusually views as missionary stock. And I remember thinking, at that time, well, maybe it isn't her fault; who knows what blood runs through her? But of course I wouldn't speak of such a thing to you, or to anyone. It wasn't my place, nor would it have served any purpose.'

I didn't know what to say. There wasn't anything to say. Kai had carried the secret about me through his childhood and adolescence and into manhood. Just as he had always known the Reverend was his father, he had known I wasn't the Fincastles' child. He'd always known there was no connection between us.

Now he pulled a round gold watch from within the folds of his shirt and clicked open its lid; even in my stunned state I thought *how odd that he carry a pocket watch*. It was such an English mannerism. Kai, who spoke of the British with rancour.

I saw my own hand, palm up, on the table. My callouses were gone.

He shut the watch. 'I must go, Pree. I've been longer than I intended.'

I was still thinking about what he had just told me. We weren't related, and he'd always known.

'Pree?'

I looked up; he was standing. 'Oh,' I said, also rising. 'You're going . . . where are you going?'

'I have business to attend to. The reason I came to Peshawar.' There was a tic on his left cheekbone. He rubbed the back of his hand over his mouth. Was I making him nervous? Or was it something else?

'What business is it?'

'Do you need a tonga to get back to the mission?' he asked.

And so it continued: Kai and his secrets.

I took his hand. 'Kai. I'll wait for you. Here.'

'No,' he said. 'I can never be certain how long things – my business – will take. I don't want you waiting hours. And . . . do you not have to return to the house?'

I nodded.

He squeezed my hand, then let it go, as he had over the table, earlier. My own hand felt suddenly cold, and empty.

'Kai, what is it that you do?'

'It's complicated.'

I stepped closer to him. There were two other couples in the room; I didn't care what they thought. I wanted to make him stay. I couldn't let him leave again, walk out of my life as he had once before.

'Tomorrow. Let me see you tomorrow,' I said.

He didn't speak, nor look at me, again taking out his watch and studying it.

'It wouldn't be proper that you come to the Zenana Mission.' I waited. Still he said nothing. 'Can I come to where you're staying?'

There was no mistake in what I was asking. He didn't immediately agree or disagree, but finally looked into my face.

'Let me come to you, Kai,' I said, softly. 'Please.' I hated my voice. I thought of the way I'd spoken to the Colonel. But this time, even though I used the same small, pleading voice, there was a horrid thread of desperation in it.

He looked away, over my head. 'I don't know, Pree. This job requires all my concentration. I can't—'

I put my hand on his arm. 'Please,' I said, in that same

voice. 'Tell me you can see me. Tomorrow afternoon. I can't leave the house after nightfall.'

His tic had returned.

I put more pressure on his arm, and he looked down at my hand.

'I'm staying at a *haveli* down the street.' He spoke as if he were telling me we should have tea and cake again. 'The door to the courtyard is painted turquoise.'

'All right,' I whispered, although I'm not sure why. 'I'll come at one o'clock,' I said, and left Kai standing there, his watch still in his hand.

I returned to the mission house, putting away my medical bag and then going to the sitting room. Aimee was there with her opened Bible. She could read English, very painstakingly.

'Come, help me, Pree. I am finding stories for the children,' she said, and I sat at the table beside her.

'Anjum's rash is now fine?' she asked, and I looked at her for just a second too long.

'Oh. Yes, yes. Well,' I said, hesitating, thinking about tomorrow. 'Not completely. I'll check on her again. Tomorrow afternoon.'

'Listen. Is good for children, this one?' She slowly laboured through a passage. I watched her bent head. Suddenly she stopped. 'Something is wrong for you, Pree?' she asked, without looking up.

'No. Why?'

She kept her head bent over the page. 'You are making tapping, always tapping.'

I curled my fingers. 'I'm sorry,' I said.

I visited Abdur Jan's *haveli* in the morning, although I reported to Helena that I was going to another *haveli* in the morning, and Abdur Jan's in the afternoon. As soon as I arrived I was summoned to the women's quarters, where I checked on the oldest wife, complaining of abdominal pain with excessive wind. After determining she'd eaten a great number of dried apricots the evening before, I gave her a mixture of bitters and water and told her to chew cardamom seeds and fast for the rest of the day. How would I pass the day until one o'clock?

I went to the children's area and played with them in a distracted manner, teaching them a little poem. I helped give them their midday meal. And finally it was time for me to leave. I hurried down the stairs. As I opened the door, Aimee stood there.

'Pree? What you do?'

'Aimee. I told you . . . I was coming here. I didn't expect you.'

'You tell me you come afternoon. So I join you.'

'I've already attended to the first wife,' I said, perhaps too loudly. 'She had stomach pains.'

'Anjum is well now? Her rash is no more?

'Yes,' I said, licking my lips.

'Where you go now?'

'I . . . to another zenana,' I told her.

'Which?'

I just looked at her, unable to summon another lie, and then turned, leaving her standing in the doorway, and hurried down the street. As soon as I was out of her sight I hailed a tonga; I didn't want to waste time walking. It was a hot, windy June afternoon; my hair whipped around my face where it had escaped from my bonnet.

The tonga let me out at the turquoise door.

When I entered the courtyard, Kai was waiting.

He simply looked at me for a long moment, and I was unable to say a word, even a greeting. My mouth trembled with nerves and anticipation.

I followed him through the square courtyard lined on all four sides with doors and windows. We climbed up wooden steps to the second floor; one of the doors in a row was ajar. He pushed it open and allowed me to pass in front of him. Once inside he closed the door and turned to me.

I wiped the sweat from my face with my gloved hand. The window that opened to the courtyard let in the sunlight. The room was large and pleasant, with only the necessities. There was a wide charpoy with a carved chest beside it, and on it was an open book and a fine-nibbed steel pen and bottle of ink. There were hooks on the wall, hung with Kai's clothing, and in one corner a large saddlebag, its flap flung back. Against one wall was a low rectangular table of the same carved wood of the chest, holding a lamp, an earthenware jug, beaded with moisture, and two cups.

'It's simple, but suits my needs,' he said. 'Would you like some water?' he asked, and I nodded, my heart thudding. I wanted to be here. This was Kai. It would be all right.

We both drank a cup of water. I handed him back the cup, letting my fingers touch his. My chest was rising and falling; I couldn't slow my breathing.

Kai set the cups on the table and turned back to me. He just looked at me, and I at him, and then I went to him, unable to be still any longer. I put my arms around him.

'I've missed you for so long,' I said, within his arms. My head was against his chest. I could hear his heart. 'You're the only person I have in this world.'

His heart thudded more loudly. 'Pree. I should tell you—'

'No.' I sensed he would say something I didn't want to hear, and lifted my head and kissed his lips. I didn't want him to say anything right now. He carried so many secrets. Why would he try to divulge one of them now? I didn't want this moment spoiled. I opened my lips, slightly, putting more pressure on his.

He returned the pressure, but then drew away, although his arms were still around me.

This wasn't how it should be. He shouldn't be able to stop; he should want me more than anything. Again, I thought of the Colonel.

'Don't you want me?' I whispered, as I had once whispered to Eddie. Why did I keep thinking about the other men?

'It's not that,' he said.

'What is it, then? Don't you . . . you care about me, Kai. I know you do.'

'Of course I care about you,' he said, pushing back my hair and looking into my eyes. 'But . . .'

'There's nothing to stop us,' I said.

'Nothing?' he asked.

Suddenly I was ashamed. 'Do you think me . . .' I couldn't think of a good description. *Like your mother?* 'Immoral? For wanting to be with you?'

He smiled, but it was a hard smile. 'I'm hardly one to speak of morality.'

Then I understood, and felt myself go limp. I stepped away and sat on the charpoy; it must have been newly restrung, for it remained firm under me. How could I have been so blind? How could I not have seen what was wrong? 'Do you already have a woman?' I asked. 'Are you in love with someone?'

He didn't answer for a moment, looking at the window behind me. 'I don't have one particular woman, Pree. But I've known many.'

I don't know what I wanted to hear. What would hurt more: that he was already in love with someone, and wanted to be true to her, or that he randomly took women, immodest, loose women, who offered themselves to him? As I was doing now.

How *could* he want me? I had so recently denied being

like his mother. I'd denied it as if insulted, and yet . . . look at me now.

Who was I? And who was he?

He was still staring out of the window. Of course he had known many women. Did I really believe he thought of me as I'd thought of him all these years? He'd said and done nothing to make me think otherwise. Disappointed and ashamed, I lowered my head. It was all going wrong. It was not as I had imagined it would be.

But as I sat there, anger rapidly replaced the overwhelming sensation of self-pity. How dare he not think of me? I dropped my hands and stared up at him. 'And you have never loved? Even one of these *many* women?' I couldn't stop my mocking tone.

He shook his head.

'Then we're the same,' I said, my voice loud and sure. 'For I've never felt anything close to love. For any man at all.'

There was silence. Unexpectedly he knelt in front of me. 'I'm sorry, Pree. My mind is . . . I'm sorry I'm so distracted.' He smiled and held my hands. 'How could any man not want to be with you?'

I looked at him from under my lashes. 'Do you, then?'

He looked tired, with the tic in his cheekbone, his hair slightly tousled. 'I'm sorry,' he said again. 'I'm sorry for being so clumsy about this. I can't explain it to you, Pree. But it has nothing to do with you.'

'I know,' I said, standing and pulling him up. Again I put my cheek against his chest. 'It's all right. I know.' I didn't know, but it felt like the right thing to say. I ran my hands up and down his back, slowly. 'I know,' I whispered, and he leaned his cheek against my head and sighed. I don't know if it was a sigh of weariness or of pleasure.

'Your hair still has its wonderful wild smell,' he suddenly

said, and those few words, letting me know he did think of holding me in the past, was all I needed.

'Don't think about anything now,' I murmured, standing on my toes so that my mouth was against his neck. I remembered his pulse under my lips once before; now I kissed that beating thread. 'Don't think about anything,' I repeated, and he pressed against me.

I was seducing him, as I'd seduced the Colonel.

Except this time I was doing it because I wanted to be close to him. To know what it felt like to belong to someone. Maybe to feel something like love. Or maybe just to feel . . . something.

As he entered me he stopped, as the Colonel had. But this was for another reason: this time it was because, as I had said earlier, there truly was nothing to stop him. Now he knew the truth.

I held my breath and opened my eyes, looking up at him. But his eyes were closed, and in the next instant he continued.

As we moved together, I let myself float. Not like that other time, when I'd left my body because I couldn't bear the sensations. This time it was a choice, this time it felt right. I let myself go.

Here was someone who knew me, knew more about me than anyone else, knew how I had been shaped, for hadn't he been shaped with the same minds, the same hands, the same soft strokes and hard slaps? He had lived my life; he had grown up at the mission with the same people. He understood. Kai was, I knew with certainty, what I needed. And I could give him what he needed.

I saw myself these last years: a swooping, directionless kite with a tattered string, held by no one. The string was brittle and dangerous with sparkling shards of glass, ready to cut anyone who would touch it. I had sailed aimlessly, sometimes dipping disastrously close to peril – to treetops and parapets, minarets and domed temples.

But here was Kai, my own Kai. And by holding me, with no concern for the glued glass, he had stopped my mindless dancing on the wind. Kai pulled me from the sky, and brought me back to earth.

It was as if I touched ground again, torn but whole, and I was home. And I knew he must surely feel the same way.

Afterwards, as we lay quietly, my head on his shoulder, I told him, 'You're the only man I've ever wanted.'

I turned my head to see his face. He opened his mouth as if to speak, then closed it.

He would say the same to me. He would say he'd wanted me in the same way. 'What, Kai?' I prompted. 'What were you going to say?'

He waited a moment. 'I'm the only one you wanted, but I'm not the only man you've had.'

I looked at the ceiling, not wanting to see his face as I spoke, knowing I had to tell him the truth. The Deuteronomy scripture came unbidden to me: *If, however, the charge is true and no proof of the girl's virginity can be found, she shall be brought to the door of her father's house and there the men of her town shall stone her to death.*

Kai was still, his arm around me. 'It was only once,' I said.

'He took you against your will? At the mission? One of the men there?' His voice was low, and filled with emotion, and this moved me, for I heard the sadness.

And how I longed to sink into his sad voice, say yes, yes, I tried to fight him, but he violated me. It would be so much easier, and Kai would understand, and would offer sympathy.

But I had lived too many lies for too long. I couldn't – wouldn't – lie to Kai now. I twisted myself so that we faced each other.

'No.' I sat up, and his arm fell away. He watched my lips. 'But it wasn't out of any feeling, Kai. I did it for . . .' Could I say the words? Could I say I did it for money? That I did prostitute myself, like your mother? 'I needed to get away from the mission. I had nothing, no one. You know that.'

He still just watched me.

'The . . .' I wouldn't say his name, 'the man gave me enough money to leave. There was no other choice. I could stay at the mission with your mother, and be used by not only him, but by many men, as your mother hoped would happen, so she could benefit, or I could lie with that one man so that I could have freedom.'

'So you took money for freedom,' he said.

'Yes. I chose freedom over a life of imprisonment. I made the choice, Kai.' I studied his face. 'Are you disappointed in me? Do you despise me for this choice?'

He sat up too, blocking the light from the window. Now his face was in shadow again, but I knew mine was lit. 'Do you, Kai? Please tell me you—'

'I have no right to judge your choice,' he interrupted, his voice even. 'I often doubt my own.'

I wanted him to say something more, something about his feelings for me. I wanted him to come to me again. But he only said, 'Lie down. Rest for a bit before you leave,' and turned on his side.

I watched his back expand and contract as he breathed.

And even though I had felt, only a short time earlier, that everything was perfect, that I was perfect, and that all would be perfect from now on, that Kai would know he had to have me in his life . . . Now, as I watched his back, those feelings were already fading.

CHAPTER FORTY

KAI WAS SLEEPING when I got dressed. The shadows in the room were lengthening, and I knew I had to be back at the house for dinner. I leaned down to kiss his cheek before I left, and he stirred and looked at me.

'You're going?'

'I have to. I'll be late.'

'All right,' he said, sitting up and running his hands through his hair. He picked up his pocket watch from the chest beside the bed and looked at it, then rose. 'I have to go, too.'

'Where do you have to be?' I asked, as he pulled on his trousers and shirt. He picked up one boot.

'You should go, Pree,' he said, in a distracted manner, looking around for the other.

'But . . . will I see you tomorrow?'

He reached under the charpoy, pulling out the missing boot. 'Tomorrow?' he pushed his foot into it. 'I can't be sure.'

'Not sure? But you're not leaving Peshawar right away,' I said, my voice rising. 'Not now. Not after—'

'No. No, I won't leave without telling you.' He came to me then, and cupped my face and kissed my lips, but rather quickly. 'I'm glad you came here today, Pree. Thank you.'

Thank you? He said it as if I'd brought him his clean laundry.

'You're lovely,' he added, smiling as he took his hands from my face, but somehow that made it worse. He was dismissing me.

'So . . . will I see you tomorrow, then?' I asked again.

'I hope so. I hope so, Pree,' he said. 'I'll be in touch. I'll send word to the Zenana Mission. A note. Can I do that?'

I nodded, unsure how this would be received. But there was no other way. I would deal with Helena.

There was nothing more for me to say or do. I smiled brightly at him, although all the light, the joy I'd felt as we'd held each other had fled. I left and made my way back to the mission house, arriving just as dinner was being served.

I slipped into my place at the table. Aimee looked at me, but was strangely quiet through dinner. I was glad; considering what had just happened I didn't want to have to chat about unimportant matters. I only wanted to go to my bed and lie there, going over every detail, pulling apart what had happened and looking at each piece.

But when the meal was over and I started to my room Helena stepped in front of me. 'Could I see you, in the sitting room?' she asked, and her tone worried me. I followed her down the hall. Two little boys were playing with tops on the sitting-room floor.

'Run along,' Helena said, holding open the door, and the children took their tops and left. 'Please sit down,' she said. I sensed she knew what I'd been doing; how could she know? Did I appear different? Was my sin written on my face?

'Where were you this afternoon, Pree?' she asked, sitting closely beside me as she had when I'd first arrived in Peshawar. 'Aimee told me you changed your plans; you had been at Abdur Jan's *haveli*, but then you left.'

I looked into her open face.

'When she went to some of the other zenanas, no one had

seen you. She told me this because she was afraid something had happened to you.'

She waited, pointedly, for my response. Had Aimee mentioned seeing me with Kai?

'I . . . I spent time with an old friend. From my childhood. I ran into him – actually at *Haveli* Abdur Jan – the other day. And so this afternoon we went for tea. And talked. I don't know where the time went.'

I hated myself. Helena was so trusting. I knew that there were only two rules of the house. Charitable actions towards the others, and no immoral behaviour. I had been here less than a year and had already broken the latter. Maybe both. I hadn't been particularly charitable to Aimee these last few days, annoyed by her questions and her presence. I tried to keep my face natural, but surely I looked guilty.

She studied me for another moment. 'Please inform someone if you're not going to be where you're expected,' she said. 'Naturally we worry if someone disappears for hours.'

I nodded. 'Of course. I'm sorry,' I said, meaning it. Yes, I meant that I was sorry. But would I see Kai again? Would I go to his bed? Yes.

I didn't sleep well that night. My body had been awakened, and I wanted to be with Kai again. I couldn't stop thinking about his touch on me, and how right it had felt. How we had fitted together as I knew we would.

But I also couldn't stop worrying that Helena might discover the truth. If she did, I would no longer be welcome in the Peshawar Zenana Mission. But if that happened, if I was turned out of the house, Kai would be there for me. It was because of him I was taking these chances on losing my home and my work.

Did I, perhaps in some deep, unspoken way, want to be

turned out so that I could be with him? He couldn't — wouldn't — abandon me now.

When he was finished whatever work he'd come to Peshawar to do, he wouldn't be as distracted. And now that we had been together, he had to keep me near him. I had given myself to him, and he had taken me. That was like a promise, wasn't it?

I sat up, staring at the window. For one terrible moment, Glory and my father came to my mind. How each fulfilled a need for the other.

Then I lay down again. What was I thinking? I was nothing like Glory, and Kai nothing like my — his — father. This was different. I thought of the future I wanted: Kai and I, together. Our own family. We would have children, wouldn't we? I kept my eyes tightly shut, creating the scenes — the made-up stories — that always came to me so easily when I let them. I did not think about the realities, about what untold work so preoccupied Kai, about his moving about India, and how that would affect our lives.

I kept my dreams happy and fanciful. They were only dreams, after all.

The next morning I didn't want to leave the zenana, hoping for the promised note from Kai. I took as long as possible helping with the breakfast dishes, washing out some clothing, and acting as though these things were important. But by twelve, when no word had come and we'd finished our midday meal, Helena told Aimee and I to be on our rounds to the zenanas. I knew Helena had instructed her to stay with me, and I was irritated with both of them. I tried to ignore Aimee's endless chatter as we manoeuvred through the busy streets. The lanes and alleys were even more congested than usual, and men stood in clusters, discussing the latest act of revolt. Two British diplomats from Calcutta had been murdered. They had been on their way to Kabul to meet with Afghanistan's king, Sher Ali, and had scheduled to stay a few days in Peshawar first.

'So terrible,' Aimee now said. 'Always one man wanting what is another man having. Too much greedy. People must listen to God. Hindu gods, Allah, Christian God, saying goodness and mercy. Why men are not listening?'

I glanced at her. In spite of the horrors she'd lived through, she was still so naïve.

As we visited two zenanas I worked as usual, talking to various women and children, helping with small ailments while Aimee tried to draw them into religious discussions.

As we walked towards the third zenana, I stopped. 'You go ahead, Aimee. I'll come a bit later.' I didn't look at her.

'No. Today I go with you, Pree. Helena says,' she said, slowly.

I hurried ahead of her, not caring that it was difficult for her to walk as quickly as I could.

We stayed for over an hour in the children's quarters of the next zenana. Aimee showed the children little painted tracts of Jesus as a baby in his mother's arms and then on a donkey, riding through the canopy of palms. I sat beside her, but couldn't concentrate, and was silent. I fidgeted, wanting to leave, to go to the courtyard with the turquoise door.

'What's wrong, Pree?' Aimee finally asked, when the children were called to eat and we were preparing to leave. 'You are being different now. Something is not the same. When you come to house first time, we all see you are not being happy. But some time pass and you are finding happiness. You smile, laugh. But now . . .'

We were walking down the stairs. I stopped, my shoulders sagging. Aimee's face – the side still whole – showed such concern. Again I was reminded of what a good person she was. Unlike me. 'I'm sorry, Aimee,' I said. 'I can't explain. I have things on my mind.' I sounded like Kai now.

'I have to speak Hindi, Pree,' she said, slipping into her own language. 'I can't say what I need to say in English. Do you feel that you're lost again?'

'What do you mean?' I turned and stared at her. 'What do you mean, lost?' I repeated. For one moment I wondered if I had called out in my sleep, talking about my past.

'Don't be angry at me, Pree. But Helena said you seemed like a lost soul when you arrived. And that's how you're acting again.' She put her hand on my arm. 'I was lost, and the man who called me Aimee saved me. And then Helena took me in. There are always kind, good people, if you let them come to you. There are those who care about you, Pree,' she said. 'Especially God. He cares about you the most. He's always looking down on you, watching you. He sees everything.'

I shut my eyes, one hand over them. I didn't want to think about God watching me, seeing what I'd been doing.

'So although you may feel lost, you're not. You're loved by God, and by me, Pree. You're loved as we love the children here, and want them to also know God's love. You've always been a Christian, so God has loved you ever since you were a little child.'

My eyes still closed, I had a sudden fleeting image of myself as a child, running about the mission, playing as any child might play.

And in that dim stairway, suddenly something lifted, as surely as if I were an ox with the yoke taken from my neck.

Since Glory had told me the story of my coming to the mission, I had felt cheated, filled with confusion and rage that I had been lied to. At times I hated the Fincastles for their deception. And for the first time since that terrible afternoon at the mission, watching Glory's beaten face as she lisped out the story of my unknown background, I thought of what might have become of me had the Fincastles not taken me in. Had not cared for me as if I were their own.

'Pree?'

I took my hand from my eyes.

'What's wrong? You . . . are you crying?'

Startled, I shook my head and brushed at my cheeks, surprised to find them wet. 'You made me think of something. From my own childhood,' I said.

Aimee nodded grimly. 'It was not being so good.' She had switched back to English. 'You know to suffer. I know you are having many sad memories.'

This surprised me. Had my uncertainty and resentment, tied to the new discovery and also to my behaviour with the Colonel, been so evident to everyone, then? Was I so transparent? 'No. I can't really call it unhappy. Not when I was young.' I stared at her, knowing what she'd suffered, and I was filled with shame. 'In spite of many things I don't like to think about, I was loved, Aimee,' I said. 'In the only way the people who raised me could love me, they did.'

She started down the stairs again, and I walked beside her. 'Helena says, always, we must be loving the children. Helena is saying to me that love is like food. We taste it. We see it and smell it and touch it. We are learning it when we are small, small, so small. If we do not learn it, we cannot know it when we are old. If we do not know it, we cannot take it, or give it.' She nodded, agreeing with herself. 'We teach to love. First for God, and then for people.'

I listened to Aimee, surprised. I'd thought of her as uninformed about the world only this morning, but now she was proving she indeed knew how to heal through the gospel. She'd shaken me from my self-absorption – over Kai, and over what I'd thought of as a catastrophic, sham of an upbringing.

531

I put my arm around her shoulders. 'Thank you, Aimee.'

She smiled, although as if to herself.

We made our way home. Aimee's words had brought me comfort for a while, but as I lay in bed that night the same fears returned.

Kai hadn't sent the note he'd promised.

The second and third day went by with no word from Kai. Helena didn't allow me to go out; she said it was my turn for cleaning in the house, and kept me busy with one chore after another. Every time I heard the front door open, or voices, I stopped, hoping it was word from Kai. Even Kai himself. He knew where I lived. As each hour went by the painful knot in my stomach grew tighter.

How had this happened? Why hadn't he contacted me? As I scrubbed the floors I played everything out in my head, over and over, alternating between sadness and anger.

I had given myself to Kai too freely. I knew that. I had forced myself upon him, even when he made it clear he didn't feel it was right. I thought not of the gentleness of his hands as he touched me, nor of the few endearments he whispered, but of the surprise on his face as he entered me. Or was it surprise? Maybe it was disgust. Now I couldn't remember clearly, couldn't re-create his expression, or even his face above mine.

Those days were endless, and I could barely eat. I tossed at night in the hot air, sure now that Kai had left Peshawar.

And again I was ashamed of myself, and grew more and more angry.

It was Monday. I had last seen – and been – with Kai on Thursday afternoon. Finally Helena let me go on zenana rounds, but again Aimee came with me. We went first to the *haveli* of Abdur Jan.

Anjum came to me and I picked her up. On impulse, I buried my face in her neck, smelling her warm baby smell, feeling the satiny skin. Thinking of Adriana, Kai's sister.

'Come,' Aimee said, holding out her arms, and I put Anjum into them. Aimee sat then, with Anjum in her lap, and combed through her hair.

'Do you remember the man you sang the song to, Anjum?' I asked. 'The Maypole Song?'

She nodded.

'Has he come again? Have you seen him?' I was sickened that I was so desperate that I would question a small child.

'*Ji-nahi,*' Anjum said, shaking her head and tilting it in my direction.

Aimee gently but firmly turned the child's head forward again, continuing with the comb. But then she stopped, and looked at me as if waiting for me to say something.

'He . . . he was a very dear old friend, Aimee,' I said. 'The man you saw, last week. I've known him all my life.'

She nodded. 'He lives Peshawar?'

'No. I was surprised to see him. I haven't seen him for a long time.'

'And now you want see him more?'

I didn't know how to answer. Helena had made it clear we couldn't be involved with a man. I said nothing.

'Maybe the old friend – he is already leaving Peshawar,' Aimee said. Her voice was emotionless as she resumed combing.

'Miss Aimee-*ji*,' Anjum complained in a high voice. 'You're hurting.'

Aimee lifted the comb from Anjum's hair and stared at me with a strange expression. Anjum turned her little face to me as well. 'You are his . . . ' Aimee stopped. 'Special friend?' she said in Hindi. 'His confidante?'

Although she wouldn't speak of it, I saw she sensed that

533

Kai was more than an old friend. Did she even suspect what had happened between us?

'I've finished, Anjum,' she said, reverting, as I did, to Urdu to speak to the child. She got to her feet, taking the little girl's hand. 'We will go to the courtyard and feed the peacocks. I have a lovely story to tell you.'

'But not the big papa peacock, Miss Aimee. He's nasty.'

'Yes,' Aimee said to her, not looking at me, 'we must be careful. You never know when you will be bitten unexpectedly.' Was she thinking of her dead husband, bitten by the snake? Or something else?

Aimee and Anjum left me, standing alone in the middle of the children's playroom, while the chimes tinkled in the afternoon breeze.

I hurried down the street to the turquoise door. Thankfully it was unlocked, and I went through the courtyard and up the stairs to Kai's room. I listened and then knocked, although no sound came from within.

I pushed open the door, my stomach churning with anxiety. What if his belongings were gone?

There were no clothes on the hooks. The room appeared unoccupied ... but no. His bulging saddlebag was in the corner. I exhaled; I'd been holding my breath. He was still in Peshawar, then. The charpoy was neatly made; I saw a bright wink from beneath it. Stooping, I pulled out Kai's pocket watch.

The gold held no warmth; it had obviously been on the floor for some time. I clicked it open. It had stopped at seven fifty-three. It was impossible to know when it had last been wound.

I set it on the chest beside the bed and left. As I was crossing the courtyard, a thin, elderly woman came from the largest of the arched doorways. Her lower face was veiled.

'You've come again?' she asked in Urdu, raising her chin at Kai's door. So she had seen me when I was here the previous week.

'Yes,' I said. 'But he's not there.'

'I know.'

I stepped closer. 'Do you know where Kai is?'

'I don't know anyone named Kai. But the man renting this room was taken away on Thursday evening. They came here, and pulled him from the room. I'm not pleased. This isn't good for my business.'

My mouth opened. I stared at the large, bristling mole on her temple. 'Taken away? What do you mean? Taken where?'

The woman's eyebrows rose as if surprised by my question. 'Where the soldiers take everyone they arrest for political reasons. To the prison at the Bala Hisar Fort.'

'Prison? He's been taken to prison? But why?'

'How would I know? I only know that I saw men – the English soldiers – tie him, and throw him into a cart.'

I clapped my hand on my chest; suddenly my heart was pounding in such a frenzy that I could barely breathe. I turned to rush off. But the woman pulled on the back of my frock. 'He hasn't paid for his room this week. It was due yesterday.'

I looked at her. What was she talking about?

She put out her hand, palm up. 'Pay me. For your man. I have given you the information you asked, and put up with your sneaking about here,' she said. 'I know everything that goes on in my establishment.' She waggled her fingers in a beckoning movement. 'Come. I need my payment for the room. And his food.'

I dug into my reticule and put some of my annas into her hand. She looked down and nodded, and something in that nod made me realise I'd given her more than she expected.

'And take his bag. I need the room for another paying guest.'

'I . . . I'll come back for it later,' I said. 'Later.' I ran out into the lane and then to the main street, hailing a tonga and climbing in, directing the driver to take me to the Bala Hisar.

CHAPTER FORTY-ONE

I T TOOK TWENTY MINUTES for the trotting horse to take me to the Bala Hisar on the outskirts of the city. I jumped out and joined the milling throng gathered around the outer walls of the fort. Many were laughing, chatting. I saw a tea-seller with his brass samovar and tray of cups. I pushed through the crowd, wondering what they were doing here, finally coming up against a ginger-haired man in English garb.

'What's going on? Why are there so many people here?' I asked. I had taken a ride along the road with some of the other women before, past the Bala Hisar, but the previous times I had passed it was quiet, with only a few guards outside the main doors. Today it had the feel of a bazaar.

'They're here for the hanging,' the man said, distracted, looking over my head.

I grabbed his lapel. 'Hanging? Today?'

He was pale, unshaven, his topi slightly tilted to one side. 'Pardon me, madam,' he said, looking down at my hand on his lapel, frowning.

I removed my hand.

'The hanging, who are they hanging? Have they done it yet?' He studied me for a fraction longer, then his eyelids lowered and his jaw tightened. 'No, ma'am. You haven't missed anything.' His voice was harsh, cold. 'You have arrived in time to see it all.'

I wondered at his tone, his expression, and then, in a flush, realised. 'I'm not here for sport, sir. I . . . I'm looking for someone. A friend.'

'In this crowd?' He again looked over my head; I couldn't see any other English people. 'Who might your friend be?'

'No.' Suddenly my face was twitching. I put my hands to my cheeks to still them. 'Not in the crowd. He's in the prison. But . . . I have to see, to know . . .'

At this the man closed his eyes for a second. 'I'm sorry. I'm distraught. A chap I know will meet the noose today. He deserted,' he said, and I was suddenly reminded of my father, the way he made such calm, ludicrous statements in the midst of utter chaos. 'He's the only Englishman dying today. I hope it's not your friend. Did he desert from the army?'

I shook my head. 'No. And he isn't English,' I said, knowing while this was a half-truth, that even when dressed as one, Kai could never pass as an Englishman.

The man's expression altered again, slightly. 'In that case, there are two others – natives – scheduled for today. They list the names on the outer gate.' He pointed somewhere behind me.

I nodded, then turned and forced my way back through the crowd. Trembling, I stood in front of the main entrance to the fort. Underneath an inscription in marble on one of the arched gates, a paper was nailed into the wood. I ran my finger over the unknown English name, Martin Sinclair, and then those written in Urdu: Kavinder Singh, who would be a Sikh, and the other, with its Persian Christian name – Nusli – and the Gujarathi surname of Tata, perhaps a Parsee. Dryly swallowing, I leaned against the splintered wood of the door.

A gunshot echoed – obviously a signal – for the crowd roared and surged forward. The gates opened, and I was caught in the crowd, and pushed along with it. 'No,' I shouted, turning against the mob and trying to fight my way back, out of the fort, but there were hundreds of people, both men and women, some surely come to mourn for those soon to be dead, and others to simply enjoy the spectacle. I was caught in their midst, as helpless as a fish attempting to swim upstream against the force of a sweeping current.

We finally stopped in a huge courtyard, across from the gallows. The men were already being brought out, shuffling awkwardly, their ankles shackled and their hands tied behind their backs. The soldiers prodded them with the barrels of their muskets. Although I could not make out the men's faces from this distance, it was obvious that none of the three resembled Kai in height or body shape or posture. Yes, I'd read the names, and yet still, at this moment, I was strangely relieved that I could actually see with my own eyes that Kai was not among the condemned.

What had he done? Why had he been brought here?

The Englishman wore a filthy, torn white shirt and army trousers and boots. The Sikh had lost his turban, and his thick topknot of hair had come unwound, and hung to his lower back. The third man still wore his round white cap.

The shouts and cries of the crowd quietened to murmurs, and then silence. In the still, hot air, nobody coughed or shifted. High above, circling in the burnt white sky, were two vultures. I watched them, their huge wings motionless as they glided round and round, as if they, too, were curious spectators, waiting to view this horrific scene. Or perhaps waiting for something more. I thought of the Parsee Tower of Silence in Bombay: how the vultures waited for the bodies left there, exposed to the elements in the Zoroastrian way.

The men's ankles were released and they were led up the stairs to the gallows, where three nooses hung. I hadn't expected it to take place with such suddenness. What *had* I expected? Surely something, some announcement, some prayer . . . but no, it would happen now, all at once. Rough burlap sacks were pulled over the men's heads.

I couldn't watch, couldn't stand and be part of it. I turned my head, closing my eyes and covering my ears with my hands as the thick looped ropes were placed around the men's necks. No. I had to leave. I tried again to push my way through the crowd, but it was too thick, an impenetrable wall of unsmiling men and covered women.

I pulled on the arms blocking my way, murmuring *please, please move, please let me through* in Hindi and Urdu and Punjabi and Persian and Pashto and English, please, please, in all the languages I knew, and yet none would let me pass. Was it because I was in my English clothes, and one of the men being hanged was English, that these people wanted me to stay, to watch? Suddenly every face I looked into was hostile, glowering, and for the very first time in my life, I felt an outsider in my own country. I wanted the comfort of a veil, a *burka*, to hide my naked face, to cover me from the stares. My breath came faster and my body was wet with sweat. For one horrible moment I felt it was I who stood on those gallows, helpless and afraid. So afraid.

And in the midst of that moment there was a terrible whoosh and thud of the bodies dropping, and then a second, sly rustle which I knew, instinctively, was the upward jerk. Now I covered my face with my hands, my mouth open under my palms, trying to breathe. Long minutes passed silently under the cruel sun; I could only imagine the dancing toes and twitching torsos as the nooses completed the act. And finally the crowd let out a collective sigh; it was done. Yet still I was trapped, and as the throng surged forward – did they intend to go even closer to the gallows? – to avoid being knocked down and trampled I was forced to turn in the same direction. Hot breath was on my neck, the pressure of a male body against my back. My arms were trapped at my sides by a tall bearded Sikh on one side and a stocky woman in a dun-coloured *burka* on the other. I couldn't even raise my hands to cover my face again. Instead I stood, wide eyed, watching as the bodies were cut down and wrapped in torn burlap. They were dumped on to a pyre of dry sticks. A flaming torch touched the burlap of the first wrapped body, and ran in a merry frenzy until it reached the second. I was completely unable to look away now. It was as if my eyes were lidless, staring, mesmerised by the flames as the bodies caught fire and burned. I felt as if the heat blew across the courtyard, scorching my naked eyeballs. I thought of the young wife committing sati, so long ago in Lahore, and the peculiar accepting slump of her body. I thought of my mother in the throes of her insanity, burning herself alive with my father's body. And I thought of Aimee, running, her flesh and hair aflame, from the death intended for her. I watched the sighing flames eagerly lap at the tangled bodies in their pitiful, coarse shrouds. I knew the Englishman would have no grave in one of the cemeteries, and there would be no place for family and friends to sorrow for him. I knew that the soul of the Parsee would not find its peace. He was not placed on a Tower of Silence as his religion demanded, and suddenly I was weeping.

My shoulders shook as I cried over the deaths of these unknown men. I didn't know what they'd done to deserve this fate, but I wept over their wasted futures. I sobbed as the crowd broke into mindless cheering, hating them all for their misguided thrill-seeking, although I understood. I knew that for these few moments their own lives held even the smallest of promises, because they still possessed a life, no matter how painful.

And I wondered how I had come to be here. This was not how I had imagined my life to unfold.

★ ★ ★

When the crowd dispersed, I had to lean against a wall for a few minutes. Finally my legs no longer quivered, and I went to one of the English soldiers who stood guard.

'I would like to enquire about a man being held in prison,' I said. My voice came out a dry croak. I thought of the vultures again.

'Go to the warden's office, ma'am,' he said, still staring straight ahead, his lips barely moving as he stood motionless, his musket at his side.

I looked around the massive courtyard.

'To your left, ma'am,' he told me.

I found the office with its title on the wooden door, a soldier stationed outside. 'I'd like to speak to the warden,' I told him.

'Your business, ma'am?'

'To enquire about one of the prisoners.'

He nodded and went inside. In a moment he returned, and gestured for me to enter. A man in uniform, with only a ring of thin grey hair, sat behind an oval desk. He rose; he was shorter than I. He bent, slightly, from the waist, in a parody of a bow. 'Yes, ma'am. Captain Gimble, at your service. How may I help you?'

'I need to find out about someone who is reportedly here.'

'The name? Have a seat, please.' He sat down and pulled a book towards him and opened it, then looked up at me. 'English or Eurasian?'

'Eurasian.'

He studied me for a moment, and for some reason this irritated me. He turned to another section of the book, flipping through pages with what felt like agonising slowness. I could barely keep still. I clutched my bag tightly in both hands.

'All right, then,' he said, when he reached the page he was looking for. 'The name?'

'da Silva. Kai da Silva.'

He ran his finger down the page, his lips moving.

'There's no prisoner by that name here.'

I sat back. The old woman hadn't known what she was talking about. I actually smiled at Captain Gimble. 'That's a relief. He's not here after all. Well,' I said, rising.

Captain Gimble closed the book and also stood. 'What made you think he was here?'

'Somebody told me . . . he's been . . . missing, since, I suppose, Thursday, and—'

His face changed. 'Since Thursday?'

'Yes,' I said.

'And he's a Eurasian? Or native?'

'Eurasian,' I insisted.

'You say his name is da Silva. Are you sure of that?'

I smiled again, shaking my head slightly. 'Of course. Do you think I wouldn't know my friend's name?' My smile faded as I finished the sentence. The old woman hadn't recognised Kai's name. 'Why?'

'In the last ten days only two men have been arrested. Natives, brought in on Thursday night.'

I swallowed. 'I see.' I looked down at my bag, clutched in my hands. 'Can you tell me their names?' What did I expect to hear?

'Yes.'

I looked at him, assuming Captain Gimble would open the book again, but he didn't. He stared into my face as he listed them. 'One was Sanat Patel. The other one goes only by the name Pavit. Both of them were brought . . . what is it?'

'I . . . I do recognise one of the names,' I said, feeling behind me for the chair. I sat down. 'Of course, it's not an uncommon name. Pavit.'

Captain Gimble sat as well. 'But you said you were looking for a Eurasian. These men gave their status as native.'

'Did he – did you see him?'

'I see all the new prisoners.'

'Did he have green eyes?'

Captain Gimble frowned. 'I'm not in the habit of studying their features.'

'If this is the man I'm looking for you would have noticed them. They're a very pale green.'

He watched my face, then closed the book. 'I suppose I did take note of that. Yes. The taller one had green eyes.'

I swallowed, breathing deeply. 'I'm sure it's him.'

'What is your relationship to the prisoner?' Captain Gimble asked now.

'Relationship? I'm his friend.'

The man's lids lowered, just the slightest, and I hated him for what his expression insinuated. Even though it was true.

'What's he been accused of?' I asked.

'You do know that all of the men held here have committed some kind of treason, or offences of a political nature? But their cases are not open to public inquiry.'

'But can I see him? Will there be some sort of trial?'

'Trial?' Captain Gimble gently explored his bald patch with his fingertips, as if feeling for something hidden beneath the shining flesh. 'Are you new to Peshawar?' he asked.

'Well, yes. Fairly new. But I don't know why—'

'If you were more familiar with our city, and our justice system, you'd know that we don't hold much with trials here, ma'am. Especially not for natives accused of crimes against the British. Your friend has a former record of wrongdoing under this Pavit name. Who knows what else he may have been arrested for in other cities, under other names? But we have enough on him to be assured he won't cause any more trouble.' He stood, as if our meeting was over.

I stayed where I was, struggling to hold on to my dignity, to make this man see that I was a woman who expected – no,

544

demanded – an explanation. I would not be dismissed easily.

'How – what can I do – to help him?'

'I would think he's beyond help. The bugger doesn't deserve to live.' He didn't apologise for his uncalled-for language, and I knew he used it purposely, as an insult.

'What do you mean?' I kept my voice steady, confident. I didn't blink as I stared at him.

He stepped around his desk, obviously annoyed, possibly angry now. 'We supply water and straw for bedding to the natives. The rest – food, clean clothing, blankets – is up to their families and friends. Those with nobody to care for them have to rely on the generosity of the others in their cell.'

I still hadn't moved, looking at him as he stood beside me. 'Yes, yes, I can do that. I can bring him what he needs. But how can I help to have him released? Or at least to see that he gets a fair trial? There's been a terrible mistake, surely. I'm certain there's a logical explanation for—'

Captain Gimble's face grew darker. 'That's all I can do for you, ma'am.'

'When can I come to see him?'

'The schedule at the fort is hangings on the last Monday of every month. Visiting the prisoners is allowed every Thursday, from ten until twelve. The guards in the native section are also native, and must be paid to gain entry. And now I have other duties.' He walked past me and held open the door. 'Ma'am,' he said, coldly, and I had no choice then but to walk through the door and across the courtyard.

I wouldn't look at the smoking pyre. The stink of what the fire had consumed hung thick in the air. I held my gloved hand over my nose and mouth, although my mouth filled with sour saliva, and I wanted to spit it out, spit out the taste of what I had seen and heard today.

* * *

By the time I returned to the mission house, having gone to collect Kai's saddlebag, dinner was over. Helena was waiting for me; as I passed the sitting-room door she called my name, and I went in and took the chair across from her.

'I'm sorry, Pree,' she said, looking at the saddlebag I set beside my chair. 'This won't do. I've told you . . .' her voice faded, and I knew this was difficult for her. I was ashamed for putting her in this situation, and yet . . . surely she would understand. 'It's the other women, of course. There are rules, you know that, Pree. We've discussed your behaviour, but you . . . I'd made it clear that you weren't to go off on your own.' Again she looked at the saddlebag.

I didn't speak.

'I thought you liked being here,' she said, not angrily, just sadly, disappointed. 'You appeared pleased to help in the zenanas.' She shook her head. 'And you provided such a needed service to the women and children. You fit in well with the others here. Why have you jeopardised all of this?'

I remained silent. I didn't know what I could tell her, what she'd believe or not believe. I had proven myself untrustworthy.

'It's the young man Aimee saw you with at the zenana, isn't it? You've been seeing him?'

Finally I nodded. 'But . . . I've just come from Bala Hisar.'

She frowned. 'Why on earth—'

'He's been imprisoned.'

'For what?'

I licked my lips. 'He's innocent, Helena. He would never—'

'For what?' she repeated.

'I don't know. They wouldn't tell me. But whatever they say he's done, it's a mistake. I know him, Helena. I've known him since I was a child.'

She waited. I spoke with certainty, and I wanted to believe

546

what I told her. And yet I couldn't help but put pieces together. Kai's obvious veiled reaction to my questions on what he did, and why he was in Peshawar. The tell-tale signs of anxiety. And of course Captain Gimble's words: that Kai had formerly been in trouble with authorities in Peshawar. And possibly elsewhere.

Everything from the past came swooping in. I knew what kind of man Kai was; I always had. He was full of anger and resentment − towards his mother, his father, towards authority. He wanted to right what he saw as wrong, refusing to accept colonial rule, fighting the repression of the natives.

He was passionate and brave and desperate. He would fight for what he believed in; he had no time to waste on his own needs. To allow anyone in.

This was why he moved me. And this was why I couldn't reach him.

'In any case,' Helena said, interrupting my thoughts, 'I don't know what's to be done, Pree. It's not only that you've been involved, in secrecy, with this man, but also that he has a questionable character. This gives me such pain, Pree. I recognise in you that you are different to the other women, although you are all tied together through the common thread of painful memories. That much I know about you, although I don't know what those memories are. But Pree, you put me in a terrible situation. By allowing you to stay it may appear to the other women that I'm condoning the very behaviour the mission is so against. I must—'

I jumped up. 'I understand the position I've put you in, Helena. But please. Just let me try to help him. What if they hang him, Helena? I can't let him die. I know it's not fair to beg you to allow me to stay. But please. All I ask is that I can remain here long enough to try to save his life. And you, Helena,' I went on, knowing I was being unfair to her, knowing her deep kindness, her own suffering, her

sentiment, 'you . . . you understand losing someone you love.'
I had never spoken the word love in connection with Kai.
Had I even thought it? I hadn't allowed myself to. 'And so I
need to stay here while I find a way to help him.'

She sat perfectly still. I knew what a terrible predicament
I was creating for her. 'And once he's free,' I said, because I
couldn't bear to think of anything else, 'I'll leave here – the
mission, and Peshawar – with him.' The words tumbled from
my lips so easily, even though I knew it might be a lie. A lie,
or just my hope, spoken aloud for the first time, like the word
love. 'But for now I have nowhere to go.' The silence
stretched. 'Helena?' I finally said.

Her face was pale and strained in the fall of evening light
from the windows behind her. 'If I allow you to stay for a
brief while, you can do no further work in the zenanas. You
cannot represent us as a woman who works for the Lord. You
will remain here, indoors, except when you are . . . doing
what you must to help this man, who obviously means so
much to you. And he'll marry you, if he is freed?'

I knew this was the only way Helena could think. I had
no answer. I rose and went to her, taking her hands in mine.
'Thank you, Helena. Thank you. You don't know what—'

She stood. 'All right. But don't speak of this to anyone. It
could ruin the good name I've worked so hard to procure for
this house. Say nothing to anyone.'

I nodded. 'Of course not.'

CHAPTER FORTY-TWO

THAT NIGHT, MY curtain pulled for privacy and a lamp glowing beside my bed, I took Kai's saddlebag from under my bed where I had hidden it, not wanting Aimee or Rohana to see it. I looked through it, not to be invasive with his private belongings, but hoping to uncover something. I told myself I was looking for a clue as to what he might have done, but perhaps I was looking for an understanding as to who Kai really was.

There were books in both English and Urdu on political matters of India, as well as a few rolled maps. I spread one on my bed; it was of northern India, with markings – crosses and stars – at various points. In a tin box there were pens and ink. As I pulled at a shirt to feel under it, it was strangely heavy. When I put both hands into the saddlebag to grasp it, I found the shirt was wrapped around something: a beautifully carved hinged box of sandalwood. Putting the box in my lap, I ran my fingers over the impressions on the lid, and then opened it.

There was a Bible, a small calfskin edition. In the front of it was written, in my father's spidery hand, *To Kai, On the occasion of Christmas of 1862.* That would have been the Christmas when Kai was alone, at thirteen. Next I picked up a bundle of strips of cloth, dyed red. It took me a moment to recognise what they were: the Maypole ribbons. There was a folded, faded paper kite I had made and given to Kai when I was eight or nine; I remember how long I had worked on it, melting yellow wax in designs over the rough brown paper.

There was a tiny smocked dress of white cotton: Adriana had worn this in her first month.

I sat quietly. It was a box of memories; precious memories from Kai's past. Memories of the man who was his father, the man who would never acknowledge his son. Of the woman who had given Kai the only nurturing in his life. Of me, when I was, to him, the little sister. And of the true, tiny lost sister.

Tears came to my eyes. Could a man who carried these meaningful memories about with him really be capable of wrongdoings serious enough to have him hanged? Could he really deny that he wanted and needed no one in his life?

And then my fingers grazed what I thought was the red silk lining of the box, but it was loose. I pulled it out. It held something; perhaps this was a memory of Glory? Surely he would have something of her.

But inside was only a strip of blanket, soft and white. In green thread, embroidered along the bottom edge, were the letters PRI. The rest of the blanket was torn, the fine wool hanging like twisted spider threads.

I ran my fingers over the letters, the beginning of my name. This would have been my blanket, then. I put it to my face, wondering if it would bring back a memory. I thought of my mother's fingers – the only mother I'd known – thick and calloused, clumsy with needle and thread. She could never have perfected this fine work. Even when I sewed Lalasa's wound – my very first stitches on flesh – I knew they were superior to hers. My mother could not have knitted this blanket with needles thin as the legs of a little house swallow, and embroidered it so painstakingly, the length of each stitch matching precisely. It was surely a prized work of patience and love. Who had made this for me? Why had only this one corner survived? I ran my fingers over and over the letters, as if to draw knowledge from them, to encourage them to speak to me.

I worked non-stop in the house for the next two days, cleaning and cooking and helping to care for the children. I was biding my time, albeit often so anxious that I could barely breathe, until Thursday: visiting day at Bala Hisar.

Nobody treated me any differently, although a few of the women glanced my way when they didn't think I noticed. Aimee and Rohana hardly spoke to me. What had Helena told them? I didn't really care; I was lost in my own thoughts. I knew I couldn't help Kai until I spoke to him on Thursday, and determined what I could do. Did anyone else in Peshawar know what had happened to him? Did Abdur Jan? If not, who was bringing him food? What was he eating?

By sunrise on Thursday I was wide awake. I helped prepare breakfast and waited on the other women, serving them. When the house finally grew quiet, with most of the women except for those on household duties away for the day, I finished my last chore and hurried to my room. I wrapped Kai's clean clothes from his saddlebag in the blanket from my bed, went to the courtyard kitchen and packed a woven basket with a jug of water and as much food as I could carry, and then set off for Bala Hisar.

I paid the guard at the entry to the prison, and waited while he opened the blanket and dug through the clean clothes with his dirty hands. He then opened the basket, having the nerve to lift it to his nose and smell the food, then slammed the lid shut and gave it back to me.

I followed him past those imprisoned behind thick bars on the ground floor; surely their crimes were light, and I hoped Kai would be among them. From their appearance I sensed they had been here some time. They walked in aimless circles or lay on the scattered straw with blank looks of despair, many coughing, all gaunt, some wracked by disease or simple starvation. In another room, this one larger and with no straw on the ground, older men sat in a circle. Dull light came from a high window, and the men were hunched over a round of wool, working with needles. As I passed I saw that the emerging elaborate patterns were replicas of Safavid carpets. Many of these ancient, original Persian carpets covered the floors of the wealthy *havelis*.

These would be reproductions; I knew they were much desired by the British in England now. Even in the dim light I saw the beauty of the jail rugs, and watched the top of the filthy turbans or caps of the men bent over them. After years of this some must surely go blind. I pitied them, but comparing them to the younger men I'd seen only moments before, I realised these were the lucky ones. They had a purpose, however slight and not their choice, and a sense of purpose must lift the despair of emptiness, of simply waiting. To eventually be released, or to die.

I followed the jailer deeper, down wet stone steps; although the June sun outside was hot, in this far depth there was no natural light or warmth, and the chilled dampness was palpable. I forced myself to stare straight ahead, breathing through a slight parting of my lips. But I couldn't escape the smells, the moans and cries and the endless deep, rattling coughing that was surely consumptive.

My instinct was to gag, to raise a hand to my nose and mouth in an effort to not smell the odours of despair and dying. The prison at Bala Hisar was Dante's underworld.

The jailer led me forward, to a cell on the end wall. There were perhaps fifteen men crowded into this small, barred room, the dirt floor covered with putrid straw. There were three other people standing at the bars, talking quietly with those they had come to visit: one woman in Hindu dress, and two men, both Muslim.

The woman wept into her hands; the man on the other side of the bars simply stood there, his own hands hanging loosely at his sides.

From the length of their matted hair and beards, I knew many of these men had been here a long, long time.

I took my place before the bars, wanting to see Kai and yet afraid of what I would find. My heart was pounding. No one spoke; did they not have the energy, or did they simply choose to remain lost in their thoughts? Some leaned against the damp walls, some crouched, some lay wrapped in blankets in the chill, their bodies taking on the shape of desolation. And then one of the men crouching in the shadows rose, stood still and looked at me, and the rapid, anxious beating of my heart increased even further.

As he came out of the darkness and towards me, I saw that Kai had changed since I had last seen him. It had been exactly a week, and yet already his chin was sharper, his cheekbones standing more prominent. His eyes, even in the gloom, burned – was it fever, or simply the intensity of all that had happened to him? A look came over his face. What was it? Relief? Joy? I couldn't tell. He came to me.

'I . . . I didn't think anyone . . .' Then I realised it had been shock on his face. 'How did you know I was here?'

'I went to your room. The woman there said you'd been brought here.' I passed the blanket containing his clothes through the bars and pulled the jug of water and wrapped food from the basket, handing them to him as well.

He took it all in a distracted manner, putting the blanket under his arm and the jug and food on the floor between his feet.

'I only discovered on Monday that you were here, Kai. And I wasn't allowed to come until—'

He put one hand to his temple, grimacing. His fingers which I had known intimately so recently – long and slender, the nails now rimmed with dirt – were so dear I longed to reach through the bars and grab them. I shocked myself by thinking of them on my breasts. That I would think of such a thing at this moment . . .

'What can I do, Kai?' I didn't ask what he'd been accused of. And I didn't ask why he was using Pavit's name.

He lowered his hand and stepped closer. His eyes were rimmed with pink, and the green irises muddied with no light reflecting on them. 'There is one man who can have me set free,' he said, so low I had to incline my head towards his to hear him.

'Abdur Jan?'

'No.' He reached through the bars and took my hand. His dirty thumb ran, slowly, up and down the back of my hand. His hand was hot, so hot. It was a fever, then, as I'd suspected from his eyes. What if I never felt his hands upon my body again? I had to close my eyes for a moment.

'You must drink as much water as possible,' I whispered back. 'You're ill, Kai.'

'Yes, yes,' he said, distractedly. 'There isn't much time. You must listen. You're the only person who can do what needs to be done. Some of these men wait years before anyone cares enough to move their fate forward. But in my case . . . you must understand. They won't give me another chance. I'm sure the authorities would be happy to see me meet the noose as soon as possible. I've used all my chances, Pree.'

I thought of the circling vultures with their cruel, curved beaks. 'I'll do whatever you ask,' I said.

'There may not be a great amount of time.'

'Tell me. Tell me what to do.'

'Find David Ingram.'

'David Ingram? Who is he?'

He studied my face. 'I don't know if he's in Peshawar right now. If he is, he can be found at the translation offices of the Administrative building. In the English cantonment. Go there and speak to him, as soon as you leave here. Tell him what's happened.'

The guard behind us barked a command, and Kai let go of my hand and stepped back.

'Go now,' he said. 'Don't waste any time.'

'All right. But you said . . . what if this man — David Ingram — isn't in Peshawar?'

Kai stared at me. 'Then there's no hope for me.'

'I'll go to him immediately. And I'll come again, next Thursday, Kai, with more food, and clothing.'

His eyes studied mine, then my nose, my mouth. 'Goodbye, Pree,' he said. 'Thank you.'

For one second I was chilled. He said it exactly as he had after making love to me, only a week ago.

'There's nobody else who knows I'm here,' he said, for the second time. 'I had no hope. But now . . .'

I nodded. His future depended on me, and I depended on him for my future.

Kai opened his mouth as if to say something more, but a man stepped beside him, leaning his face close to the bars, closing his eyes and raising his chin, a look of concentration on his face as his shoulder touched Kai's. Kai turned from me, pushing the man beside him away with his elbow, and leaned down to pick up the food and water, keeping his balance with one hand on the bars.

I turned and walked away. Later, I realised the unknown man hadn't been trying to take Kai's food. He had been breathing deeply in my direction, hoping for a trace of fragrance, perhaps to remind him of a woman he had once held.

★ ★ ★

I couldn't go straight to the office Kai had told me about; I had to present myself to the unknown Mr Ingram in the best light. I was dirtied by the prison, the hem of my frock filthy and malodorous from dragging on the unspeakable, putrid leavings of the prison floors. Back at the mission I hurriedly dressed in my best frock and bonnet, sorry that my only clean gloves had a slight tear in the stitching over the thumb.

I took a tonga to the English cantonment and went to the Administration building, as Kai had instructed. Once inside I found the double doors with *Translation* written on the glass in black script. I pushed through them, finding myself in a central office with a high counter. Around the main area there were a number of other doors, each with a name on a glass panel. Behind the counter were two square desks: a young man sat at one and a young woman at another. The man was tall and thin, with straight brown hair and a rather shabby tweed suit. The woman wore a nondescript grey frock; her pale brown hair was styled in an unbecoming manner, held back with decorative combs so tightly that her slightly bulging forehead appeared even higher. They were laughing over something, but when I stepped in they stopped.

I went to the counter. 'Good day,' I said.

The man – Mr Hooper, I read from the rectangular brass plate propped on his desk – came to the counter. 'May I help you?' No longer smiling, his face had a chilly expression; his voice matched.

'I would like to see Mr Ingram. Immediately,' I added.

Mr Hooper looked at my collar. I reached up and patted down the curled end; it must have flipped up in the breeze. I licked my lips; I was thirsty, both from the heat and from anxiety.

'Do you have an appointment?' he asked.

'An appointment? No.'

He raised his eyebrows and looked over his shoulder at the

woman. She raised hers in return. 'And what is the nature of your call?' he asked.

I stared into his face. 'It's imperative that I see him immediately. It's of a personal nature. And very urgent.'

'Personal?' he asked, slightly frowning.

'Yes,' I said, louder than necessary, for he was directly before me. 'Could I speak with him now, please?'

'Have a seat.' He didn't ask my name, nor was his voice particularly courteous. 'He's in, but not available just now. You may wait.'

I sat on the edge of a chair in a line of hard wooden chairs, smoothing my skirt over my knees, and then joining my gloved hands in my lap, keeping my left thumb over the tiny hole in the thumb of the right. I looked at the glass doors, and read Mr Ingram's name on one of them.

Mr Hooper took his seat again, turning his back to me and facing the woman – Miss Wells, I read – at the desk behind his.

He talked to her in quiet tones, and she looked around him, at me, and nodded at whatever he said.

'Will Mr Ingram see me?' I called. 'As I've said, it's very urg—'

'When he's free,' Mr Hooper answered, looking over his shoulder as if annoyed. He turned back to Miss Wells, murmured something, and again, she looked at me.

Something in her expression made me stand and say, very courteously, 'My name is Miss Priscilla Fincastle, and I have come to see Mr Ingram on a matter of life and death.' I knew I was being melodramatic, but I needed to impress on this man and woman how important it was. And it truly was life and death. I tried not to think of Kai in that stinking cell. I had never before called myself Priscilla, but at that moment I felt it carried more dignity than Pree. 'I simply can't sit here waiting.'

'Miss Priscilla Fincastle, is it?' the woman repeated, then leaned forward and whispered something to the man. I heard the words *hill woman*.

Suddenly, by her expression and the whispered comment, I was back in Mrs Wyndham's drawing room in Lahore, sitting beside the perfect Eleanor, holding my breath at the full and humiliating realisation of how my mother and I appeared. But in that same instant I realised I no longer cared, for I was no longer *that* Pree Fincastle. Too much had happened to me since then. I really didn't know who I was, but what I did know with certainty was that women like Miss Wells could no longer make me feel inferior.

And I had more important things to worry about than what she or Mr Hooper thought of me.

I went to the counter. I was frightened for Kai, and angry that I was so powerless to help him at this moment. I felt that the very blood running through my veins was popping and sputtering, threatening to burst from the intense heat in the office and my unbearable impatience and worry. Still, although they both glanced at me, they did not rise or speak to me. I straightened my bodice and stepped around the counter. It gave me a thump of pleasure to see Miss Wells sit back in her chair, to notice her thin throat constrict as she swallowed.

'See here, there's no one allowed behind the counter,' Mr Hooper said, standing and facing me as if to block my progress.

I ignored him, stepping to one side so that Miss Wells could also see me. 'I'm sure that your superior – Mr Ingram – will not appreciate it when – if – I mention how thoughtlessly I was treated while I waited to speak to him,' I now said. 'And Miss Wells?' I forced a small, pleasant smile on to my mouth. 'Is there something you wish to say to me, or to ask me?'

Miss Wells shook her head, her own lips uncertain now. 'Oh, no. No, Miss Fincastle.'

'I thought I heard you refer to me as a hill woman.' I tilted my head, quizzically, as I looked at her.

'Oh, surely you misheard—'

'I have perfect hearing, and your voice carried clearly, as you wished it to. Was this meant as an insult?'

Now Miss Wells looked at Mr Hooper, who glanced up at me and then, clearing his throat, picked up a stack of papers and tapped them together on the desk as if to straighten them, even though they were already perfectly aligned. 'I'm sure there's no need for any upset, Miss Fincastle,' he said.

Miss Wells was silent now, although her cheeks were slightly stained with pink.

'We naturally see a number of hill women,' Mr Hooper went on, 'coming down the Khyber Pass with their men. Quite striking, many with Aryan features, and a carriage that's very dignified.' He spoke quickly, nodding at me the whole while. 'They can walk for days, carrying heavy loads; they appear tireless, and have been said to display a moral fibre which could match that of any man. Not that . . . I mean . . .' his words faded.

I had kept the smile fixed in place while he hurried on.

'I have lived in India my entire life. I am the daughter of missionaries from Lahore,' I said. 'And I have lived here, in Peshawar, for almost a year. It is not necessary for description. I am fully cognizant of hill women.'

Miss Wells stared at me, her neck now splotched with colour.

I stared back at her, lifting my eyebrows slightly, as if waiting for a further comment.

But she bent her head over the paper in front of her, and immediately the air was filled with the exaggerated scraping of her nib.

'And now, Mr Hooper, if you don't allow me to see Mr Ingram, I will simply go into his office myself. It really is *most* urgent.' I turned, keeping my back very straight, and walked towards the door with Mr Ingram's name printed on it.

I heard Mr Hooper's hurried footsteps behind me, and knew he would try to prevent me, but the door opened as I approached it.

I stopped, and heard Mr Hooper stop as well.

A man stood there. He stared at me, unspeaking. He was perhaps in his forties, tall and broad of shoulder. His eyes and eyebrows were very dark, although his hair did not have quite the same depth. It was more chestnut coloured, thick, and rather long, falling in a slightly untended manner over his collar. One of his collar stays was missing. Even from a few feet away, the stubble on his cheeks and chin was apparent. He had obviously spent much of his life under India's sun; lines fanned from the corner of his eyes and were deep around his mouth. He was in distinct contrast to the very well-groomed, although rather prim, Mr Hooper.

And his face was strangely familiar, although I couldn't think of where I may have seen him in Peshawar.

I went to him, aware of Mr Hooper and Miss Wells watching. 'Mr Ingram,' I said. 'My name is Miss Fincastle.' I extended my hand. I was sorry it was my right glove which had the tiny rent, and surprised I would even think of such a trivial matter when I was here with such drastic purpose.

But Mr Ingram didn't seem to notice my glove, or even my hand. He simply continued to stand as if rooted to the spot, looking at me.

I lowered my hand. 'I'm sorry to present myself without an appointment. But may we go into your office? I have a matter of utmost urgency to speak to you about.'

He stepped back, allowing me to pass him. Once we were

inside he closed the door but didn't speak; he simply stood there with his hand on the handle.

Was this the man who could help Kai?

'Please, do have a seat,' he finally said, his voice cultured.

I sat on the chair in front of the desk. He went behind the desk and sat as well, then immediately stood again. He appeared nervous; looking away from me, then back. I needed to tell him about Kai as quickly as possible. I'd wasted enough time changing my clothing and then having to wait in the front office with Mr Hooper and Miss Wells.

He went to a narrow table under the window, where a heavy crystal water jug, surrounded by four matching glasses, sat on a silver tray. His hands shook, and the jug clinked against the edge of the glass; water spilled on to the gleaming surface of the tray.

'Would you care for some water?' he asked. What was wrong with him? I had every reason to be anxious; I hadn't had a peaceful moment since I'd found out about Kai on Monday. But what was this man's excuse?

'Yes please, sir,' I said, trying not to show my impatience.

He brought me the glass, the water vibrating because of the tremor in his hand. I suddenly thought of Mrs Lang, and her shakiness when she needed the drink, and hoped Mr Ingram did not share her addiction.

I thanked him, and after I drank I held the half-full glass in my hands. Mr Ingram had returned to the seat across from me. His water glass was on the desk in front of him, untouched. He watched me with an unreadable expression. It almost appeared he was fearful of what I might say.

'It's Kai, Mr Ingram. Kai da Silva. He has sent me to you, to help him.'

Mr Ingram rose again, his face losing some of its tightness. 'Kai? You're here about Kai? What's happened? He's here, in Peshawar? I only just returned a few days ago. I've been

561

working in the Calcutta office for the last eight months. What's happened?' he repeated.

'He's been arrested,' I said, setting the glass on the desk and leaning forward. 'I've just been to see him at the Bala Hisar. I . . . I'm not sure of the reason for his incarceration. But he implied, as did the warden, that . . . is it true? Could they hang him, with no trial?'

Mr Ingram had gone pale. I suddenly saw the line of an old scar, from the bridge of his nose, down under his eye, to his cheekbone. It had been well stitched, I thought, to leave a scar slender as a spider's web. His mouth was a firm, straight line. He didn't speak.

'Could they?'

He blinked as if suddenly awakening. 'Um . . . I'm sorry. Could they what?'

'Could they hang him without any sort of trial? He said you could help him, Mr Ingram. That I was to come to you immediately. *Can* you help him?' I asked, trying not to sound desperate. But I was desperate. And he was the only one I could turn to.

'I . . . I must think about it. The best way to deal with this. I'll have to . . .' He brushed back his hair with one hand, clearly distressed. His hand surprised me. It had a number of scars, and there was no fingernail on his index finger. It did not look like the hand of a man who used a pen for a living. He lowered his hand and looked into my eyes.

Again, I had the unsettling feeling that I'd seen him somewhere before today.

'Of course. I'll do all I can. What a mess.' He shook his head. 'Kai,' he said, the word hard, angry. 'I warned him so often . . .' He stopped.

'He's going by the name Pavit,' I said.

He nodded as if he already knew this fact.

'I'm not sure why he's taken on a false name,' I said,

although of course I knew why. And it wasn't encouraging. It was a guilty thing to do, wasn't it, to hide one's true identity? I stood. 'Thank you, Mr Ingram. I live at the Peshawar Zenana Mission.'

'Ah,' he said. 'Of course.'

Of course? Did I look so much like a Bible woman?

'You can contact me there. I'll anxiously await to hear from you. If there's some course of action I can take, anything, please, I want to do something.'

He nodded. 'Yes, yes.' He came around from his desk. 'How long have you been in Peshawar, Pr—' He stopped.

I narrowed my eyes. 'I've been here almost a year. Have we met before, Mr Ingram?'

He didn't answer for a moment, then looked away, saying, 'I'll contact you at the mission, as soon as I have some news.'

I held out my hand again. 'Thank you. We must get Kai out of that terrible place.'

This time Mr Ingram took my hand. He glanced down at it, and I pulled away, not wanting him to see the hole in my glove.

'Yes,' he said. 'We must.'

CHAPTER FORTY-THREE

I DIDN'T HEAR FROM Mr Ingram for the next few days. I expected something, possibly a note, telling me his plans, or what he had been doing to help have Kai released. But there was nothing. I could barely eat, and found it difficult to sleep, worrying about Kai, knowing I was unable to go and visit him until Thursday. And it had grown evermore strained in the house. Obviously Helena had said something to the women about me not going out to the zenanas, and although nobody spoke of anything but the usual small daily details when I was present, I sensed they were talking about me, watching me.

After four days I went back to the Translation Office, unable to wait any longer, but Mr Hooper – this time a little more civil – informed me that Mr Ingram wasn't available; he wasn't at the office.

I whirled to look at his closed door. 'He hasn't left Peshawar, has he?' I asked, holding down the panic that came over me at the thought.

'No, no. He's simply out of the office today. I'm sure he'll return tomorrow.'

I could only hope his absence had something to do with Kai. It must have; surely he cared about Kai. Wasn't his strained expression when I spoke to him about Kai's arrest proof of that? Miss Wells hadn't looked in my direction at all, turning her chair so that her back was to me, shuffling through files in a wooden cabinet.

'Thank you,' I told Mr Hooper. 'Would you please inform him I was here, inquiring as to the business we discussed.'

'I will, Miss Fincastle,' he said. He was definitely treating me with more respect today.

Finally it was Thursday. There still had been no word from Mr Ingram. I took more food and another set of clean clothes to Kai.

When I arrived at his cell, hurrying along the putrid, dim stone passage behind the same guard, I found Kai lying against the wall, curled in a blanket. It wasn't the one I had brought for him; this one was thicker, with dark stripes. Even though he faced the bars, I couldn't see whether his eyes were open or shut. I was afraid to call out his name, not sure if using his real name would cause any more trouble, although I doubted that the filthy, coarse jailer standing behind me, jingling the coins I'd just given him, cared about anything more than collecting his money.

But one of the other men looked at me – was it the one who had put his face to the bars last week? – and nudged Kai in the leg with his foot. Kai sat up; I moved into his line of vision and he rose and came to me. He was unsteady, stumbling against another man, who growled and pushed him away.

He looked far more ill, his eyes glittering feverishly in his drawn face. 'Will it be soon? Will I be released soon?' he asked, without greeting me.

'Yes, surely, yes,' I said, handing him what I'd brought. 'Mr Ingram is doing all he can,' I said, hoping it was true.

Kai clutched the food and clothing against his chest. His whole body trembled, slightly, his teeth dancing against each other. 'What has he done? Who has he spoken to?'

'I . . . I don't know, Kai. I'm not certain,' I said. I didn't want to tell him I hadn't seen or heard from Mr Ingram all week.

'This isn't good, not good,' Kai murmured. 'I thought by now . . . what day is it?'

'It's Thursday, Kai. Visiting day.'

'Yes. Thursday.' He blinked heavily. 'How long have I been here?'

'Two weeks now.'

'Two weeks?'

He sounded surprised; I don't know whether he thought it had been a shorter or longer period. It was obvious he was losing touch with reality.

'Did you eat what I brought you last?' I asked.

'Eat?'

'The food. Did you eat it?' I worried that in his state someone would have taken it.

He looked down at what he held against his chest. 'He was here, last night, with me. He had another horse for me, he said. I told him I still had the last one he gave me. The dappled mare. She's a good and sturdy horse.'

'You must eat some of the food now, Kai,' I said, gently, worried at his state. 'Eat it, and then sleep.' There was no point in me staying. 'I'll come again. I'll come again, Kai,' I repeated. 'And we'll get you out of here. Mr Ingram and I. We'll get you out.'

'Yes. He said he'd be good to you. He would take care of you.'

He was simply rambling. 'Goodbye, Kai,' I said, and left. Before I turned the corner of the corridor, I glanced back. Kai was still standing at the bars, his lips moving in conversation with an unseen person.

I went back to the Translation Offices. This time Mr Ingram was in. He stood as Mr Hooper ushered me into his office.

'Well?' I said, not caring that I was behaving rudely. 'What

566

have you done? Why haven't you contacted me? I've just been to see Kai, and he's very ill.'

'I know,' he said.

'How do you know?'

'I saw him this morning as well.'

The blanket. 'Oh. But you can see why we must do something soon. He won't . . . he can't survive much longer in that state. He's desperately ill.'

Mr Ingram nodded. 'I have a plan in motion, Miss Fincastle,' he said. 'I simply can't talk about it until I'm sure that—'

'But I can help,' I said, speaking quickly. 'I'll say he was with me that night, or whenever he was supposedly committing the crime. I'll make a statement, whatever is needed, swearing I was with Kai, and that he couldn't have—'

'That isn't necessary, Miss Fincastle,' Mr Ingram said. 'It wouldn't be of use.'

We were looking at each other across the desk, both still standing. His tone, and the way he looked at me, suddenly shamed me. And I realised that my silly attempt would indeed be useless. Which of the men in power I might try to tell my story to would actually take me seriously, or believe me?

I stared at Mr Ingram. 'What is he guilty of, Mr Ingram? I should know.'

Mr Ingram sat down heavily, not waiting for me to sit first. 'Miss Fincastle. I'm doing all I can. Please believe that. I care deeply for Kai, and don't want him to come to any harm.' He sighed. 'I don't suppose there's need for any confidentiality, any mystery. Not with you.'

I sat down as well.

'I know you feel strongly about Kai,' he said. 'For so long he's been getting himself into serious . . . I was going to say scrapes, but his actions have become far more grave.' He picked up a small round globe that sat on a glass circle on his desk. Turning it in his hands, he said, 'Kai has long been involved in acts of rebellion against the British.'

Of course I knew this.

'There are a number of young Indian men engaged in these activities, travelling about the Punjab, distributing subversive literature, making notes on vulnerable areas, passing on word to those they consider higher authorities within their own group.'

I nodded.

Mr Ingram gently set the globe back on its glass circle and shook his head. 'He's too young to remember the destruction and havoc the Sepoy Uprising brought about . . . but there are always young men who . . .' He shook his head again. 'There is little purpose to his actions, Miss Fincastle. There can be no real outcome from what Kai is attempting – has been attempting – for a number of years. The British rule the Punjab. There is no Indian power that can effectively take back that rule. And yet there are always young men, hot headed, as young men are wont to be in every country, who are outraged, and who wish to change that which they won't admit is unchangeable. Kai has been involved in these insurgent activities since he was a very young man.'

'But he hasn't harmed anyone, has he?' I asked. That's what had been worrying me the most: that he'd been arrested for violence against a person or persons.

Mr Ingram looked back at the globe. 'Last year he was linked to explosives planted on the railway line outside Delhi. There were a number of important English government gentlemen coming in to Delhi from the south for a series of meetings. It was never proven that Kai was directly involved, but he and others were held for a number of months in gaol there.'

I waited a moment before speaking. 'But it wasn't proven, you said.'

Mr Ingram just looked at me then, and by his expression I knew that Kai wasn't innocent.

'Thankfully it was discovered before the train passed over the line,' he said. 'If the plan had been carried out, many, many people would have been killed or injured. But it's apparent to me now that Kai will not be stopped. I have long tried to tell him that he can do far more good for the country by directing his energies to more worthwhile projects, ones that can help the natives instead of destroying them in his attempts against the English.'

'But Kai is half English! His father was English,' I said, loudly, leaning towards Mr Ingram. He must know Kai was Eurasian. And yet Kai was taking on the role of a native. Ironic: his mother had tried, all her life, to deny her Indian heritage and embrace her Englishness, while her son did the opposite. 'His father was English,' I said again, more quietly.

Mr Ingram nodded. 'I am aware of that. And I believe that's the reason Kai has always been so filled with vengeance.'

I sat back. 'He told me when he left the mission the last time that he was going to work as a translator in Madras.'

Again, Mr Ingram was silent.

'He didn't?' I knew then that Kai had lied to me, even though Mr Ingram didn't answer. I thought back to the scribbled maps in his hut at the mission, so long ago. The clandestine work behind the sandal shop in Lahore, printing the paper filled with outrage and calls for rising up against the white powers that held back the natives.

'And this time . . .' he stopped. 'Did you hear of the most recent murders, Miss Fincastle? Of the British diplomats?'

I closed my eyes. If he was involved, surely Kai had only given orders. He didn't, couldn't, himself, carry out the—

'I was able to convince the authorities to have him released on my recognisance, the first time he was arrested here, in Peshawar,' Mr Ingram said, and I opened my eyes. 'He was, thankfully, foiled in those last efforts.'

I watched Mr Ingram's face.

'I know many people in Peshawar, and have worked in a number of capacities over the years. But he has shown me up. I gave my word he wouldn't cause any more trouble.'

There was silence then. I studied my hands, clenched in my lap, and then stood. 'Whatever he's done . . .' I said. 'You can't let them hang him. You can't.'

He rose as well. 'I'll do everything in my power to help him, however I can. And I'll contact you the moment I know something. I give you my word, Miss Fincastle,' he said.

'Thank you, Mr Ingram.'

I made a move to leave, but unexpectedly he asked, 'You enjoy your work within the zenanas? You're happy there?'

'Pardon me?'

'I . . . they do good work. The women there.'

'Yes,' I said, and walked to the door. I realised I had never asked Mr Ingram how he knew Kai, and turned with the question on my lips. But he had followed me so closely that he almost came up against me at my abrupt stop. Immediately he stepped back, and again, I was somehow vaguely troubled.

'You're sure we haven't met previously, Mr Ingram?' I asked.

He stepped even further away. A look came over his face, a deep frown, followed by a lifting of his eyebrows, as if he were arguing with himself, and then he said, 'Well. Not as you see me here, today.'

'What do you mean?'

'I was in different attire,' he said, and I studied him more closely. His height, the straight shoulders, the dark eyes.

'I knew you from the mission. Your mission, outside of Lahore.'

His answer was completely unexpected, and a rush of

dread filled me. My heart thudded. 'The mission?' I swallowed. 'Were you . . . were you formerly in the army, Mr Ingram?' I tried to breathe evenly. Had he been one of Glory's gentlemen callers?

He shook his head. 'No.'

'Did you know Glory da Silva, Kai's mother, in some . . . capacity?'

Again he shook his head, and I released my breath. 'Oh. Were you acquainted with my parents? The Reverend and Mrs Fincastle?' Even as I asked, I knew I would remember if he had come to visit us. But perhaps he lived in Lahore . . .

He shook his head. 'It's Kai. I've known Kai since he was about twelve years old.'

I studied him, but before understanding could dawn, he said, 'I sometimes came by. On a golden Arabian.'

My mouth opened. 'But . . .' I didn't want to say, *but that man was an Afghan.* This man standing in front of me looked like an Englishman − albeit a rather rough and grizzled Englishman − except for the eyes. And it was clear that English was the language he had first learned. He spoke with the deep plummy tones that I knew, by comparing his voice to those in Mrs Wyndham's drawing room, came from a certain breeding. The Afghan − my Afghan − had spoken Urdu. And yet . . . his eyes. They held the same intelligence. The same sadness.

'The last time was a number of years ago,' he said.

'Three,' I told him, nodding. Adriana had been an infant. 'I'm sorry. I didn't recognise you. But . . . I don't understand. Why . . .' It was too confusing.

'You look much the same,' he said, still studying me.

'I used to . . . I wondered, back then, before I knew certain . . . things, if you might be Kai's father, even though he assured me you weren't,' I said.

'He spoke the truth.'

'Yes. I know that now.'

'I'm Eurasian,' he said, although I'm not sure why he felt the need to tell me. Had he understood my earlier look of confusion? 'English and Afghan – of the Pushtun tribe. I was born here, in India, and educated in England.' He continued to look at me as if waiting for me to say something more.

I nodded. 'I see. But you're Christian?' I didn't really care; I simply asked because I was uncomfortable. There seemed little for us to discuss, and yet it appeared he wanted to speak to me further.

'I don't believe strongly in any one religion. Although my . . .' He stopped. 'The Persian poet Rumi wrote that there are hundreds of ways to kneel and kiss the ground.'

I nodded.

'I hope that's not shocking to you, as the daughter of missionaries, and a Bible woman. The fact I don't embrace one formal belief.'

'It's not my business what you choose to believe or not believe,' I said, and again started towards the door. It wasn't my business, and of no interest or consequence. But again I turned back. 'I'm sorry. But I can't hold my tongue any longer, Mr Ingram. Who are you to Kai? Why have you always had this interest in him?'

He wiped the back of his hand over his top lip; he was sweating.

Suddenly I wondered if I could trust him. If Kai could really trust him to help.

'As I said, I've known him for a long time. Since he was a boy.'

I thought of this man, dressed as an Afghan, on his horse on the Grand Trunk Road, or outside the mission fence, talking to Kai, letting me sit on his horse.

'But you didn't know his mother?' I asked again.

'No,' he said, and backed up, sitting on the chair I'd been on, moments before. His movement was sudden, heavy, as if a weakness had come over him, and he could no longer stand. For one horrible moment I was reminded of my father, and his attacks.

He put his hand over his eyes.

'Are you ill, sir? Shall I fetch someone? Mr Hooper?'

'No. It's best if you leave, Pree,' he said, and I studied his covered face. He had unthinkingly called me Pree.

I stood there for another moment, and then left, as he had asked.

It was enough to consider that Mr Ingram was the Afghan from the Grand Trunk Road; it was, in actuality, disturbing. But it was Kai I couldn't stop thinking about as I rode back to the mission house in a tonga: his flushed face, his frightening gauntness, the talk born of delirium. Either his fever would soon break, or . . .

I had only been back at the house an hour when one of the women brought me a message which had been delivered to the door. It was from Mr Ingram.

It is imperative that I speak to you, he had written. *Please come to my home this evening,* was all it said, followed by his name and directions to his house.

I didn't like it. What man summons a woman to call at his home at any time of day, let alone the evening? I realised how little I knew about him. Was he married? Did he have children? Simply put, he was strange, and did not fill me with any sense of security.

It was disrespectful to ask this of me, I thought, smoothing the paper. And yet of course he wished to speak to me about Kai, possibly some way I was needed to help. And in this I did understand Mr Ingram's need for privacy, secrecy.

'Helena,' I said, still holding the note as I went to her, 'it's about my friend, and helping him. I must go out this evening.'

'This evening? You know I don't allow—'

'Could I take someone with me? Aimee could come.' I was quite aware that the other women were already viewing me with veiled looks. But not Aimee. She made it clear she pitied my fretful state; I had confided to her that without my help the friend she had met might die. She had nodded, praying for me, aloud, every night, and even for Kai, although she never said his name.

'If she accompanies me, you would know that my visit contained nothing untoward, Helena. If I don't go, it may harm my friend's chances . . .'

She shook her head as if distraught over my request, but said, 'Well, ask Aimee, then. I'll give my permission for both of you. But you must take a tonga. Don't walk about in the dark. And you must return within two hours at the very most. You must. Do you understand, Pree?' She rubbed her temple. 'You have upset the calm of our house.'

'I know. I know, Helena. But thank you.'

'If Aimee doesn't want to go, you won't be allowed.'

'Yes, yes I know,' I said again, then hurried to find Aimee. I had no doubt she would help me.

I sent a note to Mr Ingram telling him I would arrive at seven o'clock.

Mr Ingram's home wasn't in the English cantonment, as I thought it might be. But of course, he was a Eurasian. I had to keep reminding myself of this: dressed as an Englishman, and, listening to his voice, it was easy to forget he was also of Afghan heritage.

He lived just outside the cantonment in a small, neat bungalow with a wide, pleasant verandah on which sat a pair of wicker rocking chairs with deep cushions. The garden in front of the house had a number of leafy *doda* trees – the Soap Nut tree, as the English called them. I smelled their slightly pungent yet soothing scent as soon as the tonga stopped in front of the house. He was waiting for us, standing on the verandah. But he wasn't dressed as I'd seen him the last two times; this time he wore Indian clothing: white cotton trousers, a long white shirt, and woven sandals. As Aimee and I stepped out of the tonga he came to the top step. I had expected him to have a bearer to greet us at the door and to usher us in. Even though not purely English, Eurasians such as Mr Ingram surely lived more in the English lifestyle.

'Thank you for coming,' he said, looking at Aimee.

'This is Miss Aimee. She will remain with me,' I told him in a firm voice. 'Aimee, may I present Mr Ingram.'

He made *namaste* to her. 'I am pleased to make your acquaintance, Miss Aimee.'

'Good evening, Mr Ingram,' she said.

'I realise, Miss Fincastle, that it was unfair of me to ask you to come to my residence. But I'm afraid I'm not thinking clearly just now,' he said. 'I've argued with myself since . . . I simply must speak to you. But I couldn't in the office. Not in the office,' he repeated. 'And I was quite certain men are not allowed at the Zenana Mission. Come in, please come in,' he said, and Aimee and I followed him into a small yet comfortable sitting room.

'What's happened? Is Kai all right?' I asked, standing in the middle of the room.

Mr Ingram looked at Aimee again, then back to me. 'There is no further news about Kai. Please, please have a seat, Miss Fincastle, Miss Aimee.'

At least he was calling me Miss Fincastle again, not Pree as he had, in the office.

If there was no news about Kai, why had he asked to see me? Perhaps to tell me of his relationship with him; maybe that would somehow help Kai's situation. I slowly lowered myself into a club chair. Aimee sat in one beside me, and Mr Ingram took his place on a leather settee, facing us both. The room was growing dim. I smelled cooked goat, and saffron. Where were his servants? A gentleman such as Mr Ingram would surely have a number of servants.

Suddenly, even with Aimee beside me, I didn't want to be sitting in the falling darkness with this man, who although he wasn't a complete stranger – hadn't I known him in my previous life? – was now someone else. All I knew about him with any certainty was that he knew Kai. The house was quiet, and even though it was tastefully furnished in a pleasing mixture of English and Indian design, there was no sign of a woman: no vases of flowers, no screen of half-worked tapestry or basket of needlework, no delicate touches.

'Are you married, Mr Ingram?'

'No. My . . . she died. Some time ago.'

'And you . . . you said you were English and Afghan.'

'Yes.'

'Does your mother live with you?' I assumed it was similar for Afghan sons as for Indian: that they support their mothers.

'No. She lives in England.'

'Oh,' I said, surprised. 'She went there with your father?'

'No, no,' he said, shaking his head. 'That's her home. She's English.'

Out of the corner of my eye I could see Aimee's head, moving back and forth between Mr Ingram and me as she followed our conversation.

'Your mother's English? But then it's your father who is an Afghan?'

He nodded. 'Not the conventional story.'

I studied him. How odd. I had never heard of an Englishwoman involved with a native man. It was always the other way round.

'But then my mother was never a conventional woman,' he added.

'And your father lives . . . there? Or here?'

'I never knew him. But he would have stayed in Afghanistan, from the little my mother ever said about him.'

'I see.' The silence stretched. 'You have no children?' I felt odd asking these personal questions, and yet he didn't seem prepared to speak of the reason he'd asked me to come. Perhaps it was Aimee's presence, but he was obviously uncomfortable.

'I live here on my own,' he said. 'Although I currently have a friend staying for a few days; he's on his way from Jalalabad – in Afghanistan – to the south.'

I wasn't really interested in Mr Ingram's life, but there was an air of something about him. I still wasn't sure I could trust him. The house was silent; if there had been servants I would have seen or heard them by now.

Was Aimee thinking the same thing as I? Something didn't feel right. We were alone with him, in the darkening evening.

I could hear my heart; surely the bodice of my frock fluttered with each pounding beat. I looked at Aimee. She was still watching Mr Ingram's face, her mouth slightly open.

I opened my own mouth. It was difficult to breathe.

My instinct told me to leave. And yet I didn't.

I knew, with certainly, that Mr Ingram was building up to telling me something. Something he thought I needed to know. And I was filled, not with anticipation, but with dread.

CHAPTER FORTY-FOUR

'COULD YOU LIGHT a lamp, please?' I asked, my voice slightly higher than normal. Mr Ingram immediately rose and lit the lamp on the table, and another on a bookshelf, a third on a desk, and as the dark corners of the room flooded with the soft light I breathed more easily. I glanced at the books on the shelf beside me; they were both Urdu and English. I could make out the titles of the ones nearest to me: *Selections From the Poetry of the Afghans from the Sixteenth to the Nineteenth Century.* Beside it was *The Gulistan-i-Roh: Afghan Poetry and Prose.*

'Do you like poetry, Miss Fincastle? I would be happy to lend you my copies; they're—'

'No thank you, Mr Ingram,' I said, annoyed that he'd watched me reading the titles. 'I only have a short time to be here. What is it you need to speak to me about?'

'May I offer either of you a beverage?' He was rubbing his hands together in an unconscious manner.

'No. Please.' I spoke for Aimee without caring. 'Just state what it is you need to tell me.'

'Would you mind if I have something?'

'Of course not.' I tried to keep the exasperation out of my voice. I wanted him to get on with it, whatever it was he had called me here to tell me, and was causing him definite discomfort. What would I learn about Kai?

He poured himself a drink from the bottle on the table

against the wall and returned to his chair. 'I really just wanted to talk to you about . . .' He stopped.

I could hear Aimee's breathing.

Mr Ingram took a drink, just a sip, but kept his hand around the glass, gripping it as if to keep himself anchored into his chair.

'Your life at the mission, with the Reverend and Mrs Fincastle,' he said. 'Your parents. It . . . was it a fulfilling life?'

Why was he asking about my past? 'My work in the infirmary was indeed fulfilling. I did medical work, as I do here.'

'Yes, yes,' he said.

Suddenly I wished I had accepted his offer of a drink. It was awkward, sitting like this. 'Perhaps, Mr Ingram,' I looked at Aimee, 'we would take a cooling drink after all.'

Aimee nodded.

He jumped up as if relieved. 'I have sherry, or—'

'Not spirits. Just water would—'

'Cordial? Lime cordial?' He appeared so eager.

'Yes, please,' Aimee said, and I nodded as well.

He filled two small stemmed glasses and brought them to us on a tray. As had happened in his office the first time I went to see him, his hands shook.

'Thank you,' I said, taking a glass. 'Really, Mr Ingram, what is it that you wish to speak about? Surely not my younger life.'

'It's rather delicate.' He didn't look at Aimee, but I knew he was referring to her presence.

'Aimee is my good friend. She knows about Kai. There's nothing you can't say in front of her.'

'It's not about Kai. Not exactly. It's more about the mission at Lahore, and you growing up there.'

I frowned. 'What of it? Why does it concern you?'

At that moment a man passed by the sitting room, coming

579

through the front door and down the hall. We all looked at him, although he didn't turn his head. It was apparent he was a Pushtun.

'That's the friend I spoke of. He's rather reclusive,' Mr Ingram said.

Now Aimee and I were alone in a house with two men.

'But we were speaking of your parents,' he said.

'We were?'

'Do they still live at the mission?'

I gripped the stem of my glass. 'No, Mr Ingram. They both were taken to the Lord. Almost two years ago.'

He raised his eyebrows. 'I see. I'm very sorry.'

I waited. Finally I said, 'Mr Ingram. What is all this about?'

'I will explain, Miss Fincastle. I'm trying to find a way to explain. They were . . . good, and loving parents to you?'

I frowned. 'I don't mean to be discourteous, Mr Ingram, but I don't understand why that would be any concern of yours.'

He drained his glass. 'I don't recall there being any orphans at the mission the times I came by. To see Kai.'

Again I frowned. 'No. There weren't.'

'Why is that, Miss Fincastle? Every other Christian mission I've known has taken in orphans. Brought them to Jesus, so to speak, taught them English and given them a cursory education.'

I kept my face expressionless. I didn't like the direction of the conversation. I had come here to find out about Kai, not to be questioned about my own life. Especially not questions like these. Suddenly I was very uncomfortable. 'I don't know with surety. But as a medical mission, I suppose my parents didn't think there was the time needed for the care and education of orphans.' I knew my voice made my impatience clear. 'Their work for the Lord was in healing. But . . . really, Mr Ingram, I don't understand the purpose of all of this. And

I'm growing . . . I'm sorry, but I've been allowed little time here.'

He put his glass to his lips, then pulled it away, seeming surprised that it was empty. 'I'm just confirming this for myself. There were no orphans at all? No foundlings?' He stared at me as he spoke, putting emphasis on the last word.

A drop of brilliant green fell to my skirt. I set the glass on the table and stood. 'If you have nothing to tell me about Kai, there's no reason for us to be here. Come, Aimee,' I said, and she obediently rose.

'No. Wait,' Mr Ingram said, jumping up. He looked so . . . hopeless, perhaps slightly desperate, standing in front of me, that I sat down again.

Aimee followed suit, sitting as well.

'May I tell you my story?' he said. 'Please? It's important.'

I looked at Aimee. 'Does it relate to Kai?'

'Please,' Mr Ingram said. 'Could you listen, for even a short while?'

Aimee was watching his face. 'I suppose so,' I said. 'Although we must return to the mission house within the hour.'

'Two years after the end of the uprising, in 1860,' Mr Ingram immediately began, sitting down, 'was a most terrible time in my life.'

From the look on his face, I wondered what sorrow he carried that distressed him so, even now. What had he seen? Or done? I remembered my mother's old, chilling story of Cawnpore. Looking as he did now, in his white clothing of fine cotton, his hair curling over his collar, Mr Ingram appeared a gentleman, and had a certain attractive appearance for an older man. But thinking back to how he had looked when I remembered him from the past, in a turban and the rough clothing and hard boots of a horseman, his skin burned by the sun and wind, astride the horse . . . had he played some role in the Sepoy Rebellion, the terrible time also referred to as *The Devil's Wind* by Europeans and *The Folly* by natives? He referred to it simply as the uprising. Was it not sorrow on his face, after all, but rather guilt?

'I had been living in India, but after the uprising I went to Afghanistan, into the hills, and lived on my own for quite some time. I became . . . I don't know how to describe what became of me. Perhaps uncivilised is the best word. Grief will do that,' he said.

I started at the grim look on his face. 'Yes, I know,' I faltered, thinking of my mother and what her grief, aided by the calomel, had driven her to. 'I know,' I repeated. 'What . . . who were you grieving for, Mr Ingram?'

'The woman I loved,' he said, still staring at me. 'She died, shortly before the end of the Rebellion.' Before I could murmur anything, he stood, setting down his glass. 'And our little daughter. She was only two years old. I thought she had died, too.'

'You thought she had died?' I echoed, looking across the room at him. Something had started inside me, some slow but heavy beat. This time it wasn't my heart, but something else. Something I couldn't name.

'Yes,' he said. 'To lose both of them was almost unbearable. After those two years, living alone and so full of anger and sorrow, I came back to India. And then, quite by accident, I met someone who claimed she had seen our old ayah.'

I nodded.

'I always assumed she had been killed with our daughter.' He hesitated. 'It was my fault. It was because of me that I lost my family.'

'How was it your fault?'

'I had left them in Gwalior, where we were living at the time. I had ridden south, to Jhansi, only a hundred miles away, because I was summoned by the British Consulate. I was working for them. Why did I go? I've asked myself that question every day of my life since then. What was I thinking, leaving my family unprotected at a time of unrest within the country?' His hands were fists at his side. 'But all of the major fighting had stopped months earlier. There had been no more uprisings, and there was no warning of the attack on Gwalior. I trusted my family would be safe. Trusted,' he said, faintly and yet bitterly. 'It was the final battle. They were the last rebels, and afterwards surrendered; peace was officially declared on 8 July. But, for me, it was the beginning of never knowing peace again.'

We sat in silence before he spoke again. 'When word came of the sepoy attack at Gwalior, I rode back as quickly as possible.' He licked his lips. 'Daryâ hadn't been hurt.'

'Daryâ was your child?'

He shook his head. 'No. No, Daryâ was the child's mother.'

'Your wife,' I stated.

He didn't speak for a moment. 'We didn't live in the English cantonment. We were in the Eurasian quarters; they were never attacked.'

'Your wife was Eurasian as well?' I asked.

His face lightened; he almost smiled. 'No. She was Afghan, a Tajik.' Then the darkness returned. 'But our daughter . . . the ayah had taken her to another home, an English home, friends of mine, to play with the children there. And when the attack came . . .' He stopped.

I glanced at Aimee. She showed no expression. 'What happened?' I quietly asked.

It took him another long moment. 'We never knew. The ayah didn't return. She didn't return to Daryâ, to our home,' he repeated. 'After the retreat of the sepoys, fought back by the English soldiers, it was possible to be on the streets. Daryâ rushed to the home where the ayah had taken our child. All the English there had been killed. The bodies of the family were still there. They were there, but not our ayah or child. She – Daryâ – went mad, searching everywhere, asking everyone still alive. By the time I rode day and night to return to Gwalior, there was still no sign of either the ayah or our daughter.'

'But . . . she was alive?' Hadn't he said he only thought she had died?

He turned away from me. 'Finally someone said she was certain she'd seen our ayah's body being put on a cart, with the other natives who had been accidental victims in the fray, to be taken to be cremated. I believed, then, that my daughter had been killed along with her, and her body cremated as well. There was nothing else to think. It was utter chaos; it's hard to imagine the confusion for one who hasn't lived through a time of such mayhem and bloodshed. We mourned the loss of our child. And then, only a few weeks later, Daryâ fell ill. She had contracted a bronchial condition, and was unable to fight it. I believe she didn't want to live at that point, because . . .' He stopped.

There were heavy footsteps down the corridor outside the sitting room, and the clink of a plate.

Now Mr Ingram turned to me again. 'I couldn't face what had happened, or face myself. I was responsible,' he said, as he had said earlier. 'If I had stayed with them, perhaps . . .' He shook his head. 'And that's when I left Gwalior, and India, and lived, alone, in the hills, far outside of Kabul.'

Now he was standing beside the lamp on the table; as the room grew ever darker his face became more illuminated. His eyes, in that light, glittered blackly. 'When I finally had lived with my own self-hatred long enough – those two years – I rode back to Gwalior. Daryâ is buried there; she was a Muslim. I was visiting old friends who had survived the Gwalior attack. And quite by accident, one of their ayahs said she had seen the woman who had been our ayah. Alive. Crippled, but alive.' He took a deep breath.

'I found her, and was able to speak to her. She had taken a bullet in the spine, and had lain on a charpoy since the attack, unable to walk or even sit up, and with only a little use of her arms. She was cared for by her daughter-in-law. When she saw me, her face lit up. She asked about Daryâ, and our little girl. She didn't know . . . I persuaded her to tell me all she could remember. It was very upsetting for her.'

Aimee took a deep breath.

'She told me that after she felt the sharp pain in her back, she fell, still holding the baby. She kept repeating that. *I held her, Sahib Ingram. I held her tightly. I never let her go.*' He made a small sound in his throat. 'She was a good, faithful woman.

'She couldn't recall much more than that, she said. All she knows is that when she was finally able to speak again, to ask about the child, nobody knew what had happened. She eventually found out we were no longer in Gwalior; for those two years she had assumed that our child had been returned to us.'

'So your daughter hadn't been killed?'

'I still didn't know. *She was not harmed, Sahib*, the ayah insisted. *I held her, and she was not harmed.* That's all she could tell me. And it had been two years; what were the chances I could find out anything more? But still . . . it was enough. The thin hope that my daughter was still alive somewhere was enough. I began my search for her.'

'But you said you'd already looked everywhere.'

'I had looked all over Gwalior and the surrounding area. Over the next year I searched all the missions in north and central India,' he said. 'There were so many little girls. So many native and Eurasians in the Christian missions, all orphaned or abandoned. But no little girls who looked . . . my daughter could pass for a European. I never saw a child who resembled my daughter,' he said. He stared at me, and suddenly my stomach churned. I didn't want him to say anything more.

I stood. 'We have to go. Come, Aimee,' I said, as I had earlier.

'But . . . please, I'm not finished,' he cried. 'I know this is . . . please, just let me—'

'No,' I said, loudly. 'We have to go back. I thought this was about Kai. You're wasting my time.'

With Aimee behind me, I half walked, half ran to the entrance, and out into the hot night where the tonga waited for us. I didn't look back at him as we drove away.

'Pree? What he is saying? I am not understanding. He will help your friend? Why you are upset?' Aimee asked, our shoulders bumping as we rode back to the house.

'I don't know. I don't know, Aimee,' I said. I was filled with some huge feeling, but I couldn't name it. I suspected what he was insinuating. But he had been maddened with grief; he admitted that. I knew what the grief of losing a child could do to a parent, didn't I? He still hoped he would find her, after all these years. He couldn't give up. How many other young women had he looked at, wondering if one could actually be his lost child? I pressed my palm against my forehead. As well as my stomach, now my head ached. Could it possibly be . . . could there be any truth in his ramblings?

No. I wouldn't listen to any more of this Mr Ingram's wild tales. I wondered, again, if Kai was wise to trust him.

Two days later I went back to Bala Hisar. I knew I wouldn't be allowed to see Kai, as it wasn't the visiting day, but I wanted to talk to Captain Gimble again. Maybe he could tell me something. I couldn't bear to see Mr Ingram. Not now, after what had happened at his home. He had made me very uneasy. I hadn't liked his interest in me, nor the urgent way he spoke to me, and especially not the way he looked at me so intently.

When I got to the closed gates of the fort, I was stopped by a guard. 'No entry, Miss,' he said.

'I wish to speak to Captain Gimble,' I told him.

'There's been an outbreak of cholera in the prison. The fort is currently quarantined,' he told me.

Cholera? What if Kai had cholera? He had appeared so ill, delirious with fever. Had he had any of the other symptoms – the vomiting, the rice stools, the leg cramps? I didn't know. But he had been more ill the second time I'd seen him. If it had been cholera that first week, by the second week he would have either been recovering, or he would have died. Cholera didn't linger.

I had no alternative but to leave.

It was another difficult night. When I knew morning was near by the lightening of the sky, I lay, wide awake, thinking about Kai, and about Mr Ingram. I got up and went to the little shrine Aimee had made. I knelt there and tried to pray, needing to find comfort.

But unlike the other women in the house, with prayers falling easily and confidently from their lips, as they had once fallen from the lips of the Fincastles, I could not find the words. I stared at the cross propped against the wall, and at the crudely painted picture of Jesus with the children. I clasped my hands and closed my eyes, trying to remember the old prayers. Nothing would come.

There are hundreds of ways to kneel and kiss the ground, Mr Ingram had quoted.

The first call to prayer came from a minaret, and then another, and another. I rose and went to the window, laying my head on my arms, listening to the cries.

★ ★ ★

Another day passed. Still no word from Mr Ingram about Kai. I could no longer bear to cook and clean, having no information, thinking about Kai. Out of sheer desperation I returned to Bala Hisar. I knew that quarantines could go on for weeks. But at least someone might speak to me, tell me anything, give me some small piece of information I could cling to until the quarantine had passed.

As I climbed out of the tonga I saw an ensign nailing a paper on to the gate where I had last read the names of the three men hanged. This one said *List of Dead*.

'The men who have died from cholera?' I asked him, pointlessly.

He nodded.

I wouldn't look, I told myself. I had convinced myself that it wasn't cholera Kai suffered from.

But, of course, I did look at the list. My eyes ran down the names. There were eleven. The eleventh was Pavit.

Something started shaking me uncontrollably, from my feet to my head. Was there an earthquake? I grabbed my own arms, gripping tightly and closing my eyes, waiting for the end of the tremor.

No. I'd made a mistake. I'd read the list too quickly. The name wasn't Pavit. It was something else, Patel, Pasha, Palash. It was only because I didn't want to see that name that my eyes had tricked me.

The shaking slowed. I opened my eyes. The ensign stood where he had stood before. The walls of the fort hadn't moved.

I took a deep breath, then lifted my quivering finger and placed it on the first name, then the second, reading slowly, carefully, as if it were a new skill. When I got to the tenth name I stopped, thinking *it's not Pavit, it's not Pavit*.

I read the eleventh name.

The ground shook again, and I fell to my knees, putting

my hands on the earth in front of me, gripping the hard, dried mud with my fingertips, holding on. I couldn't hear anything; a roar filled my head.

Someone was pulling my arm. I swallowed, over and over, and the noise in my head receded.

'Ma'am? Are you all right, ma'am?'

I looked up blankly.

'Ma'am? You've had a shock, I take it.' The ensign pulled me up; I felt a tearing sensation in my shoulder.

I swallowed again. 'Are you certain that . . .' My voice was that of an old, old woman. 'Could there be a mistake?' I clutched the ensign's sleeve. He looked at my hand, and slowly pulled away from me.

'Are you sure these men are dead? Are you sure?'

'I posted the list, as I was told, Ma'am,' he said. 'I don't know nuffin else.'

'I must speak to someone. I want to see someone, someone who . . . someone . . .' Who would I talk to? Had the bodies been examined, or had the dead simply been hauled from the cells?

'No entry into the fort, ma'am,' he said, now staring straight ahead.

'But . . .' I looked around, seeing only soldiers outside the gates, a few horses, some carts and tongas. My own tonga, waiting. 'Where are the bodies? Have the bodies been taken somewhere?'

'They're waiting to be burnt, ma'am. And evryfink they had – blankets and such – gotta be burnt, so's not to spread the cholera.'

'But nobody was told. I wasn't told,' I cried.

'The men what had listed their families – them people was told.' He still looked ahead, and not at me. 'Because of the korantine, they can't claim the bodies. But they can watch, from the parapet,' he said, lifting his chin at the walkway,

589

reached by a wooden ladder that ran along one section of the fort wall. 'Say their prayers for 'em, if they wants to, Christian or heathen, don't matter to us.'

'But . . . I'm his family. He . . . he was my family,' I cried, my voice finding its strength, growing louder.

'Then they musta sent word to your house,' he said.

I was shaking my head, shaking it without stopping. Something wet was running down my back, down my sides.

'I'm sorry, ma'am,' the ensign said. His voice came as if from far away. 'Any of them prisoners with no family, they's already been taken to a mass pyre and burnt up. First fing in the mornin'.'

I made a sound, and the soldier finally turned back to me. 'Was he slated for hangin', Ma'am?'

I didn't answer.

''Cause if he were, maybe this way were more merciful. Think of it like that.'

'Merciful?' I whispered. 'Merciful?' but he had turned now, his back to me, making it clear our conversation was over.

CHAPTER FORTY-FIVE

I TRIED TO CLIMB into the waiting tonga, but my legs wouldn't cooperate. I finally pulled myself in, holding on to the edges of the seat to keep myself upright. When the driver asked where to take me, I couldn't answer. He kept waiting, looking at me. Eventually I lifted a hand. 'Go,' I managed to say.

I sat as if frozen as the tonga-wallah drove. I needed to tell someone about Kai. I couldn't simply go back to the mission house as if it were an ordinary day. I needed to be with someone who knew Kai. As we reached the gate that led into the city I leaned forward and told the driver where to take me.

I went into the Translation Office. Again I had to face Mr Hooper. He studied me, then spoke slowly, carefully, as if I were a person with little understanding of the language. He told me Mr Ingram wasn't well; he had received a note that morning saying he wouldn't be coming to work.

'Would you care to sit down, Miss Fincastle?' he asked. 'You appear to be—'

I left before he finished speaking, and went to his home, to Mr Ingram's home, walking slowly up the steps, breathing heavily, as if the three steps had been a steep incline. I lifted my hand and banged on the closed door with my palm. When nobody answered, I pushed the door open. As I stepped into the entrance, Mr Ingram came out of a room down the hall, looking alarmed.

'Pree. What are you—'

'He's dead,' I said, my words catching in my throat. 'Kai is dead.'

'Pree . . .'

'Don't call me Pree, as if you know me so well,' I said. 'Don't.' The entry was stifling. I wiped my forehead with the back of my hand; when I pulled it away I absently looked at the dusty, damp smear of sweat and dust on my glove. I was too hot; I jerkily yanked off my gloves, dropping them to the floor. I put my hands on my cheeks; they were hot and wet.

Mr Ingram looked behind him, then shook his head. 'Please. Let's go to the verandah. It's cooler there.'

The door Mr Ingram had come from only a moment earlier closed with a quiet thud. His Afghan friend, I thought, absently.

There was a sabre with a handle decorated with gold bars hanging on the wall beside me; it was slightly askew. I wanted to reach out and straighten it. Mr Ingram's hair was uncombed and dusty, his face covered in dark stubble. His lips looked as dry as mine felt. I was thinking so clearly about these unimportant things, noting everything around me. It was as if my thoughts were somehow standing separately, brightly, and I could see them.

As soon as we were on the shaded verandah he gestured to a cane chair. 'Please. Please sit down. The heat . . .'

I lowered myself heavily to the chair. 'Don't you understand what I'm telling you? Kai is dead.' My voice was shaking, and tears ran, unheeded, down my face. 'I loved him. I loved Kai.' The words, said aloud for the first time, shocked me. But why? Of course I loved Kai. I had loved him all my life, hadn't I? First as a brother, then a friend. And finally . . . 'And it appears you did nothing to get him out of that terrible place. You could have done something. He had faith in you, as did I. I trusted you to help. But you didn't.'

He simply looked at me.

'Kai is dead,' I said again, my voice suddenly going high and tremulous. It seemed I couldn't stop saying it, as if convincing myself of this shocking, terrible fact. 'There's nothing more to be done. He's dead.' I wanted to shake this man, shake him out of his stupor. 'Do you even care? You're looking at me so . . . what's wrong with you?'

His mouth moved, but no words came out. Had he already known about Kai's death, or was this the first he'd heard of it? Was I seeing shock? If so, it manifested itself in a silent, curious expression.

'You're upset. Understandably,' he finally said.

'Upset? Kai is dead, Mr Ingram. Upset? That doesn't begin to describe anything. But you don't appear to be moved at all. Have you no heart, Mr Ingram? No heart at all? You've known Kai since he was a child, and yet you stand here as if dead yourself. Cold and unfeeling.'

'You're upset,' he repeated. 'But perhaps, at a later time, I can—' He stepped forward and put his hand on my forearm.

'Let me go,' I said, pulling away, and rushing down the steps. A man and a woman stood on the road, staring at me. Their faces were blurred, pale ovals.

I heard Mr Ingram's voice, too close; he was following me. Again he put his hand on me, this time my shoulder. I turned and looked at him as if he were a stranger. My body was filling with an unknown and sharp pain, as if a thousand stinging ants had invaded my bloodstream.

'Please,' he said, 'let me call you a tonga. You can't—'

But again I pulled away from him and ran. I ran from him, past the man and woman, past the houses and into the twisted lanes of the old city. When I could no longer run, the pain in my side so intense I had to press the heel of my hand deeply into it, I walked. I walked and walked, until I finally reached the Peshawar Zenana Mission.

I went straight to the convenience and shut the door, taking deep breaths. I couldn't bear to face anyone.

I remained there, with the condensation from the sides of the copper vat of water hitting the floor with an endless, metered drip, until there was a persistent knocking. The rhythm of knuckles against wood slowly broke through my daze; I listened, at first unaware of what the sound was, or where I was. It was as if I had been in a deep sleep, or some dark unconsciousness, and was now slowly wakening.

My head cleared. I sat on the floor with my back against the door. My knees were up, the fabric of my skirt stretched across them, and my arms hung limply over my knees. How long had I sat there?

Kai. Oh, Kai.

I stood and opened the door. The woman – Hannah – looked annoyed, hands on her hips, but that expression fell away as she studied my face.

'Are you unwell, Pree?' she asked. She had a fleck of something, perhaps potato, on her bottom lip. I stared at it. I fixed on that tiny white morsel as if it could explain something important to me.

'Are you ill?' she asked again.

I pushed past her and walked down the hall to my room, my hand on the wall for support.

I sat on the edge of my bed, staring at my boots. Then I unlaced them and took them, and my stockings, off. I looked at my toes. They appeared strange, unfamiliar, as if they weren't part of my body.

I remember nothing more of that afternoon, or evening. I had lost all feeling – in my body, in my head, perhaps even in my soul.

★ ★ ★

The light of morning finally came. I don't know if I'd slept or not; my eyes were gritty and my head pounded. I was still wearing my frock. I stayed within my curtained enclosure while Aimee and Rohana readied themselves for the day and left.

Finally Helena came into the room, pulling aside the curtain and looking down on me.

'Were you sick this morning?' she asked. 'Hannah said she thought you were sick yesterday. Do you have something to tell me, Pree?'

'No,' I said, in a rough whisper, closing my eyes. 'It's not that.'

I heard the swish as she pulled the curtain around my bed again, then the sigh of her skirt on the floor, as she walked from my room, and I rolled on to my side, curling myself around my pillow.

I changed into my nightdress and stayed in my room all day, not eating, not sleeping, just lying on the bed. When Aimee and Rohana returned, Aimee quietly asked if I wanted her to bring me anything to eat or drink. I told her no.

That next night was endless. I couldn't sleep. I noiselessly walked about the room, looking out of the window and then going back to my bed, only to toss for a few moments and then rise again. When the morning finally came and Aimee and Rohana left again, I put on a simple sprigged cotton frock. I washed my face and ran my fingers through my hair, not having the energy to pin it up, and left it hanging loosely over my bodice.

I sat on my bed, thinking about what I would do, where I would go. How could I stay here, and carry on as I had before?

Helena came to the open door. 'Pree? There is a gentleman here to see you,' she said. 'A Mr Ingram. I asked the nature of his business with you. He would only say that it was of a personal nature.'

I didn't want to see him. I didn't want to hear his excuses about how he hadn't been able to help Kai. Or any further tedious, tortured stories of his own sad past.

I shook my head. 'Please, Helena. Tell him . . . tell him I'm not well. I can't see him now.'

She studied me. 'Is this the man, Pree? The man who was imprisoned? Were you able to help him, then?'

'No, no. It's not him.'

'It's not him,' she repeated. 'So this is another man you have dealings with?'

I stood, running my hands through my hair again. 'Helena, I'll explain everything to you. I promise. Just ask that man to leave.'

'Is he a threat to you?'

'A threat? No.' I sighed. 'All right. I'll go out and see what he wants.'

I tried to find the strength to face Mr Ingram as I walked downstairs. When I stepped into the sitting room, he rose immediately. He was wearing his English clothing. He studied my face and hair. I knew how I must appear, but didn't care.

Helena hovered beside me, and I said, dully, 'Thank you, Helena. You may leave us.'

'I shall stay as a chaperone.'

I looked at her. 'That isn't necessary, Helena. Really.'

'I will stay, Pree,' she said firmly, and took a chair to the far corner of the room, sitting behind Mr Ingram.

'Thank you for seeing me,' Mr Ingram said.

'What do you want?' I said, wearily.

'I . . . it pains me to see you so distraught. Please,' he said, 'won't you take a seat?'

I did, only because it was an effort to stand. I was so tired.

596

'Pr — Miss Fincastle,' he said. 'I have a message for you. From Kai.'

At his words, I cried out, clapping my hand over my mouth. Again tears came, and I did nothing to stop them. Kai had left a message for me. He must have seen Mr Ingram before he died, and had given him a message. He had thought of me, even while near death. Maybe now I could bear this. Maybe knowing I had been in his last thoughts would help carry me through.

I leaned forward. 'Yes? Yes? What was it? Kai's message to me?' I could barely see Mr Ingram through the blur of my tears.

Mr Ingram reached inside his pocket and took out a white handkerchief, handing it to me. I pressed it against my eyes. I heard the rustle of paper, and moved the handkerchief to see Mr Ingram pulling out a thick folded sheet, sealed with red wax. He held it towards me.

Again I wiped my eyes, and then my nose, with the handkerchief. 'Kai wrote this?'

He nodded. 'He was very specific that it was for you, and you alone. You can see that the seal is unbroken.'

'But . . . how did he manage, from prison, to write it?' I still hadn't touched it.

'Miss Fincastle.' Mr Ingram set the paper on the table beside me. 'It was impossible to explain earlier. I couldn't tell you, even though I wanted to. You must believe that. I didn't want you to suffer as you have.' He stopped. 'Kai lives.'

I couldn't understand what he was saying, even though I heard his words. I shook my head. 'He isn't dead?' I glanced at the paper. Only my name — *Pree* — was written there. I knew Kai's handwriting. 'He didn't have cholera?' What did I feel? Kai wasn't dead? Or was this all a terrible hoax? Who was this Mr Ingram, to put me through all of this?

I stared at him. I wouldn't allow myself to believe. Not yet.

Even if Kai were alive, that didn't mean he wouldn't soon meet the noose.

'No. He was ill, but it wasn't cholera.'

'But I saw his name. I saw the name he used, Pavit, on the list of the dead.'

'He isn't dead, Miss Fincastle,' Mr Ingram repeated.

'He's still in prison, then?'

'No.'

'Then he's been released? You managed to have him released? He was innocent, wasn't he? I know he was innocent.'

'No,' he said again, but I don't know which of my questions he was referring to. 'He's left Peshawar. But . . . perhaps your questions will be answered in the letter. He said to make sure you received it; that it was of utmost importance. He gave it to me before he left, last night; I brought it as soon as I could.'

I looked at the letter again. If what Mr Ingram was saying was true, that Kai was no longer in prison, the letter would tell me where he was, where to meet him. Of course he couldn't remain in Peshawar. 'Did he escape?' I asked, although that seemed an impossibility, thinking of the chained prisoners in the cells, the underground passages, the jailers.

'You might call it that. I have worked in the offices of Bala Hisar in the past. I know people there, as well as the buildings and their passageways. But, ultimately, it was the quarantine that allowed me to . . .' He stopped. 'It really isn't prudent – or helpful in any way – for you to know of certain details. It's best if you just know that he's free. He was helped by others as well.'

I thought of the Afghan I'd seen at Mr Ingram's house.

'He's been at my home for the last while.'

I thought of the door in his hallway, closing. 'He was there when I came to tell you that I believed him to be dead?'

'Yes. He needed to rest, and recover his strength enough to leave.' He looked at the floor. 'He couldn't be discovered. I was afraid that if anyone – if you knew, it might endanger him further. I hope you can forgive me. It was the only recourse.'

I rose. 'Thank you.'

'Again, Miss Fincastle,' Mr Ingram said, standing, 'I know this may not be the time . . . there doesn't seem to be a right time for us to speak. But I want to apologise for what happened that evening at my home, when you came with the other woman. I know I had no right to—'

'That's fine, Mr Ingram,' I said, almost briskly, again interrupting him. I picked up the letter. 'Quite all right. Thank you. I appreciate what you did in helping Kai.' I started towards the door, clutching the letter and the sodden handkerchief.

He followed.

I was anxious for him to leave so that I could tear open the letter and read what Kai had written.

'Please. Will you allow me to stay just another few moments?' He glanced behind him, at Helena, who sat motionless. 'Or would you agree to see me again? Won't you let me try to explain my story further? Are you not curious, if nothing else?'

'Curious?'

'About . . . what I spoke of. My daughter.'

The letter was warm in my hand. 'No. I'm sorry, but I'm not. I'm not curious at all. Please, Mr Ingram, I'd like you to leave.' I couldn't take in anything else. I couldn't.

I heard the rustle of Helena's skirt as she stood.

Mr Ingram nodded, and the moment he went through the sitting-room door I hurried to my room. Sitting on the bed, I steadied my breathing, looking at the letter in my hand. Then I pressed it to my face, inhaling deeply. There was only the faint smell of the wax.

I ripped the sealed fold open; a thick pile of rupees fell into my lap. I ignored them, scanning Kai's familiar writing.

I read it a second time, and then a third. I put it beside me on the bed. I sat there for a long time, and then, with one swift, brutal move, crumpled the letter and tossed it across the room. I stared at it, then rose, the rupees fluttering from my skirt to the floor. I picked up the balled paper and opened it again. I read it for the final time. Then I ripped it, over and over again, finally letting the tiny bits of paper flutter to the ground. They fell like snowflakes. Like ashes.

I would never read it again. The words were burned into my brain:

My dear Pree,
I know you have seen David Ingram if you are reading this. He is responsible for helping me a number of times over. He is perhaps the only person I have ever fully trusted.

Although I was unsuccessful in my attempt to help my country this time, I will continue. This work has long been my life. And in order to carry out my labours to the best of my ability, I cannot allow myself a dependant. No one can wait for me, or worry over me. I need the freedom of concentrating all of my efforts in my beliefs.

We shan't see each other again, Pree. I shall disappear into India. You will continue to proudly find your own way, as you always have.

You may rely on David Ingram in all matters. Trust his word, as I have.

I will always think of you, and the wild smell of your hair.
Kai

I lay listlessly on my bed. The rupees were still on the floor. Kai had paid me for what had transpired between us. And that truly made me what I'd pretended I wasn't while I rocked under the Colonel.

I thought of what Aimee had said, about learning to love. Had Kai ever been able to know it – to taste it and touch it – raised as he had been, with a mother who clearly cared nothing for him and a father who would never claim him as his own? I thought of the secrets he had carried, and the pain he must have felt.

And at that moment I knew that, unlike Kai, I was able to love. I had loved him, always. I can love, I thought. I can love.

And yet, I was so alone: in this room, in this house, in the city of Peshawar, in the whole of India. And I had felt alone for so long – even at the mission with Glory and her company across the courtyard, even in the busy *caravanserais* along the Grand Trunk Road, even with Aimee and Rohana breathing softly in sleep on the other side of the curtain. The only time that had felt different, for these past years, had been the one afternoon with Kai, when the sensation of being part of someone else took away the aloneness.

It wasn't fair, I thought, sitting up, to have been allowed such a tiny glimpse of happiness. It wasn't fair. How could Kai have used me?

I looked at the rupees. I was trying to deny the truth, blaming him. But I had wanted him to take me, practically begged him, and so he had. My loneliness, my need to feel that I mattered to someone had made me wanton. Kai wasn't a saint, just as I wasn't. He had told me he wasn't a good person; I knew the same of myself. But could he really have so little feeling for me that he could proclaim that he would never see me again, that he didn't want or need anybody?

He had said something to that effect so long ago, as he left the mission. I hadn't believed him then. I thought I had some power to change him.

601

I was filled with fresh anger; stiff and somehow chilled in the hot air, as if I were wrapped in a cold, wet sheet. Now I wished that Kai had died. It would have been better to live the rest of my life believing he had felt for me as I felt for him. It would be better to feel hot grief than this cold emptiness.

Filled with loathing for myself, wanting to break through that coldness, I dug my fingernails into my own cheeks, needing to hurt myself. But then I thought of my mother, with her bitten arms.

I pulled my fingers from my face. I wasn't like her. I wasn't. And yet . . . in that instant I felt that I understood her more than I had in all the years I had lived with her. I went to the oval mirror on top of the washstand and stared at myself: my drawn face with the small half-moon indents from my fingernails on my cheeks, my auburn hair streaked with lighter shades of brown and a hint of dark yellow, my brown eyes with the threads of gold, although now streaked with pink, the lids swollen from weeping. Who was I?

I hated myself. Fumbling in my medical bag, I took out the sharp scissors. I don't know what I wanted to do with them. I lifted a heavy strand of hair, then let it drop. I held the point of the shears to my neck, seeing my pulse beating beneath the silver blades. And then I picked up my skirt and slashed at it. I cut the fabric to bits, the scissors occasionally nicking my thighs, my knees and shins and calves. I cut and cut until the skirt of my frock hung from my waist in long jagged strips. I was panting, spots of blood welling on the skin of my legs.

And then I sat down heavily. The strangely satisfying zithering of the blades against fabric had brought me a brief, albeit false comfort. My breath eventually slowing, I stared at my shredded frock, my bloodied legs, and realised I had been crying about Kai — over his leaving my life — since I was fifteen years old. Was it not time to finally stop my tears? Was it not time to say goodbye to him?

I lay down again, closing my eyes in exhaustion. Then I opened them and looked at the rupees on the floor. I rose and slowly gathered the notes into a tidy stack. *You may rely on David Ingram in all matters*, Kai had written.

I thought of Mr Ingram, his dark, sad eyes, his occasional sudden smile. He was so determined, so intent, as he stared at me. He had helped Kai, as he had said he would. He had not broken his promise. And he was the person Kai trusted more than any other. More than me.

I knew it was my decision as to whether Mr Ingram was ever again in my presence.

I suddenly thought of him as the Afghan – my Afghan, as I had referred to him when I was young – and the way he had said goodbye the last time I had seen him at the mission, as I held Adriana.

Khuda hafiz, Pree, he had said, with something in his voice I hadn't been able to interpret, something deep and painful.

Khuda hafiz.

CHAPTER FORTY-SIX

T HE NEXT MORNING I made a slight effort, fixing my hair and dressing in my best frock. I hadn't cried that night, and had fallen into a deep, exhausted sleep. Some of my normal colour was returning. I wrote a short note, and sent it with a boy I found outside the house, giving him one anna to deliver it and promising him two more on his return to me, with proof that it had been received. And then I went to the sitting room, and waited.

Mr Ingram arrived in less than an hour, and was shown in by Hannah. He was dressed in Indian clothing. His hair was still damp, and he was freshly shaven.

'You're looking better today, Miss Fincastle,' he said.

'You may call me Pree,' I said.

He nodded, taking the seat I indicated. Once again Helena joined us, sitting behind Mr Ingram, but this time she held a Bible and appeared to read from it.

'Kai's letter,' I began, and he again nodded, 'told me he trusted you. And that I could rely on you. And so I decided to listen to what you have to say. What more you have to say.'

He licked his lips. There was a feather on the floor; it must have been from the children's play. He reached down, absently, and picked it up.

'So I will listen to you, but I don't see what you can say to make me . . .' I stopped. 'Just go on. Tell me why you kept coming back to the mission at Lahore.'

Mr Ingram was silent for a moment, then looked towards the window as he spoke. 'First, Pree, I need you to know that I wasn't going to disclose any of this until I knew, with certainty, that you were aware that you weren't born of the Fincastles. I told myself – when you came back into my life – that if you fully believed the Fincastles were your true parents, I wouldn't impose on you. I wouldn't destroy any memories you had.'

He really didn't know what memories I had of my parents. There were some good, but so many distressing.

'That's what I was clumsily trying to determine, at my home. But it was obvious it was too difficult. I didn't know if I'd have the chance to ask Kai; he was so ill in prison, and of course all that was on both his and my mind was finding a way to get him out. And then, when he was hidden in my house, recovering, I asked him. And he told me you had confided in him about your unknown origin.'

I nodded.

Mr Ingram took a deep breath. 'It was in 1862 that I came upon your mission,' he said.

I sat quietly, my hands in my lap.

'As I said before, I had been searching for a full year after I had returned to India from my time of . . . of hiding, in Afghanistan. And, as I told you, I had gone to every mission in north and central India,' he said. 'But I hadn't heard of yours; it was quite out of the way. Most of the Christian missions are well known and easily located.' He didn't look at me as he spoke, but kept his eyes fixed on the window. 'But yours . . . it appeared it was deliberately made difficult to find.' He seemed hypnotised by the play of light.

'When I first rode up outside the mission I saw Kai – as I have said, he was about twelve – mending the fence. I asked him for water for my horse, and he gave it to me. I enquired about other children at the mission – if there orphans. He said no, there was only you – Pree – the daughter of the missionaries. Pree? I asked, because it was similar to the name we'd given you. But I didn't think anything more of it: Kai had said the only other child was the missionaries' daughter. Why would I doubt him? But then, as if predestined, you came into the courtyard. I saw that you were about the same age as my daughter would have been. Kai returned to his work. I sat there, watching you.'

I could envision the scene. Had it been the same golden Arabian?

Now he looked away from the window, and at me. 'You were dressed in a little yellow frock, its hem drooping on one side. Your feet were bare, and your hair was in two plaits; one had come undone. I've never forgotten that moment, and exactly how you appeared. You were laughing, chasing a chicken. You caught it, finally, and clasped it against you, its wings flapping in your face. You looked at Kai, as if for his approval. You paid no attention to me. But there was something in your face, as you laughed, something so familiar, that I knew – I just knew, as surely as a wild animal can identify its offspring, even after years, by its smell. It had been almost four years; you had been two years old when I'd last seen you, and now you were close to six. And I knew you were my daughter. I didn't know how you came to be there, but there you were, alive and well. To see you, so unexpectedly, after my hopes had all but died . . .' He bit his lips to stop them from trembling.

'But . . .' my voice was a whisper. Could I believe what this man was saying? I cleared my throat. 'If you felt this so strongly, why didn't you do something?'

He waited until he had composed himself. 'Don't you think it took every ounce of willpower not to jump off my horse and run to you, gather you up and announce you were my own lost child? That was my first instinct. But then—'

'Then what?' I demanded. 'What?'

'You didn't – don't – look much like your mother, or like me. There is a strong resemblance to your grandmother, my mother. But that isn't enough to claim a child – the vague declaration of a family likeness. I had no proof. And I was . . . I'm certain that at that time I resembled a wild man from the hills. I *was* a wild man from the northern hills. What would have happened if I'd rushed into the mission, shouting that you were my child? Do you think anyone would have believed me? And what about you? I would only have frightened you.'

'But my parents – the Fincastles – they would know, surely, that you spoke the truth. They had no idea where or who I came from.'

'And do you think they would simply put you into my arms because I said that four years earlier my daughter, who was roughly the same age as their own, and with the same colouring and facial features, had disappeared from Gwalior during a sepoy attack? Do you think they would give up the child they obviously considered theirs, hand you over to an Afghan who rode into the courtyard?'

I had no reply. What he said made sense. My parents had moved so far north, to an isolated mission, for that very reason, Glory had said. So that there was no chance anyone would ever come looking for me.

'I knew where you were, but I also knew that if I acted spontaneously, improperly, they might somehow prevent me from coming again. Or perhaps even move away, if they were truly worried about what I might do. So at first, the only option open to me was to return frequently, to watch you, and make sure you were thriving.'

'And you were content with that? To occasionally watch the child you thought to be your own, play about in a courtyard?'

'Of course not. I fully believed, for the next few years, that I would find a way to reclaim you. It was all I thought about.'

'But you didn't,' I said, in a hard voice.

'Pree. Please try to understand. I moved to Lahore and secured work there so that I could be nearer to you. I so often rode by; many times I didn't see you. And I was concerned about being noticed by the Fincastles. I always dressed in native clothing and a turban. My hair . . . people see me differently when my head is uncovered and I'm in European attire. I've always been a bit of a chameleon,' he said, smiling, so slightly, as if encouraging me to smile back.

I didn't move. Everything he said made sense, and yet I was still wary. I had to be.

'Sometimes I'd leave my horse down the road from the mission. I would walk by on foot, so I could pass by more slowly, to see if you were about. But as time passed, and I grew more and more familiar with your routines, I came to understand something. Something painful, but undeniable. It was the reason I ultimately didn't try to claim you.'

I slumped against the back of my chair. 'What? What was your excuse?'

'It wasn't an excuse. I . . . I want to think it was . . . perhaps an act of kindness. I started to see that it would be selfish to take you away.'

'Selfish?'

'At first I told myself I was waiting for the right time, figuring out what proof I might present to the Fincastles. During those first years I sometimes saw you with another little girl, a native child. One particular day you were climbing in the peepul tree in the courtyard. When you both jumped down, the other child suddenly pointed at me – I was on my horse that day – and then shrieked something, grabbing your arm. You stared at me, then looked back at the other girl and screamed as if terrified, but you were laughing at the same time. Then you both ran behind the house, still shouting.'

Of course. The games Lalasa and I had played. Hiding from the Afghans who might kidnap us.

'And I realised it then. The conclusion I had to face. You were growing up in a secure home with a mother and father, living what looked to be a normal life. I considered what I had to offer you: a man alone, with no idea of how to raise a child — especially a daughter.'

He pulled apart the feather. 'I watched you, Pree, I watched you playing in the courtyard, running about with a dog at your heels, in and out of the infirmary. And I thought of what your life would be like with me. No mother, and a father who could never settle, no real home.'

'Did you think of what I might want?' I asked, after a long time. 'If I really was your daughter?'

The feather was in tatters. He still held the quill. 'I watched you grow up. There was never a time I didn't think of you. I came by on the road, walking or riding, every ten days or two weeks. As you grew older I saw how much you loved to read; you'd even walk across the courtyard with your head bent over a book. One time you had a gecko on your shoulder.' He smiled unconsciously. 'I saw your kindness with the old leper.' His smile faded. 'I watched you squatting beside the cook, your face a study of concentration as you ground spices or chopped vegetables. I heard music, pianoforte music, when I could see the Fincastles in the infirmary or on the verandah, and knew it was you playing. Then I realised, as you grew older still, that you were assisting in the infirmary. I was so proud of you, of your many accomplishments. You were learning so much more — becoming so much more — than I would have known to teach you.'

Unexpectedly it was difficult to swallow. For most of my life my parents had made me feel inadequate; I disappointed them with my inability to act as a daughter of missionaries. I wasn't virtuous or thoughtful enough. I was too unreserved, too impatient. They had never made me feel the way this man did in only a few sentences: that I was clever, and kind, and accomplished. That I was worthy of praise, of being proud of. The painful heaviness grew larger in my throat.

'And then, the last time I saw you at the mission, with the ayah's baby strapped across your chest, you seemed so . . . so happy.'

He fell silent, and I swallowed and swallowed, forcing down the obstruction. 'I was happy?' I asked, finally, when I could speak again. Yes, I remember that day, with little Adriana, and the quiet peacefulness I had felt. But it was only for that brief hour, when the baby slept, warm and heavy against me, and my mother lay quietly on her bed, lost in her own shifting thoughts, and my father bent over his Bible or a phial of tablets in the infirmary. When Glory was away from the mission. He had seen only what he wanted to see. He had only seen the outside life. He had no idea what went on inside: what I felt.

'I heard you singing,' he continued. 'You were leaning on your hoe with a dreamy expression. And I knew then it would soon be time to let go, to stop coming to the mission. I had watched you living your life for over a decade. That day, seeing you with the baby . . . it upset me. I knew I couldn't continue on, watching you but not being able to know you. And when we spoke that day, I looked into your face, and imagined what it would be like when you married, and had your own children. Knowing that I could never be a part of your life. It was too late; I had missed any opportunity to even try to explain. I had to let go,' he repeated. *Khuda hafiz, Pree.* 'You had grown up, safe and protected. To intrude then would have only confused you, and brought you pain.'

'How can you know that with such certainty?'

'What good would it have done you?'

'What good?' I stood, my fists clenched. 'Did Kai know about this? All of it?'

'Yes.'

'He knew all along? For my whole life he knew you were my father?' I couldn't believe what I kept finding out about Kai. All the secrets he carried. But this was the worst. If he had told me, I wouldn't have stayed at the mission with Glory. When my parents died I could have gone and found him, this Mr Ingram. Maybe. And if I had, everything would have been different. I thought of the Colonel.

'No, no,' Mr Ingram said. 'I only told Kai much later. He didn't know when he still lived at the mission.'

He rubbed the old scar under his eye. I realised that I hadn't seen it in the past because his skin was so darkened by the sun. 'Could you believe me, Pree? Could you ever believe, as I do, that you're my daughter? That I'm your father?'

I was silent for a moment. Finally I answered, calmly, although my heart was pounding, 'No. No, I don't believe you are. I don't wish to believe it. I know you cannot be my father. Not you.'

His face blanched, and I knew how deeply my words hurt him. And I didn't care. I wanted him to be hurt.

'But why not?'

If I was the daughter he thought he'd lost, I had been six years old when he found me. Only six. And yet he'd left me there. I didn't care what his reasons were. If he really was my father, and had known that, all through my childhood, it was obvious he hadn't cared enough about me to take me from that mission.

'Why not, Mr Ingram? Because of what's happened to me. If you really were my father, you could have saved me.'

'Saved you? From what?'

611

'Do you really believe you knew my life? The real life, not just watching me play as a little child, or walk across the courtyard or help in the infirmary? Or sit astride your horse for a few moments every once in a while?'

He pressed the tip of the quill into his palm.

'If you're so sure I'm your daughter,' I said now, wanting to continue to hurt him, as I was hurt, 'and are trying to convince me, you would have proof. Just as you said you doubted the Fincastles would believe you, why should I now?'

He reached inside his shirt pocket. 'I have this.' He held out a creased daguerreotype.

I was inexplicably frightened. I didn't want to look at it, but my hand – it shook – reached for the photograph as if of its own will.

It was him, a younger man, although looking much the same as he did now. He wore a light shirt and a decorated vest. His head was bare. He was standing with his hand on a woman's shoulder. She sat on a stool with curved sides, wearing a *salwar kameez* of a dark colour, the long shirt and full trousers worn by many of the Muslim women here. Her thick braid hung over her shoulder and almost reached her waist. On her lap was a small child with a mass of curly hair, dressed in a pale frock. All three of them stared into the camera, unsmiling, and yet their expressions were calm, peaceful.

The image blurred in front of my eyes. The sepia paper shook; I brought it closer. The woman's face – heart shaped, with wide, light eyes and full lips – appeared to be marked in some way. There was something – tattoos? across her forehead and on her chin.

I studied the child. Then I handed back the photograph. 'That's your proof?' I asked. 'I see you and a native woman and a child. A child, like any other. Isn't there something else? Do I have a distinguishing mark on my body?'

I wanted him to say yes, there is a dark stain on your right shoulder, or you are missing the second toe of your left foot. I wanted to prove him wrong. If there was no proof, I couldn't believe him. I couldn't let myself think that what he said might be true.

I don't know why I was fighting him. Didn't I want to know, didn't I want to belong to someone? Maybe it was fear that I would be disappointed. That if I let myself believe, and then found out it wasn't true, it would be even more painful.

'No. I only wish you had something that would be confirming. It would be what I needed. But you are my daughter, Pree,' he said. 'Pari Regina Ingram, born 1 June, 1856.'

'Pari Regina Ingram?' I said. 'That was my name?'

He smiled, a very small smile. 'Your mother named you Pari. That's why, when I heard your name was Pree . . . Pari is Persian for fairy.'

'I know,' I said.

'I called you my little fairy.' He picked up the daguerreotype again. 'My choice was Regina. I simply liked the name.'

I stood.

'Please. Don't rush off again. What can I do to—'

I ran out, and up the stairs. Rohana kneeled in front of the little altar in our room. She jumped up when I came in. Her mouth opened and closed as she spoke to me, but my heart beat so loudly in my ears it blocked out every other sound. I hauled Kai's saddlebag from under my bed and pulled out the sandalwood box, flinging back the lid and dumping its contents on the bed. I picked up the strip of blanket. PRI. Not the beginning of Priscilla. They were initials. Pari Regina Ingram. I sat there with the piece of blanket in my hand for a minute, or five minutes. Maybe shorter, maybe longer. I have no idea.

As I set it back on the bed, I dully noticed that a piece of the hardened yellow wax from the paper kite had dislodged, and was sitting on the red silk that had held the bit of blanket. I stared at that hard, dry sliver on the red silk; a yellow sickle moon against its red sky: the Muslim *hilal*.

Back in the sitting room, I again picked up the daguerreotype from the table. Mr Ingram was as I had left him; he hadn't moved. Helena's head was still bent over the Bible.

'It was taken when you were just a year old. I had sent it to my mother, in England. I found it among her belongings when I went to visit her only last year, and brought it back with me,' he said. 'I'd forgotten about it. To find it was a gift from God. I had nothing to remember Daryâ – or you by.'

I squeezed my eyes shut.

'I had destroyed everything, burned everything that belonged to you both. Now I don't know why. I suppose it was some form of not wanting to remember, to try and rid myself of the pain.

'As I've said, you don't really look like either of us. But you resemble my mother.' He reached inside his pocket again and brought out a small leather case. 'It's very old; I've kept it with me always.' He opened it so that I could see the image of a woman. 'Of course this was when she was quite young; I was a child when this was taken. She was delicate, but strong, like you. And you have the same eyes. Topaz, I always called them.'

Was there a resemblance? I don't know. I thought of the blanket again.

'Did she have a hand for needlework?' I asked. My voice didn't sound like my own.

'My mother?'

'No. Her.' I lifted the daguerreotype.

He nodded. 'Daryâ had the most delicate touch. She had

become proficient at creating beautiful *zardosi* – you know, the intricate embroidery using gold and silver thread. She made pieces and sold them in the bazaars.'

I gave him back the daguerreotype. 'You have to go now.'

'Yes. I . . . I'm sorry,' he suddenly said. 'This is a terrible upset for you. I understand your difficulty in believing me. But . . .'

I kept looking at his face. I think I was shaking, but I can't be sure. As it had been when I read the name Pavit on the death list, it was difficult to have an account of what my body was doing.

'I know this is unsettling. I didn't know what to expect. How you would react.'

I stared into his face. There was so much I wanted to say to him, but nothing would come out.

'I had decided to move to Peshawar shortly before I'd seen you, that last time, at the Lahore mission. It would be the distance between myself and you that I needed. And Peshawar was familiar to me; I'd often passed through it as I travelled between Afghanistan and India. I secured a good job. I've never had a problem with work in India, because of my ability with languages and knowledge of both cultures. But of course I still wanted to know about you – at least that you were all right. I asked Kai about you when he came up here the last time. That's when he told me that all was well. That he'd recently gone out to the mission, but you were gone.'

That would have been after he'd found out what the mission had become. After he had listened to the gossip in Lahore, and the lies his mother told about me.

'Kai told me', he said, softly, so softly that I had to lean forward, 'that you had left the mission. He said he'd found out that you'd moved to Bombay, and were well and happy, living near the sea. You were carrying out missionary work, and a young man was courting you. All is well with Pree, he said.

You mustn't worry about her. It's best if you leave her to live her own life. I can still remember his words. But . . . are you all right? What's wrong?'

'He lied,' I whispered.

'Kai lied? About what?' He didn't wait for an answer. 'Since he told me that, I knew with certainty I wouldn't see you again. That I'd truly lost you, finally. I had let you go to have the life you deserved, the life of your choosing, in Bombay. I tried to be happy about it, tried to tell myself it was for the best. But the pain kept coming back. It wasn't the same pain as when I thought you were dead, or when I couldn't find you, but it was still pain, the deep pain of a father who knows he won't ever again see his child. But now you're here, in Peshawar. You had come to me, back into my life, and I knew, from the moment I saw you at my office door, that I couldn't let you go again. That I wouldn't. At that moment I didn't know how, but I knew I had to find a way, a way to . . . Pree, I'm sorry. I can see how this is distressing you.'

I had been breathing deeply, trying to calm myself, before speaking. 'Kai lied,' I repeated. 'I never went to Bombay. I was at the mission, all that time.'

He ducked his chin as if startled. 'But why would he do that?'

'Because he was ashamed of what he thought I'd become. He didn't want you to know. He thought he was protecting you, much as you thought you were protecting me by not claiming me when you knew I was your daughter.'

Mr Ingram's mouth opened, but before he could speak I continued.

'He didn't want you to know that he'd discovered that your daughter may have become a prostitute.' I spat the word at him, seeing a fine spray fly from my lips to his cheek. I heard the intake of Helena's breath.

He ignored both the saliva and the bitter word. 'So you . . . you really were still there? You never went to Bombay?'

'Do you know how I lived after the last time you saw me, when I was – you said I was happy? Happy!' I repeated, sarcastically. 'My parents – the Fincastles died: first my father, and then my mother. My mother took her own life in a most hideous manner. It was a terrible, terrible time. I was all alone, left to deal with everything. Their deaths, and the . . . the horror surrounding it all. Did you know that my father – that Reverend Fincastle and Glory were . . . did you know that he was Kai's father?'

Mr Ingram sat down, putting up his hand. 'Yes, but wait. Wait. You're speaking too quickly. I don't understand. What—'

I didn't care. 'I was left with Glory, Kai's slattern of a mother,' I raced on, stumbling over my own words in an attempt to get it all out, 'and she turned the mission into a brothel. A brothel.' My voice had risen to a shriek.

He was shaking his head and staring at me with a shocked expression. Helena hurried towards us, but I put up my hand, and she stopped.

I wanted to hurt this man even more now, now that I knew it was true. He was my father. 'I had to sell myself. Yes, I sold myself to a brutal pig of a man to have enough money to escape. You decided I was happy? You decided it was best to leave me? How do you know what was best for me? Did you ask me? How could you have done that to me?' I ran at him; he stood, and I struck him – his chest, his arms – with my fists. I ignored Helena's voice, begging me to stop.

'It was easier to let someone else raise me,' I cried. 'Don't say it was because you thought it best for me. You didn't want the responsibility. And don't talk about second chances. I don't want you in my life. I don't need you now. I needed you once, but not now.'

He stood as if made from stone.

'The only person I wanted to be part of my life was Kai. And now he's gone. He's left, and doesn't care about me. He's gone,' I repeated, yet again. 'And you – you're even weaker than my *real* father, the man who was there for me when I was a child, who comforted me when I cried. Who raised me as his own. Who carried all the responsibility for me. He died and you're allowed to live.' I struck his chest again, although weakly now.

'Pree,' Helena whispered, but still came no closer.

Mr Ingram let me hit him, over and over again, until finally I fell to my knees, putting my face into my hands and weeping.

There was the afternoon call from muezzins outside the open window. I felt his hands on my arms. He lifted me to my feet.

I stared into his face, and then turned and ran out of the room again.

I was sitting on my bed, the bit of blanket in my hands. Evening had fallen, and I'd lit a lamp. Aimee silently came in and took her nightdress and Rohana's from the wardrobe. 'Helena says you need being alone,' she said. 'We are sleeping other room this night.'

'Thank you, Aimee,' I said, the blanket soft under my fingers.

As she left, Helena came in. She sat beside me, and put her arm around me. 'It appears a lot has happened to you in the last few weeks, Pree,' she said, the daguerreotype in her hand. The photograph of me, with my father and mother. 'You were very distraught,' she said, 'and your treatment of Mr Ingram, while understandable . . .' her voice faded.

I was ashamed then, ashamed for my earlier behaviour, and ashamed that she knew of my past, the life at the brothel, and what I'd done. 'I'm sorry, Helena. I'll leave immediately. Tomorrow.' I didn't know where I'd go, but I had the rupees from Kai. I could pay for a place to stay for now.

But Helena shook her head. 'This is a mission house, Pree. We have always said we are here to help women in need. And I think you're in need right now. Please. Stay as long as you need to. When you're ready, you can resume your work.'

I leaned against her, my throat raw. 'I'm sorry,' I said, again fumbling for a handkerchief. 'You're so kind. I'm sorry for all the concern I've caused you.'

'I spoke, briefly, to Mr Ingram. He's very worried about you.' She looked at the photograph. 'He left this for you.'

I took it from her, studying Mr Ingram's face, then the face of the woman, Daryâ, who had made the beautiful blanket. Who had died, unable to bear losing me.

'But don't you want to have your father in your life? I know you feel so hurt by him, and yet he appears . . .' she stopped.

I stroked the soft piece of embroidered blanket. 'He hurt me by not protecting me when he could have. Should have.'

Helena reached and touched the blanket. 'Some might argue that Our Heavenly Father didn't protect His son. Over and over again, He allowed His son to struggle on, alone. He allowed Him to die.'

I didn't want her to try to make me see sense with religious persuasion. I sighed.

'Do you really believe that Mr Ingram acted out of selfishness?' she asked. 'Out of cruelty, or thoughtlessness?'

I shook my head. 'No. He . . . he said he did what he thought was best for me.'

Children's laughter floated down the hall. 'Then he acted out of love?'

I didn't answer.

'Sometimes we make what can be seen as the wrong

choice with the right intention,' she said. 'Could you find it in your heart to forgive your father?' she finally asked. 'Is that not the true test of a Christian? Forgiveness, for those who have hurt us?'

Could I even be called a Christian? The woman who gave birth to me had been a Muslim. I had fought against my adoptive father's Christianity. Mr Ingram claimed no religion. Now, even when I tried to pray, I couldn't.

I brought the blanket to my face, and held it there. Again I thought of the woman in the photograph, the woman who had made this blanket for me, and had held me in it. And surely Mr Ingram had done the same, had once wrapped this blanket around me and held me against him.

Helena left me there, in the fading light, the children's laughter muted now.

The next day I went out into the street and hailed a tonga.

It was Sunday; I knew the English offices would be closed. I directed the tonga-wallah. When I arrived at Mr Ingram's home he was on the verandah, leaning against the railing with his arms crossed, looking out at the road in front of his house. As we pulled up he straightened, and then went to the top step of the verandah.

His face was unreadable as he watched me approach.

'I decided I would come for a visit, Mr Ingram,' I said, as I came up the steps. 'I'm sorry not to have sent word first.'

He stared at me; I could see his chest rise and fall under his shirt. '*Salaam*, Pree.' His voice was unsteady. 'Please. Sit down.'

I did, and he sat beside me. We watched the road, rocking in the wicker chairs. Neither of us spoke for some time. Finally he asked, still staring straight ahead, 'You'll stay at the mission here, in Peshawar?'

'For now,' I said. 'And you?'

'I shall remain in Peshawar for the present as well,' he said. 'Although there are many wonderful places to live in India. I have always loved being near the sea.'

I looked at his profile. He swallowed. 'I have some *kulfi*,' he said. 'Do you like *kulfi*?'

I thought of the last time I'd had that sweet, smooth dessert at the *Haveli* Abdur Jan. How it had brought back some distant memory, making my stomach churn. 'I'm not sure.'

'I'll fetch it.' Mr Ingram said, rising and going towards the door. He paused, looking over his shoulder. '*Kulfi* was your favourite,' he said. 'But we could only let you have a spoonful or two; it was too rich for a baby. Once the ayah allowed you to grow ill from eating so much of it.'

I waited for him to return, rocking slowly in the warm afternoon sunlight. The handsome *doda* trees spread their umbrella-like canopies over the garden. In the leaves of the tree closest to the verandah a little warbler hopped and twittered. I rocked slowly, watching it. It preened itself, and finally opened its tiny beak and sang its sweet song. I counted. It sang once, twice, three times. Four, five. Six and seven.

It stopped, again fluffing up its chest, and then sang out one more time.

EPILOGUE

I TURN AT THE sound of feet, quick quick, light and buoyant, as buoyant as the updraught of air that rises under the wings of the tiny sunbird fluttering outside the window. The door opens and here they are, my children. They have come to say *goodbye Mama, goodbye, goodbye, Grandpapa is here*, then there are excited kisses and hugs and the same dancing footsteps out the door and down the broad, sun-lit corridor. Their grandfather has stopped by, as he so often does, and is taking them to the waterfront to see the hundreds of Ganeshes washed up on the beach after last night's festival.

At my insistence my father moved to Bombay so we could be near to each other, and it fills my heart to watch his delight in his grandchildren. And they adore him, endlessly asking for tales of his past, of adventures in mountains and deserts, of his meeting their exotic, beautiful grandmother who recited poetry and created delicate tapestries, of ocean voyages and English cities and the names of all the glorious horses he has owned. My father says his adventures are over, his journey complete, and that theirs is just beginning.

Three children, girl and boy and girl, light and dark, dark and light, a combination of culture and blood and religion and all that has come before them. A product of their father, and of me, of the generations preceding them. Racing to grow up, their lives stretch ahead of them like the open sea. They will always know who they are, and where they came

from. It is important they do not live a life of secrets; too lo
I knew this secret life. Too long.

I lie back in the wide, rumpled cool bed and watch the white curtains dancing in the morning breeze. I am always tired, the morning after my rounds. I hear my husband's voice through the open window, his easy laughter as he bids farewell to his children and father-in-law. No matter how late I return after my medical duties, he waits for me with a cup of chai, and asks about the latest women I have treated. We sit, in the warm light of the lamp, and talk about the day, the children, the weather, tomorrow's plans, in the usual way of husband and wife.

My younger daughter's hair smelled of smoke this morning. She must already have been in the back garden, helping with the breakfast as I did when I was a child, and perhaps as my mother before me. This one loves to cook. She crouches beside the *biwarchi* and helps chop his spices, and fan the fire. How well my fingers remember the rhythm of the knife, the smell of the flames feeding upon the morning air.

For so long I could not bear the smell, but only moments ago, as I pressed my face against my girl's shining tresses, I breathed it in, and it brought me pleasure.

The once-brutal memory of fire has grown old for me, finally. Thin and colourless, mute, it can no longer bring pain.

Now it is only heat, and smoke. Nothing more.

I rise and go to the window. From our home I can see the silver glint of the sea over the tops of the trees.

I watch the silver, and begin my prayers.

ACKNOWLEDGEMENTS

As always, there are many people to thank upon the completion of this book. There are those who help shape my initial ideas and words, gently and thoughtfully urging me in directions I may not have taken. Thank you to Harrie Evans and Sherise Hobbs, my editors at Headline, for your insight and wisdom.

There are those who ensure that my words reach my readers. Thank you to Kim McArthur and the fabulous staff at McArthur and Company, not only for all your work in Canada but for the great parties. Thank you to Peter Newsom of Headline for your travels into the world with my books.

Thank you to those at the Marsh Agency: Paul Marsh, Camilla Ferrier, and Caroline Hardman, for your belief in me and all your work on my behalf.

And thank you to Sarah Heller, my agent, for your intuition as you listen patiently to my wild ideas and come up with some of your own, for your business acumen, and also for your friendship and making me laugh at myself when I threaten to take it all too seriously.

Many thanks to the Tandon family: Anita, for your motivation and for answering my many questions on life in India; Ravi, for ensuring that my Indian journey was inspiring and filled with wonder, and Richa and Priya, for your beauty and grace and support.

As always, thank you to my family and friends in so many

parts of the world who instinctively understand when to hold me up and when to let me go during the long and all-encompassing creative process. There are too many of you to name, but you know how I treasure your love and understanding.

And finally, thank you to my daughter Zalie for accompanying me to India, and bringing with you your own brand of joy and unique outlook on the world.

GLOSSARY

assalamu alaikum – 'Peace be upon you' – an Arabic greeting
atma – soul or self
ayah – a lady's maid or child's nanny
bahan – sister
Basant – festival celebrating the arrival of spring
beedi – cigarette made of tobacco wrapped in a tendu leaf
    and secured with thread
beti – daughter
bhai – brother
bheesti – water carrier
bibighar – women's house
biwarchi – cook
caravanserai – a rest stop for humans and animals, enclosed by
    walls but open to the sky
charpoy – low cot of woven rope
chattri – a memorial, usually made of stone
chee-chee – disparaging term applied to Eurasians' manner of
    speech; hybrid English
chowkidar – watchman or guard
chuprassi – messenger to greet and admit visitors
churail – evil female spirit
daal – cooked lentil dish
devadasi – girl married to a deity; a temple virgin or Servant
    of God. The practice eventually degenerated and some
    sunk to prostitution

dhobi – one who washed household clothing and linens

dhoti – a long cloth wrapped around a man's waist and legs and tied at the waist

Diwali – Festival of Lights – celebration symbolising the victory of good over evil

durzi – tailor

goli – game of marbles

hakim – an authority or wise man, often of medicine

haveli – private residence, usually containing a courtyard in the centre

japa mala – mantra meditation using a string of beads

katha – story or tale

kedgeree – dish of fish, boiled eggs, rice and butter

khansana – head bearer in charge of the other servants

khitmutgar – head table-server

khuda hafiz – goodbye

kirpan – Sikh sword, a symbol of independence, self-respect and power

koss – a measure of distance of approximately two miles

kulfi – dessert made with boiled milk, sugar, thin noodles, nuts and fruit

kurta – loose shirt to the knees, worn by both men and women

ladoo – floury round sweet dipped in sugar syrup

lattoo – game of spinning tops

mali – gardener

masalchi – one who works as a spice grinder

namaste – literally, 'I bow to you' – a polite greeting or parting phrase

Om Namah Shiva – mantra for meditation

paan – digestive of spices and fruit, chewed as a palate cleaner and breath freshener

panjammahs – men's loose cotton trousers, tied at the waist.

preta – supernatural being

puja – religious prayer ritual to show respect to gods and goddesses

punkah – overhead cloth fan, operated by pulling an attached string or rope

purdah – practice of preventing men from seeing women through a physical segregation

rani – a Hindu queen: a rajah's wife

rasoi – kitchen hut set apart from the main house

roti – flat circular unleavened bread. Also known as nan or chapatti in various regions

sadhu – ascetic dedicated to achieving liberation through meditation and contemplation of God

salaam – peace. Less formal greeting

salwar – loose, flowing trousers worn by both men and women

sati – funeral custom in which a widow immolates herself on her husband's pyre. Also known as suttee

sepoy – a native of India employed as a soldier by a European power

shnai – stringed instrument plucked with the fingers

sudra – lowest of the social castes; sometimes called untouchable

surma – cosmetic used on the eyes; also known as kohl

tambour – small drum

tikka – a red powder applied with the thumb in an upward stroke, worn by both men and women in decoration or for religious observance

wallah – a male employed in a particular occupation or activity

zardosi – embroidery done with fine gold or silver thread

zenana – the part of the house reserved for women

LINDA HOLEMAN

The Linnet Bird

'For you, I will write of it all – part truth, part memory, part nightmare – my life, the one that started so long ago, in a place so far from here . . .'

India, 1839: Linny Gow, a respectable young wife and mother, settles down to write her life story. To outside appearances Linny is the perfect Colonial wife: beautiful, gracious, subservient. But appearances can be very deceptive . . .

An unforgettable book, richly descriptive and mesmerising from the start, *The Linnet Bird* is the spellbinding story of the journey of Linny Gow – child prostitute turned social climber turned colonial wife turned adventuress. Frequently disturbing, often moving and always enthralling, it is that rare thing: a once-in-a-lifetime read.

'We use that old cliché "unputdownable" so often that it has little real meaning any more, but I can assure you The Linnet Bird *stands alone, proud and beautiful . . . I turned the final page with deep regret*' Lesley Pearse

978 0 7553 2463 7

headline
review

LINDA HOLEMAN

The Moonlit Cage

'I have always been told I was wicked'

The Moonlit Cage is the spellbinding story of Daryâ, a young Afghan girl, cursed, worthless and despised by her husband and her family, who embarks on the journey of a lifetime – one that takes her from the unforgiving valleys and mountains of her homeland to 1850s London, the heart of the mighty British Empire.

Enthralling, unusual and richly textured, *The Moonlit Cage* is a thrillingly realistic evocation of a lost world. It is a novel you will never forget.

Praise for the international bestseller *The Linnet Bird*:

'A sweeping, unputdownable saga (think *The Thorn Birds* and *Gone with the Wind*) that you'll want to tell all your friends about' *Woman*

'Compulsive reading . . . (*The Linnet Bird*) succeeds in being more than just a historical saga' *The Lady*

'Sheer bliss . . . A superb read in every way, epic, moving and unpredictable. I couldn't put *The Linnet Bird* down until I'd finished it' Lesley Pearse

'(Linda Holman) is a master of dramatic tension and of seducing a readerís attention . . . There is a beautiful imagination at work here and a touch of genuine narrative magic that makes the book a once-in-a-lifetime read' *Toronto Globe & Mail*

978 0 7553 2294 7

headline
review

LIU HONG

Wives of the East Wind

'Mao told the Chinese Communists the East Wind must prevail over the Capitalist West Wind. Liu Hong's novel tells us of the terrible cost to her *Wives of the East Wind*' Xinran, author of *The Good Women of China*

Two couples – Wenya and Zhiying, Zhenzhen and Lao Gao – meet, marry and become inseparable just as China is shaking off the memory of war, and the brightest of its youth are pledging themselves to building a vibrant new future. Yet for all that their lives embody the ideals of the new republic, they are spared none of the suffering and hardship that are to follow, through years of famine and the terror of the Cultural Revolution.

The powerful experiences of motherhood and loss only deepen the bond between Wenya and Zhenzhen, and it is their friendship, above all, that sustains them through their darkest hours. And as a new, more affluent China dawns, and the struggle for survival becomes an equally fierce battle to protect the values closest to their hearts, Zhenzhen teaches Wenya an unforgettable message about courage.

Praise for Liu Hong:

'Fascinating and very sympathetically presented' *Independent*

'A unique story, told with a sweetness and restraint that is both beguiling and illuminating' *Woman's Journal*

'Absolutely extraordinary . . . There have been so many works of fiction and non-fiction from China, but if they're this good, we're going to keep buying them' *Open Book*, BBC Radio 4

978 0 7553 0605 3

headline
review